ALSO BY ODIN ROARK

3 WAY MIRROR
MIND PUPPETS
PROSETRY AT WORK
PERCEPTIONS

ECHOSIS

ALSO BY ODIN ROARK

3 WAY MIRROR
MIND PUPPETS
PROSETRY AT WORK
PERCEPTIONS

ECHOSIS

ECHOSIS

A Novel
By
Odin Roark

For their help with this book,
the author is particularly grateful to
Danae Wilkin, Daniel Berkey, Mitch Geller,
Michelle Montgomery, Greg Crites,
Diana Hockley, Patti Yaeger, Paul Negri,
Jeni Decker, Kydd Dustyn, Dan Laker,
Stindo, Sara Basrai, Archie Hooton,
and to Sol Nasisi and the TNBW staff.

For Jordan and Kedric

"Every child is an artist. The problem is how
to remain an artist once we grow up."
                                        Pablo Picasso

"It is no measure of health to be well
adjusted to a profoundly sick society."
                                        Jiddu Krishnamurti

Odin Roark

ECHOSIS

---

iPOV Books

Ashland Oregon

Chapter 1

Little stops a New Yorker in his tracks.

But, there I was. Brought to a halt.

Caught half stride by the determination in front of me.

The overalls he wore had seen their share of grease guns and oil pans in another time, another place. Now, beneath the Washington Square Arch in Greenwich Village, the downtrodden body that had recently laid claim to the Goodwill bargain continued duct taping the punctured tire of his bike. Even the stench of old, caked hair, carried by the trace of sweat trickling into his eyes, could do little to dissuade his resolve. For this rare, cheery-eyed example of the homeless frequenting the streets of New York, the most important thing at hand was wrapping that tire sufficiently to hold the air his battered tire pump stood ready to deliver.

It's not that I'd never seen such images before; after all, this is the land of the free and supposedly the brave, but the old man's image gave me pause while passing through to the other side and my date with the 4th Street subway station, a few blocks away. The hesitation was long enough for my hand to finger the money clip, but not long enough for me to finish doing the right thing. The peeling of just one twenty would buy him a new tire—two tires on Houston Street. But there was that wavering moment, the lack of tenacity that had kept me from carrying out certain other actions in my life, an indomitable serious weakness that was unique to me and perhaps to all of us—the questioning of instinct. *You're such an asshole.*

I ran to the subway station and my appointment at Zano's, never releasing the cowardice clenching of my money clip.

***

For many, New York's conspicuous consumption was best defined by its coffee intake. And, in Lower Manhattan, Zano's coffee shop proudly stood center stage, 24/7, resonating with the cacophonous stirring of cups and the orchestrated sips and slurps of dark, light, and flavored java.

"What if..." Samara said.

"You're asking me?" I blurted out, bumping the table and spilling my meal for the day. I jumped back. "Son of a..."

"Can I buy you another cup?" she asked in her usual analytical tone.

"No. Think I'll just stay on the 'fast' I've grown accustomed to for the past few months."

She smiled and sipped her own cappuccino. "Whatever works for you, Derek."

As I spread the Times classified section across the marble slab table and let the double espresso soak through, I avoided the eye contact she used so persuasively. That, together with her trim body topping out at five-foot-seven, made it almost impossible to win any debate, at least for this man, especially when she chose to focus her green eyes on my mouth.

"At least leave me with *some* sense of identity. Okay, Doctor?" I muttered.

She nodded, smiled and leaned on her elbows, studying the dark brown Rorschach design seeping through the Lexus ad proclaiming the 2005 models *unrivaled*. "You know, after all this time, I don't think I've ever seen you so relaxed," she said. "Do you have an answer?"

"You're asking me again the same worn out stupid question that is so fucking rhetorical it's off the scale."

"Derek," she whispered, "I'm just being the way you said you liked me...curious. Remember? By the way, your body may have just tensed up, making words sound bitter, and your language gutter-prone, but... I don't believe it."

"Oh, Jesus. What? Don't believe what?" I asked.

"That you are *not* the same blissful, relaxed man that arrived back from the Far East a week ago," she whispered once again, eyeing my six-foot frame that she had reminded me ad nauseam needed the ingestion of some extra meat and potatoes.

"Why must you whisper all the time?"

"It makes you listen, Derek. Makes you listen to my *curious* questions."

I stood up and motioned for the waitress. "Could I have a double espresso to go?"

"Doppio coming at ya," the little waif of a blond shot back at me.

"I'm leaving now, Samara."

She sat motionless.

"I'm going. Do you hear me? I don't want any more questions."

Samara continued turning her head left and right gazing at the coffee stains. "I'll be finished with this little study before your take-out arrives."

2

"God damn…" I sat down, took a deep breath and leaned across the table. "If I answer the question, will you just let me leave without planting more guilt? Okay?"

"Not intended to stir up guilt. I'm not that way."

I turned on my chair. *God, can I get through this? Right now, at this very moment I want to just lose it.* "Why are you all the same?"

"You mean the gender or the profession?" she quipped.

"Both. All. Okay? Here's the answer. The answer is as it's always been, as you've always known it for… Jesus, how long has it been… two years?"

"Two years? You mean our relationship?"

"I've not accepted it as a relationship yet, okay? You screw around with my head and…"

"At your request," she interrupted.

"…at my request, and I tell you what you want to hear, and we see each other every Tuesday night at this funky coffee house, and you always manage to get me pissed. That's a relationship?"

"Oh, Derek. The best. You pay me to get you upset, just like in a marriage."

"Husbands never pay their wives, for chrissake," I shot back.

"Oh… in more ways than one, Derek."

"Okay. Okay. This is going nowhere."

"Right. You were going to give me *the* answer, remember?"

"The answer. Okay. It's so obvious. I'm scared, Doctor. I'm fearful, and I'm lonely, too. I'm a basket case, okay?"

"You forgot 'I'm horny'."

"Shit," I muttered, "that's a given."

Her eyes remained diligent as she said, "It's important you say it."

A young, black house painter tried to navigate the tables, carrying two empty five-gallon cans in one hand and lugging a full can in the other. "Excuse me," he said.

Samara glanced at the painter's backside. "You'd think he could go out the back way, right?"

The painter continued toward the front, "Excuse me, mon…sorry…thanks, oops…sorry." As he arrived at the entrance, the manager, whose body and hand gestures left little for the imagination, met him.

I leaned forward in an effort to get Samara's attention away from the disturbing painter. "Okay. I'll say it. I'm horny."

As she brought her eyes back to the table, "And what else, Derek?"

I didn't like this part. I didn't like it at all, but like a Twelve Step program, I had to admit certain things. "I'm not a normal person," I

3

blurted out, turning the heads of several Village types, one giving me a thumbs-up.

The waitress handed me my coffee, and surreptitiously leaned in. "Mister Turrel, this is not the place to be so vocal, you know?"

"Oh, come on, Patty, but it's okay to parade house-painters through while we're having coffee?"

"What? Oh, sorry. He's just working on the storeroom. Don't worry, my manager took care of it."

I reached in my pocket, threw a twenty on the table, and stood up, my eyes never leaving Samara's. "Patty, how long have you been serving me and Dr. Jennings, huh?"

Patty stuck the twenty in her pocket. "Long enough to know that these kinds of tips pay my rent every month. Five-forty for the coffee." She slipped the check under my hand with the pen. I signed my usual *swoop and spear* and took Samara's hand. "So, Samara, you want to do it, or not?"

Samara shared ever so slight a grin and hoisted her handbag onto her shoulder, leading the way to the front door. I followed, as usual.

This was always our foreplay. She had suggested role-playing as therapy, and…well, it was interesting. I had to admit it. A little crazy, I know. But, it worked for us. Truth be told, *neither* of us were "normal," especially in the romance department. For instance, I always stopped for a yellow rose on these Tuesday nights, and she always appreciated the gesture. But, she wouldn't let me buy her red roses. Don't know why. A quirk of hers. Like I said, not normal.

That's how my crazy Tuesdays always started. I still liked sleeping all day. Somehow, it was easier that way. The setting sun was my usual wake up time and Wednesday through Monday was my usual workweek. Tuesday charged me. No, it wasn't the sex. And it sure as hell wasn't the role-playing. It was a sense of recklessness, that feeling that I could break all the rules and still make it through the night.

The rest of the week was grind, grind and more grind. I hated the market, but I knew it well. I was extra lucky. My losses never caught up with my gains and, although I spent less and less time with the Dow Jones, I mildly continued in the midst of the dust and noise of my jackhammer and welding torch.

My passion was finally paying well, but not quite as well as the market. I wondered many times when I'd have the courage to throw away the earplug, the clip-on PDA, and the glasses that let me weld and watch the MSN ticker tape screen in the corner of the lens at the same time. But, next to Samara and rock, electronics were the next best turn-on I had.

4

As usual, we walked the short distance to the loft without talking, allowing for the simple ritual-like silence as she mused over the fragrance of the yellow rose. Maybe it was to counter Soho's waking-up-at-ten routine. Junkies, lookiloos, celebs, and wannabes cluttered the sidewalks like overgrown vegetation that needed pruning. Didn't matter that pockets were being picked, drug deals were going down, cops were cruising on bicycles shootin' the shit about the Mets or the Yankee games. Didn't matter. People just went their own way and paid no mind—just like Samara and me.

I leaned over and pulled the sheet up over her flawless skin. I got off on just seeing the black sheet contrasting her olive color, especially when she'd fall into a deep sleep after making love. It was always I who lay awake, staring up at the seven-hundred-pound marble and iron mobile that hung from the twenty-two-foot ceiling. The strange-looking art piece I'd playfully named "Family" had been a present to myself during the lean years when there was no one, either to buy my work or to sleep with. I thought of the years earlier when I'd turned down ten thousand and a permanent spot for it at MOCA, in LA. That act of "craziness," as my agent called it, left him speechless and me hungry for a bit longer. But, when it's your first-born, it's hard to give it up.

I glanced about the studio at the hanging plastic tents that surrounded the ladders, scaffolding and heavy stones barely removed from their mother's womb at the quarry. I still felt alone. Even with the pieces I placed about the floor like children of sorts, even—my eyes drifted back to Samara—even my lady, couldn't remove the feeling of aloneness. But that's how I understood it...the way I preferred it.

"You *want* to be alone, Derek. Just accept it. It's part of your eccentricities."

"What happened to 'abnormalities?'" I remember asking her.

"I think you've worked through the bad ones. The good ones are... good. Very good."

I never forgot her gesture that day. She pointed to my head and said, "One day your conscience will agree with your demanding friend inside there."

Oh, she left it open to continue with the therapy, but something rang true in her comment, and I opted to work on her suggestion. It wasn't long before I suggested we graduate to a new level in this *happiness quest*... another of her favorite phrases. I was insistent, but she resisted, saying, "I don't think it wise to change roles."

That's what Samara said to me on the last day I was *formally* a patient and the first day I *formally* became her lover. And... well, here we are. That's how we've been relating ever since, Samara and me. Now she provides the mental challenge of an intelligent woman, mixing in a safe amount of "psychologist" game, and I remain right where I wish to stay…alone. She still loves playing the doctor side of her genius, and insisting on a strict "therapeutic" hour, here and there, and I've insisted on paying her normal fee to carry it out. That was the arrangement. I'd pay the money, and in exchange, she would give me the therapist thing. The rest—the *mothering* thing, the *lover* thing, and the *artist's companion* thing— that was special and still a bit overwhelming for me at times. No woman I'd ever met managed power like Samara Jennings. Not controlling power, but strength of conviction.

I turned over and watched her slow breathing. Her calm face showed the occasional twitch, subtle smile, and raising of the eyebrows, all the usual sure signs she was in the final minutes before awakening. After all these months, I was beginning to think she loved our arrangement almost as much as she loved composing, which is what I suspected she did in her sleep, given the tight schedule of patients she had every day. But, however she made the time, she got everything done, including the progression of her concerto. As she started to awaken, I thought of Tanglewood coming up in the summer, the season her concerto would premier, and how it might affect our Tuesdays as the summer drew near. Fortunately for me, that was a few months away.

She turned and backed her body into me, her usual wake up routine. Then came the little whimpers, like now, until I put my arms around her—like now. These early morning habits usually exposed my backside to the "elements," as she had labeled them. I never share this part of my *aloneness* with her, though. Don't know why. I just never do. I always try to keep my mind calm, focused and loving, but this mental-backside of mine, what's behind me now in its own shadow, you know, this is when I feel cold, really cold. Strange. Whether it's summer or winter, the "elements" grip my shoulders like a cornice atop a mountain, sometimes buffeting with a curling, blowing…. I'm going off the edge again. Of course there are no winds. Of course. The air in the loft is always calm. I'm not crazy, you know. It's only in my mind, these howling winds, winds that Samara is still working on. Sometimes, she senses something is bothering me that professional experience can't calm. Those times, she addresses me with care and understanding, with mothering, with sex, whatever she feels will appropriately soothe me. I wonder many times if this is love or love's trickery.

I like the mornings—sometimes. She holds me to her breast like a mother; does her magic like a lover, and even subtly rocks me sometimes like I remember my grandmother doing. But then...

This morning was like many others. She stopped her little whimpers. Now there was only the thirty to thirty-five breaths per minute she always took just before awakening. Soon, I would be in the arms of... I didn't know, really. I still didn't have a word for it. Goddess? I'd be taken care of, gently held, and asked the usual Wednesday morning query, the question that usually kept me awake Tuesday nights, anticipating the words that always *screamed* at me, even though they were delivered in her usual whispered confidence. And, as usual, I could only stare at the ceiling with the dry throat that always followed on hearing the question once again, the question that was progressively becoming a demand.

"When are you going to do it, Derek?"

CHAPTER 2

For Samara, music was her first love. Her therapy practice was a means to an end. On completing her PhD and receiving her therapy license, she vowed she would work hard and save the money from her practice in order to someday have the bank account and the time to compose music exclusively. For now, however, fulfilling the obligations that two hundred dollars per hour demanded was the first priority of the day. She sat and waited.

Seated across from her was her Jamaican patient who spent the majority of each therapy hour staring at the floor. The rare occurrence of a question or a statement brought Samara forward in rapt attention, only to be thwarted by his seeming inability to converse beyond the singular answer to her question, "Pierre? Is there anything you wish to talk about?"

Pierre raised his thin, twenty-one-year-old torso, as if a wrecking ball were resting on his shoulders. "I don't want to talk about it anymore."

As usual, her retort was, "About what, Pierre? We've not picked a subject yet."

"He's just a son of a bitch."

"Who?"

"Him."

"Okay. Does 'him' have a name?"

"I don't want to talk about it."

"Okay." Samara looked at her watch. It was only twenty minutes into the session. She could only imagine the next thirty minutes would be more of the same. This was not the first such session he chose to just sit. She had brought the *non-communication* problem to the attention of Pierre's mother, but she was bent on Samara continuing, regardless of the silence. "He's just screwed up. Give him time," his mother had insisted. "His father is paying top dollar for the best, right? So do your best." Samara paused, re-crossed her legs, took a swallow of water, and waited some more. *Two-forty was the time when******

"Can I go now?"

"Let's try again," said Samara. "We've still ten minutes."

"Waste of time. Waste of money."

"Finding the words sometimes takes patience."

"C'mon, mon. To just sit here and have you just sit there? Jesus. I have better times with my hallucinations."

"Is that what you think they are?"

He looked up and grinned. "You have a fancy name for them?"

Samara shrugged. "No. 'Hallucinations' is the word we use too...when that's what we're talking about. Are you sure that's what you mean?"

He rose and tucked in his shirt, then pulled it out again. "Doesn't matter. I've got a long trip to make. Gotta get goin'." He turned and started toward the door.

"See you next week then, Pierre. You can call me any time, you know."

As he opened the door, he looked over his shoulder. "Why would I want to do that?"

The side door shut and Samara remained seated, her gaze fixed on the exit as she reminded herself that this was what she had spent eight years learning how to do—listen, listen, listen.

"Why would I want to do that?" continued to hang in the air as she prepared for the next patient.

***

Driving to the quarry on a Thursday was a pain with Harry being gone. No one knew the stone like Harry, but *Thursday* was his day off. I usually made this trip on other days of the week, but I had to get out of the city.

The fall colors were starting to appear. Early, I thought. Sign of a bad winter coming. Even with the fall foliage to keep my interest while driving, the anxieties kept nagging me. Taking out my aggressions with the chisel and hammer was proving not to be the way to overcome discomfort. That's what I paid Samara for, except today her schedule was full.

Another cigarette was not the answer either. But, like the addict I was, I flung the half-smoked butt out the window, and started to light up another. Like a watch dog in heat, the howl of the siren announced the pursuit of a driver's worst enemy, the salivating tan and black breed. The red and blue flashing lights, together with the wailing of the siren, brought my shoe leather gently to the brake.

I cracked the window just enough to be cooperative as the stout gentleman of *the badge* lumbered up to my truck.

"License and registration, please."

"Something wrong, Officer?" I said, the cliché phrase obviously making him bristle.

"Of course not. I just wanted to stop and chat," he replied as I handed him my license and registration. He sauntered back to his patrol car to check me out. He couldn't be stopping me for a stupid cigarette out the window, could he? No. I had to be speeding. *Dumb, dumb, dumb.* I hated traffic school and that would be the result of this stupid mistake. After waiting several minutes, I glanced in the rear view mirror only to see him pulling up alongside me. *What was this all about? Cops don't pull alongside you when they give a ticket.*

His hand reached through his passenger side window and passed me my license and registration, and a motion to follow.

Shit. Follow. Shit, shit, shit. He's taking me straight to jail. I couldn't have been going that fast.

He pulled ahead. I sat there frozen, as he gave a burst of the siren and motioned once again to follow.

Three miles later, he pulled to the side of the road, got out, and walked back to my car. Again, I rolled down the window. "What are we doing *here*, officer?"

He pointed to the mountainside. All charred. "Seventeen thousand acres, Buddy. Seventeen thousand. All with the flick of a butt out the window." He tore off the ticket and handed it to me. "Think next time." He gave a two-finger tap of the brim of his trooper hat. "Nice '88'."

"Pardon," I said.

"The truck. '88 Ford, right?"

"Yes!" And he strode back to his black and tan.

As I looked at the ticket, I had the urge to piss, shit and upchuck, not necessarily in that order. "Five-Hundred Dollars!"

It took a few moments to calm down, but then I looked up at the hillside he had pointed out. The blackened area took on a different meaning. He was right. "Think." *Nature took care of its own. Man had no right to usurp such authority. Where would my art be were it not for nature's natural process?* I looked at the ticket one last time and nodded to myself. *There are no accidents.* I pulled onto the highway.

The rest of the drive was slow and smokeless as I thought further about the forces of nature I so depended on. It was late afternoon when I turned into the Jensen Quarry.

***

"Mister Turrel," bellowed the gatekeeper. They always made a big thing about keeping the gate locked as if someone might come in and steal a couple tons of rock.

"Hello, Gavos. Like your new hat."

Gavos blushed and adjusted the beret.

"My daughter. Sent it from Hungary. Nice color, don't you think?"

I squinted playfully at the red and green plaid and smiled. "Yes, very European. Cheerful."

I pulled into the quarry and marveled at the "magic hour" light that turned the gray, white and black veins of granite into Alpine glow. I drove to the quadrant that inventoried carefully cut blocks for their special customers. Getting on the *list* had taken a lot of years of jack-hammering my own pieces and schlepping them to the studio where patrons would often marvel at the richness of pattern, believing the rock's origin was Italy.

Today, however, I had a particular size and shape in mind, so I pulled the climbing gear from the back, cinched on the harness, grabbed the chalk bag and started the climb up the back side of the four-hundred-foot slab of granite. For most, the work by the cutters was sufficient. They were good. But, having qualified with demolition instruction from their best explosives man, I had acquired a license to blast my own. I knew from years of climbing that sometimes the best veins in the rock were hidden. Today, after several climbs on the slab, I planted the dynamite. Gilanni pushed the plunger and the corner of the outcrop dropped the hundred feet onto the prepared sand mound.

For the next hour I, along with several workers, maintained a constant lean on carbon bits, further carving the rough shape and size. As usual, the percussive sound that breathed spirit into the blocks of formless mass was music to my ears. For these men of massive arms and shoulders, these artisans from Europe and South America, *cutting* was an art of birthing they had spent decades perfecting. These men, who seldom spoke save for the drone of their jackhammers, were my closest friends.

In our tradition, one that Gilanni and I had started several years ago, the quarry cutters stood around the pick-up and I stood atop my rock and handed out tall bottles of ice-cold Spaten Lager from my picnic cooler. We lifted our bottles as Gilanni gave tribute—"To nature for allowing us to rip from her innards yet another piece of her heart. May it be worthy of the sacrifice."

"Zum Wohl!" the cutters shouted and quickly tipped the first of several lagers that I continued to pass out to quench the thirst my friends had wholly earned.

Later, after the men gathered their lunch pails and headed for home, I once again climbed atop my rock and stared at the dark sky. My shirt, caked with the perspiration of the pneumatic trauma I'd given my body, felt like cardboard. Jeans that only a few hours earlier had reminded me of Samara with their Downy smell of freshness, were now stiff with dust and sweat. I peered down at my feet standing on the perfectly cut eight-hundred-pound mass now resting in the back of the pick-up. The weight all but buckling the springs, I wondered who was worse off, my wheels, or me? As I looked once again toward the heavens, my eyes caught a glimpse of the single light bulb above the "no trespassing" sign. While fireflies darted about, leaving their familiar contrails of atom-like designs above the hundred-watt playground, moths played kamikaze. Gazing at the early night stars, my mind drifted away from the pain in my shoulders and into the images of surreal thought that had obsessed me for so many years. The challenge of another piece of nature's history filled my mind, and I climbed aboard and started the long drive back.

Leaving the quarry was always a strange kind of excitement. Sometimes cathartic, but always an exhausting test of will power and focus, I anticipated the struggle I'd experience with yet another attempt to ground what Samara had spent months getting me to understand was my very stubborn and belligerent *id*. She counseled many artists, and being one herself, she believed the magic of creation was more often than not, the providence of the unconscious or *id*. "Your hands, eyes and ears either allow a *channel* for the world of the unconscious to thrive and express itself, or you become the *captor and slave master* of all the bottled up imagination and freedom the ego and superego try to imprison with a vengeance." I could see her cupped hands as a scale—her favorite demonstration. "Artist or schlock."

As I drove up the on-ramp to the 91-South, I started to prepare my mind for what lay ahead. *How many completions had I experienced? A dozen?* All were in museums or lobbies of skyscrapers, save the first born that hung above my bed. All bore the unmistakable *Derek Turrel* stamp of being *unfinished*. Sometimes appearing as a minor flaw, other times a "gross arrogance," as one critic put it, the one constant was that the various works increasingly became front-page art news. I tuned the radio to a jazz station and lit a cigarette. Here I was about to begin the nine-month vigil once again. Yes, I had turned more than a head or two over the years with my *nine-month* time frame for each sculpture. I hadn't planned it that way in the beginning; it's just the way it happened. Now, with the encouragement of Samara, the nine-month thing was habit—a mystical time clock that knew better than I when the creation was finished. It didn't matter where I was when the nine months ended, I always capitulated to the *magic*, as I preferred to call it.

I turned up the volume as Coltrane filled the cab with *his* kind of magic.

The oncoming cars' headlights flashed through the windshield like slow-motion flashbulbs of the past; snapshots of the abstract storyline of my life that now were hundreds of rock and steel impressions of my experience. If only I could rid myself of the sometimes overwhelming impatience of the chisel and torch. Samara had been working on that as well. "You're letting the tail wag the dog, Derek. Your tools are not you. You're the captain on the ship." I had usually nodded in agreement, but there was always this nagging suspicion that if I didn't respect the love affair my hands had with the tools, I might lose whatever it was that made up my so-called talent. "Your imagination with your work is only superseded by the fantasy connection you have with yourself," she was fond of saying.

As if on cue, my cell chimed in with a text message from Samara. "Know you don't like to be interrupted on a 'rock day,' but only one more patient, and then going to hang at Stefano's. Drop by if you feel like it."

I had four more hours of driving. I didn't know if I felt like hearing again tonight, "When are you going to do it?"

CHAPTER 3

As Derek began his long journey back, Samara walked the quiet streets that crisscrossed Soho, lighting one cigarette after another. She approached a man standing on the corner, stopped, snuffed out her cigarette, took his arm, and continued walking.

"You're late," he said.

"A lot on my mind."

"It's been a long time. Don't I even get a kiss?"

"Lighten up, Christopher," she said with a smile and pecked him on the cheek.

Christopher's apartment was perfect in every detail, featuring muted colors, furniture with soft textures, unpolished stone sculptures everywhere, and a lighting scheme that allowed center stage prominence to the two perfectly behaved poodles standing like sentries beneath the arched entrance to the living room.

As Stan Getz's bossa nova filled the air, it was perhaps two hours into this—their periodic exchange of philosophical ideas always scribbled on three-by-five cards—Christopher leaned back, and grinned as he studied a card. "You trying to tell me something?"

Samara, heavily involved in sorting her cards, looked up. "Which one is that?"

Christopher slipped into his James Mason imitation and lifted his voice just loud enough for her to hear. "Can love ever be defined for those who have never loved?"

"Oh. That one. I thought it a good question, given all you've told me lately."

"Oh, please..." he replied, still in his Mason voice.

"You know, Christopher, your graduate class of elitists might have some interesting answers."

"Meaning?"

"Have you?"

"Have I what?" he asked, now in his normal voice.

"Loved?"

Christopher rose, gave one furtive glance and walked to the liquor cabinet. "Usual?"

Samara peeked at her watch. "It's a bit late. Don't you have somewhere to go?"

"Like I said, usual?"

She smiled. "So...have you ever loved?"

Christopher poured two fingers of cognac in each glass and walked back to the couch. "That's like asking a smoker if they've ever tried to quit. Everybody tries."

"To love?" she said.

"Of course." Christopher sat down and took a savory sip of the golden liquid as he tilted his head left and right reading the various 3x5's. "And you're right, my class could give a variety of answers, I'm sure." He chuckled. "Especially since we just finished a rather extensive study of *Lady Chatterley's Lover.*"

She lifted her glass. "To the professor who can teach the clothes off of love, but whose students think he's never *done it*."

He grinned and raised his glass. "Best kept secret on campus."

She leaned across and patted his thigh. "That's what I like about you most. You're painfully honest."

His eyes remained fixed on her. "Most gay men are."

"Honest?"

"Likable."

He gathered up the cards and put them in order. "You outdid yourself tonight. I like these ideas... like them a lot."

"A woman's perspective can be interesting."

Christopher laughed quietly, "My mother used to say something like that. Drove my father to drink."

"Because she was a bore?"

"Because *he* was a bore."

Samara sipped her cognac and savored the taste as she stared over at the crystal bottle on the bar. "Sharing your private stock now suggests I'm still welcome."

As he placed the cards in his three-by-five box, he said, "Thought you'd appreciate that. Just a small thank you for sharing work like this. By the way, that's *Timeless*, Hennessey's best you're drinking. Bought three bottles last year when Derek passed that tip on to me. Tell him my door is always open for another."

"Thanks, but he's rapidly weaning himself away from the stock market."

"That's a surprise. He's so good at it."

"He's finding out the museums and corporate world thinks he's good at his sculpturing as well."

"Pity."

She unexpectedly downed the balance of cognac and picked up her coat.

"Something I said?" he asked.

"No, something *I* need to say."

She kissed him on the cheek and moved toward the entrance. She opened the door, allowing a stream of hallway light to spill across his childlike expression of disappointment. "You're special, you know."

He nodded, "Yeah. My mother used to tell me that."

She moved into the hallway and towards the elevator. "I'm not your mother, though. Tell Jonathan hello for me, will you?"

He threw her a kiss and said, "I will. He's so obsessed with his health lately. Every night at the gym, you know. Hey..."

She turned back.

"My love to Derek. I mean, say hello. When will I see you again?"

"As always. Up to you, Christopher. You set the rules, remember?"

The elevator arrived. As she stepped in, she glanced back one more time. He stood in the doorway, his continued disappointment in her leaving reminding her of the first time he'd asked her to his apartment. She could only think his "rules" for her visits only exacerbated the confusion he continued to experience with his sexual identity. *Had it been a full six years he'd been with Jonathan?* It was times like this that separating friendship from therapy was the most difficult. She was, after all, a human being first, and a professional with a particular skill second. She valued his friendship.

***

The walk back was short. Two blocks east, one block north. She smiled at the twisting and turning of her high heels on the cobblestone. For a therapist and composer ten to twelve hours a day, that was exercise. She turned the final corner and a freshly washed sidewalk of the small rocks glistened with the reflection of the neon martini sign for "Stefano's Bar." She glanced up at the display, then at her watch. She paused a moment. *He's still driving. Might as well make the most of a good start.* She pushed the wooden door open.

Inside, she paused to take in the scene. The regulars were at their usual stations. Marge, the Johnny Rockets waitress, whose plastic surgery had left her somewhat of a "phantom of the opera," hovered beneath the shadows in the corner of the bar. She was doing her habitual humming of Irish folk music as she played with the parasol decorations of her six-a-night habit of rum and Coke. Jersey, the bartender, was polishing glasses, his ritual in-between serving customers. Known as "Mister Clean" among the regulars, if the glass didn't blind you with refractions, he considered it dirty. Sitting at another table was Cinch. Not a pleasant man, he was known in Soho as the guy who could get you anything you wanted—for a price. Stefano's was where his "counseling," as he called it, took place. Tonight, he had a visitor unfamiliar to Samara. She was pleading with Cinch.

"Christ, even my John treats me better than you," she said.

Cinch leaned back in his chair, laid out another card to his solitaire hand. "Tina, I'm not your daddy, your lover, or your John. This is strictly business. Cash and no carry. Cash."

With fright and hurt in her voice, Tina leaned across the table and said, "You promised I could give you half now and half next month."

Cinch looked up at her bruised face. "That was before you got yourself messed up. How you suppose to turn tricks with that face? What's due, is due."

Tina stood up wanting to find the words that might convince him, but instead, took a deep breath. "I'll be back. Gonna soak this face in some good salts, put on some ice... you'll see... good as new."

Cinch threw down another card. "What's due." Tina stared a moment.

"Jack," Samara fired at Jersey.

Jersey looked up from the glass he was polishing and with another glance through the spotless polish, grinned. "Feelin' chipper, are ya?"

Tina's shoulders dropped and a distraught turning of the head from left to right kept Samara's attention, "What does she drink?"

"Tina? Coffee," quipped Jersey.

"Coffee?"

"With cognac. 12-year-old stuff."

"Damn," said Samara with a grin. "Child's got taste."

Tina made her way to the far end of the bar and slumped on a stool.

"Scrub the Jack. Two of those," said Samara as she made her way toward Tina and sat on the adjoining stool. Tina glanced at Samara, then the empty row of bar stools. "I don't do bitches."

Samara stared back at the bar mirror reflecting Tina and the tears beginning to roll down her cheeks. "Neither do I," Samara whispered.

Jersey placed the drinks down. "Compliments of the lady," he said to Tina.

Tina wiped her tears and nodded to Samara. "Sorry. Thanks...whoever you are."

Samara could only imagine the turmoil in Tina's mind as she watched the steaming cup lifted to her battered lips. Tina closed her eyes and enjoyed one, two, three, four sips before saying, "Beats shit out of sex."

CHAPTER 4

I'm not much for surprises, especially in the dark, but, well, there I was in my birthday suit, covered only by a sheet, half aroused in my sleep—a habit Samara said was healthy for her ego as long as I didn't utter another woman's name—and suddenly the mattress edge caved. I half opened one eye to see Samara sitting beside me on the bed. What was sitting next to her gave a quick rise to my other eye.

"Whoa…" I said, taking in the battered face of Tina trying to smile back at me.

Pointing her limp finger at Samara, Tina calmly said, "She insisted."

Samara leaned down and kissed me. "We've had a few coffees and well…"

"Coffees?" I quipped, fanning the air.

Both women gave out with a quiet giggle.

I decided I'd better make the next move as my prone position wasn't doing my modesty any good. As I sat up, Samara grinned at my receding erection.

"Oh, what a pity," she whispered in my ear.

I wrapped myself in the sheet and walked across the loft to the closet.

"Sorry, Darling, but this was unexpected," said Samara, her playfulness gone, and the clinical voice emerging with every drunken step she made toward the pantry. "This is Tina, and I'm hoping we've still got those herbs I left here last year."

"Beg your pardon?" I bellowed as I pulled on some jeans and slipped into a t-shirt.

"The paste, you remember, the dark brown stuff I made with that Amazon root you thought smelled like death."

"Oh, *that* herb. Sealed tight in the fridge door."

Samara opened the door, took out the jar and began to knead the paste warm in her palm. "Tina had an accident and if this does half the job on her that it did on my ankle, she'll be hooked forever."

Tina shook her head and wandered over to the kitchen, carefully navigating her inebriated body as she went, looking about at all the sculpture. "I'm really sorry to disturb you like this."

I came out from the shadows feeling a bit more in control. "Oh, don't worry. Samara is unpredictable at times."

"At times?" said Samara.

"Always. Sorry." I wasn't sure what I should do next. I was just an onlooker without a clue. Samara had brought a stray cat home once, but my allergies got rid of that surprise. Next there was the homeless guy with one leg she had to help up the stairway. After blackening the tub, dulling the last blade in my razor, and accidentally dropping a butcher knife from his grungy ankle-length coat as he dressed, I thought it a good idea to give him a meal—at a distance—and send him on his way.

"Here," as Samara guided Tina to the couch, "this will just take a few minutes to rub in and…"

17

"Damn, Girl," Tina cringed. "That smells *worse* than death."

Samara gently rubbed it into her bruised face. "Think of it as compost for the soul."

Tina leaned back, "This ain't no shit I'm gonna get hooked on, is it? I just got out of rehab."

Samara grinned, and turned to me. "See, she's bringing a little humor into our lives."

Samara, the *Schweitzer of Soho*, made sure the treatment was administered with all the care and concern I'd grown to know and love about her. Yes, she was an eminent therapist, but first and always—as she reminded many times—she prided herself in being a homespun daughter of a jungle missionary. She had learned at an early age to never turn her back on the needy. Her father had taught her, no, ingrained into her; "Goodness is not learned. It is the natural order of things." Simple statement actually, but one that had become a profound part of Samara's persona.

Wanting to get a breath of fresher air, I wandered over to the freight elevator entrance where my new 800 lb gorilla was straddling the forklift until morning. I guessed that Tina would be here a while, at least until the paste had done its job and the stench had been washed away. They were laughing together now, obviously having found more in common than the urgency of the moment.

***

Samara's fingers raced across the keyboard in an arpeggio rivaling even her favorite, Chopin. She closed the lid of the concert grand with, "No. Another." She moved to the next piano amidst the sea of ebony "jewels," as she called them, that flooded the warehouse. After yet another arpeggio, she stood up. "No. Not quite." She eyed one in the corner with its lid closed. "That one?"

Elvis, the Baldwin factory's head salesman, dropped his chin and peered over the top of his tortoise shell glasses. "Used. You don't want a used…"

Samara walked directly to the outcast, lifted the lid, quickly examined the keyboard and sat. She touched the keys as a feather might, then breaking into a series of Khachaturian chords, she smiled as she completed the test with a flurry of chromatic runs from one end of the keyboard to the next. She abruptly stood, arched her shoulders, and gently closed the keyboard cover. "This one. I'll have it tuned myself."

As she passed Elvis who was quickly jotting down some sales notes, she smiled. "Never underestimate the power of 'used,' Elvis. The word is usually imbued with the residue of experience. Tomorrow?"

"Delivery tomorrow. Yes, Dr. Jennings."

18

"And could we make it in the morning? I have a very busy afternoon."

"Yes, Dr. Jennings."

"And, oh, could you have my old one taken from the loft and delivered to 703 Thompson afterwards, top floor?"

Elvis looked up. "You're not trading it in?"

"No. Old friends are hard to part with, you know. This one will keep me company when Derek's working; the old one at my studio will pacify me when we fight."

Elvis smiled politely. "Of course."

Riding back from the factory to Manhattan, her mind became restless. First, there was the familiar skyline crossing the 59th Street Bridge, always reminding her of all that New York had given her. Then the continual chatter of the cab driver kept a contrapuntal accompaniment to the unexpected melodic line and unresolved chord progression that had begun to grab her back at the warehouse and persisted through the heavy traffic. The atonal idea needed to be dealt with while it was fresh, but something even more persistent was causing the majority of her restlessness right now.

"Driver," she blurted, "Forget the Soho address, 680 Park Avenue."

The driver politely touched the brim of his Yankees baseball cap, "Yes, Ma'am."

As she sat back and pulled out her cell, she smiled at the Middle East driver with a pride that had been nurtured often with like observations since the 9/11 disaster. She was a believer that America was a country that gave a lot, but New York was a city that gave even more to immigrants. Her eyes looked at his I.D. on the dashboard. The Iranian name was common, but she could only think of how uncommon the people were, especially the hard working ones that helped keep the cabs going.

"I like your name, Hediyeh," she said as she dialed a number.

He smiled into the rear mirror, tipped his hat again, and said, "Thank you. It means gift. Thank you."

"Doctor?" said Samara into her cell. "How's your schedule?"

***

Dr. Ivan Seegar came out to the reception and greeted Samara with a kiss on each cheek. "Please, come in. Your call was a surprise."

"To me, as well," said Samara as she entered his plush and comfortable office. She couldn't help but smile at the watering can atop the windowsill where his usual pet hybrid-honeysuckle plants received obsessive care only Ivan could administer. "I hope I'm not fouling up your schedule."

"No, not at all. My three o'clock cancelled. We're fine. May I get you something, coffee, coke...?"

"No, thanks, Ivan. This will be brief." Samara plopped down on the couch reserved for patients, as Ivan took his usual place in an armchair.

What followed was a series of sighs and apologies, as she asked her dear friend and mentor from the graduate days at Boston University to handle a few of her newer patients so she might devote some extra hours to her music. Because he had been her professor at Boston U and later her professional mentor for years, she confidently outlined the nature of the selected patients, emphasizing that their problems were such that convincing them to work with Dr. Seegar's approach wouldn't be difficult. She told him that if there was anyone who could carry on a trusting patient relationship in her absence, it was he.

"Well, thank you for the kind words, Samara, but as you well know, switches like this can be complicated."

Samara leaned forward and implored him, "It will only be for a short while. Think of it as only temporary. I must do this for me. You understand, I know."

Ivan thought a moment, then, "You may or may not know, but my practice has changed a lot. What was my mainstay roster of patients in the past has become almost extinct now. For me, the growing trend of the last century has shifted from individual therapy for the man-on-the-street patient to a corporate world of confused executives getting their boards to financially support their neuroses."

"And?"

Ivan stepped to the edge of the couch and sat next to her. "Well..." he lifted her hand and fixed his gaze on her anxious eyes. "This corporate trend is creating some very big demands for me. I've even got one patient that keeps me on retainer six hours daily, so I'm not sure..."

Samara opened her eyes and grinned. "You're kidding me. Six hours. Two thousand a day just to have you on call?"

"Well, I gave him a break. Even I have a little conscience left. Eighteen hundred."

Samara sat up and gathered her thoughts amidst her muffled snickers. "God, Ivan, that's terrible."

"Making a pun, busy lady?" Ivan retorted.

She rose and gathered her purse and jacket. "Well, you might be the best, but you are terrible, Ivan." She walked toward the door, "But not *that* terrible, are you?"

Ivan nodded. "I better not be, is what you're saying, isn't it?"

She turned back to him. "You were always the master of reading subtext. Haven't lost your touch."

"And you can still persuade a truck driver to say his prayers at night."

"I take that as a *yes* on the patients?"

Ivan opened the door for her. "I'll try, okay? This corporate thing has kept me from working with private patients for over a year now."

She didn't move, keeping her eyes locked on his.

He sighed. "Call me tomorrow and we'll set up some time to go over these 'temporary' patients of yours." He kissed her on each cheek again.

"Thank you, Ivan," she said. "You're one of a kind."

"He says so too."

"He?" said Samara.

"My *eighteen hundred dollar* guy."

"Like to meet that one someday," she quipped.

"No... you wouldn't. Tomorrow. Say hi to Derek for me."

***

Aretha Ballard was like many of the Cape Cod residents—quiet, retired, a widow, and rich. What set her apart, however, was her background in astrophysics, and men. Many men. All dead. All making her richer with every burial. Six to be exact. "Who would have thought..." wrote one society journalist several years earlier, "...that Aretha Ballard could continue such a pace, at her age?" She kept that editorial framed in antique gold leaf hanging above her bed, right next to her Michelangelo sketches of "David"—a collection that Sotheby gave up for $303,000. It wasn't that this woman of extraordinary beauty and elegance was obsessed with men, but, well, six is a hard number for most anyone to keep up with. When the *Times* had interviewed the acclaimed scientist several years earlier about her seemingly inexhaustible talent for finding celestial answers no one else could even come close to matching, she sloughed it off as luck and her propensity for staying up all night staring at the heavens—"with a little lovin' thrown in. I've always adored *good* men." That quote was immortalized in an audacious engraving on a King Louis XIV hand mirror given her by the fourth husband—also a Sotheby acquisition for a paltry $60,000.

Aretha now spent retirement walking her beachfront property, gathering rocks and driftwood, and occasionally toiling in the garage with glue and wire to pacify her favorite hobby, mobiles. Never truly drifting into oblivion, as so many other beach retirees chose to do, Aretha kept the neighbors of Truro looking forward to her bi-monthly

21

invitation to a lavish *sand dune* dinner party. The only requirement was an appreciation for the stars and her Ceylon root tea, the kind that rewarded the mind with small *kaleidoscopic* pleasures. Yes, this demure woman of the century did like her specialty tea, almost as well as her men. A close third was her monthly trip to New York City and her expensive habit of shopping the Soho galleries for yet another find, something to hang on her crowded walls, or place on a shelf or pedestal.

As she sat at her desk, preparing for the next day's trip into Manhattan, she opened the top drawer to sort the gallery mailings announcing new acquisitions. She paused as her eye once again caught the corner of the purple envelope with childish hand-drawn yellow daisies around the edges. It had been a year since the garish envelope had arrived in the mail, and it had also been a year since she opened and read it, just once. It still needed to be answered, but not today.

***

Earlier, having parked my rock and returned the forklift, I now eagerly watched as the bank teller counted out fifteen one hundred dollar bills. Given my recent good fortune, it wasn't a lot to splurge, and it was the least I could do to reward Samara and myself for the wait we had endured. The installation had entertained thousands over the past fourteen months and MOCA was more than pleased with the controversy it had created. Yes, *Dust to Dust*, had turned out to be more of a surprise to me than to the public. Three years earlier, I had started the work several times and left it several times. Finally, when I'd solved the physics involved, I gave it my nine-month challenge. Like all the others, the magical period of time served me well, never dreaming it would have the emotional impact it had on the public and European critics. Enough so, that it was now sailing across the Atlantic on its way to Amsterdam's National Museum of Modern Art to become part of its permanent collection. One reviewer had called it "...evolution through the *Looking Glass*..." Another had referred to it as "...the trans-neuter Genesis." For me, it was the collision of contemporary man into granite, half way emerging out the other side as rusty-iron, skeletal forms depicting prehistoric birds of prey.

I took a cab to 57th street and walked the sidewalks where platinum and gold plastic ruled. After many windows, my eye caught sight of a "Samara" look. I walked into the boutique with its two story ceilings and crystal chandeliers. The mannered wisp-of-a-man glided to my side, gushing with La Cage Aux Folles drama. "May we be of service to you, sir?"

I pointed. "That. How much is that?"

"*That*, sir?" he asked.

Again, I pointed, "The scarf."

The salesman looked at my granite scarred hands, my dusty jeans and sweatshirt with "Tanglewood – 2001" embroidered across the chest and said with a bit of sarcasm, "Thirteen-hundred."

"Perfect," I replied. "Gift wrap it with a yellow ribbon, please." He flashed his smile once again, reached and lifted the scarf from the angel-like mannequin, and then sashayed to the cash register. "I'm sorry, but we don't have yellow ribbon. How about silver?"

"No," I replied. "Yellow. You box it and I'll be right back."

I hurried out the door and scurried up the street to the small gift shop where I thought I could probably con a piece of yellow ribbon. As hoped, my sad story worked and the clerk cut the strip of ribbon, insisting there was no charge. Running out the door, the yard of yellow ribbon streaming behind me, I shouted back, "You're an angel."

"Whatever," she laughed, turning back to her dreary counter job. "Whatever."

I rushed to my clerk and handed him the ribbon. "Curls. Give it some curls. You know, on top."

"Curls. On top, of course," he muttered. He wasn't going to rush, either. He pulled the scissors across the ribbon over and over until I raised my hand. "My," he said. "She *does* like her curls, doesn't she?"

"It's actually a guy thing."

"Oh, lovely," he purred.

As I walked with the shopping bag containing my *celebratory gift*, I couldn't help but think back at the times years ago when I'd wanted someone to care enough to just "splurge." You know, indulge in some kind of giving that one knows will please another, and give them a moment of self-worth. Simple. Unexpected. Silly, maybe, but I missed that in my youth.

By the time I got off the subway at Spring Street, it was dark, but not too late, as I knew Monday nights were always long ones for Samara. For some reason, a number of patients preferred Mondays over any other day to wade through their hell with her. Maybe it was the weekend weight on the lonely. Only Samara knew, but, she always was to bed early on Sunday nights in preparation for the long and exhaustive Monday.

I rounded the corner of Greene Street. One of the wide-spaced street lamps beamed its circular pattern across the sidewalk, spilling into an alcove, where I was shocked to see two young guys beating the hell out of someone. I'd never experienced this kind of a moment. Inside of one or two seconds, my body surged with anger, indecision, and fear. Then I snapped. I remember running the fifty or sixty feet and lunging on top of the two attackers, my lungs bursting with a primal cry to destroy or be destroyed. I flailed with my arms, sending my shopping bag flying to the side. With my punching and kicking, coupled with my guttural demands to stop, the assailants only fought back for a few moments, then took off as if they had been vanquished by a creature from Hell. I tried to catch my breath as I gazed at the victim bleeding heavily from the head. She lay motionless beside her ripped-open purse. The contents were scattered across the sidewalk; and her diamond inlayed glasses, suggesting a lady of means, were smashed. More blood streamed from her half-severed right index finger, suggesting perhaps moments before a ring had been ripped off.

"It's okay. It's okay now," I assured her. Her elderly eyes were panic-stricken, her mouth agape with disbelief. Her shock merged with mine and I instinctively ripped open the yellow-ribboned box and hurriedly wrapped her bleeding hand.

I sat in the waiting room of the ER and stared at the TV. Amidst the smells of street people, the cries of children and groans of stressed out mothers, I had to endure another night of Reality Shows, the genre of TV that had over the past few years become 60% of all programming. There on the screen was the latest hit… a dwarf bachelor going through the machinations of deciding which of the little ladies he was going to choose. It was the million dollar, "Little People are Real People Too," show. Others sitting around me were getting off on the freak show, but I could only stare into the space the screen occupied, thinking of the split second decision that had left me close to paralyzed, emotionally.

The doctor walked up and sat down, eyeing the two bandages on my forehead and cheek. "You okay?"

I turned to him, took a breath, and said, "Yeah… yeah, I'm okay," knowing full well, I was not.

"You saved that woman's life tonight. May I tell her your name?"

"That's not necessary," I muttered. I stood up, and trying to cover my still shattered nerves, looked down the hall to my right, my left, then back to the doctor. "Okay to leave now? She's okay, right?"

24

"We're trying to contact her daughter. I think things will be okay now."

He handed me a blue plastic bag. "She thought this might be yours."

I opened the bag. The silk scarf was a blood-drenched gesture of what might have brought a few moments of joy for Samara, but now was a reminder of how fragile life could be.

I opened the door to the loft and trudged in, feeling the exhaustion of the night weighing me down like concrete. I looked around at the usual familiar comfort my space gave me. The moonlight spilled across the floor meeting up with the faint illumination of a candle at the far end of the 3000 sq. ft loft. Then the quiet sounds of a piano gilded the silence. It was the sound of a sonata only one person could play. I walked to the far side to see Samara seated at the new piano with her head bowed, and shoulders hunched as her fingers embraced the keys. Her body was draped with a silk caftan she knew I especially appreciated. As she finished, she lifted her head and turned to me. An ethereal smile vanished. "My God, Derek. What happened?"

"That was beautiful. The piano is... perfect." That's when I guess I let my exhaustion take over, because it wasn't until the next morning that I remembered anything.

Vivid? Yes. That's how it felt. Maybe it was shock that had taken over yesterday, but today, all I could see when I opened my eyes was rock. Lots of rock. That was my life, except when it wasn't. Like now. I squeezed my eyes shut. My mind filled with the woman's blood beginning to soak up the kerchief—the sidewalk turning crimson—her mouth agape with horror.   That's how the memory flooded my awakening; as I once again opened my eyes and took in the quiet, save for the pigeons swooning one another on the window ledge. I turned over, giving rise to a headache that was just waiting for me to stir. I faced a folded piece of paper. I smiled to myself, re-opening my cracked lip, as I read: "You were exhausted. I bathed your hands and face as best I could without waking you. Hope you slept well. Will see you tonight. I love you. PS – A messenger delivered an envelope early this morning. On the night table."

I glanced to my left to see the courier service envelope was addressed to *Mister Derek P. Turrel.* I never used my initial except for formal and legal references. I ripped it open wondering if it was good or bad news—the kind of moment I hate most.

***

Aretha adjusted her chair to the sun peeking between buildings onto the sidewalk cafe. "Why meet me here? Because it's only a block from your address and I didn't want to put you out."

"But, your hand," said Derek.

"Hey, once they sewed it up, what was there to do? I hate hospitals. One day was plenty. Plus, I needed to say thank you properly, without delay. So, enough questions."

I couldn't help but smile as she waved her bandaged hand at me. "They told me once this healed, they could do wonders with plastic surgery nowadays. Me with plastic surgery. Scars are always good conversation pieces anyway. You know what I told them?" she asked mockingly.

"About?"

"Suggesting plastic surgery."

"Oh, that. No," I replied.

Aretha shyly smiled, "Can't repeat it."

"That bad, huh?"

She nodded, "Oh, yeah. That quote ever get back to Truro, I'd be banned from O'Laughlin's."

"Who's O'Laughlin?" I asked.

"The village pub. Everybody hangs out there, you know, to socialize. I'm considered 'Dame Aretha' due to my reserved ways, you know. I've got a reputation."

"Okay."

Aretha pushed her copy of *The New York Times* aside and shot a gaze into my eyes that would have frozen Satan himself. "So, why?"

"Why what?"

"You could have gotten yourself killed."

I tossed it away with, "And you could have lost more than some blood."

She didn't alter her stare. "No, no. Don't evade. Why?"

I didn't know what to say because I didn't really know myself.

"C'mon. Why?" she repeated, this time with a bit more of the Irish in her.

"Because you were there?" I smiled.

Again, she held her fix on my eyes. I wasn't going to get out of this. "Don't throw that Everest crap on me," she now whispered. "Hillary stared death in the face every day he was on a mountain. You just happened along, right?"

"Yeah."

"Yeah." She leaned back and looked to the side. "That's how my husbands came into my life too."

"Beg your pardon."

"Happening along. The Universe doesn't just sit up there with nothing to do, you know."

"Okay," I said. My mind starting feeling like a carnival Dodge-'Em car, bouncing from one rail to another.

"I'm way too old for you, but were you a bit grayer..." She took my hand and turned it over, as if she were about ready to read my palm. "The Universe provides, and I've always been provided for, even if they didn't last very long." She squinted. "Ever hear of Jergens?"

I diplomatically pulled my hand away and flashed the palms of both at her. "I'm a sculptor. Rock. Granite. Rough stuff. So, bad hands."

She folded her arms and took another look at me. "Good hands. Knocked hell out of those little buggers. Derek Turrel. Haven't I heard that name before?"

I shrugged.

"Starving?"

"Starving?"

"You a starving artist?"

I didn't quite know how to answer. She was both charming and intimidating as hell; a very persuasive personality. I flashed on how interesting such a person would be to Samara.

"Well... I've had some tough days in the past."

"Just days?" she quipped.

"Ms. Ballard, the truth is..."

"Just call me Aretha, for God sake. You saved my life."

"Aretha. Those days are behind me now. I'm doing okay. Making a decent living."

"Mistress?"

"Sorry," I asked.

"You're not married. That's obvious. Muse. You have a Muse?"

I was feeling stripped of all my defenses. I was without retort. What was this woman about? "I have a lady friend."

She softened and drew me in even further. "I would hope so. Your kind dies young without a woman. What's her name?"

"Samara," I answered.

"Samara. Nice name. Uncommon like mine."

All I could do was nod.

She stood up, took my hand. "Come. Take a walk with an old dame?"

I hesitantly obliged and as we walked away from the table. She took my arm like, well, like a close friend would take a guy's arm.

"Tell me about your work," she said softly. "I've been known to appreciate art from time to time. You've been written up, haven't you? I know that name from somewhere."

CHAPTER 5

"Sounds to me like my Sir Galahad has got himself an attractive but strange friend," shouted Samara. She leaned across the keyboard and penned in the notes her left hand played across the octaves.

On the other side of the loft, surrounded by hanging painter-tarps, I slowly circled the heavily veined granite, marking various cut points with bar-soap that would begin my new obsession. "Not 'strange'," I bellowed back across the fifty feet separating us. "Just a bit different. That walk of ours loosened her up enough to reveal a lot about her seventy years."

"And *your* reveal? Does she know you're a compulsive obsessive with latent insecurities bordering…"

"Okay, Samara. I got it. We'll just let her be a… potential patron. Just that? Okay? Seventy, Samara. She's seventy!"

Samara put down her pen and played through the new sixteen bars of her concerto.

I had to stop, for the sounds, even to me, were so different from her other work that I had to glance around the hanging tarp just to be sure she was in fact playing. *Samara was accomplished. Samara was brilliant. Why does a soul like this spend so much time having her energies drained by the sick, the needy*, the *mess* of the world?

As I continued my own work, reverie took me where first we met at the library. Nothing happens by accident. I was surprised as I pounded the Evian machine, trying to persuade the four quarters to deliver a bottle of water; a hand reached over my shoulder and gently pushed the "return" button, releasing the quarters.

In contrast to my clenched fist, was a delicate, long-fingered visage that carried the fragrance of Boucheron—a perfume I was guilty of stalking from time to time at the finer department store fragrance counters, just for the hit. I flashed on an old lover, who also carried the scent about her wherever she went. It had only been *after* our painful breakup that I realized what power the sense of smell had over me. It was an astonishing realization. I spent hours at the public library, researching the sense of smell and its influence on behavior. I had always been aware my moods were affected more by sounds and smells than from my sight, touch and taste sensations; but, there was something so unique about the combination of Boucheron and Charlotte, that for months following the break-up, I had awakened from dreams of rejection with her image and fragrance in the room.

"Your quarters? In the return?" she said.

The invitation to *wake up* jostled me back. I turned to the lady belonging to the alluring hand.

"Thank you." I barely had time to take in my first impression of what was at once austere beauty and quiet assertiveness, when she was on her way. "Saw you needed some help. Have a nice day."

She went to the elevator and proceeded down. I watched the dial and when it stopped on the floor below me, I took the stairway and made it to the floor in time to see her sit back down at her study table. Since she was immediately into reading and making notes, she didn't notice me circle and peer through the stacks. On second glance, I saw she was several years my senior. She was dressed somewhat conservatively, professional, but with the aura of Boucheron, she was all that and something else. It was the *something else* that made me hesitate. I didn't know why I needed to utter it again, but after a few moments, I ambled over, sat down across from her, and leaned in.

"I just wanted to thank you again," I stammered, realizing I was being shy and hesitant—definitely, not my norm.

She finished her notes. Then with a polite, but dismissive smile said, "Duly noted."

All of a sudden, I wanted to admit I had an anger management problem and that the fist pounding on the machine was just that, but then I thought better. *Why would she want to hear that, and why was I so compelled to carry on any further?*

"What I really wanted to say was…"

She interrupted without taking her eyes from the book or slowing her note taking. "I'm really not your type."

I sat there without any sense of retort. *You've been stripped naked right in the middle of the fucking library, my ego proclaimed loudly.* Even feeling vulnerable, I had to continue. "It was really just the Boucheron. I had to tell you."

She paused, looked up and smiled. "Had to tell me what?"

"Not many wear it," I whispered, thinking a soft approach would not antagonize.

"Not many can afford it."

"Right. Well…" I fidgeted and started to stand up.

"How long ago did you break up?" she quipped.

I stopped. *Vulnerable* really seemed inadequate for the moment. I was frozen in my tracks, and *naked* wasn't the word for it, either. *Where did all this come from? I don't know her. She knows nothing of me.* I leaned back down. "Beg your pardon?" I eked out.

"Just that. Was it yesterday, or are you one to carry a torch?"

I didn't speak. I didn't know what to say. There I was half bent over in a frozen gesture, unable to move.

Her change of pace—that ability to flip a switch and *be* whatever was needed for the moment—was showing itself for the first time. "C'mon now," she said with an inviting smile. "You shouldn't be so surprised. You're easy to read." She leaned forward. "Curse of the profession."

"Profession?" I said.

"I deal with behavior, and yours is interesting. So, you got my attention. Please. Sit down before you get a cramp."

I slid back into the chair, muttering, "You're a shrink?"

"Don't you find that word demeaning? Shrinking is so *not* what it should be about. I prefer to expand consciousness, not analyze and pack it up neatly, or *shrink-wrap* it, so to speak. So, how long?"

"How long?" I mumbled.

"Your being alone? Wandering the streets, your senses on alert, your spirits pulverized, your needs unfulfilled."

There was something so frightening about the moment that I could only stare and hesitate.

After three double-espressos and some decadent chocolate mousse cups, I had garnered at least six hundred dollars worth of shrink time from her. Samara had never been to Zano's Coffee Bar, so by the time we were ready to leave, she was buzzed beyond the norm, which happened to most everyone on their first visit to the only truly Italian run, Italian built, Italian-roasted-espresso-in-a-cup in all of Soho.

"You've got enough baggage for an army, Derek."

"That bad, eh?"

"For me, the professional, that's good."

"And?" I said somewhat flirtatiously.

Samara turned away. As she seemed to bring herself back into the moment, I could see there was another side to this youthful lady who had taken the past three hours out of her regimented schedule and listened to the problems that a simple whiff of perfume had resurrected.

"For me the woman, not so good." She rose and started towards the door.

"I don't understand," I said as I threw down a twenty and caught up to her.

She took my arm and cradled it as we stepped onto the sidewalk. "Don't try to understand everything, Derek. Just let it be what it is until it isn't, okay?"

"Huh?"

"Like the Boucheron," she said.

"The Boucheron," I repeated, as if I knew where her head was.

"Yes. Like the Boucheron," she repeated in a hushed, voice...a tone I would find out was her professional trademark and a quality that inspired confidence in her from not only men, but women, transvestites and everything in-between.

As Samara finished the playing of her last notations, I stared at the rock's fissures, and allowed the veins of my own memory to recede. I lifted the soap and made a final mark.

Samara unexpectedly peeked through the hanging tarps. "You up for a Zano?" she whispered in her tired, but sensual voice.

I smiled. "Put on some Boucheron?"

"Oh. Thinking those thoughts, were we?"

***

In a less desirable part of Manhattan, Tina stood in a phone booth holding a phone in one ear and peering closely at the glass reflection of her once-battered face, touched the all-but-miraculous healing that had taken place. "Cindy, gonna blow Cinch away when he sees this, ya know? Get the money arrangement taken care of, and then it's you and me, sweet cheeks... Of course it's a miracle... Stink? My God, chica. I told you, you've never smelled that kind of shit. But, gotta say, them jungle babies know how to zing-a-bam-boom when it comes to herbs and root shit for healing, you know?" She switched ears and examined the other cheek. "So... What you sayin', Cindy? What? Now that's nasty. Wouldn't put that shit anywhere near my bootylicious, or thereabouts. What's the matter with you, girlfriend? Well, you wanna try that on one of *your* problems, go ahead. I'll get you some... Sure. We're tight. I let her think she's in control, you know. Makes her happy. So... tonight."

Click.

***

Flying back to Truro, Aretha caught herself looking at her bandaged hand over and over again. The doctors said two months of physical therapy, and then she was to come back for a checkup. She still didn't like the idea of plastic surgery, but a scarred finger the rest of her life was daunting as well. Her husbands had always commented on her beautiful hands. *I'm so damn vain*, she thought.

***

A week passed and Aretha was weaning herself off the painkillers and settling down to the task of physical therapy and decision-making. She sat at her desk overlooking the shore and finished a part of the prescribed therapy: rubber-ball squeezing. Painful as it was, she could sense progress, and patience not being one of her virtues, she was adding an extra minute of hell each day.

She placed the ball back in the drawer and paused. The infamous purple and yellow envelope that had arrived that cloudy day a year earlier was once again asking to be pulled out of the drawer. *When is enough enough?* She couldn't come to the *why* of *now*, but she was catching herself questioning her stubborn nature— that shirking responsibility and avoiding decisions was just not her. She lifted the envelope and removed the matching purple and yellow-daisy trimmed letter. Remembering her first reading, she hoped she was now ready to face it all.

Dear Mommy,
I want to come home. I am well now. The doctors don't think so, but I know. You would too, if you'd visit and take a good look at me.
Mother, the white coats, the pastel food, the striped windows (the orderlies prefer we call them "stripes") and those fucking white ducks below my window forever quacking, well, enough to drive anyone mad, let alone someone as fragile as me.
So, Mommy, I want to come home.
Please bring me home.
I love you. I miss Daddy too, but you're all I've got now.

Love,
Linda

Tears were rare for Aretha, but on occasion, she was known to shed a few—mostly at funerals—mostly her husbands' funerals. This was different. These were the embarrassing kind, the sincere ones you experience when you're a child and your parent has told you to stop crying, which only brings on even bigger tears. She attributed the raw feelings to the assault. Knowledgeable of the psychology behind attachments sometimes made with heroes and *life-savers*, she still couldn't understand the strange bond she had with Derek after just one short meeting. But, these were honest times for her, and with no one around; no doctors to tell her how to think; no husbands to tell her how to be; and no child to tell her how bad a mother she had been; she was reduced to the one problem that she kept running away from—being alone.

Holding the letter in her injured hand, she picked up the phone with the other and punched out the Rhode Island number.

"Doctor Reagan?" she asked.

"Yes," came the reply.

"This is Aretha Ballard. Is my daughter well?"

"Mrs. Ballard, what a pleasant surprise."

"Oh, please, Doctor. You know I'm a despicable mother who hasn't visited her daughter in two years. Is she okay to come home?"

"Come home?"

"Come home," Aretha repeated.

"It's not that easy, Mrs. Ballard."

"Just a simple yes or no."

"Mrs. Ballard…"

"Yes or no?"

"No."

"Would another gift of six figures help her condition?"

Dr. Reagan, who sat in his cramped office, harried by the pressures of voluminous reports surrounding him, adjusted the phone and paused.

"Mrs. Ballard, we appreciate your generous contributions, we really do, but your daughter's health is not something that can be bought."

"She says she's well. She wrote me a year ago and said she was well. Are you telling me she's worse today?"

"Over the past year we've seen some improvement."

"Improvement. What does that mean?"

"Well, improvement can sometimes go in spurts and then…"

"And then what?"

"Mrs. Ballard, your daughter has been in solitary again. She…"

"Solitary? She wrote me, you know. You let your patients in solitary write home? With pens and pencils that are weapons? So, do you?"

"She was only confined for the past week. Took an orderly down with a chair. Fifteen stitches."

"Is she alright?"

"Yes. She is physically fine."

"Don't play adjective riddles with me, okay? You like white or red?

"Beg your pardon?"

"You and your wife… white or red wine?"

"Mrs. Ballard I don't understand…"

"What you don't understand, Dr. Reagan, is that I am a woman of determination when I set my mind. My head's been in mothballs for a year, but..."

"Mrs. Ballard..."

"Let me finish Doctor. If she's well, she's coming home. If she's still a basket case, she's staying. So, to determine *that* you're going to have me to dinner for a review kind of chat, and I'm bringing the libations. Now that's easy to understand, right?"

Driving the short distance to Rhode Island allowed Aretha to review her past, when despair had threatened her life, usually with husbands about ready to go. Glancing upwards out the windshield, the previous night's moon still maintained a gray imprint for her. *If only I were as comfortable with people as I've been with the cosmos.* Up through the cloudless sky, the gray of the moon, past several galaxies and beyond, she rested her thoughts somewhere in the friendly stars of her favorite part of the universe. This was that place *on the other side* where a movie she had viewed several years earlier impressed her with enough clarity and semblance of truth that she wrote the producers and offered her consulting services free on any future project of that nature. She had received a glowing thank you letter back, but thus far, no "catch the next plane to Hollywood," message.

From behind, the blare of a horn got quick response from her foot, and she floored the 2002 Volvo, moving it closer to the shoulder lane where she could still look up occasionally at the pale moon.

It was dark when she arrived at Dr. Reagan's seaside home. Exiting the car, she noticed a full moon again. She smiled. *Wish me luck, Arnold. She's your blood too.*

***

Chung Young's was not only conveniently located close by the St. Regis, but it was also one of Tina's favorite *pre-trick* dining indulgences. Bathing in the light of a Chinese lantern, Tina giggled as she loosened her fancy wrapped fortune cookie *omen*. "Prosperity comes to those who least desire it," she said, her words sliding out a bit sideways, the result of two emptied snifters.

"Guess that leaves me out," said Cindy, a tall, mixed Latin and African American woman nursing a line of Jack-shots, "'cause I desire a *lot* of that prosperity shit."

"Now, now, Cindy. You'll upset the gods with that kind of talk." As she finished off her remaining snifter of cognac, Tina turned on her stool and gazed over at the silk suits and their couture-draped women sitting at the lacquered, Chinese-red tables. "How come them and not me?"

"Come again?" asked Cindy.

"Look at that display. Ain't that the ugliest group of rich no-good-lovin' moochers you've seen in a long time?"

"You talkin' 'bout the guys or the women?"

"Those aren't women. They're wrigglin', squirmin' little leeches, suckin' some more blood off those over-worked executives, who wouldn't know good lovin' if it bit'm on the balls."

Cindy gave a glance at Tina. "Lord girl, you all wound up tonight, aren't ya?"

Tina nodded and drew some air through her teeth. "We need to move up to more of that kind of money, you know?"

Cindy looked at her watch. "Well, we might snap-to. It ain't gonna cross the street to find us."

As they crossed from the Chinese restaurant to the St. Regis, Tina studied Cindy's walk.

"You got some sticks on you, chica. Been workin' out?"

"Stairmaster and every other night with *Boom-Boom.*"

"Oh, my God," said Tina with a grin. "He still makin' you do that spin?"

"Hey, he might be a midget, but he likes what he likes. Brings that platter with him every week; puts his fifty-one pounds on top while I do the back-on-the-bed-legs-a-spinnin-the-platter-routine, just like the last two years."

"He ever lose it?"

"You mean upchuck? Nope. Dizzy is what turns him on. What can I say? He climbs down off that thing—I ain't got nothin' left in my legs—and he just does it with that *wonder-stick* of his. $200-a-spin. I just have to call it a night after that."

Tina took another look as they stepped up on the curb. "Good sticks, girl. Need to find me a spinner. Ask him if he's got a friend."

Cindy laughed as they pushed through into the St. Regis, "Trust me. Stairmaster is less work."

The tray of empty glasses was lifted and a fresh round placed on the marble coffee table. Joseph, a paunchy diamond salesman, slipped a twenty into the waitress's hand as she left. As he passed the drinks around, he proudly whispered, "Know how to make a drink here, don't they girls?"

Cindy and Tina nodded and switched their bodies into a new provocative pose.

"What do you think, Chad? Good drinks?"

Chad, a thin accountant type with coke bottle specs and a nasty case of psoriasis, nodded as well.

"C'mon, you guys. It's party time," said Joseph as he slugged down his tequila, then swigged a gulp of beer.

Chad sipped his glass of wine and asked Cindy about her tax base, as she twisted some small hairs on the back of his neck, every so often, giving them a little yank.

Joseph leaned across and got up-close-and-personal with Tina. "You are one pretty thing, you know?"

"Joseph, you're a nice guy. Okay? But I really prefer to drink in a room where we can talk or do whatever without the noise of a bar."

Joseph looked at his watch. "But the night is still young, little one. Let's have a couple more and then..."

Tina leaned in and started to fondle his ear, then pinched it ever so persuasively. "Tell you what, Joseph," she whispered in his ear, "time is money. You understand that. You've been drinkin' here at this table for sixty-eight minutes now. That's time enough for you to get off three or four times and for me to make a living. So..." Tina let go of his ear, dipped into her handbag and pulled out a hundred-dollar bill. "... I'll buy the drinks here. You have dinner sent up to the room with some whatever-to-drink for you, Courvoisier twelve-year for me, bottle of Jack for Cindy, and some more house wine for your reptilian friend and we'll do some real 'party time.' Okay?"

Joseph blinked twice as he rubbed his ear, and came to his senses. He took the hundred-dollar bill and pushed it back into Tina's purse. "I like you, Tina." He rolled his own wad out and slapped down two-hundred on the table. "I like you a lot." He stood and put out his arm. Tina rose with a reserved grin and took his invitation, hugging it close to her bosom. "Come Cindy, Chad. What kind of party atmosphere do you like, ladies?"

"Suites," said Cindy.

"Presidential suites," said Tina with a giggle.

Chad grinned as Joseph winked at him. "I like both you girls... a lot." Pointing to the black jewelry case beside Chad's chair, he said, "Chad? Visit the front desk with that case and make sure you put it in the vault yourself."

Chad nodded, stood, lifted the case and turned to Cindy. "I'll be up in a minute, miss."

Cindy smiled, "Up where? We don't even know what room yet."

"Our other friend, Mr. Sudly, " chimed in Joseph with a grin, "is already in the Presidential Suite,".

Cindy turned to Tina, "Whoa, a five-some."

"My secretary is joining in a bit later, too," said Joseph with another satisfied grin.

Tina nodded. "What, no donkey?"

Joseph burst out laughing. "You kidder, you."

Chapter 6

It was an unusually warm night for March in Manhattan. After a tough, but short day of *worse* than worse patients, Samara felt drained and decided to take the bus uptown to the Atkinson where she was to meet Derek to see a revival of "Jesus Christ Super Star." It was 5 p.m. as she boarded the 5th Ave bus and sat down next to an itinerant sleeping against the window. He wore a threadbare tweed jacket and equally worn pants. She smiled at how clean his attire was. He snored softly while maintaining a strong grip on the ratty backpack—also surprisingly clean—straddled between his legs.

Samara looked up at the advertisement along the top of the bus for "Jesus Christ Super Star." The much-publicized revival was a huge success. Some said it was due to the six month run of Gibson's film "The Passion" that had stimulated some kind of *Jesus consciousness* in a lot of people. She hadn't seen the film, but was an old fan of "Super Star" and had bought tickets a month before it opened.

She once again gazed at the man sitting next to her. He wasn't that scruffy. He didn't smell. That was a good sign. Some semblance of self-esteem was still left in him. The strong intelligent lines in his face made her wonder what his life had been like to bring him to this. *What made me take this bus today? I haven't taken a bus in ten years.*

As she watched the shops of lower Manhattan pass by, she remembered when it had been the neighborhood of her entire family. In the fifties, she had watched as one relative after another moved from the lower neighborhoods to the upper west side. All but Uncle Jerald and Aunt Golda. With their butcher shop, they were in the center of Gramercy Park. Everyone in the tenth and eleventh street blocks made Jerald's Meats a weekly, if not daily, stop. It was even rumored that Uncle Jerald's butcher shop was the inspiration for Albee's famous monologue reference to a butcher shop in *Zoo Story*, where the meat to be poisoned was bought.

More shops were passed, shops Samara had frequented often as a child running errands for Uncle Jerald or Aunt Golda. The dry cleaners, apothecary, and the tailor were still there. Even the corner candy store still stood, although it was shrunk to a closet size to make room for the indoor newsstand. Memories.

Her eye caught the man again as he stirred, squinted, lifted some worn glasses to his eyes, squinted again at the street sign and dropped back into his cat nap. As she watched him, his eyes slowly opened, never moving from their glazed-like fix on the seat in front of him. "Why are you staring at me?" he muttered in a voice consistent with many years of tobacco use.

"I'm sorry," she said. "I didn't realize I was. I'm sorry."

He glanced over at her. It was easy to understand why he squinted again, raised his glasses, took a closer look at her, then lowered his glasses and fixed his eyes once again on the back of the seat. "People like you don't sit next to bums."

"I don't think you're a bum. Are you?"

"No. Of course not. I'm just on a longer journey than I was prepared for."

"That's an interesting way of putting it."

"What, an intellectual spin on a *failure?*" he exclaimed.

"Even better."

"Even better what?"

"Even a better way to put it. You obviously have an active mind and some interesting things to say."

He lifted himself up to a more attentive position. After squeezing some Visene into each eye, he took a small swig from a miniature plastic bottle of SCOPE. "So, you want to talk?"

Samara smiled. "I thought we were."

He cleared his throat. "No, I mean really talk."

Samara glanced out the window. "Good for me 'til we hit 42nd."

He reached inside his sweater and pulled out a ratty plastic ID pouch, the kind the press used to go wherever they go. He flashed it at her. "Sixty one, I was on top."

She looked closer and could see the resemblance of the picture to his present state, even though a beard and receding hairline made it a challenge.

"Reporter, eh," Samara said.

"*Journalist. Journalist* when it meant something." He stashed the ID back beneath his sweater. "No more. 'Reporter' is even overstating it today. Wannabe show biz aspirants at best."

Samara grinned. "Especially the weathermen."

"Especially those guys." He laughed quietly.

"So, what did you write about?"

He extended his hand. "I'm Theodore Donnaly."

She looked at the gentle fingers.

"They're clean. Just washed before I got on the bus."

She shook his hand. "I wasn't afraid of that. Just noticed how groomed your nails were."

"Yeah, well, got lot of time on my hands nowadays. Better than drinkin' away the boredom."

"You didn't tell me what you wrote about," she repeated.

"Art. Music and art."

"Really?"

"Had a column that was syndicated to forty-three newspapers. Even got a few shots with the New Yorker once. I said "no" when I should have said "yes" for a certain performance, though, and that finished my shots with the New Yorker. Big lesson, that was."

"So, what kind of music did you cover?"

He turned now, obviously excited. "You name it, I wrote about it. Just couldn't handle Country/Western though. Jazz. Carnegie Concerts. Clubs, Philharmonic, Bernstein. Gave them all their due. Mostly good, too. I was respected. Even got a card from the Beatles once after they read a review I wrote of Sergeant Pepper. You like that kind of music?"

"I'm a fan of most everything too, all except..."

"Lemme guess... Country/Western."

They exchanged a chuckle.

His eyes wandered up to the advertisement for "Jesus Christ Super Star." "I even reviewed that when it opened originally."

"Really?" Samara asked.

"That was one hellacious and audacious piece of work. Yes it was. Changed my life at the time."

"Mmm," Samara mused.

"Got me thinkin', you know. More to bein' alive than what we think. I miss havin' moments like that, you know. The little epiphanies. Don't need any big colossal ones, just some little ones. Yeah. Little ones." He smiled. "Art is an endangered species now, though."

"Lost your faith in artists?"

"Lost my denial of the truth. It's them out there that lost their faith in artists. The system doesn't want art. It can control everybody much better promoting mediocrity."

Samara nodded. "Mmm."

***

Derek looked about for Samara as he handed his ticket to the doorman of the Atkinson. Reaching his seat, he again looked around as the usher handed him a Playbill. He sat down and began shuffling through the pages. Theodore sat down next to him. Derek did a double take, then after a moment or two he said, "I think you're in the wrong seat, sir."

"Oh," Theodore said, "You must be Derek. Your lady was kind enough to... oh and she asked me to give you this." He handed

39

Derek a note. "Dear Derek, Be nice. I'll explain later. Meet me at Mickey's afterward. Love you, S."

Theodore flashed his dated ID at Derek and extended his hand. "Theodore Donnaly." Derek looked at the picture, then Theodore, then the note. *This better be good*, he muttered to himself.

"Oh, don't worry. If it's even half the show of the 60s, you're gonna love it."

Totally off guard now and flustered, Derek shook his hand. "I'm Derek Turrel."

Theodore slowly drew his hand back. "You got to be kiddin' me."

Derek, put further off guard, flushed red.

"Global-Essence-hangin'-from-the-ceiling-in-the-B-of-A-Wall-Street-Derek Turrel?"

The house lights dimmed. Derek fully enveloped in embarrassment, leaned over and whispered, "Yeah. Let's just watch the show now, okay."

Theodore beamed, straightened up, crossed his legs, and lifted his chin, looking like a proper patron of the arts. As the curtain rose and the stage lights flooded across the first few rows, Theodore looked again at his ticket stub, gave it a quiet kiss, and placed it in his pocket as he leaned over whispering, "You have a wonderful lady, Mister Turrel."

As the music swelled and the sets were revealed to heavy applause, Derek wondered. *What the hell is this all about?*

***

Following a thirteen-curtain-call ending to the musical, and a fine late-dinner at Mickey's with Derek and Samantha, Theodore left the table a minute early and flagged down a cab. Waiting in the backseat as it idled in front of Mickey's, Theodore watched the meter click once, twice, and by the third time, "Hey Cabbie, seventy-five cents every minute for waiting?"

"Yeah, so?"

"Just an observation." He turned his attention to the front entrance as Samara and Derek emerged and climbed into the cab. "Hey, I can sit up front," excused Theodore. "Me and the Cabbie are buds now, right Cabbie?"

As he slid out and opened the front passenger door, the cabbie shook his head, "Yeah. Buds."

The cab left the curb and disappeared into the crowded after-theatre-traffic.

Derek and Samara talked quietly in the backseat as Theodore engaged the Cabbie once more. "So, when did it get to seventy-five cents?"

The cabbie threw him a glance. "'Bout the time that jacket was in style."

Theodore covered his embarrassment with, "Whoa. Good one. Gotta remember that one. Yeah. Good one."

"That was still pretty weird, you have to admit," whispered Derek.

Samara smiled. "You need some surprises in your life, Derek. It felt good. Look at him. He hasn't had a night like this in a long time, right?"

Derek nodded. "He's gonna talk my head off at the loft. Why did you have to invite him tonight?"

Samara leaned up to the cabbie, "We need to stop at the wine store on Greene, okay?" The cabbie nodded. Theodore turned around. "You sure I'm not a pain in the ass for you two?"

Samara smiled, "We invited you, Theo. Derek is excited to hear what you think."

Derek returned the jab with, "And Samara will preview her concerto for you. Now, how's that for a fortuitous night, Theodore?"

"Far out," Theodore exclaimed. "Far out, eh, cabbie?"

The cabbie grinned. "Right up there with your jacket, pal."

Theodore leaned toward the cabbie. "I could have used a number of colloquial and politically correct exclamations, but I knew that little chosen remnant of the 60s would entertain the hell out of you…" he grabbed a quick glance of the driver's ID on the glove box. "…Tony Gee."

The loft was flooded with moonlight when they entered. Derek went for the light switch as Theodore said, "Oh, wow. Don't. Not yet." He peered in all directions. "Look at those shadows. My God, what are you creating, Derek?"

Derek and Samara stopped and paused a moment at what Theo was settled on, Derek's "Image Planet," as he was calling it now. The spill from the windows and skylight allowed the chiseled holes to cast shadows on the loft that gave yet another perspective of Derek's imagination that was a surprise even to Derek.

This was to be a longer night than either of them expected. A much longer night.

CHAPTER 7

Evening can serve people in such different ways," said Theodore as he hunched on the window seat, his arms casting shadows of a symphony conductor as he listened to Samara work through her concerto. Derek grinned and did a rabbit shadow on the wall just to aggravate him.

"Hey," said Theodore. "Stop that. Go mess with your own shadows there, over there, with your rock." They both laughed, and Derek topped up their glasses with another two fingers of Tequila, Derek's favorite "dream juice," as he called it.

Samara, instead of just playing the work, started making corrections. She grabbed a pencil with one hand and kept the movement going with the other, feverishly jotting down notes as she went along, the work becoming beautifully dissonant. Theodore stopped the conducting, and walked over to the piano area where he slumped into a giant beanbag chair and listened even more intently.

At the far end of the loft, Derek feeling the Tequila, wandered over to his worktable, picking up a chisel and hammer. He walked up to the rock, and peering through one of the chiseled holes, stood poised to make noise.

***

The service at the Regis was a 24/7 operation. Carlos picked up the phone at 1 A.M. and said, "Room service, breakfast, lunch and dinner. This is Carlos. How may I help you?"

Joseph was determined to get his money's worth. "Hello there, Carlos. This is the Presidential, okay? One of us wants breakfast. One wants lunch. One wants supper. And…Stop that!" he said as he slapped Tina's hand ripping away the towel covering his pear-shaped body.

"You got a duty to perform, child. My turn now!" said Tina as she scampered from the living room back into the master bedroom.

Joseph cleared his throat. "Oh, Carlos, sorry. Got a little change in plans. One of us wants oysters. All the oysters you've got, okay?"

"*All*, sir?"

"What'd I say, Carlos?" He stood up from the couch in his birthday suit and re-lit his cigar and smiled. "Hey, bring my towel back here you little piece of joy!"

"Sir?" said Carlos.

"Sorry, Carlos. Now where were we?"

Joseph continued with details, as Carlos hurriedly took down the order, going from one pad to another. "Thank you, sir, but this will take awhile to prepare… Yes, sir. Oysters will be right up. About 45 minutes for the rest, sir. Thank you, sir."

The Presidential suite was now clouded in cigar smoke as Joseph hung up the phone and like an overgrown, cherub reject, scampered toward the dining area, grabbed the discarded towel from the floor and wrapped his protruding belly.

He paused, looked at the dining table, then staggered to the china cabinet. As he bent over and started taking out plates and silverware, the towel dropped to the ground, leaving him once again, bare-assed. Ignoring his nakedness, he fastidiously started placing the settings around the table. "Everyone! Oysters coming. Oysters coming!"

From the bedroom, Tina bellowed back, "Don't need no sorry-assed oysters. Get in here!"

* * *

The rocks on the inlet glistened with the clear night's light. "I'd all but forgotten how beautiful Newport is on a clear night," said Aretha as she walked the short distance to the boathouse. Dr. Reagan accompanied her, snatching a few quick drags on his pipe, looking over his shoulder several times. "The wife hates me to smoke," he said.

"One of your few pleasures, eh?"

"How did you know?" quipped Dr. Reagan.

"Making mind puppets out of people must be so dreary," said Aretha.

"Mind Puppets. Not heard that phrase before."

Aretha leaned down and picked up a stone. "I read a novel once by that title. You remind me of what it was about."

"How so?"

"Well, you'd have to admit, the fine line is getting more blurred between reality and fantasy nowadays, yes?"

"Health—and the lack of—is, and always will be, the same."

"Yes, but what was crazy when you and I were young, is sane today, don't you think?" said Aretha.

Dr. Reagan tapped his pipe and threw the tobacco into the surf. "Well, according to the media, you're right, but that doesn't make it so."

"You really think my Linda is whacked though, don't you?"

Dr. Reagan stopped and turned. "You certainly have a way with words, Mrs. Ballard."

"Wait till you see me with a sailboat." As they reached the oversized boathouse, Dr. Reagan opened the door and flicked on the light. Aretha backed up. "Whoa. Now *that* is a boat." She stared at the forty-eight foot antique ketch, appointed in teak and polished brass.

"Like it?" he asked.

"I'm gonna have to stay friendly with you, aren't I... I mean, you're not going to let me ever sail her if I tell you you're full of shit about my daughter, are you?

"Probably not."

"Okay, I'll just say we're not calling it a night until you convince me she should stay. We'll sit right here on the deck. You can smoke all you want. Just give me your best shot, because I intend to take her home tomorrow."

Dr. Reagan gave her a long look, then pulled out his pipe and once again lit up. He looked up at the double-mast. "Ever try to buck the winds on a bad day?"

"Can't say I have," she replied.

"Get ready. Tomorrow might be one of those days. So, here are my reasons."

As 1 A.M. approached, the sea air of Rhode Island felt uncharacteristically cold. Dr. Reagan tapped out his pipe, and pocketed the well-aged Meerschaum. "Well, that's all I have to say, Mrs. Ballard." Aretha gazed at the goose bumps now appearing on her arms. "So, *that's* the kind of day you were talking about."

***

In Soho, a heavy black cloud replaced the moonlight. Shadows through the chiseled pores of the rock no longer provided inspiration for Derek as he stood holding his tools and staring into space.

***

At Stefano's, Samara and Theodore leaned across the table, deep into musical history, spawned by the resonance of her concerto and the empty bottle of Port in front of them. Their conversation wavered but a moment as the power failed and all was dark. Quickly, whistling as he went, Jersey, the bartender, lit emergency candles.

***

The St. Regis was like any New York hotel at this hour — quiet. From the outside, a burst of rain pounded the windows into blurred images of insomniacs and die-hard party animals. High above, The Presidential Suite was dark. Far below, Cindy and Tina rushed out into the rain, laughing loudly, as they tried to hail a cab. "We hit the mother lode, Cindy. Damn if we didn't," shouted Tina, waving frantically for a taxi, the hundred dollar bills clenched tightly in her hand.

***

As the thunder, lightning and pounding rain turned Manhattan into a reflecting kaleidoscope of headlights, scurrying pedestrians and romantic strolling couples, a girl of around eighteen years emerged from the Columbus Circle Subway. She was clad only in a do-rag, long t-shirt and climbing boots. Strapped around her waist was all she owned, stuffed compactly into an oversized fanny pack. She started to run, slowly at first, then faster, kicking the puddles high and singing. Not particularly unusual in Manhattan, except the lyrics of her unfamiliar song were not of a familiar language—if the bursts of non-descript sound could be called a language at all.

As the instrument of unearthly sound crossed the street, she passed a carriage standing idle in the rain, its horsepower covered in a tarp. She paused just a moment to gain eye contact with the dripping face of the steed, then whispered in his ear, "Equus Cabalus.," Continuing down the street, she sought our even bigger puddles, projecting even stronger echoes of somewhere else.

A whinny.

A flash of lightening.

A disappearance into the park.

Darkness and rain continued.

***

Sunrise.

Garbage trucks.

Street sweepers.

Shop keepers rolling down their awnings.

In Central Park, a sparrow flew from limb to limb, coming to perch high in the branches of an ancient elm tree. It peered down. Cradled in heavy branches huddled the girl, her climbing boots extended out from an anorak.

Silence.

A pathetic whine came from below.

She lifted the cover, peering toward the feline cages of the zoo. From her mouth came the identical sound. Soon, primal sounds from inside the larger cages joined in.

The sparrow took flight, landing a distance away on the animal clock at the entrance. The clock moved, bringing the 6 AM announcement of another fall day in New York. For the girl known to some as Echo, it was the beginning of another journey.

Chapter 8

The early morning Soho corner was without traffic, foot or motor. "And the Lord will bring peace to all in Jesus' name, I say, and all will be saved, I say, for to sin is to be human and to repent is to know of your humanness, I say..."

What would bring the "Savior Guy" out so early? I walked past his improvised soap-box pulpit, gave him the peace sign-a signal of acceptance that kept him half sane and off the tax payers ledger at Bellevue-then continued on to Stefano's for coffee.

The streets looked like a miniature war zone. Small piles of wet trash littered the surrounding areas of the sewer drains. Odd sized bits of garbage that couldn't fit through the gratings remain pushed aside by the all night downpour. I'm not afraid to admit it; I dream of rain in the city. The heavier, the better. Foreigners can never understand that. To them, the streets look like, well, garbage, waste, back up. To me, it's always been a kind of catharsis, breathing and tasting the air, instead of the city, after a rain. I've thought often of my first walk from Amsterdam to 5th Avenue through the middle of the park, pouring like you wouldn't believe. Hooked me. Hooked me good.

As I wandered into Stefano's, I pictured Samara's stay here through the night with Theodore, exploring her music, the history of music, his history. Smiles came out at that moment as I remembered her climbing in beside me just a few hours before. Her hair was wet from the dash up the sidewalk, and a soft quiet hum of her concerto still resonated from her lips as she kissed my ear and then faded into rest. I thought of the little guy, all but forgotten by his world of the "critique," the world of creative comparisons he had shared with the people for so long. That which was so much of him, seemingly all bottled up until a chance meeting on a bus. A bus. Samara never took buses.

"Hey, Derek," said Silver, Stefano's daytime short order cook, clean up man, and "fantastic" coffee maker.

I sat on my usual stool. The coffee came sliding down the counter, never spilling a drop. "Just made it," Silver said.

I took a whiff and turned around on the stool, looking back outside. "Mind if I take this out for a walk, Sil?"

"Hey, just don't forget where you got that antique."

I looked again at the cup. "This?"

"That, my friend, is not a 'this'. That is part of the estate of Stefano's grandfather."

"Looks like a soup kitchen cup to me."

"Yeah. Probably. With thirteen kids, he was probably well acquainted with soup kitchens back then."

***

I didn't know why a walk felt so compelling this day, but out I went. Maybe it was the cooler air of fall that tempted me. Whatever it was, a look to the left, the right, and I found myself choosing the street toward the Hudson.

***

"Oh, Jerry, I can't do that," muttered Samara as she rose on one elbow and glanced at the clock showing nine. "I just got to bed... It's a long story. I can't have those revisions ready for... you'll just have

46

to postpone a day. I'll be on the ivories by seven…polish it tonight. You'll have the whole, terrible, creation by tomorrow. Oh, it's probably not that bad. Just had someone last night remind me how good music was, and can be…eah a bit. Hey, he liked tequila. Had to be polite…Jerry! My head needs a pillow…Right. Tomorrow. You handle the flack today. G'night… I mean, morning." Samara laid back down into instant sleep again.

***

I softly whistled the concerto between sips as I wandered along Battery Park's river edge. Tugs were beginning the long haul with the daily load of Manhattan sludge. Several curious gulls left the barge's slow pace and lofted toward my path, knowing they could quickly scope out my cup in the hopes there might be something in my hand to go with the coffee. I knew the routine. They turned away, however, squawking wildly as they veered toward the subway entrance, and other gull sounds, but, there were no gulls.

Encouraging raucous gull sounds, a flurry of breadcrumbs, bagels, baguettes and tortillas came flying out of the entrance, followed by a youthful apparition. Now, I had seen old bag ladies with this routine of feeding the gulls, pigeons and all, but this was different. *What was this? A young woman/child dressed like a rainbow with layer after layer of bright colored shirts and a cacophonous bird call—all coming from the lips of an ethereally beautiful face?* Now that, was new. Walking slowly, she invited specific gulls to land on her arms. That was new. Gulls taking up a cadent pace behind her, careful not to get too close, unless invited, that was new. Like polite children, they waited their turn and she did just that, invited them one by one to perch on one of her arms. I gazed at the eight birds she carried on each arm. One to two pounds each.

***

"I swear, Sam, that's what she was doing… talking to the birds." Samara grinned. "What did *you* drink last night?"

I wandered over to the loft window and peered out. Samara was rushing to get to the office before her noon patient arrived. She wasn't in the mood to listen to my "fantasy tale" as she called it. It was obviously not the time to tell her the best part. That would have certified me. It was bad enough carrying out the therapy sessions sometimes. She didn't need to hear about nature girl walking the edge of the river; fish jumping like dolphins alongside her. "That's right," I would have to say to her when I did share this part, "…fish in the Hudson can barely swim through the pollution, let alone do acrobatics. I know. But that's what happened." Of course she would leave the room if I told her the gulls flew like Blue Angels

47

above the jumping fish without ever blinking a "hungry" eye. So, I decided she knew enough and the rest would remain my secret.

I went back to the river each morning for the next five days. Maybe I had imagined it.

***

Aretha stood at the window looking in at Linda. She knew it wouldn't be easy. According to Dr. Reagan, Linda had told everyone that she was going home. She had packed her things and was now busying herself with the basket weaving class—waiting.

Aretha looked at the small pastry box in her hand containing a chocolate éclair—Linda's favorite. For a moment, she struggled with feeling like a rueful mother, not the petulant parent of a schizophrenic. Hardly a peace offering, but she hadn't expected to be bringing a "get well" token. All the way up the turnpike, she had thought about her conduct over the past couple of years; the hasty decision to send her away to be rid of the anxiety, the guessing, and the pain of knowing she had contributed to the condition. *How could I know so much about the universe and know so little about raising a daughter?* She had thought over and over. *Was it repairable? Could I be a mother to a grown woman now?* She peered in at the frail hands weaving and crossing the strands of red and black straw. *This is going to be the hardest thing I've ever done.*

Dr. Reagan stepped forward and pushed open the glass door. "Don't wait too long," he said. Aretha stepped into the room and walked the short distance to Linda. She stood behind her for a few moments and then placed the box on the table in front of her. With the jubilance of a child at Christmas, Linda lifted her eyes, dropped her straw, and spun around, throwing her arms around Aretha. "Mommy, what took you so long? I've been packed for hours. Oh, Mommy, I love you."

Aretha patted her daughter and took her by the shoulders. "Let me see you. You are pale."

Linda smiled. "They don't have much of a sun-bathing program here." She referred to the half finished basket. "Good teachers with weaving, though. I started a basket for you... I named it 'Passion and Death.' Don't you like it?"

Aretha smiled at the innocuous shape. "Yes. I see your point. Your favorite colors, red and black. I can see you've been working hard."

Linda reached down and swept up the work into her plastic bag. "Plenty of time to finish it at home. C'mon, I must show you my room before we leave." Before Aretha could say anything, she was being ushered back toward the front door of the recreation ward. "This is my mommy, girls. Isn't she beautiful?"

Several of the patients looked on with stoic gazes, while others let out mocking oohs and ahs as mother and daughter approached the door.

Dr. Reagan pushed through as if on his morning routine. "You're looking well, Linda. Good morning, Mrs. Ballard."

Both women nodded and exited into the hall. With a panicked look on her face, Aretha looked back over her shoulder at Dr. Reagan. The doctor nodded encouragement, making it worse as they walked the short distance to Linda's room.

"Mommy," Linda said with sadness in her voice that Aretha hadn't heard for a very long time.

"Yes, Sweetheart."

"I'm sorry you couldn't have seen it before I packed. I had all kinds of decorations and projects up and..." Linda took Aretha by the hand and led her into the room, not noticing two orderlies moving casually down the hall toward the door.

"You sit down there, just for a minute. See the view. Pretty isn't it?" Aretha sat on the lonely wooden chair under the window and peered at the roof and water tank of the adjoining wing. In the background beyond the roof was the laundry building, its plumes of steam rising into the dead air and forming a wall of gray. Linda stepped to the window and gazed out. "I used to sit here for hours and count the times the steam allowed a small opening to appear and reveal the lake out there. There *is* one. Really. A lake that is so blue." She turned around, her eyes fixed on Aretha. "Except when it's night. Then it's black. I like black. The laundry never stops with such a busy hospital. Wash, wash, wash. All day. All night."

She opened the box and took out the éclair. "Oh, my favorite." She took a hasty bite. "Mmm. Here." She offered a bite to Aretha.

"Oh, that's okay. You eat it dear."

Linda took another bite, this time consuming the whole éclair, its cream slipping to the outer edges of her mouth. Not bothering to lick her lips, she stepped to the single bed, neatly made, the pillowcase now stuffed with her clothes and projects. "You forgot to bring me a suitcase. But I thought you just might have a slip of the memory, you know, like when you forgot the visiting days. Visiting hours." She picked up the pillowcase and stood there a moment, then turned around. "So..." She slung the bulging pillowcase over her shoulder. "So...Mommy?"

Aretha knew she had to say something, but couldn't.

"You're not taking me home, are you?"

Aretha was abruptly seized with paralysis. She didn't know why, but she couldn't move.

Linda's eyes became moist, her voice sad. "Dr. Reagan convinced you, didn't he, Mommy?"

"Uh...Linda," Aretha's voice cracked.

Linda stepped forward. "Yes, Mommy?"

"Linda..."

The two orderlies peered through the small glass opening, unseen by either woman.

"Something you want to say, Mommy?"

Aretha started to stand up, but Linda dropped the pillowcase in her lap, causing her to drop back into the seat.

The two orderlies quickly pushed open the door. Assuming a routine position of *inquiry*, one asked, "Everything okay, Linda?"

Linda turned slowly. "You guys are such bad actors. Of course not. I'm about to beat the shit out of my mom. Wanna watch!"

Linda whipped up the pillowcase and brought it down with a "whoosh" to the top of Aretha's head, just as the orderlies lunged, quickly pulling her away. The second orderly activated his belt alarm, the sound screaming through the halls with the impact of a prison break.

Aretha, more frightened than hurt, cried out, "Linda, my little..."

"Get back, Mrs. Ballard," yelled one of the orderlies.

Linda struggled angrily, her frail body proving a formidable opponent, even to the two strapping orderlies. "You never even visited me! You are the worst, do you hear? MOMMY! THE ROT OF MY BOWELS..." her voice lowering to a growl of graveyard hatred, "... THE LOWEST."

Dr. Reagan burst into the room. Linda, now restrained on the bed, shot a fiery blast at the doctor. "Watch your back, Doc. You're next, you little prick. Only it won't be a pillowcase!" She spit at him as he quickly escorted Aretha out.

"She's just disappointed, Doctor. I've let her down," Aretha said, her voice shaking loose uncontrollable tears.

Shutting the door behind him, the doctor quickly ushered Aretha down the hall. "That's not a disappointment, Aretha. That's a breakthrough."

Aretha found the drive back strangely relaxing. She had experienced, according to the doctor, the part of Linda that *had* to come out. The little girl that had always been the obedient, subservient child; the young woman that had always resentfully agreed when Aretha had mocked the boys that would ask the young teenager out; the grownup who had decided one day to close down, not speak, not eat, not open her eyes. That was the daughter that she had unknowingly liberated with a single visit after two years of fear. Aretha began to weep again. For the first time in her life, her heart felt more active than her brain. She was beginning to understand the world on the ground, the world that struggled every day with the tug-a-war between who people were and who others wanted them to be. She glanced upward through the side window.

No moon.

No stars.

Clouds shrouded the *only* friends, the *only* focus her eyes were comfortable with. She had spent a lifetime nurturing, studying, and believing in the infinite perfection of the universe. Now, she was faced with the recovery of a single, lost, ever-so-small imperfect wonder of that universe, and it felt overwhelming.

She allowed the tears to run freely.

CHAPTER 9

Winter was short this year and late March brought opening buds to some of the trees. No sooner had the trees sprouted, when all you could feel was the 80% humidity and subterranean odors rising up through the sidewalk gratings.

What a winter, though. A one-night event with Theodore turned into a weekly habit. Samara found inspiration, I think. She wrote, revised, wrote and revised, all in flurries following visits from Theo. Now she was in Tanglewood rehearsing. And I, well, I was nursing a bruised thumb for the moment. Too much wine and no sleep last week brought my hammer a bit too close and now I had a lot of walking time on my hands.

I began thinking about why I loved New York. From the beginning, I had been seduced by the co-existence and harmony of disparate people—clashing points of view, and the ever present energy of imagination. And then there's my vulnerabilities. Samara knows my weaknesses better than I will ever know them, but I've concluded that my greatest weakness, and at times, paradoxically, my greatest strength, is my ability to be at peace with my fantasies and realities. I mean, as long as *they* co-exist in harmony, don't get in the way of each other, I'll be okay. Samara used to accuse me of denying the real world, as if I only responded to my fantasy side and left reality behind. She believed I threw myself into sculpting for hours on end because I couldn't face the unpredictable energy outside on the sidewalk. To a degree, she was probably right, back then. I admit, I didn't have any interest in challenging the crap that pushed me the wrong way. Perhaps that's a mistake, but why allow distractions to waste your time? That itch, that idea of vanquishing all distractions was behind her incessant reminder, *when are you going to do it?*

I reached the point mid-winter when all I wanted to do was wallow in my confusion with a chisel and hammer. It was much easier to just lose myself in the stone, carving out images, some of which I didn't like, others were okay. That was the magic for me. I'd hammer and sometimes break away these large pieces and magically, a new way to appreciate the stone would appear. Much to my surprise, I'd found three dimensional Rorschach-like abstracts beginning to take on meaning, perhaps more than they should have at the time, but something good must have come out of that period because, like I said, fantasies and realities were getting along fine. Well, not fine, but better.

That brings me to why I still walk this Battery Park path along the river every day, even through last winter. It isn't that I can't accept the possibility I might have hallucinated that morning last fall, but on continued visits to the same area, trying to once again find the enigmatic girl, I often see this formation of gulls flying above. Just as before, *they too* seem to be looking for her—like today.

As I proceeded north along the river's edge, I noticed things were curiously different.

The river was quiet, save for about two hundred feet out. In that area, just beneath the surface, small ripples appeared about every six or seven feet. The gulls flying above were keeping vigil at about a hundred feet, circling in a perfect formation. I didn't know why, but I sat down on the bench and waited.

I looked to my left and right and viewed the typical morning activity; a jogger or two, a cyclist, an old couple holding hands as they walked.

In an abrupt turn, the gulls veered toward South Street as a speeding ambulance entering from State Street came to a virtual halt in the busy morning commute. I turned back toward the river. The ripples were gone. I rose and smiled to myself. I wanted to see what I wanted to see. I was a hopeless romantic. I knew that, of course, but as Samara often reminded me, I needed to *get a grip*.

I trudged back across the park. The ambulance was making its way through the traffic with siren, lights, and intricate maneuvering in and out of any momentary relief from the congestion. My eyes drifted once again to the sky. The gulls were still in perfect formation hovering over the ambulance. Perhaps they were mesmerized by the sound. Maybe it was the lights. Maybe—

I wasn't in any kind of shape to be running that fast, but whoever or whatever was in that ambulance had a grip on the gulls, and I'd only seen one person with that power. I quickly became a "whoosh" in action.

I was no match for the wheels once they started uptown, but my best guess on the destination was Coler Memorial Hospital, which was a few blocks away.

Arriving a few minutes later, my attention was drawn to the gulls moving about the overhang of the entrance with patient nonchalance. My assumption was right. I dashed past the ambulance, its doors still open, through the entrance, and into the emergency receiving area.

"That ambulance that just arrived, who was injured?" I asked.

The nurse looked at me incredulously. "Sir, if you don't know who you're looking for you probably aren't family or friend are you?"

I realized I was sounding like a patient waiting to be taken away by the white coats, but something banged at my senses to persist. "I'm sorry, Miss, but I think that might be my daughter."

Now the nurse gave me a look that said I'd really convinced her I was a kook. "Sir, you sit down over there, and I'll check for you."

As I sat down, I thought maybe I'd said the right thing, and her expression changed to one of sympathy. The girl I'd seen months earlier was young enough to be my daughter. Sure. I'd said the right thing. But, wait a minute. So, the girl is in there getting emergency treatment. *Where could I go from here? I'm just a guy who has taken on another obsession that is just what Samara said... nothing else. Oh, my God. What if the nurse calls me back up to the counter to tell me I can see my daughter?* Now that could spell problems. I barely had time to think about it when a security officer stepped up to me. "You have some ID sir?"

"Yes."

"Could I see it?"

I was flustered now. "What for?"

"Standard procedure when someone is suspicious. And you've got my attention."

"I'll just wait," I said.

The officer shook his head. "Sounds like you best be on your way, buddy."

"But, I'm waiting to see my daughter."

The officer leaned down in my face now. "You can go out nice and peaceful or not. Your choice."

"Jesus," I said, now realizing I was on the edge of real trouble, "I'm just upset. Is she in there?"

"Buddy, if that's your daughter, you got off to an awfully early start with your oats. She's in her forties, about *your* age. Get my point. And according to the nurse, only a miracle will save her. So… go home. I'm sure your real daughter will be glad to see you."

I stepped out into the ambulance area. When I looked back up to the roof of the overhang, the gulls were still there. I threw a glance toward the ambulance. The paramedics were arranging the back for the next call. I walked toward the sidewalk. The gulls began squawking, a sound I'd heard only one time before around the subway entrance. I turned back. The girl exiting, dropped her hospital-green facemask in the garbage can, then stepped out from beneath the overhang and squawked back at the gulls. This was definitely the girl I remembered.

As she walked in the opposite direction, I felt compelled to follow. *What was this girl? I mean, who was this girl?* I could hear Samara now, "You've really got to get more rest, Derek."

I kept my distance as she walked, skipped, spun around from time to time and in general acted the king of strange any New Yorker was obliged to ignore—except I couldn't. After a couple of blocks, she stopped in the middle of the sidewalk. She just stood there. Other pedestrians kept their pace, passing her. I was bumped a couple of times, "Get in the slow lane, guy," fired a *butched-up* skater, sporting a spiked collar.

My mystery girl asked, "Why don't you come up and walk with me."

Now, I'm not the kind of person that seeks out crazy situations. I mean, I've got enough neurosis to keep me challenged, you know? But, here I was, chasing, I don't know who, for whatever reason, other than my fascination with a person that causes fish to imitate porpoises arching through the water and controls a flock of gulls like a remote control airplane, and now, rides in an ambulance, and—

"What were you doing in that ambulance?" I blurted out.

"Direct enough," she answered. "Depressed artists do stupid things sometimes."

"Oh, I'm sorry. I'm… I'm Derek," extending my hand.

"Hi," she said, giving my hand a look then grinning. "Echo."

"Pardon?"

"Echo." She said again, followed by a few screeching gull sounds, sending the flock above us away.

"I was in the ambulance because she needed me."

"The woman that died?" I asked, a bit puzzled.

"She's alive. She'll be up and painting again like nothing happened in a couple of days."

"I don't understand,"

"I know. Not important… today. Gotta run."

With that, she took off like a gazelle.

Now I know I have a rich imagination, but this did happen. I think. *Could I be that far gone with my fantasies?* I couldn't let Samara know of this latest experience. She would have a hard time, a very hard time.

I started to leave, then turned and gazed at the trashcan where the girl deposited the facemask. I walked back, paused, and looked in. There were many masks. *Ambulance driver's discard? Coincidence? Was the top one hers, or...?* I turned and walked away. Up to this point I'd had no physical evidence to support my... impression. *Is that the right word?* So far, I had to admit, it was all a very out-of-this-world impression. *Would I ever see her again? Why had I been at this place at this time?* As I reached the corner, I turned and raced back, reached in, and snatched up what I thought might be the only evidence to prove it a reality.

***

I sat at the table with the surgical facemask between us.

"Okay," I said to Theo, "Let's assume there's no extraordinary reason for all this."

I'd just told the whole story, but for the moment, getting Theo to relinquish his attention from the avocado, tangerine and shrimp salad was next to impossible. So, I waited for his nod and then waited for him to finish. I'd had dinner with him before and learned. Having a conversation with Theo without giving him room to interact was foolish. His brain was such that he would remember every word you said, and then when he was finished eating, he would review anything you'd said in minute detail with his steel-trap mind.

I got up, walked to the counter, and ordered myself another coffee. Knowing Arlie's Deli was Theo's favorite—when he could afford to eat—I'd chosen a mid-afternoon lunch to explore what I thought was either the beginning of an epiphany or the end of my senses.

As I sat back down, Theo, with the exact touch of an aristocrat, wiped his mouth with the canister-dispensed napkin, and quietly sighed. One thing about Theo, there was seldom a hint of him showing his homeless position in life. Even when Samara offered both a *professional* ear and a place for him to stay, he'd declined, saying, "When we agree it's been earned, then we'll talk about such things."

"Okay," he said. "To start with, I think you're gathering the notes for a future work."

"What?" I stammered.

"Think of it this way. You first saw her after the Aretha thing, right?"

"Actually, it was the morning after I met you…"

"Which was preceded by the rescuing of Aretha a few days before, right?"

"Weeks."

"Weeks, days, months. All the same. Don't you understand, you are stretching out this time, your life, even though it's digitized in your brain as a memory… just like a computer chip. Instant access. You just choose to dramatize it all with… time, my friend. Time. We're all just spending this time remembering who we are. Vertical existence, not horizontal."

"You lost me."

"No, I didn't. That's just your cop-out."

"No, really. I don't get where you're going."

Without a blink, he continued. "Try thinking all that is happening, or happened, or is about to happen, is all happening at the same time…as memory. You're just choosing to access that *part* of the memory that serves you at the moment."

Theo leaned across and picked up my water glass. "Mind if I slug this down? Should have ordered some."

"No. Sure."

Theo didn't slug it down. He took his time and relished each swallow. "Watch. I can do the expedient thing and drink this down normal, swallow after swallow, elapsed time about three to five seconds, or, I can stretch it out and use the memory of water when it meant a lot to me, like in the mountains, in my youth. Stretch/Memory. Good for us."

He finished savoring the water, chuckling to himself at the end. "Good one. Thought I'd die rationing the canteen to the last minute coming down the Briethorn in '64, only to be met by a climber coming up with a whole goat skin full of water sitting on a trailside rock, pouring it over his head. I was ready to lick his head, you know? Anyway, like I said, memory."

"Whoa," I said. "Where the hell are you?"

"Right here, Derek. Same as you. Listen to yourself. Aretha didn't just happen. No accidents, right? We agree there are no accidents, yes?"

"Yes," I said, thinking I sure as hell wasn't on the same roll as he was, but what the hell, what a ride.

"This girl, she got a name?"

"Echo."

He grinned. "Echo. So think of this Echo, with the squadron of seagulls and jumpin' fish and whatever she was doing in the ambulance, think of it as fodder for the creative-cannon, Derek."

"Fodder? Creative cannon? It's not fantasy. Not something I imagined." I pointed to the mask. "Like I told you…"

"I know," Theo said with ginning eyes. "*That's* real. One you took from several in the can, right? Might have been hers. Might not. I'll accept it as the answer you need, if that's what you want to believe. What you believe, is, Derek."

"What?"

Theo repeated, "What you believe, *is*." He stood up. "Should we leave?"

I grabbed the mask as I glanced about the room, self-conscious. I pulled him down. "No. Continue."

He turned his chair around and straddled it to make a point. Rolling up his sleeves and extending his arms, he said, "See anything unusual?"

I looked. "No."

"Sure you do. Check out those veins."

I looked again. *Was I supposed to see some tracks.* "Don't see anything, but veins," I said.

"Exactly. Healthy, bulging veins. No marks, right? No tracks, right?" That's because I don't need drugs or anything else like that to stimulate my imagination. Without your imagination, Derek, you're just…" He pointed to the busboy. "… you're just existing. With it…"

He turned his chair back around and sat. "With it, you're all that Derek was, is, and will be… all wrapped up in a memory, some would argue an alternate universe or alternative reality. A chip of existence that is happening all at once, vertically with everything else that has ever happened, and… *she* is part of it."

"Part of my memory?"

"Part of whatever internally is happening to your existence, manifested or projected as needed."

"Internally?" I muttered. "Alternative reality?"

"Yeah," he said. "Others blame it on the soul. Others, on the inner-self, etc. Consider it this way. You might just be finding what you need, when you need it. The memory chip. The database of who you are, giving you glimpses of the totality of existence. Your existence. You're accessing this alternative reality little by little, as needed. It's all part of quantum mechanics, universes separated from each other by a single quantum event…or maybe a couple. I don't know. Nobody really knows. Hypothesis now, theory down the road."

I felt paralyzed with wonder and ignorance. *Who was this man, really?*

"Remember Aretha? Even with that anger management thing of yours, you told me you'd never even gotten close to a fight in all your life, and you jumped in, risking everything against the knives and youths that could have ended it all.

"Need," he said. "That night you met me, I invaded your privacy in the loft, spent the night with you and your lover, and what did you do?"

At that moment, all that I could think was I couldn't keep up.

"C'mon. What did you do?"

"I worked."

"You breathed new life into that rock, my friend. Samara drained me damn near dry that night, too.

"NEED. She turned her concerto upside down. Not because it was bad, but because there was more to be realized—more of the vertical memory to realize at that moment. I was just a springboard device, a jogger for her memory of who, what, and why she is the spectacular woman she is."

His eyes were now like hot rivets looking for a place to solidify. "This girl, this half- real, half-fantasy of a girl to you right now, is going to happen again. And you know why?"

"No, but you're going to tell me, aren't you?"

"Damn right I am. You will find her again when you need her. A reality sifted from your memory, the vertical memory that is happening all at once. You will create the moment as you need it. Trust it. Just as I did months ago on that bus when I met Samara and then you. Okay?"

"And that was real, right?" I blurted out rhetorically.

With an impish grin again, he stood up. "Yes. You're not crazy. Some needs are furnished to us in reality. Some..." He swirled his hand like a conductor sending an arpeggio into the air. "Some in that other reality." He smiled. "I earned a couple of bucks just now, right?"

"You mean..."

"I mean you got a grip on it now, right?"

"A grip? You must be kidding." I needed a cold shower. This guy, this man from nowhere, who seemed to be creating himself as we went along, was earning a lot more than a couple of bucks—a lot more.

"Think *I'm* crazy, yet?" he asked.

I nodded. "It crossed my mind."

"Me too. Damn, I'm still thirsty. Couple of bucks?"

I nodded, and fished out a five. "Keep the change."

He started out the door. He looked back at me. "But, two beers are my limit."

I laughed. "Until you create a new need for three?"

He licked his finger and pushed it upward as if checking the wind. "All depends on the memory chip, doesn't it?"

As we walked the short distance to Stefano's, I glanced skyward catching myself expectant of, yeah, gulls. *Was all this somehow a determined way of getting me to "do it?"*

CHAPTER 10

The clouds thickened as the train left Manhattan and made its way north. The skies darkened even further as the train pulled into the western Massachusetts town of Lenox, site of Tanglewood, summer home of the Boston Symphony orchestra.

It wasn't as if Tina had never heard classical music before, but attending her first concert, and experiencing a full rehearsal of Samara's concerto, well, that was very special, and nerve racking.

The train pulled to a stop and Tina quickly gathered her small overnight case and shoulder bag. She slipped her loafers on with a child-like smile—an occasion unto itself, given the high heel profession she spent most of the time pursuing—and stepped onto the platform. Samara had arranged for her to be picked up, but as Tina looked up and down the platform, nothing stood out like a driver. No black cap atop a black suit. She looked for someone holding up her name on a card like she had seen at the airports. Nothing.

She proceeded toward the street, when someone tapped her shoulder. "Miss Foster?"

Tina was not used to the formal identity. She turned to face a man in his 30s. Tina swallowed. She had never been this close to a Denzel-like refinement before. "I'm Leonard... Leonard Paxton. Samara asked me to pick you up."

Tina was taken aback. Standing before her was this well-groomed African American man dressed in tuxedo and holding an envelope.

"This is for you. The car is this way. Pleasant trip, I hope."

"Yes," Tina replied. "Got a lot of reading done."

"Excellent. I apologize for this costume here at the station. Hope it didn't embarrass you."

"Oh, no. You look quiet good in your...tux."

"The rehearsal is in 45 minutes, so I didn't want to take any chances with the traffic and all."

"Sure. I'd do the same."

"Over here." He extended his arm toward the curb where a classic '65 Austin Healey stood parked.

"Wow. This yours?"

"Well, mine and the bank's."

"This is so…original. Don't see them often."

"Here, I'll put those in the boot. Not much room, but I think they'll fit." He took her overnight and shoulder bag as he opened the door for her. "Yes, not many left. Winter and salt gets to them. Most of the really cared for classics like this are on the west coast."

After glancing at the impending sky, he slipped into the driver's seat and pushed in a CD of Wynton Marsalis playing a trumpet concerto.

"Like Wynton?"

"I'm not familiar."

"Wynton Marsalis, the jazz trumpet guy."

"Oh, that Wynton. Didn't recognize the tune."

"He plays both classical and jazz. Samara tells me you two are 'special' friends."

"Yeah. Kinda special. Yeah."

"Well, she speaks very highly of you, you know."

"Nice," said Tina. "This was such a nice thing she did…inviting me to a dress rehearsal and all."

"I know she wanted to get you in on opening night, but the tickets are usually sold out months before. You'll enjoy this tonight, though. Just casual, except for us in *black tie*. They like to tape this rehearsal for TV and all."

"So, you play?"

"Trumpet."

"Really. That's why the CD?"

He grinned. "Yeah. Mar's been a hero to me since I was a kid."

"You in Samara's concerto? I mean, are you in the orchestra, like?"

"Actually, I'm on the end of the program playing solo in a tribute to Duke Ellington."

"Wow. This is really a special thing, right?"

"Let's hope the critics think so. Pre-opening night invite for the press can be a bit daunting."

"Daunting, for sure."

"Yes."

The rest of the ride to the hotel, Tina turned the music up and played out her nervousness with rapt attention to the unfamiliar Telemann Trumpet Concerto.

The end of the winding country road brought them to a cluster of trees and the Apple Tree Inn. Leonard jumped out and opened Tina's door. "Samara arranged a room for you. Number twenty-three. Hope you brought an umbrella. We might get a sprinkle."

"Let's hope it's just a sprinkle. My sister lives in North Carolina. Says the edge of the hurricane dumped on her last night."

Leonard lifted her bag from the boot. "Well, we'll think positive, eh?"

"Thank you for the ride," said Tina.

Leonard glanced at his watch. "No problem. Gotta run. Oh, the concert stage is just beyond those trees. Eight sharp. It's less than a five-minute walk. Samara said she'd come to your seat afterwards. Ticket's inside your room."

As he drove off, Tina turned entered the Inn and made her way to the room. Pictures of musicians decorated the walls. The far end was equipped with a small refrigerator and hot plate. A four-poster bed occupied the corner. Across the room in front of a window looking out to the woods was a music stand and chair. The opposite side door led to a small bathroom and shower. Even there, composer's pictures were mounted on the walls.

She set her bag down and lounged on the bed, taking in the surroundings. Clouds darkened outside, and she reached over and flicked on the bedside lamp. She had never been in such an environment and didn't really understand the mood it was evoking.

***

Derek too was contemplating his current mood. Alone in his loft, he gazed at the rock which for so many months had dominated his workspace. It was now a third the size. Its form suggested a meteorite, riddled with porous holes, each containing an abstract miniature steel mobile. He had achieved a new perspective for his sculpture and was hopeful, but unsure of the feeling it would effect in others. It was 7 o'clock. In two hours the sun would be gone and he would be able to turn on stage lights, indulging in his nightly contemplation of the mobile's turning shadows on the walls. Depending on the speed of the fan, he could select a rhythm and tempo for the movement at will. This was an exercise he jokingly thought of as his "good, bad and the ugly."

He glanced out the window. With the cloudy night, there wouldn't be a moon. Rain had started to highlight the streets. His watch told him he still had time to phone.

He dialed the number, hoping his call wouldn't disturb her.

"Shed." Came the reply.

"Hi. This is Derek Turrel. Is it possible to speak with Samara?"

"Hey, Derek. Weylin here. You in town?"

61

"Oh, hi, Weylin. Didn't recognize your voice. No. Coming up for the opening Saturday. Had to finish up some work here."

"Well, it'll be good to see you. I'll patch you through."

As Derek waited to hear her voice, he remembered his first meeting with Weylin, the oldest employee of the music festival. On their initial visit, Derek and Samara had been introduced to him not at the stage, but at the local bar. He was a fixture there as well. Locals called him the "keeper of the gates" as he was stage manager for Tanglewood; night watchman for the swing shift at the local lumberyard; and on week ends, took tickets at the one movie theatre in town. Weylin liked to stay busy.

"Derek?"

"Hey, Sam. How's it going?"

"Oh, God, I'm so out of it."

"What. Not the cool, collected, master mu..."

"No, Derek. I'm serious. My fingers feel arthritic. My head won't stop pounding and..."

"Just some extreme jitters. You'll be fine once you step out there."

"To top it off, they kept it under the stars, instead of indoors."

"Not raining there, is it?"

"Black as hell outside, Derek. It's just a matter of time."

"Well, trust in the big guy up there. It'll be fine."

"Oh, how I wish you were here now."

"Hey, I'll be there Saturday and you've got Tina for support. She arrived okay, didn't she?"

"Oh, my God. I got so carried away with the time. Oh, shit. Got to call her."

Derek glanced at his watch. "Bit late. She's probably in the audience now."

"Oh, how embarrassing."

"Hey, I'll let you go. Have a great rehearsal."

"Oh...okay," said Samara. "Thanks for the call. Love you."

"Yeah. Me too."

As the line went dead, Derek mused how it must be to step out on Tanglewood's stage and play your creation for the first time in front of an audience. *Ugh. That takes guts. No wonder her fingers are stuck.*

***

Tina walked slowly through the grove of trees from the Inn to the "Shed" Tanglewood's covered concert hall, with open-air walls. From the distance of black clouds, she could hear approaching thunder. She picked up the pace, arriving with time to spare. She handed the usher her ticket and taking the program, sat down. The audience for the dress rehearsal was dressed informally, and all carried an umbrella—all but Tina. She did have a heavy sweater, which was pulled up around her neck as sudden gusts of wind blew through.

Back stage, there was panic. Management had just informed everyone the weather report suggested Hurricane Belinda's fringe winds and rain had unexpectedly turned west. They might have to cancel the performance.

Samara, dressed in an elegant black velvet dress, got word in her dressing room just as she was about to leave for the stage. "No," she said to the assistant stage manager. "Not..." Her response was interrupted by a clatter of thunder.

Tina jumped to her feet as from nowhere, a torrent of rain and wind slammed through the open walls. Everyone scurried to exit. Amidst the confusion, the load speaker came alive. "Ladies and Gentlemen, our sincerest apologies, but tonight's performance has just been cancelled. We are warned a sudden shift of a rather strong edge of Hurricane Belinda is headed our way. We ask you to vacate the Shed as soon as possible, and return to your homes or hotels and safely wait out the storm. Call the box office tomorrow to arrange for a credit on your tickets for another performance next week. Again, our apologies."

What had been an inspiring walk through the trees now turned into a dash for safety. The winds and rain came even harder as Tina, along with other Inn guests, ran the short distance to their rooms, dodging swirling leaves and small fallen branches.

Tina slammed the door behind her and shivered beneath her soaked clothing. She quickly turned off the air conditioner and changed. Moments later, lightning lit up her room accompanied by a crushing clap of thunder, sending her wide-eyed beneath the bedspread.

Samara dialed and shouldered her telephone as she gathered up personal things in her dressing room.

"Tina?"

Tina answered with a sigh, "Yes, Samara?"

"So glad you got back to the Inn. This is some storm. It was supposed to stay east of us."

As tree branches whipped against her window, Tina spoke beneath the covers. "I'm so sorry for you. You must be terribly disappointed."

"Just a bit frustrated. Listen, I'll swing around with a car and pick you up. We'll go and try to salvage the night with some dinner," said Samara.

"You sure it's okay?"

"We're tough, right? See you in five."

Derek stood at the window gazing out at the torrents of rain beating on the street below. In the background, he could hear the TV newscast. The weatherman highlighted the sudden shift in the storm's edge and said, "From New Jersey to Maine, rain can be expected throughout the night, and could become heavy at times."

Brilliant, he thought. *Could?*

Inside the Central Park Zoo, caretakers hurriedly checked entrances and exits as the wind and rain increased. Animals paced restlessly, their faces taut, eyes barely moving. Cages vibrated as their howls leapt beyond, swallowed by the torrential weather.

Underpasses leading to the zoo became flowing rivers. The echoes of panicking animals skipped across the torrents of water, ricocheting up the walls, around the boulders, to the trees' upper most branches, where they seemed to be harnessed into an even louder cacophonous echo, a reflecting mass of turbulence, gathering even greater power. Beneath what appeared like a miniature rainbow of whirling strands of color, the sounds were swallowed into silence. Stifled momentarily beneath what seemed to be an even greater energy, the echoing cries of animals joined together, reversed direction, and rushing down the trees, spewed dead leaves left and right from its path, across the stones, atop the river of water, and up to the bars of the cages.

A final shrill condensing of the eruption preceded the sudden dissipation within the walls where it had started. The torrent outside subsided into gentle rain drops. As if the eye of a storm had embraced the building, the frightened creatures behind the bars relaxed, and let their frozen eyes lower to the concrete floor. The calmer air seemed to whisper, "Shhhh. The kaleidoscopic flow of energy receded into the maze of twisted bark and branches.

In Lenox, the MARY & JANE establishment was hosting an array of visitors like it had never seen before. For locals, this particular restaurant and bar was more than just a place to *tip back* a few, satiate their hunger, and listen to a jukebox filled with jazz and classical recordings. Here, Town Meetings were commonplace, with an occasional wedding or two during the summer. It was tradition for Tanglewood visitors to have a social drink before and after a performance, but tonight was rapidly becoming *historical* for the tiny watering hole.

Within an hour of the cancellation, every table and barstool was filled with out-of-towners as well as locals whose special pre-opening night tickets were now only good for the few available seats spread throughout the festival. Mary worked furiously behind the bar while Jane worked the tables. After a few minutes, a local, Bart, took off his coat and went behind the bar to help Mary prepare the drinks. The way the crowd was throwing down the booze, no one was going to want to drive anywhere, save the mile back along the motel road.

Samara and Tina sat quietly in a corner, sipping their wine and listening to the windows rattle throughout the room.

Finally, Bart moved from the bar to the jukebox, reached behind and punched up the volume. "Sorry folks, but we need to hear more of Jarrett and less of the storm noise."

Outside, one car alarm went off, setting others in motion. Soon, the whole parking lot was a chorus of alerts and sirens. It was only 8:20. The TV above the bar was saying the main storm wouldn't arrive until later. "What the hell is this, then?" mocked Bart.

***

Stanley Huff, Lenox's sheriff, put the brakes on to avoid a fallen limb. His Deputy, Marlin, cinched his safety belt tighter.

"Damn, Stanley. This is gettin' serious."

Stanley shot Marlin a glance. "That makes seven trees. Six behind us. You could be callin' this in instead of poppin' off with the obvious, okay?"

Marlin picked up his radio mike. "Denise, get me Power and Light."

***

A "Bulletin" banner across the TV screen brought one customer to her feet. "Hey, turn the music down," she shouted as she approached the monitor hanging high above the bar. The pictures of hurricane damage brought the room to a hush. Devastation along the Jersey coast dominated the montage. The newscaster warned all residents of a four state area to stay indoors tonight, as the storm had veered inland and was still packing thirty to forty mile-per-hour winds. Rain accumulation was expected to be four to eight inches.

Customers immediately started paying for their drinks and leaving for their hotels.

Tina watched the exodus as Samara tried to make a cell phone call to Derek. Reception was so riddled with static a connection was impossible. Samara stood and walked to Mary. "Can I use your phone, Mary?"

"You could, if the lines weren't down." She shrugged. "Want a good stiff one for the road?"

"Thanks, Mary. Better stay sober for this trip."

"Tina? Gotta get back to the room. C'mon."

65

As they hurriedly crossed the parking lot, there were still several cars with their alarms mixing with the winds and rain clatter. "Shit," Tina complained. "This started out so nice."

"Yeah, well, let's hope it ends nice," said Samara.

The car started down the road normally, but within a few yards, puddles of water splashed above the running boards. Samara heard the engine begin to miss and feared the worst. "Damn. Water's raising hell with the spark plugs or something."

"Oh, please dear God, not out here. Don't strand us out here," groaned Tina.

"We'll make it. We'll make it," Samara said with frightened optimism.

"What's that?" asked Tina, as the car sputtered and coughed its way along.

"What?"

"Just ahead." Tina squinted.

"A tree."

Tina threw a glance at Samara. "I know a tree when I see it. Isn't it lying across a car?"

Samara slowed. "Don't conk-out on me now. You're right. Smashed down on something... yeah...a car. God, somebody might be in it." She pumped the gas, dropped it into neutral, and pulled to a halt just short of the fallen tree.

Tina was out of the car before it even stopped. "I'll check," she shouted above the wind and rain. "You stay here with your velvet dress." She dashed to the crushed car.

Samara leaned forward and turned up the windshield wipers. The downpour made a cascading waterfall in spite of the fast wiping. Above the rain, she heard Tina's screams and jumped out, running through the high water. "What?" She shouted back. "Is someone there?"

Tina tugged on limbs, throwing them behind her and reached through the broken driver's side window and unlatched the door. The man slumped onto the pavement, his cell phone still clutched in his hand, 911 visible in the digital window. "Oh, my God!" said Tina. "The Healey! It's Leonard! It's your friend, Leonard!"

Stunned, Tina wiped the rain from his unconscious face as Samara lifted her velvet gown to shield him. Speeding toward them in the distance was a police car's flashing lights leading the way for a paramedic van, swerving to miss downed trees and power lines.

"He's alive, isn't he, Tina? Cried Samara. "Tell me he's alive!"

CHAPTER 11

Watching the drizzle meander down the windows of the bus, Theo was inexorably connected with the rain as a friend. Sprinkle. Downpour. It didn't matter to him.

He first realized his close relationship with the weather when he was a student at MIT, majoring in math where it seemed perfectly logical to combine studies in numbers with the love affair for his keyboard. An accomplished composer on the Moog at age seventeen, he had received a scholarship to Julliard, but forfeited that opportunity to take up the challenge he felt studying through the math department at MIT could provide. His undergraduate years were confused with what he called an "atonal mix" of his sex life. In later years, he modified his "atonal mix" with drugs, plus some rock and roll. Yes, he stole the phrase, but couldn't come up with a better one, so it stuck. Theodore Donnaly had a reputation. Genius. Genius. And Genius. But, when no one would buy it—this way he had with numbers and sampled sounds converted into polytonal scales—he looked in other directions. If they, the decision makers for the public knew better, he, the creator of the sounds, needed to learn better, right? Wrong.

Two years later, after numerous essays on the tragic state of creativity in music, Theodore was asked to apply his distrust of the music industry and his sense of musical adventure to the pages of the London Review, an upstart periodical that was silently funded by another rebel, Timothy Leary. Seems Tim had a similar view of performing arts and when he read Theodore's treatise on "blackboard formulas as music," he too became a loyal follower of Theo's critical sensibilities.

Theo reveled in the opportunity to challenge the world of music, and within a year of working for the London Review, he was asked to apply his theories to the world of painting and sculpture. Many a night was spent typing reviews and essays in his converted firehouse on Houston. On occasion, Timothy visited and imbibed tiny reds and blues for a psychedelic exploration of his own disgruntled life, as Theo would walk about orating into a tape recorder—his preferred form of writing. When Theo allowed the little red and green pills to take over *his* life, he became lost in an even more dissonant polytonal world. Focus seemed to elude him. Deadlines were missed. Libel suits became common as he lost his verbal tact. Timothy invited him one night to a party at Manhattan's famous "57." Six hours later, Theodore woke up naked in a Hell's Kitchen hotel room; the words "you're fired" spray-painted across his chest. The

Kitchen became his home for many years, until that too saturated his being, bringing him close to the point of dissolution of mind, body and spirit.

Then, buses and subways served as his sometime home. One ordinary night, he happened upon a turning point; a woman offered him clean air to breath in a theatre.

The memories were becoming transparent like the water now rolling about the windows. Accompanied by the sound of the tires going over puddles and manhole covers, he became aware of counterpoint images and sounds in search of a manuscript. The memory cells under his beret became his only recording device this night. He lay on the furthermost seat at the rear of the bus and closed his eyes.

***

As morning broke, the landscape across Central Park and the zoo was strewn with garbage from as far away as Broadway. The picture was one of a declared emergency. Wind and rain had separated posters and signs from their moorings, and animals restlessly whined and squawked with caged confusion. Zookeepers busied themselves tearing down tree branches and limbs that had tried to weave their way into the cages the night before. The task proved formidable.

***

Tanglewood faired with fewer dramatics, even though for Samara Jennings, *drama* could hardly describe the harsh reality of the past twelve hours. It was raw. It was traumatic. It was like the threat of losing a brother. She dragged herself through the lobby of the Inn and into her room where she collapsed on the bed. Her cell phone rang with all the subtlety of a Chinese gong. The hospital gave the requested hourly report on Leonard. He was still in a coma.

In the next room, Tina tossed and turned in her sleep, pulling the pillow this way and that. Neither the light of day nor the rat-tat-tat on the door from housekeeping was going to disturb her anxious sleep.

***

In Lower Manhattan, darkness was the order of the day as the coffee shop remained buried in the all-day shadows of skyscrapers. Theo sat with an empty cup of coffee at the counter, waiting for the new brew to be ready. With a stubby pencil, he made notes on napkins for the unwritten manuscript.

He looked up and noticed, sitting at the end of the counter, a strange looking bundle of layered rain jackets and colored scarves.

"Been here long?" asked Theo.

The bundle remained silent.

"Hell of a night, eh? Caught the 8th Ave line and stayed on it."

68

Still no response.

"Rather calming, actually. The subway. Calming." He shrugged.

The bundle continued in mute silence.

The waitress—a rather unorthodox image for a waitress looking more like an NBA forward at six and a half feet with flats—topped up Theo's cup. "Good brew today, Sally." She turned and placed the pot back on the warmer.

"I said, good brew today," repeated Theo.

"Same shit as usual. Thanks anyway," said Sally, as she flashed a smile desperately needing dental attention. "You comin' onto me again, Theo?"

He shook his head and smiled back. "Not today, not tomorrow. Never."

Sally laughed. "How come you always think I wanna jump your bones?"

"Cause that toothless smile always means only one thing," the voice from the kitchen bellowed.

"What you talkin' 'bout? I smiles at everybody."

"And you'll take anybody you can get, right?" said the cook. "Right, Theo?" he yelled from the grill.

Theo took a big gulp of coffee. "Hey, what do I know?" he said, trying to concentrate on his notes.

"So, what's a *girl* supposed to do?" she said as she grabbed one of many hard-boiled eggs resting in a bowl.

Theo looked up. "Sally. I love ya, but you ain't no *girl*, even with that operation. Okay?"

Like a daily ritual, she methodically cracked it against her forehead, placed it on a saucer, and slid it in front of Theo. With a serious look, she said, "That hurt, you know. Really hurt." Not being able to feign any longer, she laughed. Theo followed. They high-fived each other. Sally turned and grabbed her coffee pot. "Topper?"

"Yeah, sure. What the hell. Like I said…"

"Good brew," answered Sally with a nod. "Damn straight." She placed the pot back on the burner.

"Aren't you forgetting your other customers?" said Theo, idly nodding toward the bundle. Sally followed his nod toward the end of the counter, then back. "You're the only one havin' coffee this mornin,' guy."

"Oh," said Theo, tilting his head, a bit perplexed that there wasn't a cup or dish in front of the motionless bundle. "Yeah."

As Theo peeled his egg, he continued to stare at the strange rainbow of layered yellow, pink, and blue scarves, and topped off with a purple anorak. *That's got to be hot.*

"Not really," whispered Echo, her head still bowed. "They breathe well. I like color."

Theo stopped his normal breathing for a moment, the egg half in and half out of his mouth. He hadn't said a word, but the girl was answering. He took a bite of the egg and then surreptitiously motioned to Sally. "Hey...c'mere," he whispered

Sally sauntered over. "You want me now, huh?"

"Want to know who that is?"

Sally gave a quick smile. "End of the counter? Echo."

"Echo?"

Sally leaned on the counter, exposing her lack of cleavage. "Sure you wouldn't like to maybe get some coffee after I get off or..."

"Sally. No. So what's her story?"

Leaning back up and starting to refill the saltshakers, she said, "Sits down there once in a while. Never eats...drinks. Just likes to read my dumb poetry. Always askin' for more, so dumb me, I lay more scribbles on the counter. Otherwise, quiet. Sits. Has the craziest knack for comin' in when I gots me a new poem though."

Theo paused, popped the rest of the egg in his mouth, then, "Think she'd find me too fast if I got to talkin' with her?"

Sally gave him the once over. "You back to bein' a dirty old man again?"

"Why would I do that when I've got you?"

Sally squinted. "That a compliment?"

Theo smiled and nodded as he picked up his cup, reached across for the coffee pot, and then casually moved down the row of stools to Echo. Before he could complete the move, Echo slid off the stool and moved smoothly out the door. Theo placed his cup and the pot on the counter and followed.

Outside, with Theo close behind, Echo picked up her step. Just as she reached the corner, she looked over her shoulder and said, "Not today. This isn't the time." Then, turned the corner.

Theo was no more than ten steps behind, but when he turned the corner, she was gone. He peered down the side street she had turned into, and except for the two or three tenement entrances fifty or sixty yards further on, there was no place for her to go. He paused and looked both ways. Mystified, he mumbled her last words, "this isn't the time."

A street cleaner rumbled by, sweeping last night's debris off the cobblestones of the old narrow street. Theo walked back. As he reached the coffee shop, he noticed a lone bag lady lingering over a refuse can examining a discarded cocktail umbrella from the local Asian restaurant. Satisfied it could still close and open, she carefully placed it in her hair. She continued down the street, the little plastic umbrella shimmering in the broken shafts of light sneaking past the buildings. Theo watched her a few moments, struck by his sudden keen sense of color. He glanced over his shoulder at the street corner where last he saw Echo, then stepped back into the coffee shop. He climbed back up on his stool. After a few moments of staring at the end of the counter where Echo had sat, he turned to Sally and said, "You never told me you were a poet, Sally."

"No, I didn't," she answered. "Dumb poets don't brag, do they?"

"Don't think I've ever heard of a *dumb* poet, Sally."

"You gettin' friendly again, little guy?" she asked with child-like honesty.

"I'd like to read your poetry, if that's alright. Maybe the last one Echo read. You okay with that?"

Sally rubbed her hands on her apron and grinned. "Really?"

CHAPTER 12

I was missing Samara, but the storm had done such damage that a week's worth of concerts were cancelled, and she remained in Massachusetts waiting for the clean up to finish so there could finally be an opening night. She was more than just stressed out over Leonard. For years, they'd been close. This wore on her and all I could do was send support and assurance over the phone that Leonard was going to be all right. He was five days into his coma, though, and my words had to be getting less and less convincing.

With all her sadness, the good thing happening for me was shadowed in gray. But, sucking it in, I stood before the Toyota forklift with its 9000 lb. lift capacity about to raise onto an open-bed truck my crated obelisk, "Ode to 2001." Seep, the effete gallery owner, stood at the curb, the armpits of his pink and blue striped shirt already showing the stress of the occasion.

"Jesus, be careful," he shouted at the driver.

The massive body driving the forklift moved his cigar stub from the left to the right side of his mouth. "You wanna drive it, Sweet Cheeks?"

Seep turned halfway with his back to the driver and muttered under his breath to me, "Where has our culture gone?"

I smiled. "Are you forgetting the Billy Bill's of the country make it possible to have a culture?"

"He didn't need to get personal," mumbled Seep.

"So," I said, "this woman, this, what did you call her, 'mother-load rich woman' paid an extra thousand to have me accompany it to her home and supervise its setup?"

"I told her it was highly irregular, and she pushed the bills into my hands. So what could I say?"

Her gesture made me uncomfortable, but, I said, "You're such a charmer."

"That why you sell a few?"

"What? A *few*? That's the fourth this year. You're on a roll, D.T.," Seep said with pride.

Were his eyes starting to well up? He gripped my arm. "The Ode is back home, now, and someone loves it, okay?"

"A 'piece of junk,' I muttered bitterly to help shake off a moment's sentiment. "Critics had me under attack for seven months in Europe, and now that all disappears just because some rich lady buys it?"

Seep stood back and threw me a look. "My God, Derek. Take a rest after this little trip. You just sold this 'piece of junk' for seventy thousand."

We both looked on anxiously as the twenty-five-foot crate was carefully laid to rest horizontally in the truck and secured with heavy cargo chains.

***

The drive to New England was starting off as a once in a lifetime experience. Billy Bill was a Nam vet and he attributed his heavy girth and bad smoking habits to his PTSD. "War made me sick. Never gettin' well." He was one of those hard working average guys that didn't understand why other people lived so well, and he couldn't advance.

"...I, mean," he said, "I don't hold nothin' 'gainst people, you know. Just don't get it. I work hard. Two kids—two monsters—a wife, cat, frog and a fuckin' tortoise. Don't ask. Fucker is big as a tub now. Ten years. Anyway, I get by. Wife gets by. She takes care of three preschoolers while their lawyer parents work. Pays good." He laughed. "Hell, she makes more than me. Just don't get it. I mean, how some people...gold falls out of the heaven's to 'em." He adjusted himself, re-positioned his cigar, smiled and said, "Here's a good one..."

That was the beginning of five hours, non-stop. Billy Bill didn't have just one *stand-up* routine; he had one for every type of crowd one could imagine. Now Billy was the first one I'd met—the wannabe Lenos of the world—but he had a funny way about him. I laughed, and for one that doesn't laugh a lot, it came as a relief. Only bad part was the constant cigar smell. And here I was trying to quit cigarettes. I never realized it before, but you can chew on one of those tree stumps and in a closed-in area, it still stinks like it's been smoked.

By the time we reached The Cape, I was ready for a stretch. The sign said: REST AREA AHEAD. "Hey, Billy, mind if we stop just for a few minutes? Stretch?"

Billy shrugged. "Hey, whatever. It's your clock we're on."

He pulled up to the toilets.

"Could use a piss myself."

I smiled as he rolled out of the truck and lumbered into the men's room. Turning, I wandered down the parking area. I marveled at how big and luxurious motor homes had become. As I passed a custom modified bus, I noticed the artwork on the side depicting someone's impression of Hell. I stopped and took a moment to imagine the kind of talent it took to airbrush such a landscape. Blaring out the windows was some old Frank Zappa music. Two kids, miniatures of Billy Bill, waddled up to the bus door and glanced my way, their eyes darting back and forth between me and the mural-like paint job. "Don't even think about it. Last guy touched that, my dad put him in the hospital."

What was that all about?

"Let's get it on," Billy bellowed from the restroom. I turned and walked back thinking how mixed a moment's impression could be. From art to monster kids. As I climbed up into the cab, I asked Billy, "Ever get pissed, Billy? Ever get really mad? Violent?"

He started to back out. "Shit yes. Where'd that come from?"

"Just curious," I answered. What I was really thinking, as I looked back toward the bus—*it's been a long time since anything made me angry about anything. Either Samara is good for me, really good, or maybe I'm losing something. Wasn't anger supposed to be normal?*

***

It was still light as we pulled up the winding driveway though the thick foliage to the house. As we got closer, the cover thinned. The sand, so prevalent on the Cape, was now beginning to take over the landscape. What started out suggesting the quietness of a Japanese garden, now graduated into a larger minimalist study in rock composition. We passed a large circular support frame whose center was dominated by an oversized stainless steel pendulum, the kind major science museums had. The sand beneath the structure showed the pattern the cabled chrome-pointer had carved. I leaned out the window as we passed for a closer look and saw an intricate design that would not last through the night. One thing you could always count on at the Cape were gentle winds that would remove footprints by morning and leave the beaches looking perfectly groomed, just as Mrs. Baker's ingenious landscaping would realize this night. The winds were already picking up.

As we passed the parked truck and trailer, we could see its cargo, the crane the lady ordered, behind the house. We pulled at the front door and I got out to meet this *mother-lode* person. A woman dressed like a proper housekeeper for such a manor answered the door.

"You must be Mister Turrel."

"Yes," I answered.

"I'm Sybil. Mrs. Ballard will be down shortly. Please make yourself at home while you wait."

"Excuse me, but did you say Ballard?"

"Why, yes."

I looked at the sales receipt. It clearly read Mrs. Baker. I paused.

"Yes?" she asked.

"A...this...Mrs. Ballard, I mean...she was recently in the hospital?"

"My goodness. How did you know that?"

"Oh, boy. This is something else."

"Pardon?"

"Oh, nothing," I answered. "We'll wait out here."

"Would you like a refreshment?"

Billy couldn't restrain himself. "A beer would be great. Just one or two though. Got a long drive back."

The maid smiled shyly, throwing a knowing glance my way. "Our friends manning the crane had soft drink orders."

"Well, he's had a long drive," I said

"Absolutely, " she said as she stepped back into the house.

Billy walked around the truck and leaned his head back to peer skyward at the ornate design of the boulder rock fireplace that ended some forty feet above the ground. "Is that good?

"Good?"

"Yeah. The stuff around the top. That's art ain't it?"

I glanced up. "Well, from here, I'd say yeah. Interesting." The upper ten or so feet of the chimney had a sculpted group of salt-resistant copper gargoyles, the green oxidation giving them an appropriate eerie look.

Billy turned around and looked back down the driveway. "Lot of space for sand. You think that's more expensive than dirt?"

"Probably not, Billy. Check out where we are."

I walked to the side of the house. It was obvious she had spared no cost in arranging the crane. Heavy iron slabs covered the ground where the crane had been maneuvered to the rear. I caught a glimpse of the ocean frontage on the backside that sloped some fifty yards to the shore. Tall grass and a winding weathered fence completed the image—like a Wyeth waiting to be preserved on canvas.

The front door opened again, and out stepped Aretha. She smiled a sheepish grin and said, "Surprised?"

"Up 'til a few minutes ago I was clueless."

"That's a yes and I'm delighted." She glanced at Billy. "You must be the driver."

"You betcha...er, ma'am."

"Well, welcome to Planet One."

"Yes. I noticed that name on the gate as we drove in," I said.

"Well, science won't single out the *first* planet, so I took intellectual title." She took my arm with her gloved hand. "Please. I want to show you the home of "Ode.""

"How's the finger healing?" I asked as we walked around to the back and out several yards to what looked to be a foundation for a gazebo. The crane stood ready, its two men sipping cokes.

She grinned and flashed her hand as if showing off a fancy manicure. "I bought a couple of pair from one of France's finest. Like the fit?"

I smiled. "Your finger's hardly a laughing matter, but, yes. You have good taste."

"Of course. I bought your Ode, didn't I?" She quietly grinned like Cheshire cat, reminding me once more how innocent her humor was compared to what was obviously a complex personality.

"So," she said, again focusing on the task at hand, "what do you think? Had it removed yesterday."

"Removed?" I said.

"Oh, one of those awful gazebos. My late husband insisted. Never could stand it." She looked up at me and smiled. "Better suited for a Turrel, don't you think?"

"A Turrel is good. Yes."

"I think so. So..." She walked over to the crane men. "All ready to show your stuff?"

"Yes, Ma'am," said one of the men. They placed their cokes to the side, slipped on their gloves as Derek stepped forward. "Hi. I'm the guy whose made this a complicated task."

"Nothing too complicated for the Betsy here. Bring her on," said the worker with a smile.

"How long will it take you to put it in place?" Asked Aretha.

"Billy?

"Yeah?"

"How long to bring it out here?"

He glanced at the backside and steel slabs. "Twenty minutes." He glanced up at the crane and the two men. "Hey, guys." He extended his hand. "Billy."

"Slim," said one.

"Ralph," said the other.

"Well," said Billy, "20 minutes and you can have your day."

"Sounds good," said Ralph.

Aretha said, "And how long to put it upright?"

"30, 45 minutes tops," said Slim.

She turned to Derek. "Oh, wonderful. I thought it would take longer. That gives us more time for dinner." She took his arm and escorted him a few yards to the deck chairs.

"Oh, that's not necessary," said Derek.

"Nonsense. Dinner, a hot Jacuzzi—it's right over here—and a feather bed from Finland. All for a perfect night. You'll sleep like a baby."

That was a first. I couldn't believe I was being seduced in one complex sentence. It was one continuous thought. "Whoa. We came to deliver, Aretha. He's got to get back to his family and..."

"I have plenty of room for him as well, but if he must get back, you'll not be stranded. Stanton, he's my neighbor, agreed, if necessary, to fly you back tomorrow. I thought there might be this kind of complication. But, my life is all about solving problems, so, it's settled then." She turned. "Mister, ah...Billy? You sure you can't...where did he go?"

I pointed to the truck. "He's working."

"Of course. Well, so..."

"Aretha, that's very kind of you, but..."

"No buts about it. I read the papers. Samara is stuck another week in Tanglewood—such a storm—and...just missed us, you know, turning west as it did. She'd think ill of me if I had you drive all this way and then sent you right back...in a Ryder truck."

My head was reeling as the Toyota with the heavy-duty forklift slowly lifted its crated cargo off the flatbed, "The Ode" securely strapped into place.

Billy followed the iron slabs from the front of the house to the backside and the gazebo foundation. Aretha stepped away from the deck and caught herself being traffic cop. "Oh," she said to the crane men. "I'm so sorry. Force of habit. Please...it's all yours. Please."

She stepped back onto the deck. "That was embarrassing. Anyway, always good to get to the unload phase," she said, smiling and pointing to the corner of the former gazebo area as Billy stepped down and began un-strapping the crate. She pointed at a large abstract sculpted stone. "That Moore piece took a crane also, on up over the roof to slide neatly under the eaves to the planks. I had concrete laid under the planks, but still, It's sinking about a quarter-inch a year. Now that's heavy. Four ton." She turned to me. "What you think?"

"About?"

"Moore. His *Mother with Child*? Your opinion."

"You're talking about Moore, Aretha. He's every sculptor's idol."

"Good. I hoped you weren't narcissistic."

She took my arm and backed me away. "Okay, fellows, you know what you're doing, I'm sure, but do take your time." The pleasantry of her words couldn't cover the stress in her voice. She was definitely nervous.

Billy and the crane men smiled back. Billy mouthed his cigar to the other side, and clip, clip, clip. The straps dropped to the ground. Within a few minutes, the Ode was upright and Billy maneuvered his crowbar to take care of the slats.

As he removed the heavy blanket padding, I stood with Aretha on the rear deck of the house, feeling the sun setting at my back. The windows at the back of the house reflected a broken, clouded horizon. As Billy removed the final layer of blankets, the horizon's fireball dodged the gray strands of weather, and as if on cue, broke through, laying a direct hit on the obelisk.

"My God," exclaimed Aretha. "I never..." She turned and took my face in her hands, kissed each cheek, leaned back and focused those penetrating eyes on mine. "I never imagined it this good." She took another moment and glanced across the sea at the searing ball of fire, then as she turned back toward the Ode, her eyes moistened with something beyond my expectation.

Billy and the other men stood before the Ode a bit awestruck as well. Billy removed his cigar and tilted his head from side to side as the two other men prepared the crane to tractor-back out over the slabs. "Reminds me of something. Just can't figure it out."

"You go to the movies, Billy," I asked.

"Sometimes. Mostly rentals at home though. Why?"

"You might have seen something like this a few years back on the big screen, even though my work wasn't inspired by the movie."

Still emotionally connected to the moment, Aretha whispered, "My guess is Africa, right?"

I nodded.

Aretha grinned. "Transcends even Mister Kubrick's fine taste. You've created a surreal meditation... the perfect grounding."

I beamed as the sun once again drifted behind a cloud; leaving the towering image with its part marble, part highly polished stainless steel surface reflecting a subtler array of impressions. We could see ourselves amidst a broken sky, the long grass at our backs swaying with ethereal elegance. We could even see a group of gulls coming toward us in perfect formation. The air was interrupted by the harmony of gulls' open beaks high above calling out with their inimitable screeches.

Aretha maintained a mesmerized gaze at the sculpture as I turned slightly to look down the shore for the gull I could hear *cawing* back to the formation.

The beach was barren of anything but sand, save for what appeared like a bright yellow scarf ambling across the bits of driftwood and shells.

Shortly, Billy and the crane operators said their goodbyes and started their drive back to the city.

***

Sybil served her specialty of roast quail. Consistent with the experience thus far, all was perfect. Aretha prepared brandy snifters for us and here we were, sitting opposite each other in the Jacuzzi, our heads resting on pillows; she in a conservative bathing suit, me in paisley swim trunks, two sizes too large. "Just one of my husband's *throw-aways*," she called them. Even the steaming water had been designed with Aretha's signature, coming as it did from jets carved into a solid peace of granite. Arcs of white, red, orange and blue light from beneath the water undulating up the sides had been created, she explained, to sometimes remind her of the ever-changing ripples and colored movements of the universe.

As we sat amidst her fantasy world of the planets, she pointed toward the sky. "And that over there, Constellation Zebra. Hard to see at times, but it's there." She turned toward the moon. "Full. Good for your Ode. God, look up there, Derek. A gleaming black reflection of... everywhere." She chuckled. "Even catches Stanton's house next door." She leaned a bit forward, squinting at the reflection. "Damn, I think he's... Oh, my. Good thing his wife is gone, God rest her soul. The little devil." She reached over and positioned my head properly to see what she was catching. "There...above the dune. See. The lens of his telescope is catching the reflection of the moon and he's...spying. I should slap him with a 'cease and desist,' but he is a sweetheart during the day. Anyway...."

She humored herself with the idea of voyeurism for a few moments, then reached behind her and flicked a switch, bringing all the house lights down. This activated the rising up of small translucent bowls of water from the ground. Lit from within, they enhanced the setting even further with a refracting circle of light.

"Jesus," I said with reverence. "You do know how to express yourself, don't you?"

"Something else we have in common, perhaps," she answered. "I just like to sit out here often, watch the stars, raise the planets of our system—that's what these *underground friends* are, you know—and just wonder at the *system* way the hell out there. Ah…it's so peaceful to imagine that someday I might be floating somewhere out there. Just me and God, assuming he shows himself to us heathens in the arts and sciences." She drifted off into some other space for a few moments.

I took another sip of brandy and leaned back again.

Without looking my way, she said, "You're bothered by something, aren't you?"

"No. Nothing."

She leaned forward, her eyes meeting mine. "You lie badly," she said.

I was bothered, but didn't feel she'd be interested. It was, after all, further out there than her "system."

"You've been awfully quiet since sunset," she insisted.

"Yes."

"Okay. Although I'd find myself down to earth, really down to earth in your arms, I'm at least twenty years and several solar systems too experienced for you. Relax."

I momentarily snapped out of my own daydreaming at her comment. "I…that's…"

As if she were reading my mind, she said, "Absolutely. What you see is what you never get. Another man in my bed is the last thing I need. So… its your problem to resolve, not mine."

I had to smile to keep from laughing. Damn, this was some kind of woman. "Not really a problem."

She put that look in her eyes again; the look that I was beginning to understand meant she was once again going to get what she wanted.

"Disconnection."

"What?"

"Disconnection is always a problem," she said.

"It's not disconnection. More like the opposite. A connection…to something. I just don't know what to."

Aretha perked right up. "Ooo, I like this. Where are we going on this journey?"

"It's roadless."

"Perfect. You have my interest."

I had to pause. That thought came so rapidly, I didn't even know from where. "Never thought of that before."

"What? A journey without a road."

"Kind of."

"I can relate. No roads up there, and oh, what a journey it's been."

I gave my head a good shake. "Just stuff. It's nothing. Just something I need to do."

Aretha paused for another moment to stare at me. "Something your need to do? Not unusual. We all have something we need to do and somehow keep putting it off." She looked at her watch. "Like, oh, my goodness, it is late. You must be exhausted." She stood up and stepped out.

As she wrapped herself in a towel and walked toward the house, sipping her drink like a teenager, I couldn't help but smile and flash back on my younger "oat sowing" years. She was remarkably fit for a woman of her age. She paused in front of the Ode, looking at the reflection of the moon's spill across the surf. She turned back toward the shore. "By the way, did you notice the gulls today?"

I was taken aback. *Why was she asking that question? Especially now.* "Yes."

"Haven't seen gulls here for a long time. Very long time." She strode through the patio doors. "Come along now. Let's have one more and call it a night, okay? I know you've got a lot on your mind."

Later, as I lay in my bed, I took the last sip of my third snifter and reflected on the two hours of exploration we'd just finished—all after her simple invitation for a nightcap.

She believed in God...her kind of God.

I wasn't sure about any of that.

She believed in guardian angels.

I didn't.

She believed I was on the edge of discovering a road in this *journey* I'd brought up.

I wasn't sure.

She was convinced the gulls had visited for a reason.

I didn't know what I believed.

The whole day had been a bit overwhelming. I closed my eyes. She was a living example of *what you believe is.*

Next morning, I recalled a dream I'd have preferred not remembering. The girl had visited me... with her gulls.

***

The departure from Aretha's was a strange one. We both knew I'd be back. She thanked me for allowing her to buy the Ode. She knew how important all my work was to me and assured me it had a good home.

As I boarded the single engine plane with her neighbor, Stanton, at the controls, she slipped me a piece of paper, kissed me on each cheek, and donning her traffic-director mood, gave an authoritative wave for Stanton to take off.

Airborne, I unfolded the paper. It was a sketch of gulls in formation, accompanied by a note. *"Couldn't sleep last night. Hope this helps you understand better the road that is out there. Aretha."* I stared at the paper. A compass was sketched in the corner, needle north. Gulls flying north. I remembered the gulls above the river...also navigating north. I had just traveled from Manhattan to the Cape. North.

CHAPTER 13

Premiering some weeks later, Samara's concerto was a critical and financial success, resulting in a recording contract.

Leonard remained in a coma for seven weeks, but was now slowly working back to some kind of normalcy at St. Vincent's in Manhattan. The paralysis of his right side, along with the speech impairment, was temporary, the doctors said.

Theo's visits to the loft became less frequent, citing the time he had to spend "thinking and writing."

I finished the "Planet" piece and began my waiting period for an interested buyer. I hated the in-between periods when I had to rely on new stimuli, etc. It was always fun to mold a project after it was decided. But the waiting for a sale, the waiting for inspiration, and the toll of ever-present distractions—it all made for more time to discuss Samara's favorite question... "When are you going to do it, Derek?"

"Soon," I told her. "Soon." For the first time, I was beginning to believe my words. Additional urgency had been building ever since meeting Echo, but I didn't know why.

The summer finally passed.

Theo didn't understand why he had such renewed energy. The *turning of leaves? Anticipation of a new Jets season?* No. He didn't want to think about the nagging urge he'd had for several months, but maybe that was it. Of late, thoughts of what it would be like to be out on the circuit of writing columns again had grabbed his imagination, but he'd always talked himself out of it by reading the headlines and watching the news. He was convinced that the people really didn't want journalism ever again—they wanted sound bites, synopses, and "news, on the hour" clips. Music and the arts? As far as he was concerned, *original* creativity in the arts was rapidly dying, except for a few rare exceptions like Samara and Derek. He missed them.

As he passed a newsstand at the entrance to the 8th Ave subway, he came up short and paused. *Was it what he thought it was?* He turned back and gazed at the cover of the "All Around New York." In full color, there was a collage of photographs showing a school of fish in the Hudson River arcing out of the water like dolphins. Above them, a formation of seagulls. The inscription read, "Fish and Fowl Celebrate 1st Day of Fall." Innocent enough, except, fish don't normally jump synchronously like dolphins, unless of course the picture is Photo-Shopped or a photographer has captured the same phenomena that Derek witnessed. He sloughed it off as coincidence—perhaps.

***

Leonard breathed in the fragrance and pulled back. Samara knew gardenias were a favorite of his, and in a hospital room, with its entire sterile and colorless atmosphere, flowers were a welcome relief. He nodded with appreciation and half smiled. His face and right side of the body were still mostly paralyzed from the accident, but he was nevertheless in an up-mood. After all, it wasn't every day his best friend could break away from her busy schedule and visit, with gardenias.

"You're looking so much better," said Samara.

"Thank you." Leonard slurred.

Samara reached in her shoulder bag, took out some photographs, sat down beside him, and began shuffling through.

"You're quite a celebrity, you know. Berlin, Copenhagen, Rome, and even Singapore wrote about you. Here…" she pulled one

82

particular photo out. "Here, you are on a seventy-five foot billboard in London. Your label paid for that one. Seems accidents are good for sales."

He attempted a smile. "Royalties...good...for hospital... bills."

"Now, don't you be worrying about the hospital bills. They'll get paid. How's the physical therapy?'

"Good."

"You doing okay with it? I mean, it must be tiring and all."

Leonard turned away toward the window. "Waste...of time, but...gotta do...it."

"Why a waste?" asked Samara.

Leonard shook his head and turned back with a forced smile. He tried to slur out a change of subject. "How's the...shrink business?"

Samara shuffled the pictures some more and pulled out one that she coyly slipped behind her back. "Problems will always be good business, Lenny. So, if you could have anything you wanted right now, besides a fast healing process, what would it be?"

"That would be...enough, believe...me," he said.

"C'mon. There's got to be something."

He shrugged.

Samara pulled the picture out from behind her back and placed it in front of him. Parked in front of the Washington Bridge underpass was his completely restored Austin Healey. There was a moment of disbelief in his eyes, and then he glanced up, back at the picture. "That isn't...my 'tree' car, is it?"

"Every inch, with a few custom pieces of metal replacing the old. Like it?"

Leonard's eyes welled up. "You did this?"

"Well, Derek wasn't going to pass up an opportunity to have a work of art restored. You know him."

"I'll pay...I'll pay...you back."

"Nonsense. Your insurance paid for most of it, and we want you to accept it as our appreciation that you're still alive." She leaned down and kissed him on the forehead, her own tears dropping and merging with his. "You know how we feel about you, so not another word, hear?"

Unexpectedly, Derek popped into the room, pushing a huge bouquet of latex balloons ahead of him, each with an inner balloon shaped like an instrument of the orchestra. "Ta Da!"

Samara backed away, wiping her tears and grinning.

"So," said Derek, letting the balloons rise to the ceiling for a moment, and noticing Samara wiping her cheeks, "Did I miss the good part?" He leaned down and gave Leonard a hug.

"Not, really, unless…you like to watch a couple of…softies," said Leonard.

Derek pulled the balloons down for Leonard to take a closer look. "Got all their autographs. Can you believe that? Even crab-ass Steiner signed."

Leonard turned the balloons and reveled in all the good wishes written on them with marker pen. Samara joined in, each mumbling some of the writings to the other, commenting how it was like a high school yearbook.

***

Later, as Samara and Derek waited for a cab outside the entrance to St. Vincent's, Samara shared the bad news. "I talked with the doctor. He'll never walk again."

Derek, feeling stunned, weakly raised his arm to hail a cab. "Bullshit. He can't drive that Healey without being able to walk. Cabbie!"

As Derek and Samara walked the short distance from the cab drop-off to the loft, like Theo, they too passed one of the many newsstands in Manhattan. Derek saw the magazine cover and stopped. Like Theo, he couldn't explain the coincidence that the picture on the cover suggested. He bought a copy and thumbed through to the story even before they reached the front door.

As Samara prepared dinner, Derek read the article, noting that the photographer referred to two other sightings: one more on the Hudson up by the George Washington Bridge, and two at the Battery Park area—the place where he too had witnessed the same jumping fish phenomena.

"Must be a good story," said Samara from the kitchen.

"Yeah. Could be…could be," he half whispered, his eyes wandering to the raised hairs on his arms.

Chapter 14

Summer was gone, with no regrets. Humidity had been at record highs with temperatures driving my air-conditioning costs for the loft through the roof. Early this morning, though, you'd have thought it late, rather than early fall. I threw on a t-shirt and jeans, grabbed my camera and enjoyed the forty-minute subway ride up the West Side, exiting in Washington Heights. "Damn," I mumbled as I rubbed my hands together. "Has to be forty degrees. A little bit of summer would feel good about now."

On the walk to the George Washington Bridge, I passed an old second hand clothing store and took a look inside. There had to be

84

something I could grab to take the chill off. A little lady, her hair pulled back in a conservative bun, sauntered up to me swallowing the last of a bagel, and with all the cliché accent one could imagine said, "So, you're cold, maybe bubala?"

Trying the better side of valor, I answered, "Bit nippy for September, isn't it?"

"In Russia, this be a heat wave. Sweater?"

"Sweater, maybe. Let me look a bit."

"Good for me. Longer you look, more you spend," she said with a boisterous laugh.

I fingered through the hangers of oversized shirts, thinking I might find something that after today, Samara would appreciate. Always looking for a fashion statement that didn't reek of trends, or "gender rubbish" as she called it, Samara loved to spend an occasional Sunday rummaging through second hand stores for a "find." I lifted a shirt-jacket from its hanger and tried it on. Colorful epaulets set it off, something from the Beatles era for sure. Big enough for a linebacker, but that was okay. Samara liked a smock look. "How much?" I asked.

"You'll be cold in that. Why don't you try this?" She pulled out a hand knit fisherman's sweater that had seen better days. "The real thing," she chortled.

"I'm sure," I said, "but, you know, I like this one."

"You'll be cold. But...you like $8.95?"

"I like $7.95 better," thinking it was impolite to not bargain.

She put her hands on her thunder-hips and said, "You like $9.95 better?"

"$8.95 is good. Tax?"

"No tax. I absorb. I absorb all the profits my husband tells me. He likes the extra pounds in bed, though. You like the extra pounds in bed?"

I gave her nine dollars, smiled and walked toward the door.

"Yes?" she repeated.

"He's a very lucky man. 'Extra pounds' are good. Yes."

I was out the door before she could respond, but I knew I'd made her day.

As I picked up the pace on the walk from 181st street down to the base of the bridge, the uncomfortable temperature was just as she had predicted. I was cold.

The boulders beneath the bridge provided some high points to peer out at the river. It was calm. Blowing on my hands, I knew it was a long shot to expect the fish and gulls active, but it was the only way I had to find her. The writer/photographer for the story had said he'd visited this spot several times in one week and had seen the fish and gulls, allowing him to take a number of good pictures.

The cold was starting to get to me, but there they were. A few fish at first, and then as if a whole school had come together, their arcing above the waters' surface began. I looked up along the bridge supports. No gulls. The fish did their dance, and then without warning, reversed and did their acrobatics against the current. I whipped out my camera and started snapping.

I almost dropped it when from behind me came a voice I'd remembered. The girl.

"I don't do miracles," she said.

I turned around. There was no one. I turned back. The fish were still jumping.

"Over here!" came her playful shout.

I turned again and saw the colorfully draped girl about fifty yards behind me. I shook my head. I knew I'd heard her almost at my shoulder before. She had to be some kind of athlete to cover the ground that fast.

"Hey," I shouted back as I stumbled over the rocks toward her. "We need to talk."

She disappeared behind some larger rocks. As I ran up the embankment, her words were going over and over in my head, "I don't do miracles. I don't do miracles."

I reached where she had vanished, looked left and right and saw no one. I climbed up on the boulder and looked back at the river. No fish.

Up to the sky. No gulls.

"I'm losing it," I muttered to myself and climbed down.

A voice from the bridge, high above and some 100 yards away projected back to me, "No you're not."

I looked up.

"You're fine!" she shouted. "Just spend some time at Montauk."

"What?" I shouted back.

"Montauk. Montauk Point."

With that she was gone and I was left more confused and doubting my senses. I looked back at the shoreline where first I started. I reviewed in my mind the distances this person had traveled, and...

I was definitely losing it.

That night, I tried to work. Sketch after sketch of nothingness came forth. I paced the loft, checked my watch, hoping the hours would pass quickly, anticipating Samara would be home by 9:30,

10:00, but it got to be too much. I put on my "new" used jacket and wandered down to Stefano's. Time for a drink, or two.

I merge easily with night and any kind of darkness. Always have. Samara says I need more light in my life, but I get my best ideas in the dark.

I wandered into my haunt and looked around to see no one but Jerry at the bar, and Cinch playing gin with some new faces, at least to me. At the far end of the room, I could see a shadow huddled in the corner, but it was too dark to make out. I stepped up to the bar with, "Jerry, I'm ready!"

Jerry grinned. "Should I call 911 ahead of time?"

"Let's start slow, might be a long night."

Jerry slid me a Becks and a glass. "Peanuts?" he asked.

"Good for now," I responded, looking about. "Got the Times?"

He reached under the counter. "Samara workin' late?"

"She's catching up. Finishing her first concerto is obsessing."

"Wondered. Haven't seen her in a while," Jerry said.

There was a tap on my back. "Gonna drink by yourself?"

I turned and was face to face with, "Theo. Where'd you come from?"

"Just mindin' my business in the corner."

"Sit down," I said. "Jerry, get us a couple of Tequilas." I turned back to Theo. "Why've you been such a stranger?"

Theo took the last swallow of his beer. "You two needed some time together."

"What are you talking about? We get plenty of time together. We've missed you."

"Well, I've been busy." Theo grinned.

"Yeah? So, tell me. You writing again?"

Jerry sat the tequilas down in front of us.

"Thanks," said Theo. He lifted his shot glass and downed it.

I grinned and raised my eyebrow to Jerry, then downed mine. "Might as well leave the bottle, Jerry."

I turned back to Theo, anxious to hear what he was doing. "The writing...what you up to?"

Theo grinned a moment, then went somber. "I don't know. Been kinda wanderin' again." He reached in his pocket and pulled out a tiny pencil and small spiral notebook. "A lot of notes, mostly. I started lookin' around again."

"You mean in the art galleries?"

"No." He looked up at me with sadness in his eyes. "Think Jerry would mind if we sat back in the corner?"

There was a sense of desperation in his voice, and I was suddenly more aware of his confusion than my own. "Course not. Jerry?" I raised my glass and pointed to the corner, grabbing the bottle with the other hand.

It took some time for Theo to get through the *feeling out* part. I mean, he was hesitant to really confront me with what it was that was bothering him. He told me about his tour of street preachers, performance art, kids playing under the gush of the fire hydrants, the galleries, and finally what was really bothering him.

"So," I said, "you have been busy."

"The girl."

"Pardon," I said.

"The girl, the gulls, the fish...that girl."

"Okay," I stammered. *Where was he going with this?* "You mean...that girl."

"I think she made me a visit," Theo volunteered.

"Made you a visit. And..."

"I thought she was your creation, you know? Thought you found her, 'cause you needed that kind of connection."

I shrugged. "And I think you might have been right. So, she visited you too."

"Too. Yeah. Me *too*."

I poured another drink. Theo covered his glass. "You know I'm a *two beers* guy."

"Except when you're not." I toyed with pouring it on his hand, and he uncovered.

We clinked our glasses and began a very late night.

***

I do remember it was cold as hell sitting on the bench waiting for the sunrise on that Sunday morning. The Hudson River was rough as well. Clouds moved across the horizon as the sun waited to rise behind us and make its way above the buildings of Lower Manhattan.

Theo was trying his best to keep his drunken eyes open, but they kept creeping shut. "She's not coming today, old buddy," I said. I was past trying to convince him any further. Three hours earlier when Jerry closed up and kicked us out, I had said, "Let's grab some *zzzs* up stairs, Theo. We're wasted." Looking up at the fourth floor windows of the loft, he shook his head. So we wandered and he kept saying it was good to walk and work off the alcohol, all the time guiding me—here.

"Yup. Think you're right. Not today," he wearily confirmed.

I stood up. "Good. Now that you got me here, and now that you're ready to leave...could we just...leave?"

He staggered to his feet and saluted me. "Absolutely, Captain."

Without warning, a plop of white gull wash hit him on the shoulder. His reaction was as slow as mine, exercising great effort to lift our chins. We both stared at the three gulls flying erratically. "Garden variety. Definitely, not her," Theo said.

"Definitely," I followed.

The gulls veered to the east, gathering together with another dozen, and crossed over the East River and toward Long Island, forming the now familiar double-arrow. I watched for a few moments while Theo leaned against a lamppost, trying to stay awake.

"Ever been to Montauk, Theo?"

"What?"

"Montauk. You've been there, haven't you?"

"When I was a kid. Remember a lighthouse."

"And a few left over concrete bunkers from the war?" I asked.

"Bunkers?" he said as we stumbled across the lawn, and I took my last look at the formation heading east in the direction of Montauk.

"Yeah," I said. "My grandfather told me about them. Spotters sat in them for days...looking for German U-Boats."

Theo stumbled and fell down and began laughing as he pulled himself up. "U-Boats? How the hell did we get from gull shit to U-Boats?"

I nodded toward the gulls as they disappeared into the glare of the sun.

CHAPTER 15

Linda squinted, trying to see out from beneath the basket atop her head. She had been weaving with a passion Dr. Reagan hadn't seen before. She had completed forty-three baskets in all.

The day following the encounter with her mother, she had chosen to sit in her room staring at the wall. Efforts to get her to eat and engage others had proved futile. Now, five months later, she had gained back the weight she'd lost and was determined to finish two hundred baskets before Thanksgiving.

From inside the basket, her words shot across the room, "Too much light, God Dammit! Too much light!"

Other patients involved with crafts and playing board games stopped and stared. Linda continued, as if in conversation with someone inside the basket. "I need to pull tighter, don't I? Of course, I'm being lazy. Rushing. Getting sloppy, aren't I?" Her voice dropped to a whisper. "You know what rushing did to you before, so slow the hell down. Yeah, I will. Good point."

As she lifted the basket slowly from her head, the other patients gazed a moment, then went back to their routine. She stood there, her eyes moving slowing about the room at each and every one of them. "How many do you think you could do? Any of you? Zero, zip. You know why? Because you don't have any discipline." She strutted over to her table, and laid the basket down. She tilted her head from side to side, eyeing the work. Without warning, she whipped a chair up and brought it down on the basket with a "thwack," sending basket shrapnel flying in every direction and patients running for the doors. She stood there and stared at what was left of the smashed basket.

Two orderlies stepped into the room. The head nurse casually walked over to the table.

"Didn't like that one, eh Linda?"

Linda curled her mouth and grinned at the nurse. "On the contrary, Ratch. It was the best I've done."

"Oh, I'm sorry," the nurse said.

Ratch, as Linda had nicknamed her, lifted the broken remnants of the basket, but Linda stepped forward.

The orderlies took a step forward.

The nurse motioned for them to back off.

"Don't do that," Linda muttered.

"Okay, dear. You want to keep it?"

"No. Just don't want you fingerin' it, okay? And I'm not your 'dear.'"

Ratch walked back toward her station. "I agree. I think that was your prettiest one, you know."

Linda gave her the bird, and then looked back at the basket. "Too much light."

It didn't take long for Dr. Reagan to hear of the incident with the "Basket Case" as Linda was referred to by some of the other patients. Usually, the intensity of her basket weaving was contained within her corner space in the recreation room, but lately, she had been wandering among the checker players and the TV watchers with a basket on her head, spouting four letter words at the light bulbs and window illumination.

Dr. Reagan knocked before entering Linda's room. Lying on her bed, Linda glanced up, rolled her eyes, and went back to reading her book, "Atlas Shrugged."

"How are we doing, Linda?"

Without looking up again, she said, "About the same as Galt."

"You mean you find society lacking?"

"He didn't find society lacking; he found the institutions *controlling* society lacking."

"That *is* a difference, isn't it," he said.

She looked over the top of the book. "Look, Doctor, you know and I know I got more smarts than you, so rhetorical analysis is going to get us nowhere. Why don't you ask me why I think there's too much fucking light?"

Dr. Reagan nodded. "Okay. Why is there so much fucking light?"

"Because we're downing our trees with axes and throwin' shit in the air faster than they can grow; because God's got to work overtime, daylight saving time, and all that crap because the system, the institutions are mutilating life."

"How about we just talk about the baskets?" Dr. Reagan said.

"Oh, now that's a very interesting subject. You think that up all by yourself?"

"I'm just curious. Who acted out of line to get you upset?"

Linda sat up, placed the book on her lap. "Either the weave is tight enough to be good, or it's not. Good baskets have tight weaves. Light can't get through good baskets. I like to make good baskets. Now what do *you* want to talk about?"

"The Head Nurse quoted you as saying it was the best you'd done."

"What, the basket I destroyed? Nurse…Ratch, takes me and her whole life too literally."

"It wasn't?"

"Wasn't what?"

"The best basket you'd made?"

Linda stood up and approached the doctor. "You bring your smokes, or just that pipe stickin' out of your pocket?"

"You know smoking isn't allowed in a patient's room."

Linda leaned down, eye to eye. "Unless under supervision. Aren't you the big dude supervisor?"

Dr. Reagan reached into his pocket and pulled out a pack of Turkish cigarettes. "These are strong, you know."

Linda smiled as she took one. "Wouldn't expect anything *but* the strongest for my Doc. Light?"

As he lit her cigarette, she touched his shaking hand, "Relax, Doctor. I only smash baskets."

He smiled. "Too much coffee and not enough sleep."

She exhaled. "Whatever. So…best…" She coughed. "Damn. These are…different." Clearing her throat, she continued. "Best basket? Probably, but still not good enough."

"Aren't you a little hard on yourself? It's just for Thanksgiving."

Linda leaned against the wall, and rested her elbow in her hand as she took another drag. "When the institutions limit one's world, the simplest achievement can mean a lot, but 'best basket' doesn't mean I'm satisfied."

He nodded. "Understood."

"You satisfied, Doctor?"

"My work is very rewarding."

"I mean satisfied. Fuck rewarding. How's your sex life?"

"We're getting off subject, Linda."

"We've already covered fucking baskets and fucked rewards. Let's talk about fucking *fucking*."

"Were you always resentful with your mother?"

Linda turned on her heels and stomped out the cigarette. "Oh, you're so pathetic." She hopped up on her table and sat in a lotus position. "Look, I put up with you 'cause you hold the strings and the real basket cases in the rec room are hardly capable of engagement, but let's get it straight again for the…how many times have I told you, six or seven…for the eighth time, I'm high strung, pissed off at my mother, lacking any psychotic symptoms, loaded with neuroses like all the rest out there on main street, and I'm going to make the best of my time here until you wise up and stop taking the barrels of money my mother gives you to keep me here. Hey, you know why she wants me here? Do you really know?"

He smiled. "Why don't you tell me?"

She hopped off the table and went to the door, gave it a knock and yelled at the top of her lungs, "Help, help! Damn it HELP!"

The doctor jumped to his feet just as two orderlies swung the door open. "What's going on? You okay, Dr. Reagan?"

"Yes, fine. No problem."

Linda sauntered to the middle of the room, leaned over and picked up the cigarette stub. "You don't want to leave your butt behind, Doctor."

He took the smashed stub from her hand. "I made a phone call before our visit. There's a Nigerian palm frond that is purported to be the most flexible and easiest to manipulate…*tightly*, according to the museum. I've ordered you a couple of bundles." He nodded goodbye, turned and left.

Linda squinted at his exit. After a moment, she turned back to the window and stood still for a long moment, her back to the door. "That's one for you, fucker," she said, her voice trembling.

One of the orderlies peered through the small glass door window. "Crackers," he muttered.

Linda continued to gaze out the window at the flock of gulls in formation flying over the grounds—heading northeast.

***

Theo blew into his cold hands. "I don't know who is crazier," he mumbled. "I don't need to see my breath in September, you know. Whole damn winter for that. And especially not in Montauk."

I pulled my red scarf tighter, rubbed my hands together and peered out to the ocean from the bunker's small opening. Grumbling was part of Theo's makeup, largely due to his unwillingness to complain. He had explained to me months before that there was a difference. "Grumbling," he had said, "was a means of staying honest. Complaining was a victim's choice."

"You complaining, Theo?"

"Damn, haven't you learned the difference yet? When I'm ready to complain, I'm ready for the box."

"The box?"

"Pine."

"Oh."

I reached down and lifted my cold coffee container. "Sure you don't want some?"

Theo laughed. "Two hours out here and you think that's still worth drinking?"

I looked into my daypack and brought out two Energy bars. "Still good enough to wash this down." I threw Theo the second bar.

He shuddered. "*Anything* is good enough to wash that crushed cardboard you eat." Theo read the ingredients and shook his head.

I looked out to sea again. "It won't be long."

Theo glanced out, shoved the bar in his pocket, and sat back down on some newspaper covering an old cinder block. As he patted his pocket, he said, "Just in case it's longer than you think."

The center of the bunker was piled high with beer cans and half-burned pieces of driftwood. Theo's eyes wandered to the graffiti on the block walls. He turned his head from side to side trying to read. "What makes you so sure she's gonna be here? Didn't she just say to *visit* Montauk?"

"You met her," I said. "You think that's all she meant?"

Still studying the wall, Theo nodded. "What, to visit? Sure. Don't know why, but..." He pointed at the red and black series of typical block lettered graffiti. "Why the hell did they choose those symbols?"

I glanced. "Greek."

"I know it's Greek, but why? Graffiti in Greek?"

93

"Why not?" Asked Derek.

"What's Greek doing in 'street' talk? Ever think about that?"

"Shivering our asses off is not the time to get into a heavy intellectual thing, Theo."

Theo turned his head once again to the side. "Yeah. Of course. We got bigger fish to fry, right? Any dolphins jumpin' out there?" He stood up and looked out at the sand surrounding them.

I asked once again, "Think that's all she wanted us to do?"

"What? We back to *visitin'* again? What do I know? She told *you*, not me. How the hell she going to know we're here, even if she wanted to come up and…and kiss us, huh?"

I turned to him. "If she's *real*, she just might do that, you know."

"Jesus. Why did I agree to come out here? Derek, she's…did you forget all I told you? *You* need her right now. Not me. I'm keeping you company, remember? That's all. If the need is strong enough, she'll be there for you. Now…" He turned back to the graffiti. "I'm curious." Theo took out his little notebook and pencil and started sketching the graffiti.

"How can you be so indifferent? She visited you too," I replied.

"That was then, Derek. This is now. The only thing I need right now is something warm enough to thaw my balls."

I had to slip in some humor to this old guy right now. "Well, if she is real…"

Theo waved me off. "Get outta here."

I turned up my collar. "Not a bad idea. Goin' down on the beach. Can't be colder than this cave. Wanna come?"

Theo, now involved with trying to sketch with his numb fingers, shook his head. "Send me a postcard."

I slipped out of the bunker, walked past my pickup truck, and began to move down the dunes to the shore that was now glistening with the early sunrise.

I had decided to drive out to Montauk after a tense Sunday in the loft. Theo, the critic, and I the artist, had our differences, and heated debates were the norm. Theo—who never knew where his mind was headed—was the proverbial question mark, unpredictable, and always thinking. Even when he wasn't, he was. Here was a debate, however, that was going to be our first real clash. Real versus unreal. Enigmatic versus enlightenment. Echo and the gulls had pushed me to an edge I wasn't sure I wanted to peek over, but I dragged him out of the loft around 4 a.m. and pushed him into the pick-up.

Arguing during the entire drive, my imagination continued to be in chaos. As I now walked down to the shore, I thought back to last night and how I had reluctantly admitted to Theo that years ago I'd gone to a New Jersey landfill in search of stone. Knowing that this particular dump was one where loads of debris from the 9/11 tragedy had ended up, I was hopeful of finding something worth the trip. And I did. A broken and jagged marble pillar, amidst the mountain of rubble, caught my attention. It wasn't because it was particularly special in size or shape. It was because when I first spotted it, atop the column perched a gull, surrounded by other gulls, all motionless, and all staring at me. Ever since that time, I caught myself ruminating often—*What's with this gull thing*?

Although, no obvious answer came to me, once the rock had been transported to the loft, I began chipping away. Week after week, month after month, faces I didn't know, faces of children and adults started coming to me, each with a unique expression of disbelief and sadness. Now, years later, the one project I had created outside my nine-month trademark, was all but finished. The eight-foot pillar was now a mass of some 200 embossed faces that attempted to help viewers find closure to the senseless act.

Theo didn't like it at all. To him, it was politically incorrect. "You're going to make a lot of people pissed at you," he had said.

I had argued. Why? "They're just faces from my imagination."

Theo wasn't so sure. "What if they're faces of some of the people who perished? What if? How can you be so sure, Derek? Faces come from somewhere, don't they? How do you know these aren't people you passed every time you visited your broker down there? He was in one of the Towers, remember? Faces of workers in the building, yes? Possible?"

The argument that started in the park lasted all Sunday night had ended in the loft. I was sure the faces were just from my imagination. Bothered, however, by Theo's challenge, I spent the better part of the late night walking around the totem pole-like edifice, riveting my focus on the small expressions, convincing myself that none of the images were from books or newspapers, or anywhere else but my head—my imagination. This of course, proved to be yet another experience where my love/hate relationship with imagination raged on long after I tried to put it to rest. It wasn't that I feared imagination, it was the freedom I felt when creating without regard for either the work's salability, or its critical acceptance. Servitude and compromise were my enemies—adversaries that history deemed the proper societal goals of the artist.

By 2 a.m., I wasn't so sure of myself anymore. The empty Tequila bottle suggested I might have clouded judgment. Theo, wanting to sleep, had glibly suggested I go to Echo for the answer about my totem pole faces. The suggestion had cost Theo the

Sunday night sleep he wanted, and now the Monday that wasn't proving to be any better. The four-hour drive to Montauk had forced him to listen to my historical battle with work, my imagination, and the critics. By the time we arrived, we were ready to give each other the benefit of the doubt—even the possibility that critics might be right once in a while. "Anything," said Theo. "Can we just put a pin in it? This much arguing gives me a worse hangover than booze sometimes."

Still being a bit woozy, the cold sand between my toes was giving me a jump-start on the *new-day* process. Even though I had been too involved in the argument all night, I nevertheless drank my share. *Got to get off this Tequila stuff*, I told myself over and over as I walked the half mile of beach to The Point and a view of the lighthouse high above the surreal clay cliffs. As the sun rose higher and around the point, deep shadows cut into the sculptured weathering of the clay shoreline, carrying me even further into my imagination.

The wall of broken knife-like erosions took me back to the Jacuzzi at Aretha's house, her words of evolving life in the galaxies; my sense of time and motion merging with the sound of surf, wind and—the sound of gulls. I looked up. Not one, but two formations. Two perfect arrows, side by side. I followed their course, spreading now, arching out and then coming back into one massive arrow. I stood motionless as the tide washed up around my ankles, the cold immediately relieving my sense of fatigue. I began to walk, then jog, as the gulls came to rest atop the lighthouse. Inside the arc light's glass enclosure, a blur of color floated, like a residual afterglow of intense illumination, playing tricks on the irises of my eyes. I turned away and looked again. The gulls were now creating a sentinel-like formation along the edge of the cliffs. At the far end, the wings fluttered and moved aside, giving what appeared to be an opening to the lighthouse.

High above in the dome, the eastern sun's ascension carried with it the refracting light. The heavy glass surrounding the lighthouse's dome now became void of the vivid colors. Within its walls the brass lamp now showed bright. Standing in front of the arc's massive lens was a figure. *Echo?*

Having filled several pages, Theo kneeled closer to the wall, penciling in the smaller patterns of Greek letters in their oversized and ballooned overlaps. "Crazy shit," he mumbled to himself. He turned around, and stood up, stretching his kinked back. Looking out the portholes, he idly shook his head. *Where the hell you go?* He took another look out the other side. Nothing. He turned back around, checked his watch, and then leaned out the entrance. "Hey, Derek! You out there?" He could see a faint outline of footprints that led down to the surf, then disappeared. He shoved his pencil and notebook back into his pocket and jumped down to the ground. "Derek? Derek! God damn it! Derek where the hell are you?"

CHAPTER 16

"Dr. Reagan. Didn't expect to hear from you. How are you?" said Aretha as she turned to keep the wind from raising havoc with her cell phone.

"Fine, just fine. Bit jammed with work, but that's normal. You doing alright?"

Aretha sat and took a moment. "I'm fine. Anything wrong with Linda?"

"She's progressing, Mrs. Ballard."

"One thing I learned about you, Doc, when you start being formal, something's wrong."

"Oh, not really. Just wanted to invite you over for a chat."

Aretha stood, stretched her back, looked at the flowerpots still needing attention and walked to the bags of polished pebbles.

"Mrs. Ballard?" Dr. Reagan asked.

"Yes, I'm still here." Tucking the phone under her chin, she reached down and spread some pebbles around the potted flowers. "What has she done now?"

***

"Damn," said Theo as he tried to maneuver the shoreline rocks that stabbed at his tender feet. He dodged left and right, seeking what little sand and clay was available. "Derek!" He gazed at the cliffs and the shadowed mini-canyons of eroded clay. The sun now glared straight into his line of sight. Ducking his head, he peered around to find small patches of sand that appeared to have given way to footprints among the rough, rock-strewn beach. *Derek's?* Once again, he glanced up toward the cliffs, and now, seeing the lighthouse, noticed the gulls as well. The flock began screaching, setting up a chorus of discontent. Then, with one loud distorted blare of dissonance, they lifted off from the cliff's edge, and like a swarm of bees, swooped down, surrounding him.

Gently coming to rest on the rocks, they waddled side to side, their tone, one of cooing. Silence followed, save for the occasional flutter of a wing. Not sure of the meaning behind this strange behavior, he remained stationary. After a few moments, his hand fumbled through his pocket, feeling for something that would perhaps cause them flight. He smiled as he lifted from his pocket the energy bar. As the gulls moved closer, he quickly peeled the wrapper, and crumbled up the bar. "Good cardboard. Good food. Yeah." With one grenade-launching thrust, the crumbs flew through the air, scattering the gulls right and left to muscle for the bits.

"Damn, damn, damn," he exclaimed as he hurriedly ran over the sharp rocks toward the cliffs. As he reached the sand and clay mixture at the base of the cliffs, he stopped, leaned over, caught his breath, and peered under his arm at the frenzy of wings and beaks clashing for the morning treats. *I'm losing it...running from seagulls...Jesus!*

He looked up at the height of the cliffs, then down at the sand. A few yards away, he saw the trail continue up a craggy ravine of clay and loose rock. He looked at his bruised and cut feet. *Real smart, Theo.*

Not believing there was any way his battered feet could go on any further, he took a deep breath and peered back up through the eroded crevasses to the top of the cliffs. The wind abruptly changed. His eyes transfixed on the slow undulating twists and turns of a red scarf floating over the cliff's edge down toward him.

"Derek? Derek?"

***

Samara paced her office with the phone tucked under her ear, nervously stirring coffee with her free hand.

"... leave a message," came the familiar answering machine. "Derek? If you're there, pick up. Derek? Okay, I dropped by before coming into the office. Got yourself a new all-night interest? Well, wherever you are, 'phone home ET'." She hung up and sipped her coffee as she walked to her window over-looking the street. A garbage truck made its way from can to can, the hoist thrusting more future landfill into the back.

From the intercom, her part-time receptionist said, "You have Mister Humphreys waiting, Dr. Jennings."

"Oh, thank you. Forgot today was your day in the office. Yes, send him in." She turned from the window, and then paused. Turning back, she peered once more at the garbage truck.

Mister Humphreys sauntered in with his usual saccharine sweet greeting. "And how are you this beautiful fall morning, Dr. Jennings, the salvation of my life, my teacher, my..."

"Mister Humphreys. I'm sorry, but not today. Tell me, Mister Humphreys, answer me this, before I start with the session, okay?"

"I'm here for you, Doctor."

She turned back from the window. "Yes. I know. Do you think there's beauty in waste?"

"Waste?"

"Yes. Like garbage. You see beauty in that?"

He responded cautiously. "Is this like those ink blots? A trick question?"

Samara smiled. "No. Here, sit down. Coffee?"

Mister Humphreys shook his head.

"Is that 'no' on the coffee or 'no' on the waste?"

"Both."

"Interesting." She topped off her cup and sat down. "It just hit me a moment ago. Just as bio waste is toxic, so too is mental waste."

"Toxic," chimed in Mister Humphreys.

"And emotional waste," continued Samara.

"Definitely, toxic. Yes."

"That's what we work on here, right. Getting rid of emotional waste?"

"I think so. Yes, you're right. Emotional waste," said Mister Humphreys.

"So, it's safe to say in order to realize beauty, we have to rid ourselves of emotional waste, yes?"

Mister Humphreys nodded. "To make room?"

"Yes. To make room for beauty."

Mister Humphreys beamed and shifted his position. "I did well?"

"Yes, Mister Humphreys. Could I now speak with Clarence?"

"He didn't come today."

"Robert?" asked Samara.

Mister Humphreys sat back, crossed his legs and folded his arms. "Fuck you, bitch."

Samara nodded. "Hi, Robert."

***

From Dr. Reagan's third floor office, Aretha stood at the window and watched the leaves drop on her car. Parked beneath an ancient birch tree in front of the Institution, she followed the autumn colors float down and cover the hood.

"She's crying out like all of us, Aretha," said Dr. Reagan from his desk as he calmly rolled his pencil between his fingers, occasionally looking up at her immobile stance at the window.

"That doesn't mean she's crying out for me."

"How can you be so sure?" he asked.

Aretha turned back with the all-knowing confidence that was her trademark. "Because you cry out for something you can't have, and she knows I'm available."

99

As Aretha made her way to the couch, Dr. Reagan stood and walked to join her. "May I?"

Aretha nodded. "So cavalier, you are."

Dr. Reagan sat. "Aretha, I'm telling you that the defecation in her room, the smashing of all her baskets, the food throwing at dinner, well, all that is consistent with you not being available. And the relatively common behavior for someone we believe is controlling much of her behavior to give the seeming impression she's psychotic. It might continue and could get worse."

"Psychotic. Heavy word."

"I said seeming. She's really done no harm to herself or others, even though she chooses to make others believe she would. It merely serves her purpose for getting attention. True psychotics find it very difficult to appear normal, and your Linda loves to be normal when she's feeling content. So you see..."

"Could get worse? Unless?"

"Well, it's not just 'unless'." I want you to invite her for a weekend break. Take her somewhere you know she likes to be. The Cape? Vineyard? She talks of the seashore a lot. Is that one of her favorite places?"

Aretha turned, her squinting eyes reflecting both regret and fear. "She talks of the shore?"

"Not with me as much as with the other patients."

"God. She used to love the beach, but she got so..."

"So?"

"So hostile. At the beach, I mean. When we lived in New York, my late husband and I had strict rules. No running into the surf at high tide. Currents were so unpredictable. She got to the point that all she'd wait for were those damn high tides. She'd claim the water was her only true friend and then just defy us."

"And?"

"She was too old to spank, for God's sake. We'd make her sit by herself on a blanket we'd put back from the shore, up against the cliffs."

"Cliffs?"

She laughed. "Not really cliffs, just some clay erosions that I loved to be around. Montauk Point. You know them?"

Dr. Reagan paused. "Is there a lighthouse?"

"Why yes. You're familiar."

"No. But Linda says..."

"Says what?"

Dr. Reagan leaned forward. "That she was born there...in the lighthouse."

"Oh, sweet mother of God. She is over the top. When she was a little girl, we used to go there and lie on the beach and watch the stars. Once in a while, the lighthouse would be operating, and we'd kid about the 'beam of the space ship that put us here...' just kidding around, fantasizing with a child. Making stories up." Aretha sat at the edge of the couch. After a moment, she glanced at him, and then drew back into herself. "She's never said that to *me*."

"She's shared that with me and some of the patients," said Dr. Reagan. "She also said she has no father. That you conceived her from..." he pointed above him, "from somewhere up there."

Aretha flopped back in the couch. "Up there? Better throw away the key, Doc. Take her for a 'weekend break' at the beach? You've got to be kidding."

"No, I'm not. There's a lot of fantasy and *ungrounded* imagination keeping her from improving. A break with her mother...well, I think there's a good chance it will help."

Aretha sighed. "Help. You're the doctor and you think I can help?"

"More than you might realize."

Chapter 17

Samara sat on the edge of Leonard's bed reading from a book of Pablo Neruda's collected poems. "...I like for you to be still: it is as though you were absent, distant and full of sorrow as though you had died. One word then, one smile, is enough. And I am happy, happy that it's not true."

Leonard smiled. "Thank you," he slurred. "That's one of my favorites."

She quietly closed the book, wiped the dribble from his lips, and gently kissed them. "You sleep now. I've got a patient at one o'clock. See you tomorrow."

As she silently left the room, the final smile she sent back to him turned to uncontrolled sobbing once she reached the ladies' room.
***

Theo sat in the truck eating the last of the energy bars Derek had left in the glove compartment. He pushed his shoes aside and squirmed with the ache of his bruised bare feet. Gazing out at the grassy edge, and then to the left where the clay cliffs started, he could see the lighthouse in the distance, now partially covered with the fog that was beginning to move in. He picked up the red scarf and folded it.

There was nothing left to do now but wait. He was satisfied that he had made a gallant effort six hours earlier to reach the top of the cliffs and explore the entire bluff. He had checked the padlocked lighthouse several times, re-reading the tourist sign indicating that the lighthouse had closed for the season two weeks earlier. He had retraced his steps to find Derek's footprints vanishing into the hardened sand and rock atop the bluff, and he had returned to the truck to wait. He wasn't ready to fill out a missing-person report yet, but—he looked at his watch—1 p.m. He assured himself. *Derek had just tripped out on his anxiety, the Tequila, and his imagination.*

He closed his eyes and retraced the last words exchanged just before Derek's departure from the bunker. "If she's real," Theo had told him... "*If* she's real?" Derek had responded, the tone of his voice dismissing any speculation. Theo had continued with, "...did you forget all I told you? It's a need you have. That's all. If it's strong enough, she'll be there."

Theo's intellectualizing had been so thorough; even *he* believed she was nothing but a projection, rememberings—a muse incarnate. The only perplexing part of that theory was how she had become part of both their imaginations. It was the duality of it all that gave Theo the hesitation to make a report. That is what he hoped was the reason as he peered out the window at the increasing fog layer. He wasn't ready to accept the worst, but his emotions were now on the surface, and he began to feel the creeping urge to weep. *Where is my friend? Is there more to the Echo experience than even I'm ready to accept?* He let out a loud purging shriek, "DEREK! GOD DAMN IT! DEREK! ENOUGH!"

From the distant fog-embraced tall grass sloping down toward the ocean, a horse rose up from the beach. Its bareback rider, a young girl in jeans and a hooded sweat shirt, gazed toward the fogged-in lighthouse. Theo squinted as the horse hoofed the sand. The girl turned toward the truck. Theo quickly stepped out and ran toward the rider waving his arms. "Excuse me!" he yelled. "Excuse me. Have you seen a man anywhere down there?" Before he could reach the edge, the horse and its rider turned and disappeared down the slope of the dune. Theo stumbled and grimaced with the pain of his battered feet as he reached the edge. On the sand below, the horse stopped once again, its rider motioning, not with a wave, but a beckoning gesture of her shoulders. What seemed to make him willing to endure more pain was the thrust of the horse's head in synchronous harmony with her gesture, the mane of extraordinary length catching the offshore breeze that seemed to be escorting ever-thickening fog.

He turned. In the distance, the swinging open door of the pickup also seemed to be urging him as it waved begrudgingly against the gust of ocean breeze, the grinding of rusted metal on metal hinges sending a foreshadowing sound—a sound that was slowly swallowed up in the dense fog and sound of the surf.

As gusts ushered across the truck's floorboards, the crinkled wrapper from the last energy bar struggled to hold its position atop Theo's old shoes.

The engulfing mist began to merge with the shrouded landscape as the creeping gray swallowed the tenuous strands of green leading to the shore. Where moments before Theo had stood mesmerized by the rider and the stallion, there was only the soft undulation of fog—and from behind, the truck door's rapidly fading pendulum-screech of rusted metal.

END OF PART ONE

PART 2 – ECHOSIS OF WILL

CHAPTER 18

The fall air was inviting, and Lincoln Center buzzed with anticipation as the opening night's elite entered the glass façade and made their way to seats reserved for the black-tie premier of Samara Jennings' Trumpet Concerto in E minor—a special 5th Year benefit for the families of 9/11.

As the orchestra tuned up, Samara scurried back and forth from the back stage ladies' room to Leonard's side. "Are you sure you're all right," she asked on each return.

"I couldn't be better," said Leonard sitting in his motorized wheel chair. "How about you?"

Samara, adjusted her sash. "Aside from working up a sweat that is definitely not good for this gown, I'm fine." She peeked at the first row from the wings. "I hope Tina is comfortable sitting there alone."

Leonard smiled. "That girl is comfortable anywhere, anytime."

"She worried about wearing that dress you bought her," said Samara.

"Well," said Leonard with a shy grin, "there's always a first time for everything, right?"

"Two Minutes!" announced the stage manager.

Samara leaned down and kissed Leonard on the cheek. "Leonard. This is your night. Enjoy it."

He gripped her hand. "You too. I've said it many times, but right now, well it's special.   Thanks."

As an aid tapped her shoulder, Samara smiled back and stepped away.

"Thank you Ms. Jennings. I'll take it from here."

Samara blew one last kiss to Leonard and quickly exited to the hallway.

"All set, Mr. Paxton?"

Leonard nodded, cradled his trumpet and took a deep breath.

Samara discreetly made her way from back stage to the side entrance and to the aisle seat next to Tina. "You okay?" She whispered.

"Worse than getting clean, I can tell you," said Tina.

Samara patted her hand as the applause continued and the conductor made his way across the stage. He shook the hand of the First Violin and stepped up on the riser.

"Your rock looks especially good in these lights," Samara whispered.

Tina gazed at her engagement ring with special pride just as Leonard was wheeled out to rising applause to take his place in the solo position.

As the baton came down and three years of work began filling the hall, Samara opened the gold leaf program for the night. The cover was embossed with the pillar sculpture Derek had completed before disappearing and which Samara had allowed to be put on display in the lobby of the Center for the premier. She gently touched the many raised images. A moment of sadness quickly vanished as she read the dedication on the inside page: *To the spirits working silently for beauty and peace.*

During the featured event of the evening, the audience experienced more of what gave Samara the composer status she enjoyed. Critics in the past had tried to describe her with *"...this century's lyrical Americana...the mystery and meditative influence of Ligeti...and the mesmerizing pendulum mist of Philip Glass."* This night's audience was being exposed to yet another layer of Samara's chameleon soundscape.

At the concerto's conclusion, Samara stood next to Leonard among roses, applause, and bravos, feeling the full impact of the past three years. The conductor took her hand and raised it, then stepped back to join in the applause. Samara's tears fell on the bouquet of roses she held in her arms. As the applause continued, another bouquet was handed to her by a stagehand. This dozen was pronounced even further by the yellow rose in the center. Stunned, she was torn between the tears of joy and those of shock. Her blurry eyes darted from stage left to stage right, to the audience, even lifting her chin to the balcony. Stifling the urge to scream out his name, she struggled with the whisper, "Derek?"

Throughout the champagne celebration afterwards, Samara maintained a mood Tina and Leonard knew to be unlike her. Even as they asked why she was so quiet, they knew that in spite of the assurance she was fine, there was an unmistakable uneasiness about her. As Samara moved about the reception hall, accepting good wishes and accolades from guests and the visiting press as far away as Paris, she kept looking around expecting to be further shocked with Derek's presence.

The limousine ride back to the loft was quiet and reserved. Tina and Leonard talked of the night's rewards, and Samara joined in politely, but they knew she was still preoccupied. Placed next to her on the limo's floor was a vase containing the three dozen roses, the yellow bud catching the light of every street lamp's spill through the windows—as if winking at her.

Finally, Tina tried to break the awkwardness. "So, Samara, secret admirer we don't know about?"

Samara took an unsteady deep breath. "Probably not a good time to address that right now. Okay?"

Tina politely dropped the subject, and the car wound its way through the deserted streets to the lonely loft that Samara had refused to abandon. As the driver helped her out and lifted the roses, Leonard reached his hand to hers. "Thank you again, and don't let whatever's on your mind take away the memory of such a beautiful night, okay Samara?"

Samara smiled back and took the flowers from the driver. "This night's memory is forever. You two take care now."

"I'll call you tomorrow," said Tina.

Samara opened the heavy door with reservation. As she stepped inside, she placed the vase on the floor and switched on the lights—first the kitchen area, then bedroom area, the living room, and finally, Derek's work area just as he'd left it three years before. She paused a moment more, then picked up the roses and walked to the living room and placed them on the coffee table. She straightened a couple that had fallen away from the grouping and then lifted the yellow rose slightly. She closed her eyes and leaned over to take in its fragrance. Leaning back on the couch, she glanced about the loft once again, then stood and went to the light switches. Dimming them all to a low effect, she walked to the refrigerator and opened the freezer compartment. Lifting a bottle of vodka, she poured herself a nightcap and walked back to the couch. Once more, she leaned back, looked around the room, took a sip, and then placed it on the table. Reaching into her pocket book, she retrieved the card for the flowers. She turned it over. Breaking the seal, she paused, fearing the unknown. Finally, she carefully lifted the flap and read the card:

Congratulations. Enjoy.
By the way, I finally did it, thanks to you.
You're very special to me,
Derek.

Samara sat down on the couch and slowly curled into herself. Rising from a smile of pride amidst a steady flow of tears, she said to herself, "Oh, I can't believe..."

If Derek was doing what she hoped he was, it was worth all the pain she had endured and the anticipated anxiety ahead. The weeping settled into a peaceful resolve by the dawn. Still curled in the corner of the couch, she gently pressed the yellow rose to her cheek, embracing the memory of her love.

Aretha slowly sat on the weathered bench and stared up at the "Ode." Glancing out to sea, she closed her eyes and remembered the past three years and the last time she had seen the man she spent many months and thousands of dollars trying to find. Even beneath her eyelids, his face reflected indelibly.

"Mom...these roots are messing everything up."

Aretha opened her eyes and glanced across the way where Linda was on her knees tilling the soil. "Don't fret, honey, I'll have Delbert take care of them when he comes."

"You know he hates digging," said Linda.

"He likes the 'Executive Maintenance Man' pay though. Why don't you take a break? Bring us some lemonade. It's such a perfect temperature today." Aretha smoothed the glove on her left hand and took a deep breath. "Perfect fall day."

Aretha closed her eyes once again and thought back over the years as she gently touched the scarred finger hidden by her glove. *I lost a friend, she lamented, but... every loss has its gain.* The quiet words beneath her lips reflected the pleasure she was feeling. *Oh, Derek, if only, if only a clue to your whereabouts could have been uncovered. If only.*

"As long as you're going to have Delbert get dirty," said Linda, "have him check out the freezer. The icemaker is acting up." She placed the tray of lemonade on the table beside Aretha.

"Oh, yes, of course," said Aretha. Opening her eyes, she saw that Linda had brought the mail as well. Sipping the lemonade, she fingered the envelopes and magazines. "Perfect. Just enough tang. You didn't put any sugar..."

"No, Mom. Of course not."

"Good. Just look at this junk. Thank God for the Architectural Digest. It's the only magazine worth..." She hesitantly stopped and gazed at the letter in front of her. The return address was Samara's.

"What's wrong?" asked Linda.

"Oh, nothing, dear. Just a letter from an old friend."

Linda skewed her neck and caught the return address. "Old friend, huh? You forget you told me about *that* old friend?"

"Well, we both loved him. Guess that's a good reason to be friends."

Linda grinned. "And *I'm* the one they locked up." She leaned over and kissed her mother on the forehead. "I'm going to take a shower. I'm a mess."

Without looking up, Aretha nodded. "Sure, dear. You get cleaned up and we'll decide on dinner. Okay?"

Linda gathered up her gardening tools and retreated to the house. Aretha stood. Holding the letter, she gazed out at the ocean, then glanced back at the Ode. It had become her habit, as often as the sun permitted, to sit in the reflected light of the polished obelisk. She didn't know why she had started the practice, but it always provided solace and peace. Perhaps it was the warmth of the reflection. It certainly wasn't the mirrored evidence of her aging. Perhaps it was the symbolism of it all. Its indomitable strength and simplicity of purpose. As she glanced again at the letter, what she *did* know, however, was that she needed a touch of his strength. She stepped over to the walkway leading toward the beach and sat down. A beam of reflected sunlight cut across her body and once again she allowed whatever it was to affect her once more and think on the artist she so admired.

She opened the letter and much to her surprise, there was only one sentence. "I think I've found Derek. Samara."

Aretha stood, confused. She didn't know whether to shout for joy, or cry. "Oh, my God," she murmured to herself.

The candle was dripping steadily onto the plate as Linda glanced at the melting and then her mother. Aretha sipped her wine and stared into the flame, her plate of vegetables and Cornish hen untouched. Linda continued picking morsels of meat from every bone with surgical precision, obviously enjoying the challenge. As her eye met the blink of the Cheshire at her feet, she said, "Only in your dreams, cat."

Still staring at the flame, Aretha corrected her, "His name is Arnold..."

"I know," said Linda, "named after your second."

"He was a good man."

Linda sucked the last bone dry. "Of course." As she placed it on the plate and glanced at Aretha's untouched meal, she asked, "You going to eat that?"

Aretha snapped out of her reverie, and answered. "Oh, no dear. I'm sorry. Think I'll just have another..." She motioned for the bottle.

Linda passed the wine and placed Aretha's plate on her own. "You know, I used to hate chicken."

"That's Cornish hen, dear. Different."

Linda nodded. "Yeah. Maybe it's the fun in eating such a small bird. Ever eat pigeon?"

Aretha lifted her eyes and smiled. "Once in Southern France."

Linda smiled. "Ginseng used to brag about how good it was, 'cause I used to send the chicken back to the kitchen and that would get the patients talking and..."

"Ginseng?"

"She was a crazy coot always wanting to sit next to me. She claimed the key to her long life was the fresh air under the Brooklyn Bridge—her address before the nut house—and pigeons." She began to devour the hen. "Said they saved her life, the cooked ones, you know."

Aretha took another sip and smiled at Linda, seeing the child once again. "You happy now, dear?"

"This is better than the white halls. Especially the food."

"No, I mean, really *happier*?"

"We used to talk about this a lot, but that was two years ago. Didn't I convince you then?" said Linda.

"Oh, I know it's easier for you now." An unexpected tear came to the surface. "I know you know I wasn't that enthused then."

"You mean to bring me back here? Sure. I know. But I also know you hated those phone calls from the Doc, right?" She topped up her glass."

"They were disturbing, of course." She surreptitiously drew her hand across her cheek.

Linda stripped off a tender bite of the hen. "You know, mom, I don't think you would have taken me back if we hadn't spent that time at the beach looking for, what's his name?"

"Derek."

"Yeah, the sculptor guy. Don't think you would have. Nope. Right?"

"The time we spent at the beach was coincidental with his disappearance. That's all."

"C'mon. Doc told me you weren't happy taking me to the beach."

"That's right."

"Fooled you, didn't I?"

"It was cruel."

"What, me jumpin' into the drink and making you think..."

Aretha raised her hand. "Stop. We don't need to visit that little prank again."

"Worked though. Doc told me it would."

"You're getting better now. That's all that matters."

"Cause you let go. Let me grow up a bit. Let me tell you off once in a while, right?"

Aretha took a swallow and topped up her glass once more. "Yes. I had to learn a lesson. 'Lessons are important.'"

Noticing her mother's moist eyes, Linda wiped her mouth and sipped her wine. "The Doc had a way with words, didn't he?"

Aretha nodded.

"We haven't talked in a while," said Linda.

Aretha took a deep breath, composed herself, and gave back her usual cover-up smile.

"About?"

"Oh, how about whatever is bothering you?" said Linda, her voice showing genuine concern.

"It's nothing. Just some old memories."

Linda smiled. "Dad?"

"No, not your father, although I think of him often."

Linda continued sipping her wine, maintaining her gaze at Aretha.

"Oh, well, I see you're insisting." Aretha reached into her pocket and pulled out the letter. "Here."

Linda, taken by surprise, hesitated. "What?"

"Read it."

"But..." Linda glanced at the return address. "It's from the female shrink...music writer person?"

Aretha nodded. "She's a gifted psychologist and a talented composer, Linda. A very nice, but overly insecure lady. You can read it."

Linda opened the envelope, read the line, and folded it back.

"Okay. Reads like a happy ending to me, right?"

Aretha put the envelope back into her pocket.

"So?" Linda continued. "So, what's the problem? She's found the guy."

Aretha leaned on her elbows and fingered the melted candle wax. "You, see, Linda, when someone is dead, or you understand them to be dead, there is a closure to connection with that person. You understand that?"

Linda nodded innocently, but somewhat indifferent.

"And when it appears that the person might still be alive...I've never had this experience before. You can understand that too, right?"

Linda again nodded, this time noticing her mother was genuinely disturbed.

Aretha continued. "So, thinking the person dead and then alive again..."

"Mom...isn't this *Samara's* experience?"

Aretha nodded, "Yes. And mine." She stood, and turned toward the window overlooking the Ode. "It's not easy bringing that reality back into focus. "Would you join me for a brandy?" She moved out the door to the weathered bench. "Tell Sybil to serve us out here."

Calling after her, "I'll take care of it, Mom. You forgetting Sybil's off tonight?"

110

The night was clear and cool. Aretha stood at the edge of the railing, looking down at the beach. The long grass of Truro's sand dune coastline moved in waves like the fine wisps of a giant caterpillar back. Thoughts raced through her head uncontrollably. *What do I talk about? This is not normal to be so disturbed over... over a woman writing me about finding her lover.* "What's the matter with me?" she said out loud as Linda approached her from behind with two brandy snifters and cradles.

As Linda prepared the flame to warm them, she asked, "Would you rather be alone?"

"No, dear." Aretha paused. "Linda, it's been almost three years since Samara and I had our one and only contact...over the phone. Telling her you and I found the truck was traumatic for her and...the whole incident was confusing to me, Linda. Your *doctor ordered* the trip to the beach...just you and I together, walking the Montauk dunes. Then, spotting the truck, notifying the police, remember how...oh, it was so strange. Derek and his friend Theo just vanishing...people searching everywhere, and we just stumble onto the truck on the bluff, the rocks, the cliffs, the failure to find any bodies and the authorities concluding they must have had an accident off the cliffs into the..."

"Mom, slow down," said Linda, as she adjusted the snifters above the flame.

"No, Linda. There's more to this than just a woman finding her lover. He's not just a *guy*. He's an *artist* for God's sake!"

Linda stepped up to Aretha and touched her shoulder. "Mom, I'm here to listen if you want me to, but..."

"I know," said Aretha, calming herself and patting Linda's arm. "I know. What's an old woman like me getting so upset over?"

"Yeah," smiled Linda gently. That's kind of how I'd put it."

Aretha stood up and walked to the Ode. "We've never talked much about this piece, have we?"

"You've told me you really like it. You've spent a lot of nights— and days staring at it."

"But, I've never told you what it means to me, have I?"

"Mom, you've got so many works of art around this place, it's not unusual that you've not told me all about this piece."

Aretha looked up at the stainless steel tip. "Not just a piece, Linda. This was chiseled and carved and polished from the inside out."

"I don't understand," Linda said cautiously.

"Neither did he. He only knew...he could only describe *his* process. He explained to me a process that was from the inside, out. He saw...he worked on this as if he were on the inside looking out, through the stone, the steel. Seeing the world through his imagination. Do you understand?"

"Shit no, Mom."

Aretha took her daughter by the hand and sat down, trying to reason with her like a student. "Dear, dear, Linda. Maybe none of us were destined to know and understand this kind of thinking…this kind of being. Your father, I loved him so, was such a simple, sweet, uncomplicated man. You got his genes, thank God."

"Simple?" joked Linda.

"You know what I mean. Not to make light of your difficulties, and me understanding them, but…" She turned to the Ode again. "This sculpture is about a man that was tormented with complications, he only wanted to let his sense of life, his sense of…creation break out and be understood. He was so humble, this Derek person. He was *so* humble. A modern-day Michelangelo, Linda. So much into living futures we can only dream of." She began to weep.

"Mom, it's…I'm sorry. Don't cry. I understand."

"No, you don't, darling, but thank you for saying so. Hell, I don't even understand it. I just keep trying to figure it out." Aretha sat up and wiped her eyes. "Perhaps his destiny might have been fulfilled in death, but now…Samara…if she knows where he is…she will…"

"Will what, Mom?"

Aretha slowly shook her head and once again, composed herself. "The brandy should be warm now."

As Aretha stood, Linda gave a quick glance at her mother, her stare fixed on the Ode. Behind it, an early moon began to take shape.

With sadness engulfing her face, Aretha sat reflected in the waning light of day.

"You said you had an encounter with Samara. What went on? Mother?"

Linda, feeling helpless with Aretha's silence, could only idly turn the snifters in their cradles and shield the flames from the offshore breeze ushering in the night.

CHAPTER 19

Theo leaned over and picked up a gold and green leaf. He turned it over in his hand several times.

"Had to have been dropped from a tourist's pocket or backpack," the clerk said. He smiled. "Don't see elm leaves around these parts. That be all?"

Theo folded the leaf into his paperback of Henry Miller's "Stand Still Like a Hummingbird" and slid it back into his jacket. "Yes, Orel. Just the apples."

As Theo left the small general store, he breathed in the October air. Fog was starting to move inland and he smiled as he tasted the salt. He looked up and saw the distant lighthouse sending its warning signals out to sea. Unlike the tower at Montauk that served tourists more than the mariner travelers, Grey Cliff Island's lighthouse was the lifeline for dozens of small fishing vessels and the occasional freight ship that would venture further north to the Maine waters to dodge around the unpredictable East Coast weather. No, he thought as he walked the short distance to his cottage, island living, even on such a desolate rock as Grey Cliff, has its rewards.

"What's up," bellowed Arnie Rose, the island's fix-it man, as he rounded the corner of the quaint street where Theo lived.

"Hey, Arnie. Not much." He lifted his bag of apples. "Last of the good ones till next year."

Arnie looked up at the fog-concealed sky. "Another couple of weeks."

"What?"

"Couple of weeks till we start seeing those ice storms."

Theo nodded. "It is that time of year, isn't it?"

"You better let me check your pipes again. That sealin' I did last year could need some repairin' before winter sets in."

"When you have a minute, Arnie."

"Have a good one." Arnie waved.

Theo had spent the better part of his life in and around the small buildings and homes of Greenwich Village, so entering the small stone building he now lived in was just like home. As a boy, stonewalls were common. As an adult, bare brick walls became trendy, and as he moved around, he inevitably rented a room with sand blasted brick walls. Even the recent past, living at times under the Manhattan Bridge nurtured his sense of home with its massive limestone foundations.

Inside, he arranged the apples in a modest bowl and placed them on the slate-topped crab cage he used for a coffee table. Surrounding the room were books. Every summer for the past three years, Theo had taken weekends to travel by fishing boat to the mainland, haunting small bookshops and antique stores, and buying any book that had merit. Now, his collection, some five hundred strong, was the source of many-a-night's entertainment and relaxation for him, and the *colony*.

He polished one of the apples and stepped to the window overlooking the cove. Waves lapped gently against the chunks of granite lining the shoreline. Eroded from the island's highest point next to the lighthouse, the rocks were a constant source of adventure for the children of the island and a constant source of worry for the parents. All in all, though, Mother Nature had treated the long-term population of four hundred twelve seasonal artists and their families gently. His first bite of the apple sent him to another place. "Mm," he muttered to himself, "let's hope it keeps the doctor away a few more years."

***

Jamie shouting over a bullhorn shattered the gathering dusk across the choppy sea. "Jesus, how am I supposed to keep the boat level in this chug-a-lug high tide?"

"Unlock the head and hold it steady!" bellowed the figure dangling from a fixed rope high up the jagged cliff. Several hundred feet below, bouncing with the erratic waters was the small boat, breaking through the gathering thick fog, trying desperately to keep a high beam light focused on the rock high above.

"For God's sake, give it a rest. There's tomorrow, you know," shouted Jamie through the horn once more.

The figure motioned to point the arc light closer to the work. Jamie loosened the head and lifted the forty-pound light onto his lap and pointed it up through the fog.

"Better," shouted the man from above. "Just another minute or two."

"Just another minute or two," Jamie muttered to himself. "Freezing wind, slap happy waves, and this nut says…"

From the boat's radio, came the Asian voice of Singso, "Mis'er Jamie… you come back soon? Over."

Jamie carefully lifted the light, keeping it steady as possible, as he awkwardly straddled the teak railing and fingered the radio. "Yes, Singso. Coming soon as crazy man comes down."

"Oh, he still banging rock?"

"When isn't he?"

"What, Mis'er Jamie?"

"Nothing. Have the dinner out for him in thirty minutes, okay?"

"Going to be overcooked, Mis'er Jamie."

"Won't be the first time," Jamie said as he almost dropped the light.

"Hey!" came the shout from above.

114

Jamie, both hands occupied now, simply yelled back up at the top of his lungs, "Hey, yourself. This fucker is heavy!"

Fingerless-gloved-hands cinched up the harness between his legs, then placed the last charge in a small crack. After checking it twice, Derek lifted the lower edge of his balaclava and placed his fingers in his mouth, exhaling rapidly to get them warm. After adjusting his hood, he wrapped his hands around the rope for the slow rappel down. His image moved in and out of the fog bands as he slid to the razor-sharp outcrop jutting up from the sea at the base. Jamie watched as Derek stood there a moment, peering up through the fog at the two hundred foot wall that was about to have another dimension removed. Then, double-checking his remote control, he slid into the small motorboat moored securely between two rocks and headed out to Jamie, who was now pointing the light directly across the fifty yards separating the two.

Once Derek tied off the motorboat and came aboard, Jamie immediately turned the small fishing vessel north and put another hundred yards between the boat and the cliff. "You've got your distance now," said Jamie.

Holding the remote like a precious bird in his palm, Derek pressed the red button. KABOOM! This was the love-hate relationship sound he dreaded. *How many times have I done this same thing and always returned home to wait till the next day to see the results? Twenty, thirty times?* "What do you think, Jamie?"

"I think I'm inviting myself for dinner. You know what time it is?"

"The rock, Jamie. Lucky this time?"

"Sounded same as usual...KABOOM. You're always lucky."

"Not always."

As he took off his climbing gear, Derek thought back at the first time he'd used ordinary dynamite on an unsuspecting cliff on the other side of the island; how the lack of control had splintered the fissures; how he'd ruined an important section of the cliff and only after scouting for three months had finally stumbled onto this two hundred foot high wave forged saber of granite bursting from the ocean floor. He remembered his first impression...like a giant stalagmite from some forgotten world whose subterranean ceiling had been blown away. This was where he had painstakingly acquired the proper permits, hoisted the generator to a safe ledge to power the mnemonic drill, and determined to not make the same mistake again. This time he invested in sophisticated explosives that could be controlled for measurable power. He pulled the balaclava off, revealing a close-cropped beard and a deep gash across his cheek. The blood was dry, but nevertheless gave Jamie a start.

"Jesus, Derek. You're bleeding."

"Just a reminder to stay humble."

Jamie shook his head and pointed to the small cabinet. "The first aid kit...some peroxide."

"That stuff stings like a..."

"You gonna get it or do I?"

Derek stepped to a cabinet and retrieved the first aid kit.

"You're not getting any younger, Derek," Jamie lectured.

Derek smiled as he took out the milder red Mercurochrome instead of the peroxide. "Kids never get older."

The fog dissipated for a few moments and both men watched as the last sliver of sun disappeared on the horizon. Derek looked back at the cliff. The elusive floating gray mist partially shrouded the fractured rock, but through momentary clearings, he could see the rough outline of a left eye and forehead taking shape. It had been a year since he started, and only now was he beginning to see results. Scanning across the top of the fending rock, the beam of the lighthouse sliced glimpses of what with time would become a full image. To him, the face in his mind was a 21st Century Mona Lisa.

As the boat rounded the cliffs into a cove, the magic hour faded into the twinkling lights of Derek's dream—his isolated *Magnum opus*—his secret place where the artist Samara had dared he find and risk making real his dream. This was the unique artistic laboratory concept Theo had reluctantly agreed to help him realize— the desolate oceanic enclave named Grey Cliff Island that three years earlier, a young woman atop the Montauk Lighthouse had suggested he travel some 400 miles NNE to find. His only regret since that day was the long absence of the young woman in colored ribbons who had caused it all to happen...and his missing Samara.

***

Leonard leaned his head back as Tina gently massaged the shampoo into his hair. The specially built shower stall was always a welcome relief to Leonard. For someone thought of as ultra-anal, staying clean, *ultra clean*, had always been a priority. And, following his body was his car. It was the concern for his car that had caused him to make Rye, New York, a forty-mile trip north of Manhattan, his home. A guesthouse, belonging to Velma Myran, an adoring "old money" fan, had become available the spring before his accident. Now, three years later, he not only appreciated the elder lady for allowing the guest house to be modified for his wheelchair-bound life, but also her insistence on putting a security camera in the garage so he could keep an eye on the restored Austin. Leonard couldn't get over the generosity and love he now enjoyed. Even the fact that Tina religiously bathed him every night, and Velma brought him food three times a day whenever he was at home alone; none of that gave him as much of a rush as being able to click his TV remote anytime, and a bank of lights in the garage would light up his prized possession.

"Good?" Tina whispered in his ear as she worked the shampoo.

"As always...the best," answered Leonard.

Tina continued the ritual of sudsing up for three minutes, then the rinse. The loofa scrub and the hot and cold shower rinse always followed. For Leonard, the greater the shock, the better. Closing his eyes and measuring how much sensation he might be getting back into his body had become the major anticipation of each day.

The atrophying of muscles had taken its toll, but now with feeling to his left leg, and some assistance, he managed to hobble from wheel chair to bed and his showers.

Tina helped him rise onto his left leg that was getting stronger and once draped with his terry cloth robe, he motored his little 6 H.P. wheelchair to the living room. There, as usual, Tina had lit candles and a fire. With Telemann's trumpet works playing on the stereo, she flirtatiously announced, "sushi coming up!"

"I could go for some sake," said Leonard as he stared into the fire.

Tina lifted the Pyrex pan from the stove showing a Japanese antique sake vessel inside warming.

"Thought you were feeling chipper tonight," said Tina.

"Not really. It felt like something...just something different to do."

Tina looked across the room at Leonard now fingering the equalizer on his stereo setup.

"Well," she said, "works for me."

Unseen, Leonard closed his eyes momentarily. He allowed himself a subtle nod as he watched the bouncing lights of the equalizer. "Like most everything," he said in a monotone fashion.

"Beg your pardon?"

Leonard raised his head and turned, "Oh, just that it's...I'm very fortunate to have you."

Tina beamed and went back to preparing the sushi.

Leonard motored over to the kitchen and parked, maintaining a calm, but disconcerting gaze at Tina.

"Whoa," said Tina. "That look is dangerous."

"Is it? Why?"

Tina blushed. "You know what your eyes do to me."

Leonard maintained his stare.

"What?" she said blushingly.

He shook his head. "Need any help?"

"No, that's okay. Not much to do but lift it from the box onto some plates."

As he wheeled back to the fireplace, he said, "Why don't you put the rest of the bottle in there to warm too."

Tina half smiled then nodded. "Sure, if that's what you want. I'll be flat on my ass if I have…"

"You'll get slightly inebriated if you have more than six ounces."

"Yeah," said Tina. "That word…ineeb whatever."

"Sloshed to some, inebriated to others." Leonard picked up the Times. "How about some Handel this weekend?"

"Sure. Works for me." Tina walked up to him with a tray and a decorative layout of the sushi. "You first."

As Leonard took a smaller plate and chose a few pieces, he asked, "Were you always this way?"

Tina smiled with the compliment. "My mommy taught us girls well. Take care of your man."

"No, I was thinking of…you know, the *dating times*. Were you always this attentive to your dates?"

"Yes…well, maybe, but you're not a date, my darling. You're my fiancé. You're my man."

She sat down on the couch and placed some pieces on her own plate.

"Forgive me," said Leonard. "That was an inappropriate question."

"No bother. I understand," she replied.

He took a sip of the sake and lurched back just as Tina took a bite of Sushi. Startled, she dropped a small piece of the fish on her lap.

Sliding her plate aside, she picked up the morsel and quickly moved to the kitchen. "Oh, I'm sorry. I know how you hate it when it's too hot."

Leonard took a small sigh. "It's okay, Tina. It will cool."

"But didn't you say the alcohol evaporates with the cooling?"

"Evaporates. Yes. But, I'll get by. It's fine." He jerked open the paper. "Handel. Yes. Then some arias at the 'Back Stage' and some oysters at Sergio's, okay?"

Tina paused a moment. "Sure, honey. You know I'm not much for oysters, but…"

"You'll learn. They're a valuable part of the diet," he said with encouragement.

Tina walked up to him with the sake bottle and two small cups. "I think this is cooler." She knelt at his feet and poured the liquid slowly. She lifted her eyes to his. She wasn't sure of herself in this, or many other situations with him, but she took the chance. "I love you, Leonard."

"I know," said Leonard.

"And I'm grateful," she continued.

Leonard lifted the cup to toast. "Let's toast something different, Tina. How about, 'to independence'?"

"Sure. Did you hear me?"

He clicked his cup to hers. "Yes. Yes I did."

"I really am...grateful."

Leonard looked aside for a moment, then brought his eyes back to hers. "Tina...I got a call from Samara today."

Tina smiled. "Good. How is she?"

"Derek's... doing *it!*"

Tina looked confused. "Derek? Doing...I don't understand."

"He's alive, Tina. He's doing it."

"Alive? How...I mean, how does she know?"

"He sent her roses the night of the premier."

Tina tried to compose herself and took a sip of sake. "He didn't drown, obviously...then."

"He's somewhere out there finally doing what she urged him to do for years."

"You mean...?"

Leonard nodded. "Yes. *His Place*. He's free at last, Tina. That's what keeps running through my mind tonight. He's free."

Tina downed her sake and poured some more, offering him another cup as well. "So, where is he?"

Leonard nodded toward the window. "Is it important where?"

They both sat in silence and sipped their sake.

Chapter 20

It was after midnight when Aretha pulled her car up to the front of Derek's loft. She glanced up at the windows. A flickering glow told her Samara was still waiting. As she rode the freight elevator up to the top floor, she found herself compelled to pull out her pocket mirror and check herself. As she reached the front door, she paused. *The scarf... too much color?* Into her shoulder bag it went. *Now, just me. Just the lonely old lady with a penchant for art and all that goes with it...including the neurosis she's sure to spot.*

The door opened and both stood a long moment taking in the other. "Aretha, please come in."

"Sorry it's so late. Traffic. Where is everybody going this time of night, you know?"

"Yes. Seems visitors to Manhattan travel at any hour. Care for a beverage, coffee, wine?"

"Some water, please."

119

Samara walked to the kitchen as Aretha scanned the open space with its orderly arrangement: piano corner, conversation pit, kitchen, what appeared to be an entrance into a bedroom, and then the magic area to Aretha, Derek's work area, somewhat hidden behind twenty-five foot hanging sheets of clear plastic.

"I'm going to have some sherry. Sure you wouldn't care for a spot?"

"Oh...thank you. Perhaps just a bit...and some water." She turned. "Do you mind?"

Samara looked back from the kitchen and saw Aretha staring at Derek's corner. "Mind? Make yourself at home. That's his unfinished piece behind the plastic. Dust still blows around, you know."

Aretha moved toward the enclosure and reverently lifted a corner of the plastic, revealing a wall sized collage panel. Thousands of pieces of chipped and cut stone made up the left profile of a woman's face, the other half, an open cross section of the brain with welded wires suggesting the synapse activity from left-brain to right. Suspended by short pieces of monofilament throughout the chasm of neuron frenzy were small etchings, paintings and photos.

"Flip that switch to the right. The lighting *makes* it," said Samara.

As the small intense spotlights came alive, the heat immediately gave movement to the small images. As they slowly turned, Aretha stepped back. The central light beamed outward toward her from irises of the sculpted eyes, coalescing the viewer with the work's visual thoughts in photos and miniature paintings, slowly rotating with the heat.

"More than just *interesting,* isn't it?" said Samara as she handed Aretha a glass of sherry.

Aretha turned and allowed a long moment of introspection as she gazed into Samara's eyes.

"Here," Samara beckoned. "Let's sit. There is much to discuss."

The Sherry went down smoothly. The smoked clams that accompanied the second and third glass helped stave off the sleep that normally came to Aretha after far less wine.

"You still haven't told me how you two met," said Aretha.

"Vending machine."

"Vending machine?" Aretha said with a grin.

"It needed a woman's touch."

"The drink? I'm confused."

"He was wrestling the machine, and I pushed the coin return."

Aretha nodded and smiled. "The woman's touch. Yes. So...how long afterward did you..." Aretha paused.

"You mean how long did the patient doctor relationship last? Not long, by psychoanalysis standards. He was a terrible patient anyway, and I wasn't fond of the guilt I was anticipating by cohabitating with a patient, so…life's better without anymore guilt than necessary, don't you think?"

Aretha nodded.

Samara smiled.

"What?" asked Aretha.

"All those months we separately spent searching for him, all the time for a common cause, yet…we never had a personal conversation, did we?"

"Yes. You're right." Aretha nodded again. "Best to not ask sensitive questions at such times."

Samara lifted her glass as a toast. "Derek always prided himself in knowing a wise woman such as you."

Aretha paused, the moment sinking in. She lifted her glass as well, and then took a sip of sherry. "Doesn't share much, does he, except through his art?"

"You noticed."

Aretha thought a moment. "And the only word from him all this time was through the roses?"

"Through the roses," echoed Samara.

Aretha walked to the window and peered up at the clear sky. "You know so little about me; just a phone call years ago. But, you felt compelled to ask me here. Why?"

Samara gathered her thoughts. "Several reasons. After Derek's initial description of your mugging and the surprise meeting in Truro, I was curious. He's generally not so generous with his time…to strangers at least. And…there was the female thing."

Aretha smiled. "Oh yes, *that* thing. Did I meet up to your expectations, or are you disappointed?"

"You are…formidable, Aretha."

"Oh, I've been called handsome, bitchy and caustic. Never formidable."

"You're beautiful, as well. Never been called beautiful, Aretha?"

Aretha turned back at Samara. "Many years ago, when being beautiful meant something. My husbands all died with that word on their lips."

"Beautiful?"

"All three. Haven't heard it since. Thank you. Goes a long way for an old war horse like me."

"Most important, Aretha, you're here because I'd like to find him. I don't want to undertake it alone. There's no one else, besides Theo that would care enough. But, he's...I don't know about him. I just assume they're together, you know?"

"I think I understand. So, where would we start?"

Samara kept her eyes locked on Aretha's. "That was rather quick. Are you sure?"

Aretha slowly nodded.

Samara let her shoulders relax for the first time since Aretha had arrived. "To start? His note to me with the roses just said, "I'm doing it." That means, he could be anyplace where there's rock."

"That narrows the field, doesn't it?" said Aretha.

They both laughed, using the light humor to release a tension that had built for hours.

"'Doing it'?" Aretha asked.

"It's a long story, but for now, I think we need just be concerned with our 'woman's' thing."

"That being?"

Samara smiled with reserve. "Instinct. I may be wrong, but he may need me. Hell, what do I know? He might need both of us."

Aretha, both flattered and embarrassed, excused herself. "Maybe you, but not..." She smoothed her dress and re-crossed her legs. "But surely he spoke of places he felt were right for such a...disappearance, a what? Venture?"

"To Derek, the only criteria for realizing his long avoided commitment would have been isolation. In those later months, he was convinced that he and a community of artists could only realize their dreams if the better part of the outside world was removed. To him, the artist's nemesis has always been distraction."

Aretha walked once more to the collage built into the sculpture. "Colony? Artists realizing...I'm sure you've studied the photos hanging here. Notice anything?"

"Only that there seems to be a thread line joining pictures and the abstract paintings. Yes. There's a theme to it all."

"Yes?" Aretha asked.

"Family. Just a lot of family. Always with a glimpse of water somewhere in the frame of every photo," said Samara.

"Montauk Point...did he speak of it?" asked Aretha.

"I knew nothing of that trip he took out there with Theo."

"Ah, yes. Theo. Never met him, but...and you think Theo's with him...now...wherever?"

Samara stood motionless at the window as the early sun started cutting across the tops of the adjacent buildings. "I hope so. I hope it's not just Derek alone with strangers. You know?"

"I think so. I mean…yes…I know," said Aretha as her eyelids became heavy and once again she allowed herself to see his face etched inside her closed eyes. "You know I know, don't you?"

The sun broke through; spilling day's first light into the studio. Samara closed her eyes as well.

***

"You can't do it that way," bellowed Theo. Derek stood above the weathered table that served as his drawing board. In front of him were several bank passbooks for saving accounts and two safety deposit box keys.

"What's left is still more than enough to begin with. A year or two from now, we'll be self-sufficient," said Derek, as the ambient spill from the lighthouse arc lamp drifted across his face and continued along the stonewalls.

"*You'll* be self-sufficient," Theo corrected.

"Theo, you know when I closed all the old accounts after Montauk, it was for this, for both of us. There's more than enough to last us. My stocks in Germany and Japan are golden, if we ever need them. Capital makes things happen."

"I told you, one more year of putting up with this pipe dream and I'm out of here."

"You're out of here? Who you kidding?" Derek said as he shook his head and arched his hand in a wide sweeping headlines gesture. "*Cynic and post-homeless New York critic abandons book on the 'Disintegration of Art…'*"

"Oh, stop it, for Christ's sake, Derek."

"How many pages do you have now, a hundred, two hundred? You're no closer to leaving here than you were three years ago, Theo. In your mind, art is a failure, therefore, *I'm* going to fail and that is the only ending your book is looking for. Right?"

Theo grumbled under his breath, "Fuck you."

Derek once again picked up his paperwork. "Exactly. Now if…"

Theo interrupted, "Even if it was enough money, what makes you think just letting these *artists* know they can come here and 'create' is going to make them drop everything and run. Grey Cliff, Maine is the most God forsaken outpost this side of Alaska—and an island to boot. No one in their right mind is going to want to live here."

"Permanent population of a few hundred fishermen and *you're* here," said Derek with a grin.

"Like I said." Theo tapped his temple.

"I warm dish twice now," yelled Singso from below, her Asian accent taking on a curt edge. "Should I throw out, Mis'er Turrel?"

"C'mon, Theo. Before *she* tries to leave me too."

"Been meanin' to talk to you about that."

"About what?" asked Derek.

"Later."

They stepped away from the table and descended the lighthouse's corkscrew metal stairwell that wound down from Derek's bedroom, through the 3rd floor bathroom, 2nd floor studio, to the 1st floor kitchen and living room. Amidst the clattering footsteps on the stairwell, Theo maintained his determination to dissuade. "Lanagra, Mariel, Hensky, and oh, boy, you try and get Touleur to venture up here and..."

"You crazy?" jabbed Derek. "He'd give his left one to be here if he knew he'd be close enough to punch out *your* lights."

"That's yesterday's... Christ, yester-*year's* news."

"Review a writer's ten year project with two words, he doesn't forget," quipped Derek.

"It was one word."

"Spelling it 'tear-able' is two."

"That's how I saw it. Quite frankly, not even worth the energy to rip it up," Theo said dismissively.

As they walked into the kitchen, Derek tried to get the last word in.

"What you believe IS?"

"That's right, Derek. That's right."

"So, *his* belief versus *your* belief?"

"Right again, Derek. You're good! No, not good, just getting better. There's hope."

Having only been in America six months, Singso, maintaining her Asian inbred sense of politeness, slid the microwaved plates of food in front of them. "You might want use some philosophy on this goulash, Mis'er Turrel, Mis'er Donally."

As they sat down, Derek patted her shoulder. "It's all good, Singso. All good."

Theo could only stare at what looked like a *plastic cast* of food. "Ketchup, Singso."

"Sure, Mis'er Donally."

"Mustard," he called after her.

"Any thing else, Mis'er Donally?"

"Better bring the Tabasco, too."

Derek gave Theo a look.

"What?" said Theo.

"Your 'later' moment. What's on your mind?"

"Oh, that. She didn't leave you."

"I don't understand."

"Samara. You left her, remember?"

124

"Hey, where's that coming from?"

"I don't know. It just came out when you suggested Singso might leave you too."

Derek adjusted his seat. "You're forgetting, this is what Samara goaded me to do for...hey, this doesn't look that bad." He waved a waft toward him. "Smells good."

"It's none of my business, but..."

"That's right, Theo. It isn't. But since you're making it your business, and because knowing you, you're now going to badger me until you get a response, I'll give it to you in one sentence, even though we agreed never to talk about this again. She once told me that she would feel like a, and I quote, 'a greedy bitch' if I sacrificed what we both found out in therapy just to have a cozy affair. She's the one that pushed my ass to do it, *this*, without her as a comfort zone companion." Derek began to eat.

Theo forked a mouthful, chewed a few moments. "That's it?"

"I said one sentence."

"Yeah. You did. But you used two to remind me you left her thinkin' God knows what. You upped and disappeared, remember? Guess all you found out in therapy got too sensitive. Right?"

"Singso?" yelled Derek. "My man here needs..."

"Can't find damn Tabasco, Mis'er Turrel."

"I'll live," yelled Theo. "Just the ketchup and mustard."

Derek picked at his food a moment, then laid the fork down and locked eyes with Theo. "I wouldn't be here, Theo, were it not for Samara's constant reminder that Derek Turrel was never going to be happy until he chanced his dream."

"Dream? *I* know this is the dream, but, she said..." He shook his head. "I don't understand women."

Derek began to eat again. "She is *more* than your average woman, Theo. So don't feel bad."

Singso hurried back to the table with the ketchup and mustard. "Sorry, Mis'er Donally. Find Tabasco. I promise."

Theo looked up and smiled at her. "Hey, Singso. It's just Tabasco. Don't fret."

"What mean 'fret'?"

Derek smiled understandingly. "Worry. Worry, Sinso. Don't worry."

She bowed, smiled, "Okay" and returned to the kitchen where they overheard her chastising herself.

Theo shook his head. "Like I said, don't understand women."

Derek continued to eat in silence, his eyes staring vacuously at the food.

After a few moments, "Miss her?" said Theo.

He moved the food around with his fork. "What do you think?"

Chapter 21

Joseph Hensky didn't care for boys, girls, men or women. He was known as the consummate choreographer of modern dance in New York, as well as the man who only related to the stage. Theodore Donally had once reviewed a new work of his called "Done 203" with *"...Mister Hensky's imagination behind the proscenium is beyond comparison, even though his social image among his colleagues in the art community is more akin to a spayed animal or a flower without pistils or stamens..."* Needless to say, Theo had not been one of Joseph's favorite people to socialize with during the late 80s.

Now, a man of extreme power and influence, in spite of rheumatoid arthritis slowing him down, Joseph found himself caught up in the increasing economic squeeze unions and sponsors were putting on the performing arts. As a member of the Board of NY Dance Choreographers, he welcomed any opportunity to speak to the needs of sound fiscal reform in the arts. Such an opportunity presented itself on a cold night in October as leaders of the stagehand union and show producers met to discuss the expiring contract governing the majority of performing arts in the city. The five-hour ordeal left tempers flaring, and, as usually happened in early contract negotiations, a stubborn resistance prevailed on the part of both sides.

Joseph stormed out early from the meeting, suggesting that the parties could save a lot of time and union money by reading some history of the theatre and especially the golden era of Broadway during the forties and fifties. "Just as Washington thinks leadership is about political power, lopsided economics, and the puppeteering of its constituency, so too are you gentlemen sinking deeper into proliferating film and TV mediocrity onto the sacred stages of live theatre. That is unacceptable. The more you allow Hollywood to dominate the upper marquee with name over title, and allow their obscene salaries to shorten the preparation time and out of town try-outs, you encourage that mentality to seep into our opera, our concerts, and our dance. Divas and prima donnas are not needed or wanted, gentlemen. I've proven for years that the seats can be filled with paying patrons without relying on glitz and gimmicked marketing to attract Platinum cards. You really need to give it a rest, gentlemen; otherwise you're courting a revolt. Trust me on that, and I haven't even begun to address the CEO salaries you're slowly creating for the stagehands. You want a bankrupt Broadway? You want that real estate unable to pay its rent? You want our theatres converted into strip joints and peep shows? That's what you're courting with your latest demands."

Joseph, working both his canes, moved slowly off the stage and handed the podium over to Sol Berkowitz, Broadway's most successful producer. "Jesus, Joe, how do I follow that?" Sol muttered as they passed amidst balcony hisses and boos.

"Go break a leg, Solly," he said with a confident smile as he offered one of his canes. "I've got an extra one of these."

Later that night, Sol and Joe gathered along with several other producers at Benny's, a 9th Ave. bar with a "speak easy" type back room that only the insiders of Broadway were invited to use.

"Christ," said Sol, "we're just thought of as money mooching tyrants by the unions. You're not going to change their way of thinking."

Fritz Crindolf, known for his production of groundbreaking Performance Art shows jumped in. "You want a socialistic theatre, Sol?"

"It's not about capitalism versus socialism or state supported arts, it's just about common sense. The average person can't even afford to go to an *off*-Broadway show nowadays. You remember Fritz, Joe, Tony, you too, you remember when we could at least sit up in the rafters and see the show for only six bucks. Try that now. Thirty, forty bucks if you can *get* a ticket. Small corporations are buying the 'luring' tickets out by the aisle-fulls now to give away as Christmas bonuses. Even the heartier who stand in line on performance night for the discount tickets, are nothing but a minority now."

Joseph stood up, balancing on one cane, gesturing with the other as he spoke. "Dance is attracting more and more of an elitist audience and less young people. You know why? It's not accessible. Forty dollar discount tickets, on up to hundred and twenty seats close enough to '*see the sweat trickle'*. What does that mean? Ten, fifteen years from now, old ladies and crippled reluctant octogenarians like me are gonna be asked to donate more and more money to keep a show going. Young people will be bleary-eyed with iPhone, web, TV and movie zombies. They'll be largely uneducated, un-moved and emotionally deprived of history's great redeeming factor and antidote for violence...artistic expression." He dropped his cane and chugged down his bourbon. "I gotta get some nitro before the pharmacy closes. Can't afford to die yet, God Dammit."

127

The group compared a few more complaints and left just before closing. Splitting up for their various destinations, all passed through the ever constant 2 a.m. scene adjacent to the Great White Way; street sweepers, empty cabs, and the occasional homeless pan handler taking refuge atop the sidewalk gratings while the ubiquitous subway steam rises to form the cocoons of warmth around them for their few hours of respite.

"What the hell you doing up this late?" Joseph asked the tall vixen brunette exiting the stage door of the Ambassador.

She pulled her collar up and pointed to the marquee with a respectful smile, "Your show...don't want to embarrass you, Mister Hensky. The end of the 3rd scene is still sloppier than shit. I really need to get it right."

He looked at the marquee and sighed. "Opening isn't until next week. C'mon, here," lifting his cane and extending his elbow out, "let the old dancer help a young and beautiful artist find a cab."

She took his arm and they moved toward Times Square. "Let me tell you what's happening to your world of dance, my darling," he said with renewed vigor.

**

Morning sun kicked off the highly polished bumper, as the big-rig pulled to a stop in the center of a small blacktopped area adjacent to a high-rise construction pad. It being Saturday, work was idle, but remnants of the demolition still surrounded the site whose billboard designated the area to be another fifty-story apartment building pushing into the skies of Soho. At the wheel of the truck was Nathan Wollzak, not your ordinary actor—more of a modern day version of Zampanò from *La Strada*.

Skilled in both classical and contemporary theatre, he had, at a youthful thirty-one years of age, opted to further his love of the stage in a most unusual way. Following the death of his father, he liquidated the Long Island property left to him and put a down payment on a motor home to house his troupe, and a big-rig semi with a trailer large enough to transport a theatre-on-wheels. Behind the driver's seat, his sleeping cab proved sufficient to house all the belongings he now chose to support his life style. Armed with his Yale Drama School credentials and Amagansett upbringing, Nathan was ensconced into the world of mall parking lots, weekend corporate parking lots, and now, *any* parking lots that were available.

The watchman sauntered over with his clipboard.

"You Wollzak?" he asked.

Nathan climbed down from the cab and greeted him with an outstretched hand. "That's me."

"Sign here. Mister Talbot said out by six, right?"

"Six. That's right."

"Give yourself time to clean up any garbage, you know."

Nathan nodded. "You bet. We'll make sure everything is just as we found it."

The watchman eyed the truck. "That's a theatre, eh?"

"Well, we like to think of it that way."

The watchman walked alongside the trailer reading the painted billboard—*Theatre of the Road - Chekhov to Post-Bogosian – Coming to a parking lot near you / 866-212-1287.*

"You're welcome to stay and watch," said Nathan.

The watchman gave a somewhat dismissive glance and gestured toward the construction trailer. "Bruins and the Kings playin'. Got a dime on the Bruins."

"Well if it gets boring, come on by."

Laughing, the watchman countered with, "Hockey… boring? Always a brawl or two to keep you interested."

"Yeah. A couple of fights can do it. Well, thanks. Gotta get busy now."

The watchman walked away as Nathan's motor home lumbered into the parking area behind the semi.

Nathan motioned back to the driver, "Okay, Larry, park it to the right." He looked at his watch. "Our flyers read 4 p.m. sharp. That gives us only two hours. Let's move it."

The door to the motor home opened and out stepped forty-eight-year old Cynthia, thirty of those years on Broadway—Unemployed; Rodney, sixty-one, former director of the London Theatre of the Absurd—Unemployed; Arnold, Frank, Stephan, Weylin, Thompson, Bruce and Betty, all award-winning actors—Unemployed. They were there because Nathan offered them a chance to work for money as it came in. It wasn't coming as he had hoped, but not catering to the masses, business had remained a struggle. This was but another week for his small troupe willing to work for partial pay. They, at least, could console themselves with knowing they were doing what they were passionate about.

Dressed for the unusually warm October afternoon, several dozen New Yorkers with a penchant for "donation" entertainment filled the fold-up chairs formed in a semi-circle in front of the trailer's broad side. The thirty-eight-foot length allowed for the wings and entrance areas to serve a twenty-five foot performing area. Motorized extensions resting on telescopic supports gave an additional fifteen-foot depth down stage for this afternoon's glimpse at the kind of theatre Nathan had grown up loving. This was the theatre experience that was all but forgotten, replaced by escapist

129

entertainment masquerading as Broadway's finest; Off-Broadway's best; and even some of Off-Off-Broadway's attempt at experimentation.

Nathan, fully immersed in the role of *"Zoo Story's"* Jerry, moved around the potted trees and park bench, taunting his adversary, Peter, who tried to remain calm and private, just trying to read his paper. Edward Albee's first work of prominence was new to a portion of the audience that had been bussed in from the Bronx; the thirty to forty young adults being part of a drug rehab program. Today was their monthly field trip, and by the quiet attention they were giving the stage, *Zoo Story* had captured their imagination.

That's all Nathan wanted, really—to present theatre that would stir people into paying attention to their lives. As he performed with his usual pride of training, he used some difficult personal experience to maintain an inner monologue for Jerry, reminding himself of the many graduate friends who had bought into the Hollywood offers. He remembered their donning the *I want it 'cause I deserve it* sun-baked mind set of tinsel town entertainers in lieu of the *'cause I have to* tradition of most east-coast artists preferring freedom over everything. Since graduate school, the trade papers had maintained a close watch on several of his old buddies, rendering a chronicle of their thinly veiled sinking beneath the lower bar of mediocrity—the very curse he had warned them of. These actors were part of the crème de la crème that Yale's Drama School routinely produced, leaving the integrity of what they had learned behind to become, in many cases, the darlings of studio heads and TV network power brokers. As Nathan's character, Jerry, entered the close of the play, he allowed this inner monologue to reveal its essence in the form of a silent thanks to the cosmos for all he had retained, all he had appreciated, all he had become.

Jerry, sighing heavily, said, "So be it!"

With a rush he charged Peter, impaling himself on the knife Peter held in front to defend himself. For just a moment, there was complete silence, then with Jerry impaled on the knife at the end of Peter's still firm arm, Peter screamed and pulled away, leaving the knife in Jerry, who motionless, screamed with the sound of a fatally wounded animal. With the knife in him, he stumbled back to the bench that Peter had vacated. He crumbled there, sitting, facing Peter, his eyes wide in agony, his mouth open.

Peter whispered, "Oh my God. Oh my God. Oh my God."

Peter continued repeating these words, very rapidly as Jerry completed the play.

The curtain dropped and the audience sat a moment in stunned silence, until spotty applause became contagious and even the reticent rehab group joined in to bring Nathan and his fellow actor Bruce out for several curtain calls. After a few moments of the two appreciating the applause and the setting sun, Nathan motioned for the other repertory actors, serving as stagehands for this performance, to come forward for a bow as well. As he stood aside and allowed them their moment, he gazed into the eyes of his audience and knew, with little compensation or not, he and his troupe were doing the right thing.

Chapter 22

"Yeah? Well, you can think what you want, but from down here, there's nothing but blobs of paint. Nothing else," said Cheryl standing back, dodging another spray of salty droplets mixed with yellow and blue glops of paint from on high. She raised her head, and stole another look at the top of the thirty-foot canvas whose upper ten feet curved diagonally outward like the page of a book in the process of turning. "Must get hot as hell painting up that high," she quipped.

Lanagra was not humored. Lying on his back atop the scaffold, he placed a final swath of the mop-like brush, mixing a crimson red into a background of pearl gray and coal stained clouds, while his emaciated black body continued to sweat profusely. Cheryl tilted her head, studying both the painted image and the painter, whose diet had become two Hershey bars and a coke three times a day, chased down with the usual four cigarettes in succession.

A massive open-book-like framing of fourteen giant canvas pages, each with their upper corner turned down, dominated the twelve thousand square foot warehouse. The fourteen-page installation called "*Inevitable*" conveyed a surrealistic history of man's greed for power, from Genesis through what he believed would represent the final moral decay of civilization—the twenty-first century. As if artists from the past had been resurrected, Lanagra had painstakingly used the canvases to capture slices of history's most painful hours, depicted in the various styles of art's greatest painters.

Unexpectedly, Lanagra swung down through the crosshatched scaffolding and stood on the paint splattered concrete.

"What do you think, really?" He asked in a soft voice whose accent was definitely of French heritage.

Cheryl craned her neck once more at the mix of images, all parts of bodies Lanagra had explained to her were partially discernable images of Gauguin, Dali, Picasso, Van Gogh, DeKooning, stepping, running and crawling upward over each other toward the foreboding red streaked clouds at the top of the canvas.

"Watch it!" said Lanagra as he pulled her aside, allowing the residual *plop* of red paint falling from the clouds to mix with the Pollock-like accident on the floor.

Cheryl looked at the floor, then up to the canvases.

Shaking her head, she said, "I don't know if they'll get it."

He stepped in front of her. "My God, what are you sayin' woman? I've done everything but paint words."

Cheryl, needing a cup of coffee, walked away from the canvas and strode to the opposite side of the warehouse that served as both home and studio for Lanagra. He was an established artist whose work hadn't been seen in five years.

Cheryl turned back toward the work and took a sip of her coffee. "And this fifteenth page... ascent into heaven?" Cheryl asked.

He sat down on the concrete like a collapsed harlequin. "A triptych ascent and return to the beginning. There's a sixteen and seventeen."

Cheryl reared back on her heels. "Sixteen and seventeen? You've got to deliver this installation in three weeks and the fifteenth canvas isn't even done. What are you talking about?"

Lanagra now tilted his head. "Simple. All white and black."

Cheryl nodded sarcastically. "White and black?"

"Not to worry, madam." Lanagra grinned, "Just a little black."

***

Touleur Gaubert looked forward to his *special* students everyday. The New School had given him the opportunity to teach his rich traditional writing approach to a group that truly wanted the secrets to rich character building, unique plot lines and structure. Like Lanagra and Nathan's rebellion against the commercialization of artistic expression, literature's influence was rapidly becoming the toughest challenge would-be novelists were facing in cracking the market with something that could rival the established icons, and the mediocrity-suffocation of the best seller lists.

It wasn't that structure was the end-all to novel creation, but the technological age had trickled into the psyche of the readers as well, and trendy formulas—not to mention bite sized menus being offered by new digital platforms—had all but quashed serious story and heart in most of the buying public's priority. So, while keeping tenure by giving those of the "other" appetite what they wanted in commercial-story classes, teaching this small group of talent was the highlight of his days.

***

It had been Theo who had recommended Touleur be put on "the list," even though he had little hope that he'd join the Grey Cliff group. All together, Touleur had spawned half a dozen "in-demand" screenwriters as well as a near-equal number of important published novelists, but Theo did not think it likely Touleur would come out of the comfort zone of a full professorship to join them.

"I should get a letter off, anyway, just for the hell of it," Theo said to Derek during one late night of Courvoisier indulgence.

"Why?"

Theo answered, "Just in case. He's a motivator. I wrote a piece on him way back when he was teaching writing 'Boot Camps' in the Poconos. He was turning housewives into fully matriculated university students back at Columbia and NYU. Plus, I know something about him he doesn't know I know."

Derek turned to him. "And that helps?"

Theo smiled. "Always. Think what I'm gathering about you."

"You can be such an asshole when you want to be, Theo."

"And, it took a lot of educating to get there." He gestured to the near empty bottle. "You going to share the rest or what?"

***

It was after-hours that Touleur became the man lurking behind the professor façade, the man Theo knew as the unique writer, *Tito Gaubert*. His name had become one of the publishing world's favorite topics of conversation. Tito had written a compilation of essays about New York and its people that had become a windfall success, all from the point of view of a homeless man known only as Tito. In spite of his open disdain for the way publishing promoted pulp, his insight into the multicultural, multiethnic nature of the city's dwellers—its movers and shakers, its losers, its dreamers—took him to the top of bestseller lists and kept him there for twenty three months. No one knew the true identity of Tito, save his friend Theo. His agent only knew him as Tito Gaubert, the man who submits his material through the mail, and receives his royalty checks at a PO Box. Professor Touleur Gaubert remained a ghost, except to his classes.

Even as days passed, and Theo and Derek continued to research and debate the final list, Touleur, aka Tito, dressed in his usual non-descript thrift store rejects—his imperceptible fake beard, and the ever-present hidden lapel microphone wired to the digital recorder beneath his coat—continued to fulfill his *need*. Sitting on

133

the curb of 59th Street at Central Park, cutting wedges of an apple and feeding them to a carriage horse, he ruminated and continued composing yet another compilation of contemporary impressions.

"Here," he said softly as he lifted his palm of apple wedges to the horse. "It's a wonder I don't snap, ya know, girl? Ever feel like people aren't people anymore? Sure you do. Feels like they're somethin' else, don't they?. Look at your buggy. Standin' here for hours, right? Nobody takin' rides in the park like they used to. Why? Why we losin' that? Same reason." He glanced at the oats bucket beneath the horse. "You can't even count on that bein' oats, ya know? Synthetic this and substitute that. Test tube designer babies, Virtual Reality love making. What happened to the real thing, Mister Ed?" He stood up and gazed back over his shoulder at Central Park. "Where's the real thing, man?"

He patted the horse, gesturing to the driver sitting atop the carriage, waiting hopefully for a customer. "You got it okay, girl. Your old man ain't gonna do nothin' to screw up his rent, and the other stuff you make possible for him. You take care now. Tomorrow, bring you one of those Jonathan apples you like."

Tito strode off into the darkness of the park, speaking into the microphone, "Tuesday, October 14, 2006. *Fall of the Horseless Empire, part one.*"

CHAPTER 23

Sitting here at my desk, pen in hand, paper blank, I'm not myself. Today, maybe I'm off the charts. Samara might think it healthy. Aretha? She'd probably see this as "perfectly normal." Theo? "Making anything personal, makes it unchallengeable," he'd remind me. I can just hear him saying, "don't dismiss it as just a whim, dummy. Like I said before, you push Echo away or dismiss her as illusion; you may never find her again."

Familiar words.

Except for this morning, I'd only seen him this serious once before, some three years ago as we sat at the base of the Montauk Point lighthouse. I was white with fear. He, after six hours of searching for me in the fog, trembled as he goaded me to break the lock and walk the stairway to the top. "You don't believe she's there," he said as he flicked the padlock, "but if you believe you saw her there, she must be there, *Dreamer.*"

That was the first time he called me that. Now, he pesters me with it whenever I get discouraged with the project, accusing me of being the *Dreamer* and dragging *him* into it. "You're not going to reduce me to living a nightmare you created, *Dreamer*," he's said on more than one occasion. I guess I'm doing something right, though. His one-year limit has moved toward its fourth. He grumbles more, but it feeds his book. And, without something, anything, to excite his writing again, who knows where his disappointment with the art world might have taken him? So, enough fear of rejection. Time to fess up, Derek. Pen to paper...move it across the page...

Dear Echo,

As I begin this letter to somewhere... someone named Echo, twilight descends in colors of purple and gold across this island you sent me to. It is indeed a strange feeling to feel I know someone so well, but barely know your name.

I'm writing because I'm at a point now with the rock where your memory is starting to fade. That's not good. Your colorful scarves, clothing, those tiny ribbons you had in your hair, "angels I've inherited" I believe you called them. Do you remember what you said that day in Montauk as I stepped up on the lighthouse landing and you appeared from behind the Fresnel lens? "They'll make you pay for that lock, you know?" Do you remember that? I was smiling to myself and thinking, how the hell did you get in here? When I told Theo, he grinned from ear to ear. "Another entrance, stupid," he replied. "But," I said, as he pressed his finger to his lips. " 'Buts' get you in trouble, Dreamer."

So, what's with you, Echo? Send a guy to a God forsaken island, two guys, actually, and never visit? It's been a long three years. I've gone many times out to the rock and waited for you to show up. Somehow, I think you've snuck a peek or two, right? What do you think? The rock, I mean. Is it how you see yourself? Lot of work, especially with the state of Maine sending inspectors out every three months to assess the damage I might be causing. For a chunk of rock that for the moment nobody ever sees or cares about, save the occasional fisherman drifting too close to the choppy shoreline, you'd think they'd leave me alone. You know what's surprised me the most all this time? I wasn't all that good with demolition at the quarry, so when I started here, and the inspectors warned me that one slip up—if I destroyed the cliff, you know—I'd get a fifty thousand dollar fine and a boot off the island. I just shrugged, thinking why should my luck change? Then I'd think about why I was doing all this crazy stuff, and—either you're the guardian angel Aretha labeled you as, or a necessary figment of my imagination as Theo put it, or— you're the most real thing that ever happened to me. Which is it? Maybe it's that very question that caused me to start sculpting you into the rock. Between the fog and the remoteness of this end of the island, it will take some kind of guided tour to bring the curious here. And then the world will be asking, "Who is Echo?"

In case you've been wondering, I'm starting on your right eye sometime this month. Left side is almost done, but now my time isn't as open as it's been. I've got to push forward with the bigger reason I'm here—The Project.

I've sold some of my stock in Germany, so that will take care of the funding for a good while. I did follow the papers and Samara and Aretha's push to find me. Bank accounts are in Zurich along with the safety deposit boxes now so for all intent and purposes, I'm dead. But...but maybe its time to open up. That brings me to the next point. I'm probably all over the map, but the thoughts are piling up now. Where are you? I don't know where to send this?

That little boy in me—the one who kept a cigar box with all his secrets in it so many years ago—he wants to put this in a bottle and float it out to sea. You'd find it, wouldn't you? I could always copy it and send it to Montauk, but then, what would they do with a letter addressed to Echo, Montauk Point, Long Island? Not a good idea, right? So...

I'm thinking now, maybe I'll start this as a journal. What do you think? Keep it with me until we meet again, or tear the pages out and send each in a bottle?

Trying to picture you. Give me a minute to just—yeah, you leaned against the glass of the tower, the Fresnel washing you out as it rotated. But each time, I remember each time it rotated, you softened. I mean, your smile, your voice, like a polarized impression, the features softened to a whisper. When you said "Grey Cliff Island, that is where you need to go," you became one with the light. I mean, it got bright in there. I couldn't see anything, but light. You said, "Go now. Leave the truck. Take Theo with you. He is needed." And I went. Like a dummy, I went down the stairway and dragged him kicking and screaming to the road, hitchhiked to the ferry station and ended up after five hours—and two more ferry rides—here. You know we had been drinking a lot the night before, don't you? You also know, I'd been in analysis for four years some time before, so, well, just wanted you to know I don't do a lot things conventionally even when I'm sober. How wiped out was I?

Hey, if you ever want to have a unique experience with feeling nuts, try doing what Theo and I did. When we got here, we didn't know where we were, other than the name. Didn't know Charlie, the painter of ocean water like you've never seen. We didn't know there was a group of six artists who lived here year round and that the summers would bring dozens more just for the warm months of work and selling of their labors to week-end tourists. We didn't know how

136

lonely it could be, just being pure artists without distractions. It's what I've always believed was the right kind of surroundings for creation. But, damn, it has its down side.

So, you've probably guessed, I'd like to see you. By the time this somehow might reach you, the need may have passed. You know how I am. But, well, give it a shot, Echo. Bring the gulls. Bring a whale or two while you're at it. Hanging on that cliff chipping away at your face, I've spotted a couple over the years. So, visit, okay?

The nut case with a chisel,
Derek

So, here I am, writing to God knows who, sealing the envelope and mailing it to Echo - Montauk Point, General Delivery. I know it's crazy, but it would really be admitting to illusion if I just kept it, right?

I walked the short distance from the lighthouse to the post office, a quaint little shingled house with a row of post office boxes. As always, Sheila, the postmaster and Mayor of Grey Cliff, stood behind the counter ready to make mailing a letter the highlight of the day.

"Derek," she said as I walked up to the counter. "How are the drafts coming?" Having been the lighthouse keeper in her younger years, she always asked about the drafts that whip up and down the three floors of the lighthouse.

"Gettin' colder."

"You best have Seth re-weatherproof those windows when he services the *Fresnel* next. Freeze your keister off in another month."

"You know, Sheila, I'm going to do that. Yes." I dropped the letter in the slot.

"Won't get picked up 'til Thursday, you know."

"Yes," I said. "That'll be fine. You take care of yourself, now."

I walked out knowing by tomorrow morning, half the town would know I'd sent a letter to Montauk Point... to Echo. "Who the hell is Echo?" the boys down at the boat yard would be saying over their morning coffee. There would be the usual speculation on anything that happened out of the ordinary in Grey Cliff, like a change in the weather, or a shingle or two coming loose on someone's house. You know, the big stuff. By nightfall, I might be called by the local two-page paper to comment on the rumor I was sending mail to an *Echo?* "So Derek, you want to help the busy bodies in town solve their mystery of the week?" Something like that.

I didn't have to wait till nightfall.

Imelda, *The Village Diner*'s only waitress slid the plate of beans and franks under Milton's nose. "Just like you like'em, Milt. Charred and crisp."

"Much obliged, Imelda."

She poured him water as he fanned the aromas and took a deep breath. "Perfect."

He picked up his knife and fork and leaned back to Imelda. "Hear about the Rock Man?"

"What. Hear what?"

"Sendin' mail to a one-word somebody."

"One-word? What you talkin' about."

"Talk is he's sending mail to something called Echo."

"Echo who?"

"That's just it. No last name. Doesn't that beat all hell?"

"I used to send fan letters to Liberace. No big deal." She walked away.

"I ain't never heard of no Echo," Milton muttered to himself. "Hey, this Echo some kinda rock and roll singer or somethin?" he shouted at her.

"Rock Man looks a little old for R & R fan mail," Imelda shot back.

The simple sign said, "Tavern." Several trucks and a couple of mopeds were parked outside. Inside—

"Echo?" grunted Samson, the local car mechanic. "Never heard of him."

"Maybe it's a she," whispered Louise, the scrawny waif sitting next to him.

"Rock Man ain't got no time for women. You see how far he carved that eye?"

"No. How would I see that?"

"Take a boat out there like the rest of us, you ding a ling," said Samson.

"Why I wanna do that? You and your crazy friends gonna kill yourselves. They don't call it "shipwreck point" for nothin', you dummy. 'Sides, you know I get sea sick."

"Louise, you get sick just breathin'. Why don't you eat some chocolate bars or somethin'... put some meat on?"

"Okay," came the cry from behind the bar. Nate wiped his hands on his apron and opened the cash register. "Okay. Beers for everyone. Leave the Rock Man alone. Deal?"

"I can handle that," said Mario, the local butcher, peering at the draft beer handles to check what kind of beer he was up for.

"Nothin' beats a free beer," said Tyson, Grey Cliff's lobster crate maker.

Several other customers wandered up to the bar as Nate slid the drafts down the counter, each finding a welcoming hand.

In the corner—an always comfortable choice—was Theo, nursing a tall glass of Gallo. He paused for a moment, taking in the clamoring for free beers, and then walked toward the front door.

"Hey, Theo, Echo mean anything to you? You're his buddy."

Theo shook his head as he left. "Nothing to me."

When Theo reached the lighthouse, he could see the light on in the bedroom. He rapped on the door. From above, Derek leaned out the window. "Hey, Theo. Kind of late for you, isn't it?"

"Can I come up?"

"Sure. Just finished the list. I was going to call you in the morning, but... I'll be right down."

Theo thought about the best way to bring it up. He didn't fancy himself a watchdog for his friend. He didn't fancy himself as anything but a companion for the artist that had captured his imagination and given him reason to live a bit longer. But, all he could think was Derek wasn't sleeping, working twice as hard on the rock, making the list over and over and...Theo was concerned with the letter and all and... was somebody going over the edge here? That was the question he posed as Derek pressured, and Theo finally acquiesced to the list of creative people Derek wanted to have at Grey Cliff.

"These are the people I think can make it all happen and the ones I want around me when I die, Theo."

He sat down. "Yeah. Sure. You dyin'? Fat chance." He looked out the window into the pitch black. "The town's goin' nuts with this Echo thing, you know. They're gonna think you're loony soon."

Derek knew what he meant, but didn't want to admit it to anyone but him. "Soon?"

Theo shook his head and grinned.

"Think she'll come?" asked Derek.

Theo sighed and shrugged. After a few moments silence, he said "Been thinkin' about her myself, you know."

Chapter 24

"Look, Tony, stage door guards always make a fuss. Whoever was on that night had to sign for the flowers. He might—just might remember what he signed—from where they came, you know?" Samara, the usually calm and professional staid woman, was more excited than usual as she confronted the little man sitting atop the stool next to the downstage wings.

Looking at his time sheets, "Miss Jennings, that was weeks ago. Benny was on that night, but he's..."

"What's Benny's last name, Tony?"

"Oh, God, I don't know. He's just Benny. He's a sub for nights when Jose calls in sick. I'm just a stage manager, not the yellow pages."

"Local 403, right?" asked Samara.

"Yeah."

"So, he's got a last name. How many Benny's could have been working stage door on the premier night at Lincoln Center?"

"Okay. I'll give them a call in the morning."

"You're a saint, Tony."

"Well, I've been called... never mind. What's your number?"

***

As I waited quietly for the balance of the city council to arrive, I scanned the room for faces I knew. I'd been here for over three years now, and with the exception of Sheila, Singso, the resident half dozen artists, and a handful of utility workers, repair men, etc., I was pretty foreign to the population of 1100 year-round residents making their livelihood off lobster and crab export. All I could think was *they would see me for the first time, this mystery guy known as THE ROCK MAN, and think I was as crazy as they'd heard.* The letter I'd sent out to Echo had set all kinds of rumors flying. The local paper had given it an inch column just below the obituary and astrological predictions for the day. My chances of everyone knowing about the notorious letter were far better with word-of-mouth than with the town gazette, whose unread copies, more often than not, were used to wrap Tillie's "world famous" fish and chips. Superstition and mysticism weren't high on the list of interest for these simple people with basic food and shelter aspirations. Theo had made a few friends of the regulars at the tavern, but Theo being Theo, socialized just enough to pacify, get a "drinks on me" pint, and then slip into his corner and continue to write notes for his book. Why the bar atmosphere stimulated him, I've never known, but that was where he went night after night.

"Might be easier than we thought," whispered Theo as he sat.

"What took you so long?" I murmured, checking my watch.

"Everybody is on the furnace repair kick, I swear. You'd think winter was here."

"Well, it is November, you know?" I answered.

"And warmer than any October on record. So Donaldson was late getting there and then I had to help him with his broken down ladder and... oh, it was a mess."

I listened with half an ear as he continued with details of the chimney sweep, the filters, the thermostat rewiring, and etcetera. I was much more concerned with the strange faces that paraded in and took seats on the other side of the room; the occasional polite nod of the head as if they knew me, and the quiet way they sat as if in church, making Theo's soft explanation sound like a barker at a carnival.

"Shhhh," I cautioned him. "I think they're about ready."

Sheila took her chair at the head of the table, surrounded by the six other council members—all men, all fishermen, all straight off the boats.

"Hi everyone. Got a few things to cover before we get into Mister Turrel's proposal."

And so, Theo and I sat for the better part of two hours as those "few things," most of which affected no one but the crab and lobster hunters, went on and on. A final vote on lowering the island tax for fresh crabs versus frozen crab export got four yeas and two nays. Passed.

"Mister Turrel, you may present your proposal," said Sheila. "Sorry for the delay."

It was of no value to present the philosophy behind the venture, as the only interest the town had was the tourist impact and the tax base. I spoke little of the need for artists to have freedom from distraction and the right kind of solitude for their creative process. I emphasized the growing tourist trade and that having a group of highly diverse and talented artists, covering both the fine arts and the performing areas, would bring in many more tax and merchant dollars from the summer months. I remember seeing many nods from the council during the explanation.

It was another thing when I asked the city to give me the old boarded up cavernous cannery down on the docks. Its tin roofs and sidings were rusting away and the foundation—without some underpinning enforcement—would be next in the total deterioration of the landmark building. I outlined how with time, it could thrive as a gallery, museum and performing arts center for experimental work and a major attraction for tourists. I closed with "this could turn the island into a *tourist destination,* not just an afternoon ferry excursion from the mainland." There were, of course, those who wanted the island to stay just as it was, but the majority—after hearing their neighbors from the floor—determined that if I took on the building at my own expense, it was a go.

Now, all I had to do was hope the artists on my list saw it the same way. Like me, they would need to renounce their lifestyles of yesterday. The Project, if successful, would do more than shake the foundation of the arts. After three years of thinking and debating the risks with Theo, we both realized we could be on the cutting edge of a revolution, a solid effort to nurture art back to its rightful place of freedom, where creation is unbound from the restraints of commercialism and mediocrity. Of course there was always the threat it could all fail. With the technology we intended to install, the project would be accessible and visible for the masses, or—we could find ourselves more alone and isolated from mainstream influence than ever before.

As we walked out, Theo reminded me of his favorite quote by Frederick Franck : "*An artist has an obligation to question the conditions that rule all our lives... and to cause his audience to do the same.*"

It was a timely utterance. "...and how many on the list will buy into that thought when we ask them to live here?" I asked.

He shrugged. "When are you sending the letters out?"

***

"That was a while back, Miss Jennings. I sign for lots of flowers on a premier night," said Benny Kay as he checked to see if there was one more swallow left on the bottom of his beer bottle. Standing in a one-room apartment with peeling wallpaper and a radiator that was whistling distorted revelries as he tried to talk, he went to the icebox and retrieved another Bud. Keeping the phone propped under his chin, he popped the cap with his key-ring opener and sat down on the edge of the bed.

"But I bet you would remember these, Benny," said Samara. "One yellow rose in the middle. Three dozen red, with a single yellow. How many bouquets do you sign for with one yellow rose?" She asked, sitting on the edge of her desk chair, the knuckles of her grip on the phone white with anxiety.

"Delivery boys come and go and...oh, boy. Am I embarrassed."

"What?" asked Samara.

"I'm really sorry. Man, how could I...Miss Jennings, I remember this one big bouquet...you said three dozen and it got me thinkin'...this limo driver, gorgeous she was, brings in this big bouquet with the one yellow, yeah, I remember. She said I should take good care of...yeah."

"So, do you remember where they came from?"

"No."

"Oh, Benny. Think. She was gorgeous. She was dressed in black, I bet. Blond?"

"Red Head. Wow. It's all coming back now. She was some looker and a limo driver. Boy, I..."

"She wasn't just an ordinary limo driver, Benny."

"You can say that again."

"No, Benny, maybe on her hat...a logo, a name, a..."

"Wow. On her left boo...Sorry. On the hankie pocket, there was something. I noticed cause...well, she was gorgeous, you know."

"And she had lovely bosoms, right?"

"You got that right."

"And on the left bosom was...?"

Samara waited, but no reply."

Benny took a big swallow of beer.

"Benny, on the left..."

"A butler. Yeah, damn. I remember 'cause I thought what a..."

"A butler...her patch...emblem...a butler?" She paused a moment. "Concierge? Concierge, Benny. Concierge Floral?"

Benny's eyes lit up and he slapped his knee. "That's it! Con...whatever. How you say that?"

"Con-see-erge," she phonetically pronounced. "Thanks Benny. You've been a big help." As Samara hung up, the dial tone buzzed in Benny's ear.

"Conci...." He hung up and muttered to himself, smiling. "How could I forget conci...ah, shit." He finished the bottle in one big gulp. "Thought I had it."

***

Aretha sat back in the chair, her tired eyes wandering to the Obelisk beginning to take on the "magic hour" glow. It was that time of day when she most liked to sit and watch the reflecting colors shift from yellow, to orange, to light gray, to the blue black of night. Cloudless nights in front of the Ode took on a meditative mystery when coupled with the moon reflecting off its needle-like sense of permeation into the heavens. Clicking off the excited answerphone message from Samara made her hope for such a night. She needed to spend time now with the message and the idea that the man whose work had caused such an impact on her was alive and—what was he doing sending flowers from an isolated island off the coast of Maine? The sun created a reflected ray off the Ode across the garden, slicing through the small square panes of the French doors, coming to rest on the table before her. She placed her hand beneath the reflection and closed her eyes. The warmth was good. It was very good. She drifted off.

***

Linda drove the dune buggy with reckless abandonment the short distance along the shore line to the house. It wasn't often she would take the shoreline route, but today was special. She had reason to be shamelessly excited. The Truro post office had left a certified mail notice for her at the front door that morning as she and her mother shopped for provisions in town. Her hopes of good news had been answered. The application for the Rhode Island School of Horticulture had been accepted. What she had learned while in the institution had been just enough to qualify her. She was going to perfect her ability to make plants and flowers grow *anywhere*. With all the stress and pain of being in the hospital behind her now, what she had learned with miniature pots, soil, seeds and water served her well.

She threw the buggy into a 360-degree spin, revving the engine, its high pitched squeal competing with her hoots of joy as she finally pulled to a stop at the base of the property. She killed the engine, cupped her hands and yelled at the top of her lungs up over the weathered fence she had so carefully repaired and nurtured as a support for the plants she'd grown from scratch over the past three years. "I'm going to be a God Damn Horticulturist, Mom. You hear me. I'm gonna be something!" No response came from the house behind the Ode basking in the late sun.

She jumped out of the buggy and ran into the heavy surf, leaping and playing like the child from days past. With one big gesture of exaltation, she dropped into the wet sand, prostrate and carefree. As the salty waters washed across her, she smiled a quiet moment into her memory. Lifting seawater to her face, she whispered as if to an invisible spirit. "I'm gonna be something, Daddy. I gonna be somebody for you."

It wasn't until several hours later that the patience with which Aretha had first greeted the news finally waned and she felt she had no choice but to state it bluntly, "You're not ready to live away, alone, on your own, and that's that. I don't understand why you didn't tell me you were applying for this so we..."

Linda burst into tears, wringing the napkin tighter and tighter as she refused to accept her mother's condemnation and proclamation. "Why must you always hold me back?"

Aretha cleared the table and placed the half-eaten food in the sink. "Control yourself, Linda. If you had talked to me about it before secretly running off with your application to..."

"It wasn't a secret. I told you I wanted to learn how to grow plants, really big plants."

Aretha looked over the top of her glasses, wiped her hands and went to the cupboard for some brandy as Linda continued.

"You even told me over and over again that nothing ever grew on the back garden, that the sun, or the wind, or the salt always killed them, and I was the best thing that happened to your garden, and..."

"Second best thing, Linda. Second."

"Oh, Christ," Linda exploded. "You going to tell me that fucking piece of phallic metal and rock is the best thing that ever happened to your precious garden again. Are you going to hit me with *that*, MOTHER?"

Aretha stopped pouring a moment and then began again. "This will calm you, I hope. Would you get out the..."

"You want calm? You want fucking calm?" Linda leaped over the couch, colliding with the Giacometti. A deep gash appeared across her cheek. Without pausing, the adrenalin eruption filling her body with unabated anger, she picked up the three foot spirited bronze figure and like a creature possessed, pushed open the door to the garden and swung the piece full force at the Ode.

Aretha dropped the two snifters of brandy and stood paralyzed. Her mouth sprung open, but sound was locked away in the pain. Her eyes glared with fire and hurt like a Goya from the dead, the bulging veins on her neck like the vines of her Hyacinth now flying in all directions along with the broken limbs of the Giacometti. The relentless succession of blows to the Ode, the screeching metal on metal, was like gasoline to the fire raging within her and with a gigantic leap through the door, Aretha clamped her thin arms around the flailing muscular limbs of her daughter, pulling her away, toppling them both over the hedges onto the sand below. The kicking and writhing nightmare who had committed the unthinkable, mutilating the very underpinnings of Aretha's soul, was breathlessly heaving like an alien beast, an aberration from the darkest of darks, smirking, gloating over the removal of her mother's connection to God.

A windmill of strobe-like images fluttered past Aretha's eyes as the mother and daughter's love-hate relationship seared her heart, sending the blood boiling through her body, as if—

Aretha's anguished face winced, her mouth opened wide, letting out a trembling "Linda!" Her eyelids flashed open as she yanked her hand away from the reflected ray of setting sun. She sat a moment, her disorientation finally coming to rest, the bewilderment at what she had experienced in a dream, grounded. She looked toward the source of the mirrored heat upon her hand. The Ode stood as always. "Oh, Jesus. Thank God."

As if to say, you're welcome, the Ode relinquished its watchful presence as the trailing orange upon its surface rapidly gave way to the gray of dusk. From the distant sands, Aretha heard the familiar sound of Linda's dune buggy. *Curious,* she thought, *why is she revving it so much?*

Chapter 25

It was a typical day in Manhattan. Fast, focused, paranoid.

Like any other day, no New Yorker worth his or her weight in hand-cart-hot-dogs was going to let anything obstruct the goals, the interview, the job, the date, the sale, messages, phone calls and the mail. Mail—the kind that gets delivered on foot by a man or a woman—has lost a lot of its edge over the years. If there's urgency, communicating by e-mail, IM, or cell phone works much better. A letter? That's to announce something like a death in the family, or a dear-John, or invitations.

But, as if propelled by the urgency of a dying time, another era, post office employees worked habitually, feverishly sorting the heavy bags of letters and packages streaming into the main depot. Occasional brightly colored wrappings suggested the early mailers for the holiday season were out in full force.

Trucks backed in and pulled out of the main loading docks, their bright red, white and blue markings highlighting the "MAIL EARLY— avoid the Christmas Rush!" banners.

Of the fourteen million pieces of mail delivered that day by post, Fed Ex, UPS and an assortment of minor carriers, only twelve were invitations from a remote island off the coast of Maine.

Postmen, some behind the wheels of their mini-trucks, others laboring on their feet in the traditional manner, moved to and from buildings with the precision and swiftness of professionals well conditioned to the *fast lane* expectations of city dwellers.

One such New Yorker, Simon Greco—a Bogosian-like personality and host of WOZ's fastest growing Liberal talk show— fingered the envelope with suspicion as he waited out a commercial break. Middle America, as well as both coasts, had embraced his radical approach to "freedom of expression" with unprecedented support, generating unheard of controversy in the process. For two years, he had prophesied the precipitous downward spiral of meaningful and constructive expression in journalism and the arts. The impact of his widely syndicated show was to Broadway, Hollywood, the Art, and Publishing worlds, what Rush Limbaugh's show was to the apathetic and subservient populace of America. To many in the entertainment, and so-called "business of the arts,"

Greco was their worst enemy. His reputation was nothing short of a reversal of Brave New World—"Down with mediocrity, up with selectivity…" was an oft-heard cry from his microphone.

If it was material recently created for a screen—wide or small—or anything other than straight news reports in newspapers, magazines or books, Simon was saying—as he did this night coming off a commercial—"AVOID IT! Boycott this trash! Demand journalism that is unbiased. Demand *more* music be played and sold which addresses a standard that has some empowering value, not just the usual in-one-ear and out-the-other degrading, life-mocking crap which is becoming the daily diet.

"Where the hell is any preference, now days. We are wallowing in a dusty drought of expression void of any depth because we refuse to support the *passionate thinking* writers, poets and humorists; the *passionate thinking* painters, composers and filmmakers. Instead, we run to the nearest quick-fix *substitute/escape* to pacify our deplorable inability to address and solve the complexities of societal demands. Hollywood! Why aren't you cultivating a new Fellini, Goddard, or Antonoini? Where's even your 21st Century *Woody*? And Christie's! Why do you gloat over the obscene prices your auctioning of fine art to private collectors brings into your coffers? You just had your half-billion dollar record-breaking auction. A dozen or so people will hoard those works of art away and only an additional dozen or so dinner guests will ever see them again. Are you proud of taking that accessibility away from the people? It's *bleep bleep* shameful. Hey, Christie's, have you heard of Janus Films? *Mister Hulot's Holiday*? *Wild Strawberries*? They recently took the last century's greatest fifty films, packaged them in DVD and made them available to anyone. Who has a right to the artistic creations of the world? The world, of course. Artists don't create for one collector! I'm sorry. No… I'm not.

"It's gotta change people. Repeating the old as if it was new is out. Plowing fields is out. Pounding steel is out. Unionizing the masses for dues and pension kick-backs to line the pockets of union bosses is out because letting someone else run your lives, making your decisions, and taking away your choice… is out! Anarchy is just waiting to pounce on us, and why you ask? Because the system of so-called free enterprise is controlled by the greedy, obsessed with controlling the minds of all those who make their profits possible. The broken system obsesses on bringing you to your knees where better control of you is possible. And what you are told to read, watch and hear lacks fundamental stimulation for your mind so you have the fodder to think for yourself! Do you hear me America and the rest of you all around the world? Have you all but forgotten

147

Paddy's historical message… 'I'm mad as hell and I'm not going to take it anymore?' Well, that's good for starters."

He took a sip of tea and continued. "But what can we yell, what can we throw out there that will *be* how we really feel, not just *sound* like we feel? C'mon, people. Limits? That's what we're workin' through here. Take out your hammers and your bats. Break up the logjam. Let something flow which has no limits. Let the establishment of safety nets know you're out to free the captured, to let the risks of passion and reason forever find an open sea, an open sky, 'cause if we don't, who will? It sure as hell isn't gonna be the control mongers. They want to see you forever shackled to their galleon bowels of rowers. And don't think I'm bashing any one party. Plenty of greed-blame to go around. Uh-huh. But, hell…"

He took another sip of his tea. "You know, all you people with your mouths open and your ears perked up like bobcats, you're not hearing anything you haven't already thought about, or you wouldn't be tuned into this rabble rousing platform for action and discontent. But thinking isn't enough. Discontent isn't enough. In fact, discontent with the media's agenda to foster glad-handing of *any* power as long as it has advertising dollars is cliché today. It's cliché because we sit back and just listen to the complaint, the *reality*, while we chug another beer and jam another handful of butter-laden popcorn down our gullets. It's time you used your mouths for something besides an overused trash receptacle, folks. Jesus, I'm seein' the edge of Niagara right now, but there's more than one falls were gonna challenge tonight. I'm just getting started. I'll be back after we satisfy the brave *bleep* advertisers who pay for this. Don't go away. But if you do, please go away mad."

Simon took a deep breath, grumbled to the engineer behind the glass, "Preachin' too much?"

The engineer shrugged, smiled and gave a thumbs-up.

"Yeah, thanks a lot, God Dimmit!" He gulped down some of his favorite tea, and picked up the envelope again. He wasn't used to getting letters from a place he'd never heard of. Grey Cliff, Maine was not on his list of "frequent" call-ins. *Turrel? Why do I know the name? Do they even have a radio station there?* He turned back toward the engineer. "Hey, you know…?" He caught himself, and shook his head as he slid his thumb through the overlap and pulled out the letter. His assistant handed him some fresh tea. "Thanks, Ellen. How come this was on my desk?"

She shrugged. "I put it there, but I don't have a clue why the mail boy slipped it under the door this late. Must have thought it important."

He stared at the return address again. "Why do I know the name Turrel?"

"Turrel? There's a giant mobile hanging in the lobby by a guy named Turrel," she said.

"Oh, yeah. What's he writing me for?"

Dear Simon, You don't know me yet, but I'm very aware of what you stand for. I'm writing you because we both see the problem in the world, in the United States in particular. It can't be solved with you remaining JUST the talk-show host the country knows and listens too. As you read these several pages of reasons for our mutual discontent, I hope you will consider joining us and helping us design an approach to lift the masses out of their diet of—one of your favorite words—mediocrity.

There is no greater influence in the world today than that wielded by the manipulators of public opinion and taste in America. You are one of them, but one of the few who subscribes to a higher standard, a standard of preference and need. That is why I'm asking you to join us.

No ruler or military general or crowned prince ever wielded power even remotely approaching that of the few corporations controlling America's mass media of news, opinion, entertainment and art.

With TV as the primary delivering platform, their power and message is not remote. It reaches into every home in America, and it works its will during nearly every waking hour. It is the power that shapes and molds the mind of virtually every citizen, young or old, rich or poor, simple or sophisticated, and, it promotes mediocrity and ignorance for the sole purpose of controlling us. Because it robs the minds of the innocent—rendering them sheep without ability to think, feel and act as individuals—journalism, entertainment and art is rapidly turning into an insidious form of viral infection to undermine the very survival of the planet.

The mass media forms the images of the world and—

Simon sat down behind his microphone and read the final paragraphs with a sense of—he didn't know *what* it was. When he got to the final lines, he realized he had just encountered another side of himself, a side he had never met, the side he never thought of value. *"Would you join us for a week-end and express the side of you never expressed?"* There was a plane and ferry voucher attached, dated October 24, 2006.

***

Derek's letter and vouchers were held this day by many passionate hands which customarily gripped pens, chisels, balance bars, trumpets, scripts, batons, and brushes. But October 24 was about to be remembered as the day all their instruments of creation, all anguished thoughts of failure, all hopes for opportunity, all the elements of an impoverished creative diet were about to change.

The sun dropped behind the stone and glass catacombs of lower Manhattan, bringing shaded cover to the hundreds of gray and white-feathered gulls perched atop the Manhattan Bridge.

Above, a double arrow of flight began to form, North-Northeast.

CHAPTER 26

"Enough, Theo!" I said with a shiver as I coiled the ropes in from the overhang. "You can philosophize it all you want, but not being here to pick me up...well, he *did* just lose a job. Find me another skipper by morning, okay?"

Standing on the docks and looking north toward Derek's rock, Theo turned to shield himself from the wind as he shouted into the radio mouthpiece. "By tomorrow. You've gotta be..."

"By morning. Think I'm going to enjoy even one night here in this cold?"

"Got it, Derek. By morning. You gonna to be alright for the night?"

I adjusted my position beneath the rock as the moist laden winds whipped the rock face. "You're breaking up. Can you hear me?"

"Barely."

"Get someone out here by sunrise, okay? And bring some coffee."

"And croissants?" Theo said sarcastically.

"Mañana, clown."

I lifted the headset off and placed it, along with the small two-way off my belt, safely into an old amo-can's protection. Pulling the sleeves of my sweater down around my hands, I reminded myself once again how dangerous wind chill could be on the body, and the mind. This was not what I planned. Five-thirty, I had told him, very explicitly. Five-thirty before the tide goes out and these fucking seasonal cold winds come for their nightly visit. All I could think was there was an empty bottle of rum somewhere either in a bar, or at the bottom of the ocean with him and the boat. One explanation I could tolerate. The other...I didn't want to carry that on my shoulders right now.

I checked my pockets for any overlooked snacks. Two peanuts—very old—and a stick of gum. Save for the half bottle of water and core of an apple—whose stem I'd nibbled around earlier—I was in for a hungry night, and...damn! It was cold.

With nothing to do but wait and keep warm, my eyes wandered, noticing details of the veining. Granite at this end of the island was darker than anywhere else. The veins of white and gray intersected and opened like an oscilloscopic reading of time. *How long had it taken to change colors? How long had this monolith of time been submerged before the oceans receded and revealed the many peaks of mountains and hills that we now appreciated as islands?*

I blew on my fingers and looked out to sea and realized I was crouched not only beneath the *eyelid* of my work, but one of the primary geological protections the island had from the ravages of erosion cascading below. No wonder the town council, the state, and the BLM had been so restrictive on what I could and couldn't cut out. I looked at the calendar on my watch. In another twenty-three days, the Federal inspector would arrive to assess and enforce the restrictions placed on me. Funny, in a way. Here I was, crouched beneath the lid of my muse's left eye, ready to huddle in the corner of the tear duct for the night and try to keep from freezing. While water below and winds all around me continued to slowly carve their millennia timed, hair-like intrusions upon the rocks. Wind, water, eruptions—centuries of making life and taking it.

How miniscule we are. How insignificant in terms of it: the all of "it." Isn't it ironic that this small piece of three-pound matter between our ears can affect the course of history with little more than a thought or two? Have the capacity to work with nature and alter this tonnage of significant matter beneath my feet into...into...into one of man's ways of creation. The power of the brain, versus the might of oceans and wind. With the idea of creating a monument to my muse, I had convinced dozens of decision makers to allow a vibration of my brain to hasten the changes on the face of this ancient rock—changes that would take less than five years, compared to millions that had preceded me. I closed my eyes wondering if nature was pleased with me. As the cold penetrated deeper beneath my parka, my mind began to wander. *Was nature pleased with me, or about to render some severe punishment?*

***

"Oh Christ, Nate, what I'm sayin' is that our drunken sailor friend really up and did it now. Left Derek stranded out there for the night," grumbled Theo. "You know how cold it's going to be out there in another hour or so?"

Nate nodded. "Not like the old mariner to get himself plastered before his work's done. You sure that's what happened?" said Nate as he polished the beer mugs and continued his neat stacking for the night's business.

"Yeah. Yeah. Checked out his mooring. Boat still there with him sprawled on the bunk below."

"Passed out?"

"Passed out is an understatement," said Theo. "I couldn't get him awake with the ice bucket. He'll have one hell of a head in the morning."

"So who you gonna get to go out there?"

Theo downed his cognac and stared into the mirror behind the bar. "Good question. Jamie was the only boatsman in town fool enough to battle those rocks and breakers every day."

Nate stacked the last of the mugs and leaned on the counter. "I can help you out tomorrow. I'm off."

Theo laughed. "Sure. Thanks anyway."

"Hey, don't just wave me off. Been awhile, and rocks ain't my specialty, but Merchant Marines served up some pretty hairy assignments for me in Nam."

Theo turned to him. "You sly devil, you. Vietnam? You that old?"

Nate threw him a playful punch and continued preparing his glasses. "What time?"

"You don't have to do this, Nate. I can find another fool to do the job."

"Not if you keep chuggin' those Courvoisiers."

Theo smiled at him. "You don't look old enough to have been in the war?"

"Eighteen I was. Fresh out of high school and nothin' but bad gambling debts to keep me in Boston, so…" He proudly rolled up his sleeve, revealing a huge chunk of indented scar tissue. "Purple Heart. How about that, Mister Fancy pants writer?"

Theo nodded. Lifting his glass to Nate, he said, "Might as well take Jamie's boat. Derek's already paid him."

Nate grinned. "The way you described him, he'll probably sleep right through it."

***

With the wind chill factor still trying its damnedest to ruin my night, I crouched in the furthest corner under the eyelid and blew cautiously at the small kindling beginning to catch fire. I pushed my climbing and chiseling gear up against the rock, making the most God-awful pillow thinkable. *What else am I going to do?* I blew once again, watching the splinters catch the flame. It was really cold now

152

and it was only 8 o'clock. I had to hope I could use some reserve mind-over-matter for the night. The small stack of weathered brush and roots I'd been able to gather from the only accessible ledge above seemed hardly enough to keep me comfortable, so I blew a bit more. The fire rose slightly, doing its best with the mixed kindling as I placed some of the more weathered roots on the edge, blew some more, and curled up as best I could. Above, I could see the stars; millions of tiny reminders of where our imagination could take us. *Who needs anything more for the mind when you've got this?* I closed my eyes and listened.

The breakers below—mixed with the wind whipping the hanging carabineers against the rock—orchestrated an accompaniment to the sparkling show on heaven's black screen; a sort of percussive dominated Rite of Spring for a crazy rock man. Opening my eyes once more, the galaxies began to dance their syncopated light show across my mind. It was all just too…. Breaking the magic, as if a star had stepped downstage, a sharp flash of light lit up the precipice outside and held for a long moment. *Wait a minute. Where the hell's any storm? Sky's clear as a…*

I slowly rolled out of my fetal retreat and stepped outside. The whole sky was ablaze with stars. What was the bright flash? I rubbed my eyes, making sure I was still seeing straight. I turned around squinting to see to the right where Echo's partially carved nose stood innocently alone without a full face; to the left, her scarf, chiseled into a forty foot ledge that the authorities had so restricted that I had to blueprint the whole project based on this outcrop as my fulcrum point.

By the time I noticed the winds had unexplainably calmed to a still and the waves below were silent as lapping surf on level sand, I was beginning to think I'd really fallen off the wall earlier and this was all just a prelude to meeting *you know who* at the pearly gates. I was now hearing humming voices, or a voice. Starting. Stopping. I stood still, waiting for the next round.

The voice was clear, succinct and right behind me. "I waited for a message in a bottle to wash ashore, but your post arrived first."

I wheeled around, but there was no one.

"Up here."

I heard it, but I wasn't ready to believe it. I paused a moment, then shot a glance upward to the brow. There, protruding out from above the eyelid were long yellow and light blue scarves floating in the breeze. Craning my neck back to see further up, I carefully stepped to the edge of the eye. All I could see were the blue and yellow colors, like undulating fins of some giant angelic tropical fish from the deep, a mesmerizing ballet of color and movement.

"Echo?" I ventured to utter.

"You're going to freeze to death out here."

"It is you. What...when did you..."

A sudden gust of wind reinforced the prophetic words. "You're right. Damn. That was an icy burst."

"We can talk back inside underneath this. Okay?"

I shook my head in wonder.

"Okay?" she repeated.

I nodded. I didn't understand how she got there, and I sure wasn't going to try and figure it out standing in the cold. *Where the hell did the sudden wind come from?* "Sure. Sure. Inside."

Momentarily coming to my senses, I didn't waste any time getting back under the overhang. My first inclination was to catch the fire before it went out, but when I reached the corner, it was ablaze, the brush burning more like a gas log. I stood there awkwardly, wondering if I shouldn't throw my canteen water on it.

"Too hot for you?" came Echo's voice. I wheeled around and some thirty feet away, she was sitting on the very edge above the ocean; her scarves still dancing *the dance*. I turned back to the fire, to her, and once again to the fire, now down to a reasonable flame. I nervously chuckled and pointed to the fire. "How'd you...?"

"Chalk it up to the tricky winds up here. It's of little consequence. The bigger question is: Are you ready?"

"Ready? Ready for what? Hey, you're going to freeze out there, why don't..."

"Come in?" She moved closer to a small boulder just inside the overhang and sat. "Are you ready for the response to your letter?"

"The one I sent you? What? Did I say something..."

"The other one. The letter of invitation."

I sat down next to the fire, purposely placing my hands close to the flame, just to make sure I wasn't dreaming. "Ouch! Damn!"

"Didn't your mother ever tell you about 'hot'?"

"The fire. Yeah. Well..."

"Derek, relax. We're just talking, right?"

"Talking. Yes."

"The letter," she said again.

"The letter, yes. Am I ready? Sure. Why wouldn't I be ready for a few artists of my choosing to...? How'd you know about *that* letter?"

"It's more than inviting a few buddies to join you for a weekend, and you know it."

"I think it will take some time, but...why do you ask?" *Talk about nerves. I couldn't formulate a simple sentence for Chrissake.*

Echo stood and moved back to the edge overlooking the ocean. As she talked, she unraveled more and more of her scarves, revealing a longer and longer trail of color blowing out to sea like the giant tail of a kite. "You're going to be hurting soon. All that you hope for is going to take time and...pain. Again. Do you really think you're ready?"

"You make me feel like...I'm not sure how I should answer. Pain? Again?" I slowly muttered.

She turned back to me, her rainbow of colors, like her tone of voice, slowly and patiently catching the moonlight like the unfurling of a maypole. "That is something you need to answer, Derek. Your peaceful fantasy on paper is about to slap you with some reality. There are many expectations you will need to fulfill. Are-you-ready?"

"Okay," I said, "It sounds like you think I'm not. So...you know how you've..."

"How I've influenced you? Yes. Of course," she said. "But, you have to come to grips with the fact *you're* responsible for you, not me. Leave the rock, this project, for the moment. You will need all the time you can cram into the next few days to think and consider the ramifications of their arrival. Think. Meditate on it. Be prepared for personalities that will challenge you, fight you, and may even try to sabotage you." She smiled. "You're one scary dude, you know."

I wasn't ready for this kind of consideration. She just stood there, again imploring me. "Get ready, Derek. You invited them. They're coming. You have no idea what's ahead."

A sudden burst of wind and the fire from behind me lit up. I spun around to see the flames flaring erratically, going in all directions. "Oh, shit!" I shouted. "My backpack! Shit! Shit! Shit!" I quickly kicked the pack aside, stomping the fire and cursing. The walls became dark again. I turned around.

Echo was gone.

It wasn't until hours later, while pulling my cold and aching body in closer to the fire's dying embers that I allowed my eyes to close again. Surprisingly, with so little flame, I was warm, comfortable and the sense of fear all but gone. Like a little kid, I squeezed my eyes closed and focused on the brightly colored sparkles — sparkles in the sky that seemed to stretch and move about like a rainbow of connected comets, a rainbow of ribbons. I smiled to myself. *She's something else,* I thought. *Something...*

CHAPTER 27

Theo hung over the side of the boat, trying his best to purge one last and final time the result of Nate's warnings the night before. The only saving grace for his embarrassment was the ocean hitting him in the face more often than his Courvoisier disgrace.

Nate helmed the boat with a perpetual grin; an obvious missed pleasure since his war days. "How's it goin' there, Captain?" he yelled to Theo.

Theo was too busy to hear the concern.

Down below, Jamie, just as prophesied, bounced around on the bunk like a burlap bag of potatoes, oblivious to the rough waters.

As the boat rounded the point, Nate picked up the cell phone.

Derek sat calmly before the opening of his sculpted eye, studying the darkened rock from the fire's smoke. He finally stood up and stepped back, allowing another perspective to formulate. He wasn't sure the darkness would be visible from the sea, but there was something intriguing about the depth blackened rock gave the eye. Having never been that close to Echo's eyes, he was unsure of himself. Her voice and overall persona were his only reference.

From below, he heard the boat's horn just as his cell phone beeped. He looked over the edge and saw Jamie's boat as he quickly put on his headset. "Hey, Jamie."

"Sorry, pal. Nate here."

"Nate? What the hell you doin' steering a boat?"

"Later. You wanna start down. These waters aren't apt to wait much longer. Storm coming in from the east."

"Yeah, on my way. What's with the body hanging over the side? Jamie?"

"Got myself two sickies. Hurry up."

Derek anchored his rope into the piton and began the rappel down the two hundred foot wall of granite. With his gloves having gone up in smoke with the backpack, he took his time maneuvering the descent, his harness and hardware belt heavily laden with the surviving assortment of climbing gear. Taking advantage of the slow decent, he made some strategic mental notes where future detonations could be placed. As he reached the bottom and pushed his small inflatable dinghy into the waters, he wondered when he would return. His sleepless night had been used to contemplate and meditate, just as *she* had suggested.

As he revved up the dinghy's small outboard motor, putting distance between the rock and himself, his eyes wandered to the top once more. He wanted to believe his focus was secure, his thoughts through the night sound, but…. *Am I expecting too much of Echo?* He had a momentary fear. *Samara would surely think I'm mad to even think such a question.*

The ride back was uneventful. It wasn't until they were within the harbor that Derek asked the question. "Theo, what's going to happen?"

Theo, barely able to sit up during the voyage back, popped another Dramamine from the First-aid kit. "I'm not sure what you mean, and I'm not sure if I did, I'd be able to give you a coherent answer."

"Over dinner, then," said Derek.

"Oh, God…" muttered Theo as he made another lunge for the prow of the boat. "Keep the food to yourself. Arghhhhh."

"Oh, Jesus, Laddie, try the stern," bellowed Nate as he maintained a steady-as-you-go toward the docks.

Derek leaned off the starboard, away from Theo's domination of the portside. He pressed his face into the mist of the wake; his mind sorting the men and women he expected might join him. The shoreline with its cottages and mooring posts were coming up fast now. He wiped his face and took a deep breath of late autumn air, its salt stinging his nostrils and eyes, its taste reminding him once again of the "no retreat" zone the sea symbolized. He glanced over his shoulder at the impending storm coming from the east. "Nate?"

"Yeah."

"Were the winters always like this, I mean, this unpredictable?"

Nate held the wheel and glanced back as well at the wall of black clouds moving its way toward the mainland. "You've been here long enough to assume the answer. Winters are a good time to be indoors with a good wood pile by the fireplace."

"What would you do without wood piles?"

"Can always go modern with a fancy electric log, you know."

Theo thought a moment. "That builder, what's his name…the one Sheila insisted we use to re-build the cannery?"

"Lawrence. Lawrence O'Hara."

"Is he really as good as she says?"

Nate grinned. "The best, when he's sober."

"Another one? You got your share of boozers here, don't you?"

"Derek, me lad, I'd be out of business if it were any different."

***

Theo cupped both hands around the mug as he slowly blew to cool it down. The steaming aroma of chicken broth agreed with him.

Singso stood at the table holding a box of saltine crackers. "You want eat some of these too, Mis'er Donnaly."

"Just leave them on the table, Singso. Thank you."

"Leave him a couple of bottles of water, too, Singso," said Derek.

"Jesus, Derek. I've downed three bottles already."

"And you spewed twice that amount back on the boat. Drink up."

Derek rose and glanced out the window. It was dark and cloudy outside, but it hadn't passed four o'clock yet. "If you hurry, Singso, you can probably get some of that soup down to Jamie before the storm hits."

Singso looked a bit surprised. "You want that I take Mis'er Turner soup?"

"Yeah. If you wouldn't mind."

"Okay with me, but Mis'er Turner usually sleep a couple of days after binge."

"Whoa. Didn't know you were so up on your *village talk*."

Singso poured a few saltines out on a plate. "Everybody know everything about everybody here."

"So I'm finding out," quipped Derek.

Singso grabbed a quick look out the window. "You okay, I leave now."

"We're okay, right Theo?"

Theo sipped his broth. "Leave some more crackers, Singso. Wanna make sure there's enough down there to soak this up."

Within the hour, Singso returned, just beating out the storm. Theo and Derek were retired to their favorite talking space, the workroom just below the Fresnel. As the rain danced across the domed glass, the light rotated through refracted magnification, cast a kind of "ballroom" ambiance across their faces. On the table were files on the twenty-two artists who had been sent the letter. Attached, were various newspaper and magazine clippings attesting to their established controversial image among the public. Derek continued to yellow highlight the clippings as Theo sipped from his water bottle and listened.

"No, I think you're wrong, Theo. So far, all *these* different critics and editors have basically said the same thing about them, a...'temperamental, anti-social, unavailable, arrogant'...here, here is a good one, pigeon-holing Mariel and her poetry, '...she writes...' he says, blah, blah, blah, wait a minute, ah here... 'She writes with no regard to punctuation, incantatory effects alliteration, assonance...'"

"'Assonance,'" Theo mumbled. "Most critics wouldn't know one if it bit them on the ass."

"Theo, don't you see, it doesn't matter whether it makes any sense. Even these anal retentive poetry critics want literal, translatable material to communicate with their readers, and it doesn't fucking matter. They're paid to garner eyeballs for reading. Plain and simple."

"Whoa, you lost me. What doesn't matter?" asked Theo.

"What they think of us, the poets, the artists. The Project is not about *us, you, me, the artists*, and this Mariel poet. It's only about how effective we are in getting other people to use their own imagination, their own creativity…empowerment, Theo. Empowerment. We've talked about this for…"

Theo jumped in. "For a long time. But the fact remains, these people, the public, most of them don't *know* they need to be creative like us. They don't give a shit about being creative if it means less time spent making enough money to *acquire stuff*."

"Let's not go there again, Theo. We've beaten that to death a dozen times. You know well enough the difference between acquiring stuff and a sturdy roof, some clothes on your back and nourishing food…the essentials, not stuff. Look, consider it this way. This *stuff*, as you call it, is still just a means to gaining access, right?"

"Access to what?"

"To that which makes them, us, *feel good* for God's sake," answered Derek, his resolve obvious. "That's all we're in search of…the nectar, the panacea, the mental vial of something that will make us *feel good*." He picked up several clippings from the table. "Theo, that's all these creative minds are doing: practicing the art of feeling good. For them, you and me, we access that spot where we feel best by expressing, grounding, call it what you will…a search…the search. We reach out for a place to plant our words, the notes on the piano, the brush stroke, the …you know what I mean. We just keep layering our thoughts and expressions until we…until we've accessed that place inside us. Here. Where we feel our particular 'ah hahs'." Derek patted his stomach, then his heart, then his head, then reached over and attempted to carry out the action on Theo."

"Don't be touchin' my stomach, God damn it."

"Sorry."

Derek shuffled through the clippings again. "These artists all have the same thing going for them. They're scaring the hell out of the critics because they're only there doing it for themselves, and they don't give a shit what the critics say."

"Van Gogh died just doing it for himself. Jesus, Derek. Some of us would like to eat too."

"And we will eat, but we're going to have to first put up with barbed wire and quicksand around every corner, Theo. No comforts of stepping out onto a yesteryear Greenwich Village or a Williamsburg Street in order to feel the vibration of a creative-hungry community. No recording studio working the stanzas until the producer thinks it's familiar and watered down enough to sell; no writing the perfect box office hit just because the writer knows how. We've got to make sure it's *them* not us that makes this what it is; the millions out there, not the dozen or so that are here. If we don't get the...you remember Chayevsky with that line that's now a cliché, 'I'm mad as hell and I'm not going to take it anymore!' If we don't get them to lean out their mental windows and shout out something akin to that, well, then we've failed. My rock, your book...it doesn't matter if it's *perfect* art. Does it fire *them* up? Does it empower *them* to exercise their *own* creativity? Otherwise..."

Theo leaned back in his chair and waited. "Otherwise, Derek? Need I ask?"

"Otherwise, continued perpetuation of art's most destructful nemesis, Theo.

"Mediocrity," they said in unison.

"You've defined it all, haven't you?"

Derek took a moment, then calmly heaved a sigh. "I didn't invent this realization. It's been there as long as I can remember, but...but somebody has to raise some kind of a bar, any kind at this point. Theo, we live in a bankrupted society. And yes, there is too much emphasis on stuff. Few know what it's like to be moved...really be moved by imagination, creation. Your creation, my creation...it doesn't matter whose. What matters is that there's at least one group of artists that really gives a damn about losing the most precious gift they, we, all of us have."

Theo looked up at the rotating Fresnel, paused and looked back at Derek.

"So? You dragged me up here to look at clippings, and rant. So, where are we? What if these people in the clips are real assholes to work with? What if trying to get them to conform to *your* standard is impossible? What if when they get here—assuming there are a few coming..."

"They're coming."

"If those few get here and listen past that letter you sent, then tell you to your face that you're a fool, a hallucinating...Jesus, I don't know what. Without anyone to drink this *Derek Turrel nectar*...what if? What if they look at you and say, 'you're fucking nuts'!"

"Precisely, Theo. That's the moment. The moment when the right one's will join us."

Chapter 28

"You still haven't told me why, Samara," said the middle-aged white haired man sitting in his Eames chair, calmly fingering the kidskin upholstery. On the wall were several degrees and honorary degrees identifying him as Jeffrey Calder, M.D.

Samara sat with apprehension, as she gazed through the glass bricks behind him that separated the therapy office from the waiting room. Her sense of intrusion rose as the distorted image on the other side of the wall paced back and forth, obviously anticipating the time that he or she would be sitting here as well.

"Could we close the curtains, Jeff?"

He rose and pulled the curtains shut, massaging his kidney as he moved to the small refrigerator. "Care for a V-8?"

"No thank you. The reason I haven't told you is…I don't know."

Jeff popped the can's tab and shuffled back to his chair, sipping his nourishment for the day and continuing to massage his kidney. "Getting too old for this. A 10 K maybe, but this training for a marathon again… ever get kidney spasms?"

"Jeff, for Christ's sake."

"Sorry, Sam. Just giving you some time to answer."

"Time. I've had all the time I need. Like you, I just don't *know* why."

"Okay. From the beginning. He disappears. After a reasonable period of time, the authorities classify him as a missing person. Then…three years later, you get flowers. Passion implodes when you find out they were sent from a florist in Portland Maine, who got the order over long distance from Gray Cliff, Maine. And then the invitation comes. And here you are. Don't know why you can't get on a plane and…"

"He's sent that same letter out to God knows how many."

Jeff put his V-8 down. "Mea culpa. But so what, Sam. You knew from the beginning your effort to dominate with your little game…pardon, your *strategy,* might backfire."

"It wasn't strategy, and it sure as hell wasn't a game."

"You sure?"

Samara now rose, walked to the curtain, parted it slightly and peeked through the glass bricks.

"Why the bricks?"

"What?"

"Why such a tentative separation?"

Jeff swiveled in his chair. "Hadn't thought of it that way, actually."

"I can't be the only patient who feels violated."

Jeff smiled. "Whoa. Violated? Samara Jennings? And hardly a patient any more."

She wandered back to her chair. "You should keep them closed."

"I'll consider that...friend. Why not get on the plane?"

"You're still the bulldog you always were."

"That's why you're here."

"I love him and...I just don't know."

He leaned forward. "Okay. After eleven years of our sitting here, fifteen feet apart on occasions, when your shit would hit the fan, I've grown to understand...no, I've actually learned to cope with the therapist *and* the woman in you. Not an easy task, even for a shrink, you agree?"

"Go on. I know you're busting a gut with what's on your mind."

"Coping is good...up to a point. Perhaps this is one of those points," he said.

"And?"

"And...the *woman* in you says if I go and he is beyond me, beyond the *woman*, and my love, and only wants my composing talents to further *his* dream, then the *therapist* jumps in to save the day and whispers to the *woman* that he was always a self centered, egotistical narcissist using you to anchor his emotional fears, and that's not what the *woman* wants to hear from the *therapist*, so...is this the reason you don't want to go?" he said calmly. You goaded him until he finally "did it." Now...

"Shit!"

"I guess I'm close." He toasted her with his can. "You could have had a V-8."

"Cute."

"So, you want to go out and get hammered? I haven't done that in a while."

"He is enamored, maybe obsessed with this Echo thing, you know," Samara said quietly.

"Ah, the other woman"

"She's a fantasy for him."

"And?"

"It makes him feel special."

"Like what the slow decaying timbre of low C on the Steinway does for you?"

"That was years ago," she said.

"You still use it, though. Discovering a form of inspiration earlier in your creative life than Derek is only *your* fortune. He's maybe trying to catch up."

"It never took on *these* proportions," she said.

"Accept it as a means to an end for him," Jeff said.

"What if she's more than a fantasy?"

"Why do you throw that out *now*?"

"What if she is?"

" 'What you believe is.' I believe you're the one that convinced *me* of that axiom, yes? With all you've told me, she's a bit too...what? Too good to be true?"

"As a real-life person... I hope so," muttered Samara.

"You're letting that old fear-crap creep back in."

"Well, for a forty-three year old woman trying to hold onto some kind of prime...thing, fear is easy to come by."

Jeff looked at his watch. "Look, I've got the *pacer* behind the wall. Give me thirty minutes. Meet you at Scandy's and we can work on your *prime* over a martini."

Samara rose and shook her head, smiling. "You're still the letch you were in med school."

Jeff opened the side "patient" door, leaning in to whisper, "*Perpetual* prime, kid. You know what that can do."

He patted Samara as she exited, then opening the main door, greeted his patient.

"Monsieur Jenour. Come in."

The pacing man stopped. Straightened up his six-foot-four frame and marched past into the office. "Colonel Jenour today, please."

"Oh, delightful. We haven't visited with him in a while."

"Been strategizing the demise of those insurgent assholes in Iraq."

"Ah, yes," said Jeff as he closed the door. "You have been busy."

***

As Samara left the building, all she could think about was how best to use the thirty minutes. Jeff would not only get the two of them drunk—he loved the libation-escape with colleagues—but use the opportunity to drag *admissions* she guarded passionately. No one knew the secrets of her need to delve into other people's minds and hearts; the need to express all her own anxieties through the music she composed; the need to love someone, anyone, with like needs. No, no one knew how badly she wanted to have it all, to be part of Derek's dream of an artistic movement that transcended any pseudo-intellectual definition, any critiqued assessment of his

163

deepest of deep purposes for art. The truth be told, she lusted after Derek's spiritual connection to life and especially, his art. She acknowledged her excellence as a composer; she accepted her place among the accomplished creators of sound that did, in fact, move people. She at least took solace in that accomplishment. But the part that would not stop haunting her psyche was she loved the man, wanted to consume the man, and was fearful of her own self-destruction, should she dare.

She passed the storefront galleries, the bookstore, and the homeless woman propped in a doorway, her wrinkled hand at rest on the concrete, still in the cupped position for a handout, snoring her way through the worlds of her past. As she came upon the bus stop, a single child held tight her bus pass in one hand, while with the other, clenched a plastic bag revealing an apple and a cookie— perhaps the uneaten portion of lunch destined for additional comfort during a few hours of TV watching before working parents returned. Samara could only wonder with awe at how Derek could witness similar sidewalk experiences and translate their meaning, transcend their obviousness, into blasted, sculpted, chiseled art. *Why does he want me back "there" on an island? Where can I fit into such a man's world? Is that my only worth to him? A musical translation into art? Or am I of normal significance to him? Is Derek beyond loving anything normally?*

***

"Of course I'm afraid of the answer. Don't be so naïve with me," said Samara as she rolled the olive around the empty martini glass.

"*If* this love you say exists between you..." said Jeff as he looked for Scandy's waitress.

"*If*, Jeff? What's this *if* business?"

"Mea culpa, mea culpa," he exclaimed.

"Jeff! For Christ's sake. Speak plain English. You're not in a lecture hall."
Jeff lifted two fingers for refills to the waitress and shooed her on. Leaning across the little round cocktail table, he whispered, "I *fucked* up. Better?"

"Much."

Leaning back, he smiled and continued. "You used to down a half dozen of those before you became crusty."

"What if I go and he's changed?"

"What if you don't go and he's not changed? You'd never know, yes?"

"You're so damn logical," she grunted.

"Look, Samara, if you don't go as invited, you're going to wait, suffer, and then go another time, right?"

"Stop it. You're impossible."

"What about Leonard?' Jeff asked.

"He's going. Says it's just to take a look and get away from Tina."

"Thought you said they were…"

"They were. Now they're not."

"Funny how that happens," Jeff quipped.

Samara leaned across and took his hand. She fingered the pronounced veins, remembering how many times in her mind he had held her hand and given counsel. "That's just it, Jeff. The *awful* didn't happen with Derek and me. Everything remained constant till the day he disappeared."

"You act surprised. You nudged him, remember? Hell, for all I know, you might have threatened him to *do it*, right?

"Never a threat."

"You sure? Holding back the sex is a threat to a man."

Samara placed his hand back on his knee and looking right and left, whispered, "Jesus, you remember that?"

"Four years ago, if my aging mind serves me correctly."

Samara laughed. "You're worse than a tape recorder, you know that? Was it really four years ago?"

"Give or take."

"That was a mistake. Even I know now."

"Failed strategy?"

She corrected him. "Not strategy."

"Okay, label it as you like. But, you told me you didn't do it for damn near a year."

"Twelve days, not twelve months."

The waitress placed the martinis on the table and removed the empties. "Anything else, sir?"

"Some oysters. Bring us some oysters."

Samara shook her head. "Not even in your dreams, Jeff."

The waitress blushed. "How many sir?"

Jeff shrugged and smiled, "One for my friend, just to keep her sociable, and twelve for me."

As the waitress nodded and left, Samara leaned across. "Where's this going?"

"You get hammered and I'll get horny, then ask again?"

"Rhetorical as hell. Why don't I call Tina. She's got friends."

Jeff took a deep breath. "Just kidding. Too old for the hookers."

"Jeff, you'll never be too old for the hookers. Tina say's they dream of the old guys. Steadier. Pay better. Tip better. What else is there to a hooker?"

"My heart of gold?"

"Yeah, sure." She sipped her drink and thought carefully as she nibbled the olive."

Jeff, enjoying the process, grinned, "That olive is having a good time. Sure you don't want me to up the order on the oysters?"

Samara kept her straight face. "Sex, Jeff, to a woman, is... "

"Is this going to get serious again?" he asked.

"Damn it, Jeff. Yes. Sex to a woman isn't like sex to a man. You know that. God knows how many patients over the years have told you the same. I never really kept it from him. He got off whenever he wanted to. I just..."

"Didn't...get off. Right?"

"Right."

"And you don't think that's any part of the sex act for the guy?"

"Not to us. Jeff..." She leaned across again. "Jeff, I composed in my head the entire 2nd movement to the concerto in one continuous weekend of Kundalini sex. He was sore and worn out, and I was with nirvana. He was pleased. I was enraptured. But he thought he'd failed because my reaction was sublime, not visceral. You guys have a problem with that kind of sex, now don't you?"

"Yeah. Probably. We're base creatures."

"Derek's beyond us both, Jeff. His rapture is beyond us both."

Jeff took a swallow. "So, you going to the island?"

CHAPTER 29

As Samara pursued her quest for answers, Aretha labored at her own. Although the two had experienced a common goal to find Derek, now that his whereabouts were known, both were left with new questions. Aretha was consumed with protecting the one man who had personified *creative* wealth for her, a gift she cherished and would do anything to protect.

For Samara, the stakes were different. Consultation, even from a colleague of eleven years, didn't help the dilemma she faced. Derek had *done it*! Now, was she worthy of his love? Was his love still there? Had the act of doing it, of completely immersing himself in his art with no regard for remaining safe and commercial—had that replaced his need for her? Was she truly capable of doing what Derek had resisted for so long? Could she confine herself to pure creation? She remembered one of her favorite movies in which "If you build it, they will come," was an oft-repeated line. She now wondered, *if you do it, Derek, will they come? The artists might, but would the people of the world see it as you see it? Could all this succeed in stimulating the creative juices in others? Is there such a thing as a mass creative nirvana?*

It was a time for Samara to be alone with herself. Walking late at night wasn't foreign to her, so to see the unusual, the unexpected, the sometimes, unbelievable, well, that was just New York late at night. As she approached the images in front of her, however, she had to admit, this was a first.

He lay with but a piece of plastic sheeting across his fetal position. The steam rising through the grating offered the only warmth for this cold October night. The mongrel companion was sitting on his hind legs, ears pricked, focus still and straight. In front of the dog and his homeless master, a vigil party of rats paced back and forth, protecting two other rats feasting on the remains of a large bone. Samara's first reaction was to yell and frighten the rats away, but on second thought, she realized the bone was probably a butcher shop scrap the dog had finished with, and the sleep of the man was not being interrupted by the thievery. *So why meddle?* That's when it hit her. *My God, why meddle?* Her first reaction was probably the honest one. Her maternal instinct with the dog, the man was the honest one. Why then was she hesitant? No, worse than hesitant, why was she being dishonest? *Okay*, she told herself, *you're making a big deal out of nothing. Just a dog, a man, some rats, all co-existing. What was wrong with that?* Nothing, except she was intellectualizing her heart.

Samara's fear of her heart had been her nemesis for many years. She knew she had betrayed it many times in her quest to insulate herself from being hurt. Natural instinct, she told herself. After all, how many people have to listen to other people's broken hearts all day, every day? She stopped, standing perfectly still some twenty-five or thirty feet from the scene. She found the ticking bomb before her fascinating. The dog could turn on her. The man could awaken, panic, attack the rats or attack her. Even the rats, veterans of many a cold night's survival in Manhattan, could turn nasty quickly. All she could think of now was the memory of a paranoid woman spending days in her office several years before recalling her experience as a child waking up to the gnawing of her sock as a rat in her tenement vied for a stolen meal.

The feeding rats stopped abruptly, casually moved to the front of the guarding rats, and sniffed the paws of the dog that didn't move. It all became surreal. Was this some kind of normal routine... the sleeping man, the patient dog, the grateful rats? The rats didn't scurry away. They sauntered away. Samara realized at that moment that she was the anomaly. She was the foreigner. They were comfortable. This was her neighborhood, but they were the ones occupying its boundaries without fear. Occupying it with the only word that came to mind—understanding.

She walked up to the dog maintaining watch. He lowered his ears for a stroke of her hand. She paused. The sound of the man's snoring brought an unexpected realization. She was weeping. She missed that snoring sound... the sound of the man she loved, the man she too would stand guard over, if only there was another chance. As she continued down the sidewalk, she placed her hand over her chest. It wasn't often she felt the beat of her heart. She allowed a subtle smile and wiped her cheek.

***

Aretha looked over her shoulder and down at the shoreline as the Piper Cherokee banked and flew north toward the coast of Maine. She adjusted the headset and microphone, then... "Stanton, how far is Portland from the islands?"

Stanton leveled and checked his horizon. "Lower group of islands, maybe ten minutes."

"Mon... what's it called?"

"Grey Cliff."

"Ever been there?"

"Nope."

Aretha reached into her purse and pulled out an envelope. As she opened it and removed the letter, "I believe Samara said it was a two hour ferry ride."

"Could be. Probably sixty, seventy nautical miles," said Stanton.

Aretha reread the last paragraph of the letter. *"I'm not sure whether now was the time to go. I know, he sent me an invitation and the long description of his dream...but I just don't know. Maybe we should wait. Give him time.*

Call me.

Samara.

Aretha folded the letter and placed it back in the envelope. Peering out the window at the early morning sun's reflection on the water, she heaved a sigh and folded her hands in her lap. "You ever think about getting married again, Stanton?"

"What? You losin' your senses Aretha?"

"You once told me you missed having that part of your life taken away."

"That was only a thought of when it was good. After thirty years, there wasn't much good left."

"That's sad."

"C'mon. You had three of them. Never had to put up with the long haul, right?" quipped Stanton.

"Oh, they more than made up for the chronological deficit. Intensity makes up for a lot of years."

"How long?"

"What?"

"How long was the longest?"

"Ten. Then there was the three and the seven."

"Intensity, huh?"

"Oh, yes."

"Well," banking to the left, "it's good to have all that behind us isn't it? Kennebunkport down there."

"Been thinking a lot about that lately, Stanton." Peering down at the coastline, Aretha paused. "Now that was intensity, or something else. Berthed a 48 ft. schooner in that harbor. Harry, dear Harry. No, Stanton, leaving it behind isn't good. Miss him sometimes."

The remaining minutes of flight into the beginning of the many islands and inlets off the coast of Maine found more memories shared between the two. There were the constant periods of separation between Stanton and his wife as he carried out his career as an airline pilot. The many parts of the world discovered and never shared in his life left a longing Aretha could sense; a longing to see his wife with him there in his memories. But for Stanton, most of life was what he experienced from a cockpit. He remained fascinated with Aretha's passion for life, relationships gambled and sometimes lost, and especially her unwillingness to let memories dominate her senior years.

"Okay. Okay," he laughingly said after hearing her tale of being chased by a bear while berry picking in the White Mountains with husband number two. "I can do without that much passion, okay?"

"Stanton, sounds like you need a little jump start, eh? When's the last time you went out?"

"A date?"

"Think they still call it that."

"Oh, boy. Few years."

"Jeeessssuuusss, man! You have that nice house next to mine, this plane, God knows what other attributes you might have, and you haven't been...I mean been on a date for years? Well, consider it done."

"Now don't you go and play match maker with me, Aretha."

"Who said anything about matchin' and makin'? We got the rest of the day and night, don't we?"

"You?"

"Yeah. I'm askin' you out. We'll cruise these islands, have ourselves some food, and go from there."

"Gotta have the bird back by nightfall, Aretha. Flight plan..."

"Flight plans can be changed. I know about those things too." She reached over and slapped his thigh. "So, let's get some searchin' done, okay?"

That's how the day proceeded from seven AM to eight AM. Stanton took the plane in low over the islands, while Aretha with binoculars and camera, had him circle Grey Cliff several times. From up that high, she found it difficult to understand what such a remote island would do for Derek...this urban Don Quixote, this man who wanted to influence the world with his art. *From here? Why?*

Once they landed in Portland, and had some breakfast at a seaside café, they boarded the ferry for the 90-minute ride to the island.

"So, Great White Hunter, what are you going to do when you get there?" asked Stanton.

"Been wondering that myself. Maybe a little undercover work, I don't know."

"This Samara lady, sounds like a..."

"Yes?"

"I don't know. Like a good woman."

"Yes. I'm sure she is," said Aretha.

"Ah, huh."

"What?"

"Well, oh, never mind."

"C'mon. Don't get off that easy," challenged Aretha.

"You two sound like friends and all, but..."

"Hell no."

"You're not?"

"Two stubborn women with separate agendas for the same man. That does not make for a friendship. That's something else."

"What?"

Aretha looked out the window at the breaking waters. "Don't know yet." She turned toward Stanton and gripped his arm. "But it's got passion, my friend. Lots of passion."

Stanton patted her hand on his arm. She slapped his, and placed it in hers. "We're on a date, remember?"

Stanton smiled tentatively, and then broke into the kind of smile that cracks lips. "Okay."

The sun was high when the ferry started its final approach to the dock. Seagulls repeated their daily exercise of flocking behind the boat, swooping in for the scraps being thrown by passengers and the occasional illegal dump of garbage from the ferry. As the boat neared the mooring, Aretha's first impression was that of a green tarnished statue atop the nearby hill. She whipped out her binoculars and on closer inspection, "Nice work. Not just a city hall memento. Here." She handed the glasses to Stanton. "You know real art when you see it, don't you?"

As he peered, "If your collection is any measure…yeah. That looks like it should be in a museum. I agree."

He handed them back to her. She pondered the statue a few more moments as the ferry came to a stop. "Maybe I was wrong."

They rose to disembark. "About?" he asked.

"Maybe there's more to this island than just crabs and lobsters."

From the docks, it was a short walk to the main street. October was not with the usual tourist trade, so most of the shops were closed. They sauntered up one side and down the other, asking merchants about the island's attractions. Most were sleepy-eyed and without much knowledge of anything, but the fifty or sixty square feet of their shop and living quarters overhead in most cases. When asked about artists, and a man named Derek Terrell, they all shrugged. "Lots of artists all over the island," was the usual reply. By the time they reached the Village Diner, both were famished. "Give it a try? My treat," said Stanton.

"I thought I asked you out."

"From what my granddaughter tells me, the times they are-a-changin'. I'll buy lunch and you can grab dinner, okay?"

Aretha smiled. "Fun being on a date, now isn't it, Stanton?"

They entered like a couple on a second honeymoon, least that's how the island "gossip-central" saw it. They sat down in a booth, immediately attended to by, "Imelda's my name. I'll be your waitress today." She slapped down two heavy plastic coated menus. "How you two doin'?"

"Fine," said Stanton. "Doin' fine. What's your special today?"

"Same as every day."

"Okay. What's that?"

She flipped open the menu and pointed with her pencil. "On the right. Crab cakes, with crab soup, side of slaw or spud salad. Drink extra."

Aretha leaned back and eyed Imelda. "What do you recommend darlin'?"

"Not the special." She leaned over the menu again, and flipped to the next page. "If you've never had our tuna salad sandwich, you haven't lived."

Stanton gave a quizzical look. "Tuna, huh? Well...guess if you recommend it..." He gestured to Aretha, who was still leaned back, a pleasant smile enveloping her face. "How's that prepared?"

Imelda, grinned, and then broke out with a laugh, "You kiddin' right?"

"Go on, tell me," urged Aretha with another burst of laughter.

"Shit, lady, I usually charge extra for an explanation."

Now all three broke into laughter.

Lenny, the short order cook peeked over the top of the warming counter. "What's up, Imelda?"

"How you preppin' that tuna sandwich on white or rye with tomatoes, lettuce and chips today, Lenny?"

"Huh?"

More laughter.

Aretha patted Imelda's hand. "Just bring me whatever you think is good, darlin'."

The lunch wasn't a complete bust in gastronomic eloquence. The tuna was fresh, even though the bread was without taste; and Aretha's BLT was perfect, grease and all. They said their goodbyes, and as they left—with just plain dumb luck—Imelda shouted after them, "If you're interested in art, try and get one of the fishermen to take you out to the Rock Man."

Aretha paused. "Rock Man? What's that?"

"We got ourselves a resident nut case whose carvin' rock up two hundred or so feet above the breakers. Guys on the dock know where it's at. Worth the trip. He's got some kind of face goin' on up there. Gonna be our big attraction next summer if he don't kill himself first."

"His name isn't Derek, is it?"

"You got it. Rock Man Derek. How come you know that?"

Aretha turned and escorted Stanton out the door. "Thanks, Imelda. Word travels fast."

After gingerly walking off the lunch with Stanton along the shoreline, Aretha had to accept that the net-maker was the only local left to do business with.

"Hi," Aretha cheerfully acknowledged the wrinkled man repairing the coils of hemp in his lap.

"Yep?" he replied without looking up.

"You wouldn't happen to know of a boat for hire, would you?"

He looked up, eyed Aretha and Stanton, then returned to his fingering pattern. "All out fishin'. Mine's slow, but all that's around."

Stanton stepped up to him, "How much for the afternoon?"

The old man looked up once again. "Where you fixin' to go?"

"The Rock?"

"The Rock," the old man repeated. "My boat? Out to the Rock Man's waters? Gotta be kiddin' me. You got to be nuts like him to go out there."

Aretha now stepped forward. "We need to see the Rock. Would $200 make you nuts enough?"

"Nope."

"Three?"

"Nope."

"Five ought to cover all three of our nuttiness, yes?"

"Yep."

He dropped his nets, stood up and stuck out his hand. "Five."

Aretha opened her wallet and gave him five one hundred dollar bills.

"Weylin Felder at your service." He folded them with the same careful precision he used in his rope repair, and then shuffled over to the tie line of his relic crab catcher sloop. "Let's be movin' you two. That high tide isn't gonna wait for our sightseein'. Got some dram?"

"Pardon, Weylin," Stanton replied.

"You get sea sick?"

"Oh... yeah." Stanton reached in his pocket and pulled out a small packet of pills, handing one to Aretha and taking one for himself.

"This the end of the fun?" Aretha said with a smile.

As the boat completed its roller coaster journey to the Rock, Aretha's sense of "an outing" with Stanton waned. The Dramamine had worked well, and he was no less pleasant to be with, but her sense of purpose was moving back to the primary reason for the trip—the partial image of a woman's eye and what appeared to be irregular folds of a scarf as if blowing away from her neck. She tried to steady herself and adjust the binoculars. "Stanton?"

"I see it," he responded.

"I'm..."

Stanton moved to her side. "You're surprised?"

"An understatement of profound proportions, Stanton. Thought the waitress was exaggerating, but that's got to be a couple of hundred feet up."

"At least."

Aretha turned to her helmsman, now busily navigating the offshore winds raising havoc with the water. "It's an island, isn't it, Weylin?"

"Not attached to anything but these damn waters. Seen enough, lady?"

"How does he get up there?" she said as she shot off several pictures with her pocket camera.

"Word is he's some kind of climber. Look lady, these waves aren't going to get any better."

"Just a little closer," yelled Aretha above the toiling engine.

The old man shook his head, and eased the boat in another fifty yards. "That's it. Get your pictures, whatever, I'm turnin' 'round."

The boat bucked and heaved with each round of surf letting it be known a bigger and heavier boat was needed for anything closer in. Aretha pointed her glasses once again at the carving in the spire of rock. Even from this distance, she could feel his presence. "Is he up there now?"

The old man nodded. "Probably. He's got a boat picks him up everyday at sundown."

Aretha looked at her watch.

"No way, lady. Time to leave." And with his last comment, he turned the boat away from the rock and headed back to the harbor.

"Impressed?" asked Stanton.

Aretha looked back over her shoulder, lifting the glasses one last time. "No. Worried."

"Over?" he shouted.

Aretha motioned for his pillbox. "Got another one of those?"

From atop the scarf, Derek looked down on the small boat now navigating slapping waves as it headed back to the shore. He wondered how many in the years to come would actually challenge the waters once the work was finished. He hoisted the jackhammer over his shoulder, snapped into his safety harness, and began climbing with his ascender hardware back up to the scarf's edge.

***

As the boat entered the harbor, other fishing vessels moved slowly into the area, their nets hung off the sides, their bows heavy with the catch. Most waved at the old man as they passed, some giving thumbs up on the catch of the day, others shaking their heads. As he eased his craft into his mooring, Aretha snapped out of her reverie. Stanton helped her step ashore and after thanking the old man and tipping him generously, Aretha and Stanton walked the short distance to the main street again.

"You think it wrong for me to try and contact him?" asked Aretha.

"You asking me?"

"Oh, come on. I'm not invited into this project. I'm just an old patron of the arts wanting to say hi. You're a guy. Would you want to be bothered?"

"If I went to this much trouble to get away...probably not. But I don't know him, you do."

Aretha smiled. "I only know the part nobody else knows." She looked at her watch, then at the sun dropping rapidly. "We going to make it?"

"Sure." Stanton took her arm and they quickly made their way to the Ferry Station. "What part is that part nobody else knows?"

Aretha smiled. "Maybe the part of you that comes out when you're flying."

Chapter 30

On the morning of October 23rd, Derek and Theo stood silently before the cannery sipping their coffee. Derek walked to his right a few steps, looked down the outside wall, then strode back next to Theo, who started nodding. After a few moments, Derek ventured a guess. "Too clean?"

"Nah. Too green."

"It's a kind of tie-die effect, don't you think?"

"Too green."

"Not painting this monster again," Derek said.

"It might be a turn off."

Derek took another look. "Just the early sun. Nobody is going to see it this early in the morning. Mid day, it'll take on the shade from those trees... break it up... be a better green."

"I tried to tell you," Theo said.

"At two bucks a gallon, green is good."

"You've got the money. Why didn't you paint it..."

"It's done, Theo. Green. Two bucks. Done."

"Dare I go inside?" asked Theo.

Derek made a grand gesture and opened the door.

Theo stepped inside the gutted tribute to a bygone era and stopped. "My God, it's still rusty."

"Yeah. Looks better that way, don't you think?"

"Rust, Derek. That's not good."

"I sealed it so it wouldn't get worse."

"Sealed rust. Now that's a new decoration idea. Maybe we can market it."

Derek walked over to the wall and opened a high-tech junction box. "Here's the money." He took a remote control and started pressing the buttons. The thirty-foot ceiling came alive with high intensity quartz lamps moving up and down the lattice network of tracks, creating an almost disco-like atmosphere.

Theo stood back. "Jesus, what is that?"

"Enough lighting, outdoor at 5500 Kelvin or one can have indoor 3400, or down to candlelight 1500 Kelvin with a press of the button. Enough for fifteen thirty-by-thirty foot spaces. He pressed a different bank of the remote and a series of floor to ceiling baffled walls started folding out from the far end on the larger tracks. "Sound proof working spaces. Like it?"

Theo smiled. "Now I know why you hired those guys to keep watch over this...so I wouldn't see it till now, right?"

"Right. Wanted to...well, you know, surprise you. Theo, we have working environments that are insulated from the outside world, if that's what they want...indoor or outdoor."

Theo pondered a moment, then "'...insulated from the outside world.' Interesting choice of words."

"Imagination doesn't want to be distracted, don't you agree?" Derek said a bit hesitantly.

Theo slowly walked the length of the four hundred and fifty foot floor space as Derek accompanied him, moving the walls with his remote like a kid at Christmas. "From giant installations to composing rooms, to paint and sculpture, to writing... it can all be here if they choose, or out there if they like."

Now a hundred feet ahead of him, Theo stopped at the far end and turned. "Are you really prepared for this?"

"I've spent a lot of time getting this ready and thinking..."

"No," interrupted Theo. "Are you ready for the *rejection*?"

"The artists? I know it's not for everyone. That's why we sent out twenty-four invitations. Some threw them in the wastebasket. Some didn't. Some will be here tomorrow. Some won't."

"And some will be on the next ferry out of here, give or take twenty minutes into your spiel," warned Theo.

Derek stopped the remote walls and the two of them walked silently back to the junction box. He paused, then without turning away from the wall, said "I feel like a child. I've spent my money like a child. Tomorrow, I hope enough children of heart arrive to join me in this adventure that only the innocent of heart can understand." He turned and faced Theo. "Do you understand?"

Theo placed his hand on Derek's shoulder. "I'm here, am I not? A group of dedicated individualists who just happen to be artists living and working in a rust sealed cavernous building on an island removed from all who would have it otherwise." He smiled. "I know. I too know what it's like to return to a childlike innocence where the entire world is a wonder and only a few of us know what to do with it. I know. I know. So, tomorrow you will find out if there are more of this... truth and wonderment. You will also find out other things. Are you ready for the *rejection*, Derek?"

Theo stepped away. "I'll leave you to work through that thought. Remember...this reality you long for might only be an illusion...including Echo. What then?"

As the rusty door creaked shut and the space became hollow with silence, Derek turned and gazed at his prelude, the yawning space that was to be a beginning. The wise old man, the homeless sage, had once again warned Derek of himself—a warning he had experienced many times with Samara. It was a warning he somehow felt comfortable with, even as the longing for her pulled at his loins, and memories flooded his senses. It was the kind of moment he'd not had for months.

He would be at the ferry's arrival tomorrow afternoon—a child hoping to be strong.

***

The rising sun fluttered across my face; sheer curtains of the open portal released their frosted layers from the night before. Fog had engulfed the lighthouse as I went to sleep, the patch quilt comforting me through another damp and cool night. October had always been an unpredictable month, warm one day, cold the next. As I rose and rubbed life back into my tired eyes, I hoped today would be comfortable. I wanted the best of everything to be present today. Sunshine, cool breezes, and most of all, calm seas. Ferry trips could be rough. Today was not a day for seasick arrivals.

I quickly left the lighthouse and met Jamie for an early morning trip to The Rock. Yes, Jamie was back on as Captain of The Rock Boat, a new name he had recently painted on the hull. As we made our way across the bay and into the open sea, I was reminded of a week earlier when he made himself sober and came to the lighthouse, asking to be heard. As a peace offering, he had brought me a coil of new rope he had used his last month's pay to secure from Weylin's Hardware.

We talked a while, and I realized the very *essence* of my dream for the island through this unassuming man named Jamie. His animated fishing tales were Performance Art. He wanted me to feel secure with him at the helm, so it was this storm, and that wind, and this rescue, and that catch that almost capsized the boat—a stream of imagination surrounding a simple man's memory—a painting of his experience. As he worked my small dining room like a massive stage, he discovered he could move me with his storytelling, and I could reach him with my attention and understanding, not to mention

177

the forgiveness he longed for, and which I never withheld. It was a duality of revelation for an artist accustomed to a Soho version of creativity, and a simple boatsman who never had a listener such as me. I smiled at one point and said, "You remind me once again that we are all creative." He waited a long while, then said innocently, "Really?"

As we approached the rock, I peered up to notice the scarf and eye in deep shadow, a single dark cloud hovering above without movement.

"One cloud, Jamie. Got a tale to fit that?" I laughed.

"Telling you something, Mister Turrel. It's telling you something."

"Storm?" I offered.

"Not likely."

"Winds?"

"Not today."

"What then?" I asked.

He shrugged. "Freaky, but it's not about weather. Look around you. Clear skies everywhere else."

I pondered a moment, but realized he had nothing more to say. He went about maneuvering the boat in his usual fastidious way while I prepared the inflatable for the final twenty-five yards through what Jamie had named the "mine fields," for the half submerged outcroppings that could sink anything but a reinforced dinghy.

"Now, don't forget the early pick up today. 3 p.m. Okay?" I shouted as I pulled away. He nodded with usual assurance, while I crossed my fingers and prayed. Today would not be a good day for him to fall off the wagon.

The cloud wasn't moving. I leisurely climbed the route I'd now made semi-permanent with fixed anchors of expansion bolts, thinking by the time I reached the top, even a stubborn cloud would find it pretty boring to stay in one spot. Pulling myself over the final ledge that would soon become the right cheekbone, I sat down, drank some water and waited. I was in the shadow of more than a cool cloud. It was dark. The temperature gauge on my watch read thirty-five degrees. Even for Maine, this was cold for an October day. I slipped on a yellow windbreaker, double-checked the gas supply on the generator, neatly coiled the cable to the jackhammer, and waited. Still no movement of the cloud's shadow.

After another ten minutes, I stood up and jokingly yelled skyward, "Hey, got work to do. What's the deal cloud?" I started to traverse the scarf to where I wanted to work. Three steps into the approach, a two hundred foot drop below me, and with my back to the cloud, and my face buried in granite, the cold was replaced with that heat flash called fear, the kind I hadn't experienced since I was ten and had snuck into an R rated movie called *Alien.*

"Like your jacket," said the voice I couldn't believe I was hearing.

Was it? No. Not today. Not here again. I eased my way back the three steps onto the ledge and slowly turned. I don't know what I expected to see with that turn toward the cloud, or the sea two-hundred feet below, but out of the corner of my eye, there she was, sitting on the bridge of the nose, a rainbow of scarves blowing in the wind—her wind, as it was dead calm where I was standing.

She repeated, "The jacket. I like it. Good color for you. Probably look even better without that cloud shadow."

As I leaned back to glance up to the top of the crown, the top of the head-to-be, looking for a rope, I realized very quickly how stupid that thought was as the cloud decided to move. At least that is what I chose to believe. There was a split second thought *Oh shit! Had I slipped and fallen and this was the weigh station stop before the big guy, or was I having a serious bout of what Samara and I had discussed—schizophrenia?* Before I could finish the thought—

"Are you pleased?"

My fear stood still as she broke the silence and I tightened my grip on the small outcrop I found my hand clinging to. "Pleased. Yes. About?"

She shrugged. "Is there nothing you're pleased about?"

I was aware that the rock I was gripping was real. It was cold. My feet were solidly planted on rock. I was alive. I heaved a quiet sigh. "I'm pleased with lots of things. Why do you ask?"

"The temperature?"

"Temperature?"

She gestured to the sky.

I looked up. The cloud took less than a few seconds to disappear, allowing warmth once more to return. I smiled. Okay. Not out of the question, I thought. "That too... I'm pleased."

"I knew you were anxious about today. Thought it would be a good time to visit," she said.

I was beginning to feel very uncomfortable—the kind of discomfort that comes with a climber's first venture onto a high wall—the kind of bewilderment that comes with knowing you are experiencing something reserved for very few people.

"That's okay," she said.

"What?"

"It is reserved for 'very few people'."

I couldn't move at that moment. I just stared into space.

"Look, Derek, we think and talk alike. Accept it. It's okay."

"Who are you…eally?" I finally blurted out.

"I'm who you believe I am. Isn't that what it's all about? What you believe is."

"Hindu," I said. "It seems to be going around."

"Oh, like a dis-ease?"

"Haven't thought of it like that."

"Cosmic," she whispered back to me…a whisper that I shouldn't have been able to hear from where she sat…a whisper that was…

"Loud enough for you to hear?" she said.

I tried calmly to reach for my water bottle, but fumbled it off my belt. I picked it up.

"Water?" I gestured toward her.

"I'm fine," she said, and stood up, standing on the razor edge of the scarf, her own multicolored fabric reaching out like ribbons of a Wyeth May Pole dancing with the breath of the sea.

I took several swallows and moved closer to what was obviously an illusion. I was hallucinating—something—

"No…it's as real as you need it to be. Sit down and let's just talk. Don't worry about the how, why or what it all means or how I know what you're thinking. Can you do that? Forget trying to figure me out, how I got here, why I pop up when it's necessary, and especially why I think and speak as you think and speak. Okay?"

I nodded, shook, nodded, cleared my head, and said, "Look, I…If I could touch you, you know, if I knew you weren't real, it would be easier, okay?"

"Harder, Derek. It would be harder. I got your written message. Does that make it easier?"

"Really?" I said. Unexpectedly, it was easier. I'd mailed that to Montauk. Not that many people there. Possible an envelope addressed to "Echo" might find its proper receiver?

"Yes," she said. "I'm able to receive your messages…anytime. That does make it easier for your reality, so…I'm here. Gather your thoughts and tell me…why the letter?"

I felt a bit strange trying to gather my thoughts when it seemed whatever was on my mind, she was aware of anyway. But, as I ruminated over this two-way mirrored phenomenon, she smiled as if to say, *I won't say a word.*

"I'm scared," I mumbled.

"Of course you're scared. Trying to influence the world's thinking, the world's soul…well, I'd be scared too."

"In less than six hours, I'm going to be greeting…least hope I'll be greeting…"

"You will," she said. "I'm sorry. Go on."

"There will be artists I've never met. Artists whose work I think I know well enough to know they are special and capable of empowering creativity in others. Well, Samara might think…"

"For right now, forget Samara. You have her blessing and as you well know, her insistence that you *do it*. Continue."

"Echo…I'm obsessed with this. Do you understand that?"

She laughed. "I'm sorry."

"Of course you understand it. So…"

"So?"

"So," I continued, "is it crazy to think such grandiose thoughts? To have such unrealistic dreams?"

She paused, her face taking on a much more serious expression. She stepped down the ninety-degree rock as if her shoes were glue. Glancing down, I noticed they were ancient climbing shoes. She sat down cross-legged, only a few feet from me. It was the closest I'd ever seen her. At the hospital, it had been so brief. At the bridge, so far away. And on the barge, just the scarves. The lighthouse had been so surreal with the glaring light of the Fresnel—even her last visit to the cave had been upstaged by the flames of a fire.

"And now you see better, yes?" she said. "That's good. You're ready for a better image of *us*."

Her last word hung in the air. *Us. What does she mean, a better image of us?*

"We're all one, Derek. You've always known that. You're just…*remembering it.* Your friend Aretha knows it as well. Were you aware of that?"

"I…"

She interrupted. "I'm sorry. We can talk about that later. You were saying you thought you were possessed with grandiose thoughts and unrealistic dreams."

My mind felt like it was on fire. I didn't know where to go. I had so many questions and I felt that she already knew the questions and the answers and—

"Derek. Your thoughts and dreams are necessary to express. It is who you are. It doesn't matter whether you are accepted or rejected by others. It is *who you are*. And…you believe there are others like yourself and that is why you've sent out this test…this invitation to come and hear about…" She paused. "Have you a name for it?"

"What, the project?"

"Yes."

"No."

"Derek, what happens when you loudly express yourself in a walled canyon?"

"I don't understand," I answered.

"Vibrations that reflect off surfaces, surfaces that are enclosed rather than open, or call it vibrations that bounce back to you, rather than be absorbed and muffled. They become what?"

I smiled. "You?"

She returned the smile. "Us."

"Echoes."

"Echoes," she repeated. Put a world of echoes together and you have its essence: Echosis.

It was five hours later when I rappelled down the wall and stood on the rock, gazing back up for a last glimpse of her. Only the floating colors of her scarves, drifting over the edge two hundred feet above, confirmed she was actually there. As Jamie guided the boat back to the bay, I realized another level of my obsession had been revealed to me as if by a living sculpture, or painting, or symphony, or soliloquy—moving and breathing an expanded energy into me. It was all so real and unreal at the same time.

As we pulled into the slip, my watch said 3:25. I was five minutes away from another reality, one I wasn't sure I could handle. Then, as I stepped up onto the boardwalk and viewed the arrival of the ferry just a few hundred yards away, my eye caught another arrival—a double arrow of gulls drifting lazily toward the Rock.

Chapter 31

My eyes stayed focused on the weathered planks of the ferry platform, watching the shoes of the disembarking. I expected a bizarre collection of visitors, each with his or her statement of independent thinking. Remembering my own image statements or lack thereof, I expected to spot telltale shoes. There were, after all, practical and political purposes for shoes. Early on in NY, when my long subway rides from Washington Heights to a shared art studio on Houston St. would take forty-five minutes, I had made up a game to bide my time. "Guess The Occupation." Based solely on the shoes, usually extended from crossed legs into the aisle, I would stay focused on the shoes, never looking up at the face or balance of the dress code. Oh, occasionally, I couldn't help but slip into a cheat, a look up to the knees, but most often, I kept my eyes on the floor until they sat down, and the shoe would come into the top of my frame of vision—like now.

As I usually did in NY with the Times, I was sitting on a bench, the local paper in both hands covering my field of view except for the mingling shoes that dragged, pranced, danced and shuffled between what I could see above my knees and below the paper. From there, I made mental notes of those that might qualify as my guests. There were the obligatory tennis shoes on many a passenger, and a few dirty shoelaces—always a clue, a check mark.

Then there were the Armani cuffs lazily shifting from side to side atop the Johnson and Murphy Wing Tips—Berkowitz? Had to be. Another check mark. An assortment of spanking new, as well as worn out weekend walking shoes and sandals followed, each getting a consideration in my attempt to ward off the fear of failure, and the welcome of joy for guessing correctly. Artists. Old shoes. Yes?

I counted only forty-three passengers stepping onto the walkway, causing a gripping ache in my stomach. Law of averages suggested that less than a third could possibly be my invitees. That would mean less than half the twenty-four invitations had come. I didn't want to drop the paper, even after five minutes of sitting there. In times passed, these were the kind of odds I dreaded on a day of falling Dow Jones Averages, the kind of numbers that could panic me into the sudden selling of perfectly good long-term stock. I knew the debating in my head might only make worse the reality.

Just as I was about to walk away from the big board, I heard the heels, the high heels of a lingering passenger walking from the ferry's metal landing platform to the wooden planks of the dock. Her path crossed my letterbox view and I froze. What I dreaded and hoped for—what I knew might be good for me and could also destroy me—what my time with Echo had made me realize could feed or douse the fire deep in my gut—was walking past me in her favorite, no, my favorite, light gray kid skin Italian imports. No mistake. Loosely bouncing around the left ankle was the miniature 24k chain I'd purchased in the village one night for her, the links having been hand forged into interlocking S's.

***

"Fuck" mumbled Theo to himself as he pressed the remote over and over again. Trying to get one of the walls moved to a more revealing position had become a problem. He motioned across the cannery floor to Samson and Jamie.

"Hey, guys, see if you can push that wall along the tracks another ten feet."

Samson looked at the thirty-foot wall and shouted back, "Hey, Theo, don't take my name literally, okay?"

Jamie shook his head and walked across to Theo, grumbling, "Jesus, Theo, fix the damn remote. I ain't gettin' myself no rupture for this thing. Here." He reached out and took the remote from Theo, popped the back, pulled out the batteries and walked off toward the other end of the building, complaining to himself. "The batteries, dummy. Gotta be the batteries."

Theo glanced apologetically at Samson. "Let him do his thing. My God, I'm a writer for Christ's sake, what do I know about technical crap?"

Samson smiled as he took in the cavernous sanctuary. "Boy, this place sure is somethin' else. Clever, you converting those tracks that used to move the barrels of fish around overhead. Hangin' walls. Who would have thought? When I was a kid, I used to work in that corner down there choppin' fish heads. Fifty cents an hour. Big money in those days. And stink? Man, you could smell this place all the way back to town on a no-wind day." He looked around again. "But, it kept this little town alive for a long time." He shook his head.

Theo nervously scrubbed the concrete with the sole of his shoe, trying to remove a splotch of green paint that had been carelessly dropped. "Well, let's hope this crazy idea keeps it alive for another fifty years."

"Old cannery was here seventy-six years."

"Yeah, well I'd settle for..."

Jamie burst from the other end, yelling like a kid who'd just found a giveaway in a cereal box, "Got it! Damn I'm good. Guessed that one right away!" He pressed the remote as he walked and the big wall moved the remaining ten feet.

"Stop, Jamie! Jesus, you'll fly it off the rails," said Theo.

"Moves faster with new batteries," beamed Jamie.

"Yeah," said Theo sarcastically. "Gimme." As he took the remote and shoved it in his pocket, he continued working on the paint splotch. He glanced at his watch. *Three twenty.* "They'll be walking through the door any minute."

Jamie walked over and sat down on one of the fold up chairs that had been placed in a semi-circle facing the stacked crab traps that made up the podium. He stared and said, "Just like a counsel meeting, only in a big motherin' cave."

Samson stepped over to Theo, and politely moved him aside, popping the top of his flask and pouring a bit of the liquid on the spot. As Samson rubbed with his own shoe—

"Whiskey isn't going to..." Theo leaned down and took a closer look. "Well, I'll be..."

"Damned," said Samson with a smile as he knelt and wiped it clean with his grease rag.

Theo shook his head, smiling. "They don't serve that stuff down at the tavern, do they?"

Samson put the flask back in his pocket, chuckling. "Only to strangers." He winked. "Nah. My own bathtub distillery. Aged."

The front door flew open and in popped one of the local children. "They're comin'. Whole bunch comin' around the corner." He slammed the door and left the three of them in silence. Theo jumped to attention. "Whole bunch?" He whipped out the fancy remote, and taking a piece of paper from his pocket, quickly programmed the lighting. "Whole bunch. All twenty four?" he mumbled to himself as he fumbled to create the setting that Derek had rehearsed with him. "Okay, you guys did great," he said to Samson and Jamie. "Thanks. Slip out the back. Can't look like a last minute panic, you know?"

"Sure you don't need anything more?" said Samson.

"Perfect. Thanks. Thanks so much, both of you. Now shoo!"

Within seconds of turning the lights on, Theo saw the room transformed into shadow and light, surface and angle, history and history to be. *Green isn't all that bad with enough white.*

The air hung heavy with apprehension as the front door was opened slowly, and a hesitant voice said, "This Derek Turrel's project?"

Theo filled his lungs. "Yes. This is The Project."

The late afternoon sunlight spilled in as the door was opened fully, and one by one, the daring, the brave, the curious stepped in and stood in various challenging and defensive stances. Like a surreal leap into somewhere never before reserved for the imagination, their long shadows fashioned across the end of the hall and started to move cautiously forward, crawling up the walls like an invasion. Theo held his breath. *Friend or foe?*

He stepped up and greeted them, recognizing most with memory acuity once mandatory for journalism, but long retired from today's raft of "sound bite" hurry/scurry reporting.

With each recognition, his greeting became more animated. By the time he'd introduced himself to all *eight*, he was both pleased and a bit disappointed. Most of the best—in his opinion—had come, but as he reviewed in his mind those that hadn't, the door opened one more time, and in stepped Samara. She didn't see him, even as he nevertheless was overcome with an onslaught of emotions. Time and recollection of the bus ride meeting with Samara rushed across his mindscape and he was left choked up. As she sat, Theo wondered how her presence would affect Derek. But she was here now, and... *Damn, it is good to see you.*

Still working through the shock of seeing Samara arrive at the docks, Derek glanced from his notes to the road, and back to the notes, as he approached the cannery. He carried a sense of fear and confusion. Had he gone too far with his treatise? Had Theo edited or over-written again? A sudden panic attack brought his stride to a stop. He stood in the middle of the road and took several deep breaths. Finding himself mentally paralyzed, he instinctively turned around. He didn't know what he was looking for, but out of the corner of his eye he caught the double-wedge shaped formation of gulls high above him. A sudden sensation of colored scarves flashed across his mind. With the mission statement clenched in his hand, he opened the door and stepped into the space and time he was sure would be long remembered.

His first eye contact was with Samara, sitting dead center in the circle of chairs. He didn't know why, but all he could think at that moment was *the therapist is back, the composer of great music is sitting in front of me. Why am I avoiding any other thoughts of her?*

The other eight took their time looking him up and down. Derek had been able to pluck them out of their routine, convince them to come to his "imagined" world for a day, and now, they saw he had the courage to arrive visibly humbled.

It was Joe Hensky that first sat up, adjusted his once agile dancer's body, and curled his feet behind the legs of the fold up chair. Once, twice, three, four and five times he began the rhythmic stretching of the Achilles. For him, his legs were like worn pistons of ageless imagination. For Joe Hensky, mind over matter was not a choice. Age made it mandatory.

Touleur sat hunched in his chair. Attired in his customary creative mode of threadbare clothes, less the lapel microphone, he comforted himself with a stubby pencil and small notebook to record the contrasting reactions of people he had either met somewhere in the past, or was aware of from his world of teaching.

Nathan Wollzak, his intense actor's eyes darting about, seemed about to pounce on any and everything that might resemble material for his *observation* process.

Leonard Paxton, now almost in complete recovery after years of physical therapy, was using but a cane for balance, as he sat down next to Samara.

Sol Berkowitz wore his perpetual *producer* smile. Was it contempt or awe? thought Derek.

The serene traveling poet, Mariel, sat next to Simon Greco and quietly finished explaining her recent poem, *Reflections of what once was*. Greco chuckled to himself at what might evolve in the next few minutes to be yet another "Reflection of what once was."

It was Lanagra, however, that garnered several glances from Derek as he stepped to the makeshift podium. It was an expression that kept Touleur's pencil busy, as well, recording the observations of one of America's preeminent painters. Seated close to the podium, the painter's eyes maintained a fix on the background of remote walls, his arms stretched across the adjoining chairs, fingers moving with their own language, as if placing images and impressions upon the various right angles to the floor, orchestrating his palette, projecting what could be.

Derek centered himself, stood motionless for a few moments, and then said, "Thank you for coming. I'm Derek Turrel. I'm not a speaker; I'm a sculptor. Words don't come easy for me like the hammer and rock. So, if you will, bear with me, as I try and put some thoughts out there for you to consider."

He took from his jacket a stack of sealed envelopes. "There are twenty-four here, but you are but nine. At some point, you will be either tempted to open your envelope, or not. It's kinda that simple. I'll not be boring you with a dissertation of *trite* reasons for joining me here. If, after filling your five senses with impressions of what this island might mean to you, there is still doubt, consider the contents of the envelope. As artists, words are not necessarily everyone's chosen or first language. We fortunately know and understand that. Words can, however, when needed, fill in the void... no offense to Touleur, Mariel, Simon or..." gesturing to the sidewall where Theo stood respectfully anonymous... "my dear friend, Theo."

A welcomed round of nervous laughter from everyone eased Derek's tension.

"To begin with, should you decide to join us, I am now, and will always only be, just a fellow artist. What does that mean? Well, look around here for starters, and then consider what might be your greatest *by-product or calling*. To create more renowned pieces of art? No. You'll do that anyway. It will be to create the need, the desire and passion in others to express *their* creativity, *their* art.

"A world of honest expression may not please or excite everyone, but everyone can be pleased and feel a growth with the releasing of their own creativity. Remember, *we are all creative*. Some know that, some don't. Picture a world less voyeuristic and vicarious in its emotional, intellectual and spiritual experience. Picture, for a moment, a world where its people are more steeped in personal, creative expression—*doing*, rather than *watching, or listening*. Whether one is in Ethiopia or Paris, the tools for expression are everywhere, and the canvases both real and metaphoric know no boundary.

"I'm talking about a place where people will draw inspiration from museums, concert halls, radios, stages and screens, those venues where *your* treasures of expression, if you will, are represented. Regardless of their venue, works of art should be owned, maintained and appreciated by the public at large, not trophies for private collectors or egocentric corporations. I'm talking here about all the disciplines, from cave drawings to pop music, slam poetry to Kushner, subway entertainers to Christo installations, and concertos to the chiseled granite—expressions that are original, free from commercial formulas and without compromise. Picture all that, and you begin to see why we can't continue to remain satisfied. We can't allow creative concessions, and all that goes with it, to remain the standard. The creativity in every mind, heart, and soul of the world population risks being impoverished and imprisoned because somebody didn't act; something wasn't made to happen.

"Finally, I am asking you to embark upon a project that might fail. We're only, how many, eleven here today, counting Theo and me. That's hardly an army. Power mongers presently manage the world's creative arts, and they *do have* armies. Big ones.

"Power merchants want to maintain the status quo and continue their stifling of originality for the masses, because that's how they retain control. Avoid risk, and you preserve the obscenity of today's bottom line, made generously profitable through maintaining the status quo. Celebrate risk, and you insure the future of healthy, if not greedy, bottom lines. They prefer to label risk and originality, as elitist. Who invented the image? The media at large. They're all in this together. But, as Theo reminded me, they substitute the accepted demeaning word *elitist* for the champions of originality through risk...the *artists of no compromise*. Today, anyone can call themselves an artist, because the media says it's okay. Mention the word, 'original creation,' however, and something else happens. 'Artists of *originality* are elitists, crazies, unnecessary risks... trouble,' the power cries out. Keep artists and patrons anesthetized with compromise, and they'll never know of integrity.

"Trouble? I'm proposing we prove them right. I'm proposing we start a movement that will empower the world's bounty of *original* imagination. Just as there aren't any two people alike, so too is the uniqueness of creativity, and the right to nurture and express it.

"Our greatest obstacle is commercialism. Artists didn't invent it, the media did. By employing the point-of-least-resistance, they invaded art and freedom of expression with the cancerous growth called mediocrity. It's 2006, and we now have a malignancy called commercialism, the fast food diet of the uninspired. I don't buy into that. I say it again: *we are all creative.* To let the invisible malaise go unattended to is to risk the complete erosion and death of man's *spirit* and *passion*...humankind's essence."

Thus began the late afternoon that, now found the group deeply involved in their digestion process, each in his own way, each with separate questions that, as Derek suggested, should be of their own language. Pointing out his primary responsibility was to provide work and living space; he was respectful of their inner needs and private demands, both financial and emotional.

Only they could determine if pulling back to an island off the coast of Maine would allow for them, as it did for him, the opportunity to create art for art's sake—and to be part of a movement to empower others. Not in place yet, he emphasized the inclusion of a privately financed TV, radio, and Internet operation with satellite transmission as a major goal. He emphasized he wasn't suggesting the demise of communication and presentational venues as we now know them, but the creation of an alternative choice through the exponentially growing Web, "...to reach a global populous that for the most part is conditioned to get their motivation from only commercial radio and TV."

After a little less than an hour of presentation, he surmised by their facial expressions that they were in accord. *Were they sufficiently dissatisfied with the status quo, however, to join him?*

He suggested they take the afternoon to explore. "There's a Q & A in your folder to cover anything I may have left out. Feel free to wander through the various interior and exterior environments, the lighting set ups and flexibility... Theo can answer all your questions on the lighting choices, interior or exterior color temperature... and he's certainly capable of answering any other questions about the project as well. As I said, the walls in here are all hanging, and remote-controlled for size and placement. Visit the bungalow accommodations, as outlined in your letter. They're just outside, down the street to your right, follow the maps, and...well, get the feel of the island. We'll meet back here at five for any questions you might have. The ferry leaves at 6:30, your plane back to NY at 8."

For Derek, glad-handing, even hanging around to schmooze, was not an option. He excused himself, and after nervously asking Samara to join him at the Tavern, left.

Chapter 32

"I think you should have gone," scolded Linda as she continued weaving her latest basket project, a creation that looked more like a frog than a basket.

Aretha moved about her indoor plants with a spritzer bottle, gently spraying each leaf of each plant. "Linda, there are some things better left to their own timing, and besides, I wasn't invited."

"He doesn't own the island. You went before."

Aretha leaned over her favorite rhododendron. "Look at that. A bug dining on my Rhoda."

"Hit him with some of that Devil spray," said Linda

"One bug? Said Aretha, looking over the top of her glasses. "Bit of overkill isn't it?" Aretha stared at the tiny black creature gnawing on the tip of the leaf.

"So?" asked Linda.

"So?" repeated Aretha.

"There's more to it than not being invited, isn't there?"

"Did I ever show you the 'Powers of Ten' film?"

"Yes, but what's that got to do with going to Grey Cliff?" answered Linda. "Damn, I screwed up." She quickly unraveled several loops of the basket.

"How about the video, 'What the Bleep Do We Really Know?"

"Yes. It's been on cable."

Aretha reached into the leaf and let the bug crawl on her finger. She got up and walked to the door, opened it and stepped to the edge of the deck, flicking the bug over the edge onto the sand below. As she walked back into the house and continued with her spritzing, she said, "We are all so insignificant compared to the whole of things."

Linda gave another glance. "Okay, I'll give you that. All the more reason to have gone. Your presence probably wouldn't have meant anything, compared to the whole."

"Oh, with Samara there, I'd have been noticed."

"I don't get it. This Samara you speak of...you two rivals, like for the same man?"

"Not the way you're thinking, my dear."

The phone rang. Aretha jumped. She looked at the clock and answered. "Yes."

"Aretha, this is Samara."

"I...well, a pleasant surprise. How is it going?"

"I haven't much time. I'm in the Tavern here waiting for Derek. He asked me to meet him, and...I'm thinking, well, I'm not quite sure why I'm telling you, but I think I should leave."

"I don't understand," said Aretha.

"He's not the same. You'd notice too. He's distant. Not like I know him...knew him. His distancing, you know, when he works, from me, I mean, it's all over the place today, but...far away. He's in another zone, Aretha. I think he needs help."

Aretha knew she was hearing correctly, but was taken aback by the apparent confusion Samara was conveying. She carried the phone and continued spritzing. "Well, that's right where you come in. The help, I mean. That's what you do."

"Not with Derek. Not any more. He needs...oh, I've got to go. He just came in."

"Well, if..." The disconnect sound buzzed in Aretha's ears. She hung up, the strangeness of Samara's voice staying with her.

The antique clock chimed four times. Linda put her basket down. "Cocktail hour. I'll make. More rivalry? Sounded like it might have been Samara," said Linda as she walked to the bar.

Aretha looked at the Ode. "It was Dr. Jennings."

Linda looked up from her pouring of the Port. "Dr. Jennings? Do I know him?"

***

The Tavern was having its usual busy Friday night. Locals lined the bar, staring into the walled mirror behind the kaleidoscope of colored bottles. They weaved new stories of the day into the air that never exchanged with the outdoors, seeming to acquire its own musty, recycled life every few days. The few candle-lit tables catered to those preferring their libations and conversations eye to eye—*private* exchanges like that taking place between Derek and Samara occupying the furthest corner. It was a favorite table Derek had grown to love as it sidled up against the old Wurlitzer loaded with 45 rpm recordings of '50s classic jazz.

"I don't know. That's as simple as I can state it. I don't know," said Derek as he pondered the sounds of Miles playing 'Round Midnight.' His face now relaxed over a glass of wine, showed the fatigue of months of planning and today's pressure.

Samara was not comfortable. "Are you trying to tell me I shouldn't have come, after sending me an invitation? How does that equate?" she uttered through tears and clenched jaw. Dispensing with manners, she lifted her glass of wine and filled her mouth.

Derek leaned forward, his own misty eyes trying to formulate clarification from somewhere, anywhere.

"I'm trying to say I want you here for the right reason. Look, you *deserved* an invitation, Samara. You are one of twenty-four I would have here. One of twenty-four that I know is still connected to the honesty of their creative energies... "*that place we all long to experience, and that place few dare reside.*" You first uttered those words to me and asked I consider them and '*do it.*' Do it. Remember? But, I think you're here for *another* reason."

Samara wiped her tears, took out a pack of cigarettes. "You can be so arrogant when you want to be, Derek. God damn it! So what, if I'm the one that pushed you here? I'm the other person, too. The one that used to sleep with you." The tears welled up. "Oh, Christ. You came. You fucking conquered..."

"Not yet," said Derek in a quiet voice.

She tried to compose herself and took a cigarette from the pack. "But..."

"But?"

"Yes. Yes, I'm here for you. Why is that so hard to understand?" She leaned into the candle to lite up the cigarette.

Derek took her hand. "I understand, Samara. I just don't want you here only for *me*. I want you here for yourself."

She leaned back and took a deep drag.

"Listen a minute. Listen to Miles. You think he ever played for anyone else but himself? No. That's why he is, and will always be, a one-of-a-kind. And it's also why so many listen to him and feel alive with their own soul, their own spirit. You have that too. But it's got to be your *first* priority. You can't put me, us, ahead of that. There's a reason why your music brings tears to people's eyes. You have a gift, and what you do with it is what your existence is primarily about. You... me... us. We're important, but only to the degree we help nurture that single most important reason for living: our creative gifts. There could be rest time for us, but..."

"Who is she?" Samara asked quietly and without emotion.

Derek started to sigh, but thought better of it and took her hand again. "She? You think there is someone else?"

In a monotone voice, "Christ, Derek. I'm a woman. It's crossing my mind."

"Samara, for God sake, that's your lower-self talking. Do you really believe I've got another woman on my mind? Do you actually think I'd be here on this...place...if it were another relationship I wanted? Have you checked out the talent?"

"You've had your irrational motivations in the past," she said.

"Glad to see you've not lost your sense of humor, but what you're really asking me is do I still love you."

"And?" she said hesitantly.

"How could I not?" He raised his hand for the waitress.

Samara was momentarily confused. "So now you're going to run, right? That's what you've always done with conflicts and unanswered questions."

He paused a moment and reflected. "I don't always run. Remember our first meeting at the Evian machine?" He took out his money clip. "And, I think I just answered the biggest question for both of us, Samara."

"You answered it with other questions, God damn it."

"How could I not love you and still believe you're the most important human being in my world? If that's insufficient, well, I don't know... I don't know how better to say it. We're artists, Samara. There's something that transcends everyday love there. You brought me to this state. I am in love...with you...and everything around *us*...now. You taught me that. Don't you remember? Don't you understand?"

He stood up, peeling off a bill as the waitress placed the check on the table. "And, I'm hardly running. Back there is the biggest conflict of my life right now."

Samara sat a moment, lost in a whirlwind of emotions.

"The biggest. Will you join me? Us?"

Samara stared at the candle, but said nothing.

"May I walk you back?" said Derek, extending his hand.

***

"I've never thought about it before, but maybe," said Nathan. "Actors don't usually seek out isolation... I mean, not like you."

"What books have you been reading?" said Mariel with a twinge of sarcasm, her digital camera held firmly as she touched off a series of images in, around, and through the stacked lobster traps along the shore. "Just because I travel and write poetry, doesn't mean I'm out of touch. I'm forever looking for the subtle action, the movement that most people miss."

"Action? Movement? You write. You sit at a computer, a yellow pad, whatever, and you write. That's being alone with your thoughts, isn't it?"

"Here," she patted the lobster trap next to her. He sat down, as she pulled another trap closer and joined him. "You act. I write. But, we don't do either until we have reason to, correct?"

"Maybe. Don't have to look very far for reasons when rent and food stare you in the face."

"Ah, c'mon," she said. You obviously don't need much to satisfy that hundred-forty pound frame. She patted his chest. "How about your acting, though?"

"What?"

"You've got a reputation. Didn't get it from spending your days in a deli getting fat."

"Your point?" he said.

"Soul food. You feed off soul food. Then you package it inside a play, a monologue, a script, and you persuade people to pay attention. People come to see your performances for unique reasons. It's not special effects. It's not 'gotta see this actor who's such a scandal in the Inquirer', right? No. They pay attention to *you*,

Nathan Wollzak, because you're good for little else, but your art. They don't understand that, but you do. Get it?"

"No. I'm a plain wrapped actor delivering wherever and whenever I can."

"Sure. That's why Derek sent you an invitation, Mister Plainwrap. Pay attention. What are you delivering, Nathan?"

He rose. "C'mon. You working for Derek? Entertainment! Just old fashioned entertainment."

She stood up, clicked a picture of him and turned the screen. "Take a look. That's the face of Nathan Wollzak who delivers entertainment to New Yorkers, even though, to the rest of the world, it would be seen as art. The problem is, it's *inaccessible* art to the rest of the world. Theatre isn't turning-on New Yorkers any more. At best, it titillates, maybe even arouses them, but the world of the stage in Manhattan has reached a point where the patrons are so glib, so spoiled by the availability of it all, or cynical by the lack of depth in most offerings, that a night at the theatre is nothing more than recreation time for them. Entertainment. There are exceptions, of course, but, hey, even my world, the world of poetry, has gone *slam*. Nothing against it when it's good, but what happened to the Sandburgs, Blakes, Tennysons, and Pounds?" She turned and faced him, eye to eye. "Nathan, hamburger can be made to taste good a hundred different ways, but filet mignon needs nothing but a flame. You serve the public hamburgers all their lives, they never get to know a filet, right? The few that sit in front of your truck and soak up Shakespeare or Chekhov, who are they? A few college students and some die-hard patrons of yesterday's theatre. That's all you've got. And you know why?"

"I think you're going to tell me," said Nathan.

Mariel shook her head. "Because the rest *don't know any better*. Burgers. *Your* audience may only feed their soul once a month, but it's going to be filet mignon, because they *do* know better." She looked at her watch. "Time to get back. You staying?"

Nathan got up and shuffled along side her. "Burgers?"

"That's what he's all about. Derek's here asking us to be the flame for each and every one of those potential steaks out there."

Nathan shook his head. "You just traveled a long distance to go a short way. You know that, don't you?"

"Of course. But you never got off the train, did you?"

Their images, like innocent children from a black and white calendar, rounded the corner of the sand encrusted walkway. She elbowed him playfully and said, "You ready for a two year rehearsal?"

"About as ready as you are to travel another long distance."

"To go a short way?"

"To go a short way."

***

Theo anxiously stood outside the cannery door and snuffed out the last of his smokes as he heard the end of the impromptu forty-five minute Q and A with Derek. He peeked through the crack in the door and eyed Samara, who now stood in the shadows, having abandoned her chair. As he gazed on, the memories of that first night with her and Derek, and the subsequent weeks and months of getting to know both of them, left him with an ache in his stomach.

He didn't need Samara to tell him that her conversation at the Tavern with Derek had not gone as well as she wanted. She was visibly distant with the man she had taken years to successfully persuade to accept his failings and strengths—the man she had confided to Theo was the only man she could picture as a father to her child, if, and when. Today, however, had obviously confirmed her worst fears—Derek had followed her advice, her goading, her pushing. He was prepared, determined, and now, independent. *He was doing it.*

Theo knew, just by looking at her, that the *independent* part was the most painful. She had wrapped so much of her self-validation up in being any and everything to Derek and his art. It left her unprepared to witness the results in one fell swoop. The pulling away, his weaning from her maternal instincts—instincts she had perhaps quashed with professional denial—were now scorching her insides. She felt self-betrayed. She was desperately in need of child—the child in him.

Derek concluded with one last thought. "I have tried to answer your questions as honestly as I'd have expected from any of you, were I sitting out there. The fact is, only *you* can answer any of these questions concerning your reason for living the way you've chosen. Only you know the answer to your needs. That's all I want to encourage in you. Be true to your needs. It's for the reason of need, that I've named this commitment, the Echo Project. That's what it is all about, echoes as empowerment. Don't compromise, whether it's here with the Echo Project, or back where you came from."

He stepped down from the podium and individually thanked everyone for coming and hoped they'd give serious consideration to permanently returning. As everyone shook his hand and thanked him for the presentation, Theo hurriedly ushered them toward the door to catch the ferry.

As Samara approached Derek, he put his finger to his lips. "Don't say anything now. Think about it."

195

Their eyes locked. She composed herself, fighting back the emotions she knew she might have to control for a very long time, and smiled. "I will. I will." She kissed his cheek, and with one last glance at the eyes she had gazed into for years while persuading him to be everything he was, she bowed her head and slipped through the door.

Derek stood silent with his back to the door, and listened to her heels gradually become distant with the sandy street. Abruptly, the exit was silent—an exit he hoped was only temporary.

Having quietly absorbed the afternoon, Simon Greco lingered outside, searching the faces of the artists as they left for some kind of indication. There was none. If any decisions had been made, they were not showing them.

As Samara passed him, her contained emotions starting to dismantle, he too found himself feeling strangely out of control. He quickly shook his head and reminded himself that he was supposed to be beyond this, the "voice of confidence," as his radio station promoted him. Right now, however, he felt vacuous, a man with anything but confidence, and that bothered him.

He quickly stepped back into the hall just as Derek was leaving. "Derek, I need to ask you a question."

"Of course," said Derek as he locked up.

"So... would it be all right to sleep over night in the cannery?"

Derek, a bit taken aback, gave Simon a raised eyebrow. "You don't look like the type loving the cold and uncomfortable. There aren't any blankets, or even a mattress..."

"Yeah. I know," Simon replied. "That pile of old canvas at the far end will do fine."

Derek smiled and shrugged. "Hey, if it gets unbearable, the lighthouse is just five minutes away. I've got a spare..."

"No. I'll be fine. Could I buy you some dinner first?"

Off-season restaurants were a rarity, so Derek suggested they walk down to The Nordic Star, a family eatery the natives vouched for, and a place that would be quiet. After ordering a bottle of Nordic Star's best wine, the "reserve" Gallo, Simon smiled and toasted Derek. "From one crazy dude to another."

"Well, that's easy to drink to... I mean speaking for myself."

"The craziness?"

"Yeah," said Derek.

"Touché. Three radio stations. Two firings... both over my 'lack of sanity' as one put it. The other told me I was 'fucking nuts. Get out!'"

"Come here and you can avoid a third firing," quipped Derek.

"How do I avoid leaving the girlfriend, her two parakeets and tortoise?"

Derek grinned. "Oops."

With that, they drank from their wine glasses, both savoring the lack of vintage.

"In your letter, you asked me to express the side of me never expressed," said Simon after pouring another glass.

"Yes."

"And I didn't," confessed Simon.

"We've got all night."

"I guess you're right." After pondering a moment, Simon quietly asked, "Why me?"

"Why did I send you a letter?"

"Yes."

"Did you see the *in progress* recording booth in the corner of the cannery?"

Simon nodded.

"Trying to do something like this has no guarantees," said Derek. "It needs a voice for as long as it lasts."

"You've got Theo… the best damn voice around."

Derek agreed. "Yes… on paper. We'll need that too. But chronicling the process, hearing the voices of the artists, your questions, and most important, the answers given by the audience… their voices… that's a special kind of barometer."

"The common man's reaction?"

Derek shook his head, "No. The common man's participation."

"I don't understand."

"Sure you do. At the risk of this phrase rapidly becoming a cliché, 'We're all creative?' Yes?"

"You really believe your own shit, don't you?" said Simon.

"What would you say if I told you that you're the only artist in the bunch, including me, fulfilling your destiny?"

Simon blushed. "I'd say again, you're one crazy dude."

"But it's true. You challenge your audience each and every night. You push them to look at themselves and their choices… how they live. Ever notice how they call in and angrily denounce you as, oh, God, a heretic, the Anti-Christ, the…"

"…the Devil incarnate, and quite often, a real asshole."

Derek picked it up without missing a beat, "They respond, Simon. They echo. You stir up the war inside them with words. They fight back… and with what? With what, Simon?"

"Okay, words. Lots of words and… "

"Yes, but what kind of words? Simon. Say it."

Simon shrugged. "Hate?"

"No! Passion! It's passion they respond with. Creative energy crying out to be freed. We rarely experience that kind of purging because we *are* free...you me and the other nine that were here tonight. We've learned how to channel that energy onto a blank canvas, a barren stage, an empty radio booth...and it works sometimes. But, Simon, a Nureyev, a Bernstein, a Sandberg, they bring chills to even our spines, tears to all our eyes and hope to the spirit, but there've been so few of them... so many of us."

"Some would say you're one of them as well, Derek."

"The minute I get wrapped up in that thought, it being about me, well, that's what we've got to fight against. It's about them...your audience...my museum junkies...the watchers and the listeners not knowing that they too can ignite dormant fuels like Nureyev, Bernstein and Sandberg did daily." As Derek took a breath...

"And together we can create a better world, Derek? Is that what you really want me to believe, you crazy fucker?"

"Christ, yes!"

Simon raised his glass. "Absofuckinlutely!"

The waitress, a Rubens come alive in sheared dress, battleship hips, and a mismatched dour-cheeked demureness stepped up. "You gentlemen look ready."

Both smiled and raised their glasses, chiming in unison, "Got that right."

Chapter 33

The rough ferry ride and plane trip back was quiet for most of the eight. The ferry delay had caused them to take the next commuter flight, and with seasickness still rendering healthy headaches and nausea for some, few exchanges took place, even though everyone politely acknowledged each other with nods and patronizing smiles. Their eyes said it all. Processing what they had heard and seen was not going to be easy.

***

Politely excusing herself from Leonard's desire to talk, Samara had tried to sip her *rock-'n-roll* coffee on the ferry, and was now up to vodka and cranberry midway through the plane ride. She had chosen to sit in a bulkhead seat, further isolating herself.

As the passengers departed, the group gave each other cordial nods, remaining somewhat aloof, the day's experience still weighing heavily. Leonard stepped up to Samara in the terminal. "Share a cab?"

A cold rain began to fall, interrupting her distant gaze. She gripped his arm. "I guess it is time to get practical again, isn't it? Sure."

Before the cab was out of the airport, Samara, staring straight ahead said, "How does a symphony realize itself without a conductor?"

"Pardon," said Leonard.

"It shouldn't be this way. I've never understood love to be so intolerant, so independent. Why does it have to be either or?"

"You're losing me," he said, patting her hand.

"Are you going to join him?" she said.

"I don't know, yet."

"Would you leave, or take Tina?"

"Don't know yet." He turned to her. "Quite a decision to make, yes?"

Samara leaned toward the driver. "Not the tunnel. Could you take the bridge?"

The driver nodded as Samara asked Leonard, "You don't mind if we drive awhile do you?"

"Sure. Beats walking around in the rain."

Once over the Queensboro Bridge, the cabby wound his way through the East Side toward Central Park. "Just take your time," said Samara.

As they entered the park, Samara rolled the window down. The late fall air was heavy and cold as she inhaled winter's preview. "Do you ever play your trumpet when you're making love, Leonard? I mean in your head of course."

"Where the hell did that come from?" he asked.

"I do my best composing just before I peak." She pulled her head back into the cab and rolled the window up. "Now, he wants to take that away from me."

"Hey, not to be too personal, but…"

"Oh, please do. Be personal. I'm missing that. Missing that a lot today." She muttered with a bit of tearful anger in her voice.

"Did you two call it quits, or what?" he continued.

Her eyes welled up, the pressure of the day about to cascade. "It's all about something else with him. We don't really matter anymore…Derek and me. He wants our relationship to be no different than that of Berkowitz, or Hensky, or Lanagra, or you. Just be a part of his 'Echo Project.'"

Leonard sat quietly the rest of the rainy drive around the park and then down the East Side Drive to Soho where they stopped. As

Samara pushed the door open, she offered to pay, but Leonard waved her off. "We'll talk tomorrow." He held her arm. "Samara?"

"Yes?"

"How does a conductor realize himself without his orchestra?"

She pulled her collar up. "You going to tell me it's all *one* too?" she said.

"I think so. At least that's what I'm going to have to explain to Tina. She's going to feel like the odd-man out, but..."

"You're going to do it, aren't you?"

He nodded. "I'm not sure why yet, but..." He stepped out with his cane and covered her head with his jacket as she walked to the building door. She kissed him on the cheek.

"I'll call you tomorrow," he said, and stepped back into the cab.

As the yellow and green colors sped away and disappeared into the blur of the night, she took out her keys and peered up the wall to the dark windows of the loft. Her thoughts once again returned to the anticipation of another night without her reason for waking each morning—without the only connection to love she had—without the validation only he could give her. She counseled others about love. *Why was it so hard to accept changes herself? And why after three years was attachment such an issue?*

***

As midnight became early morning, and the drying cobblestones once again became their true selves, the one-fingered melody rising to the open skylight found company with the counterpoint of her left hand. Finally there was harmony out of the dissonance, order out of the chaos, and the layers of love's loneliness became a serene orchestration. At least, that is what she wanted to believe.

The broken-cloud sunrise peeked through the refraction of the last remaining droplets of rain clinging to the skylight. Samara sat hunched over the manuscript paper atop her lap. Her shoulders arched like exhausted boughs—her hands felt exhausted, wanting only respite. Her eyes remained transfixed on the manuscript paper riddled with frenetic Pollock-like blobs and lines. *"What's it all about, Derek? Why can't I know like you?"* She quietly quivered. *"Why?"*

Not yet fully aware she was answering her own question, Samara remained focused on the manuscript as the voices of the strings, then horns, reeds and percussion began resonating as one, forming a path of sound, pulling her inward to the audible core that for Samara was her white heat, a conundrum unraveled, her cauldron made drinkable.

She drank in the tempos and rhythms gently, finding her inner spirit of calm. Her eyes lifted to *Family*, Derek's first-born mobile hanging over the bed some thirty feet away—hanging as it had all those years. On several occasions before his departure, she had fought off sleep to observe his seeming worship of the giant work from his pillow, his closed eyelids fluttering with a vibration—"my connection with the *Family*"—he had called it, the reason he couldn't part with it even when earlier times had been hard. *Is he missing it now, or has something or someone taken its place?*

As her eyes found their way back to the manuscript, she felt a sense of understanding working its way to the surface. *Is it as simple as Theo professed that one night, "all you have been and will ever be is within, and a connection to someone else is unnecessary to know love?" Are those I care about most trying to tell me something I just can't get? As a doctor, have I hardened my heart with so much objectivity that the simplest of personal answers is out of reach?*

From above, a single gull feather fluttered to the top of the Grand and lay in ebonized sunlight.

As Samara glanced upward, there was only the sound of arching wings lifting from the skylight.

CHAPTER 34

"Why can't they be specific? Why? Why? Why?" Derek sat before the radio, talking to himself as his fingers fumbled for another news station, but the vague report remained the same: Amid heavy fog, an American commuter flight from Maine to NY crashed into Long Island sound. No survivors.

Again, Derek's "Why?" emerged through his constricted throat like the last breath of a condemned man. On the other side of the tiny room beneath the Fresnel, where only the bed, table, radio and reading light broke the harsh white reality of the historical walls, Theo remained standing, unable to bend the necessary distance to sit, his body a freeze-frame contortion of grief and disbelief.

The repeating "buzz, buzz, buzz" of Derek's cell phone came more as a death-march dirge than an alert that someone wished to speak with him. "Yes, hello," he mumbled, clearing his throat.

"Derek, it's Leonard. You've not heard the news, I hope."

"The news," whispered Derek, still dazed from the shocking reports.

"Oh, thank God. You would have freaked. We're fine. I mean, the group, Samara, all of us. The ferry hit choppy seas and was late. We missed the plane. We caught the next one. Derek?"

Derek squinted, trying to focus back to the moment. "Leonard?"

"Yeah. This is Leonard. I'm sorry I woke you, but..."

"Everyone. Everyone caught another plane?" came Derek's broken words of disbelief.

Theo stepped to Derek's side. "They're okay?"

"Caught another plane," Derek sighed.

"Derek. I'll call everyone and let them know I've spoken to you. No worry, now, okay? Everything's fine."

"Thanks, Leonard. Thanks." Derek closed the phone and then grasped Theo's hand. "They missed the plane, Theo. Missed it."

Theo slowly sat down. "Something to think about, eh?"

"For a hell of a long time. Hell of a long time."

***

Relief showed itself differently among the group. Berkowitz had not found sleep a friend that night, too caught up in the decision making process. From Scotch to early morning TV movies to cigars to ice cream (his favorite vice) the night had dragged on until the moment he flipped on the news. It was then that he realized his luck was not unlike that of his injured cat, Cindy, who lay curled up beside him, the splint on her leg reminding him she too had just recently avoided a black angel.

Lanagra awoke to his cup of coffee and usual ten minutes of CNN news. Upon hearing his good fortune, he climbed to the top of his scaffolding and hunched over the top railing, directed drops of paint to fall; a large sky blue *pladop*, followed by slowly decreasing drops of yellow, green, gray, black and red. Not a praying man, he chose to give thanks to *whoever might be listening...don't know why me, but, thanks for the dumb luck. Yeah. Thanks.*

The red spilled over the can and increasingly wider on the offering, beginning now to consume the yellow, green, gray and black. The droppings stopped, replaced by the stream of tears merging with the surreal benediction.

In his Ave. C flat, Wollzak, upon hearing the news, stoked up his two-burner, brought the kettles of water to a boil, removed the plywood table top from his tub, and after pouring water far too hot for a normal human being to enjoy, began lowering his body. Acknowledgment of his worth had always been a never-ending quest. Today, confirmation of his existence would suffice.

Hensky stumbled upon the news from a student arriving late to take a make-up lesson for his absence the day before. Knowing Hensky had flown to Maine, the dancer broke into sobbing on finding him safe and alive there in the studio. Holding the mirrored reflection of the girl in his arms, he tearfully uttered, "Life is good, Jennifer. Life is good."

For Mariel, the one most akin to travel, the accident left her both sad for the victims and joyous for herself. Surviving the numbers was a constant concern, given she clocked over two million miles a year in the air. Upon watching the TV coverage of the dismal search and rescue for the unfortunate, she cut short her normal daily routine of saving digital pictures from the previous day and dashed to the nearest ATM. She quickly drew out a large stack of currency and made the short train ride to lower Manhattan's under-the-bridge homeless population.

This was where she had taken numerous pictures and written countless verses about the *Rag Soldiers*, as she called them. Here was a sleepy world of the hopeless, where many were usually just a few winks from the darkness themselves. Leaving the subway, and walking several blocks to the Brooklyn Bridge, she immediately found the all too familiar images everywhere, huddled in cardboard, rags, and each other—a lattice work of those just thankful to survive another day.

The ten dollar bills slid into the pockets of the sleeping gave the promise of waking up to a more positive day with the means to put food in their stomachs, and perhaps a reminder that luck is sometimes handed out unexpectedly.

Touleur stood in front of a Broadway *going-out-of-business* electronics store, gazing at the multiple TV sets carrying the coverage. Next to him stood another passerby, shaking his head. "Damn, one minute you can be alive, and the next dead, eh?"

Touleur held his gaze and shook his head. "Or… one minute you can think you're dead, and the next find you're alive."

"Huh?" said the man.

"Fate or luck?" said Touleur as he stepped away, and continued down the Great White Way.

***

The balance of the day for Derek was one of introspection and thanks, as he sat at his desk and faced a blank piece of paper. The intermittent screech of a gull mixed with the tides' flirtatious swooning over the rocky shore below reminded him even further of the isolation that was his, the remoteness that was his, the choice—that was his. Finally, he wrote: *Dear Samara—I don't know if a day like today was meant to be through and by some higher power. I'm far from being realized to the point where I can portend the answers. I do know that my mind and heart has wandered aimlessly today. We must all be wondering why? Why, the choppy seas? Why the missing of the plane's departure? We're not the first to face the question of divine providence dictating when we go. So, why this experience now? Why such timing? Does it have anything to do with the group, us…really?"*

Theo broke the quiet as he bounced into Derek's room, jovial and excited. "Your friend Simon just woke up. What did you pour into his veins last night?"

Derek looked up hesitantly, "What?"

"Simon. He's catching the next ferry out of here and wants you on his show tonight."

"What are you talking about?" said Derek.

"Simon ran to catch the next ferry and said you had to be on his show tonight. Wants you to be available, special guest, and all that. Said to be stay your phone, nine o'clock."

Derek stood up, folded the letter and put it in his pocket. "What the hell *did* I pour into his veins last night?"

"Whatever, he's psyched and…"

"Why the hell you so excited, Theo?"

"You can push the envelope, dummy. The crash. Fate. Death can happen anytime. 'Where will *you* be Mister John Smith?'"

"Mister John Smith? I don't get you, Theo."

"Here, I'll spell it out for you—he's probably going to ask you why he's still alive? Why the others are still alive?"

"So. I don't have a clue, for Christ's sake. Luck. Wasn't their time…what other clichés could we use?"

"Derek, you can't explain Echo either, but there's a reason why she exists. She's not waiting around to nudge me, but she sure as hell has got it in for you."

"Meaning what?"

"Meaning that when the student is ready, the teacher will appear."

"Oh, that's original," quipped Derek.

"Says it though, doesn't it?" She made you move. Made you seize the day. In turn, you took heed and here you are. That rock you're creating is out there waiting for the next day. My book—bad as it might turn out—is waiting for me to chip away at it. Derek, those eight that left here last night, weathered the seas, and caught a lucky flight…they're primed. They're waiting now for their nudge…for answers. You got yours. I got mine. Give them theirs. There's even more out there in that audience of Simon's. He's expecting you to do something with this experience."

"You two talked about more than just telling me to be on the show, didn't you?"

"Huh?"

"Knew you couldn't be trusted," said Derek with a childish grin.

***

As early evening came on, the associate producers and production assistants for Simon's show were busy making calls on a bank of phones.

"Well, tell Mister Hensky to tune in at 9 p.m., WOZ, Simon Greco's Show. Important, okay. Thanks."

"That's right. 9 p.m. Thank you Mister Berkowitz."

"Okay, but if he comes in, tell Mister Wollzak, 9 p.m., WOZ, Greco's Show."

"I know your work so well, Mister Lanagra. I'm so… well, I'm sorry… That's right, 9 p.m."

Simon made his way to the studio, the excitement of his plan staying contained in spite of the speculating buzz among the staff from his early morning phone call and instructions. A perky new production assistant bounced up alongside him. "Coffee, Mister Greco?"

Not missing a step, he mumbled, "No… the usual."

She backed off, bowing and stumbling through a half Geisha, half Victorian response. "The usual. Yes. Right away." She scurried down the hall and into the production office. "Bill, he wants 'the usual.'"

Bill looked up for a moment, then grabbed the phone. "Shit. The usual isn't the *usual*. That's reserved for Friday nights. He really must have something going on tonight." Turning in his chair and covering the mouthpiece, "Sally, brew up 'the usual,' okay? I know it's Wednesday." He hung up and turned back to the PA. "Give Sally five minutes, then take it to him."

Looking lost, "Sure. Take him what?"

"His *usual*. That's all you need to know. Sally makes it, you deliver it."

The hot tea *usual* was delivered at precisely 8:20 p.m., ten minutes before airtime on Fridays. Simon sampled the brew, then placed the cup back on the saucer. He looked toward the control booth and pointed at the cup, making a plus sign with his fingers. Dizzy, his producer, smiled and picked up the phone. "Sally…he wants more. No, just a sip so far, but he wants more…Just brew the shit and bring it up here. Controlling him is my job."

CHAPTER 35

The first thirty minutes of the program was getting its usual high listenership. Phone banks were fully lit up with an average of fifteen calls waiting on each line. Every minute or so, Simon warned his audience that what he was going to share with them at nine may not make them happy, "...so if tonight was your 'I just want to be entertained and informed by Simon,' turn me off. Don't listen. Don't even think about it, 'cause this is not going to be just a sit back and listen night." Every minute or so, a variation of the same alert was pushed out to his nightly audience of 11,000,000, world wide English speaking audience reached by satellite.

At the nine o'clock station break, Simon sipped the last of his second cup and gave the plus sign once again to Dizzy. He then sat back, looked upwards for a moment, then leaned toward the microphone and said, "Ladies and gentlemen, and the rest of my audience who hopefully haven't earned the distinction of being labeled according to the old broadcasting political correctness... this is a special night that I hope I can do justice to."

He took the list of telephone numbers and placed them in front of him. "A few days ago, I was asked to join with a group of ten other artists on a remote island in Maine to hear about a purpose, a destiny, if you will, designed, or perhaps the proper word is encouraged, by a man who will remain anonymous for now. There is a good reason for the anonymity, and it's not secrecy. This is a man many of you would know, if I mentioned his name, but because he convinced the ten of us that the idea was not about him or any of us, the artists, but about you...I'm getting ahead of myself. Suffice it to say, this man voiced a gut wrenching dilemma he was having, not unlike a dilemma we're having ourselves, but don't know it: we've been sleeping through the *undeclared* war on art.

"Okay. Okay. I know that sounds like a subject that you're all anticipating a yawn over, but listen a few minutes before you pull the sheet up over your head. For those of you who missed this broadcast a few weeks ago, I'm going to replay a portion. This is what aroused the interest in an artist—this man of mystery—who, we found out very quickly, has more than a dream... he has a question. He might even just have the answer. Anyway, let's start out with a replay...just a few pieces of it, so you who missed that night can get involved with us tonight. Hold on, 'cause just like Ms. Davis said, 'It's gonna be a bumpy ride.'"

The recording of Simon's previous broadcast was piped in, catching him at an impassioned apex of the broadcast..."Boycott this trash! Demand journalism that is unbiased. Demand that music be played and sold that addresses a standard that has some redeemable value, not just the usual in one ear and out the other degrading, life-mocking crap. Down with mediocrity, up with snobbish selectivity.

"Where the hell is any preference, nowadays? We are wallowing in a dusty drought of expression because we aren't demanding the thinking humorists, the thinking painters the thinking composers and filmmakers. Instead, we run to the nearest quick fix to pacify our deplorable inability to deal with the complexities all around us. God help us. That would demand some thinking, wouldn't it? Hollywood, for instance! Where's your Fellini? Where's your Goddard? Where's your Renoir? Where's even your 21st Century Woody?

"Who's conscious that we aren't creating icons of art like we used to. It's gotta change, people. The system is obsessed with controlling your minds. With your minds in their pockets, guess what? Your heart goes next, then a piece, if not all of your soul. This 'big brother' control needs to bring you to your knees where it can better control you. And what you are reading, what you are watching and hearing lacks fundamental stimulation for your mind so you have the fodder to think for yourself! Do you hear me America and the rest of you all around the world? Have you all but forgotten Paddy's message... 'I'm mad as hell and I'm not going to take it anymore?'"

Simon came back in live. "Well, gang, that's what started it all...for me, that is. An artist I'd never met, but whose name is known in art circles around the globe, sent me a letter after hearing that broadcast. He sent the same letter to a small group of artists he considered on the same page with him. Quite frankly, it took me a while to figure out why he even thought of me. I'm just a radio hack to a lot of people. To some, I manage to squeak through some thought provoking ideas. That's what he told me had arrested his attention. So, me, and a few others, all received this letter, announcing a little get together on an island off the New England coast. We all met for just one afternoon. For some, I'm sure it was love at first sight. For others, *yours truly* included, it was downright scary. That's right. He was scary, and you know why? Because he might be right. And if he is, me, and the others, have no choice but to join him. But, damn, I'm getting ahead of myself again.

"What this is really all about is you. That's right. You guys out there using, or may not using your creativity. This is not a figure of speech. Many of you are all out there sitting on your asses—most of you—listening to me and doing nothing, right? Well, I sit on my own fat ass a lot and sometimes, I don't do anything either. But...and this is the big one, gang, SOMETIMES I DO. SOMETIMES I GET CREATIVE.

"Now, it doesn't matter that I can't even re-paint my bathroom wall with any talent, but I get out the oils and throw them around every once in a while, and you know what? I feel...better, not because some pop psychology has been laid on me that says, 'do anything you want, as long as it makes you feel better.' That crap is nnough to make you snap.

"What we're talking here folks, is feeling better because *we've* exercised some creativity...done some of our *own* thinking...created some *interactivity with ourselves*...in short, TAKING THE POWER BACK.

"So, understand this. Our mystery artist believes that the process of allowing your juices, those creative microbes lying dormant in all of us, allowing them to be expressed, is paramount to survival. Otherwise...implosion. And that implosion comes in even scarier forms, like car bombings, suicide bombers, fascist takeovers, and yes, genocide. But don't get him or me wrong. We're not about politics. We're just convinced that politics, as we know it today, both in Washington and the entertainment capitals of the world, and the constituencies it controls, is existing this way because of far too much stifled imagination and creativity. Obviously, there are the rare exceptions.

"It's energy, gang, energy that needs an outlet. Don't open the spigot, and it backs up. Okay. Here's where it starts to get bumpy. Don't switch the dial now, just because I might be pissing you off. I'm going to be paraphrasing, but this is the gist of his message.

"We all work at something. Some to pay the bills. Some to pay the bills and fulfill something. Some of us have to be productive, because that, for many of us, is the acceptance of morality, our acknowledgement that we must live, not just exist. But in order to live, really live, one has to be productive, translate raw energy into something alive on that big white, blank canvas we're all born into...the life canvas.

"So, think about it. Housewives, take that kneaded bread and roll it into a new shape, any shape but the standard, uncreative loaf, okay? Those of you dining on a can of beans tonight, spoon it out in small mounds, lines, squares. Create something that feeds your eyes as well as your stomach. Any of you down on your hands and knees scrubbing the tub? Take the Comet, sprinkle that green stuff all over, then for God sake, swirl it into something that takes you somewhere else. To a Van Gogh painting, Starry Night in green, I don't care. Try anything, but don't just scrub the tub. Okay?

"Now for all you night workers in the markets, the wholesale warehouses, the…well, any place that asks you to stack stuff *properly.* If your boss tries to fire you tomorrow morning, tell him to call me, I'll explain. But I want you to stack that stuff in a way that fires you up. Don't think about whether that's the way it's always been done and so that's the way IT IS DONE. Do it your way. Make it different. Make it creative. I'll be back in two minutes."

The station break took over, and Simon sat back, checked his pulse. *Shit like a marathon runner!* He looked up toward the control booth.

Simon's producer, Dizzy was pacing. The researchers, normally scouring the databases for references Simon was always asking for, were sitting transfixed on the man.

***

Theo, sitting across from Derek at the kitchen table, turned the Scrabble board around. "Your turn, and I'm penalizing you after sixty seconds. Derek reached over and turned the radio down. "God, I hate commercials. Sixty seconds. You're merciless." Derek looked at his letters, then the board. "Fractious… F-R-A"

"Too many letters," said Theo, looking at his watch.

"Fraction works, though, right?" Derek leaned in and placed the letters on the board. "Go. You got the same sixty."

As Theo examined the board, Derek stepped to the port window and looked out on the sea in the distance. A full moon painted the tips of the breakers. "He's surprising me, Theo. I think he gets it."

Theo placed five letters on the board, "Transillumination. How's that?"

Derek still gazing out at the white caps, "Pretty accurate. Yeah. You're right. I'd say he's passing light through the walls of a lot of people tonight. Now we have to see what the medical inspection reveals." He turned and cranked the radio up again, as…

"…and that's just the beginning," said Simon. "So, what this man said to us was, 'we are nothing.' Yeah, me and the others, we're nothing. We're icons in our respective fields, me being the runt of the litter, but you know what I mean. Composers, musicians, painters, sculptors, actors, artists all. 'You're nothing,' he says. 'You're whole purpose is to just *empower?*' he says. 'Just because someone is world famous, makes a lot of money, has people bowing at their feet, they're nothing…' And he's right if…" Simon's voice lowered to almost a whisper. "Nothing if you don't empower others to explore their own creativity! So, is it working? I'm a nothing, but did I empower you? You whipping up some awesome bread shapes? How are those stacks coming? Bet there's some geometric wonders out there tittering on the tip of a needle, right?

Tubs. How many of you were scrubbing tubs? How many of you went and started scrubbing your tub with some Comet, eh? Simplistic and innocuous, right? Just a tub. But what did you see in that tub?

"So, it's all about empowerment. Your tubs, your bread, your stacks, all about empowerment. Somebody else is going to see your imagination and say, 'what the hell you doing, guy?' What are you going to say in reply? 'I'm creating. What you doin' besides nothing while you gape at me? And don't even think about firing me, 'cause I'm doin' my job, just my way'

"So, that's what the meeting on the island was all about. I'm going to stay somewhat vague, so don't light up the lines asking specific questions, okay?

"This guy wants me to quit my job here at WOZ, split to this island, broadcast whatever I want as long as it's my creation, you know. As long as I throw out enough, something will stick, that's what he thinks.

The control booth became a group of gaping, mouth-open *shockafoids*.

"So...I threw a mouthful at you tonight. If you did the bread, the stacks, the tub, call me. Tell me what you think. I've told you all you need to know in order...in order for you to tell me if you think I'm nuts for listening to him? Am I nuts to go? Am I nuts to stay? And, hey... am I nuts to begin with? I'll be right back."

Dizzy came storming out of the control room. "Quitting? You are nuts. NUTS! Jesus, man, what about the show, us, all of them?"

Simon looked perplexed at Dizzy and said, "You've been my producer for 15 years and I just met you...just now. Fuck Off!" He looked up at the control booth, lifting his cup and gave them the plus sign for his tea. "And I'd appreciate it in a hurry, okay?"

Dizzy answered his cell phone and paced in front of Simon. "Jesus. For a station manager, you're... look, he don't mean none of this shit. You're what? Yankin' it. Yeah. Well, hey, take a Midol, stop your bellyaching and listen up. If your sponsors call tomorrow and want an extra block of time, you'll be kissing both our asses. Take that Midol, Christopher. Give your loins a break." Hanging up, he shot one last jab at Simon as he made his way back to the booth. "Simon, this better be just a ratings ploy. Ya hear?"

Simon smiled. "Christopher must be reeling from that assault. The creative bug got ya, Diz?"

The next two hours saw the fifteen lines of his call-in board stay red, red, red. Dizzy was racing between his cell phone, and the monitoring supervisor, trying to keep the nuts off the air.

One after another, the jabs came over the hot lines.

"You are nuts, Simon."

"If I could empower like you, I'd scrub tubs for a living."

"Take a vacation, Simon."

"Can I join...I mean I'm no icon, but my stuff's so original, drive a sane man mad. You get it?"

"Simon, I think you are just...I don't know. My tub is so beautiful. I don't want to rinse it. My husband said leave it. He told me to leave it till the party this weekend. My husband, Simon. You understand what I'm saying?"

"I put a flashlight in the middle, Simon. The blue and white boxes are all lit up like stacked apartments in a Greek village, you know? It's so damn beautiful. I don't think my boss is going to appreciate the condom section arranged like a geophysics experiment though. Could you talk to him in the morning? I really think this will sell like crazy."

It was the third hour that Simon decided to turn it loose on the other seven invitees. He called Berkowitz first, thinking that as much as he didn't want to put commercialism in the thoughts of his audience, Berkowitz could be good sometimes, really good. He had the reputation of being what hadn't been seen on Broadway for decades...the new David Susskind...a breakthrough producer with plenty of angst for any producer or writer who catered to the 'expense account' audiences, at the expense of the ordinary people.

"Is Broadway inaccessible?" asked Simon.

"Somewhat of a rhetorical question, don't you think? At $125 a ticket, what do you think?"

Then came Hensky. "Women used to move down a sidewalk like ballerinas. Checked them out lately? Where do they get that 'truck driver' swagger is sexy? Yeah, I believe like the rest of the group. My focus has always been on movement, but this guy, this artist...are we gonna tell your audience who he is?"

"Not necessary," said Simon. "Continue."

"Okay. This guy, this artist of uncanny reasoning ability, yeah, he hooked me. I'm all for getting women moving creatively again, without the 'I'm so freakin' insecure, I've got to be something I'm not' attitude. That's not too precious, is it?"

"Just women?"

"Okay," said Hensky, "not to slight the men, but...the kind I generally do not deal with, you know what I mean, those men out there who *are* truck drivers, well, think of it this way, for every ballerina who moves like a wisp of grass floating through space, there has to be an opposite counter energy giving it meaning. Too oblique? Yeah. Too oblique. Men? I'm going to join this venture and I'm going to be looking to do something, I don't know what, but something that will make you take a look at the way you move. So, think, no, study men as they walk about. Next time you pull into a truck stop and order up a corn beef on rye, check it out—the other guys in there. See any John Waynes? How about Mick Jaggers? Kobes? Even Letterman has a unique movement. Ask yourself, do I move like I feel, like I'm capable of imagining? Am I doing anything about it? Am I so frickin' scared of myself that…oh, hell, I'm talking about creating only who you are. Movement. Guess it's obvious. Damn, I love what I do. And, oh, truck drivers move with grace just as a ballerina, only with weight coming from a different fatigue from long hours. And for all the rest of you out there, make no mistake about it, truck drivers are creative too…waiting to be empowered."

One after another, Wollzak, Mariel, Lanagra, and Paxton, all had something to say about their experience. Some made public commitment to the project, others still not sure, but all with a testimony that their world was turned upside down on that day at the island.

Simon finally took the last ten minutes and asked his audience to bear with him as he was about to bring on a woman many of them would recognize for her musical accomplishments, but who represented a special kind of knowledge and experience with the creator of the project—the guy. "I'm talking about the man whose vision has connected with our guests tonight, you, me and this woman. Well, let me ask *her* to tell you more."

"Samara, are you there?"

"Yes, Simon."

"This has been some night. I've still got every line backed up and… hey, gang, I'm sorry I couldn't get to you all, but we'll hear from you again, I know. So, Samara, is this what it seems to be…a possible answer to a lot of problems?"

"If you mean does stimulating creativity in everyone have validity? Yes. Do I think setting a course to cause this to happen is going to be easy, my answer is no."

"But you do believe in the project?"

There was a pause, then Samara spoke quietly. "To all of you out there…this man whose identity we've kept from you is not an ordinary man. He is not an ordinary artist. And—as Simon has tried to respectfully intimate tonight in his own brand of artful persuasion—this man we speak of may be, just might be some kind of messenger we've all been waiting for. Then again, what if he's not?"

Simon, caught a bit off guard, cleared his throat. "Could you explain that…"

"…that last question?" Samara said, finishing the sentence with a tone of speculation no one expected, especially Simon.

"Yes. Please. Would you?"

Derek sat crouched on the floor in a corner of the kitchen with his knees tucked under his chin and peered at the radio's dimly lit dial. Theo tired to idle his time organizing the Scrabble letters as he listened.

Samara continued. "We've spent three hours listening to all the good this man's vision could bring to the world, but what if it turns the ordinary lives of millions into turmoil? What if he's not that kind of messenger? What if he's something else?"

"Yes," said Simon, "He touched on that."

"Touched may not be enough," said Samara.

Derek sat up, a series of wrinkles appearing on his brow like shrinking paint upon a burning wall.

"Why would stimulating creativity cause 'turmoil' as you say?" said Simon.

"As you know, I am a composer and a therapist. The composer in me is as excited as the other artists in the group…you included. But, it is the therapist in me that sees it as…potentially something else."

Derek rose to his feet and stood over the radio, his stoic face now bristling with attention. Theo, aware that Derek was more involved with what was being said, sat back and paid more attention himself.

Simon asked, "Something else?"

"Yes," said Samara. "As a therapist, I think it is dangerous…*potentially* dangerous. There are professionals who would argue that for some people, there's a risk in turning unbridled creativity loose. With, let's just say the, more intense ones, not knowing the disciplines and understanding of the course creativity can take, can have a down side. This is not what you expected, Simon, I know, but it needs to be said. Creativity unleashes so much from within. Your listeners with the bathtub experience tonight, the stacked boxes, all of them, stepped through a threshold they might have never experienced before. Granted, a minor one in comparison to… well, let me say it this way, it's like when we, as therapists, cause a breakthrough with a patient, and they choose to finally step over the line, it's sometimes very frightening for them. If the care and love of a guide, a professional guide, is not there for them, well, that patient might not feel confident with the risk. Do you understand?"

Simon paused. "Yes." He motioned a plus sign to the booth. "Yes, I understand. With all due respect...you are an accomplished professional and an artist, but is it possible you are afraid to swim? *Personally*, I mean."

"Swim?" said Samara. "What has that got to do with what we're talking about?"

"I'm just a radio hack, Samara, but I know what it's like to be thrown in a pool with all your clothes on...especially if you can't swim. Frightening. And, if you refuse to be creative, you might drown. So you look up at the light above the water, and you paddle and panic, paddle and panic, and you...break through, in a manner of speaking.

"So, I have to ask you Samara. Aren't most rewards fraught with danger of some kind? The breakthroughs you speak of have all had their risk, have they not? Hell, not to imply disrespect for your profession, but my pushing some oils around on a blank white canvas, many times making mud, had a lot of danger. Personal danger. It looked like failure to me, and who likes failure? But, then I looked hard and I thought, *under all that mud, there's something I'm trying to say. I'll find it. I'll find what it is.* Wasn't I stepping 'through a threshold,' 'Over the line,' to use your words? Wasn't I breaking through on my own, because that's what I *needed* to do? Sounds so simple, but...what if it's true? I survived that muddy expression because I was finally ready to take the risk of failing. Like our man on the island, I believe we *are* all creative and imagination is not without its danger every time we dare express it. It's a lot like love, don't you agree, Samara?"

Samara didn't respond, but sat back from the telephone, her mind swirling with hesitancy and uncontrolled thoughts.

"Samara?"

"Yes."

"You were there on the island. This project is first of all about love, isn't it?" said Simon.

"Of course it's about love, but...."

Simon waited through a long pause. "But? Samara? Seems we've lost our connection. Samara, if you can hear me on the radio, I want you to know you've brought a very intelligent perspective to the surface. You've made us ponder some important considerations, but let me close with this. I believe *our man on the island*, and his project, is first about *love*. Then about helping us find that kind of love within ourselves. Maybe...maybe my mud was an effort to find a place to experience love, yes? Dare I say, *you* experience love in that place called music, Samara? Samara? Yes, I'm afraid we have lost our connection. Well..."

Simon took a deep breath. "Time is gone, Gang. Three hours of...Hell, I don't know. My producer doesn't know. It's been different hasn't it? Maybe even creative? This is Simon Greco hoping all of us will make time for our own creativity and breakthroughs—maybe even with a little danger on top? We'll see you tomorrow."

Derek remained hunched over the radio as the closing commercials gradually brought him back to the present. He switched it off and walked back to the corner, slid down the wall and peered across the kitchen through the window and into the vacuous darkness.

Theo stood up, walked calmly to the door. "I'll call you in the morning, okay?"

Derek didn't answer.

As Theo left, the night wind hurled a screech through the opened door. Then, he squeezed it shut, leaving Derek and the room in silence.

CHAPTER 36

"He picked himself a handful, didn't he?" said Linda.

Aretha continued washing the dishes. She lifted her head. "You want to tune that in to eighty eight point zero. 'Jazz through the night' just started."

Linda adjusted the dial and brought in some *Terrance Blanchard Jazz for Films*.

"Better. Really not one for talk shows, you know."

"So, that's it? You told me this Samara was the love of his life," said Linda.

"Would you hand me the pans off the stove, dear," said Aretha.

Linda smirked quietly and handed the fry and saucepan to her. "I thought jealousies were reserved for us younger ones."

Aretha glanced up coldly. "Meaning?"

"You don't want to talk about her."

"Linda, you are my daughter, and you have never lacked in the aggression department, but... not now. Okay?"

Linda stepped up and put her arms around her. "Not trying to make a fuss. You're just not yourself right now and I think you want to get something off your chest."

"And I should unload on you?"

Linda grinned. "Why not? One neurotic to another?"

"You...neurotic? Little more serious than that."

"The doctor said I was on the mend, remember?"

"Guess that deserves a *touché*." Aretha turned the faucet off, reached for a towel and walked to the window where outside the Ode stood before the clear sky. As always, it reflected whatever light came from above or off the ocean surface. Tonight, mixed with the other night-light, a lone campfire on the beach sent miniature reflective slivers of gold and orange at the obelisk.

"We're always on the mend, Linda. All of us."

She turned back to Linda and took a moment to gather her thoughts, sat down and patted the cushion next to her.

Linda joined her. "Is this going to be heavy? I could retract my aggression and we could watch an old Laurel and Hardy."

"If I told you, Linda, that once you know of love—I mean of the depth of love in general—once you've known that, you can never be the same again."

"So?"

Aretha leaned back on the couch and listened to the music for a few moments. "Nothing like a trumpet to bring out the torch in me." Turning back to her daughter, she said, "I'm not jealous of Samara. I'm not jealous of Derek. I'm sad that time seems to always go in the wrong direction. Have you ever thought what it would be like to be born old with all the experience of a life time, and as you aged, you actually aged backwards, discovering the reasons for your state of mind, and state of heart and soul...all the way back to a baby? Think what it would be like to come upon the moments of learning, the moments of knowing what caused so many realizations in your life, hmm?"

"Now that's really...out there, mother."

Aretha laughed. "Not really. Just a piece of imagination that doesn't have anywhere to go except back into my heart. You see, I don't know where my sense of understanding of love comes from. For most, I'm a failure in the love business. But..."

"You had a good ride."

Aretha pointed her finger and smiled. "Now, you watch your words here daughter. But, actually, you're right. I did have a good ride, except I'm not ready to get off the train. I think...I want to see this love thing carry forward with Derek. Not in the way you think. If he could realize his faith, his belief, *that* conviction that the purpose for all art is to empower—such a huge word, empower—but if he *could*...I would be ready to step off the ride. Do you understand?"

"Huh?" said Linda.

"You don't. Okay. You might someday realize a love, with a man, a man that opens certain doors in you that have been locked since birth. When they open, demons and angels take flight. A battle of passion ensues, where *right* and *wrong* surfaces and you—

the one whose doors have just been burst—you have to engage this force and through that engagement, you find that something of beauty—beyond beauty—can, and does, emerge. From that day forward, love transcends men, women, the sexes, and the attraction that introduced you originally. Beauty and love merge and... an *expression* transcend the two of you. *Expression*...the essence and all of us, the part of us so many are fearful to engage, and..." She turned toward the Ode and closed her eyes. "It becomes very personal. But when it happens. You know it."

Linda wiped her eye of a simple drop of emotion she wasn't prepared for. "That's love?"

"Maybe," offered Aretha. "To me...maybe."

The trumpet sounds hitched a ride on the night breezes and drifted down to the ocean. The fire on the beach backlit the waving colored scarves draped around the neck of the huddled figure before it. The rainbow colors reflected onto the Ode as a lone gull hovered above, its motionless wings defiantly holding onto the shallow stream of air and the subtle hue of moonlight.

By the time burning wood became mere smoking embers, the moon had arched through its nightly presence and rested on the edge of the horizon, waiting for its sister sun to rise. As the fog billowed across the dunes and enveloped the landscape, Echo stood motionless next to the Ode, save for the energy that invited the colors about her neck to gently embrace the brushed reflection.

From above, Aretha peered down from the parted Spanish brocade curtain. Her breath was short and paused, allowing barely enough exchange to create the small patches of condensation on the windowpane, arresting the gathered energy below. Echo's turn upward was a cool sip of water to the parched lips of someone feeling lost and frightened.

Their eyes held the silence in abeyance.

The moon dropped below the horizon.

Linda rose sharply up from her sleep and turned toward the window to hear shouting from below. "...but you have no right to accuse me of such things," blared Aretha. "You of all people!"

Her mother's voice had not been this shrill in years. For Linda, this was a sound pushed to the outer reaches of her memory, the sound of castigation and reprimand only the small girl in her could remember. Thinking it a dream, she blinked at her clock. It was 4:30. She pulled the covers up and buried her head in the pillow.

Echo moved through the grassy hillside down to the barren beach and the flameless coals of the fire. Aretha followed at a distance, her long white dressing gown cutting through the undulating grass like a white-hot branding iron in pursuit of its mark. "Don't ignore me, damn you!"

Echo turned sharply at the fire pit, and dropped into a flexed position, her scarves moving to folds beneath her knees.

"You chastise yourself, Aretha. The pent up energy you refuse to channel where you know it belongs is imploding."

"What would you know of my pent up energy? Just because I know of you, what you are, why you come to me, us, what gives you any right?"

"This has nothing to do with rights, Aretha. I'm here because you need to give yourself the permission."

"Permission? Permission for what?"

"To remain the woman you've chosen to be. Have you any idea the degree to which you manifest energy for him?"

"Derek."

"Of course, Derek."

"I don't understand. You come in the middle of the night and chastise me for remaining in my place and…"

"Damn it! Give yourself permission, Aretha. He needs you." Echo turned and passed her hands over the dead coals. "Getting cold again." With an eerie transformation, the coals slowly flamed and the warmth seemed to fill Aretha with clarity. Beneath Echo's eyelids, the blue of cobalt seemed to swirl around her pupils, sending Aretha's memory back to some remote galactic memory, some distant telescopic moment from a dark night long ago. The blue disappeared, replaced by green…

"How can that be? Your eyes?"

Echo smiled. "You see what you need to see, Aretha. Just as the Ode atop the hill is to you a glorification of simplicity, to others, a miniature Washington Monument, still others see it as an affront to art."

"Impossible."

"Quite possible. In fact, the Ode was dismissed in Germany and Austria as a waste. In Belgium…a mockery."

Aretha turned toward the house and the obelisk, all but lost in the black of the now moonless night. "Mockery? Mockery of what?"

Echo dropped her head. "Of art."

"What?"

"Before you knew of the work," Echo continued, "Derek had it on display at the World Bank Plaza in Frankfurt. The press attacked him for arrogance—foisting a 'support beam on the art world,' as one critic put it. By the time it arrived back in NY, he had nowhere to go with it. The critics had made their decision."

Aretha shivered and then slowly wrapped her arms around her shoulders. "I need to get back to…"

"Nonsense," said Echo, as she once again passed her hand over the fire, giving charge to even higher flames. "Here, come closer."

Aretha grinned to herself, not believing the experience, but enough of a stargazer to want to believe.

"That's how it should be. You only have to want to believe."

Aretha's grin became even wider. "You're something else."

"So is that," Echo said as she nodded toward the hill again, the Ode now reflecting the flames that seemed to get higher and higher. "He needs what you are, Aretha."

"And what's that?"

Once again, Echo nodded toward the Ode. "Help him mirror beyond even that. That's what he is all about. Reflection…essence…Echosis. The group will learn from him…and indirectly from you. Can you understand that?"

Aretha paused a moment, filling her lungs with the early morning's brine-soaked molecules that she knew all too well was the origin of life. Her face was enveloped with peace and contentment as she savored the moment, then turned back and was met with only the fire. Echo was gone.

Aretha exhaled and walked back toward The Ode, its surface reflecting the flames like a firestorm searching for fuel. Her nightgown pressed against her body as if trying to peel away the layer of resistance that had, only a few moments before, stood defiantly before the—*what*, she thought.

She turned and looked back. The tide moved quickly up the sand like a battlefront preventing any possibility of the next moment turning to doubt for Aretha. It sucked the flames into its wake, disappearing into the darkness of the sea.

The single *screech* of a gull broke the silence as she looked up at the quiet sky and the morning sun began to break the darkness.

From the bedroom window in the distance, Linda stood motionless, holding her pillow close to her.

CHAPTER 37

All, but Samara, had made the decision to join the Echo project.

The winter months saw Derek evolve into even deeper complexity. Using an investment brokered by Sol, massive

219

construction and technology installations busied not only the artists, but the residents of the island, whose menial talents were greatly appreciated in speeding up the work. In taking charge, Derek made sure the group had all they needed in order to *be* and *do* what he had promised them was possible.

The cannery was packed with projects moving forward in unexpected speed. The sense of freedom seemed to expand the artists' ability to work long hours and experience parts of their imagination they had not realized before. Even Simon was busier than he'd ever experienced. Having convinced both Derek and his radio station that he could still broadcast his regular show from the island, along with video broadcasts of interviews and artists-in-progress, he was so stretched for time, that a futon in the small cannery recording booth became his sleeping accommodation on many a night. As inclement weather had stopped any work on the Rock, Derek continued fine-tuning the organization, and designing the Internet video programming of Artists-at-Work. Theo's book was now beginning to take the kind of shape he had dreamed. Everything was progressing as anticipated. In late spring, subscriptions to the Internet site began to come in; Simon's radio show realized substantial increases in listenership; and artists were readying for the summer tourism and sales. All seemed right.

***

Samara checked her watch. The e-mail invitation she had received was tinged with urgency, as well as a flattering "...your talent is of much interest here at OST." Her *inviter*, however, was fifteen minutes late. Biding her time, she nervously tapped on the linen clad table, constantly peering at the entrance. Unbeknownst to her, Samara's lunch date had chosen The Tavern On The Green because it was the kind of place that had just enough noise, enough panache, and enough drama for what he wanted to make happen.

The man in a tasteful champagne silk suit entered and stood in the doorway. Or perhaps it is more accurate to say, he *loitered* in the doorway, giving acknowledging lifts of his chin, an occasional nod and a one-time wink at the lady passing him on the way to the powder room. To stand still and appear to be waiting would have given those who knew him a suggestion that he was ill, perhaps terminally ill, for this GQ image of impeccable grooming and charm had never stood still in public. Some said it was a learned political MO of always working a room. Others dismissed his behavior as the insecurities of power. Still others suggested it was the fear a bullet might find its mark if he remained motionless for more than a moment or two. The maître d' stepped up and exchanged a few words, then ushered him to Samara's table.

220

"Ms. Jennings, I'm Stoppard Denning." The man with premature silver hair graciously shook Samara's hand. "A pleasure, indeed."

"Likewise, Mister Denning."

Stoppard quickly turned to the maître d'. "The usual, Lawrence. Ms. Jennings, will you join me for some wine?"

"Thank you," said Samara.

"And some goose pâté, Lawrence."

"I'll have Roger bring it right away, sir."

The maître d' walked back to his station, nodding to a waiter, Roger, as the meeting began between Samara Jennings, accomplished composer and therapist, and Stoppard Denning, Chairman of OST Media, the most powerful conglomerate of publishing, television and motion picture distribution in the world.

"Your e-mail suggested my little blurb on the Simon radio show was the reason for us getting together, Mister Denning."

"Hardly a 'blurb' my dear. More of a declaration of war."

"Sorry?" said Samara, donning a cautious smile.

Stoppard picked up the menu, "The Halibut is fresh today. A good choice."

Samara nodded, "I'm sure. War, Mister Denning?"

Roger walked up with a rare bottle of Chardonnay, received a gesture from Stoppard, and proceeded to remove the cork.

"Oh, please, call me Stoppard," he said. "You see, war is a catch phrase to mean many things, don't you agree?"

Samara eyed the shrewd man whose presence assumed the vortex of power in the room and continued to attract head turning. She quickly surmised this was going to be his show, unless, "As a word, it can represent a strategy ploy as well," she parried.

"You mean to arouse attention? Very good." He tasted the wine, and nodded for the waiter to continue pouring.

"All the more reason to sit back and sip the nectar of a fine libation. 'Make love not war,' what a period in history! You agree?"

Samara took a sip. "The '60s, yes, in spite of the war."

"Because of the war. It was Vietnam that brought the country back to its rightful place in thinking it had finally protested enough to the government, the people's representatives, to get the troops to close shop and come home."

"A rather simple way of putting it."

Stoppard smiled. "Simple is good. You know that all too well. As a therapist, you've simplified lives…like me."

"How so?"

"My simplifying lives? The media is charged with a duty to do just that. We have an enormous responsibility in gathering data and talent, and making the kinds of decisions in programming and publishing that the people want. It's not enough to just be the world's largest supplier and distributor of entertainment and publishing. To remain as influential as OST is today, I have to bring companies together under one umbrella and eliminate the obstacles inherent in the *Davids* trying to slay the *Goliaths*. Business simplification. Not unlike your ability to neutralize behavior so life can be less complicated, yes?"

Samara smiled. "And if I said no?"

"Oh, I like a perceptive female. You'd be wrong." He smiled back.

Humoring him, she retorted with, "This is definitely your lunch!"

He lifted his glass to toast. "Before we leave, it will be yours."

As he took a sip and placed his glass on the table, his eyes narrowed, and the charm switched gears. "There is a virus starting to spread in Maine, and you have the means of preventing it from becoming cancerous."

"This isn't about an offer for my professional talent, is it?"

"Quite the contrary," he said. "Without your personal talent, we wouldn't be sitting here."

***

It was several hours later, after having finished lunch and a limousine ride back to the OST skyscraper, when Samara was given a tour of the six floors occupied by the executives managing the fifteen companies listed as subsidiaries of OST. Here was the foundation for the corporation's third stock split in two years, an achievement that Stoppard boasted about as the two sat in his office over a "cup-o'-joe," as he so charmingly put it. It was hardly a plain cup of coffee. Served up by a white-aproned maid, the silver coffee container and bone china occupied a particular part of the antique coffee table in the conversation-pit, a few steps down to the lower floor of his lavish office atop the sixty-story building. Stoppard continued to stroke and prime the pump for the long awaited question.

"You're wondering what I'm willing to pay for all this, correct?" he said standing before the wall of windows looking north over Central Park.

"You mean, what does it take to buy me?" said Samara.

"Yes."

"You want me to do something that goes beyond the protocol of a professional and certainly beyond the boundaries of integrity."

"Oh my, Samara, never that far, please. I'm just a businessman anticipating obstacles in the road and wanting to address them as problems, not crises. All you have to do is divert the train before it goes too fast to stop." He turned back to her and waited. "Come now. It was you, after all, that introduced a medical opinion of Derek at lunch, remember?"

Standing in the middle of the room, she remained motionless. "A professional opinion. I'm only a therapist."

Stoppard ignored her qualification. "Regardless of the compensation you're thinking about...I'll throw in an extra bonus, just to show you I'm fair. We'll arrange payment for any hospital in the country, or 'health spa' as they're sometimes referred to in Switzerland. You name it. We'll help you arrange the "incident" to warrant his confinement. I know you would want him well taken care of. Your choice."

Samara stood another moment, then as her eye allowed one tear to converge on her cheek, "He's only a *possible* danger to himself. That's all. Not to others."

"Oh, but he *is* dangerous to others. Such poisoning of minds could irreparably harm Media and its responsibility to the public. He's only been broadcasting for two months and there is uncomfortable writing on the walls." He raised his eyebrows, soliciting a response. None came. "My dear, we are both professionals in our chosen field. You know your work well, as do I. So let me tell you: Eliminate the taste of the masses and you invite selectivity, even elitism. The collective is what's built this country and its numbers are many. The *country* can't have someone trying to take that choice away from them. The *world* can't have it, either, and, my dear...one-way or another, OST *won't* have that. "

Samara wiped the tear away and composed herself. " 'Won't have that.' May I have time to think?"

With a gratuitous smile and an outstretched arm he took her by the shoulder and ushered her to the door. "Of course. Take all the time you need. In the meantime, we'll take good care of you."

As she left, Stoppard remained facing the closed door. With a deep breath, he turned and walked to the fifteen-foot wall of corner windows that overlooked the Hudson. The sense of pride he felt for the accomplishment was short-lived, as the intercom announced, "Mr. Denning?"

"Yes."

"Ms. Haweisi is on the line."

Stoppard turned, "Take a... never mind. Shit. Put her on."

He picked up the phone and coated his voice with his professional charm. "Tanika, how are you?" He brushed some dust from his desk. "Oh, I'm sorry. Nothing serious, I hope." Slowly, his face took on the seriousness normally reserved for his enemies as he said, "How long has he been back?"

***

Samara's mind and heart was twisting out of control as she left the building. Now, walking the short distance from the OST building to the subway station—the black limousine he insisted on leaving at her disposal keeping back a few yards—she could only swallow hard several times to try and relieve her dry throat. *What have I caused with my jealous mouth? Where are the earlier days of counseling him, his simpler days, when only a common neurosis of mother-dominated-insecurity had been his problem? When telling him to break away from the insecurity and just 'do it' had given me such a sense of accomplishment? Had it all come to just this, a veiled threat by a power monger to destroy him? Why had I stayed and listened for so long?*

She waived the driver off and walked down the stairs of the subway as the rush hour began to congest, to abuse, to make her feel more like the ordinary person she often times longed to be—not the complex and seemingly strong professional person she was expected to be. Few knew her as the often-confused person that was really her.

She didn't know why, exactly, but this understanding about herself—a very private feeling of commonality with the working class, the everyday people, as well as people of unusual accomplishment—was a layer of her complexity shared with no one. She looked up and reminded herself that this feeling could always be dealt with better on a simple subway ride. As she continued the descent into the arteries of the city, the past few hours began to feel evil. *Am I being asked to destroy a man because of my love for him?*

She reached the platform crowded with 9-5 workers. Their faces showed the end of the day, and the beginning of the night, where some would tend to families, some to themselves, even some, she thought, to their creativity.

She gazed at her reflection off the windows of a speeding express train as it passed through the station. She didn't like what she saw.

Chapter 38

Derek sat on the deck overlooking the boat harbor, and idly fingered the stem of his wine glass as he took in the sunset. His host, Sheila, moved rapidly from the kitchen to deck, shuttling plates, napkins and utensils for the place settings she had prepared for the two of them.

Her pet parrot, Captain, was perched erect, firing off comments as she rushed about. "Gotta go...gotta go."

"Yeah, I know, Captain. 'Gotta go'. Think you could do a little less flappin' so I don't have to clean up your mess again," she said.

"Gotta go...flappin' flappin' gotta go," squawked Captain from the converted diving cage that housed him.

"You're missing a beauty, Sheila," said Derek as the last rays began to fall below the horizon.

"Yeah. Yeah. Seen one, seen 'em all. Hope you like your meatloaf well done."

"Anyway is fine." He glanced back through the doorway to the kitchen as Sheila lifted the meatloaf from the oven. "You never stop, do you?"

"Never stop...never stop..." screeched Captain.

Sheila shook her head. "Gonna shoot that bird one day. Got no time to stop, Derek." She stepped onto the deck with the meal plates complete with meatloaf, mashed potatoes and peas. "If I had time to stop, I'd learn how to cook something besides meatloaf, but..." She placed the plates down and sat, lifting her wine glass and taking a much-needed gulp. "Had to catch up, you understand. Now..." She raised the glass. "To a summer that's gonna make us rich...oops...sorry...to a summer that's gonna make the island rich and Echo Project famous... sorry..." She took another gulp. "Know how sensitive you are about that."

Derek clinked his glass to hers. "Like I told you earlier, I've got nothing against money, I just don't want to suggest we're *in* this for the money."

"I know. I know," said Sheila as she salt and peppered her plate.

"I know. I know," squawked the parrot.

Sheila bolted from her chair, grabbed a blanket and threw it over the cage. "Give it a rest, Captain." As she sat back down, "There...now...can I get you anything else?"

Derek stared at the disappearing sun. "One of those every night would be nice."

"Every night would just add boredom." She sighed. "Can't tell you how excited I am about this summer. Since your group came here, the town's another thing, you know? Even this early in the season, it's somethin' else. Now I got somethin' to really be Mayor about."

As he took a bite of the meatloaf, "Well, it goes two ways. Now we have something to keep us busy as well. Hey, good meatloaf."

"Can't beat a packaged mix to spice up that frozen burger meat. Taste the difference?"

"Difference?"

"Moose. Moose meat. Still got a freezer full since Arnie bagged that big one last year on the mainland."

Derek took another bite. "Tastes like burger to me."

"Glad you like it. A-1?" She shook the bottle over her plate.

"No thanks. You seasoned it just right."

"Know how to charm a woman, don't ya?" Sheila leaned back and loosened the belt on her jeans. "Don't mind me. Time to relax." As she leaned forward and piled another load on her fork, "So, think you'll have it ready next week? Them ferries are gonna start arriving with the *real* summer vacationers in force."

"Think so. The cannery's all set, except for some vents that still have to be finished for the air conditioner."

"Damn. That's some generator you got workin' your power, you know. How many gallons of oil that sucker take?

Derek grinned. "Well, suffice it to say, New England winter-costs got nothing on me. Wish I had some stock in oil about now. The TV equipment, the up-link to satellite, even just keeping the temperature at seventy-two in that twenty thousand feet of floor space, pushes the generator to the max."

Sheila wiped her mouth and leaned back again. "Well... I'm sure lookin' forward to this. Really... lookin' forward. After that monthly counsel meetin' last week, almost every shop was out in the streets next day coatin' those old shake sidings with a new coat of paint. Haven't been able to get them that ambitious since Nixon scheduled a stop here on his yacht in June of '74... three months before he resigned. He looked like hell, you know."

"Sad what some people do to keep their status quo," said Derek.

"Been there, done that. Hell, before he kinda put us on the map, we were just a way-out-there island for crazy lobster hunters. Now you come along and turn us into a...what do you call it when you run a satellite TV station and all?"

"Satellite TV station and all, I guess," said Derek.

They both laughed.

***

Sunsets were never seen from Tanika Haweisi's Jamaican Café. In fact, the greatest sense of day's end was conveyed by the rickety, rickety, rickety clack of the L tracks as the over-head trains transported their daily rush hour passengers through Long Island City and onto distant parts of the borough.

Inside the café, Tanika listened on the phone and continually wiped her hands on the apron loosely tied to her waist. For an attractive forty-five year old Jamaican native, the urban sounds of New York continued to be an adjustment, as did the continual phone calls for take-out. This call, however, wasn't a take-out. "You've got to straighten up, son," said Tanika. "This has been far too long for you to…I'm not being ignorant. I'm being your mother…that's not true…I've given you all I have…Son? Son?"

She whipped her head to the side and banged her forehead lightly several times into the wall before hanging up. No sooner had she replaced the receiver, than the phone started ringing again. She turned to her cook and said, "You need to take these calls for a bit. I need to get out."

"Hey, mon, I'm just the cook in this place, not the…"

"You're an employee, Tommy. I need a break and you need to watch things a few minutes, okay? Why is it so difficult for you to…oh, never mind. I'll be back in a few minutes." Tanika hung up her apron, as Tommy picked up the phone. "This be the Jamaican. How can I help you?"

Tanika lit a cigarette and stepped to the side of the building where for two summers she had been repairing the small patio that had once been a dingy alley. Brick by brick she had patiently repaired and relived the simpler days of her youth by painting the gay colors and moods of Jamaica into the inlay. She had left the tourist destination twenty-three years earlier, arriving on a much different island with high hopes of a new and exciting life. Even though she stepped off the plane a six-month pregnant, single mother-to-be with only two hundred dollars in her pocket, she had a promise from the father of her unborn that would take care of them.

She glanced around at the few old tables that fulfilled the sign hung prominently inside; *Outdoor Patio Seating. She* reminded herself that the tabletops covered with faded green plastic and the little centerpieces of weathered plastic palm trees needed replacement. Canal Street would provide for the yards of plastic, but she would have to write Dolores, her oldest friend still living in Jamaica, and ask her to forward a box of new souvenir trees. The *Jamaican* just wasn't *The Jamaican* without these little trees. Many a customer had lifted the centerpieces on leaving. Visiting friends at Christmas time, Tanika had seen some become tree ornaments, while others provided dreams of another kind for the customer's small children. She fingered the little palm leaves, allowing memories to flood in.

"You've got to be just about the prettiest girl on this whole island," the dashing sportsman said as he picked up the volleyball that had gone astray. The waitress blushed and smiled back as she gathered up the player's empty beer cans and strolled back across the beach gathering whistles and hoots, as she made her way to the poolside bar. Later that night, the young American again crossed her path as she walked the short distance from the bar to her home, a shack on the beach she shared with four other siblings and her

227

mother. Two nights later, the sophisticated Yale graduate and the West Indian succumbed to each other's charms and slept the night away under the stars, listening to surf and fantasizing futures they dreamed of living.

He went on to fulfill his, but she had been left as a "kept" single mother all these years. As she snuffed out her cigarette and rose from the rickety chair, its plastic upholstery breathed a sigh of pwoooosh, reminding her of her own exhaustion, all the years of struggle, and now the return of her son, a struggle unfulfilled yet again.

"You can take off now," said Tanika as she re-entered the cafe.

Tommy glanced at the wall clock and smiled. "It's only 8:45. You sure?"

"Yeah. You get a jump on that earlier bus. Sorry for the bully tactic before."

"Oh, that's okay, Miss Haweisi. I got a big mouth sometimes."

She patted him on the shoulder as he rushed toward the front door. "You're a good man, Tommy. See you tomorrow."

As the door slammed, sending the overhead tinkle-bell into spasms, Tanika watched the happy cook run toward the bus stop, reminding her she had something to be proud of—when everybody else turned him down, she had given the parolee a job. The mother instinct was still strong, she reminded herself, as she tied the apron back on and started in on the sink of dirty pans.

It was a gentler tinkle of the bell when the front door opened and in stepped Stoppard. "Hello? Stop's here!" He turned back to the limousine driver and waved him on.

Tanika looked in the mirror one last time, tucking a lock of hair behind her ear. "Be right there." She tied a brightly colored kerchief around her head and stepped from the restroom into the café.

Stoppard stood eyeing the ceiling and walls, not paying any attention to her. "You've painted since last I saw you."

"Yeah, walls need some paint every ten or so years."

"Oh, it hasn't been that long...has it?" He looked down at her now. "You look...well."

"It's been eleven years, to be exact. Eleven next Thursday."

"Like your red head band."

"A wrap. It's known as an 'Island wrap,' remember?"

"My, you do like details, don't you? Wrap, band, whatever makes you happy," he said as he took a napkin and brushed off the seat and sat.

"Seat's clean. I wash them every night about this time." She eyed him up and sat at the table next to his. "You...*don't* look so well, Stoppard. Being the King has its drawbacks, I guess."

Stoppard smiled and took from his pocket a blue box from Tiffany's. "Here," he said with studied strategy. "Just a little something." He placed it on the table in front of her.

Tanika looked at the box and chuckled. "You never change. Do I still look like a kept woman to you?"

"No...yes. Please open it. It's practical. Nothing fancy."

She pulled the blue ribbon off and lifted the lid, revealing a platinum crescent shaped clock attached to a like chain of quarter-moon shaped links.

"I know you don't like jewelry, but...well, it will help you keep those chronicled details of yours in order. Do you like it?"

She casually lifted it from the box, held it up and placed it respectfully back in the box. "My Timex still runs fine, but thanks anyway. Might come in handy for rent sometime."

"Now, now. Let's not get off on the wrong foot. I came all the way out here just to see if there was anything I could do."

"Could do? How about being a father?"

The smile disappeared from Stoppard's face momentarily, then another, more calculated smile enveloped the man Tanika knew so well. "We don't talk about that, remember? You get your five thousand every month; this little business is paid off; and you live quite comfortably for a Jamaican immigrant without an education...correct?"

Tanika turned away and wiped the quivering tear from her eye. "He's still depressed...more than ever."

A deep guttural bark from the kitchen broke the awkward silence. Tanika wearily rose. "Titan needs to go find a tree."

A skate boarder swished past, as Titan, a strange looking mixed-breed-smashup of wolfhound and mastiff, remained fixed with his leg lifted to the elm tree.
"Jesus, that hound can piss," said Stoppard, standing at modified parade dress as Tanika held the leash loosely. A few yards away, the Mercedes Limousine idled in wait.

"So that's it?" said Tanika.

"The boy?"

"The boy," she repeated, is twenty-two next Thursday, remember?"

"And he's still acting like a teenager. He needs to grow up."

"I hear fathers help that process."

Stoppard sighed and reached into his breast pocket, retrieving a bank envelope. "Here," he said. "I'm not paying for another 'spa,' as you call them. Christ, four 'treatment' clinics in that gray and icy Switzerland could depress anyone. Here. At least there's enough extra in your monthly deposit to get him his own apartment. This way, you don't have to put up with his nonsense under the same roof."

"He's our son, for Christ's sake, not a stranger from the street."

"He's your son, Tanika. I provide the means because I feel for your plight."

"'Plight!'" Tanika jerked the leash. Titan moved his hundred and twenty pound body up along side her. "That's a new way to put it."

They strode off once again toward the café in the distance. "That's the only way to put it. He isn't mine. He looks nothing like me. You should be thankful."

"You're a bastard, Stoppard. A real bastard."

Stoppard stopped and turned toward her. "Yeah? I'm the guy that has supported you for twenty something years. I'm the provider that's kept you from the poor house."

"And the bastard that refuses to be a real father because he's a coward," she screeched back at him.

Stoppard raised his hand and motioned for the limousine. "The only *real* bastard among us is that son of yours." As he stepped into the car, he shot back one last evidentiary of who he was. "And for the last time... don't call me at the office. You know my cell number." The driver tipped his cap to Tanika as he scurried around the front, jumped in and drove Stoppard away.

Tanika stood for a long time as the car disappeared into the converging old pre-war tenements of this, her neighborhood, her "plight." As she walked off toward the café, she opened the envelope. The deposit slip in her name read eight thousand. A sticky read: *You, and the first and last months rent for an apartment for him.* She folded it back into the envelope and walked. "A one-room for him, if he's lucky." She glanced down at the dog. "He's all heart, Titan. All heart."

***

Stoppard shuffled into Mickey's, the watering hole for him and his "yes" men, as well as the habitual glad-handers looking to score points with the right people. Lining the bar were the usual Jr. Executives—the ones wearing Armanis they couldn't afford, the obligatory dress code of sacrifice necessary to impress the power-brokers-charged-with-monitoring-the-ascent-of-pecking-order-ambitions. Stoppard, having long left such observations to underlings, remained addicted to the idolatry thrown his way each night—an ego *fix* that cost his expense account several thousand in cork popping each month. Tonight was no exception.

He made his way to the balcony floor reserved for VIPs and sat down at his private slab of marble within a glass enclosed separate piece of real estate. It was permanently reserved for him as *private*, not *public* space to accommodate his smoking habit. The waiter immediately acknowledged his presence with a chilled bottle of Dom Perignon and a flame for his Churchill cigar.

"Thank you, Cedric. Would you bring another glass please, and send Elizabeth over?"

"I've not seen her tonight, Mister Denning."

"That's because she's warming up that dark corner of the balcony with her charm and very pricey French perfume." He touched his nose and gestured to the spiral staircase leading to the upper floor. "Like my Churchill, Cedric, a distinctive bouquet such as hers is difficult to avoid."

Cedric smiled and politely acknowledged Stoppard's radar. "Yes, sir, Mister Denning."

As Cedric carried out his assignment, Stoppard scanned the room, nodding occasionally to those he thought worthy of his attention. Engulfing his corner with a hanging moat of cigar smoke, his mind wandered back to the time he occupied bar stool number seven, night after night. He too knew of the "Armani" rite of passage. Many a late hour had been spent at Mickey's nursing one very dry martini with extra olives as he watched and studied those who could make or break his rise to the top. And rise he did, very rapidly. Stoppard learned early that there was nothing like using the threat of scandal to make things happen fast. He fostered and generated "knowledge" of questionable behavior among his co-workers whenever he could, giving rise to easy promotions and power for himself. Generating scandal was what Elizabeth was good at, as well.

"Good evening, Stoppard," came the smoker's voice of Elizabeth, as she leaned down and kissed him on each cheek, a favorite affectation stolen from her favorite screen siren, Sophia Loren. Cedric smiled and closed the glass door behind her.

"My, we are cozy tonight, aren't we?" said Stoppard.

All eyes from the balcony bar were fixed on *her* for the moment. A turquoise Baby Jane silk dress draped her body like a magician's silk sheet, luring her admirers into abracadabra *centerfold* fantasies.

She flashed a 2-carat cocktail ring at him with "Like the new trinket?"

With an arrogant puff of smoke across the refracting glare of her finger, he lifted her hand and pressed it to his lips. "Am I on my way out of your life?"

She laughed as Cedric re-entered, poured her champagne, and left. "It would take a half dozen of these to do that."

"Ouch!" He smiled. "You've learned well. There's always a price for everything, isn't there?" said Stoppard.

"Of course, darling. But you must be willing to pay the price, as you broke up my little balcony party, correct?"

Stoppard puffed another cloud, further enshrouding their corner and leaned in to touch her ring. "How would you like to own the mine where that came from?"

With a conspiratorial grin, Elizabeth allowed her perfect face to risk a wrinkle or two. "Oh, you do know the way to a woman's heart, don't you?"

Stoppard smiled. "You have no heart, my dear. That's why we get along so famously."

From the bar, a young Adonis with too many empty shot glasses in front of him lifted another and shouted a slobbering toast to their corner. "Hey! Whatever he's got, I've got more of, beautiful!" Two very distinguished black suits quickly lifted him from the stool and before Elizabeth could even respond to her admirer, he was gone.

As she turned back to Stoppard, she lifted the thin shoulder strap back into place. "The price I have to pay. This better be good."

Stoppard touched his lips with his index finger. "Quietly stopping a revolution good enough?"

"Revolution? Ooo, you're so sexy when you're serious."

Chapter 39

Playing a foreign journalist wasn't new to Elizabeth. After twelve years of private investigative work, she figured she had used every a.k.a. appropriate for any well deserving beautiful woman. The Italian accent took a bit of brushing up, but within a week, Elizabeth, a.k.a. Valentina Cochesi—music correspondent at large for "Ciao," an Italian magazine whose image was any and all things promoting romance—was ready to become Samara Jennings' best friend. Tailing was a PI's MO, so tail she did.

In the heart of the financial district, Green Dolphin Street was a club mix of jazz, blues, and rock and roll, where musical invention was spawned and gambled with by both the established and the wannabes. Agents, record executives, and producers—they all came to GDS whenever they were ready for the new, the different, the bad and many times, the ugly.

On this spring night that brought the temperatures down to unusual winter levels, Samara was still not feeling herself. So, wrapped in her cashmere trench, she stepped quietly into the club and took a stool at the bar. Not a steady customer, the bartender didn't recognize her, which was as she wanted it. Tonight, she just wanted to listen to music and try to get her focus back. The meeting with Stoppard was two weeks old, but trying to act as if that was the beginning and the end of it was impossible. Oh, he was good, she could admit to herself—flowers, limos, show tickets *given to patients*, etc., but even putting aside the obnoxious assumptive attitude he was famous for, she still couldn't bring herself back to feeling she was in control of herself. He wasn't letting go. That bothered her—bothered her a lot.

"Could I have a glass of Chardonnay, please?" she asked.

The bartender nodded. "House, or you want the list?"

"Not the house. I'll let you choose. Dry, though."

He nodded once again. "Dry it will be, Miss."

As she slid into the stool next to Samara, Valentina smiled and said in a subtle Italian accent, "You can always trust the Deloach."

Samara turned and nodded to the elegant woman in crimson red and dark glasses. "Thank you. That is a good choice."

"In fact," said Valentina, "that sounds just right for me as well. Bartender?"

"Got it," he said grabbing another glass.

Valentina continued, "Who's playing tonight?"

"Hugo, it said on the door," replied Samara. "Lester Max and that guy he found in New Guinea on the drums... Kollader or Kolada, something like that."

Valentina shook her head and smiled, "Max is always finding the catches, isn't he?"

She then turned once again to Samara. "You hear his last session here a couple a months ago?"

"No," said Samara, her eyes starting to scan the house for another stool.

Extending her hand, Valentina headed her off, "Oh, how rude of me. Valentina Cochesi. I work for Ciao in Milano. Are you familiar?"

Samara felt suddenly trapped, so she smiled and shook hands. "No, but seeing we're shoulder to shoulder, why don't you tell me about... 'Ciao'."

Valentina used the bit of sarcasm to her advantage and politely responded. "The magazine is legit, Italia's answer to Gramophone, Billboard, Rhythm, you know. I'm legit too. You legit?"

"Pardon?" said Samara indignantly.

"Sorry, didn't mean it that way. Just, flying around the world covering music leaves one a bit tired of getting hit on all the time, you know?"

"And you think I'm…"

"No. No, I mean it's usually guys, but sometimes, well, anyway…I didn't get your name."

"I didn't say it."

"Oh," nodded Valentina.

Samara took a sip of her wine. "Sam."

"Nice to meet you… Sam? Incognito?

"No. Just shorthand for strangers."

"Ooookay. So…I…I really enjoy coming here. Every time I'm in New York, GDS is the first place I come. At least this is one place where the integrity of music invention is still alive, even in New York. Sadly, the concert halls are banal with stodgy repeats of the old sounds. Few real artists left trying to raise the bar, you know?"

Samara took another sip. "You sound like a die hard."

"Die hard?"

"You write for the magazine?"

"Uh huh. Supposed to find the new, unusual, not-yet-famous type. I'm expected to find the unknown gem and give them some good press. There was this group in London last month that…"

Samara listened and gradually became relaxed with the help of two glasses of Deloach. By the time Max played his second set, Samara found herself tapping her foot and adding a comment here and there to Valentina's copious notes and ravings about Kolada. Valentina was so excited about what she thought was her find of the next Coltrane; she took out her Platinum Express card and ordered a bottle of Dom Perignon. By the second bottle, both ladies were happy and best of *music* chums. Valentina had her "find," and Samara felt liberated, having purged all her closed down feelings about the blocks in her own music. With champagne aplomb, Samara offered, " …and I think I'm finished now."

Valentina leaned forward and wagged her finger. "No, not yet, my little drunk Sam…"

"You're not doing so bad yourself," giggled Samara.

"You share all your gripes about not being able to compose, and, well...who are you, really?"

Samara giggled again. "No…nothing in your magazine, alright?"

Valentina crossed her right breast. "Hope to die."

"It's the left side."

"What?" said Valentina as she wavered.

With a bit of a Gloria Swanson accent, Samara said, "Your heart, darlink."

Crossing her left side, Valentina guffawed, "That too."

"Okay," said Samara, her voice feigning an over-serious tone. "I actually am a disciplined composer of 'fine' music." She allowed a *gottcha* pause, and burst out laughing.

"I'll bet," giggled Valentina back.

Serious again, Samara said, "No, Lincoln Center, Tanglewood, and..."

"Wait...wait a minute. You're shorthand thing...Sam...Samara...I know it...it's...Jennings? Samara Jennings."

Samara lifted her champagne glass into the air and clinked it too hard with Valentina's, sending broken glass everywhere. "Yes... by Jove, I think she's got it." Samara said, continuing to play-act serious. "How would you know about classical gigs anyway?"

"You think just because I write about jazz and R & B I don't listen to death marches?"

"Death Marches?" feigned Samara with a *Gloria Swanson glare*.

Valentina stood up, giggling, while Hugo swept up the glass and wiped down the counter. "Good death marches."

"And I thought you were a friend," proclaimed Samara with an even heavier *Sunset Boulevard"* accent than before.

They both broke out laughing again.

"I am. I am the best friend you have right now, 'cause..."

" 'Cause'?" mumbled Samara.

" 'Cause' I'm going to get us out of here while we can still stand up...to get...out of here. Capish?"

"Capish," said Samara. "But first, *andare in bagno*..." She slid off the stool and made her way back to the ladies room.

"Cash me out, Hugo. Cash me out," grinned Valentina as the sober side of her focused a keen eye of her real 'find' for the night, Samara Jennings, composer, drinking buddy, and ticket to a diamond mine.

***

Expecting her newfound friendship to continue at a break neck speed, Valentina wasn't ready for the rejection that took place over the next few days. Polite enough, Samara had thwarted all attempts at another meeting and was immersed in her composing, making up several weeks of lost time.

She couldn't get Derek off her mind, using his imagined presence to fuel her fire that, thanks to the Valentina experience, was re-ignited. By the end of the week, Samara was once again, worn out. She had managed to fulfill her heavy therapy schedule

235

and complete an entire movement of a new ballet she was determined to finish on schedule.

***

With the weekend approaching, Elizabeth felt frustrated, having made what she considered an excellent first night contact as Valentina, only to be batting zero for the rest of the game. Her call the following morning to Stoppard had been received with congratulations and hints of even more rewards. Now, having rewound the memory tapes of that night several times, she made notes and looked for some way to get Samara's attention again. She wasn't anticipating the answer would come from her employer, but at 4:30 on Friday morning, it was Stoppard's call that broke her short night's sleep.

"Meet me at the Carnegie Deli. I need some coffee," he bellowed over the phone. Elizabeth grabbed the clock. "Jesus, Stoppard, it's four fucking thirty. And the deli isn't open at this hour."

"It is for me. See you in fifteen." Click.

***

"Tina? Tina who?" said Elizabeth.

"A hooker gone straight that Samara helped out of the gutter," said Stoppard as he sipped his coffee and grimaced toward the counter. "Jerry, this coffee is the shits."

Jerry, setting up for the start of a new day, bellowed back, "Sorry, Mister Denning, but… never mind. The fresh should be just about ready. Gimme a minute."

"So?" said Elizabeth.

"Tina's getting the butt-end of the stick. Her boyfriend, some Leonard Paxton, the guy that turned her clean and straight, a long time friend of Samara, has joined the trouble makers in Maine and Tina…they were supposed to be getting married…well, she's pissed to say the least."

"How come you know so much about this group of 'trouble makers' you think are going to cause this *revolt, anarchy*, whatever you called it last week?" said Elizabeth.

"My business to know it all…except what *you* find out for me." He patted her on the cheek.

"And I'm supposed to do what with that little bit of info?"

Jerry stepped up with a new batch of coffee. "Sorry, Mister Denning. This should do the trick." He poured a new cup, then turning, "Miss?" Elizabeth waved him off. "Lousy coffee wakes me up faster. So?" she continued with Stoppard.

"So, another fact finding night on the town. You don't mind that now, do you Elizabeth? This Tina is ready to fall off her monogamist wagon. I'll arrange for some deep pockets to give her a call.

Arrange a meeting, say, at the Carlisle. You can hang with the piano player."

"Piano? God, that's still the Carlisle's trademark even with Bobby gone?"

"A fixture. Stay on point. I'll let you know the hour. Deep pockets will arrive an hour or so late. You will keep her company during the wait."

"And? I don't get it. What's her getting laid got to do with this Maine thing, this Turrel character?"

Stoppard leaned across his coffee and picked up Elizabeth's ring finger. "History is full of men who did unexpected things at unexpected moments." He patted her finger. "You're about to make Derek Turrel one of those men. Pay close attention now."

***

As Elizabeth and Stoppard emerged from the deli, a Times Square street sweeper moved slowly down Broadway, swirling the night's trash and party-people's used liquids into the bowels of his truck.

"Gonna be a beautiful day, Elizabeth. Beautiful."

"Jesus, how do you do it? When the hell do you sleep?"

"During boring status reports and excuse sessions of those who don't keep up." He winked. "Better get some rest now, 'cause it's going to get demanding soon."

"Soon? What do you call this?"

"This last week? A briefing, my dear. A briefing. Have a happy!"

CHAPTER 40

Stoppard wasn't accustomed to his driver pulling to the curb in the middle of Park Ave., but today he calmly picked up the Journal and read while Siebert properly removed his driver's cap and coat, went to the trunk, retrieved some paper towel and Windex and proceeded to wash off the bird droppings from the windshield and hood of the Mercedes. No sooner had he used half the towel roll and was giving the final polish to the windshield, when another round of white wash missiles bombarded the hood, roof and this time, both the front *and* rear window.

Stoppard stopped his reading with, "What the fuck is going on, Siebert? For Christ's sake. Get us the fuck out of here!"

Siebert lunged into the driver's seat, carrying with him the remnants of gull-shrapnel on his shoulder. "Son of a...Sorry sir...Very sorry indeed, but..."

Stoppard interrupted, "No buts. Get us out of here. What the fuck kind of crap those birds eating, anyway?"

Siebert squealed away from the curb, as Stoppard peered up through the whitewashed back window at a group of gulls forming a double-wedge and veering north over the tops of glass towers lining Park Avenue. "Why the hell can't you shit on the big targets? God Damn birds!"

From his outside rear view mirror, Siebert watched the double-wedge formation distance itself. He sighed. Looking now at the inside rear view, he watched Stoppard grumble some more and sink into his seat.

"There ought to be a campaign launched in this city... a major campaign to eradicate the dirty little creatures," grumbled Stoppard to Juan the elevator man while he waited to arrive at his Penthouse office. "Christ, they do nothing but fly around scrounging for crumbs and shitting."

"Si, Mister Stoppard. Si."

The doors opened and Stoppard stepped onto his floor with a Pattonesque swagger, his eyes bringing rows of secretaries front and center, their fingers immediately goose-stepping with the Stoppard standard of work ethic...*every idle moment is a misuse of the stockholders hard-earned money.*

As he entered his office, his assistant, Myra, handed him his messages and mail. Shuffling through the mail before reaching his desk, he stopped short, stared at the greeting card envelope, turned it over, then sat down and stared at it another few moments. He reached for his phone. "Myra, what's this unstamped envelope about? And who opened it and taped it back up?"

Myra paused and said, "It was left with the security guard station downstairs early this morning."

"By whom?" said Stoppard.

"The guard said he was maintaining the monitors when it arrived and didn't notice. He apologized, but he sent it through inspection... you know the usual. Nothing suspicious, so it was resealed and sent up. I'm sorry if..."

"Only a handful of people even know about the "P" nickname. Okay. Thanks." He turned it over again and stared at the initials...*S.P. Denning only*. As he slit the scotch tape open and peeked inside, the threatening image on the card made him think of his postgraduate law professor at Harvard that labeled him with the *Panzer* nickname. "Slow down," Professor Abrams would say, "slow down, Stoppard. You're like a *Panzer*"

238

It wasn't just that the card struck him as odd. For a man who didn't like to be subjected to surprises, unless he created them, it was a bit frightening. There, in his hand, was an embossed gray-on-gray card depicting his building, the OST MEDIA tower, a mass of cracking walls, with its top story—the penthouse floor he occupied—rendered as a floor crumbling over the edge, like strata atop a shifting plate made unstable by an earthquake.

He thought back at that moment when several fellow students grabbed onto the *Panzer* image. It stuck through graduate school, and on through the early years in New York. Wherever he worked as the ambitious lawyer he was, fear of his methods followed. He was known as the man who would pop up when least expected with a surprise that usually meant a head would roll, or an undesirable project would be sent to the project graveyard. This image of fear became iconic, a moniker of his law school personae. But, few people new of the "P" initial. He picked up the phone. "Myra, get me Sanders."

"Sorry, Mister Denning, but he left for his vacation yesterday."

"And today it's ending. Get him."

***

Adam had worked steadily for sixteen months, so even with the jet lag of a twelve-hour time change, the smell of freshly laundered sheets and an orchid laid invitingly on his pillow made it all worth it. His tired eyes relaxed as the Geisha girl pulled back the disposable bedspread of pressed flowers and paper and lifted the Kimono from his shoulders. He smiled with the thought of what was about to happen. He'd paid handsomely for the premium ritual of deep tub bathing, oiling and massage, but as she turned the bedside light out and lit a candle, then slid beneath the covers with him, all he could think was *I earned this*.

His secretary had researched thoroughly and yes, he was satisfied. She had truly followed his orders. "Find me Shangri-La." Kyoto was still as impressive today as in feudal times. Little had changed, excepting the modern utilities that made the five hundred year old Inn as comfortable as some of the more state-of-the-art, high-rise hotels in Tokyo. As he allowed the jet lag to take over, the fragrance of the orchids adorning his room drifted into his subconscious. He took a deep breath and smiled as the hand of his pleasure-host for the night gently stroked the erection he had diligently disciplined his mind to wait for.

RINGGGGGGGG!

Adam rose with a start and groggily lunged for the phone. "What?...Jesus...Didn't I tell the desk to..."

"Adam?" said a familiar voice.

"Myra?"

"Adam, I'm so sorry to disturb you."

"Disturb me? Disturb me? I'm just about to…what's wrong? Something's wrong."

"Yes…well, not sure how wrong, but Stoppard insisted on my reaching you immediately."

"For Christ's sake, I'm on vacation, God damn it!"

The Geisha girl rolled quietly out of bed and retrieved the sake from the small table in the center of the room. She quickly poured the liquid and presented it to him as Myra continued. "You want me to tell him that?"

"Hell no. What does he want?"

"I'll connect you. Sorry Adam"

Adam sipped his sake and smiled sheepishly as he realized he was nothing but an overworked executive with a withered specimen now. She smiled. "No, worry, sir. Finish phone, then we happy again." He pushed his sake cup forward for another shot just as *the* voice came on.

"Sanders, how are you? Nice flight? Treating you good? So…we got a problem," said Stoppard, as if it were only natural to interrupt a key man on his vacation.

"I would have never guessed," sighed Adam.

***

Theo walked his thinking pattern in the sand… left, right, left, each print directly in front of the other. He called it his *sobriety walk of concentration*. In his left hand was a group of notes. His right, a large marking pen poised and ready to blitz his writing with editorial genocide—a self-destructive process, many years in the making.

Gulls swooped and glided past him, curling a pattern of enclosure just in case a tasty morsel might be dropped. In the distance, Sol Berkowitz walked as well, but with his hands jammed in his pockets and his head dropped to his chin. This was not a man using the beach for inspiration.

"Sol!" shouted Theo.

Sol didn't turn.

"Hey, Berkowitz, wake up!"

Sol paused and slowly looked up. He stared for a moment, and then trudged the fifty yards to where Theo had seated himself on a rock. "Scare the fuckin' scales off the fish with that seal call."

Theo smiled. "So what brings you out at 6 AM?"

"Same thing that kept you up all night till 6 AM…worry."

"Worry?" said Theo with a less than smiling tone.

"Yeah. You gonna tell me you're not worried about this thing going belly up before it even gets started?"

240

"Couple of months is hardly enough time to fail don't you think?"

Sol picked up a smooth stone and rolled it over with his fingers. "Takes a few thousand years of influence for this kind of perfection. With us, we think we're gonna change the world in a few months."

"You watching too much TV, Sol?" asked Theo with a chuckle.

"Like it or not...the slimy tube is still the fastest place to see what other people think about things. Even with subscribers we got now, that schmuck King threw us a jab last night on his show saying, 'the little group of artists in Maine was starting to give the networks and studios an itch. An *itch,* he called it."

Theo smiled. "You think after just a couple of months that two hundred sixty thousand subscribers and God knows how many hits the website is getting, isn't worth a little 'itch' to the suits? I think that's great."

Sol threw the rock across the lapping surf. "I didn't make this commitment to provide those assholes some scratching time. I have a Swede and a German banker ready to pluck down enough to take us off the month-to-month satellite rental, and put our *own* up there. We have Walcott at MIT ready to throw in his holographic software to make every computer monitor in the world perform like a 3-D live stage, and King's calling us an 'itch'?"

Theo slashed through some notes with his marker and stood up. "Maybe King needs something bigger and better to get his worn brain to react to your liking."

"You know, Theo, you and Derek have to understand that in the business of getting this concept to the masses, we're making enemies right and left. Enemies tend to stand in your way, you know?"

Theo paused and then spewed another yellow strike across the page. "You knew that when this all started."

"But I didn't think so many would respond so fast. Supporters and attackers all at once. At this pace, and with our own satellite up there opening up their creative juices, the whole globe is going to be 'creating' their own art and entertainment like...Hell, you can forget *everyday streaming video* and *myspace*...dinosaurs, when this gets rolling. Papers, magazines, TV's and movies are going to be choking to death on their own dry heaving. Do you honestly think the corporate world of voyeuristic art and mundane entertainment is going to stand for that?"

Theo idly kicked the sand. "The world of entertainment masquerading as art? No. But that is why we're here and not in New York. What are they going to stop us with, a ferryboat full of angry journalists?"

"It might get done with one man," mumbled Sol.

"Pardon."

Sol sat down on the rock. "If you own all the major corporate power in publishing, movies, TV, and stage, and your earnings of forty billion a year keep your stock holders happy, you find a way to keep the status quo."

"You're thinking of Stoppard?"

"You figure it out." Sol pulled a letter out from his pocket. "This is supposed to be an irate stock holder, but I have my doubts. I think it's Stoppard, and the beginning of something much more destructive than the hue and cry of an investor."

Theo opened the letter and read.

Dear Mister Berkowitz,

It's common knowledge now that you and your cohorts, and that rabble-rouser Turrel, are bent on changing things, but you are hurting people. Don't you understand that? My stock in OST Media is down four more points today. That's a cumulative drop of thirteen points in the last four weeks. As I understand it, you've been doing your dirty work for just over two months now. Sounds successful, and if I weren't a simple man with traditional values and INTEGRITY, plus a life savings in OST, I might be tempted to invest in what you're doing.

Are you aware that OST's latest monthly letter showed book sales down 3%? Not much, you might think, but given it has been gaining on average 2% upwards for the past two years, that's significant. Pulp fiction has been a lifesaver to the publishing world, and you're trying to kill it with encouraging every Tom, Dick and Harry to write their own expressions and throwing it up on the web. What are you, nuts? Record sales down 3%, movie distribution another downward trend with three of their four releases this past six weeks garnering just fourth, eighth, and fifteenth place on the charts. And TV...you and that Turrel are killing the ratings with your pushing of everyone to stay home and create for themselves. We've lost 8% of viewership. Cable subscriber cancellations are ballooning. At this rate, it's going to be another dot-com disaster for stockholders. You're profiting off the naïve fantasies of your audience...and at our expense. There's only a gifted few who can create pop culture for the masses, and the "few," sure as blazes, don't mean you guys.

What the hell, or who the hell, you think you are in robbing the public of their established habits?

Fuck Off before something bad happens to your little island.

You damn betcha this is sincere.

A Grandfather and impassioned protector of my rights.

"Well, as they say, 'you couldn't buy that kind of PR.' Let's publish it," said Theo with a grin.

Sol stood up. "You're out of your mind."

"Hell, I know that."

"Theo, this is serious. This is probably just the beginning."

Theo looked at his notes. All but two sentences were yellowed out. "Or the end."

"What?" said Sol.

Theo folded his papers and stuffed them in his pocket. "Oh, just some of my writing madness letting off steam. You're right. Probably is the beginning. But once our own satellite is up there...Oh, boy!"

"Yeah, well, philanthropic or not, my bankers are going to have second thoughts if they get wind of this kind of angst. They don't give a damn about the money. For them, it's a write-off. It's the *guns in the night* they might have a problem with."

Theo walked toward the water. "C'mon. Let's walk barefoot in the sand. Get our feet wet. Get in touch."

Sol didn't move. "Get stuffed, Theo."

Theo turned back and gestured, "C'mon. It's not as bad as you think, really."

Sol hesitated, then stood up and joined him.

Theo reached down and took off his sneakers. "C'mon. Shoes off."

"My feet are too tender for this sand," Sol bellowed.

"Okay. Up here, then." Theo moved down the beach another fifteen feet where the sand was finer. "There."

Sol shook his head and followed. "Nut case."

The two of them walked the length of the inlet, putting several hundred yards behind them as they swung their arms and gestured several times, with less than admirable finger protrusions at each other, before Sol finally stopped and plopped down in the sand.

"Jesus, don't those legs of yours ever get tired?"

"Spent a lot of time training," said Theo. "So, are we doing better now?"

"You mean do I think I'm a bit more crazy now than a half hour ago? Yes."

"Good," said Theo. "Without the insanity they choose to label us with, we have no identity. Identity is good. Oh, my. Just thought of something..."

Theo whipped out his notes and quickly jotted down an idea, then stuffed them back in his pocket.

Sol starred at him. "You always this focused?"

Theo grinned. "Only when provoked. You're good for that."

"Glad I'm good for something," said Sol.

"Sol, did you *mean* what you said back there…you know, about feeling pissed and whipped sometimes, but still committed?"

Sol leaned back on his hands and gazed out at the sea. "Christ. I don't know. Forty years in the business and you'd think I'd have learned right from wrong."

"Meaning?"

"Meaning, Theo, I can talk to just about anybody I want in the performing arts, excepting those assholes in Hollywood, and they listen and most of the time respond the way I want them to. Right now, if I picked up the phone and called Pierre in Paris, Malcolm in Frankfurt, and, oh, God, if I called Pino in Madrid, they'd all listen, but they'd probably say, 'I love ya, Sol, baby, but let's wait and see if you survive, then we'll revisit each other."

"You really believe that, Sol?"

"What they'd say? Yeah."

"No," said Theo, "I'm talking about survive. That was the operative word, was it not?"

"Do I believe a contract could be issued on me or you or Derek? Yeah. You're damned right. In the hard core business world, people who upset the flow, the status quo…well, bad things sometimes happen."

Theo wasn't expecting that kind of answer and stood perfectly still for a few moments, only the surf breaking the dead silence. He looked down at Sol.

After a moment, Sol looked up. They held their gaze for a few moments. "Stoppard is not a nice person, Theo."

Chapter 41

"Generous," Valentina said with a flourishing swipe of her arm, "He's built his empire on just that. You can say a lot of things about a super achiever like Mister Denning, but without his generosity to the poor, the charities, even the employees he's fired—severance pay like you wouldn't believe—well, you can't fault him with that word. Generosity is his middle name."

Tina spread her hands over her crossed knees, smoothing out the form fitting silk skirt and reached for her champagne glass. The Carlyle Room was abuzz with its usual clientele, and Tina, with her well-schooled ability to work a room, had her eyes wandering unconsciously.

"So," said Tina, "Doing a story for your magazine on Mister Denning must be a challenge."

"Very. Of course, he's rather busy right now, what with all the stock holders screaming for his hide, but I'm sure that will blow over."

Tina grinned. "THE Mister Stoppard Denning is in trouble?"

"Haven't you read the papers, watched TV? Yeah. Seems that crazy project up in New England is doing damage."

"You mean the Echo Project?" said Tina leaning slightly forward.

"Of course. That group of artists up on some island brainwashing the world into believing they're being dealt a bad hand with entertainment and art. They're building a huge subscription base for their 'Art for Art's Sake' radio station, satellite broadcasting of 'art' of the world, *to* the world, and on and on it goes. All a bunch of propaganda to damage Stoppard's company and his stockholders. And, it's spreading. Smaller media conglomerates are starting to suffer as well. You've not heard anything about it?"

"Well, I'm..." said Tina, as a well-dressed middle-aged man casually stepped over to the table and kissed Valentina on both cheeks.

"Valentina. My God. Fancy meeting you here," he said taking her hand, leaning back and gazing at her. "I was supposed to meet someone here...Look at you. As radiant as ever."

Valentina blushed. "You take away the need for makeup with comments like that, Gino." She turned to Tina. "Let me introduce you to my friend, well, actually we just met, but we're becoming friends. This is Tina."

"Tina?" quipped Gino. "The Tina meeting Gino, Tina?"

Tina blushed. "Oh, well..." She laughed. "Yes. The Tina meeting the Gino."

Gino leaned over and lifted her hand to his lips. "My pleasure, Tina. Such a surprise." He turned back to Valentina, "And...you. I've not seen you here before."

"Oh, not often, but once in a while I need my 'cocktail piano' fix," said Valentina.

"Shame about Bobby, but isn't his replacement something else?" said Gino. "Guy plays and plays. So, some drinks." He motioned for the waiter.

"Oh, I..." said Valentina.

"No, I insist," Gino interrupted. "Tina won't mind, will you?"

And thus began a night that, as Tina lapsed further into her old way of being, the hurt of Leonard leaving her for the project became more pronounced. Trying to hide beneath hotel sheets only pushed her jealousy and frustration into deeper claw and bite marks. Gino's passions exploded and as he rolled over, he gasped, "Goddamn, Tina. Goddamn you're somethin' else."

"Yeah, Goddamn Tina," she tearfully whispered in his ear. "I am somethin' else."

***

Early summer was long coming, and all Derek could think was it didn't arrive with a bang—at least not the right kind of bang.

Mayoral duties had always been routine for Sheila. During the week, she had her job at the post office to shore up the routine boredom of managing a sleepy island of summer tourist escapes. But, on this Saturday, she strode up the lily-lined path to the lighthouse carrying a letter in her hand and an expression on her face that was anything but bored.

Derek poured tea from the pot, spilling herbal buds over the top into her cup. "Adds that *organic look,* don't you think?"

"This is serious, damn it," she said.

"Of course. You'll feel better after some tea and…"

"Hell, I will," blurted Sheila. "This letter from Atlantic Ferries says high cost of gasoline is cutting the number of ferry trips by 75%. That could close us down if it were true, Derek."

"What do you mean, '*if* it were true'?"

Sheila sipped and jolted up, crossing the room and opening the window. As she held the cup out into the chilly morning air, she said, "Damn, Derek. That's hot."

"Helps to brew the herbs." Derek scanned the letter on the table.

Sheila continued holding the cup outside, and leaned against the sill. "How can they be claiming high cost of gas when OPEC keeps bringing the barrel cost down, huh? You answer me that."

"Up one quarter, down the next. Seasonal. Anticipation?" Derek replied. "I don't know." He shrugged. "We've been at the whim of OPEC forever, it seems, it'll probably never stop. They've got to do what they've got to do."

"My ass," said Sheila. She checked the tea and stepped back to the table. "I checked two other islands that damn ferry company services, and they haven't received any such letter."

Derek looked at the date. "Only four days old, Sheila. Could be getting theirs any day."

Sheila slapped his hand, then took it and held it gently. "Derek, this is about you."

"Me?"

"You…and probably Theo and the rest of your group. No ferries, no tourism. No tourism, no island. No island, and where's your dream? Adrift!"

Derek picked the letter up again and studied the words. "Well, I hope you're mistaken, but… You know, Sheila, this *isn't* a form letter.

246

'Dear Sir or Madam' or 'Attention Head of Tourism,' would fit, but, 'Dear Sheila'? And why do you think this is directed at my activities?"

Sheila's apprehension rose. "Did you notice the CC?"

Derek glanced at the bottom. "A. Sanders?"

"That's why this letter is really about you. OST's VP Public Relations is Adam Sanders," said Sheila.

"A. Sanders could be anybody," said Derek.

"It's easy to believe when you watch late night TV as much as I do. That A. Sanders, Adam Sanders, is on talk shows a lot, always promoting OST's interests. You don't have time for radio or TV, but my bet is that CC is for Adam Sanders, Stoppard's mouth piece... and not a very pleasant one at that." Sheila leaned closer. "You really want to wait another four days and see if the other islands get theirs?"

***

All Derek could think was the cliché, "When it rains, it pours." Within two days of Sheila's letter, Derek received an envelope with no return address, postmarked New York City. Inside were photos he didn't want to see—Tina in bed with another man, obviously taken from a hidden camera behind a vase of flowers. A simple typed anonymous note said, "Just one man's woman, but there are many more ways to bring the morale down on your island. You might want to reconsider."

All he could think was, *Reconsider what? Abandoning the project? What am I supposed to do with these pictures?*

***

Working out of a "garage" atmosphere wasn't new to Simon Greco. His early radio days had started with tin cans stretched from his parent's garage to his best and most hated friend Bobby's garage across the alley. Besides Maryland Blue Crab, Baltimore was famous for its alleys. Fine homes, poor homes, all had their alleys— a kid's paradise. Simon had spent nights from seven years on with a small radio strapped to his bedpost and an ear peace hidden in his pillow until he discovered the *two-way* fun of a tin can and wire. "This is more than cool, Bobby, this is *really* cool," he used to say over and over in the early days of his *tin-can interviews,* as he called them. From tin-can interviews with made up kid celebs, to radio mikes with real celebs, and now, digital with ordinary people. Simon had spent forty years making it to the top-rated late night radio show, but still he chose to call his show, LATE NIGHT IN THE GARAGE WITH SIMON GRECO. Now, a long way from Baltimore, Simon sat before his microphone and sky-cam video camera in a corner of the cannery warehouse on Gray Cliff and sighed. "I'm waiting Charlie."

"Charles," corrected the call-in voice. "Charles."

"Sorry, Charles, but you did introduce yourself as Charlie."

"That was before I got serious," the voice boomed through the headphones.

"Of course. We're serious now, aren't we?"

"Why do you radio guys have to be such wise asses?"

"Oh, c'mon, Charles, you're the one with the identity crisis."

"Fuck Off, Simon. *You* guys are the ones trying to get some kind of handle on what *you're* all about. Ain't got nothin' to do with us. Talk about identity crisis! You love to just try and make your listeners squirm...make them think they're the ones with the problem."

Simon re-crossed his legs, "Charles, I liked it better when you let me call you Charlie..."

"It's Charles, God damn it!"

"Charles, you're listening because something here in the Garage sparks that small lump of mass lodged between the lobes of your ears. You're so damn set on being important, you can't see the synapse war going on between your *beep* ing ears. You said you only *listen* at night, and you bitch and moan, but tomorrow morning, do yourself a favor and turn on the TV or your computer monitor. I know...I know...our tube broadcasts ask you to interact, but you can still sit there with your Bong, or your six or twelve pack, or whatever it is that makes you so *beep* ing obnoxious, and you can sit on the vicarious perch OST and the rest of the main stream media ask you to nail yourself to, and you can put on a mask or hood over your freakin' head, or, Charles, or...you dumb *beep*, you can believe you're as creative as you allow yourself to be, and you too can have a *beep* ing ball looking at a Pollock and maybe grab some paint and express *yourself*, or you can word cluster your ass off with Miriam Stanton when she splits the screen and asks for you to focus your web cam and talk with her and create at least that ONE great poem we've all got, or, Charles...Charles...you still with us?"

"You're such an asshole," groaned Charles.

"Good, you're still looking in the mirror. Charles, you can do any of the above, or you can even pick up the phone and rant with the artists...ask the impossible questions to your *beep* ing heart's content. Ask any of the artists up here what the *beep* they're doing and why you should watch and experience some real creation, and heaven forbid, get involved and be creative yourself...yeah..." Simon leaned back in his chair and stared at the ceiling with its glass panes open to the star clustered sky. "You can do that or switch me off now and do whatever you do at 2:30 in the morning to get off, or...if this is a planted call Mr. Denning put you up to, well...pass on the good vibes to him as well."

"CLICK" echoed into Simon's earpiece. He leaned forward and pressed another toggle and brought in…"Mary…from Toledo. Are we creative or scared?"

"My God, Simon, that creep was so bad. You really shouldn't waste your time with that kind, you know? You've got so many of us that *get it*."

Simon sprang forward in his chair. "Good to hear, Mary." He moved the joy stick that maneuvered the camera that scanned the cannery continuously, spotting the middle-of-night creators working, digitally recording their efforts onto DVD disks for the next day's "Extended Experience" as the subordinate channel was known by— the place where devotees of *Echo Life*, as the network was called, could remain connected for as long as they wished, 24/7, to get whatever they wanted to revue. "Tell me, is your monitor on?"

"Of course, Mister Greco. It's never off. My husband even has a set of headphones he puts on at night to sleep by. You and Derek, and he especially likes the replays of Wollzak's original soliloquies, and Berkowitz and his art of…" she whispered "'Screwing the Broadway Establishment' lectures. So…where are you taking us now?"

Simon stopped the remote scan and zoomed in on Lanagra perched atop his thirty-foot scaffold, detailing the roots of grass that made up the uppermost part of his latest exploration, LIFE, WORM STYLE. Trailing down the yards of canvas were the worms that inhabited the soil of brown, cobalt blue, and gold—an ethereal perception of the underworld, the world void of sun, the space where only imagination could create visions of light and color.

"You know Lanagra's work, Mary?"

"I'm…well, I'm embarrassed to say it, but…I think…I just don't have the experience to…well, you know…?"

Simon leaned into the microphone and directed the remote camera to Lanagra's hand. "I understand. There are some in the art world that love to intimidate and alienate, but that's not what we're about. Check that out. Lanagra's world is some place most of us avoid going to… underneath. You spend some time with his work, you find…and, Oh, Mary, he's on tomorrow with, well, you won't believe where he'll take you, but…you'll find layers way down in your own world that you really can appreciate. God, look at…I don't know where he's at right now, but…" Simon zoomed in even closer. "…makes you think twice about pulling them out of the ground for a fishing trip, doesn't it?"

On the screen, Lanagra's brush touched in the eyes of the brown creatures, each with his trademark…the ever so subtle blue teardrop.

"It almost makes you feel like you shouldn't be watching, Mister Greco," said Mary.

"That's been the trouble for so long. We not only couldn't watch the making of the creation, but most of us never had the opportunity to even see the finished piece. *Echo Life* is about that... is only about that. The process. Their process. Your process. The finished process. Enjoy, Mary."

Simon looked at the clock. "Time for some recognition of those that make this possible. *Echo Life*'s IN THE GARAGE WITH SIMON GRECO will be back in just a few moments."

He swiveled in his chair and leaned his head back, once again taking in the density of the star-filled sky through the ceiling's glass. Over the speaker on his desk came, "Simon, the *usual*?"

Simon smiled, his eyes reflecting the upward sparkle of distant galaxies. "What would Gray Cliff do without you, Sally?"

"It would have one less temperament to deal with. Hot and challenging. Coming right up. You're really on, tonight, you know?"

"Yeah...feel it. Wish I knew why," muttered Simon. "Give me an extra slug, okay?"

A faint kiss could be heard over the speaker. "Of course."

Derek, having spent the past couple of hours walking the many paths around the island alone, now walked past the cannery. He adjusted the earpiece to his MP3 and continued down the path toward the lighthouse as *Echo Life* commercials continued, each providing information on several museums featuring works of *Echo Life's* group of artists. As he reached the base of the long path up to the lighthouse, the commercials broke and Simon returned.

"We're back," said Simon. "I want to ask a simple question, if I might. I know, *simple* and me don't seem to go together, but indulge. Those of you with Internet, give me an e-mail answer and those of you without, our 800 number will record your answer. It's simple enough. Do you think media is a major malady of our society right now? Just give me your answer with a simple yes or no, but first, let me try to give you some thoughts to contemplate. You're listening to this broadcast, or watching it on your web screen, because all the other choices to occupy your mind tonight were less important than tuning in *Echo Life*, right? That's because the malady, or at least one of the major contributors, if not the primary, is the *ubiquitous passive* media. TV or movies, or, and I hate to say this, the theatre, the *stage* for those of you with that kind of access, even books and museums are experiencing the slippery slope. Not that it's all a waste, but let's face it people, how many of you can remember tomorrow morning, with any modicum of detail, what you experienced tonight through any of those mediums?

"Of course there are exceptions, don't think me unreasonable. I like to escape too…once in awhile. But if escape is the order of the day…if starting off in the morning you find yourself counting the minutes to the next coffee break; the lunch break; the afternoon coffee break, well then, you need to take a close look at what you're doing with your time, especially if the next break is the five to seven cocktail hour, followed by another anesthetizing exercise, the evening meal, followed by more escape into commercial TV, the multiplex movie house, or the Great White Way in your town. And yes, that latest pulp fiction bestseller. For some of you, the day might be one big escape, yes? *Echo Life* doesn't believe it has to be that way. In fact, we believe your life should be one big enjoyable battle to *overcome* escape."

Simon worked the remote sky-cam around the cannery until he picked up Nathan Wollzak crumpled in a corner of his work area atop a much used beanbag sofa. "Now, you see, that's exhaustion I'd bet, not a drunken' stupor, or a…Mary, he's not drunk is he?" He chuckled.

A click from the modest control booth brought Mary's voice, "Hardly. He finished his work. I've got it on disk."

"I hoped you'd say that. Put it on."

"Simon, I've not had a chance to revue or edit or anything, you know."

"That's understood. Thank you. I'm sure, Nathan was okay with it or he wouldn't have turned it in."

Simon turned back to the broadcast microphone. "So, now, we're going to broadcast some of Nathan's last, oh, hell, I don't know, maybe nine or ten hours of work, a play, performance art… he calls his *time* a lot of names. So, let's see if it sounds and looks like he's escaping. Now, I've not seen this, so we'll be experiencing it together… a sort of eavesdropping on the creative diet of one Nathan Wollzak. As usual, those of you just listening, enjoy your imagination. Those watching, you get a double helping of that imagine food, his and yours."

Simon nodded toward the booth, and Mary pushed in the DVD.

"Here we go," announced Nathan as the familiar piano music-bumper reached across the *Echo Life* broadcast…a reach that now exceeded eight million a night. "So, how many of us are there…really *there*?" said the savvy and natural urban street voice of Nathan. "Enjoy. Be stimulated and find out." He leaned back, pulled the mike to him and whispered his trademark phrase, "It's time to soar."

As was usual each night, there were the new listeners and watchers who learned that *"There,"* was that place in everyone where a creative voice *hangs out* and longs to express itself. Nathan spoke of the global malaise, as he saw it, through a group of ethnically varied characters. Through a series of tableaus, he played all the characters, speaking their frustrations as if sitting on fold-up chairs in a surrealistic group therapy circle—the green-screened background suggesting they were on a tiny island of sand, surrounded by the surf.

At the broadcast's conclusion, it took little time for the call-in lights to start flashing.
   "…and that is only a small portion of what we miss," said Simon. "You can't know your neighbors, your community, without spending time with them. You might think that CNN or Fox News is doing it for you, or God help us, one of OST's propaganda machines that invade our living rooms all day long with one *escape* after another. I said it before, and here again…the real world is one big abstraction that cries to be met head on…to be concretized and made workable for each of us. You have to go outside your viewing and listening habits for that. You too can go where Nathan went. Pull out your video cameras, sit down and tell us your frustrations and appreciations, and…your imagined answers to happiness and fulfillment. After all, as Derek has said many times on this network, '*so-called* therapy doesn't have to be invasive and painful. Expression and imagination is what cures, not a set of behavioral rules or another person's need to control us.'
   "The private corridors and passageways of your imagination are what make up your free pass to life, people. That's Life spelled with a capitol L. Then, once you're out there, use whatever works for you, but take it in, record it, assimilate it, and use it. That's all I do, Derek and the rest of us here at Gray Cliff. Be creative with what you expose yourself to. You don't' have to be an actor like Nathan, or a host like me to justify that time to observe and store impressions. Just keep in mind what Frederick Franck proffered: *"An artist has an obligation to question the conditions that rule all our lives—and to cause his audience to do the same."*
   So, here's a short clip of an interview I did with Nathan. Listen carefully."
   Simon took another sip of tea as the interview was rolled in. The video showed Nathan sitting cross-legged on a coffee table, talking directly to the camera. "I bring these memories and experiences to the stage to hopefully stimulate *you* out there, and all *your* needs to express yourself, but primarily, I do it for myself. 'Cause, if *I* don't do

it, how can I expect you to believe it's important? I think once you try it, though, you too will find the same kind of joy as I do in studying the behavior out there and interacting with it. Role-play to your heart's content. Just don't hide behind the screens in your living rooms that promote the mass *dumbing down* of your creative senses. You weren't created to be passive. Remember that."

For the next hour, Simon exchanged with call-in viewers and listeners, and asked them to go to the Blogging site to exchange their impressions, thoughts; anything they thought represented a change in their perspective on being creative. "Let the little boy or girl inside you out once more."

Chapter 42

It was just another night of *Echo Life*, but for Stoppard high above Manhattan, ensconced in a comfortable easy chair of his penthouse, it had been anything but "just another night. The gray clouds of cigar smoke rose slower than usual, as if intimidated by the weight of the man's seething release of hatred. As it drifted to his right toward the windows overlooking Central Park, its hovering swirls reluctantly dissipated into the late-night skyline.

Directly in front of him, the ten-foot screen continued to bring the *Echo Life* broadcast images and words of Simon Greco. He grabbed his phone and punched in the number, bringing little interruption to the persuasive *Call-to-Arms* that continued on screen. He glanced down at his vid-com screen and saw it come alive with a bedside light clicking on, and the illumination of a very tired and drunk Adam Sanders.

As Sanders picked up his cell phone, Stoppard grumbled, "What the hell you doing drunk?"

"It's Friday for Christ's sake."

Stoppard looked at his watch. "No, it's Saturday and you're due in the office in four point three hours."

Adam leaned on one elbow, rubbed his eyes, held the cell phone's camera lens at arms length and said, "Mister Denning, I am your humble servant. Have been, even on vacation, and will be for God knows how long, but right now…according to you, I've got four point three hours left before I have to kiss your ass. So until then, I'm…" CLICK. Adams screen went black.

"That's my guy," mumbled Stoppard confidently as he took his gaze back to the wall screen. Smiling, he sent another plume of smoke to cloud the close-up of Simon's face. *Don't know who I hate more Simon—you or that little prick, Derek.*

Early morning sunlight cascaded across Stoppard's face. "You little shit," he said as he reared back on his executive chair of Kangaroo skin, and folded his fingers into the pointed steeple, his favorite childhood finger game.

Adam shifted his tired body from side to side in the plush arm chair and took another gulp of coffee. "Why?"

"*Because* you were sleeping while those assholes in Maine were increasing their subscription base by God knows how many, that's why."

"Oh, come on, Stoppard. I recorded the program. Caught most of it shaving and driving in here. David is hardly slaying Goliath up there."

"I don't think you realize what's happening *here*, Adam. These people are *life* evangelists. They've got a grass roots base and it's moving like primordial ooze. Last month, three and a quarter million subscribers and eight million listeners. This month...do you even know what that number is?"

"Haven't checked today's update yet," said Adam.

"Adam, get with the fucking program, pal. If I can get the number from a low-life secretary, you should have it tattooed on your fucking dick, or at worst, that manicured hand you grip it with. It's you job, no mine, to announce any and all details that might but me into orbit over this island shit!"

"You mean like now?"

"Yes, like now."

Adam rose.

"No, not now. Sit your ass down."

He sat.

"They upped their satellite time as well. Broadcasting 24/7 now and yes, they did increase the numbers this month...by another quarter million. That's three and a half million, total. At this rate, they're going to have our viewers so fucking *challenged* they'll begin to know the difference between art and shit."

"Meaning," quipped Adam, "Shit might lose?"

"Yes, Adam, 'shit,' the stuff that puts you in silk suits might dwindle to nothing but dehydrated fertilizer for the inner-city idiots that can't afford our cable, or can't read our paper-backs, or won't spend twelve bucks for a movie. Yes, that kind of shit might lose and reduce our audience to watching our free network plan. Do you remember five years ago we thought it was a good PR move to give something away in the free network plan...to lure paying subscribers? You remember that?"

"That's bad," chimed in Adam.

"What? Bad because you might get reduced to jean suits or bad because the company you work for could lose everything?"

Adam cleared his throat, took one last gulp of his coffee and said, "You're serious, aren't you?"

"You notice I haven't offered you one of my Churchills."

***

This wasn't the kind of morning I enjoyed holding onto ropes. The wind, 15 knots. The mist and fog, suffocating. Visibility, zero. Not your usual early June sunrise.

"You okay up there?" came the bullhorn voice of Jamie from far below in the boat.

I tugged on the rope, giving Jamie a sigh of relief. "Hey," he said, "Give me a break once in a while and not make me yell up at you. Doesn't take much to yank it."

"Sorry," I yelled back down, as he yanked the rope again.

It had been seven long months since I'd had my hands on the fixed ropes. Winter had brought a sudden stop. With spring lasting longer than usual, this unusually cold morning became a sudden unexpected awakening for Jamie, and an unwelcoming first day back on the rock.

My fingers ached and my grip was weak. I should have worked the handball more these past months. By the time I reached the ledge, I was exhausted. Looking back over the edge, the fog was still socked in. "Jamie!" I shouted. "You hear me okay?"

"Yeah! You on top?"

"Sure as hell hope so," I laughed. "Yeah, I'm here. You ready to send that God awful generator up to me?"

Jamie checked the straps one more time and bellowed back up, "Yeah. That winch still solid"

"Yeah. No problem"

"Send the rope on down."

I took the extended coil from the storage box I'd placed back in the overhang for the winter and checked it out for any signs of deterioration. I knew nothing obvious could happen to it up here, but old climbing habits were hard to change. The Matterhorn had taught me that—long ago. Save for the spider that quizzically gazed at me from the inner coil—its eyes seemingly larger than expected—I was satisfied that nothing had impacted the rope. I looped it over the winch, securely anchored in the rock, and shouted down, "Coming at you!" The sound of my voice was swallowed into the dense fog like the drop of an anchor into the deep idle waters. It was the sound of fear. *Why was I thinking this way, at this time, this place? I hadn't any reason to feel insecure—not on the Rock.*

I looked once again at the spider, gently brushed it away and heaved the rope over the edge. Its multi-colored webbing reminded me of Echo and her colorful presence. I longed to speak to her, but the long winter away from the cliff, and holding the fragile infrastructure of the group together, had kept me distanced. I couldn't help wonder at that moment if perhaps I was without need for her—as Theo defined her—and only with a desire to revisit, just for old time's sake. I was, after all, well into the sculpture and didn't feel I could ever forget her face, or her impact on me. *Was I now without need for a muse?*

"So, why would you think your need is gone?"

The sound of her voice pummeled me like a sudden hailstorm. *Okay,* I thought. *I want to hear it. That's why I have heard it. But it's not there...the voice. It's just the wind and my...* I whirled around. She sat on the rock where only moments before I had flicked the spider. Coiled around her neck and flowing skyward with the updrafts was a new and brighter array of May Pole invitations.

"Like your new...colors," I cautiously eked out.

She smiled and reached upward. With a slight twist of her wrist, the ribbons froze in space like a fragmented rainbow. "Too many colors can get in the way, can't they?"

"Hey, Derek! A little help would be appreciated!" bellowed Jamie over the bullhorn.

I jumped to the edge. "I'm ready. Sorry!" I yelled back. "I was checking a couple of things."

"Well, pay attention! Winds are picking up. Last thing you need is a generator slamming into the rocks."

"Gotcha. We're okay," I assured him.

"Are we?" came the calm voice behind him.

"Yeah," I answered, as I adjusted the winch, allowing another six inches away from the rock face for clearance.

"I'm talking about something else, Derek," said Echo. "Are *we* okay?"

I cinched the rope and turned around. "Sorry...you were saying?"

I looked left and right. She was gone. "Echo!" I called out.

***

"Why?" Derek said incredulously once again. "Why? Why the first time I'm back on the rock in months she visits me just long enough to ask if 'we're okay'?" C'mon, you're the guy with the answers."

Theo raised his finger. "No. You said she *asked* if everything was okay. That's what you said."

256

"Yeah, you're right. She did ask if 'we're okay,' meaning us, the island. But, why would she ask and then leave?"

Theo turned over his notebook and put down his pen. Standing up, he stretched and stepped toward the window where the fog showed heavy across the bay. "Derek, if there's one thing I've learned over the millennia…"

"Oh, c'mon. You're not that…"

"OLD? Oh yes I am. And the one thing… just when you think things are going well, your creative juices are churning, the troubles in front of you are *other* people's… they turn out to be *yours* as well."

"I don't get you sometimes, Theo."

"Well, we've had a relatively good winter. Now, with the summer knocking on our door, subscriptions are up, transmissions are maintenance free, it seems, and everyone has had a productive few months. Everything is as we planned, except for that *pesky* thing."

"Pesky?" Derek queried.

Theo turned back from the window. "Don't lull yourself into thinking *he's* going away. We very well might not be 'okay.' Just a matter of time before he tries to thump us harder with either the gas thing or some far more serious morale *ripper* than Tina's night out. By the way, you ever tell Leonard?"

"Hell, no."

"Think you should have?"

"Hell no."

"I guess, 'hell no,' is the answer to those questions."

"So? What's the Tina thing got to do with Echo?"

Theo continued staring out the window at the fog. "You're aware, but maybe not enough. I don't think Echo is without better things to do than cater to your cold-assed-rock."

"You think she resents coming here?"

Theo smiled. "Jesus, Derek. How long is it going to take you to get it? She doesn't come to you, my friend. You go to her."

Derek paused a moment, and shook his head. "Sometimes I think I'm going mad." He glanced down and found himself thinking only about Theo's book. He fingered the note pages. "How's it going?"

Theo sat down. His eyes fixed on Derek's. "It's where it should be. It's where it belongs, for now. And Derek, Echo's is always going to be where she belongs too. That's what Echo's about."

***

The windshield blades tried, but they too were impotent in washing away the mind reflections of Echo cascading through the June rain onto the rental Toyota. I was sure my head would clear up after Theo's relentless exhausting of my "misunderstandings" of

Echo. But, even after convincing himself that I was finally facing my reluctance to accept Echo as "…a Derek-created muse of imagination," I was actually no closer to understanding my obsession than before. Well, maybe a bit closer. At least I didn't go running back to the rock right away. No. Instead, I was driving from the ferry dock to the airport, a short distance that would allow a fifty-minute flight to take me back in a familiar direction.

Chapter 43

The placid Cape Cod beach was a welcome contrast to the rocky shoreline of Gray Cliff and the rains that I'd left behind. Having parked the rental car down the beach, I enjoyed the warm sand. With winter's icy cover gone, left behind were fresh dunes from spring blown winds. The kernels of soothing sand, massaged my toes, calmed me as I prepared for what I anticipated were awkward moments ahead. *Strange,* I thought… *the erosion of rock is so easy to understand. Yet the friction of time on our minds is so elusive, so indeterminate.*

I looked down the beach toward Aretha's house. I was a man now committed to an imagined dream…perhaps a chimerical longing. They were different. I knew that. I didn't want to separate the dream from the fantasy, but I knew they were not of the same cloth. My simple quest to make accessible a world exposure to the arts, and in turn arouse the creative spirit in all was more daunting than I imagined. The venture had brought me to a place with myself I didn't understand. *Were the exalted expectations in jeopardy? Why was I not dealing better with the complexities of my nemesis the commercial world? Perhaps I was just depression. That's probably what Samara would suggest. And then again, maybe I relying too much on Echo?*

Then there was Theo. We had left each other after three hours of challenging questions and few answers. His last words hung heavy on my mind, "Are you sure you want to go all the way with *Echo Life*… with this Echosis?"

I was uncomfortable with his suggestion of uncertainty. I was challenging the very convictions I'd so vehemently professed to artist after artist. It seemed I was unsure of the right and wrong of it all. I tried to walk-down my anxieties before dumping on Aretha who felt so much like a sage to me now.

"My God," Aretha blurted out as she lifted herself from the kneeling position, a weeding fork in one hand, a trowel in the other. "What a surprise."

"It's been awhile," I clumsily said.

"Yes," she replied as she laid the tools down and began slipping off her gardening gloves, never releasing me from the grip of her eyes. "What brings you…? My goodness. Please. I'm due for a cup or glass of… something. Care to join me?"

The moments between the slow motion walk into the house, and the first sting of the Irish whiskey trickling over my wind-chapped lips, allowed my mind to organize, or so I thought. "I didn't know if you would be here."

"And if I hadn't? Would you have at least left a note? Or would you have turned around and retreated to your rock again?"

"You're angry I'm here."

"No," she uttered with little sympathy.

As I sipped the whiskey, I could only think she pitied my laborious period, back when everything seems out of reach, when nothing seemed possible, when my actions seemed on occasion, *not* my actions. But I had gotten through them. I had created in spite of it all. Yesterday's time on the rock, the ribbons, the voice, the trip back to the lighthouse, the words and sighs of Theo…they all had compelled this visit. I had allowed them all to sink in, to remind me once again that I was just a man trying to create purpose, and yet, I finally blurted it out. "Sometimes, I think they expect too much."

"They?" she said.

"The artists, the town folk, the mayor…"

"Oh. That. And Denning? What is *he* expecting from you?"

"My *head*, if one believes the strange happenings of late."

She picked up a stack of periodicals and newspapers from the coffee table, and from the middle, pulled a copy of The Inside Track. As she quickly thumbed through it, she said, "Read it?"

"I have on occasion."

"Once in a while I read something that…" She slid the magazine across the table and turned it. "… Here. Kaufmann thinks he might resign."

"Kaufmann… the film critic?"

She nodded. "Lee, the TV eye for the mag got in on it as well. Second page. Seems he's got some flies-on-the-wall of his own. Denning's been keeping some late hours in delis, coffee houses…middle of the night kinds of meetings…anyway, it's all there."

I quickly scanned the pages and got the gist of the article as she stood and poured herself another whiskey. "You?"

"No...I'm..." My eyes locked onto a closing paragraph alluding to "...a purported nefarious lady about town, keeping company with a 'lady of the night' about town." The article closed with *"Echo Life may be bringing the average man and woman to their feet in praise, but it is pushing one Stoppard Denning to his knees. Resignation may be what the stockholders want, but what does the unstoppable Mister Denning really want? Perhaps the two ladies know?"*

"What's this you've underlined?"

"Oh, a reminder I needed. Making a phone call or two was the least I could do to help."

"Help?"

"You."

"I don't understand."

She took another of her elegant sips of whiskey and reached across, patting my hand and smiling. "I'd hoped you'd get in touch so I could tell you that you've reason to be extra cautious."

"And?" She wasn't usually this oblique.

"Phone calls. I've made several. It helps to stay in touch with your friends, you know."

I was getting it.

She patted my hand again. "Mister Denning has forgotten perhaps that the city doesn't sleep any more than him...especially his deli of choice. We all go there. We all know the boys behind the counter there. They all know us."

"And?"

"And...especially Jerry. It wasn't common knowledge, but certain circles of inside information knew him as a.k.a. Wallfly. Every rag paper's biggest silent reporter. Denning made quite an impression on him a few weeks ago with a middle of the night meeting with a viperous—' nefarious,' as Lee put it in The Inside Track—lady named Valentina. Seems conspiracies run in strange circles."

I found myself sipping away three more drinks as Aretha played Deep Throat, allowing just enough information without causing me to go berserk. She was a surprise, as usual. She not only knew Jerry's *Wallfly* alias, but knew who else to call, who to question, and who to trust.

"And finally, Derek, there's my broker, Robert. Simple man, actually, except when his clients are unhappy. Fortunately, I'm not one of them, but those whose portfolio contain large amounts of OST stock, well, that's another matter."

I finally had to rise and deal with the rage going on inside. "Aretha, I didn't advise anyone to play with glamour stocks. I didn't coerce anyone into putting their life savings with that creep."

"But, nevertheless, those people exist, and as Robert quietly whispered to me, 'They're pissed.'"

"I already knew that," I blurted out.

"So..." she said, obviously quieted by my outburst, "that's all I know. Anything else I can help you with?"

I smiled. She knew me. She knew me well. "Sorry for the outburst. Sometimes...Look, you know I didn't come here to hear fact sheets on the entertainment economy."

"Yes. That would have been a wasted trip. But, now that the prelims are over, how do you expect me to contribute to this visit? Dinner? I have some wonderful squab ready for the oven."

I looked out toward the ocean and watched the domino effect of the cappers. "Do I lean into the collapse, or let it go?"

"Collapse? You're hardly there, yet. But, conversely, you've never been one to 'lean,' Derek. You either fight, or you hide. That *is* your MO, unless of course..."

I turned back to her, but she was off to the kitchen, muttering, "That squab would be perfect. I received a rare bottle of Pinot Noir as well from..."

"'Unless of course' what?" I said as I swirled the air of my empty glass. "I hate it when you bait me."

"You love it, Derek. Come on. Your mind shuts down when the air is full of facts and gossip. You live for the 'what ifs' in the world."

"So..."

She opened the fridge, took out the squab and began her ritual of preparing a meal as if it were her last. "So, what if you bought OST?"

I had to look into my glass and shake my head. "I know what I've been drinking. What the hell you sipping?"

"Even the threat would send shivers through Wall Street," she laughed.

"Yeah...that is kind of funny," and I started laughing as well.

"But," she started giggling now as she gathered her spices and prepared the roasting pan, "relatively easy to do."

I pulled up the reins of laughter and pushed my glass toward the whiskey. "If you're going to continue with this English humor, I'm going to have another one." As I poured, she buttered the squab, sprinkled the perfect combination of flavors, and slid the pan in the oven. I took a sip and gave her the questioning look she'd been waiting for, I suppose.

"Still don't get it? Look, Derek, it's no harder for a financial man to consider the take over of a company than for you to entertain the attack of a rock. How is face coming, by the way?"

"Fine. Just fine. A *takeover*. I'm not a financial man and unless you've got a string of insanely rich investors lined up to buy my work, I don't have the means of a Stoppard Denning buy out, either."

"Of course not," she said, now turning her attention to the bottle of Pinot Noir. "Paul Hobbs, 2002. My friend said it was Napa Valley's finest. Smoky black fruits and Acacia flowers... his description certainly sets it up, yes? Oh, and he used the phrase, 'hedonistic and intellectually satisfying,' just what we need about now." She took out her wine bucket and placed the bottle on the tabletop. "Don't forget to remind me, twenty minutes before we take the squab out...into the fridge for a lightly chilled cellar temperature." She turned and faced me. "What if I could arrange the purchase, well, at least a believable bid to purchase? Something to distract Stoppard, and to appease—for the moment—this gloom and doom consideration of the stockholders? What would you do with that time? Consideration by stockholders for a buyout does take time, you know."

"Whoa. You're going a bit too fast for me. I'm debating whether to give it all up. Let the public go to hell, and you're saying I should buy, pretend to buy, the very thing I'm so against? What are you talking about?"

She poured herself another healthy glass of whiskey and ushered me out to the deck, seating me in front of the obelisk. "If you didn't believe in illusion as I do, we'd both be just another one of *them*. But illusion is what we both know controls everything. This sculpture of yours. What is the essence of its beauty if not illusion? I paid a healthy sum to have my illusion next to me. It's nothing but metal and granite, reflecting whatever is out there for it to mirror, allowing me to create whatever illusion I desire from its light, shadow, texture, temperature, all the elements of art. All elements of that Pinot Noir as well." She leaned over onto her knees and stared into the sun's reflection on the obelisk. "What I'm talking about, Derek, is affording you the time to complete your masterpiece and Echo Life's growth...without the encumbrance of a force that would have you abandon both...abandon your illusion...your Echo...your dream."

"You don't know if it's even worth finishing, let alone pronouncing it a masterpiece," I said.

"I've flown past it several times this past year." She turned toward me once again. "Yes. Stanton still thinks a single engine plane is romantic, so I let him believe in his illusion and get him to fly me past your rock whenever..."

"You've seen it?"

She took my hand and cupped it with hers. "Derek, whatever is driving you, whatever persuades you to climb that edifice and God knows…risk your bloody skin to pound away at that inert mass of earth's resistance, well, that is something else I don't understand. But…you mustn't lose it. You mustn't fragment that focus with worry and concern for your flock or whatever you call it…the group. I know Echo Life is important to you, but that rock is exclusively about you and you alone, and it's worth anything necessary to maintain its impetus."

As my head reeled with surprise and even more confusion, the critical moment of decision was saved as the upstairs window was pushed open and a woman wearing a frilly peasant's dress leaned out with, "Hey…'what man art thou that thus bescreen'd in night so stumblest on my counsel?'"

Aretha, taken aback, smiled. "I think it's my company thee 'stumblest on' daughter, but you could come down and introduce yourself."

"I already have. And you are?" chimed Linda.

I smiled and said, "Oh…I'm Derek…old friend of your mother's."

Linda laughed loudly, "My mother doesn't have 'old' friends. Derek, huh? The rock man?"

"Well…"

"Of course," she continued. "How the hell are you?"

I smiled again, "I'm…" But before I could continue, the window was closed, allowing only the faint strains of La Boheme being vocalized off-key.

I looked to Aretha and she patted my hand. "My daughter, most of the time; Juliet, some of the time; and of late, an attempt at Colline's 'Vecchia Zimarra,' although vocal lessons are definitely in order. Sleeps all day, sings all night. Earplugs have become my bed partner lately. I love her though. Crazy is as crazy does, right?"

I politely shrugged. "You only briefly mentioned her before."

"Well, she has some problems, and I deal with the problems…alone." She got up to check the squab. "I better throw in an extra bird and make another setting. Never know when she's going to be awake. Care to freshen your drink?"

I glanced at my glass. Jesus, I thought. I've emptied another.

It wasn't until fog became apparent outside that I realized it was getting late. By virtue of the two empty bottles of wine atop the coffee table, I realized dinner was far behind us and it was probably very late. For Linda, however, it was midday. I looked at my watch.

"Oh, don't even think about it," bellowed Linda. "You're sleeping here tonight."

"Linda! Perhaps it would be proper to ask first," whispered Aretha before she burst into drunken laughter.

Feeling no pain, I looked at my empty wine glass, and joined in. "My God, I'm drunk."

"Drunk?" said Linda. "You're shit faced," sending us once again into spasms of laughter.

Aretha stood up, got her balance and started for the liquor cabinet. "Well, as long as we're doing it, let's do it right. Courvoisier anyone?"

"Just bring the fucking bottle and some *snufters*, mother."

"Will snifters do, dear?"

"Only this once, mommy dearest."

Aretha had to lean against the wall for balance as the triumvirate of laughter filled the room once more.

"So…" slurred Linda as she wiped the smile from her face, "time to get serious."

"You mean we haven't been?" I said with more laughter.

Linda composed herself and then, as if by magic, took on the look of a fem-Nazi. "I'd kill him."

I looked up at Linda just as Aretha returned with the Courvoisier and snifters. "Pardon?"

"Stoppard. Mother says he's a real prick trying to destroy you. I'd kill him."

Aretha poured the cognac. "Sounds like I have to get serious too. That was rude, Linda."

"Oh, cut the crap, mumsy. Just sit down and let's get this thing planned out."

Aretha finished pouring. "We should perhaps let this be our last drink."

Linda reached across the coffee table and picked up the bottle, cradling it against her breast. "Suit yourself." Turning her attention back to me, she said, "I wasn't rude, was I? Don't tell me *you* haven't had such thoughts."

"Killing someone," I replied. "I don't think so."

Aretha leaned forward. "Linda, darling, I know you mean well, but we've got this in control and…"

"Mother, I know you mean well, as well…such English…but, you don't. You really don't have a clue to his might. I read the papers. I watch TV…even C-Span had him last week cryin' the blues 'for my stockholders' he called it. Let me tell you something, rock man…Damn, it's hot in here." She rose and stepped to the French doors, swinging one open. "If my mother thought enough of your work to feature it on her deck, you can trust you're good." She turned back toward me. "And if you're that good, good enough to make my mother happy, then she'll be expecting more from you.

And, that means you've got to be rid of anything or anyone that might threaten your work. So...I'll kill him for you."

I smiled politely. Aretha flushed with embarrassment. Linda walked to the stairway with her snifter. "I'm going to do some planning alone now, while I'm still fresh. You two enjoy yourselves." And she was gone up the stairway.

Aretha stayed transfixed on the open door, swirling the cognac in her glass. "Like I said, she...I've got some problems."

"She was just drunk," I said, trying to humor her.

"Yes. Perhaps." She rose and stepped to the stairwell, "She loves to fantasize." As she continued up the stairway, "You'll have to excuse me. This shouldn't take too long."

Once again, I was faced with one of my compelling weaknesses—dealing with adversity. Aretha was amazing. Here she was juggling several balls in the air because of my unexpected visit, and now she had just added another. *How did she do it? And with such ease and confidence.*

I listened, but could hear nothing from upstairs. Little did I know.

Aretha squeezed the door shut and walked up to her daughter, now fully involved in her "planning." Sitting at her desk overlooking the ocean, she held her quill several inches off the parchment paper, watching ever attentively for the ink drop to fall. The paper, along with the writing instrument, had been Linda's choice of new tools, determined several months ago, about the time she stopped weaving.

The walls were covered with all shapes and sizes of baskets Linda had made since coming home from the institution. After several months of quiet crafting in her room, Aretha had brought lunch up to the room one day to find her weaving a mask.

"Do you like it," Linda queried.

"Very nice," Aretha replied. As she placed the lunch tray down, however, she took a closer look to discover woven into the eye sockets were small portraiture photographs. Lying to the side had been the snap shots from which she had cut out the faces. Faces of fellow patients, the doctors, even some of her prized photo-album memories. "That *is* original, Linda. Whatever made you think of that?"

Linda only said, "Death."

When Aretha tried to engage her in conversation regarding the masks, Linda became totally silent. Aretha hadn't challenged any further.

One wall now, however, was covered in masks, all containing eye sockets with pasted faces from photographs.

The ink drop finally found its mark on the parchment. Linda began moving the quill in a circular motion from the middle of the ink spot, outward, creating a spiraling effect to the outer edges. "I don't want to argue, mother. I can do this myself."

"What, dear?"

"'What, dear'?" Linda repeated, never missing a swirl of the pattern she was creating.

"Yes. What can you do yourself?"

"You're sure as hell not thinking *you* can help, are you?"

Aretha sat down on the bed and stared at Linda's backside. "It would help to know what you mean."

"Mother...if I figure out the *perfect situation*, I'll kill him and we'll all live happily ever after. Okay?"

Aretha rose sharply and walked to the wall of masks, trying to contain herself. "This notion of yours that killing Stoppard...well, it's not the way."

"For you, maybe not. For your lover, it's perfect."

Aretha spun on her heels. "Lover? You are..." She caught herself. Wiping her hands down the sides of her dress, she tried to appear calm again. "You are wrong on that one, Linda."

The swirls continued, creating a denser vortex, the center now becoming solid black. "Mother, you've never seduced anyone in my memory using your bed, but, oh, *your* ways put traditional sex to shame."

"Linda, that is uncalled for. You apologize."

"No. It's true and I won't say I'm sorry. No. No. No. I'm a big girl now, and I don't need to say I'm sorry. No. No. No."

Aretha turned her back to the child-like statements that were coming with lightning speed, sending Aretha back to all her fears the day she brought her home from the institution. After a few moments, she turned back to her. "Am I really that good, dear?"

Now, it was Linda's turn to take notice. She swiveled in her chair and gazed at her mother's backside. Sitting in her lap was Guildenstern, her stuffed bear. "Don't throw that reverse psychology at me, for God sake. You don't need me or anybody else to tell you that you are a cunning woman who always gets what she wants, one way or the other. This time it's Derek Turrel and you'll stop at nothing, short of killing Stoppard yourself, to make sure your discovery continues providing you with pleasure."

Aretha lashed out, "You are..." She caught herself again, and then in spite of the control she knew was necessary at times like this, her eyes lifted from the Teddy bear and finished, saying, "You are in need of help, again, my dear."

"I'm only in need of…" Linda turned back to her quill and paper. "A little time."

"Perhaps it's best I call Dr. Reagan."

"Yes. He probably could help you work through your obsession."

"Pardon?"

"Please, mother. This is Linda talking to you. Crazy daughter of yours that knows you only too well."

"You said it. I didn't."

"What? Crrrraaaazzzzyy? Hardly a stranger to you, mother. We both have the spike in our genes. You channeled it into the stars and art. I'm still working on mine, but…you know, mother…I think there's a lot I'm going to learn about my craziness…very soon. Now…." Linda placed Guildenstern on the desk top, rose from her chair and like a diplomat who had just allowed an arch rival to feel confident of her negotiating powers, quickly escorted Aretha to the door. "I've much to think about. Thank you for the visit." And Aretha was urged out the door.

Cachunk.

I glanced upstairs as I heard the door shut and locked. Within moments, Aretha walked down the steps, her shoulders slumped uncharacteristically forward. The usual vibrant, energized face was now sallow and pale.

"I'm sorry for all this," she said as she stepped into the living room.

"Is she alright?" I asked.

Aretha paused and sat down, then chuckled. "No. But then, who is?"

I tried to lighten the mood with, "Well, just a bit too much to drink. I'm sure she'll…"

"No. She won't. It will take more than some overnight sleep to deal with it. I know this pattern. Hasn't happened for some time, but…I know it."

"That…" I said, stumbling to find the right words. "That whole thing about Stoppard was just the booze talking, right?"

Aretha looked straight at me. "Wrong. Linda could drink us both under the table." Then, as if not wanting to believe it serious, she chuckled. "Hell, under the house."

"I didn't know," I said, trying to be sensitive to the situation, but not wanting to pry.

"Linda is a fragile child. Much like I was. But a liver of cast iron. The difference is she doesn't accept the fragility as real. There's a part of her that seeks out the primitive to counteract that delicate femininity." She rose. "I'm afraid I'm done. Got up at six yesterday, so I'm a bit tired. I'll make up the bed in the guest room. Just be a minute."

"You sure? I mean, it's nothing for me to drive into town and..."

"Nonsense," she said. "You just relax. Won't take me but a few minutes." As she reached the stairway, she turned, showing the familiar confident smile. "Drive into town? You'll be lucky to make it up these stairs."

A few minutes later, Aretha bade me goodnight with, "We'll talk in the morning... late morning?" But, I wasn't sure talking would cure the problem that must have gnawed at all our psyches this late night. It was close to sunup when I finally closed my eyes and let sleep have a run at my quandary.

Chapter 44

"I know, Doctor, but you can understand my concern," said Aretha as she walked the edge of the surf with her cell phone pressed tightly to her ear. "I don't want to sound that way, but she did utter the words...understood...role playing has been her salvation. You've reminded me many times. If it's so harmless, why does she hold onto it so vehemently when she knows it's hurting me. I mean, she not only threatened to kill someone, but said some very nasty things about me last night...Alright. Alright. I'll bite my tongue and call you in a few days. Yes...'just to check up.' Of course. No...it's rather lovely today. Just a light breeze. Thank you. You too. Oh, and I'm sorry I got you up so early. Okay. Thank you."

Aretha closed her phone and continued walking the mile stretch of beach she liked to call her own, even though her frontage was only seventy feet. In the distance, she could see her sanctuary above the dunes, the Ode, catching the eastern sun and kicking it back against the house in a rainbow array of refracted colors. She looked up to the sky. Last night's moon still hung as a translucent reminder of the anxious fear she still carried with her. Heavy thoughts continued to prey on her as she walked. *What if Dr. Reagan is wrong? What if this wasn't role-playing and she is really convinced that she could fix it all... looking out for me... for Derek? But, why? Why is she showing so much concern for me now, after all this time? I should be oh so grateful. What would I have done without her these past years...institution and all?*

Rising up over a dune in the distance, I saw Aretha walking through the sand, hands shoved in her pockets, obviously in deep thought, as I was. I wound my way down toward the surf. By the time she reached me, I was walking lighter and she could see the smile that she knew was rarely exposed. "Derek! You're up early."

"By the looks of those tracks behind you, I'm up late," I countered.

"Oh…had to call Dr. Reagan and let him know what was going on. Better she doesn't overhear."

"So…everything okay…with the Doctor, I mean?"

Aretha took my arm and we continued to walk. "For the moment…with him, anyway. I'm just not as comfortable with her words as he is."

"They were pretty…what, scary?" I said.

"She's a strange woman…a person that usually walks around fearful, like an ant crossing a sidewalk, but can say certain things."

I squeezed her arm. "Why don't you just let it settle for a day or two. If the doctor isn't worried, you probably shouldn't be."

She returned the grip on my arm. "Okay. Better we keep our focus on the legitimate ways to get this guy, anyway." She took a deep breath and said, "I did do some 'proper' thinking about Stoppard last night, in spite of everything. I have some I.O.U.'s I can call upon. One in particular."

***

Aretha stood before the glass encased Picasso and smiled to herself. The sculpture was insignificant to museum curators, but to a wealthy businessman, beating the odds and owning a work of art that had garnered the covetous lust of fellow collectors, was "…better than sex could ever be. And, I owe it all to you and your scandalous tip," he had said. Behind the center-stage placement of the piece was his company's name, CHANDLER-TRONICS. From the ceiling came multiple laser beam detectors forming a circle around his precious Picasso. Natural sunlight flooded the reception area from three walls of ceiling to floor windows overlooking the Hudson River and the Statue of Liberty.

"They might steal my technology, but not my Picasso," came the voice behind her. She turned to face the tanned and graciously smiling Wurden Chandler, owner of the world's largest supplier of GPS technology.

"Even if they did, you'd have them GPS'd to the ends of earth, wouldn't you?" Aretha answered as she exchanged a European embrace on each cheek.

"Please," he said, stretching out his arm to escort her back his office.

"I'm honored. Such a busy man doing his own ushering?"

Flashing his charming smile, he said, "Never too busy for my 'partner in crime.' That's the first time you've seen it, right?"

Aretha shook her head, "It has been too long. Last time we actually saw each other was the night we planned that little conspiracy."

"Almost two years now," he said as they reached his office doors, two mammoth Chinese-carved slabs of Mahogany. "Like my newest acquisition?" He nodded toward the doors.

"Impressive." She squinted a bit, paused, and then said, "A Hu person watering an animal... Chinese unicorn drinking from a well. Yuan Dynasty. Especially valuable."

"What don't you know about art?" he asked.

"What a friend of mine is trying to teach the world," she answered as he swung the behemoth doors aside and welcomed her into his art museum-like office.

"Sounds interesting."

"Very," she said. "Need a big favor."

"It's about time. That Picasso changed my life. Anything."

"Anything could change it again."

"Ooo! Tell me more."

As he closed the doors, Aretha asked, "Still friendly with Bernard?"

"The retired FBI agent? Play poker every Thursday with him."

***

The reports were stacked before him like pick-up-sticks. And like the challenge of lifting one element in an effort to not upset another, he too was reduced to a child-like dilemma. Which one next?

Stoppard wasn't one to back away from a challenge, though. He'd even been known to put on the gloves, as he did at the Friars Club Roast several years before. It was there that many learned that even in jest, you don't ruffle Stop's feathers.

The ring bout, coming as it did at the Athletic Club just two hours after the roast, offered the press some additional froth of gossip for even the most tight-cheeked columns, such as The Times. Showing a picture of Stoppard standing over Harold Simms, like Ali over Liston, the caption read, "Stoppard Denning KO's OST's Executive VP in a two round reprimand." For Harold Simms, however, the broken nose was hardly just a reprimand. Looking like a reminder of Nicholson's "Chinatown" image, complete with nose bandage, Simms, needless to say, not only took the punch to heart, but took the two-month healing period to formulate a more acceptable repartee. Today, however, the implied mockery was very serious— very serious indeed.

His staff, in preparation for the annual shareholders meeting, had prepared reports that if leaked out, would make Stoppard the laughing stock of Wall Street, bearing out all the rumors. Not only were profits dramatically down according to report number three, but report number six, using Stoppard's tried and proven opinion poll, showed the public perception of OST had fallen three points, an all time low.

Stoppard stared at the remaining reports and wondered which one held the balance to his teetering OST. Which to pull now, he thought. Report two, the P & L statements of all seven divisions? Or should he really allow himself to get depressed by reading Report number one—the cost cutting recommendations he'd only heard about, but if confirmed, would give the appearance of real panic, the most dreaded Achilles Heel, collapse of the stock. He didn't want to even entertain the thought. Instead, he picked up report number nine, trying not to disturb the untouched for fear he might be tempted to jump in, head first.

This was the first time a report number nine had been prepared. This was also the first year that OST's future was at risk, so it was only natural to get a clandestine report on the competition, a report that would tell all about the hammer that was poised to pound. He fearfully reached under and carefully slid out the half-inch-thick testament—remembering a saying more than one woman had reminded him of, "Nothing lasts forever."

***

Two hours later, a depressed Stoppard Denning was dropped off by his driver at "Vinny's," a little known bar in Brooklyn...the bar his father had built and owned until his fatal heart attack in 1965. As he walked in, he looked up at the polished ship's bell carrying the engraving, "established in 1951." *So many memories.* The mirror stretching the full length of the bar was still standing, its aging swirls of discoloration growing over the years. He smiled as he climbed on a stool, laid his arms down on the brown marble inlayed mahogany and stared at the corner of the mirror. As a child, he had tried to scrub away the discoloration with a Brillo pad, only to make it worse, its scratches continuing to pay homage to the industrious nature of Vincent's boy, Stoppard.

"What'll you have?" came the effeminate voice of the bartender. Stoppard looked up, forced a smile at the young man whose nose ring sent shivers through him. "Oh, how about some Johnny?"

"Black or Red?" the emaciated one asked.

"Black...double, okay?"

"Double it is. Water on the side?"

"Sure. Might as well try and prolong it."

The bartender extended his hand with nails painted black. "Haven't seen you around. Shino is my name."

"Yeah..." fumbled Stoppard. Not knowing why he was even there, he clumsily reached over and shook his hand. "Just call me Bob."

Shino smiled and began preparing the scotch. "It's okay, Bob. I get a lot of your type in here. Don't know why, but this place seems to make people feel safe."

Stoppard turned on his bar stool and peered into the darkness. Antique walls of ships' wood his father had carried by cart from the dockyards still made up the walls. He remembered helping his father hammer them into place and laying the first coat of varnish. Even the floors were still layered in peanut shells and saw dust with beer kegs remaining as tables—smaller ones, mixed with wrought iron chairs, as seating. Candles in old wax-encrusted Chianti bottles still provided the atmosphere, illuminating the only other three people drinking at this early hour.

"Here ya go," said Shino as he placed the double Johnny on the bar with the side of water. "Opened up a bottle of Pellegrino for ya. Figured you'd appreciate that."

"Thank you. That was thoughtful."

Shino smiled. "Maybe, but I pretty much pay my rent with tips, so..." He winked and went back to polishing the glassware.

Times have changed was all Stoppard heard in his head for the next few minutes as he finished the double and ordered another, and another. Memories started flooding in faster than he could field. He took out a hundred dollar bill and gave it to Shino with, "got a bottle of that stuff?"

"Black? Sure." As he reached into the cabinet and took out an unopened bottle, he said, "I can give you a break on a bottle."

"Don't bother, Shino. Keep the change and pay your rent." He picked up the bottle and glass, swiveled on his stool, picked out a table in the furthest corner, and stood.

"Here," came Shino's voice. Stoppard turned around and there was a full bottle of Pellegrino with a fresh glass.

"Might 'prolong' it a bit longer," offered Shino.

Stoppard smiled. "You know your drinkers, don't you?"

"Know my bar. People come here for only one thing. Depression is never fun. Enjoy."

Son of a bitch, thought Stoppard as he sauntered over to the table in the corner. *Why can't I have that kind of understanding from my own people?* He passed the three bodies slumped over their tables, each with a defining characteristic of youth: green hair on one, triple ear rings on another, and sitting two tables away from his destination, a shaven head tattooed with the names of Mary, Sue and Esmeralda. *Unrequited love.*

It was the last name that kept Stoppard's attention as he sat down. *What the hell is Esmeralda to this apparition?* He poured a half glass of scotch, the glug-glug-glug causing the shaved head to rise just long enough to focus on Stoppard's full bottle of Johnny Walker. With a smile that stretched across his face like a shrink-wrapped porcelain mask, he giggled "all of it... you're gonna drink that whole fuckin' thing?"

"If I can, buddy. If I can hold out."

"Well, you let me know if you need some help, okay?"

"Deal." Stoppard smiled back as the head slumped back into the crutch of his arm, this time allowing one eye to take in whatever Stoppard might not drink from the bottle. He slowly sipped the next glass, his eyes once again taking in remnants of a past he had all but abandoned.

"Stoppard! Enough a'ready. Got enough nails in that wood to sink a battleship," his father bellowed from the other side of the wall.

"Just a few more," yelled Stoppard, the hammer gripped by both his little hands, relentlessly urging the next ready-to-smack nail into the old wood planks. For the six year old, this was more fun than burning ants on the sidewalk, a pastime his friends lived for, but a game he felt overqualified to play. After all, his father was giving him a nickel per plank nailed to the wall. Excepting the struggle to reach high, even when standing on the fruit box, this was easy money for the small child—a lesson he took to heart and morphed many times on his way to becoming OST's largest minority stock holder.

"How many you got up now?" chimed his father.

"How many am I supposed to have up?" answered the young Stoppard.

"Don't you be hustling me. How many?"

Stoppard looked to his left. "Four, but I'm almost finished with the fifth."

"Almost is good enough for some, but not for a Denning. Get it finished. It's 3:26 p.m., and you're three behind by my calculations."

That's how he remembered his father. A man of unnerving expectations. Once the walls of the bar were built, there was the mirror. Stoppard spent the rest of his summer spackling in the edges of the mirror. The boards that were to make up the frame were not the best of measurements, so it was with reluctance that he accepted the job. Even at one dollar a day—more money than he had ever earned for a day—moving clay around, as he called it, turned out to be the most boring work he had done up till then.

He looked up at Shino. Shouting across the room, he asked, "Hey, Shino, you ever have to repair that mirror?"

Shino paused from polishing his glasses and gave the strange man in the corner a look. "What mirror?"

"The one behind you."

"Oh," said Shino. "Guess it is the only one in the room, isn't it? Well, Bob, tell you the truth… shit, I don't know. I only bartend."

"Yeah. That's okay. I think I know the answer."

"So, why'd you ask?

Stoppard thought a moment about the right answer for his alert *Goth* bartender. "Age, Shino. Age. When you get a little older, you'll be asking your *own* stupid questions."

"Hey, old man, no disrespect intended."

"Hey, skinhead, no condescension intended."

Shino gave Stoppard a two-finger stab and said, "Got cha. How's that bottle workin'?"

"Okay, by me." He looked to the man whose eye had never shut since laying his head down at the next table. "How about you? Think I should order another bottle so we can talk?"

The man lifted his head, took his hand and slapped his face, immediately beaming with smiles. "Best offer I've had today, guy."

Stoppard gestured for him to come to his table. "Best offer you ever had, you mean. I'm Bob. You're?"

The man stood up, worked to maintain his balance, then carefully, very carefully walked the three steps to Stoppard's table. "Jonesy, just plain Jonesy."

"Fine. I understand the *just plain* part. Me too."

The two looked into each other's eyes, knowing what the other meant without any further explanation.

"Hey, Shino. Let's have another bottle of that Johnny stuff and a couple of fresh glasses," shouted Stoppard.

Shino grinned. "You some kind of guy, Bob."

Jonesy smiled. "Don't see you…"

"…around here very often? I know Jonesy. Old haunt. Very old haunt," chuckled Stoppard. "I halfway built the fucker."

Jonesy, rubbed his eyes, slapped his face again, glanced at Shino, who shrugged, and looked back at Stoppard. "You be fuckin' with me, aren't ya?"

Stoppard smiled. "Before we start on that new bottle, you go over there and count the nails in that plank, any one of them makin' up that wall. Twenty-three… the highest one's at a real angle toward the ceiling. I was a little guy then."

Jonesy smiled again, looked toward Shino, who once again shrugged, and then pulled himself up. "Damn... I think I can still count." He stepped to the wall and started.

Shino came with the new bottle of Johnny Walker Black and placed it on the table, looking at the other bottle that was still half-full. "Planning on staying a while, Bob?"

Stoppard patted his hand and gave him another one hundred dollar bill. "As along as these last."

Shino took the bill and rushed back to the bar, returning with a Pellegrino lodged in the ice filling of an old dented champagne bucket.

Jonesy returned just as Shino said, "You yell if you need any more water now, ya hear?" Shino shot back to the bar as a new customer entered and Jonesy sat down at the table. He licked his lips as he said, "You're right. Twenty-three. I counted two of them to be sure."

Jonesy sat down, straightened up and said, "I'm no drunkard, you know. Just a bit tired and come here to catch a few winks. That's all."

Stoppard poured him half a glass of Johnny. "Sure. I know. Water?"

"No, thank you. Just a cube."

Stoppard reached in the ice bucket and dropped a cube in his drink. "So, let's talk about your future."

Jonesy straightened up again, then burst out laughing. "You're... you're serious, ain't ya?"

Stoppard reached in his pocket and stuck a one hundred dollar bill under Jonesy's glass.

"Damn, mister. You some kind of...somethin." He raised his eyebrows and glanced again at the one hundred dollar bill as if to ask, *that's mine?*

Stoppard slowly nodded.

Jonesy, like a kid stealing in a candy store, surreptitiously stuck the bill under his shirt and into his pants. "If I wasn't a gentlemen of sorts, I'd be sayin' 'You're out of you mind, BOB!'" Then he burst out laughing again, and slugged down the half-a-glass of scotch without another blink of his eye.

Stoppard slugged his own down and looked Jonesy straight in the eye, whispering, "So, Jonesy, your future. What would a guy like you do to get a thousand of those?"

Jonesy looked quizzically, then tapping his pants, "Thousand of these?"

Stoppard nodded.

Jonesy leaned across the table, looked to his right and left, then, "I ain't no math guy, but I think that's a hundred grand, right?"

Stoppard nodded once more.

Jonesy let out another burst of laughter, then in a straight-faced animated comeback said, "Shit, I know a lot of people would kill for that kind of money," followed by another burst of laughter.

Stoppard wasn't laughing. "Probably so, Jonesy. Probably so."

Chapter 45

Sheila peered out the window to the *Atlantic Ferries* loading and unloading activity of several tanker trucks.

"For God sake, Paterson, you've been coming to my Gray Cliff barbecues for what...ten, eleven years now? What the hell am I to you, just an island escape and a summer spare rib?"

Paterson lifted his pear-shaped body and went to the coffee maker. "Sure you won't have a cup?"

Sheila shook her head and sighed. Paterson's office was hardly the place to expect good coffee. Equipped with but meager practical necessities like a desk, filing cabinet, couch, hat rack, corner table for donuts and the java.

"Suit yourself," he grunted. "And when did you stop calling me Patty?"

Pouting, she shot back, "Since you started sending me into bankruptcy."

"Ah, c'mon, Sheila," he answered, returning to his desk with another cup of the mud he liked to call coffee. "You're getting far too excited about all this. You know how OPEC works. It's probably only temporary."

"You've cut back to three ferries a day, Patty. And this is just June. What if it gets worse? What if you go to one a day in July. Shit. I'm history."

"Look, Sheila, the price of oil and gas is the price of oil and gas. Whatever they charge, I pay. Hell, I'm still packin' the boats to capacity since Memorial Day. You can't be hurtin' that bad."

"When you're used to six trips a day, *packed*, you hurt."

"Well..." He scratched his head and walked to the window overlooking the harbor of Port Clyde. "Wish I could do more, but those storage tanks out there are carrying gold right now." Down below, a tanker truck unloaded its gas into *Atlantic's* storage tanks. The high noon sun bounced off the lettering on the side of the truck's container...*Benson Trucking*. "Tanker trucks run on gas too, you know. Unions. They all add onto the price you pay for car gas. I'm gonna be hurtin' too if this runs through the summer."

"So what's all this, 'probably only temporary' crap?"

Paterson turned. "Because I don't know. Damn, woman, OPEC might or might not lower the price per barrel…oil companies might or might not lower prices. Shit look at those profits Exxon had last year. Did they budge to lower anything? Hell no. And then what do I know? The truck unions might or might not strike if the oil companies keep raisin' prices to where long truck hauls to places like Port Clyde can't afford the run."

Sheila jumped up. "Okay. I get the point. And unions are supposed to *be for the people*."

"And with six boats to fill up everyday…"

"Damn it, Patty, you sound like an old woman."

"What the hell does Harry say at Bar Harbor. He's got four boats servicing the islands."

Sheila shuffled to the door. "Same, Patty. Same. Oil prices and our beloved unions. What else is new? Thanks for listening. We'll talk."

Paterson rushed to the door, opening it and leaving her with, "I know that *Echo Life* thing you got going is bringing more tourists, but…"

She patted him on the arm. "I know you'd do more if you could." She gave an understanding smile. "Maybe you could install some solar panels on each boat and stick it to them."

He smiled back.

"Not a good idea, I know," she said with a sigh of resignation.

He closed the door, walked back to his desk and picked up the phone. As he waited, he glanced out the window at the tanker truck still unloading its gas. "Make that return call to Benson's office now, will you?"

***

Theo wasn't used to hand holding. That was Derek's job, and he wasn't back yet, so with reluctance, he arranged to accommodate the meeting several artists had arranged to talk about the problem. The group sat around, some wiping their faces from the lack of air conditioning—a temporary compromise for the cannery due to a power ration, due to oil and gas ration.

"Not getting food to the island is the problem, not the fucking tourists," said Nathan. "I've got eight actors to worry about. She's threatening to shut the island down if this ferry thing continues. Not enough tourists to pay the bills, she claims. Shop owners are talking too."

Theo shook his head. "I've listened for an hour now while a bunch of you have shared the rumors. And that is just what they are, rumors. Until she comes to me or Derek and announces her intentions, we're going to proceed as usual."

"And what if they're not rumors?" said Simon. "It's great having the satellite up-load here for the channels, but I don't think Sol is looking forward to asking his investors to plunk down God knows how much to move the operation."

"Who says we would have to move the operation?" chimed in Lanagra. "I can grow my own food." He looked around for support.

"Don't look at me," said Rodney. "I'm just an actor. Gardening passed me by a long time ago."

Theo stood up and started to gather his notes together. "Ferry boat service and tourists…the jury is still out. The only real threat we have to worry about right now is oil and gas. Those power generators don't run on water, but…" He took one last look at the group. "And this is a big but… if she brings the island to a halt, we'll not fold. One way or another, we'll keep the generators humming and keep your stomachs from growling. Right now, I've got to get back to the apartment. Derek's calling at one o'clock."

As he stepped toward the exit, Sol stepped up beside him. As they reached the door, Sol said, "You've got a lot to handle with Derek away. I'm here."

Theo turned to him. "Thanks, Sol. We'll get through this."

"I know. We've been without much food before. Some haven't."

Theo stepped out into the 85-degree day. "Didn't stop us, did it?"

Sol nodded. "Let me know what Derek has to say."

Theo waved and was down the wooded path that avoided the town with a circuitous route toward the lighthouse.

Sol gazed after him, feeling he knew why Theo had skirted the town.

***

The mouse wasn't particularly different, and yet it was. Its calm stare at the page of words was disconcerting to the man who had had his share of mice and rats in one-room dumps and under the bridges. He held the receiver still, close to his ear, not wanting to startle the creature. "What? Yes. Yes," whispered Theo. "I'm not whispering…just listening…quietly. I know you do. Yes, of course. You take care, Derek. I mean that." As Theo hung up the phone, he thoughtfully held his gaze on the mouse that remained perfectly content, poised as he was atop one of the many notebooks stacked on the old oak table. Penciled words, he thought. So many tablets of words. The mouse tilted its head as if saying, "Is that it? You just going to stare? I'm outta here." As he scurried off across the stacks, making a leap to the chair, then to the floor, then to a small knothole in the old planked floor, Theo smiled and stepped over to the tablet the mouse almost seemed to be reading with his rapt attention to the page.

As he picked up the notebook, he smiled. Had it not been for the wind through the window, the notebook might have remained closed forever. But a gust had disturbed the pages, and an innocent mouse had brought him to this paragraph of thought, one of many from his past, before he had met Derek. He sat down and read it carefully. *"There are few rewards living this way provides. One, however, is knowing that all good efforts are their own reward. When the news was broadcast over the radio, I was standing at the shipping table, preparing a box of books to be shipped to the Harvard Medical School. The sound of Cronkite's voice brought it home. He was fighting back the tears. You could tell. You could only picture him in a TV studio, his coverage being sent over the CBS radio and TV affiliates everywhere. He needed to be strong. A nation was counting on it. This was journalism's hero in the country's saddest moment as he announced that President Kennedy was dead. He calmed so many people. He was the grandfather to us all and that deed of compassion and understanding, seen by millions of people, shall stay with me forever."*

Theo moved to his desk and opened his present notebook, number seventy-eight. *"To my fellow artists,"* he began. *"It may seem hard right now, but we must stay focused and determined, even though our friend and leader Derek must be away for a while longer. He trusts we will remain steadfast in our original goal, but he feels, and I concur, that he's of greater value addressing some issues head on...in New York. You deserve some further explanation, so let me see if I can say it as he would have it said."*

That is how he started his thoughts that carried well into the night. It was 2 a.m. before he looked up and realized he was hungry and tired. He closed the tablet. "My God," he murmured to himself, "fifty-two pages." As he opened up his favorite peanut butter jar and spread a good amount on the crackers pulled from the box, he glanced over to the knothole and smiled.

***

"Write your congressman!" shouted Aaron Benson into his speakerphone as he pushed back into his desk chair and slurped from his *Benson Trucking* promotion mug. Standing in the corner cleaning his nails and glancing at the New Haven street below was Leroy, a not very intelligent looking "suit." Benson dribbled a bit of his coffee on his tie and angrily motioned for Leroy to get something.

279

As Leroy lunged forward, pulling a not very clean hanky from his lapel pocket, Benson listened.

"Yeah...that's going to do a lot of good," said Paterson at the other end. "Your union probably has *him* in your pocket as well."

"As well?" said Benson as he rubbed his tie. "What's that supposed to mean? Nobody's in my pocket. I just adjust. Adjust, that's what I do. Those fuel costs are not only higher; they're makin' it difficult to tank up, too. You want somebody to throw rocks at, look to the oil companies. They haven't built a refinery in this country for over thirty years. Crude comes in and gets backed up. My truck drivers got nothing to say about it...except they're tired of waitin' in line for fewer loads and they're tired of the union not gettin' them raises for all the hassle they got to go through. They think everybody is makin' money except them."

"We have a contract," bellowed Paterson over the speaker.

Benson leaned in. "With a force majeure clause. Call your attorney. The raise per gallon stays. Nice talkin' with ya." His chubby finger pressed disconnect. "Leroy... you might need to get yourself a clean hankie now."

Leroy retrieved the stained handkerchief, glanced at it, folded it inward, and stuffed it in his lapel pocket. "Works fine. You want lunch?"

"Jesus, Leroy...that's all you think about. Get me some more coffee and don't be so damn stingy on the sugar."

"Don't forget you got that call from New York waitin' on five," said Leroy as he opened the door.

Benson looked at the flashing light, and mumbled, "Yeah...wait'll he hears about Paterson's shit storm."

CHAPTER 46

Tuesday, July 5th was like every other year. Independence Day had left a few more with hangovers than usual, but otherwise, just another day. Stoppard got off his elevator at the usual time, greeted his floor staff with the usual aplomb, and sat down at his desk for the usual kind of day. On his credenza, the ongoing electronic chess game, now in pause, was always his first action. It was not unusual for him to take a moment to study the board from yesterday's move, then deftly place his fingers upon a piece, and making a move that would serve to set his day of numerous other strategies into play. He smiled at his right choice, leaving the computer with a longer than usual retort. He then sat down to go through his mail. "I'll have some tea today, Myra. Some herb tea," he said into the speakerphone.

"Herb tea, Mister Denning?"

"Yes. Maybe something soothing. Okay?"

"But you always...yes, sir. *Soothing* tea. Be just a minute."

"Thank you," he said as he thumbed through the opened envelopes, a task he always had his secretary do for him, unless the envelope was marked personal like the one facing him now. Strange he thought. No return address, but laser printed address. Looks like a business letter, he thought. He opened it to find a plain piece of water marked stationary with a short message, again laser printed.

Dear Mister Denning,

This letter will serve to alert you to the imminent threat of a Proxy fight at OST's annual meeting of August 1. If you wish to talk about this, I'll be having my lunch on the east side of the lake in Central Park tomorrow at 12:30. I'll bring some extra in case you show up and are hungry. I'll be wearing a Yankees cap. Shouldn't be too hard to find me as there are only a few benches.

Mister Smith

Stoppard turned the envelope over several times, looking for a return address, even going so far as to smell it. He put it down next to the letter and wiped his palms against his trousers. After a moment, he picked up the phone.

"Yes, Mister Denning?"

"My schedule tomorrow...lunch. Anything for lunch?"

"Why...no. Just a moment. You've got Mister Thomas at 4, but, no. You're open."

"Not anymore. I'll be out for lunch."

"Should I mark a reminder?"

"No. I'll remember," muttered Stoppard as he flipped off the speakerphone and dropped back down in his chair, staring at the letter lying on his desk.

***

Unlike the past, the streets of Soho seemed strange to me— foreign. I'd not been back for the better part of three years, and so much seemed different. Like a tourist in search of new impressions, I looked up at the tops of buildings. The sun was low in the west, and for me, the highlighted tops of buildings now stood like hot cinders atop burned out coals; a fire gone dead. I rounded the corner and paused. Ahead of me was Stefano's, the once peaceful, as well as unrelenting, din of repose. Even with a couple of sections out, the neon martini glass held its own against the waning colors of magic hour, enough, at least, to send an onslaught of memories cascading through my sober head. Not for long.

Inside, it was unusually quiet. I couldn't see even *one* of the old customers. As I approached the bar, Jersey did a double take and put down his forever glass-polishing towel and said, "Derek! Good to see you. Damn, *great* to see you." He extended his hand and I gave it a warm shake. It was good to see him as well.

"So, the usual?"

"No, I've got some business to attend to. Make it a beer."

Jersey smiled. "Must be some *important* business, eh?" and popped the lid of a Grolsch. "Glass?"

"No. That's fine." I chugged a couple of big swallows and took a deep breath. "Where's all the old gang?"

"Oh," answered Jersey, "you know. Soho is still somewhat transient, even with the real estate boom. Most of our friends couldn't afford the rent any longer. Yuppiedom all over again."

"Yeah. Guess shit continues to happen."

"That it does, Derek. That it does." Sensitive, but also curious, he said, "I do see Samara once in awhile." He let his eyes drop to the polishing glasses again, just in case.

"Well, some of us just can't pass you by, old buddy."

Jersey lifted his head. Relieved with having not said the wrong thing, he continued. "She sure talks about you a lot. Says your project is going great. *I* even bought a subscription."

"Yeah? That's what it's all about. How do you like it?"

"Well, you know, bartendin' can get to be a bit of a bore. When I'm not bushed, I... it's kinda silly, really."

"What?" I asked.

"Oh, you know. Jersey Barrett, he's just a bartender."

"Okay. C'mon. You're gonna tell me, what?"

"I fuck around with some water colors now and again."

I reached across the counter and patted his hand. "That's what it's all about. You work along with Alonzo?"

"Yeah...as long as he keeps doin' that 11 a.m. web cam class on week ends. I catch that once in a while. He's a good teacher. Where'd you find him? "

"He was already on the island. Just joined us."

"Yeah, he really got me goin', you know? Learned a lot from him."

I smiled to myself. *That's really what it's really all about.* I swigged down another gulp and wandered over to the jukebox. "Still got the oldies on here?"

"That's never changed. Wouldn't be Stefano's without the old jazz collection," said Jersey.

I scanned the listings and found a song I'd not listened to since, well, since I was with Samara last at Gray Cliff. I dropped in a quarter and stood there a few moments as Miles played *'Round Midnight* like no one else could even attempt. As I wandered back to the bar, I looked at Jersey and finally popped the question. "See her much lately?"

"Last night."

"You're kidding." I finished off the Grolsch and said, "guess I can afford one more." The strains of Miles filled the bar, and I found myself debating more than I'd anticipated.

***

At the front entrance, the security phone still had both our names on it. I stared at the keys in my hand, then put them back in my pocket and lifted the receiver. After four rings her voice startled me, "Yes."

I turned around and faced the security camera. "Oh, my God," came her voice and the sound of the buzzer a few moments later.

As the freight elevator rose, the familiar scrape of the wood sidings against the concrete shaft brought back further memories. That first night we rode the elevator together was like yesterday, even though it had been four years now. I closed my eyes and could still recall the subtle smell of her perfume, the child-like breath drifting through her smile, as I had pressed my lips gently to hers. The touch of her hand beneath my shirt, the curve of her back beneath my fingers, and the sudden burst of passion that enveloped us both, driving our hands and arms into an embrace that deferred only to our mouths that explored beyond what any words could possibly express.

With the familiar jolt, the elevator came to a halt. I lifted the double doors to see the entrance to the loft open ajar and the strains of a soft piano sonata filling the background. As I stepped up and entered, I found myself trembling. *This was my loft, after all. Why was I so nervous?* I stepped further in and saw, through the shallow pin spot lights framing small circles on the hardwood floor, the familiar form of Samara sitting at the piano playing. I quietly crossed the loft and stepped up within a few feet of her.

She stopped and turned on her stool, revealing the sweet, gentle smile I'd missed for so long.

"Hi," I said softly.

"Hi, yourself." She continued to smile back.

I shrugged, trying to appear casual and said, "Just passing through the neighborhood."

"Little off your course, aren't you?"

"Well, you know, homing pigeons always return."

283

"Yeah, so I've heard."

She stretched out her hand. "Are you okay?"

I cupped the soft fingers into my palms. "I am now."

"It is good to see you, you know."

"Yeah. I mean, me too...seeing you." As she took my arm and guided me into the sitting area, the pools of light continued to remind me of so many mixed feelings that by the time we sat, I wondered if it wouldn't be best to leave. "I wasn't prepared for this, you know."

"Neither was I. So there must be a good reason for you 'passing through the neighborhood.'"

I scrunched myself into the corner of the couch, took out a cigarette and tried to appear relaxed. "It's only been a few months since I saw you at Gray Cliff, but...four years since being back in here."

My trembling hands betrayed me and she picked up the lighter from the coffee table saying, "May I?"

That's how the late evening started. By the time the familiar rays of sunrise cut through the skylight, it appeared we had satisfied all the personal catching up, apologies for distancing ourselves, and a vowed determination to not repeat the pattern. We understood that we were both at fault: her for sending me away to pursue what she knew, both personally and professionally, would not be accomplished with her as a distraction; and me out of a determination to not let her or myself down.

"So, you haven't mentioned much about Echo Project itself all night. Simon keeps your audience informed, at least. Sounds...well, sounds like it's not without problems. What are you going to do now?" she said.

"I was hoping you could counsel me, Doctor."

She wagged her finger at me. "We covered that a couple of hours ago. This is between you and yourself, Derek. I'm of little value to your processing now. Sometimes, we have to let creativity be our guide, not muddy it with so-called counseling."

"And if it fails?" I said.

"Creativity never fails. *You* taught me that, remember. 'It is sufficient unto itself,' you said."

"And do you believe that?"

"It's served me okay, I think. I finished my 1st."

"Symphony?"

She nodded and smiled.

"I'm happy for you, Samara."

She returned the smile. "So, what are you going to do?"

True to her professional instincts, I realized she wasn't going to let me off without *me* fully addressing *my* problem. "Well, like I said, if this tourist problem doesn't right itself, and quick, this will be our last summer with a 'live' island of artists. They have to eat too. Makes you wonder. I sure got myself into it, didn't I?"

"Yes you did… and them."

"You're really not going to give me an answer, are you?"

"I don't have one to give." She rose and walked to the kitchen. "Coffee?"

"Yeah. Yeah." I looked at the empty bottle of wine. "You realize this is the first time we ever had an all-nighter with only one bottle of wine?"

"Only bottle in the house, that's why." We both laughed.

Somewhere between the first cup of coffee and, I don't remember, I must have fallen asleep because when I opened my eyes, I was under a blanket and in need of a tooth brush. I arose and looked around.

"Samara?" No answer. I walked about; taking in some subtle changes to the minimal décor and realized, most everything was as I had left it. She hadn't really made it hers, it seemed. I called out again at the bathroom door. No answer. I opened the door, hoping my toothbrush was still in the cabinet. On the mirror was a note.

"My love, hope you slept well. I had early appointments, so I didn't want to disturb you. I enjoyed last night. Been a long time since we just talked about us, save that little skirmish over Echo Life. I need to let you iron that out yourself. You know that, don't you? When you've got it settled, please get back in touch with me. This is not shining you. This is still the time you need to be your creative self…alone. I love you, Samara."

I wasn't prepared for this. I opened the cabinet and took out the toothbrush…still in its usual place. The tap still squeaked as I wet the brush and applied the paste. As I went through the routine, I looked hard at myself in the mirror. *What kind of love is this that lets a woman ask her man to make his mistakes and achievements…alone? I love you Samara.* I continued to brush as moisture from my eyes dropped onto the porcelain.

***

Samara sat stoically in her chair and once again waited patiently for the young man she hadn't seen in several months to express himself.

Pierre, dressed in his paint-splattered overalls, sat on the chair — one leg over the arm — like a marionette at rest waiting for its strings to be pulled. His only movement was the picking of speckled paint from his fingernails with a nail-clipper.

"You've moved on to brighter colors since we last met," said Samara as she focused on his hands.

"Yeah," he mumbled.

"The trip abroad seems to have been good for you."

He didn't answer, but instead continued to pick at his nails.

"Wall painting doesn't have to be mundane, right? Your customers must have very interesting rooms."

"Little shops, yeah. Corporations still ask for the bland pastels, though," he answered. He looked up with a grin on his face and pointed to a large splotch of cobalt blue on his coveralls. "This here… from the yearly repainting I did last week at that place you said you had coffee all the time, Zano's?"

"Yes. Zano's. Funky, Zano's," she said, momentarily musing over old memories. Samara adjusted herself in the chair and casually picked up her pad, jotting down a note. "Do you still work long hours?"

"Less."

"Tell me about Europe."

"You know all about it. You sent me there, remember?"

"It wasn't a matter of *sending* you there, Pierre. Your mother and I just thought it might be helpful."

"Before you, there were two others who thought it would be 'helpful' too. Sent me to Phoenix and Seattle. They're all the same, though. They test and test and talk and talk and…"

Samara waited, but the sentence was never finished. "So, do you feel any different?"

He chuckled. "Yeah. *They* thought I was on drugs, too." He chuckled again.

"How did that make you feel?"

"That was pretty cool, mon. I came back and my mom was happy 'cause the letter, like the others, said they hadn't found any drug use and my depression was 'improved.'" He looked up at Samara and shook his head. "How do you improve depression? Huh? I guess because I threw around some bright colors in the arts and crafts lounge, I was an okay guy…improving." He softly giggled. "Should have seen some of the other wacko's throwing paint around."

"'Other wackos?' Do you really think you're a wacko?"

Grinning and shaking his head, he looked up from his nails, the whites of his eyes flashing above his high cheekbones like beacons in the night. "Do you?"

"It's not a term we use. But, no." She nodded toward his hands and pants. "Why did you change?"

"Change?"

"Looks like you switched from your favorite dark colors…the browns and blacks you were so fond of…why the change?"

"Oh, that. Working on a new kind of idea."

"Some new house painting project?"

He grinned and put his fingernail clip away. "Yeah. You might say that." He lifted his leg off the arm and stood up. As he held up his hands, "Check it out. Looks weird, all clean and all."

"Nice. Are you needing to go?"

"Yeah."

"We still have fifteen minutes."

"I know, but…I prefer forty five, to sixty, okay?"

Samara put her note pad down and rose. "If that is what you prefer. Next week?"

"Yeah…sure. Long as you're getting' paid, guess I'm obliged to come, right?"

"Your parents just want the best for you."

"You mean my mother?"

"Sorry. Yes. Your mother." She walked across the room to open the door. "We should talk about him sometime."

Pierre smiled, a familiar gesture of denial Samara understood very well. "Who?"

"You have a nice week now," said Samara, not missing a beat.

"Always do. Us depressives always do."

She closed the door after him and returned to her desk. Sitting down, she penciled in *45 minutes* next to his name, *Pierre Haweisi.*

CHAPTER 47

Central Park in July was a *whirling dervish* of activity. Children roamed freely, exploring hill and rock, tree and shrub, water and concrete. Wherever there is escape from the congestion of city life, New Yorkers will seek it out. Today, the lake was dotted with an armada of remote controlled sail and speedboats. Dotting the edges of the lake were balloon and ice cream vendors, passed occasionally by a nanny and a carriage. All looked normal to Stoppard, a frequent visitor to the park, using the paths to walk off the frustrations of running OST.

As he approached the man sitting on the lake bench wearing the Yankee cap and munching his sandwich, he thought to himself, *Proxy battle, indeed. Who does this person think he is?* He sat down and gazed out over the lake. "Perfect day for a toy boat, wouldn't you say?"

It only took Mister Smith a quick glance from his sandwich to get started. "OST was worth fifty two billion according to Wall Street estimates, first quarter last year. The stock has dropped eighteen points in the past six months. You own thirty-eight percent of the stock that is continuing to drop. Selling now and stepping down would be an intelligent move for you. Staying on would be corporate suicide. Your thoughts?"

Stoppard allowed himself to take a breath, given he'd stopped breathing about two sentences in. He cleared his throat and looked over at the man who continued to carefully navigate around his sandwich like a squirrel with a prize catch. "Thoughts? I think this is a joke."

"That could be a dangerous assumption, Mister Denning."

Stoppard waited for more, but that was all Mister Smith had to say, given there was still half a sandwich to eat.

Gathering all the authoritative timbre he could shove into his clenched throat, Stoppard said, "'Dangerous.' *Obviously*, you're just a messenger. Prove it...sir."

Mister Smith reached into his knapsack and pulled out another sandwich as he asked, "What? The dangerous part, or that it isn't a joke? My apologies, care for a sandwich? It's your favorite, pastrami on rye, light on the Dijon."

Stoppard's eyes darted between the sandwich, and the nonchalant way Mister Smith maintained his presence, including his fix on the lake. Their eyes were yet to meet. "The dangerous part. I'm not hungry."

"Well, you're right," he said as he dropped the sandwich back in his knapsack. "I'm just a messenger, so I don't have details for you. Suffice it to say, however, once one has been served with a challenge, it does beg for a defense, yes? Without a defense, my client's guess is that the 'annual meeting' challenges can get dangerous when they come from thirty two and a quarter billion dollars worth of angry stock holders."

"Please. Do I look like a fool? There are answers to all your client *supposes*."

Mister Smith wiped his mouth, folded the plastic wrap from his sandwich neatly, tucked it back into his knapsack and said. "Excellent. Then it should be an interesting experience to see who prevails." He rose, strapped on his knapsack and straightened his cap. "With you having all the answers, there probably won't be any need for the dirt."

"Dirt?"

"Oh, just some laundry in your hamper, Mister Denning. Hopefully, it won't be necessary to air it soon. Good day." Mister Smith moved away with a jaunty step and was gone.

Stoppard felt the corners of his lips, eyebrows and nostrils begin to quiver as deep inside, wells of anger fought against the suppression. "Son of a bitch," he mumbled under his breath. "Which fucking laundry?"

***

July breezes made for an opportune gardening day on her beach deck, so Aretha was down on her hands and knees again, this time planting some of her favorite purple coneflower starters when the call came in. She carefully put down the bag of potting soil and stepped to the phone. "Hello."

"Just wanted to let you know the message has been delivered, Aretha."

"Oh, thank you Wurden. Hope it wasn't too much trouble for you."

"Well, like I said… I owed you one for that Picasso. Bernard, uh, Mister Smith, complained a little bit, until I told him who the target was."

"He was okay?

"He was more than okay. Said *he* had heard some dirt on Denning as well, but I told him we didn't need any of that. Just a business message."

"Well, I do thank you.

"Probably should give Stoppard a couple of days to think things over. Bernard can be somewhat intimidating when he wants to be."

"Well, let's see how he responds. We'll talk soon, okay?"

"Anytime, Aretha. Anytime."

She hung up the phone and knelt back down, reaching in a bucket for some polished pebbles to spread around the flowers. As she pushed the stones in place, she couldn't help but wonder. *What dirt had Mister Smith heard?*

***

For the next couple of days, Stoppard's usual focus was fragmented. Even though his preparation for the annual meeting was progressing—thanks to a fearful and highly motivated staff— there were several times they had to repeat themselves during meetings, as his mind kept wandering off. He was definitely distracted with Mister Smith. A proxy battle didn't bother him nearly as much as that little tidbit of threat with "dirt" as he called it. He couldn't figure out why that bothered him so much. He only knew that his fix on getting rid of Derek Turrel wasn't nearly as consuming as this. It was only after racking his brain with endless reruns of business dealings in his long climb to the top, that he finally concluded it had to have been a slip of the tongue with someone inside his small circle. Someone close, but not directly involved in his business. *There was Stella, his barber. No, never shared anything personal with her, other than his sordid taste in jokes which she loved to hear. His secretary, Myra. Nosey at times and she could be overbearing with reminding him of everything, but, unless she listened in on telephone…No,* he thought. *Shit, I'm really starting to feel paranoid. The only other person…*

***

"Siebert, how long have you been with me now?" asked Stoppard as he scanned the stock pages of the Times. He looked across the seat. "Siebert?"

His chauffeur was grinning as he glanced back and maneuvered the limo through rush hour traffic. "Well, long enough to know you've never ridden in the front seat before. Kinda strange."

Stoppard smiled back. "Oh, just thought it would be interesting to see what things looked like from up here. So, how long?"

"Well, started out steward on the yacht. That was two years. Been…" he counted on his fingers, "…been nine years you count the yacht."

Stoppard put down the paper and gazed out the windshield. "Nine years. Been through a lot together."

"Yes, sir."

"You've opened the car door for a lot of important people."

"Yes, sir. Sure have."

"Served a lot of important people on the boat, too, yes?"

"For sure, Mister Denning."

"Heard a lot of things, too, yes?"

"Pardon?"

"You've heard a lot of conversations I've had through all those nine years."

Siebert gave Stoppard a confused look. "I've…I suppose there's been some talk I've overheard. I don't remember." He looked again toward Stoppard, who held his gaze out the window. "Something bothering you, Mister Denning…something you want to say?"

"No. Just reminiscing. You reminisce some times, don't you?"

Siebert shrugged. "Yeah. Everybody does, I suppose."

"Have I been a decent boss, Siebert?"

Embarrassed now, Siebert blushed. "Yes, sir. You're the best."

"Treat you good at Christmas?"

"Absolutely."

"Loaned you the money for your kid's prep school?"

"I'm gonna pay that back as soon…"

290

Stoppard reached over and patted Siebert's shoulder. "Not worried about that. You're not going anywhere, are you?"

"Long as you want me. I'm here for you, Mister Denning."

Stoppard turned to him. "I want to believe that."

Siebert did a subtle double take. "Well, it's true. Mister Denning...there is something bothering you."

"Naw." He pointed to the Hudson. "Let's take a quick look at the boat. Haven't checked it out since Marco and the crew brought it back from the Hamptons."

As Siebert signaled and got into the turning lane, "Sure. Be good to get out of this rush hour anyway."

As Stoppard got out of the car, he nodded and approached *The Katherine*, a motor yacht measuring seventy-two meters from stem to stern, replete with fifteen suites to accommodate thirty guests. *The Katherine* was among the elite of the world's motor yachts, proudly displaying opulence fit for a king, which Stoppard felt was an appropriate surrounding for his self-image. He enjoyed entertaining friends, and even strangers on occasion when cruising, just for the sheer joy of sharing his wealth with those less fortunate than he—at least that was the inference commonly suggested by Adam Sanders when Stoppard requested some publicity. After all, there were only three boats of this caliber in the world, and two of them belonged to sheiks that chose to treat them as just another toy. For Stoppard, however, this was art. This was award winning engineering and esthetic superiority. And, in Stoppard's model of the world, the sixty-three million dollars he paid for it was proof.

Standing on deck was one of the ship's security guards, who tipped his hat. "Good afternoon, Mister Denning."

"Afternoon, Renaldo. Looks like *The Katherine* arrived back safe and sound."

He nodded. "The captain left a full report in your cabin, sir."

The word "cabin" was a gross understatement, but one that Stoppard excused given Renaldo was from a "Bronx" school of boatmanship with certain verbal habits that were unbreakable as they were charming. Stoppard and Siebert boarded and walked to the aft where he proceeded below to his suite, a setting that would rival that of any royalty. He lifted a bottle of Pellegrino from the mini-fridge and moved to the couch, where he idly thumbed through the Captain's report. "Siebert, you haven't said a word since we boarded."

Siebert smiled with diffidence. "I've never been aboard *The Katherine*, sir. A little different from *The Princess* and my old days as steward."

Stoppard passed a glass of the sparkling water over to him. "Well, let's toast to your first exposure to my queen. A trusted chauffeur deserves rewards as well."

The humble man, whose black uniform unexpectedly made him feel awkwardly out of place, adjusted his position on the baby Gazelle covered sofa and returned the gesture. "You're very kind."

Stoppard nodded back. "Yes. I am, aren't I?" He took a quick sip, then, "That was rather arrogant. I apologize. It's just..." He rose and walked to the other end of the suite's forty-foot playing field of corporate indulgence, and then turned back. "I've begun to realize something, Siebert. All this is very nice to have, you know? But, like everything else in life, it could all disappear. Perks." He chuckled, the essence of his thoughts hitting home. "Perks come with the job, but the job comes with risks. Know what I mean?"

Siebert nodded. "I think so."

"Risks you aren't even aware of some of the time. And you know what, Siebert, you know what?"

Siebert, feeling a bit uncomfortable from the edge in Stoppard's voice, shrugged. "What?"

"That's the biggest risk of all, saying or doing something you're not even aware you said or did. You know, in the heat of the moment kind of stuff. And even if you think you're alone, you know, like at a quiet corner table in a restaurant, or on a park bench, or... even in the back seat of your own limo... well, sometimes, you might say or do something that might be used against you, or you might be overheard or seen, and then you wake up one morning to find you've been betrayed." He sipped his water. "You think I've been discreet?"

"Discreet, Mister Denning?"

"Yeah, you know, blabbing like I do sometimes in the back seat with passengers."

Siebert took a swallow of his water. "You've always been discreet as far I can see."

"Or hear?"

"Pardon," said Siebert.

"Hearing me blab. Ever think I was saying things I shouldn't?"

"Mister Denning, you've only had me keep the glass partition open a couple of times when you've been in the back seat, so I haven't heard you say much."

"I can be such a big mouth sometimes though, right?"

"Not that I've heard, Mister Denning."

Stoppard swallowed the last of his drink, his eyes remaining on Siebert. "Good. That's good. You know the lady in Jamaica is an old friend, right?"

Siebert, knowing the *lady* was a sensitive issue, paused a moment. "The lady with the café?"

"Yes."

"Yes. She's an old friend. You told me that a long time ago."

"She's nice to visit with sometimes," said Stoppard. "Old friends are special, don't you think?"

Siebert smiled, "Yes, sir."

"Well, guess we best be getting back." Stoppard reached down and picked up the report, and as he walked toward the cabin door said, "And trusted friends are even more special. That's why you've remained employed by me for so long. You know that, don't you?"

"Well, I hope you trust me and I hope I always drive safe for you."

Chapter 48

OST's talk show answer to Letterman and Leno had taken two years to mature. In the beginning, launching another such late night show seemed risky. The strong TV ratings battles were legend between CBS and NBC. Both seemed to accept the constant pressure, knowing between the two of them, their 11:30 to 12:30 slots garnered the vast majority of that hour's viewing public. But, Stoppard Denning had ambition, and toppling the two nighttime giants was a challenge he enjoyed. Six months earlier, OST's NIGHT TALK was within four points of becoming the leader. The game of the top three networks duking it out at midnight was "business as usual," until it wasn't.

Like an old replay of the '90's political race where the renegade Ross Perot caused havoc with both the Republicans and the Democrats, so too was Derek Turrel's *Echo Life* project making the three competitors angry as he fragmented their ratings with his success. ECHOES IN THE GARAGE WITH SIMON GRECO had, after all, eroded the late night TV audience by taking an impressive thirty-two percent of its viewers and converting them to interactive radio and TV/computer junkies.

This July night, however, was special for OST, as they expected to pull over to their side of the ratings board a good portion of the thirty-two percent that would normally be listening to or watching Greco. Through a massive 2-day promotion blitz, anybody who watched TV, read newspapers, or listened to the radio was aware that tonight Adam Sanders was about to generate a lot of attention to his personage as OST's Public Relations VP. OST was announcing on NIGHT TALK a concept that Stoppard hoped would demonstrate to Wall Street that his company was far from being a "share holder risk," as the journal had recently suggested.

Adam made his way from the Green Room to Stage Six where OST's NIGHT TALK host, Denny Cullen was finishing up his opening monologue before the commercial break and his first guest. Tonight, however, his only guest would be Adam Sanders.

"It will be just a few moments, Mister Sanders," said the Assistant Stage Manager, as she held her arm out and pressed her headset with the other hand. "Yes, he's here. Anytime you're ready."

Adam nervously straightened his tie and toned the gathering tension in his throat with a spray of some Binaca. "How do I look," he said kiddingly.

"Like an executive about to go on national TV," she kidded back. "You look fine, Mister Sanders. Denny is so easy to talk with. Don't feel nervous about anything."

"Anything? If only you knew."

"Commercial," she said as she dropped her arm and escorted Adam to the stage where make-up awaited his sitting for a final touch-up.

Denny stretched out his hand. "Good to see you, Mister Sanders. We're all on the edge of our seats for this one."

"Well, I hope the viewers are as well."

"No doubt. That blitz you guys did has got to land us the night. Running four plays of the promo during the lead-in hour was priceless."

"Thirty seconds," said the Stage Manager.

Denny nodded and took his seat behind the desk. Make-up finished Adam and did a quick check of Denny.

"You never sweat," said the make-up lady with a smile. "How come?"

Denny smiled, "It's the ice in me veins, lassie."

Break music swelled and the show was back on. After an introduction fit for the Pope, Denny asked the big question. "What's this all about, Mister Sanders?"

Fifty minutes later, the show signed off and many of the studio audience went to the local bars and taverns to kick back, have a few, and laugh or worry about what they had witnessed.

All around the country, similar discussions were going on in both homes and bars.

"He's gonna get his head blown off"
"That stunt should get him a few rating points."
"Hope his insurance is paid up."

"The President's gonna love this."
"They're gonna be lookin' for a new CEO real soon."

***

Simon Greco had a different take as he fielded questions the rest of his all-night show. By 2:30, the lights on the switchboard had cooled down, but the conversations were going just as hot and heavy.

His caller wound down, saying, "If that's only the beginning, where's Stoppard going with this thing next?"

Simon sat back, sipped his tea and answered, "You mean pre-supposing he *comes* back." Pushing another line, "Mary in Toledo. You told my producer that you thought Mister Denning was grandstanding to pacify his stockholders. How so?"

"Look, Simon, I'm just a little guy, girl actually, but I've got a few shares, you know. Dividends were good till a couple of quarters ago."

"Shares of OST, I presume. You pissed?"

"At you guys? Naw. Win a little, lose a little. Hell, way I see it, the ones that *can* afford a *lot* of investment in OST should be smart enough to diversify. If they aren't, then they need a broker, or a *new* broker. I can barely afford to pay the rent, but some inheritance got me a few shares, what the hell. Say...about my call. That shareholders' annual is comin' up around the corner, ya know, and, hey, forget me, but he's gonna have a lot of *big* guys to pacify. Goin' to Darfur and puttin' himself in harms' way, I don't know. He's got a ton of reporters to do that kind of stuff. He's head of the largest media conglomerate in the world. What kind of a gimmick is this anyway?"

Simon leaned forward into the mike, as the sky cam angled toward him. "Mister Sanders quoted Stoppard as saying, 'I'm going to get down on the ground and live a little where it's happening.' Sounds to me like he's tryin' to let his audience know that he's just one of them, that he's not afraid to '*be*' with the people, that he's not above the masses. Hell, maybe he's even giving TV more of what they want."

Mary chuckled. "You mean serve himself up dead?"

"Working the front lines is not foreign to correspondents. He'll be well taken care of," said Simon with a chuckle.

"So what you think he's doin' this for, really?" asked Mary.

"I think you may be right—that stock holders are going to give him a different kind of attention if he pulls it off. A man of his stature risking it all, joining front-line reporting with all its inherent dangers will probably serve him well...momentarily. Those nightly live telecasts and one-on-one exchanges throughout the day with the net

295

and cell phone text messaging, the probable constant flow of play by play analysis he's sending back via web video feeds...yeah, I think he'll get some attention."

"Hey, that sounds like an *Echo Life* schedule," said Mary.

Simon grinned. "Yeah. Does, doesn't it?"

"But is it what he claims – 'another example of giving the people what they want'?"

"Well, I'm no soothsayer," said Simon. "So, let's see what happens. If I were a fortuneteller, I'd probably say it's all a test, albeit a dangerous one. He's got more in mind than he's letting on is my guess, and...this Darfur stunt is probably targeting *Echo Life* as well as his stock holders."

He pushed another line. "Hi out there in Provo, Utah. What's up?"

A squeamish man's voice came on. "Mister Greco, your show is strange, you know that? You get everybody thinkin' they're not usin' their brains enough, not doin' enough creatin'...that all we do is passively use the day watchin' or listenin'. Why Mister Greco, don't you know our job here on earth is to serve the almighty creator? We're not supposed to challenge our leaders. We're not supposed to do that kind of thinkin' or creatin'. We're put here to listen and watch. Listen and watch. That's all I have to say. God bless you." Click

Simon sat forward and gazed at the switchboard. "Well, okay. Another listener not bothered by just sitting there...listening, or watching, or...anyway...anybody out there wanting to listen and do something while we talk? Hey, there's one. Vernon in Costa Rica. Says here you're filming and...well, you tell our audience what you're doing."

"Hi, Simon. I'm whispering so I don't disturb the turtles. God, what a sight, even with the green tint of night lenses. I'm down here in Costa Rica filming thousands of sea turtles covering the sands...Oh, I'm sorry. Just so damn many of them. Every third quarter of the moon, females hit the beach each night for four nights, bury their eggs, then whoosh. Gone. Seen no more. Just wanted to tell you that me and my buddy, Temple Southern, are putting this film together, oh, he's up the Florida coast with the Talitrids jumpin' all over the place. Sand hoppers, they're called. Anyway, nocturnal creatures. That's all we do. Gonna send you a cut when we get it together...might interest your *night owl* audience. Anyway, been listening and watchin' your satellite show with my portable TV and just wanted to say, if that guy thinks I'm going back to *his* kind of TV, he's crazy. I don't care if he rides a Humvee with the windows out in Darfur and lives through it. Nothing beats makin' somethin' and doin it, know what I mean? I watch damn little, but when I do, better be somethin' you guys are sending out, know what I mean?"

"Yeah, Vernon. Guess I know what you mean. We'll be looking out for your film. So, about time to wrap up. If you're staying up, tap into the cannery, 'cause even though I'm tryin' to get some sleep, as usual, there's always someone creating into the wee hours. Thanks for listening and watching. And as far as OST is concerned, we're not going anywhere, right?"

***

The paint splattered latex gloves were removed, and two light brown hands fingered several keys of the Mac. The screen changed to the interior of the cannery where the cycling sky cam paused at Lanagra's work area. Having completed his "Inevitable" installation that was now on permanent display in the lobby of a Manhattan office building, he was feverishly applying the parchment texture to a giant canvas suspended from the ceiling. Standing on the scaffold thirty feet above the ground, he deftly pushed his wide brush upwards giving yet another sense of wrinkled age to the foundation of his next work.

"Using a wall paper brush," said the young man as he peered at the screen. "I'll be God damned. A wall paper hangin' brush! Mon, you be somethin' else." As he saw his face with its splattered paint reflected off the screen, he said, "I'm going to be in that space someday, Lanagra. Do you hear me?" He leaned closer to the reflected image on the screen. "Do you hear me? 'Course not." He chuckled. "You be listenin' to Shostakovich again." He turned the volume up on the laptop, amplifying the Russian master that always accompanied Lanagra's work time.

Picking up the paint splattered spherical speakers in one hand and grabbing the portable rolling lighting with the other hand, Pierre walked back into the cavernous fifteen thousand square foot floor that had once been a Brooklyn sewing factory.

The boarded up windows and walls of the disintegrating floor were painted with Lower East Side New York and Brooklyn history. The style of the young black man suggested that of magnified scribbles of a crude pen and ink drawing. Realism seemed to gradually reveal itself as the black and white broad stokes merged into muddied pastels and further into clashing vibrant colors. Painted beneath the historical images of late nineteenth and twentieth century New York that surrounded him on the four walls, was a moving continuous plume of dust suggesting fragments of previous annals—raw nature with animals, their skins, the birds and vegetation of a more primitive Native American time—floating up past recent times into the sky.

Scattered about the floor were dozens of empty five-gallon paint cans and brushes. He placed the speakers down and walked into yet another corner of the immense floor, being careful to avoid the breaks in the rotting hardwood. He reached over and touched the paint, satisfying himself that it was dry, turned the light toward the other walls. They too depicted more of the neighborhood history moving through time to a 22nd century metropolis exploding into an apocalypse; the finely detailed rancid-colored dust billowing upwards along the bottom, along with the floating fragments like the frayed pieces of a jigsaw puzzle depicting erosion, reminding the viewer of the city's former years.

He smiled as he glanced at the fifteen-foot ceiling where the rising dust converged from the four walls into clouds beginning to shroud the sun's rays, giving rise to painted shadows that spread across the farthest end of the floor. He walked to where the crisscrossing shadows had been worked into even broader strokes of his magnified pen and ink style, curving down from the vertical walls onto the floor.

"A paper hanging brush," he mumbled once again to himself with a smile and sat down on a five-gallon can. He slowly turned to take in the full 360°. He returned his eyes to the curving shadows of the sun and gazed at a large gaping hole in the floor. He rose, walked over and peered through the opening, which revealed nothing but darkness. He looked around at the paint cans. Abruptly, he rushed to inspect the color identification on the cans. Pulling aside several, he quickly lifted the lids and once again, looked at the hole in the floor, then back to the open cans of black, white, yellow, orange and red paint.

Moving from one side of the floor to the next, he searched impatiently, finally finding the wide push broom. He rushed back to the cans and the hole and stood quietly listening to Shostakovich music coming from Lanagra's broadcast. He took a deep breath and then, as he reached to dip the broom into the black paint, he found his mind and senses unexpectedly flooded with a bright explosion of light, like a giant flash bulb. As if a white-hot branding iron had been pressed to his eyes, he filled the building with a sustained screech that only he, his demons and his angels understood.

CHAPTER 49

"Going it alone" isn't what I counted on. Growing the group and its goals is turning into a business competition. When have I ever said that's what I wanted?

I walked along the East River reminding myself how simple life had been only a short while ago. I had my work, my loft, and yes, a woman who loved me and was always there for me. *What happened? 'Going it alone', she had said. Why had that become necessary for her to lay on me?*

I sat down on a bench and gazed out over the water. It too was going in multiple directions, currents clashing, ebb, tide, high, low. What direction was I to take? Traveling up the river was a motor sailboat, its mast pulled in tight, clearing seven or eight knots. College age girls lounged aft. The captain, looking like a college jock, held fast the wheel while his Dalmatian standing forward, pointed its body like a determined compass.

Steering the opposite direction toward the bay and Atlantic was a barge loaded with garbage. As the two passed in the low light of late afternoon, I had to contemplate my own directional choice. I wasn't comfortable with making decisions for others. I thought I would be. Theo thought I would be. Even Samara suggested early on that I was a natural leader. But, here I was, slumped on an anonymous perch watching youth and its awkward grappling of newfound power challenge the upstream currents, while the inevitable by-product of conspicuous consumption floated lazily toward its final resting place.

"Interesting composition, wouldn't you say?" said the man I'd not noticed sit down at the opposite end of the bench.

"Pardon?" I responded.

"The shit barge and the love boat."

I chuckled, half embarrassed, half amused. "Okay."

"Can't appreciate one without the other, can you?" he said, his eyes narrowing as they followed the wake of the barge.

"I suppose."

He turned toward me, then away again, smiling. "Suppose hell. You know exactly what I'm talking about. You are him, aren't you?"

I caught myself rolling my eyes. Oh, boy, I thought. Sounds like another disgruntled OST shareholder thinking I should walk to the nearest bridge and jump. "Him, who?"

He extended his hand. "Derek, I'm just a convert. Don't mind if I shake your hand, do you?"

Now I was really embarrassed. I wasn't used to recognition of this kind. Galleries and museums were common places to shake people's hands, answer questions, explain your art at times, but, here on a walkway bench? I felt like a front-page item. Maybe I was. "No, I don't mind," and shook his hand. "You know about *Echo Project* then?"

He nodded. "Let's hope OST doesn't throw its weight around anymore than they have already. Gets kinda old, ya know."

"How so?"

"Just the big business bullying that seems to get worse."

"Oh, that," I answered. "The great American way. Competition is supposed to be good."

He chuckled. "You really want me to think this doesn't bother you? Hey, I don't wanna pry, I'm just a subscriber and convert, you know, but...how do you avoid the press? I mean, his PR guy, what's his name?"

"Sanders," I answered.

"Yeah, that guy, he's got to be driving you nuts."

I smiled and stood. "Hey, I really appreciate your loyalty and support. I really do. But, I've got to get to another appointment. It's been nice talking with you. You take care now."

"Likewise. Hope I didn't bother you."

I started walking away. "No. Not at all. You have a great day now."

"You too, and good luck!"

I picked up my pace, glancing at my watch to insure he didn't take my leaving personally. I was, however, feeling like I might go a bit nuts if I couldn't get this stress out of my system. I started to jog along the river. After a few minutes, the endorphins kicked in and I got the little high associated with the blood starting to move around. I felt better. I ran now, dodging around the baby strollers, the other joggers and cyclists, finding myself working up to a sprint...fatigue...anger.

***

The morning sea air filled Linda's room, as Aretha stood transfixed on the note in her hand. She pushed back the hair from her face and turned the writing toward the light of the open window, *"Mother, I've tried, but haven't found the perfect situation like I said I thought was necessary. Terribly frustrating. Going to New York for a few days. Don't worry, everything is going to be just fine."*

She lifted her eyes from the paper and gazed out to the surf lapping the shore. She wanted to believe it was just the wind fluttering the note, but she painfully knew it was her trembling. Her eyes wandered to Linda's bed. Something was different. Among the many stuffed animals, Linda's favorite, Guildenstern, the bear, was gone.

***

Stoppard was laughing contemptuously into the phone mouthpiece. "What do you mean I can't, Adam? I own..." He started coughing, the laughter beginning to get out of control. "I own this on-its-way-to-bankruptcy-piece-of-shit conglomerate…" His face reddened and he sat down at his desk, picking up the phone and disconnecting the speaker. "So, you listen to me. It's your job to keep the press happy, the whining stock holders pacified, and that fucking brokerage house thinking it's them that are going to lose if they keeps this up…I don't care if they're advising their best clients to sell. Look, you tell that little bald headed chicken fucker to advise his worst clients to sit tight then. Get it? …Jesus, Sanders, the fucking meeting is in three weeks and I'm catching that fucking plane tonight. You know what it took to get the assholes at the State Department to give me clearance? …Well, hell no. I'm counting on *you* to keep the boat afloat. …Vice Presidents? No, *you*. How the hell can I trust VP's?… So that was a gratuitous mistake, for Christ's sake. You're *more* than a VP. You're my right hand, Adam. Now act like it."

He hung up the phone gently and took a deep breath. He remembered his cell phone had rung while he was on with Adam. He flipped it open and punched up the message. He immediately recognized the voice being that of Mister Smith. He smiled as he listened, "yeah, yeah, yeah…get on with it." And, *get on with it* he did. Stoppard felt a trickle of sweat run from his armpit as the last of the message left him feeling impotent and anxious. He fumbled with the phone's keypad, running the message back a bit and grabbing for a pencil. He slowly hung up and slumped to his chair, fixed on the address he'd written—105 Moore St, Brooklyn.

***

Sitting in the cab, Linda didn't really understand where the feeling was coming from, but what she did know was that she felt somehow empowered. Growing up with all the inhibitions and withdrawn personality had given her nothing but self-doubt. She was angry with life. *Why not?* She thought often, like right now. *I'm tired of wasting away because there's nothing to live for.*

She had tried to express her sense of rotting away to Dr. Reagan, but lost her nerve on several occasions. At least once a year, she'd call a "family meeting" with her mother, wanting so desperately to purge the sense of worthlessness, but each time, she'd find herself making nice and just thanking her mother for being the best mother any girl could ask for, etcetera, all the time hating herself and her mother for not seeing she was faking it, concealing the awful reality that she was nothing.

Today, however, she sat calm and confident in the cab parked two cars behind the black Mercedes limousine with the unmistakable license plate, OST 1. She glanced at her watch, peered out the window toward OST's pharaoh styled office landmark, and recalled how the pyramid-like structure had been built with the windfall money Stoppard realized when he took the company public fifteen years earlier.

The cabby, a typical New Yorker, was quick with speaking his mind and no matter what, always delivered his comments with a smile—of sorts. "Hey, lady, don't want to sound like I'm not appreciative, but you sure you want to continue to wait? That meter is getting' up there."

"We're okay. But thanks for asking. It's four ten and…" she glanced out the window up toward the Mercedes, the chauffeur now getting out and going toward the passenger rear door. "Yup. Cocktail hour, I'll bet." She watched as Stoppard exited the building and moved with an urgency that was foreign to him, but seemed normal to Linda. She chuckled. "He's thirsty."

"Sorry?" said the cabby.

"Oh, nothing. Just stay close to that Mercedes, okay?"

He glanced at the meter reading $46.75 and said, "Sure. You're the boss."

The cab pulled out behind the limo as Linda nodded. *Yeah. I am.*

Traffic was unusually heavy that day. "No explanation for this congestion," said the amiable cab driver, "But, what are you gonna do?" He grinned and looked over his shoulder at Linda. For a lady who was usually in hiding, she looked anything but withdrawn. *Having purpose makes all the difference.* With the debit card she rarely used—but was always with a balance of five digits thanks to the trust deposits every month—Linda had enjoyed the Bonwit Teller splurge that was now still garnering a smiling admiration from the cabby. She felt both giddy and nervous over the acknowledgement. Wearing designer silk wasn't her comfort zone, yet she continued to revel with anticipation over the next phase of her plan.

"Siebert?" asked Stoppard. "How familiar are you with Brooklyn?"

"Well, can't say I've spent that much time there, but where is it you'd like to go?"

Stoppard moved tightly into the corner of the back seat. "I don't know."

"Pardon," prompted Siebert.

"I mean, I don't know if I want to go."

Siebert glanced in the rear view mirror. "You okay, Mister Denning?"

"I'm not sure, Siebert. You ever feel like…" Stoppard stared at the note.

"Sir?"

"105 Moore St," said Stoppard. He glanced out the window. "Got another couple of hours before it's dark, right?"

"Yes, sir." Siebert glanced at his watch. "Actually, another three hours."

"Good. Take your time."

Siebert grinned. "This time of day, that's not hard."

Stoppard turned his stare to the sidewalks and building facades passing ever so slowly through the rush hour.

"Hey," yelled Linda. "Don't lose him."

"Doin' my best, lady. It's the 'dog-eat-dog' hour, remember? Everybody is trying' to steal some real estate, okay?"

Linda passed a twenty over the seat. "There's another one of those in your tip if you *don't* lose him."

The driver glanced at the twenty, and smiled. "Yeah, well, if I get a ticket for honking' or driven' crazy, this won't…"

She passed a hundred over the seat. "Will this?"

He smiled a different grin. "Yeah, that will pay a bribe…probably." He laid on his horn and leaned out the window. "Hey, move it asshole. Ain't no fuckin' parkin' lot, ya know." He turned back to Linda, "Sorry for the language, miss, but…"

"I know, I know. Anger's what it takes sometimes." Linda now leaned out the window. "You heard the man, move your ass."

The driver in the van ahead of them looked in his rear view mirror, threw "the bird" back at her and continued moving the snail pace like all the rest of the cars.

"You still got that Mercedes in your sights, right?"

"Yeah," said the driver. "'less he sprouts wings, we're joined at the hip for a while longer."

The normal twenty-minute ride to Brooklyn took over an hour that day. For Linda, the industrial Williamsburg part of the city was not what she expected. She knew from the tabloids that he frequented his favorite bar around the corner from his office each day around 5 p.m. The corner of Bushwick and Moore St. was anything but a 'favorite bar' location. As she had the cabbie pull to the curb, she watched the on again off again rhythm of the limo's brake lights. *Was this a mistaken address Stoppard had driven to?* Still the lights went on and off. Then the limo started backing up.

"Back up!" shouted Linda. "Back up, damn it!"

"Okay, lady. Take it easy. How far you want me to…"
"That's good," said Linda. "Don't want him to see we're waiting, you know?"

The cabbie stopped a couple of car lengths back and waited. After a few moments, Linda went to get out of the car. "Hey, lady. Didn't you forget somethin'?"

Linda leaned back in. "Just looking around the corner, for God sake." She shook her head and walked to the corner. As she peered around the edge of the building, she jumped. Leaning there was Siebert. "Jesus! You scared me," said Linda.

"Is there something I can help you with, Miss?" answered Siebert.

Trying to compose herself, Linda shook her head. "No. Why do you ask. Just turning the corner."

Siebert smiled. "Yes, ma'am, but you *have* been following us, right?"

"I don't know what you're talking about."

Siebert did a curtsy, and said, "Well, then, my mistake. Proceed. Don't let me stand in your way. You were turning the corner, yes?"

Linda could only walk with a purpose and hope she could round the next corner and not have to face him again. As she passed the building where the limo was parked, she tried to grab a surreptitious glance through the windows, but their dark tint made it impossible to see in. All she could think was, "Is he still sitting there?" She picked up her pace and hoped her over-dressed appearance wasn't going to be her downfall. She was, after all, in a neighborhood of condemned buildings.

As she rounded the next corner and out of view, she took off her heels and broke into a run, trying to get back around to her cab before he was freaking. Little did she know he *was* freaking, but not over her absence.

Siebert stood at the driver's window.

"Look, buddy, I'm just a cabbie. What the hell do I know what she's doing here. Gave me a hundred to not lose ya, that's all I know."

Siebert shrugged. "Well, we shall see. When she returns, I'd strongly suggest *you* suggest that…" He glanced down the block, nodded, obviously figuring she would be back and pulled his black gloves tightly. "No. On second thought. Let's see what she does. Ta Ra." He strode off to the corner, where he glanced up the street at his limo, then leaned against the wall and folded his arms.

Within a minute, Linda came running down the street from the opposite direction, saw Siebert at the corner, paused, put on her shoes, and calmly walked to the cab and got in. As the door shut, she said in a hushed tone as if someone might hear her, "Get the hell out of here...now!" As the cab drew away, she looked over her shoulder. Siebert hadn't moved.

Chapter 50

The note in Stoppard's hand was limp now with sweat. As he peered at the writing one last time, he muttered to himself. "I'm either in for a revelation or I'm gonna die...or maybe both." He tried to quietly place each step up the old rickety service stairwell, but being a building over a hundred years old, he was less than successful. Each step sounded like a mini earthquake to the man that was about as far removed from his element as his memory could recall. *Why am I here? I'm following the instructions of a Mister Smith, someone I don't know...risking life and limb to see what the hell this is all about...allowing fear to rule me...and..."*

Above him, he heard what sounded like a motor, a compressor, maybe. He paused. The noise continued. *At least it drowns out these fucking creaks,* and took the steps more rapidly. As the sound of the motor drew near, he slowed down. He stopped. The motor stopped. The sweat that had been reserved for his hands was now drowning the starch in his shirt. He wiped his brow and continued as quietly as he could.

As he reached the top floor and entered the hallway, he had to blink several times, wipe his eyes of sweat, and take another look at was before him. The walls and ceilings were completely covered with depictions of people dressed like the 1920's, going about their apartment routines, children running about, a mongrel dog, generations of immigrant families, grandparents and uncles, aunts. It was all simple to understand with its similarities to pictures he'd seen of his German relatives when they immigrated at the turn of the century.   Then at the double-door opening going into the main part of the floor, the place where the motor continued to run, the images became blurred and stretched, as if in a morphing process. For Stoppard, it wasn't comfortable. *What the hell am I doing here?* As he stepped closer to the entrance, the images became even further distorted, as if evaporating. For the man who dealt with crisis everyday, the exigency of this moment made all other routine dangers pall in comparison.

The motor abruptly stopped. He paused, unwilling to move. The floorboards betrayed him and the squeak—the movement of his weight. He felt himself swaying. He hugged the wall, gathering his composure, hearing his breath skipping a beat, then another. Just as abruptly as it had stopped, the motor started up again. Only now, it was closer. He wanted to run, but his rational side knew that was out of the question. He cautiously moved his face to the edge of the wall. Rolling his cheek around the edge of the doorway, he peered into the gapping hollow of what he thought hell must look like.

In the center of the sparsely illuminated room that stretched out like a cavern of broken shards of stalactite and stalagmite sheetrock, stood the scaffolding. Three dimly lit work bulbs rendered the room pale of light. The portable generator and its cord stretched to the top of the scaffolding. There, the artist in paint splattered overalls, air-mask, goggles, miner's hat and head lamp stood with an air-brush finishing a detail of what appeared to be the open mouth of God; the lips and white beard spreading to the outer edges of the sixty foot ceiling and then fading into a dark angry cloud that spread to the furthest dark corner of the cavernous room. "Jesus," was all the Stoppard could eek out.

As the artist continued his painting of what appeared to be the aft of a yacht being sucked into the mouth of God, Stoppard felt his dry throat closing with the downward pull of quick sand. The moment he dreaded was unfolding. The motor stopped. The silence was jolted by the wild fluttering of a pigeon swooping from a gaping hole in the ceiling. The artist turned, lifting the paint splattered facemask and goggles, showing his dark skin. He caught sight of Stoppard. They stared at each other. The artist didn't move. Stoppard cowered, thrusting himself against the wall, allowing the moment to give release to his pent up anxiety. "Aieeeeee…God damn it!"

The gentle voice of the artist said, "Perhaps he already has."

Stoppard squeezed his eyes shut, his breath all but stopped.

The man climbed down from the scaffold and walked toward him.

Slowly, Stoppard turned his head from the wall, and lifted his eyelids. He was staring straight into the black eyes of the six-foot young man, the light from his miner's hat beaming straight at him.

"Who are you?" the artist inquired.

Stoppard's jaw remained clenched.

The eyes of the man narrowed. "Do I know you?"

Stoppard shaded his eyes and slowly answered. "Not 'til now."

The artist gazed at Stoppard's dickey collar framing his silk tie. He rotated the blinding light on his hat away. "What are you doing here? This is a boarded up building."

"What are *you* doing here?"

"I…maybe I live here."

"Maybe? You can't live here. This is…"

"Condemned?" He smiled. "The signs outside have established that. You're from the building department, sent to ask me to leave or you'll press charges, yes?"

"No." Stoppard stood up and straightened his tie as he took a calmer look at the man who remained at ease. "You live here?"

"Will that go for or against me?"

"I'm not a building inspector…obviously."

The young man turned and walked back to his scaffolding.

"Well, do you?" said Stoppard hesitantly.

"I *work* here…until I don't." He turned back to Stoppard. "You are a weird one, mon. I don't know…"

"*Me* weird? You're the one…" Stoppard glanced left and right as he walked forward. "Jesus. The walls…it's like a tornado or something. All this…stuff."

The artist shrugged. "Yeah, I suppose for some it's just 'stuff'."

Stoppard continued to gaze around the room with its air-brushed people, their clothes suggesting different decades from the depression to the present. Miscellaneous objects from push-carts to automobiles, wooden chairs to leather couches, all swirling in the upward pull of a whirlwind emanating from the giant mouth painted on the ceiling.

As the artist climbed back up onto the scaffolding, he said "I don't know who you are, mon, but if you're not the building inspector…" He turned and looked down at Stoppard, who was at the scaffold now. "Hey. That's far enough. You might want to leave, 'cause when I start this gun again, it's going to get mighty messy."

Stoppard stared up at the artist.

The artist tilted his head. "You a crazy mon, maybe?"

"You haven't lost your West Indies accent," said Stoppard.

The artist paused. "How you know I'm from West Indies?"

"You have another one of those masks?"

"How you know?"

"Could you loan it to me?"

The artist paused a moment, then reached in his overalls and retrieved a mask. "Why should I give you a mask?"

Stoppard started climbing up the scaffold. "This hold me?"

"Of course, mon, but your suit…"

"Don't worry about it. It's just a suit." Stoppard reached the top and the painter reached out and pulled him onto the platform. Stoppard, still nervous but determined, peered closer at the details of people and things disappearing into the mouth of the bearded image that he assumed was God. He turned toward the painter, who pulled down his mask and removed his miner's hat to wipe the sweat from his shaved head.

"If you're from immigration…"

"I'm not immigration," said Stoppard, his voice reflecting his insecurity.

The painter smiled and turned with a confident air toward his ceiling. "Well, then you must be a *crazy*, comin' here to get some kind of kicks?" He laughed.

"I just want to watch," said Stoppard, as he pulled the mask over his face.

The artist let out a burst of laughter. "Hey, Stan. We've got a *watcher* tonight."

Stoppard squinted in the direction the artist shouted.

"There's somebody else here?" stammered Stoppard.

The artist chuckled.

"You want to watch? Watch. Just mind yourself, understand? I am a US citizen, you know. You come here to *watch*, remember I have my rights too." He started to adjust the mask back to his face.

Stoppard's emotions started to feel tenuous. His eyes shot back to the darkened corner, then to the artist. "Rights? Rights to live in a condemned building?"

"Look, I grew up here…"

"Not here, Pierre. In Queens." Stoppard squinted to read the word "Stan" tattooed on the back of the young man's head.

The painter held his gaze at the ceiling, his mind now cluttered with confusion. As he pulled his mask back down from his face, "How do you know my name?" Who are you, mister?

"Who is 'Stan'?" answered Stoppard.

Pierre whipped around, his eyes now ablaze with anger. "You don't wanna play games with me, mon. You know all about me? Who the fuck are you? Stan be my friend, mon, but he's a big mother fucker of a friend, and he's got a mean fuckin' temper."

"He be telling you the truth," came a raspy, yet somewhat effeminate voice from the dark far end of the room. "Especially when I'm tryin' to be patient waiting for my Pierre."

Stoppard held his breath. He felt his lip tremble. "My Pierre?" he mumbled. Another glance at the tattoo and he understood the buried card Mister Smith said he didn't want to have to play. "Pierre? Oh, my God. I think…"

"Yes. You think what?" asked Pierre. "And how come you know me?"

Letting his chin drop to his chest, Stoppard crouched and sat on a paint bucket, his hands came up to the sides of his head. His shoulders slumped and he felt spent. "My God. No son of mine would be a…"

"What? A gay? Or does your type prefer *fag*? Maybe *your* son wouldn't be, but you're lookin' at one, so as long as you're gonna be a watcher...that's what you're watchin. Okay, you twisted fuck?"

Silence once again filled the cave like room.

Pierre shook his head. "So...I got work to do. Okay, *Mister Watcher.*"

Stoppard heard the sound of a Zippo lighter. He looked up to see Stan emerge from the shadowed corner taking a heavy, long drag on his cigarette. His bare-chested, six foot five body was chiseled and heavily tattooed. "Don't be too long, *watcher.* Okay?" He smiled and stepped back into the shadows.

The silence was broken with the crack of Stan's knuckles.

Stoppard abruptly rose and started climbing down the scaffold. His voice trembled as he said, "I'm not ready for this."

"Not ready for what?"

"All of...*this,*" answered Stoppard, sweeping his arm in an arc, his eyes darting from the mouth of God to Pierre, to the dark corner.

Pierre shook is head. "Whatever, mon," and switched on his airbrush gun.

After a few more words were exchanged, "crazy fuckin' pervert," were the last words Stoppard heard from Pierre as he reached the floor. He paused, his head swimming with all the thoughts he felt seething inside. *Am I wrong? Can't understand why I feel this way about gays, bastards...and art that borders on the sacrilegious.* He wanted to punish Pierre, as well as himself. The words were hard to utter—very hard.

Chapter 51

Jonesy slugged down the last swallow of his whiskey. "You sure you don't want me to pull that trigger you talked about before?" came the hushed voice of Jonesy, well along on his daily drunk.

Looking haggard, sitting on a stool staring into the mirror behind Vinny's bar, Stoppard said, "Jesus, no. I've got bigger problems than pulling a trigger for Christ's sake."

"Bigger than one hundred thousand dollars? Shit, you *are* carrying a load."

Stoppard pulled his gaze to Jonesy. "Want another?"

Jonesy smiled. "Hey...I've never been known to turn down a drink."

Stoppard motioned to the bartender. "Shino. Give him another. No, hell. Give him the bottle."

Jonesy smiled even bigger. "Now...you've got class, mister. Class."

"I got shit," said Stoppard.

"Pardon," said Jonesy.

Stoppard threw down a jigger of Tequila and chased it with a swallow of beer. "Hey, Shino..." he managed to slur out. "I deserve a bottle too. That full one... the Gold, no, the Black Cuervo." He slapped a hundred down on the counter and slid off the seat, the bottle in one hand and his shot glass in the other. "C'mon, Jonesy. Time to tie it on."

"Want a pitcher of beer with that?" asked Shino.

Stoppard lumbered toward the corner with Jonesy in pursuit. "Hell, no. Can't get a good drunk on diluting it with that piss water." He threw his arm around Jonesy and pulled him down into a seat as he slumped into the other. They both started to laugh boisterously, then slipped into a whisper. Stoppard playfully pulled Jonesy's ear toward him. "How about I give you *two* hundred thou and you pull *two* triggers?"

More laughter.

Jonesy staggered to his feet and drew from his imaginary six-gun holsters. "Bam, bam. Shit. I'm good."

Another blast of laughter.

"So," said Stoppard, "What's your take on gays?"

Jonesy wavered. "Hey...shit, mister..."

"Relax," slurred Stoppard. "Just a simple topic for conver... conversation, okay? You're a young man. Gay or straight...shouldn't matter, right? So...help an old drunk get a grip, will ya?"

Shino continued to polish his glasses.

The voices of Stoppard and Jonesy graduated into whispered tones, getting quieter and quieter as both bottomed-out their bottles over the next hour.

Shino thought he heard whimpering, crying...but he wasn't sure.

***

"God, damn it!" came Pierre's voice in the darkness as he slammed Linda against the wall and flipped on his miner light. "Who the hell are *you*, now? What's with this fucking night?"

Linda, her eyes tearing with fear stuttered, "Oh, God. Don't hurt me. I'm just...I was looking for...I'm sorry. I needed to see why he came in here, that's all."

"Why who came? You mean the *watcher*, ma'am?" came the voice of Stan as he crept from the shadows and turned a work light straight onto her.

"The man that was here earlier. Please. I just thought maybe he was still here. Where did he go?"

"That's none of your business," said Pierre.

"Yeah. None of your fucking business, ma'am," followed Stan.

"Okay. Okay. Just don't hurt me. Please."

"No problemo, long as you leave the same way as you came." Pierre looked at her cocktail dress. "What's with you fancy assed people peepin' 'round here, for Christ's sake?"

Stan stepped forward. "Enough. This ain't no peep show. Get the fuck outta here."

Linda pulled her shaking body together and hurriedly backed away, catching glimpses of the painted images as Pierre's headlamp bounced off the walls.

"And don't you come on back. You hear, lady? Don't come back," threatened Pierre.

As Linda reached the opening into the halls, she burst into a run, stumbling, falling, getting back up and cautiously descending the stairway. From above her, she could still hear them.

"And tell that other creep, when you see him, that next time we won't be so accommodating," bellowed Stan. "Tell him Stan sent him a big *wet one*." He laughed.

Pierre turned and silently walked back to his scaffolding. He paused and looked up, the beam of his head lamp centering on the mouth of God. "You didn't need to say that, Stan."

***

Street lamps hummed with the cacophony of mercury arcs zapping moths that dropped to the ground. Bushwick was deserted now, save for the occasional heavily woofered Honda low-rider blasting its way through the late night and the all too infrequent cabs, whose dark vacancy signs signaled yet again how dangerous it was to be a single woman walking the streets after midnight. As a taxi pulled up and dropped its passenger at the corner, Linda lunged from the comfort of a heavily shadowed alcove and flagged it down.

Once inside, the piercing eyes of the East Indian driver reflected in the rear view mirror reminded her of the evening's earlier nightmarish events. He turned down the radio. "Where to, ma'am?"

She glanced at the dashboard. The cab license read: Ohmar Shukta. "Ohmar, I'd like to go to heaven, but that's probably out of your zoned area, right?"

Ohmar's face lit up with a smile. "Very out. But, I know all the nice smooth roads that won't upset your sleep."

"That's nice, Ohmar. That's nice. Sleep is good. I'm at the Peabody...across the street from OST."

"No problem. Rough night?" he said.

"And day."

"Pardon?"

He turned back, but her eyes were closed, her hands clutched tightly around the beaded cocktail bag whose bulging outline of cold steel reminded her that there was always tomorrow.

Ohmar rounded the corner and turned his radio up just loud enough to not disturb his passenger. He hated missing any part of the Greco show.

***

For all concerned, the previous night had been unsettling.

Derek slept with Samara, but laid awake most of the night undecided on what his next move should be.

For Theo, not having Derek back had left him unsettled. He tried to ground himself by writing through most of the night. He didn't like what he had written.

Stoppard continued to get very drunk and had been helped by Siebert to the elevator of his apartment.

Pierre stayed up until dawn painting, concerned as to who the man in the silk tie was and the woman that followed.

Linda returned to her hotel and spent most of the night staring at the small compact Beretta she had taken from her mother's storage cabinet.

Aretha sat gazing at the storage cabinet most of the night, not knowing where her daughter was with *her* gun, a weapon her first husband, Linda's father, had always insisted on keeping on premises... "Just in case," he always said. "Just in case."

***

The toilet bowl was clean, but Derek continued to flush. Samara stood stoic at the doorway. "There's nothing to come up, Derek."

"Jesus, don't you think I know that? What am I supposed..." he purged yet another dry heave. "I'm sorry. No need for me to bite your head off."

Samara contemplated a moment, then "You've had these anxiety attacks before. Maybe it's time to get back to what you miss."

"And that is?"

"The rock," said Samara as she turned and walked back into the kitchen area. "Coffee?"

"God, no. Some chamomile maybe."

"Chamomile it is. You haven't mentioned Echo since you've been back. Still part of your routine?"

Derek rose and wiped his mouth, then reached for the Scope. "Hardly a routine, but, yes, no…well, I've been trying to just be…you know, like you said, work this out myself."

Samara concentrated on scooping just the right amount of coffee to brew as she waited for the water to boil. "And? Working with Echo is just *that*, Derek. It's real to you, and it's very personal. Consistent. That's what you need to keep focused on. That consistency you're so famous for. Want some dry bread for your stomach?"

Derek walked into the kitchen buttoning his shirt. "You don't like her, do you?"

"Who, Echo? It's not a matter of like or dislike. I suppose I'm a bit jealous of her presence in your life. Probably, that's true. But, that's a woman's prerogative with the man she loves."

Derek nuzzled her neck as she poured the hot water into his cup of chamomile. "Not while I'm pouring, you."

"So," quipped Derek, "should I tell her it's over?"

Samara chuckled. "Derek, darling, you don't tell a muse it's over. She, it, or he, not you, will utter those words *if* they are ever to be uttered."

"You're jealous. You really do believe in it, don't you?"

Samara poured the remainder of the teakettle into her French press and turned to him. "Did I ever tell you about Zelphon?"

"Zelphon? No. Who's he?"

Samara lifted the French press and Derek's cup and walked into the sitting area. "Oh, just a little experiment I've had going to a long time."

Derek sat down and lifted his cup of tea. "Zelphon. You've never mentioned him before. A patient?"

"Hardly." She laughed and pointed over at the grand piano. "He sits on the lid most of the time, occasionally sits by my side when I've taken a page of manuscript to bed with me."

Derek grinned. "Trying to humor me?"

She turned to him and matter of fact said, "Zelphon is working out well, so far. My sub-conscious is alive and well, just like yours. Picked me up out of many a down day, you know?"

Derek nodded, acquiescing the necessary *points* in their long history of one-upmanship competitions. "Okay. You've got one too. What does that make us both? Loonies?"

Samara put her arm around his shoulder and stared at the piano. "No. Just two people with like needs for their inner voices. My patients would think otherwise," she said, chuckling once again, "but

313

I'm the doctor and they're the patients, so I can get away with it, etc, etc, etc." She poured her coffee and took a sip. "You're up against some challenging times, Derek. Were it me, I'd take all the help I could get…including my muse."

Derek's cell phone rang, taking him by surprise. He looked at the screen's telephone number notation. It read, *unknown caller*. He pocketed the phone and smiled. "Don't need an interruption from somebody I don't know, so…"

"Unknown callers are half the time just people you don't have in your directory. Might be from the island. Never know, you know," said Samara as she took another sip of coffee and rose. "I've got to get rolling. You listen to the message and I'll get dressed. You can walk me to the corner."

Derek shrugged and sipped his tea. His eyes wandered to the windows where a couple of pigeons were in the preliminary stages of a mating ritual. Finally, he lifted the phone out and saw there was a message. As he listened, the pigeons continued their rowdiness on the windowsill, and Samara hummed the strains of what sounded to Derek like a work in progress. *"Derek, I'm sorry to disturb you, but it's important we talk. This is Linda, you know, Aretha's wacky daughter."* She laughed nervously. *"But, well, I'm really not… wacky. I'm needing to talk to you about something that is wacky though. Could you spare a minute, assuming you're still in Manhattan? Mother said you were heading that way. You can reach me at 617- 400-1212. It's important to both of us. Thanks. Good by."* Derek listened again and then stood up and walked to the window, staring aimlessly at the windowsill. Only one pigeon remained, the other was gone.

Samara walked in, fastening her wristwatch and noticed the windowsill as well. "Oh, that one again. Horny as hell. She ruffle some of her boy friend's feathers for you?" Derek turned, half-smiling, half-serious. "Yeah…kinda. Samara, that was Linda…Aretha's daughter."

"Oh," she said chidingly, "you're not messing around now behind my back, are you?"

"She sounds upset. She's never called me before. I don't even know how she got my number…probably from Aretha."

"Look, Derek, I'm really running late. Could we…"

Derek grabbed another sip of his tea, and then said, "Yeah. Of course." He walked with her to the freight elevator.

"So, what was she upset over?"

"Didn't say."

They stepped onto the elevator. As Derek pulled the strap down closing the heavy door, Samara casually asked, "Okay. So what are you going to do with that complication?"

Chapter 52

The espresso arrived as usual with just the right amount of froth still floating on top. Patty, in her usual sarcastic, but charming mood, said "Two cubes, right Mister Turrel?"

I maintained my laid back, calm listening mode and waived her off with a smile.

"I really appreciate you seeing me, Derek. I know I'm not one of your favorite people," said Linda as she stirred cream into her espresso.

"Well, you sounded like it was important." I wasn't sure I was starting off this get-together properly, but the elitist in me burst forth without warning. "That is the best espresso in all of New York, you know?"

Linda smiled back, a bit embarrassed. "I'm sorry. Old habit from childhood. Any coffee has to have cream for me to..."

"I've got to catch a plane, Linda. Could we get to the problem?"

"Yes...Yes, of course." She took a quick sip to gather her thoughts. "I'm really just a simple person, Derek, you know? I'm not prone to drama."

"No. Of course not," I said with a slight grin.

"Oh, that. When I took you on at the house...well...that was the liquor ranting. I weave baskets, you know. And masks. I'm usually very calm."

Oh, boy, I thought. From panic to basket weaving. "Something tells me you don't feel calm right now. What happened?"

"I met someone."

"Linda, with all due respect, is this a man problem we're about to talk about, 'cause I've really..."

"Not that kind of man. Oh, God. It's long and ugly...the whole story, and I..."

I refrained from saying anything more as she began talking faster in an effort to hold back the tears. I listened, and found myself pulled into a cat and mouse drama fit for a new soap opera, but then again, *scary* real. I glanced at my watch only once, and that was forty-five minutes later.

"Oh, Jesus."

Linda, now with a pile of tear drenched napkins stacked in front of her, jumped. "What? I'm sorry. Did I say something that..."

She was not in good shape at all. Not wanting to embarrass her any further, I said as calmly as I could, "Oh, forget it. Just have to catch a later flight. I'm sorry for interrupting you. This is utterly...*unbelievable*. Is that the word?"

"Oh...it happened, Derek. I wish it hadn't, but it did. I just wanted to follow him into his favorite bar and slip quietly into a bar stool...and get him to take me somewhere so I could...but then, he goes to Brooklyn. That rude chauffeur...my going away, then slipping back later and...then..."

She had spent a long time telling me how the only answer to *my* problem and the only way to insure her mother and I would be happy was to put a bullet in Stoppard. To say I was troubled—again—as if the beach incident wasn't enough, would have been an understatement of monumental magnitude. Even though she had spent an inordinate amount of time explaining her rationale for killing Stoppard, she insisted on revisiting the "painter" experience with more details than I was really ready for. As she gave me the minute-by-minute terror she felt in a condemned building, she kept interrupting herself with, "I realized this painter and Stoppard thing was none of my business, you understand. None of my business..." over and over.

It was three espressos later and a large tip for Patty when I heaved a sigh and patted Linda's hand. "I find it hard to believe Stoppard is a...one of those types..."

"Oh, they were definitely gay. Definitely."

"But, Linda, that doesn't make Stoppard..."

"Gay? What the hell would a man of his stature be doing in a...a...God, those walls were like things, people, moving, like a movie..."

"Linda?"

"But they were weird like...and...when I stumbled out of there...their voices...yelling from the fourth floor to 'find some other way to entertain yourself, bitch'...and calling me all kinds of...oh, it was horrible."

"Well, you did kind of take them by surprise."

Linda blew her nose and seemed to be gathering her composure. With a big purging sigh, her eyes became clear and her expression, resolute. "Yes. I suppose I did." She took out her compact and dabbed her cheeks and nose. "It definitely makes it potentially messier. It could have been so simple." She put the compact away and looked up, projecting a different Linda. "Well, you have a plane to catch and I've got things to do. You failed to tell me what to do, you know. That's what men do. They tell Linda what to do. Well?"

This was a Linda I didn't like and I wasn't ready to tell her anything, except "I think you should probably go home, Linda. Your mother will understand."

She stared a few moments at me with a look that was impossible to read. Finally, she rose, I followed, and we walked to the corner. "I really can't go back home now," she tearfully said. "She'll never trust me again...taking the gun and all. Besides, how can I just turn my back on this...well, my trip has a purpose, you know."

Derek took her arm and consolingly said, "The gun is not a problem, Linda. You didn't use it, remember?"

As they reached the corner, Linda raised her arm for a cab. "Not last night." A cab pulled up.

My anxiety level rushed over me at mach speed now. Fear, I told myself, fear is the enemy here, not the gun. "Linda, you sure you don't want to let me take the gun back to Aretha? I could explain perhaps..."

"No." Gripping her shoulder bag, she stepped into the cab. "Thank you for listening. It's important that somebody close to mother knows I love her and have finally realized I haven't shown it much...need to make it right...something to make her happy...this will help."

"Help? Help with what?" I stammered, not knowing how to react.

With a convincing smile, she seemed to be all together. "And that coffee *is* very good." She closed the door, as I blurted out a plea much too late. "Linda, where are you staying?" But the cab was gone. I stood there, somewhat in a daze. "Fuck. I just let her...Fuck!"

***

I don't know how long I walked, but by the time I reached Central Park, I had managed to start talking to myself, giving one homeless man his entertainment for the day. Pushing his overloaded grocery cart, he sidled up along side me, copying any cadence I chose to use, and mumbled along with me like a parrot, until, "Mister... you just don't look like..."

It was enough to shake me back to some reality. "Like what?"

"The *type*, you know?"

I peeled off a five-dollar bill and stuck in his shirt. "Why? You think you've got a corner on the *talk-to-yourself-market*?"

The man held the five up to the sun, then smiled. "Nope. Have a nice day," and was off down the path circling the lake.

I sat down on a bench and stared out over the water. The only right thing to do was call Aretha, but then all I could think was we didn't know where Linda had gone, so what could she do… then it hit me. Linda had said she had waited for him in front of OST and wanted to just somehow …*quietly climb on a bar stool and get Stoppard to take me somewhere so I could…*" I looked at my watch. It was 3:30.

***

Standing in the doorway across the street from the OST headquarters skyscraper was perhaps the most un-Derek action I'd ever engaged in. I had to allow, *really* allow that little voice that is oft times referred to as the sub-conscious to speak. I had to let it tell me what the hell this was all about 'cause the conscious me sure as hell didn't know. *Why hadn't I just gone to the authorities and told them that I was concerned with Linda and her apparent determination to kill Stoppard? And for what? For me? For her mother?*

Confusion reined heavily as I peered across the street at the black limo with the infamous license plate, OST 1 standing idle, the chauffeur leaning against the passenger door. My watch teetered on 5 p.m. *Where was he?* The unanswerable questions came at me again. *Why didn't I go to the police? Did I think I could somehow stop her if she showed up…as I hoped? Did I think it might give me some kind of advantage to stop his murder?* "Damn!" I muttered.

Looking up and down the street revealed nothing of Linda. Maybe she had come to her senses. Maybe she was on her way home. I looked at my watch. Well, five straight up. It was now or never. I hailed a cab and gave the driver twenty bucks to just sit and wait. The back seat was cramped, and even with the air conditioning, I felt hot, sticky…no, wet. That's how I really felt. "Hey, could you push that air a bit?"

"Yeah. Sure for a few minutes. Idlin' like this makes me overheat, you know?" said the driver.

I wiped my palms, looked out the window, up and down the street, even at the three cabs also idling in front of us, but no Linda. I took a deep breath and tried to calm down. I was an artist, not a stalker or a private detective. *What was I doing playing out this clandestine game?*

Ahead, the chauffeur stepped forward and opened the back door as Stoppard walked up and climbed in. Now the test. "Just follow the limo," I said to the cabbie.

The driver grinned. "Follow that car? That still goes on?"

"I know. Sounds corny. I don't believe it myself, but…I have to."

"Hey," chuckled the driver, "you pay. I drive."

We pulled out into traffic. I took a quick look behind me to see if any other cab pulled out, but I was the only one, at least the only one following the OST 1 car.

318

"You thinkin' I'm gonna keep behind him in this crazy traffic?"

"Just do your best. Don't lose him."

"'Do your best' but 'don't lose him'." He shook his head and smiled. "What I have to go through."

***

Fortunately, I'd dressed fairly conservative for the flight back to the island, so merging into Mickey's crowd of Happy Hour customers was easy. I had kept my distance, entering behind Stoppard, but now he was walking up to the VIP lounge and dressed conservatively or not, I wasn't likely to get in there. "Hey, bartender, what's the key to getting in upstairs?"

"Membership, or know a member you're meeting."

"You mean, if I tell the little guy in the tux up there that I'm meeting someone inside that he knows..."

"You got it."

It was time to relax and gather some courage. If Linda showed up, that was the only thing I could do.

Stoppard made his way through the suits of Jr. Execs and the power brokers that were the bread and butter expense tabs for the Mickey's high-end costs, including the tux -attired stanchion man that now unclipped the crimson rope and greeted Stoppard with, "Good to see you again, Mister Denning. Your guest is already seated."

Stoppard paused, "Guest?"

"Yes, Mister Denning, Miss Parks."

Stoppard craned his neck to peer back to his glass-enclosed corner table, but all he could see from the overhead pin spot were two hands atop the table resting on a purse. "I don't know any Miss Parks."

"But..." The host looked back at the table again. "I'm sure she said Mister Denning was... oh, I'm terrible sorry. She did say that your secretary neglected in reminding you of the appointment. I trust I haven't..."

"It's okay, Hiram. It's okay. I'll take care of it." He slipped Hiram a tip and proceeded back toward his table. As he passed the tables, two, then three cronies made comments, "Not bad, Stoppard, for an old man!"

"Let me know if she wants some company later."

"Need some help, Mister Denning?"

His waiter, Cedric, greeted him. "Good evening, Mister Denning."

"Hello, Cedric," he said, squinting at the lady sitting inside. Cedric opened the glass door, and he stepped in.

"Don't take it out on your secretary, now," came the voice in the shadows, her spotlighted hand lifting. "I'm Jennifer Parks, your Event Planner."

Stoppard took her hand, gave it an acknowledgement and sat down. "Event Planner? This is all...I'm sorry, but I'm in the dark."

She chuckled and said, "Yes... we both are. Let's get acquainted." She leaned into the overhead spot's rim, revealing the face of Linda. "Your shareholder's meeting? The reception?"

Stoppard remained in the shadows. His confused voice eked out, "Okay. But, I don't remember making an appointment with you. I usually..."

"...Have Mister Sander's office take care of that. I know. But, he thought it best I speak to you in person about my idea. He felt you deserved to hear it first hand. He has a high respect for you, Mister Denning. You know that of course."

"Of course. Okay, I don't know what the hell...but..." He relaxed, smiled and raised his hand which immediately brought Cedric.

"Yes, Mister Denning?"

"The usual. Uh...Ms. Parks?"

She raised her empty tumbler. "Another ginger ale. I'm working, you know."

"Very good, Ma'am," said Cedric, and he was off.

"So...what is this idea that Sanders thought I should hear 'first hand'? Uh, mind if I smoke? The room is well ventilated."

"Of course not. Please." Linda lifted the maraschino cherry from her glass and slid it into her mouth. "This could take a while. Is that okay?"

Stoppard watched her maneuver the cherry, as he lit up a Churchill. "Am I supposed to respond to that?"

Linda smiled. "You already are."

Stoppard's eyes stayed with hers.

After an hour, *Shit,* was all I could think as I sat at the bar, grabbing glances of the upstairs VIP area, and back down to the front door. *What the hell am I doing here? I obviously guessed wrong.*

"Another?" said the bartender.

"Yeah. Sure." I threw a futile glance upstairs again. "No. Cash me out."

***

The sidewalks of Central Park South are pretty much a surrealistic experience at two in the morning, so I found myself sitting on a bench on the park side of the street, fixed on Stoppard's

320

building entrance, and imagining all the people walking in and out of one of the most prestigious apartment houses in the city. I could picture all the types that, in their own inimitable way, were perfectly suited for living here with Stoppard Denning. *Strange,* I thought, *even a man of his power, couldn't resist publicizing his purchase of the twenty-six million dollar penthouse, knowing with it, went his ultimate privacy. Maybe privacy—that kind of privacy—didn't mean much to a man like him. God knows, I wasn't the first to watch the front entrance for a glimpse of one of the richest men in the world.*

At the time, a spread in the Magazine section of the Sunday Times, which included a picture of the building front and its address, was like announcing to the world that his home was on the *sightseeing* list. I remembered one of his statements for the interview, "I may be one of the richest men in the world, but I'm no Enron. Investor confidence will always be my deepest concern." Public trust and corporate suspicions being what they were, countless others, I was sure, had gazed at this building and wondered as well— "When will he hurt us?"

Right now, however, the one that was maybe about to get hurt was Stoppard himself. The limo pulled up and came to a slow stop. I waited for what seemed like minutes for the driver to get out and open the door, but all I could see was the silhouette of the still seated driver who raised his hand to beg off the doorman. The red-coat attired man retreated into his small enclosure.

I was standing now, still not knowing what I was doing there, really, or what I thought was going to happen, if anything. I only knew that I felt duty prone to at least give him warning that his life might be in danger. After another few moments, the driver finally got out. I began hurriedly walking across the street, as the limo door was opened and out stepped Linda, followed by Stoppard. *Oh, my God. How? Where?* I ran ahead for the final few yards.

"Stoppard!" I blurted out. "Wait!"

Stoppard turned in bewilderment, as even in his drunken state, he recognized the man now leaping over the curb. He chuckled. "Whoa! Derek? Derek Turrel?"

"I know. This is one hell of a way to meet, but..." I don't know where they came from, but the words burst out in a not very soft whisper. "Your life might be in danger. Please, can we talk?"

Stoppard gave me a quizzical look.

I could see Linda having only just a slight moment of weakness, then putting on the smiling face I didn't know, but I presumed had been working for her for God knows how long that night. *How the hell did she meet him... get him to bring her to his apartment?* "I'm serious. Dead, serious," I blurted out.

Stoppard smiled. "Well, quite an entrance. You are a man of ever-revealing talent, Derek. Let me introduce…"

"Don't bother. I know who she is. Could we talk alone?"

"Excuse me, Mister Turrel, but have you been drinking?" asked Linda. Mister Denning is very tired and…"

Denning gave a double take on the two of us, then took me by the arm, and threw some drunken charm. "What the hell. At the risk of the cliché, eh…you know her? Well, so do I, now." He glanced at his watch, "I thought it was late, but I guess the night is young. Come. Please, Mister Turrel…join us. We were just going to have a nightcap." Still amused with himself, he quipped, "We'll have some sherry and you can tell me all about this imminent danger to my life. You're not trying to kill me, are you, Mister Turrel?" He laughed.

The doorman slipped out from his cubicle and caught the door for us, but I was catching something else—the troubling stare of Linda. But, which Linda?

CHAPTER 38

As we approached the elevator, my mind was racing for an answer. I had stupidly managed to back myself into a corner. *How could I continue my bungled mission? Stoppard has to be confused as well, with the presence of Linda. Yes?* I didn't even know if she was bluffing, or just playing out a scenario she felt was worth experiencing for God knows what reason. The one thing I was sure of, Linda was not stable, and my experience with her thus far had suggested she felt duty bound to do whatever necessary to keep her mother from being disappointed or hurt.

Stoppard's cell phone rang just as the elevator arrived. We stepped on as he impatiently said, "Jesus, it's two fifteen. What…hey, slow down. Look, I'm on my way up the elevator. I'll ring you back from the apartment." He closed the phone and smiled as if nothing was wrong. "So, how did the two of you meet?"

I glanced at Linda, but she had a face on—a face that was flirtatious in its intent, almost daring me to make up a good story. "Oh, that's much too long a story," she said.

"Pity," said Stoppard. "I'm always interested in unusual relationships, and the two of you, well, from what Miss Parks has revealed about herself thus far, you two would seem like water and oil. Know what I mean?"

Fortunately, the elevator arrived at his floor and saved me from answering.

"Oh, but we can discuss that inside. Welcome to my little hideaway," he said, escorting us off the elevator and into his ultra classical 30th floor penthouse apartment, complete with marble floors, fourteen-foot ceilings of windows overlooking Central Park, and an art collection to rival The Guggenheim. "Please make yourself at home...the bar's to your right. I've got to answer this pesky phone call. Won't be a minute."

I walked to the bar followed by Linda, who maintained her chosen attitude suggesting I was the intruder.

"Just what do you hope to gain from this little drama," asked Linda is whispered tone.

"Me? Drama?" I replied. "My, God, Linda. Look at yourself."

Linda took a proud look in the bar mirror and smiled. "Miss Parks. Everything is going to be just fine."

I stood behind the bar knowing any moment he could return. "Linda, I appreciate your..."

"Miss Parks. Jennifer Parks. Get it straight."

"Oh, Christ, Linda. Stop the charade." Her gaze told me she didn't think it was a charade. "Jennifer... you have only one choice." I extended my hand. "Give me the weapon and leave now, or we'll have one hell of a conversation that is going to end up creating a lot of unnecessary trouble. I appreciate your concern for me and your mother, but..."

She looked at my hand with a sense of betrayal. "Derek, you have no right doing this, but you're probably right. Trying to accomplish my mission like this is going to become complicated." She laughed. "He actually invited two of his worst enemies right into his living room. So, I'll leave and you can have your little talk. Just tell him...the headache line. You know. That always works, doesn't it?" She smiled, turned and started walking toward the front door.

"Jennifer. Your purse. Haven't you forgotten something?"

Ignoring my words, she stroked and patted her purse. "No. It's still here." She opened the door and was gone.

These are the kind of moments that remind one of how bad TV can be. No one would believe it if I told it, so... I poured myself a glass of water and waited for Stoppard. I had only a few seconds to ponder what Linda might do next. Aretha had once told me that Linda's personality switches were very unpredictable and very convincing. Yeah. I was in agreement. It was frightening, however. *Was she okay? Would she attempt this again? I could only hope for the best, yet there was a part of me feeling I might have betrayed myself in not insisting on the gun being left with me.*

Stoppard stepped back into the living room from his study and looked around. "Where's Miss Parks?"

"Oh, she apologizes, but a sudden migraine. She did ask me to say thanks for the evening, though."

"Migraine. Yes…well, perhaps for the best." He stepped to the bar and began pouring a scotch. "But, you were saying, Derek, about my *life*?"

I felt relieved he wasn't pursuing her leaving any further and then quickly realized again, I didn't know what I was about to say or do.

"Derek?" He said again. "You were saying?"

"Mister Denning…"

"Stoppard is more appropriate, don't you think?"

"Stoppard, I really don't know how to deal with this."

He sat down, sipped his scotch and made a sweeping motion of his hand. "Well, the ball does seem to be in your court."

"I don't hate you, you know. I've not the courage or the daring to take up such a thought. Just understand that."

He nodded and sat quietly.

"Others might not feel that way. I mean, there are probably some out there that would do harm to you," uttered Derek carefully.

"Like the one you allude to that wants me dead?"

I hesitated. "No," I said. "Like the one…trying to protect others."

"I don't understand, Derek. You said my life was in danger."

"And well it could be. That *someone* thinks they are doing the right thing…the protecting and all. Protecting might cause harm. War 101."

"Some strange pathology, eh? A psycho?"

"Well, I wouldn't say it that way."

"But, you would say it…another way?"

"Stoppard, you, your network, your conglomerates, they all have their people with vested interests. People who are always thinking how they can protect their investment."

"You're making a point, I understand, but can we stop with the riddles? I thought my life was the issue."

"I think I will have a drink."

"Help yourself."

As I walked toward the bar, I knew I could take the easy way out and admit I was the reason for the potential act. After all, it was common knowledge that Stoppard and I stood in each other's way and for different reasons, and both of us felt everything was at stake. Yes, I could use myself as the cause for this, but that wasn't the case. At least I didn't think so. No, Linda hardly knew me. She was concerned with her mother. Even though Aretha was double my years, Linda knew that age had never been a criterion in her mother's effort to create friends. Linda knew I was more than just a friend, and was an important contribution to her mother's happiness.

Revealing the same would have been the direct answer to give Stoppard, but one which would take too much explaining. So, with but a moment or two to think… "Your life is the issue, yes, but…"

"I guess it is late, Mister Turrel, because my patience is waning. Do you have a reason to believe my life is in danger? And if so, might it not justify a call to the police?" He flipped open his cell phone.

I walked back to the couch with a stiff three-fingers in my glass. "It's not as bad now as I thought…I think. In other words, a call to the police right now might be blowing this out of proportion. A threat to somebody's life…your life…is maybe in check now."

Stoppard smirked, "Okay. I get it." He nodded and chuckled. "You're good. But, don't you think it a bit elaborate to use a death threat to get an audience with me? A simple phone call would have done just fine. Did you think I wouldn't see you?"

I sipped my drink, trying desperately to formulate the right thing to say. *Maybe I should be calling the police. Maybe I'm being too presumptuous in thinking I can prevent Linda from carrying out her crazy notion. But, then again, he's right… I have worked my way into a meeting with my arch opponent.* "The fact you haven't thrown me out would suggest you would have seen me. Yes. Actually, I had thought many times about sitting down with you and reasoning this out, but I convinced myself that you were too far into OST to hear or understand me."

"I'm doing alright, wouldn't you say?" He shook his head and grinned. "Son of a bitch. I'm listening, even though you're not the easiest man to understand, so far." He leaned forward. "Good scotch, eh? Tell me, what is it you want; besides my Neilson's to continue dropping? Or is that only the tip of your iceberg. You're costing me a lot of time and money. You know that, don't you?"

"Whoa, Stoppard. I'm not here to be chastised. I'm just doing what I think is the right thing to do."

He rose and walked to the windows, cracking his neck as he walked. "So am I. Tell me, what do you think I'm all about, really? Just some power monger sitting in perhaps the second most powerful seat of persuasion in the world? Well, there is *more* to it than that."

"'Second most powerful seat.'"

"The White House I think occupies the first, right? But, when it comes to supplying this country, and many parts of the world, the necessary information and entertainment… to maintain global sanity, you understand… OST is unrivaled."

"The Whitehouse notwithstanding, you sound to me like you see yourself as having it all."

He turned from the window. "All except *that* which *Echo Project* is trying its damndest to steal from me."

"Steal? Giving people freedom to choose is hardly stealing."

"Choice? Hell, man, you *tell* them what and how you think they should use their time. You're hardly giving choice. Unlike OST, you're proselytizing my friend. *We* give them what they want, and that in turn gives them pleasure, gives them satisfaction. In other words, Derek, we *serve* them. We don't tell them what to read, listen to or watch."

"*Exposing* options is different from *telling people to do something*. Have you watched our programming?"

Stoppard sat down, pulled a Churchill from his humidor atop the coffee table, and prepared to smoke. "Care for one?"

"No thank you."

Stoppard lit up. "You know, Derek, I've watched your flagship show, that vulgar little program, *Late Night in the Garage*. Now, that's real sophisticated programming, Derek," he offered with a sarcastic cigar-roll between his lips.

"It's not meant to be sophisticated. Just a simple show that let's people speak their mind about their imagination."

"Oh. 'Imagination.' Yes. I'd almost forgotten you think that OST and everything it stands for is void of imagination."

"When did I ever say that?"

"Ah, that's where you *are* sophisticated. You understand the value of *inference*, so do some members of the media who listen and pick up on your strategy."

"But, hardly a tool of proselytizing."

"Quite the contrary. A very effective way to make your audience think you're just a man looking out for *their* best interest. That's proselytizing, evangelist style. It obviously has worked. You've taken over thirty percent of my audience away. Bible thumping big time."

I slugged down the scotch and stood up. "You don't mind if I have another drink, do you?"

Stoppard looked out his windows at the horizon, as he extended his own glass. "As long as you're pouring. You know, Derek, I wonder every day now whether I'll see tomorrow's sunrise. I've worked a long time. It's probably taken its toll. Could end any day, you know?" He turned. "But, of course you do."

I stood over the ice bucket and dropped two cubes in each glass. "Guess we all wish it could go on forever."

He chuckled. "Only in your dreams, right? Only in your *imagination*. Reality is a crass, harsh son of a bitch, wouldn't you agree?"

"It doesn't have to be. It is what you make of it. Crass and harsh aren't necessarily bad. It's how you choose to deal with crass and harsh...your *choices*."

"Unless you don't have any means, smarts, hutzpah to choose. Do you think for a minute that the people out there..."

I handed him his drink.

"Thanks," he mumbled. "Do you think for a minute that the people out there really want to make choices? Hell, that's taken from most of them at such a young age they don't even remember it. Do you?"

"Your third person reference suggests you see yourself apart from *us,* but no, I don't remember because I've never believed I was without choice."

Stoppard spun on his heels. "So, big deal. You *are* like me then. My apologies. But, I made the choice to lead. I took it upon myself to know all I could about the people around me, and I chose to serve them. I'm a servant, Derek. You don't understand that, do you? You're too busy choosing to control the likes and dislikes of people under that...that guise of art. 'You are all creative.' Oh, how that pet phrase of yours curdles my fucking blood. Let me tell you about *creative*, my friend."

And he did for the next hour, non-stop. Much to my surprise, he was more than just well read in all the arts, his background was more akin to a professorship in the arts. He had started off wanting to be an architect. Then law. Then back to architecture. He'd even done his postgraduate studies at the Cornell College of Architecture in Rome, one of the most prestigious institutions in Europe. He'd taken a second degree in economics and had stumbled into the world of media through consultancy. *How could he have so much understanding and end up where he was?*

"And, so you see Derek, I'm not without empathy for what you're seeking to do. It's just that I happen to have a different take on what's right and wrong. I don't believe, like you, that *everyone is creative.* I think you keep pummeling the public with that kind of nonsense and you'll have everyone thinking they can draw, paint, write, compose, etc., and the messy end product will be a whole society thinking they can take the place of the *real* artists, the *real* professionals. Yes, and even the bean counters like you think I am. Derek, OST leads the world in digital technology, and that my friend, is what, if not controlled, will lead to our downfall. Digital gives everyone a tool to paint, write, compose—a tool for just about any creative discipline you can imagine. All those people you keep brainwashing into believing they're creative, well...it's just a lateral arabesque for any of them to now think they're a competitive force in the world of imagination. Bullshit! Aren't you going to ask me why I think that is bullshit?"

"Why is it bullshit?"

"I'm glad you asked that question," he smirked, "because OST, and all its millions in R & D, its contracts with the government, its digital expertise, second to no one on the planet, makes it so. Coverage. Penetration. Exposure. You think I'm going to allow you to bastardize *my* creation? You know what I'm talking about?"

"Yeah…maybe I do," I answered, thinking that maybe our differing points of view were destined to be the yardsticks of choice with no one winning any battle for the "I'm right" trophy.

He took a long moment, then "You want to discredit the likes of me and what I stand for, but is it really so bad? Is it so bad to build a mega-corporation from a little book publishing company into the largest media conglomerate in the world, and do it honorably, without scandal, without losses…?"

"Without soul," I interrupted. "I hear what you're saying, Stoppard, and the word that threatens that kind of thinking is mediocrity. You proffer what you think is right…what they *want.* But who are you? Who am I to think either of us know what they *need*? Since when was having your wants satisfied the panacea for happiness? If one could figure out the formulae for supplying the needs for mankind, would we be closer to that *something*? I'm not sure. But, I think somewhere inside everyone is a crying out to create, to express their imagination no matter the consequence. That's a real need.

"So what if the whole fucking world becomes *camcorder* minded, digital pen minded with infinite colors for the palette, and Samara is upstaged by a GarageBand composition on the Mac. Is that really so bad?

"Does the grandchild think any less of the grandmother who presents a number-painting as her expression? No. Of course not, Stoppard. It is an expression of imagination, even if it is mechanical and confined to *any old brush to canvas* kind of reward. At least the grandmother is *doing* something…not waiting for someone to *serve her needs into passive comas on the couch with a bag of popcorn for company*, as you suggest.

"We're not a species that loses imagination. We are a species that allows people like you and your conglomerate empire to deprive us of the real sustenance of *doing*, and in its place feeds us Pablum all our lives, never placing the means in front of us to test and discover what our bodies and souls need to fulfill that individual inside us. No, you just continue to offer the same, old unchallenging ideas that need no digesting because they have been reduced to liquid, the masticating process done for us, the translucency apparent from all the processing, so that you and your stockholders can console yourselves that you are the *servers* of the safe diet of life, diluted liquid pacification, the purveyors of happiness, the martyrs of justice, the *givers*. Yet in reality, you are the takers, the hypocrites and bourgeois rapists of individual creativity, gathering trophies immortalized as carcasses of lost purpose, death. You thrive and profit from decay of the soul."

Stoppard hadn't moved. From pursed lips, he said "Are you finished?"

It would have been so much easier to gather my marbles and leave, but something told me he was starting to see something… not what I was saying, but *from* what I was saying. "No. But, you're trying to say something. Please. Go ahead."

Stoppard wasn't ready to relax his lips. He wasn't used to allowing his instincts to rule without deliberation. This wasn't a man, after all, who made an empire from knee jerk management style. He waited. Poured himself another drink, raised the glass to his lips and in three successive swallows, prepared to *allow*. He moved deliberate and fearlessly calm, like an approaching tsunami.

"Why do you think I'm staying up all night listening to you? Why would I ever give my enemy an invitation into my place of solace and retreat? To hear about some alleged threat to my life? Do you somehow think you are the first to warn me of such an attempt? Do you think I've risen above the average without the anger and envy of those I left behind? The difference between you and me, Derek, is not that you are the creative one and I am the… how did you put it, 'rapist of the individual creativity?' Without my creativity, I'd be dead from so fucking many threats to my life."

He rose once again. "You see, my pompous, arrogant little friend, to survive what I am immersed in is the quintessential act of creativity. I have to be more imaginative everyday than you and all your artist friends combined, because we're not just talking about the preservation of an ideal, we're talking about the preservation of modern mankind.

"Yes, Derek. Like it or not, without what OST represents to a world population, there would be depression like the world has never known. They, from the far reaches of the Australian outback on up to the Park Ave. elite, read our pulp fiction, wallow in our Reality TV shows, fill their ears with our Howard Stern-a-likes, and they do it by sitting or standing or riding some form of support, the chair, the fender, the porch, doesn't matter what is holding up their weary asses, just that they choose to give their worn out bodies a rest and to recharge their survival instincts with OST's brand of escape.

Escape is what it's all about—what everyone really wants to engage, Derek. Who the hell is really interested in running head on into the Mack truck of your belief system? Losers! You're so blinded by your own vanity and ego, you can't really see that only a few in this world really want to commit psycho-suicide. Most want to get away from the pain. They just want to survive.

"Let me tell you, creative friend, for over thirty days after 9-11, forty-three percent of all US citizens were tuned to OST radio or TV and twenty nine percent of the rest of the world's TV and radio sets followed suit. You know why? Because we were, and continue to be, the desired big brother to the world. Even today, in spite of your efforts to change the tide, we enjoy on average thirty-two percent of the worlds readers, watchers and listeners, twenty-four hours a day. I didn't plan it that way. OST just represents any kind of escape needed today from the excess unhappiness and discontent that plagues our planet. Those people out there, all over the fucking world, know that our networks, our publications, all that OST offers can lead them out of their exhaustion, can recharge their batteries. And you know what they are trying to escape, Derek? The exhaustion of their worn out imagination. Their fatigued souls from just trying to cope with it all...whether it's Iraq, Sudan, Katrinas or just plain drive-by shootings. We sit here forty-eight stories above the ground, fearless of those few radicals who would have us both buried just like those hordes of innocent Twin Towers victims, not because we are impervious to fatigue, but because we both refuse to give in, because we are driven to a will power few understand, because we both think we have the answer.

"The truth is, neither of us have an answer. They...those walking forty-eight stories below have the answers...walking to the subways, walking to the corner for a cab, walking to the bus stops, walking, walking, walking...to where? Their homes. For what? Escape! As big as OST is in their lives, we only have a small percentage of their attention. The rest of their retreat-from-reality is focused elsewhere. No, my friend, I'm not the enemy, I'm a provider. You think you're the provider. We've locked horns, haven't we?" His arms opened in grand gesture to the windows. "Indulge yourselves, or escape yourselves? That is the question for all of you out there." He turned back toward me. "Have I made myself clear?"

Perhaps I was a victim of the malady as well, because I felt exhausted and wanted only to escape. "Oh, yes, Mister Denning. You're something else. Something else."

Chapter 54

As the morning sun spilled across her face, Linda held the phone loosely and tried to enjoy its warmth. With her shoulders slumping forward and her feet dangling over the edge of the bathtub in a pool of warm water, she blurted out, "I didn't do anything, for Christ's sake. I just let it happen...badly. I couldn't even... "

"Stop it, Linda," said Aretha, as she tried to steady her shaking hands. "I'm just glad you called. You're okay now, Linda. You've talked about it, and you're okay." She quickly sat down on the bench in front of the Ode. She had just started her weekly ritual of polishing when the call came in, and now, she was trying to steady herself. All she could think was *Linda needs my support. I have to be strong. Jesus, I have to get in touch with Dr. Reagan at once.* "There's no need to throw rocks at yourself, sweetheart. You did a stupid, pardon me, you acted impulsively. Now it's time to forget it and come back to your home. I'm sure Derek appreciates your meaning well, but, and I do as well, but, it wasn't the right thing to do. You really do need to put it behind you now, dear." She nervously chuckled, "My God, I don't need any more frights, okay? It really is quite amusing in a way. I love you, my daughter. I really do."

Linda moved her feet over the bathtub's edge and with the phone held in the crick of her neck, patted her feet dry. "I still don't think it's right. I don't like him and what he represents, especially to you, mother."

"We'll talk about it when you get home. Now, call me when you've made the arrangements. I've got to get on with this before the sun bakes...oh, this stuff is so hard to work with."

"What are you doing, mother?"

"'The Ode'."

Linda paused. "I'm sorry...I'm really sorry I couldn't do it, you know. I'm really sorry."

Aretha listened for more, but there was none. She cleared her throat. "That's okay...I think. Perhaps a visit...no, we'll talk about it later. Just hurry home, dear. We'll have your favorite tonight, okay? I'll have it ready. You are going to come right away, now that you've got it...in perspective, right?"

Linda's eyes slowly moved to the bed of her hotel room and held her gaze on the gun, its four parts spread over a white towel amidst the can of gun oil, swabs and a small toothbrush, and an oil stained washcloth. The cartridge lay beside the open box of shells. "Sure, Mother. Sure." As she hung up, from somewhere deep inside, perhaps from that place she could not "escape," came a guttural, cry. "Why?"

The maid passing the door with her cleaning cart pulled up short, paused, listened, shrugged and lumbered slowly down the long, empty hall, leaving behind the somber yellow light of the art-deco sconce illuminating the tarnished brass numbers of 1102.   As she arrived at the far end and inserted her key into 1160, she thought she heard a pop behind her—like a firecracker.

***

I know I shouldn't still be affected by the sound of New York traffic, but I am. Perhaps it's the unlikely marriage of somnolent pedestrian cadence and the start and stop of auto engine aggression that keeps me intrigued, or the harmonics of horns and cursing that usually rises above the mantra of drumming chuckhole resonance layered with the vehicular power, but ever since childhood, the orchestration of city traffic has had the ability to lull me into sleep as a carefully listened-to sonata might do for others. The cab ride to the airport was no exception.

"Hey, buddy, we're here," was the real noise to my ears that brought me forward out of my respite—a much needed respite, as the brief morning hours had been futile in my quest to catch some shut-eye. Racked with tossing and turning over the events of the night before, I felt like a zombie for the ride to the airport, but, thanks to the cacophony of motorist sounds that had lulled me to sleep, arriving at the terminal had allowed me a good hour of rest.

After taking care of the cabby and checking in, I decided to call Aretha to see if she'd heard from Linda. I didn't know why I felt guilty, but whatever the reason, I needed to address it. Aretha had said she was prone to mood swings, but that they usually passed harmlessly. *Had this one?*

Aretha's response was perplexing. The empirical scientist in her usually dominated her style of expression, but today, she was different. After cautiously relating in as matter-of-fact a way as I could about running into Linda, and without frightening her about the gun, I tested Aretha's willingness to maybe hear more. "I think Linda might still be harboring a somewhat aggressive attitude, Aretha."

"You mean Stoppard? She called me this morning, Derek. Yes, she is impulsive at times, and I think you're right about her not managing her emotions very well... *again*, but I think once she gets home, we'll let Dr. Reagan deal with it. She's on her way here, you know."

"Really. I didn't know...when is she due back?"

"Probably later today. She told me all about meeting you, and…even spent time explaining the feelings she has for both of us. She's very fond of you, Derek, and only wants the best. Unfortunately, she seems to be giving far too much attention to this fantasy of hers that my *happiness* somehow depends on *you*." She giggled. "I'll have to admit, however, you do have this ability to excite me even more about the arts lately. But, well, as long as I have my Ode I have the right amount of *you* mixed in with the rest of the collection. Do you understand?"

I smiled. Aretha was the consummate politically correct patron of the arts. "I think so. What are you going to do when you run out of space for more of 'the rest'?"

"Were it not for the Ode, I suppose I'd move. But…anyway, you have a safe trip back to the island. I'm sure you've been missed."

"Well, if Theo's grumbling about dealing with everyone is any indication, you're most likely right. Aretha, let me know everything is alright when Linda gets home, okay?"

"I'll call you."

"Don't forget, now. I feel responsible for her running to New York and…well, I've already explained that."

"Yes, you have. Dr. Reagan will straighten her out."

"Thanks. Gotta run, now. Bye."

***

Shrieks echoing through the halls were fairly uncommon, even for a *barely* three-star hotel, but the housekeeper was unaccustomed to surprises like this. Oh, she had seen most everything else in her twenty some odd years cleaning up after tourists that frequented the last of a few hotels still willing to cater to tight budgets, but, "Shit!" She grabbed the phone and punched in *housekeeping*. "Sara, this is Lisa. God damn…there's a freakin' teddy bear propped up in the over-stuffed chair here with…with pins, I mean lots of pins, stuck all over the little fucker, and… shit, a raggedy-assed hole dug in its head."

"What you talkin' 'bout, girl," said Sara, lifting her cup of Joe with the air of floor supervisor who was not in the least bit surprised at anything that might be found in a room cleaning.

Lisa stood back and looked at the mirror where the guest had scrawled the word, FAILURE. "And that ain't all. Jesus…" She stepped closer to the mirror and hesitantly touched the child-like crimson-colored lettering. She sniffed the residue on her finger. "Damn…just lipstick. Shit, I thought…"

"Lisa?" interrupted Sara, "You sound like somebody that just stepped off the boat. Get the fuckin' room cleaned up and get yo ass

back on schedule. You're supposed to be down other end of the hall
by now."

Lisa hung up the phone and lifted the bear by its ear and
dropped it in the trashcan. "Fuckin' weird just gets weirder and
weirder." As she pulled her cart into the bathroom, she failed to see
just how weird it really was. Lodged in the bathroom door was the
bullet that had torn the "raggedy-assed hole" in the bear's head.

***

"If you were that bothered, why didn't you call me earlier?" said
Samara.

Pierre sat in the chair and picked at the dried paint on his
coveralls. "Trying to work it out myself, you know. You're the one
said that taking on my own problems was good even in failure,
right?"

"Right. But, anytime a patient gets this strung out, I expect him
to call...at any hour, Pierre. Why did you wait two days? I know, you
wanted..."

"This is scary shit, mon. How would you react if a stranger
stumbled into your life and said, 'No son of mine is a...' He couldn't
even say gay. Fucker. How would you feel? Son. Bullshit. How
would you deal with it? Playin' like he's my father. Fuckin' pervert.
My father is dead, you know. Dead. What's he talking about?"

"Pierre, why does it bother you so much? Like you said, just a
'stranger'."

"I don't think so. Something about him."

"For instance?" asked Samara.

"Just his way... his confidence, his... eyes."

"Yes?"

"Just his eyes. They were different."

"How so, Pierre?"

"Like eyes I've seen before. I don't know. Maybe a job
somewhere. Maybe I painted his office or somethin', you know?"

"Anything else?"

"Anything what?"

"Was there anything else that made you feel you might know
him?"

Pierre squirmed and crossed his feet. "He knew I grew up in
Queens, and...he said something about the mural as he left."

Samara sat motionless, waiting.

"He said 'you're right, you know. You're right'," muttered Pierre.

"Meaning?' asked Samara.

"He was running out the door, when I asked him what that
meant, he stopped and just stood there, said something like,
'...some of us can express it and some of us can't.' When I told him

334

again, that he was a crazy motherfucker, he said 'part of me is sad, and part of me is proud.' He smiled and went to leave. Pervert, fuck. Those eyes again...he said, he even thought he didn't get it, or, no, he said he didn't *want* to get it, but he hoped I would find a way to preserve the work so it didn't get destroyed with the building. Then he looked toward Stan who was still sitting in the far corner and asked how I found out...you know, how I knew I was gay. I told him that I'd never known anything else. And then he turned, like he wanted to leave again, then he didn't, you know. And I think the crazy fuck had tears in his eyes. He paused once again, and then he left. He didn't say goodbye. I don't think he be a kook."

"Who then," said Samara.

"I think he's a crazy son of a bitch like me."

"Does it bother you?"

"What? That he might be...it's fuckin' crazy. My father's dead. It's crazy, you know?"

"What if it were true? How does that make you feel right now?"

Pierre stood up, grabbed a tissue, spit on it, leaned over and used the moisture on the tissue to pick up the flakes of paint he'd nervously peeled from his coveralls. He then folded the tissue and put it in his pocket.

Samara watched, saying, "that wasn't necessary, Pierre. You don't have to..."

"Yes. Yes, I do. I don't like chaos."

Samara waited a moment, then "You described your painting as chaotic, didn't you?"

"Yes. That's why I paint them."

"Them?"

"The people...the immigrants...the mixed blood. God is maybe crazy, you know, letting all that mixed stuff go on. Stan helped me find out at the library about all the peoples that had lived in the neighborhood...all the changes that had gone through the building, the neighborhood, the city. Chaos...disorder, you know? Just like in my life. All those people, desperately trying just to live."

"Why do you tell me this now? We were talking about the man...by the way, did he ever give you a name?"

"Something about him was like the people I paint, that's why. I don't know. And no... no name."

"Did you ask?"

"No."

"Not even after he made the '...no son of mine...' accusation?"

"Accusation?"

"I'm sorry. Accusation, slur, insult."

"No. After the insult, he left, except for all that bullshit talk at the door."

Samara watched as Pierre turned away again, then after a few moments, sat down.

"We've only a few more minutes, Pierre. You sounded a lot more anxious when you called and asked to see me, I mean, than you do now. Is there anything else you wanted to talk about?"

Pierre stood up, slid his hands in his coveralls and turned toward the window. "I don't know if I'm any good. I mean, I know I do good walls for people, but am I any good as a *real* painter, you know?"

After a few moments, he turned back toward her. She was still sitting, waiting. "Well? What am I supposed to do with that? Maybe I should save the city some expense and burn the fucker down."

Samara leaned forward. "We've been working together for a number of years, Pierre. Burning down the *chaos* isn't going to solve anything. We're trying to deal with it, remember? And besides, you might be very good."

"I'm just experimenting, but…that friend of yours…Derek Turrel. He'd know. He'd know if I was good."

"Do you want me to say something?"

"I don't know. I'm just a house painter, you know?"

"But a house painter that has spent a lot of time and effort painting something he feels and cares about. Derek has always got a moment for the kind of imagination you described, and especially dedication. He's a real sucker for that." She grinned.

"What? You makin' fun?"

"Oh, no, Pierre. I just couldn't help but see a bit of him in you. The dedication. The sense of doubt. Every artist has that, you know. Why don't you see if someone can take me some pictures and I'll send them to him. That would be a start."

"I don't want to be a bother."

"You're the one asked me, remember?"

Pierre smiled with embarrassment. "Okay. Yeah. I'll get some pictures. Thanks. You're sure it…"

"No trouble at all." She picked up her appointment book. "Would you like to come next week again?"

"I know I'm not a very good patient, but…yeah. That would be good."

"Are you okay with the stranger?"

Pierre nodded slowly. "Yeah. For now. Thanks. Good to talk with you about it."

It was hours later, as Samara walked home, when the full impact of Pierre's visit hit her. She realized today had been a minor breakthrough, but a breakthrough nonetheless. Not only had a man—quite possibly his father—provoked Pierre's calling her after many months of avoiding appointments, but in addition, until today, he had never been willing to mention Stan's name since he first brought his "friend" to her attention five years ago.

Chapter 55

Aretha walked the dunes, accompanied by the full moon, and reflected on the years she had spent trying to figure out what had gone wrong. *What have I done to foster this abnormality in Linda? What could I have done different? Linda, after all, is the product of a tumultuous marriage. Perhaps all the violence I've tried to keep from her has somehow been experienced. Is it possible that the same energy I suspected was either my curse or gift—that same energy I suspected of pushing three of my husbands to early heart attacks and one fatal stroke—shit, is it possible that Linda, my only daughter…my first husband has also fallen prey to my unbridled zest and passion for life? God, I can fuck up when I let it happen.*

She paused, leaned over and pulled up a handful of beach grass. Drawing it lightly across her cheek, she began to hum an aria she'd heard Linda try to sing many times. How sweet, she thought, was the sound of a love song when heard in the privacy of ones reverie and regret. How many times had she thought of a husband number seven? Many. How many times had she fantasized the merging of art and science in one relationship that would—in her unavoidable appreciation of the romantic—transcend the imagination of even the most gifted magus?

She knew how magical love could be and that its essence had little to do with the reason her daughter had assumed a mission on her behalf. The curse of the young, she thought… the "delusion" of passion…a delusion even she had indulged in over six husbands. But for right now, all that mattered for this woman of surprising energy and supreme knowledge of life's galactic origins, was her appreciation for the sand her feet managed to displace in poetic rhythms, as she strolled the curvature of the dunes, humming the song, and allowing the caress of the grass upon her face to remind her of days gone past when the long auburn hair of her daughter brushed across her cheek as she carried the child and told her stories of the sea and its mirrored universe above them.

The thought that she might have unknowingly created an anomaly, a daughter with distorted perceptions; a being of her own flesh and blood that might feel *taking*, rather than the *preserving* of life was an answer. *That* was more than she was prepared to consider. She turned and looked toward the house, then, looking at her watch, started back. It wouldn't be right to not be there when Linda returned.

At half past midnight, Aretha turned the remaining coals of the dying fire and waited out their desire to be stirred one last time. She chose to cradle the poker until the last twitch of desperate flame vanished. All was quiet. The room was dark, save the reflection of moonlight off the Ode slicing across the room like a line in the sand. She waited another few minutes, then stepped across the line and disappeared up the stairway, questioning all her resources as to why Linda hadn't returned. The fearful answer was unthinkable.

***

For Derek, the flight back to Maine had passed uneventfully, save for the war of thoughts that played about in his head. Tomorrow morning the words would have to be clear and precise. The group would have expectations and questions. He would have to be focused, free of any indecision.

The last ferry delivered him to the island where he chose to walk the back way and slip into the lighthouse, unnoticed. As he removed his clothes and lie down for the night, his eyes drifted to the window and the clear sky. Even though he knew they didn't fly at night, he was sure he heard the distant sound of seagulls.

***

By 3 AM, Linda, having driven from the airport, now wearily sat before the Ode and watched the stars reflected on the polished surface. All was quiet. Even the surf was without movement. In the silence, she wondered, as she had so many times before: what magic this simple obelisk creation held for her mother. She had watched from her upstairs window many a night when her mother had sat just staring at the Ode. *How could something so starkly unreal make such a real impact for her mother?* She could understand a canvas of paint with its layers of texture, veins of life, colors of mood, images to contemplate. She was even aware of simplistic impressions such as her baskets and masks conjuring up imagination in viewers, be they everyday pedestrians, or schooled professionals, even a fellow mental patient. But—her eyes began to well up. The thought that the Ode was something more than an abstract index finger thrust to the heavens in defiance was beyond what she wanted to admit. *How could this—as so many other works of art her mother had collected in the past—take precedence over human connection—human appreciation—human family?*

338

"I love you, mommy. I really do," she whispered to herself as she turned toward the ocean. Repressing the sobs that churned beneath her lips, she couldn't understand why clutching the cold steel in her handbag gave such comfort as she watched and listened to the surf now coming alive. Whatever *it* was, it lessened the overwhelming feeling of despair—the sense of worthlessness that had haunted her for so long and finally found the beginning of its *grounding* on a lonely mirror in an everyday Manhattan hotel. She glanced over her shoulder at the Ode one last time. The reflection joined her with the heavens and ocean. She became aware of the completion of the *grounding*. A sense of belonging, of merging with something as eternal as space and water. She was calm. She felt at peace. She loosened her grip on the steel and let the non-reflection of her backside against a dark universe quietly usher her toward the calm surf.

***

The Eastern seaboard was experiencing unusually cool weather for July, so it was with boyish anticipation that Stoppard asked Siebert to stop as he reached the park entrance, saying he needed some exercise. He exited and waved him on.

It had been some time since his feet had been asked to just shuffle and the rest of the world be damned, but this morning, for reasons unknown to the man, Stoppard was feeling different and needed to walk. He reasoned this sudden need to be alone was possibly the impending trip to Darfur, or the more distant shareholders meeting, or perhaps the memory of the night in Brooklyn.

As he walked, he flashed on his picture occupying the recent cover of Forbes Magazine. He was known not only as one of the richest men in the world, but as one of the most influential. This same man that had been humbled—*was that the right word*? He wasn't sure. What he did know, however, was he didn't feel the same as usual when he stood before this younger man, this much *younger* man who had once been the boy Stoppard never knew, and who was now a reminder of the many paternal experiences the man of power had never known.

He walked among the confined beauty of Central Park's nature, but the recent night's images painted on the decrepit walls, the crumbling ceiling and the collapsing floors—all were now floating among the blowing leaves, undulating through the pools left by last night's rain, and blaring through the tempered horn blasts of chauffeur driven power mongers riding in their gray, white and black insulations of escape. Just as the boy had asked him to leave *his* territory, so too did Stoppard feel the claimants of Central Park's

339

early morning roads for the rich were asking him to move aside and make room. He stepped up on the curb, taking himself out of *one* harm's way and into *another* that wasn't as easily avoided.

He paused, looked around, and realized he was alone on a path, save for a wayward seagull perched atop the walkway bench. The feathered company stood motionless, it too with eyes querying the solitary terrain. Stoppard gave a curious second glance, realizing he was within arms reach of the bird's brazen steadfast perch. He thought, but couldn't remember ever being this close to one of New York's dominant populace. His wandering fingers found a pocketed unopened fortune cookie. He slowly opened the surprise package and laid the separated cookie onto the bench, curiously reading the inscription. As he rose, his eyes stayed fixed on the passage... "If you don't know where you are going, any road will get you there." - Lewis Carroll.

As he walked away, the cookie remained untouched. The seagull remained undeterred in its choice to ruminate over the park's surroundings. With glances over their shoulders, both found the unblinking stare of the other.

***

The stroll from the lighthouse to the cannery had always been invigorating, but today, as Derek made his way through the flower-edged streets, he counted eight cottages presenting *For Rent* signs. With only twelve in all available when he left, the numbers now suggested yet another sign the tourist season had not improved. All he could hope, as he passed the curio shops and souvenir stores, was that the traffic of normal weekend get-a-way travelers was better.

He glanced at his watch. He still had twenty minutes to spare before joining Theo for the meeting. Coffee at the Leeward Café was always a great excuse to catch up on the island gossip, so with a smile of optimism plastered across his face, he pushed the door open, entering a room whose total occupants numbered eight, four of which represented the precious tourist-type the island depended on and were probably occupying one of the four rental cottages. The other four were familiar shop owners.

"Well, thought you deserted ship," said Moby, the former professional wrestler turned t-shirt shop retiree.

Derek, maintaining his air of confidence, climbed onto a counter stool and nodded. "Oh, come on Moby, and miss seeing Shaumu do her wiggle?"

Moby lifted the sleeve of his t-shirt and flexed his twenty-inch bicep, giving Derek his due with the tattooed overweight hula dancer

340

bumping and grinding as the old man of the ring whistled *My Little Grass Shack*.

"Derek," acknowledged Velma, the waitress, as she placed a coffee cup and saucer in front of him.

"Morning, Velma."

"Same?"

Derek nodded. "Thanks. They don't make it like you in New York, you know."

Throwing her trademark sarcasm back, "Yeah, if I believe that, you've got a Brooklyn Bridge to sell too, right?"

"Better jump on it. Price is goin' up, you know?" Derek said jokingly.

"Yeah, well, won't find many buyers on the unemployment line."

Derek chuckled and lifted his chin to the tourists in the corner. "Ah, c'mon. Business isn't that bad."

Velma leaned in and poured. "Hell it's not. Drink up, pilgrim, 'cause old Juan Valdez is gonna be served *instant* soon."

Derek, respecting her candor, wiped the grin from his face. "Sorry. Business *is* down?"

Still whispering, Velma started refilling the napkin holder. "Them ferries are only three times a day now. You lose half your visitors to the island and you lose your business. But, hell, I don't need to tell you. You gotta be shittin' your pants 'cause they're not delivering enough oil to run *your* generators either, right?"

"Haven't got the report yet. Just on my way."

"Theo didn't look too good last night when he came in to fill his thermos. Said he was gonna be up all night gettin' ready for you."

"Getting ready?"

"The report?" she chortled. "You know those summaries we all love to read every month."

"Sorry, Velma. I'm really sorry."

"I'm not a casualty yet, but a lot of other islanders are. Ferry schedules on the other islands haven't changed, you know. Still gettin' their six a day. Mayor is really pissed."

"So the ferries are running as usual all around us. Kinda looks like some conspiracy, doesn't it?"

Velma nodded and turned toward one of the few customers raising their hand. "Be right with you. Be a shame to see everything close up."

She walked over to the woman.

"We just came in this morning, such a lovely morning, wouldn't you say?"

"Absolutely, ma'am."

"Well, my husband and I wanted to visit this." She pulled out a flyer whose headline read: ON YOUR VISIT TO GRAY CLIFF, BEWARE OF ECHO LIFE PROJECT, because… "We're curious why somebody would want to hurt a group of artists, you know?"

Velma glanced over the four reasons why the tourist should boycott Echo Life. "I'm curious too. Well, at 1p.m. they open up the gallery. That's just down the road a way. There are signs. Mind if I show this to my friend at the counter?"

"Why, no, Miss. You can have that one. We've got more. The kids gathered a bunch. They were on every seat on the ferry. Ought to distribute nicer messages for the visitors, don't you think?"

"Yes. Yes I do. More coffee?"

"Thank you," the woman said.

"Could I have some more hot chocolate," asked one of the teens.

"Be right back," answered Velma.

As Velma made her way to the hot chocolate machine, she laid the flyer in front of Derek. "Doesn't get easier, does it?"

Derek glanced down. "Color. Mine was plain white." He patted his shirt pocket holding a folded plain white flyer.

Derek and Theo stood before a massive wall of the cannery. Plastered from floor to ceiling were e-mails and letters. "What the hell is this?" asked Derek.

Theo, douching his eyes with Visene, looked down, blinked the excess away and said, "Friends…fans…art junkies. You know, the ones that *aren't* trying to bury us."

"Just since I left? Hell, it's only been a week."

Theo took his hanky and scrubbed his teeth. "Seems longer to me."

"Why didn't you brush your teeth when you got up?"

"Haven't been to bed in order to get up. Capish?" He handed Derek a manila folder and walked toward the end of the building. "That wall's nothing. Wait till you see Lanagra's piece."

"He finally took down the tarp? Thought he was never going to let us see it," quipped Derek. They walked through the various cubicles of artists, some working, some curled up on whatever was handy for a nap. Reaching the far end, which was dark, Theo walked to the side and lifted the breaker switch, lighting up Lanagra's latest.

Derek stopped short and gazed in awe. Before him was what looked like a giant three-story installation of a microscope, fractured, broken, as if the result of an explosion. Beneath the beam of light emanating through the eyepiece, like a spotlight through one of three rotating lenses, was the specimen plate of some twenty square yards of floor space. Scattered about were specifically placed pieces of debris among broken oversized glass slides. "I think...I think I get it."

"Probably not. I had to have him explain the whole thing and then let me see five minutes of a rehearsal...it's too much." He pointed to the stack of glass slides. "Wollzak's actors provide the live specimen thing."

"And?"

Theo smiled. "Wait till you see it. He's broadcasting it Saturday. Phone-in music from the audience, etc. Whole thing is revolutionary. Too much to explain."

"Okay." Bewildered, Derek shook his head and looked at his watch again. "Try. I've got a few minutes before the meeting."

Theo sighed, "Lanagra'll kill me for this. Asked me to keep it under wraps till Saturday. This all came to him in a dream, mind you. So...anyway...the actors, working as dancers, come out like cells, mutant, damaged from the explosion, dividing, replicating, etc. But of course, they don't look like people. The arms and legs function like appendages growing from the cells, non-descript abstract shapes. They seem to move about aimlessly looking to become something, trying to survive."

"That's not too hard to understand. What was so hard about that?"

"That, my friend, is just the beginning." He pointed up to the top of the microscope. "Housed up there at the eyepiece is a digital projector, compliments of Ernest...you know the guy no one ever heard of before he came to us?"

"Yeah...the kid that left Tech U in Boston."

"Because," Theo continued, "the powers-that-be insisted he share the profits of his holographic invention with the school, whereby he politely told them to fuck off. Anyway..." Theo walked over to the corner, "Ernest's already created thousands of shapes from the footage he took of the dancers. Their animation is projected down through the lenses onto the floor in holographic form and change shape and movement according to the music and or sound effects picked up from this."

Derek stared at a pile of debris. "That...what?"

"That, my friend, is a big assed computer looking like a piece of rubble, but in reality, the brains of the work. Ernest's AI pal called Igor, sits in there waiting. Somebody punches in a digital piece of music or any sample of sound and we sit back and watch the show. This Saturday, anyone viewing the channel can e-mail in a digital sound or piece of music and Igor—Lanagra's 'Hal'—will analyze it and feed in what it thinks works."

"What *it* thinks...Igor?"

343

"Igor. Not like some random piece of consumer electronics here. Igor has been programmed with pretty much the history of music and Ernest suspects Igor, with time, will come up with a new genre of musical taste. *It* has already created a new atonal scale. But for now...*it* just does a sort of American Idol thing in choosing what *it* thinks is best for the theme."

"And the theme is?"

Theo nodded. "*There is no life without death first.*"

"Just your everyday 'American Idol' theme."

"This is no joke. Actually, according to Ernest, Igor thinks it's the most rudimentary element of existence."

"And all dramatized with interactive music and sounds from subscribers?" Derek muttered.

"Interesting, isn't it? People empowering a computer."

Derek paused a moment. "Makes you wonder how it will all end."

"It's like nuclear energy in a way. The community of imagination just keeps getting larger and larger, getting compacted smaller and smaller. Long after we're gone, the digital world will still be redefining 'small,' you know?"

"A rather voracious appetite, wouldn't you say?"

"That's one way to look at it," said Theo. "Wait 'til Kurzweil's nano bots start creating."

Derek smiled and shook his head. "Sure we can't get Lanagra to give us a preview?"

"Hey, you made the rules. Any artist can present or sit on anything they create. Whenever they want, they can broadcast radio or video as they choose, long as it doesn't disqualify itself as lewd or distasteful. Your words."

"My words. My words."

Alicia, one of the apprentice assistants, stepped up. "Oh, here you are, Mister Turrel. We weren't sure you got back. It's noon."

"Thank you. It's time, isn't it."

She smiled anxiously. "Yes. Everyone is up front waiting."

"I'll be right there."

Alicia left the area, and Derek took one last look at Lanagra's creation.

"I know you're worried, Derek," said Theo. "So are we. But, decisions have to be made. The island is...well, you know. By the look on your face, the week away didn't produce any solution, right?"

Derek's face took on the solemn look that few people ever saw. "Right. But..." He turned back to the microscope installation. "This kind of work has to be..." He took a breath and exhaled. "Ass-on-the-table-time, isn't it?"

Theo gripped his arm. "Ass-on-the-table-time."

Chapter 56

The forty some odd artists were spread about the floor, on chairs, with some on ladders and scaffolding. Derek greeted those he passed on the way to the front with a cheerful nod, occasional handshakes, and for the younger ones, fist bumps.

He stood before them and stated the pleasure he was feeling in being back. "There are few places that truly qualify any longer as 'the place I'd most like to be,' and this is one of them. It's been a hell of a week, and we've got a lot to cover and discuss. But, first, let's get this out of the way." He reached in his pocket and pulled out the flyer. "As you're probably all aware, seems the ferries are carrying propaganda targeted at getting us ignored. Let me just read from whoever designed the four reasons why they're advising tourists to boycott us. 'One—Because Echo Life arrogantly proclaims to know what people *need* to satisfy their entertainment time. Two—Because Echo Life recklessly ignores the economic hardship it is causing other honest hard working people.' I love that one. Guess we're being blamed for the corrupt ferry line service. 'Three—Because Echo Life is polluting the minds and hearts of viewers with their non-censored broadcasting of supposed creations of artistic merit. And fourth—Because they are trying to play God with their sanctimonious proclamations of superiority over your established media giving you what you ask for...all you want.' That's my favorite. That had to come straight out of the mouth of one, Stoppard Denning," said Derek.

And so the meeting proceeded for the next two hours, giving an open forum for discussing the options and potential results. There were those who were for "going down with the ship" and there were those who felt to abandon the inevitable now was "...to go out while we're on top."

By 2:15, as Theo finished summarizing the financial report, everyone was tiring and beginning to feel irritable, the result of expended energy in directions they were not used to. It was apparent that they were still financially healthy, even though subscriptions were leveling off; a dip Theo felt could be attributed to the summer season. What concerned him the most was the drop in tourist traffic, a reality that didn't mean that much to them, but was essential for the economic health of the island. "I suggest we sleep on it," said Theo. Try and spend a bit more time with some of the suggestions voiced today and let's meet again tomorrow for a short meeting to finalize our thoughts and maybe take a vote...if we're that far along. We just can't continue as if nothing is wrong." He turned to Derek. "You have anything to add?"

Derek stood up, his hands jammed in his pockets, his shoulders back, giving his familiar air of confidence. "Only to say that whatever we decide, let's make sure we don't lose our will to be and do what we believe is *right,* not succumb to what someone else thinks is *wrong.* Tomorrow, say noon again. Thanks. Thanks from me...and I think there are more than a few subscribers who are thinking about us right now and thanking us for being there for *them.*"

***

Back in New York, however, the Echo Project was a fact of economic life that some wished didn't exist. "They're very close to getting enough subscribers to kick in that bench mark commitment for additional satellite space," said Boswell Clark, Stoppard's CFO. Allan Gentry, President of OST, and Terrence Kensington, President of Broadcast, along with the other board members gathered around the table, sitting tense for the few moments it took Stoppard to respond.

Stoppard turned his unlit cigar over several times before taking it from his lips. "And you're sure their satellite contract is bullet proof?"

Boswell nodded. "Legal assured me it's automatic. By luring Berkowitz to run the business side, it appears that Turrel isn't just an artist."

Stoppard unconsciously began grinding his cigar into the ashtray. Once there was nothing left in his hand, he stood up and calmly said, "And I'm not just a chairman. Gentlemen, ladies, this board meeting is over. My plane leaves in four hours. I will stay in touch, obviously both as your CEO and as reporter. Darfur is our answer. Thank you."

Stoppard walked calmly from the room as eyes cautiously glanced from side to side, begging for someone to tell them *how* Darfur was the answer.

***

As the preceding months had been spent carefully planning Stoppard's PR leading up to the shareholders meeting, Adam Sanders watched from the control booth as OST's seven o'clock news began with the announcement that their Chairman had embarked on a goodwill mission to Darfur.

The anchor continued. "He will be reporting via satellite twice daily, 7 and 11 p.m. His goal: make sure that in the event international efforts fail, he will be there, along with our OST team, to step in with whatever financial aid and other resources he can call upon to help buffer the genocide and starvation running rampant.

346

Mister Denning sends this message to all our viewers, 'If for any reason, the peace process bogs down, OST's imagination and commitment to the needs of people, the real needs, will be addressed with all the resources at OST's disposal.' Following this broadcast, OST will present a one-hour special on the history of the Darfur crisis and will repeat it after the eleven o'clock news. Stay tuned. And now…"

Sanders checked off the first entry on his list of carefully programmed public awareness releases and stepped from the booth to make his first of many phone calls to Stoppard. Reaching his cell phone message service, Sanders oozed out, "The beginning is launched. Good luck. Looking forward to your reports."

***

Derek sat at his desk and watched as the lighthouse beacon swiped the dark horizon with a swath of light, catching the upper edge of the Echo cliff and his unfinished work. Before him on the desk were several sketches exploring the lower reaches of Echo's granite foundation. The scratched out and erased areas of the base weren't going as he hoped. On the top of the cliff, his pencil had carried the carved flow of Echo's scarf high above the reality of the work, drifting into a cloud dotted sky and disappearing. As he slowly began erasing the obvious impossibility of the scarf's heavenly assent, the phone rang.

"Are you watching the tube?" bellowed Theo.

Derek tucked the phone under his chin, sipped some coffee with one hand, and continued to erase with the other. "Sure. Like I always do."

"Okay. Dumb question. You better take a look at your Tivo recording of the eleven o'clock OST news. Stoppard's trying a one-eighty."

Derek smiled down at his paper and quipped, "I'm really enjoying my fantasy. Must I?"

"Yeah. I'd say it's a definite must over your fantasy."

***

Several hundred miles south, Samara had also been called, but not by Theo. She had been alerted to the newscast by a patient, Pierre, who in a monotone voice of bewilderment had said, "That's him… that's the suit guy."

***

So too had Simon Greco become aware, keeping one eye on the news cast and one on the board that was lit up with dozens of calls about Stoppard's latest ploy to appear in Darfur as the man most in touch with peoples' *needs.*

***

As the sun rose the next morning, sound bites of the previous evening's broadcast were also being watched by OST's Boston remote news crew inside their broadcast van.

Helicopters crossed over the Cape Cod house and down to the shore, as the drone of swirling police and ambulance lights outside flooded the control monitors with red and blue urgency.

As Aretha stood at Linda's bedroom window high above the cluttered shoreline of local news crews, emergency vehicles, volunteer and Coast Guard search boats, she clutched the surf-stained note that only hours earlier had been found by an early morning runner atop Linda's clothes stacked neatly on the beach. There had been a gun weighting the note down.

As the morning progressed, it appeared that the local beach story of life and death took precedence over Sanders and Stoppard's philanthropic international staging. By midday, Aretha, being a world famous scientist, had mention on the front pages of most newspapers around the globe. Sighting her accomplishments in terrestrial study and assistance to NASA, most of the journalism was sympathetic to her tragedy, but there were some who couldn't resist the obvious *rag paper* approach, sighting Linda's many years under institutional care, and emphasizing the lack of a corpse. "Although no foul play is suspected, the local authorities are holding back any comment until the body is found."

Aretha, still in yesterday's clothes, sat beside the Ode watching the continuing search of the off shore waters up and down the coastline.

Sybil stepped out from the kitchen with a tray of coffee, toast and a boiled egg. "Mrs. Ballard?"

Aretha didn't move.

"I thought you might like some nourishment."

"That's very kind of you, Sybil. Just put it down on the bench. Thank you."

"Is there anything else you might like?"

"No. That's fine."

"I'll be inside if you need me." Sybil nervously wiped her hands with her apron and backed into the house. "Got some cleaning up to do."

"Of course." Aretha lifted her dark glasses and put her hand in her pocket, retrieving the suicide note. Opening it slowly, she fought back the tears. *Suck it in, woman. Suck it in.* She wiped her eyes and once again read the last words from Linda.

"Mother, it's better this way. So much better. You'll not have me as a failure in your life. I don't mean that to hurt you, but I guess I got the bad daddy genes, didn't I? Like you told me so many times, all you can do is try to be the best you can. I tried. I failed you. At least, this is something I can succeed at. I do love you, mommy. Linda."

***

On another beach, Derek and Theo walked toward Jamie who worked feverishly on his boat's engine. "Doesn't really matter what you think, Theo. I still feel involved, if not responsible for this."

"Jesus, Derek, she killed herself. You just don't flip out like that over night. It's been coming. It has to have been coming for a long time."

"What's a long time to you, Theo? To me? Time is so damn relative. Who knows why? I only know she was on a mission that night… maybe to kill him, maybe to just frighten him… anybody's guess. It's very possible I didn't handle the situation the best way."

Theo, trying to be the *listening-friend*, nevertheless felt compelled to *right* what he felt was a *wrong*. "You listened to her disclose her intent. You saw what you thought was a gun bulging from her purse. You dissuaded her from any action with the gun. How can you suggest that was wrong?"

"I could have done more."

"What!" Theo snapped.

"You don't just send someone on their way with a pat on the head when they have murder on their mind."

Theo's voice became quiet. "She left on her own free will. You told me that. How do you know she didn't have suicide on her mind then? She wasn't stable, Derek. You convinced me of that from all her mother told you. I'm no professional, but what if her ploy was to purge a final volley of supportive words for the cause she thought you were so committed to, and one supported by her mother, and… *pop*. Ever think she might have wanted to blow her own head off in front of him after such an evacuation of thoughts? Use her death as a call to arms against the…what was it, 'Emperor of waste' I think you quoted her as saying? Was she thinking that would prove her worth to her mother…to you?" Theo shrugged. "Of course it's a theory of little use for someone who just bagged it all and walked into the ocean."

"And all because of me."

Theo stopped and turned. "Derek, you can do what you want about this. I mean, beat yourself up, blame yourself, they're your choices. But if you want my opinion, taking on the responsibility for her suicide is a bad choice. You've got real responsibilities here.

Her death is what it is; the end of a life that was eroded long before she met you."

Derek began walking again. "Aretha won't even take my calls."

"Derek, give her some time. She's not thinking about you right now. Until they find a body, we, she, none of us know if Linda even did what everyone thinks she did... right?"

As they approached the boat, Jamie looked up. "Hey, you two."

"Jamie," said Theo.

"How's it looking, Jamie?"

"Nothing some oil and nut tightening can't cure."

"Well, that's one good thing happening today," offered Derek.

"You wantin' a trip to the rock today?" said Jamie.

Derek looked toward the sea and nodded.

***

As Jamie steered the boat through the choppy waters around the Cliffside, Derek's hand cut through the wake. "We're a bit further out, but will this work for you?" said Jamie.

Derek lifted his hand and let his gaze move from the top of the cliff and down through the mist. "Nothing like a roller coaster ride to wake you up." He stood up and began freeing the dinghy. "I think I'll be awhile today, Jamie. I cancelled the group meeting until next week, so you go on back, do whatever you've got to do, and I'll give you a ring on your cell when I'm ready... probably two or three."

Jamie looked skyward. "Okay by me, but keep your eye on those clouds east of here. Don't want to be messin' with a storm now, do we?"

Derek lowered the boat and glanced up to the sky. "No. Suppose not. Don't need another complication today."

Jumars work well on a rope in all conditions, but moving up a sheer wall drenched in heavy mist made this particular ascent surreal. Derek's feet slipped in and out of his loops well enough, but sliding the Jumars up the wet rope was a constant reminder of how tenuous life could be. He remembered his days in Hawaii scaling the rock behind a waterfall giving him a similar appreciation. He had slipped and without the anchors, it would have been his last slip. When he began climbing, his mother had wondered. His father had shrugged. But, when he was younger and took up the sport, there was nothing that gave him more joy than to take on the challenge of a rock that was beyond his experience. His habit of always calculating the angle of each wall he attempted, making sure it was at least five degrees greater risk than the last, had become his trademark.

Challenges had served him well, and, as he made his way once more to the top, he came upon his scorecard carved in the granite with hash marks. He paused. This would make one hundred thirty-nine ascents of the same wall. He smiled and thought what his climbing friends would say. "Weenie, lost your nerve? You were working on overhangs, remember?"

The top was slick with mist. He took off his gear and stepped into the shallow cave containing his storage. He checked the gas tank of the generator, noting he'd have to haul up a five-gallon can of gas next time. Feeling unsure of what he wanted to work on, he sat down and pulled out his recent "fantasy" sketch of a few nights ago. He examined the changes of what he hoped would be the finished product some day. Then, looking at the smudges where he'd erased the unrealistic extension of Echo's scarves, he smiled. "Only in your dreams," he muttered to himself.

"Why?" came the all-too familiar voice of Echo.

Derek spun around, facing the cave's entrance. There, dangling in the opening, were the familiar strands of colored material, their graceful, dance-like movement undaunted by the heavy mist. He rose and walked outside, looking up and behind him. There, perched high on the eyebrow, was Echo. She looked unhappy. "Why the sadness?" asked Derek.

"Oh, I wasn't aware."

"Kind of heavy, huh?"

"What?"

"The fog," said Derek.

"Not unusual for this time of year."

Derek cast his eyes at the ribbons again. "You've changed."

"Changed?"

"The ribbons are different. You never had mustard, brown and grays before."

"You weren't as depressed before."

"Oh. It's my doing, eh?"

"Who else?"

Derek nodded. "Okay. So, I'm depressed. What's wrong with that? Don't you ever get depressed."

"I don't know. Do I?"

He slowly shook his head as he stepped to the edge of the cliff. "Gonna be one of those days, is it?"

Echo shrugged. "Going to be what you need it to be. You know that."

Still looking over the edge, he shoved his hands in his pockets. "Sometimes you're not much help, you know."

"Contemplating suicide?" she said with a grin.

Derek turned around. "Not a good joke."

"You mean, not a good joke *today*?"

"No. Not today. Not any day."

"Okay. So why me? Why the thought?"

Derek sighed and quickly walked back into the cave. He started unraveling the extension cord to the pneumatic hammer drill. "I wasn't looking for you today."

"Strange. Could have sworn you were."

Derek spun around. Sounding as if she were in the room, all he saw were the gently waving mustard, brown and gray strands outside the entrance. He lifted the compressor and walked its hundred pounds out onto the ledge. Pulling the cord out to him, he said, "I'm very inspired today."

"Understandable," she said from up above.

"I need to do something, but..."

"Theo was right, you know. She was pre-qualified for that suicide before she ever met you."

Derek straightened up. "I..." He wandered over to what was becoming the cheekbone and sat, folding his fist under his chin. "This is fucking everything up. I don't like where it's going."

"What, the Echo Life Project, or this rock?"

"The project. Nothing seems right anymore."

"You merely got through the easy part. You're into the real work now; keeping other people from destroying it."

"And the first effort in that direction put an innocent girl to death."

"She put herself there, Derek. Stop dwelling on *other* people's reaction to you and Echo Life."

"What else is there to dwell on?"

Echo drifted down the opposite side of the face and stood on the chin of the rock face. She looked down at her feet, the tip of the chin, then back up to the eyebrow. "Bit protruding, don't you think? The chin, I mean."

"Needs work. So what am I supposed to do with this mess? The island is about ready to pack it in. The group is feeling the pressure and probably thinking the humidity and claustrophobia of a New York summer would feel pretty good about now."

"You're jumping the gun. They haven't voted yet."

"They would have today, if Linda hadn't..."

"You sure you're not more concerned over Aretha not returning your calls than anything else right now?"

"Of course not. Her daughter just killed herself. Why would I be so concerned about that?"

"Derek, sarcasm doesn't fit here."

He looked up toward the protruding sculpted scarf pointing north. "Am I ever to finish this?"

"If you don't…"

Derek waited, but the sentence trailed off, unfinished. He turned back. She was gone. "Son of a bitch. Why'd you leave?" He stood up and shouted. "What the hell kind of muse are you?" He turned back to the scarf and then looked over at the protruding chin. He picked up the extension cord, threw it over his shoulder and walked over to the chin. "Fucking ski slope of a chin." He slammed the hammer into the rock and began the chiseling task. "That's how you look to me, damn it. You're worse than a real live one, you know. At least Samara would let me keep my impression, even if I saw her chin different than she did."

From above the rock, a gull swooped down and rode the updraft from the ocean. Hovering over him, it relieved itself. Hitting his hand, the droppings oozed down onto the gun.

He turned off the power and wiped the white comment from his hand. "Always have the last word, don't you?"

Chapter 57

On the other side of the world, Stoppard Denning was having his own kind of "last word." Standing on an airstrip in the middle of the desert, he watched behind him as four cargo planes unloaded transport, food and medical supplies. Clad in a white baseball cap and jumpsuit with the OST logo and the words, *Flight for Needs* prominently displayed across his breast pocket, he worked to keep a calm demeanor in the hundred-degree temperature as he faced the news camera. "I know this will confound some people and make others angry that the CEO of the largest media conglomerate in the world is standing in the middle of the Sudan Desert instead of being back at the office. Well, there's a war here, one that most of the world is less aware of than Iraq or Afghanistan. Here is where there is an innocent *need,* a real innocent *need* to consider what we all have and what these people don't have."

The camera pulled back, further revealing the large cache coming out of the five cargo planes which also carried the OST logo and the added *Flight for Needs* inscription running along the length of each aircraft. Surrounding each plane were many similarly white clad armed guards standing as sentry-watch over the nourishment and medicine.

"While the UN and their peace keeping efforts work through the endless politics involved in these genocidal acts of terrorism, I have decided to personally donate enough essential supplies to keep the two hundred thousand Darfur refugees in Chad from starving and dying due to lack of medical attention and food. Along with over fifty doctors and nurses, plus a volunteer force of five hundred veterans of Iraq and Afghanistan campaigns, we will distribute and keep watch over the supplies, insuring that Chadian rebels don't get their hands on the them.

"As the UN works out the hopeful peace treaty enforcement, I'll be here for the few weeks we trust it will take, bringing you images and sounds that should help us all understand the true essence of *need*. I'm Stoppard Denning, CEO of OST."

Stoppard unclipped his sound mike and handed it to a PA as he walked toward his veteran officer in charge, Boone Wright, a retired three-star general. "Boone, you okay? Running smooth, are we?"

"No problem yet, sir. Once we get everything from your planes, our choppers should have a slam dunk time."

"Well, let's hope we don't have to ever use that artillery you brought along."

Boone smiled. "Rebels take one look at our arsenal and gun ships, they're not likely to mess. Fortunately, they're working with simple rifle and hand gun weapons."

"Well," Stoppard gulped, "Still, there's a shit load of those smaller weapons out there. Glad you're along Boone. Glad you're along."

Stoppard, along with his African American assistant, Dana, continued toward a waiting OST Range Rover. The black native driver rushed to open the door. "Where to, Mister Denning?"

As Dana climbed in, Stoppard looked over his shoulder at the two Range Rovers behind him loading up the camera crew and armed detail. "Get me to the older part of the camp... where the earliest refugees are. Hear they're in pretty bad shape."

"Yes, sir. That be very bad corner of camp. Many dying. Many orphans." He jumped in and, leaving a cloud of dust behind, sped past the planes as they continued to unload Stoppard's unorthodox weapon against the threatened proxy battle for his company. He enjoyed the sound of his voice as he lifted a Churchill from the Rover's custom humidor. "You know, Dana, I'd love to see Mister Smith messenger *this* back to whoever. Shareholders are gonna love the twelve, maybe thirteen share this is gonna give us through sweeps."

"Could make a fifteen, if we get a little luck, Mister Denning."

He smiled, and placing the cigar between his lips, lovingly prepared his oral habit. Dana glanced over her notes as the Rover sped out onto the lone road to the largest refugee camp on the Chadian border, Oure Cassoni.

As he applied the Jojoba cream to his battered hands, his eyes stayed glued to the TV screen. It had been a particularly trying day for Derek and arriving back at the lighthouse after sunset, he had once again left Singso venting one of her cooking bad moods over cold food. "You know how long I cook for you, Mis'er Terrel? Mis'er Terrel?"

Derek stopped the nursing of his palms for a moment and acknowledged Singso with a wave of his hand.

"You wave me away now, you wave me back when taste cold soup."

"…and as counter to UN policy as it may seem, tomorrow we at OST will be reporting on the efforts to get the warring rebels to sit down and discuss giving some peace to this refugee camp in exchange for filling their own need for food and medicine. This is *Flight for Needs* and Stoppard Denning reporting from Oure Cassoni on the eastern border of Chad."

Immediately, the phone rang. Derek picked up. "Well that undoubtedly got him some extra points," said Theo.

"Bastard is making a mockery of the word *need* and most of the viewers don't even know it," replied Derek.

"*Need* is a motivating word," said Theo. "That's why we chose it, remember?"

"And why he's sticking our noses in it."

"Hey, Derek, he didn't get to where he is without knowing how to bare-knuckle it."

Derek finished rubbing in the lotion as he watched the newscast end with more images of refugees. He switched off the TV and looked at his soup bowl. "Hey, Singso? What the hell is this?"

From down below, Singso yelled back up, "I tell you it get cold. I tell you. Three hours it simmer while you beat rock. Now cold. You eat. I go home."

As he heard the door shut below, he lifted the spoon from the bowl. "Hey, Theo, what could a gray stringy looking thing with eyes be doing in my soup bowl?"

"What are you talking about?"

"This soup Singso made for me… three hours simmering, she said."

"Gray, string like, with eyes? Mm. My guess is it's not meant to be questioned, like most things with Singso."

Derek pushed it aside and leaned back in his chair. "Damn. You know, this whole Chad thing's got to have something to do with his annual meeting coming up, wouldn't you say? I mean, a multi-million dollar aid program, personally financed…for what? For rating points, that's what."

"Didn't you say Aretha had some friend of hers prepared to stage a proxy battle to take him down a few pegs?"

"That's what she said. Wish I could get her to…" Derek looked at his watch. "I'm going to try again. I'll talk to you later." He disconnected and immediately punched in Aretha's number.

***

"And this is natural? Natural you say?" Aretha waited for the spontaneous response, thinking it took forever.

"Yes, Aretha," said Samara. "Yesterday you denied everything. Natural. Today…"

"Today," Aretha interrupted, "Today I'm angry, pissed, enraged is probably the better word." She continued even though the *call waiting* clicks were starting to annoy her. "God damn it! And you want me to think this kind of mourning is natural?"

"I know it's hard…"

"Hard? *You* didn't have to identify…I was fine 'til they pulled back the tarp. God…she looked so…" Aretha dropped to the couch and began to weep. After a few moments, "Just a minute, Samara, I've got to get rid of this call." She pushed the keypad. "Hello, who is this?"

"Aretha. I thought I'd get your… it's Derek."

Aretha sat up. Her hand tightened around the mouthpiece. Squeezing her eyes shut one last time, she switched ears and in matter a fact tone, said, "Derek. How are you?"

"Well…I'm fine. I'm so sorry for…"

"Yes. Yes. Oh, thank you. Just…" She swallowed hard. "Just one of those things no one can do anything about, right? It just is."

"I tried to call…"

"I'm sorry, Derek, but I'm going to have to call you back in a bit. I'm on the other line. I won't be long." She switched over again. "Samara, I'm sorry. Derek. Derek, the dear boy."

"Are you okay?" questioned Samara.

"Yes. I'm fine. We were…the anger thing." She chuckled. "Crazy. I'm feeling better. I mean…" She looked out the window. "It's a full moon coming on. A full moon. Maybe we can talk tomorrow. I feel better now."

"You're sure? That's good. If you have any need, though, you can call me anytime, any hour. Okay?"

"Sure. Any time. Any hour. Sure. Tomorrow," she said in a seemingly *lost* tone. She placed the receiver down and walked out to the deck and peered up at the moon. "We are so small…so small."

356

She kept her eyes fixed on the moon as she sat down beside the Ode.

***

It was several hours later as dawn began to spread across the horizon that Derek finally sat down, took out a piece of paper and began making notes for the vote-meeting that would take place in just a few hours.

He had taken a shower—that didn't help. He had spent another hour on the phone with Theo making sure he wasn't overlooking anything for the meeting—that didn't help. Another late night call to Samara only reminded him again that no one was going to make *his* decision for him. He'd even spooned the mysterious soup, and although he concluded the liquid with the gray stringy thing actually tasted great cold, that only served as a diversion from his task.

The final revue of all he'd managed to confuse himself with proved fruitless as well. Anguish dominated his heart. Guilt continued dominating his thoughts, as he feared he might be doing harm to himself and others by not accepting the responsibility that he, and his Echo Life project, was most likely the cause of Linda's death.

The fading gray of night turned to purple and orange as the rising sun reminded him that it was down to this—a sheet of paper with letters, words, and doodles. As he studied his clustered thoughts, he challenged his own need. *How do I reconcile this guilt? Has my ego run amuck? Have I attempted too much, or am I giving up prematurely?*

As the light worked its way through the window and sliced across his scribbling hand, his throat squeezed the sound deep within that reached upwards, wanting to wail away all the doubts and fears. Nothing came forth. The island may be facing economic disaster with the oil price conspiracy, but regardless of the group's vote to stay or leave, *he* needed to decide as well.

***

It was a kind of hot Stoppard had not experienced. There was something about the smell that made the desert temperature unworldly. As a boy, he had always been sensitive to certain smells—his father many times having to carry along surgical masks, like some fathers carry along tissue for the occasional runny nose of a child. By his early teens, Stoppard's tolerance for certain odors, usually garbage, was such that the faint smell of a dumpster on the side of the road was enough to send him into a dash to the other side of the street, many times leaving his small group of friends laughing and sometimes provoking one of them to grab a piece of the garbage and chase him with it. In his latter teens, the discovery of cigars surprised him, for the pungent aromatic was, for reasons he never understood, intoxicating. Bothersome odors were usually no match for his Churchill defense—until this day.

"People shouldn't smell like this," he said to Dana as they walked through the tent city of refugees. He refused to be the only one to take a hanky from his pants and cover his nose. "Could you pause the video, Jerry... just a second."

The cameraman lifted the camera from his shoulder and took advantage of the moment to clean the dust from his lens as Stoppard looked to his left and right, only to be met by innocent fly infested eyes of children—smiling. He smiled back and leaned toward Dana. "I'm gonna barf. I'm gonna..."

"I have something." Dana sifted through her butt pack and came out with a tube of Mentholatum. "Here," she said. "Put some of this under your nose. Old mortician trick. Kills just about any smell."

"Mentholatum?" Stoppard whispered, still smiling and nodding to the children who were giggling, and staring at the strangers in white. "That's a kid's ointment."

"Works," Dana replied. "Used it all the time on that Tsunami assignment two years ago."

Stoppard took the tube and smeared a glop under his nose, much to the enjoyment of the children. As they giggled even louder, occasionally brushing the flies from their faces, Stoppard joined in. "What the hell," he said laughing. Leaning down, he gave each of the children a small smear on their noses, each taking the gesture as a friendly *hello*. Stoppard lifted his arm and waved to the now long line of children forming behind the favored ones, each holding out their hand, and touching their noses.

"I've got more back at base camp," said Dana. "You won't need anymore for awhile."

Stoppard nodded and began putting a smaller and smaller dab on each of the now dozen or so children lined up. All but forgotten by the usually *all business* Chairman was the "smiley face" yellow badge affixed beneath the OST logo on his hat. One little boy missing his right arm and dressed in bright blue only pointed at Stoppard's head and put on his own imitation "smile" ear to ear. Finally, having squeezed the last bit from the tube, he jokingly chuckled as he dabbed the last child's nose. "That's a very handsome blue shirt you're wearing, young man." He positioned himself to the camera. "Might get a commercial out of this, Jerry. Keep rolling."

By the time they reached the makeshift burial ground located several hundred yards beyond the camp, the children had thinned out, their laughing faces gradually turning passive and stoic as grim reality set back in. As the last of the young refugees turned and shuffled back to the tents and lean-tos, Stoppard said, "How do they do it?"

"What," said Dana.

"Cope." He gazed out over the endless mounds of sand in every direction—hundreds, perhaps thousands of graves.

"They cope like most in this part of the world. If it's not drought, famine or war, it's rape, AIDS, and plain old depression."

Stoppard turned to her. "Does it get to you? I mean, you've been around this a lot."

Dana sighed and lifted the water bottle from her belt. "Actually, I was relieved when I was assigned to assist you on this trip." She smiled and took a swallow. "I thought I'd have a cushy job just using what I already knew and had experienced. Obviously, it's *different* exposing someone like you to all this."

"Different?"

"Yeah." She put the bottle back on her belt. "I was born south side of Chicago. Poor was an everyday thing. So…this doesn't affect me same as someone who, you know, someone not from the same kind of background."

Stoppard moved the Mentholatum a bit closer to his nostril. "Wind's changed. Let's get it done. You're right. Hey Jerry, set up so we can get this with some late daylight. Shadows on those graves will be good for the camera, right?"

"Gonna be a while for the light to be how you want it," said Jerry.

"Yeah. I know. Time for me to get used to it, maybe."

Dana walked down a small embankment to a flat area, as Jerry motioned for the assistants to set up some chairs and reflectors. Dana sat down on the sand and took out a cigarette. Stoppard came up behind her and sat down. "Smoke?" asked Dana.

"Only the big ones." He took out another Churchill. As he looked at it, he paused and then put it back in his leather cigar case. "Maybe I will have one of yours."

As they sat smoking and looking out over the endless small grave mounds, Stoppard asked again. "You never did answer."

"You mean am I used to it? No. She lifted her dark glasses back into place.

Stoppard quickly looked away, as it was evident Dana was not coping well either. She was thinking of other things.

"Mind if I ask how much you spent on this trip, Mister Denning? I know it's none of my…"

"Off the record, about eight and a half. And, it's really okay to call me Stoppard or Stop… off the record."

Dana didn't move. "For my ears only. I know."

Stoppard glanced over at her as she took another drag. "You're wondering why, aren't you?"

"Kind of. You don't have much of a philanthropic reputation."

"I give to charities, but I know. This looks like a bit of a grandstand for a guy like me, doesn't it?"

Dana hesitated.

"You can speak freely, Dana."

Dana turned to him. "Anybody can have a change of heart. Did you?"

Stoppard now took the long drag and exhaled slowly. "Good question. I am who I am, Dana, so if you'd asked that yesterday, probably different answer. My life has been a different answer every day. Always depends. Usually on what's good for the bottom line or ratings, you know. Share holders like ratings."

Dana pondered his answer. "You carry a lot of responsibility."

"Yeah," he said with a nod. "Yeah."

"You've never exposed yourself to this kind of thing have you?"

Stoppard shook his head. Hesitation wasn't part of his style, but for the moment, he knew why. Death always robbed him of his edge. He glanced up and knew there was no escape, at least not until after the segment was taped. "Boarding schools, Prep Schools, Yale, Harvard... not much time to expose yourself to the everyday stuff."

"So why now?"

"I'm asking myself that same question. I thought I knew." He looked to the west. "So... another hour, maybe. If this Mentholatum holds out, I should be able to catch up on a bit of jet lag. Gonna grab a few winks. Give me a ten minute warning, okay?"

She nodded as he leaned back, snuffed out the cigarette and covered his face with his baseball cap.

Standing on the ridge behind him was the young one-armed little boy blue... still grinning and staring down at the man in the smiley white hat.

***

The next few weeks brought unexpected changes.

Nightly OST broadcasts delivered unique coverage of the Darfur crisis and the staged good will efforts of "...our charitable Stoppard Denning." Momentum increased each night, turning *ten* shares into *twelves*, into *fifteens*. By day ten—after Stoppard brought Santana over for a series of concerts in several refugee camps, segments of which were aired each night following the 11:00 p.m. news—OST was courting a *twenty* share of the nightly news audience—a feat not seen since 1993 by NBC.

By the time Stoppard returned to the states and his shareholders meeting, his personal monetary commitment to Darfur had grown to twenty million dollars. He had shown his stockholders and the rest of the world that NEED was a four-letter word that could be addressed his way and still satisfy the "human interest" WANT of his media audience. OST's continued high newscast ratings remained impressive. The board awarded him a high seven-figure bonus and a renewal contract of unprecedented yearly income and stock options. The board also insisted on personally contributing to his philanthropic mission to the tune of ten million, thus insuring that the name of OST and Stoppard Denning would remain synonymous with the media's coverage of the Sudanese genocide and its one-man savior-like efforts. All this enthusiasm for OST and its ratings spike hadn't yet broken the Echo Project's back, but it hung by a thread.

***

Earlier, after a difficult vote, a few of the Echo Life artists returned to their homes to wait out the fuel crisis, hoping it would favorably resolve itself soon so they could return.

Gas prices soared to an all-time high, rendering many airline and summer car travelers home bound. The limited ferry arrivals on Gray Cliff's shores delivered disappointed tourists, who, were it not for the advanced reservations being locked in, would have stayed home as well.

With Derek being one of the few determined to stick it out, an effort was made by residents to make ends meet by converting their fishing boats for trips to Echo Rock. On days with calm seas, they packed in the tourists, taking them to vantage points where Derek could be seen through binoculars working away on Echo's face—a commitment that occupied all his time now, save the nights he would spend with Theo who was writing a book he called "ECHOES... *a work in progress.*"

***

Aretha Ballard still grieved her loss and traveled every other day to Dr. Reagan for help through her crisis.

***

Samara continued her practice, using her spare time to work on a symphony she questioned would ever be finished.

***

Pierre continued his *Walls of Infamy* as he now called his project—each night painting well into the morning hours, save the nightly break to sit on a paint can and watch the OST news and the occasional repeated Darfur broadcasts of the "suit" man he still couldn't accept as his father. Fortunately for him and thousands of other all-night fans, Berkowitz held the investors at bay, kept the satellite lease active, and Simon Greco did his Echo Life broadcast, thanks to Derek's generosity of extra cash for the high costs.

All in all, it was a gallantly fought experience for everyone—an experience that few knew was just beginning.

A stage was set, but no one was quite sure what was ready to play out behind the curtain.

CHAPTER 58

The black limousine crept slowly down the pot-holed pavement to 105 Moore St. just as it had each night for the past month. Always arriving at the same time and always leaving the same sized box of food and drink at the boarded up side entrance, Siebert was getting used to his new last chore of the day. Dropping Denning at his apartment always preceded the excursion. On nights when the "master of media" had remained sober enough to hold a pen, Siebert waited for a hand written note, roughly composed in the dim illumination of the limo's vanity light, and then carefully folded and sealed in a plain white envelope and addressed to Pierre. Siebert was never told the contents of the notes, and he never asked.

Walking across the street with the box, he noticed light bleeding through the blackened windows of the fourth floor... an oversight that might be noticed by others, resulting in a phone call to the police or other authorities suggesting the building might be the home of crack heads, etc. He paused just long enough to anticipate what Stoppard would say if such an oversight caused the arrest of the man inside. "Why didn't you warn him, you fucking idiot?" or "What the hell I pay you for, you fucking idiot?" or even worse, "You *are* a fucking idiot."

Siebert was aware that the man inside was special to Stoppard. He also knew that since his return from Sudan, Stoppard had never missed a night of dropping off provisions. He knew that the many gallery opening nights he had driven Stoppard to were highly unusual as well. That, coupled with the frequent after-work visits to MOMA, The Whitney and The Guggenheim, had added considerable time to his daily driving chores. These were new activities for Stoppard. New activities Siebert suspected were connected to his nightly delivery to the dilapidated tenement building.

He slid into the shadows and stepped up to the cross-thatched side entrance, noticing for the first time, the boarded-up look was fake. The door was ajar. He looked about, peered upward to the top floor, and looked at his box.

Stan fingered The Arts pages of the Sunday Times. "Asshole gets his face into every opening, it seems."

Pierre remained hunched over, laying down wide swaths of orange paint with his hand made "mop-brush," as he called it. Backing his way into the middle of the floor, he lifted his head to double-check his pattern. "So what? Why does that bother you? Could you move your lazy ass and reposition the lights?"

Stan shot him a look no friend or lover ever wants to see.

"Please?" said Pierre. "I can't see back at the doorway."

Stan rose, reached up and moved the hanging pipes closer to the opening. "You know, you don't need to be so snippy."

"You try and keep this up, and run out of paint as well, and see how your mood is," answered Pierre.

"Nobody said you had to kill yourself with this thing, you know. So, you run out of paint. We'll find a way to get some more. We always do."

"Ever stop to think what would happen to me if you got caught?"

"Stealin' paint? Hell, get less time than stealin' money. Besides…"

Pierre stooped over and whipped the mop furiously, making the floor an eruption of flames atop an undercoat of black rocks and ash. "Less time? Any time without you would be…God…sometimes I think you've got the sensitivity of a rock…like my fucking rocks of hell…the castoff molten shit…the primal ooze of…sorry. It's just…" He stood up and gazed over the small explosion of flames he'd laid down amidst the other crawling colors of the inferno, leaping up the walls toward the clouds of the other kingdom. "Sorry…not your fault." He laid his mop down, picked up the gallon can, shook it, and dropped it on its empty side. Walking back toward the corner where Stan crouched, he gathered up the scattered newspapers. Placing his hand on Stan's shoulder, he said, "I don't know what I'd do without you."

"You'd do fine. You're some kind of freak genius. You'd do fine," said Stan, looking up.

Pierre sat down and pulled his knees in. "You live this squalor life with me…why?"

"How many times you gonna ask me that? Keeps me out of trouble…'cept if I get caught stealin' your fuckin' paint." He playfully punched Pierre on the arm. "Wouldn't have it any other way. Figure I'd rather be doin' somethin' makes somebody feel good about themselves than fuckin' with the old habits. Shit, you don't have any idea what it was like all those years."

"You've told me. And yes, I don't have any idea what it's like to live in a cell. Just glad you're out."

"So…looks like I get to be second-story man again." Stan stood. "What you out of?"

Pierre looked up at the room. "Jesus…three floors of…how many gallons so far?"

"Probably sixty…seventy," said Stan.

Pierre smiled. "Enough to get us both a few years in a cell if you got caught."

"Enough to get you an agent, maybe?" said Stan cautiously.

"Nah. We'll take pictures one day, then…"

"Then?" asked Stan.

"I don't know." He looked up at the ceiling where, in addition to the open mouth of God sucking in the surroundings, he had painted a perfect replica of the *finger of God* touching what he imagined Lucifer's finger from Hell would look like. The devil's hand rose out of flames that scorched and singed the flowing robes of the Creator.

Stan repeated, "So, how many? What colors?"

As Pierre began taking inventory of the empty and partially filled cans, he heard the sound of something sliding on the floor outside the entrance to the hall. "What the fuck…" Skirting the freshly painted area, he dashed to the entrance as Stan grabbed a ball bat and followed.

In the darkened hallway, Siebert jerked away from the box he'd slid across the landing and quickly started running toward the stairway, slipping on the fresh paint and colliding with the wall. "Son of a bitch!" screamed Pierre as he lunged out the entrance, trying to dodge the paint and slipping himself. Not far behind was the flying body of Stan, the bat jettisoned from his hand and tumbling down the stairway, barely missing Siebert, who by now was crouched in the corner with his hands up to shield his face.

"Who the hell are you?" yelled Pierre, now hobbling down the stairway. "You fucked up my…bastard…" Pierre cocked his hand to do damage.

"Just delivering your food. I've got an envelope too. When I saw the boarded up effect was phony, I didn't want to just leave it out there in the dark for somebody to steal. "Never liked leaving the food there, and…"

"You walk all over my work, you asshole…fucked up my fire."

Siebert's hand caught the brunt of Pierre's slap. "Please, Mister Pierre, I'm sorry. I didn't know."

As Pierre pulled back to hit him again, Stan grabbed his arm. "Hey…don't blow a good thing here, bro. Food, man. Food. He didn't know." He reached out his hand to Siebert. "Sorry, partner. Yeah, that back door fakey wasn't gonna fool you no more, was it? *You* didn't know the stairway was wet with…"

Pierre grabbed his arm. "My work, Stan! What you protecting him for? Kill the son of a bitch."

Stan turned and grabbed Pierre by the shoulders and through clenched teeth whispered, "You be good now *to your fuckin' meal ticket* or I'm gonna do something I don't want to do."

"He..."

"He fucked up. A mistake." He motioned with his eyes over his shoulder. "That box got food, man. And he says he's got an envelope. You crazy?" Stan turned around and offered his hand to Siebert.

As Siebert stood up, he reached his trembling hand into his breast pocket and pulled out the envelope, handing it to Pierre who was still heaving with anger. "He said to make sure you got this. Glad I could do it personally. I'm really sorry... whatever I did. Can't see on these stairs and...."

Pierre stood there holding the envelope, his eyes fixed on the destroyed flame patterns creeping up the stairs that were now but smears resembling finger paintings of a child.

"Hey, Pierre! Wake up, man," said Stan. You can repaint the fucking stairs. What's in the envelope?"

Pierre slowly gathered his composure and opened the envelope as Siebert said, "May I go now, gentlemen?"

Stan waved him off with, "Yeah. Yeah. Watch your step, okay?" Stan quietly giggled and leaned over Pierre's shoulder, as Siebert crept carefully down the stairway. "C'mon, bro. What's in there?"

Pierre lifted out five one hundred dollar bills.

"Shit," said Stan. "Holy shit? Five big ones. Buy a lot of paint, man."

Pierre opened the letter and walked around the slippery mess and into the large room, taking the letter to the light of the work lamp.

"So, what's he say," said Stan.

Pierre's eyes darted across the paper several times, re-reading the first couple of lines. "Personal."

Stan leaned back with, "Oh... now it's personal. Gonna give me up for the rich dude?"

Pierre slowly lifted his eyes to Stan. His voice was resolute and strong. "Don't talk about him that way."

Stan shrugged. "Hey...he's your dude, man. He's your guy." He turned and slipped into the shadowed corner and sat down. "I'm just your..."

With quiet resolve, Pierre interrupted, "You're my best friend...and I love you. Remember? Now let me finish this."

Dear Pierre,

I know you don't think much of me. All the little notes until now were just my inept way to say I was sorry. I'm sure I didn't leave much of an impression the night I lost it and insulted your feelings. I'm sorry about that. I had no right to speak that way. I've enjoyed sending you the food each night. Hope it's helped. I know you are proud. Your mother has reminded me of that many times, so this little bit of money is just a gesture of goodwill. I know it might be too late for that, the goodwill that is, but never too late to try.

I don't know what you're doing in that building, but you made it apparent you weren't about to leave, and from the look of the walls, you're into something that's important to you. So, just use this money to maybe buy some paint or for whatever you might need. Siebert will be back tomorrow, as usual. If there's more I can do to help, let him know, and maybe if you feel like it, you could send some words back with him, or if you have access to e-mail, write. Anyway, I hope you'll leave yourself open to maybe exchanging a bit more. Oh, I know you're wondering why now, right? I don't really know, Pierre. Seemed like the right thing to do after I got back from some traveling. Wishing you well, a friend.

Pierre slowly walked over to the darkened corner. From the shadows could be heard, "Maybe this will buy enough to finish. Really finish. Get us one of those disposable cameras, okay?"

After a few moments of silence, Pierre looked up. "I'm not ever leaving you, Stan."

Chapter 59

Early fall on the island was always one of the best times of the year. Not because of any foliage change, for except for the patch of forest between the lighthouse and Main Street, Mother Nature had skipped trees when she designed Gray Cliff. As had been the tradition for years, for most of the natives and the few artists still remaining, the fall represented the time of year when the scent of the air introduced clear foreshadowing of the winter. Red noses and mufflers became part of everyone's early morning adjustment. Although the gas prices had sent some artists back to the mainland, and many of the natives to relocations up and down the New England seacoast, the few that remained embraced the changing season with anticipation and hope that winter months would be kind and not bankrupt the island with heating fuel costs.

As Theo passed the boats that were for the most part now in dry dock, going through their yearly maintenance and prep for the harsh winter that was around the corner, he fingered the e-mail he held in his hand. Samara had sent it the night before from a Boothbay Harbor hotel. His asking that she come as soon as possible was a bit out of character for the calm man of words, but her response within twenty-four hours suggested his purpose made sense to her as well. He quickened his step as he heard the ferry horn announce the approach.

Samara was already feeling rejuvenated from the sixty-minute trip. The crisp fall air, mixed with the mist of the boat's wake, had given her a refreshing sense of power. She enjoyed such feelings perhaps more than she would ever show. Oh, she was quick to admit the rush she got from understanding other people's emotions—an often shared thought with her own analyst—but when it came to getting a handle on her own emotional makeup, she felt as though she were destined to be a student for life.

Seeing Theo in the distance, quickening his gait to meet the ferry, gave additional rise to her already peaking sense of control and focus. After all, receiving an urgent message from a friend suggesting there was need for some deep understanding was what she was all about. She lifted her arm to wave and reminded herself that what Theo may be about to ask of her, might take all the courage she could muster.

***

The canvases were enormous, measuring thirty by forty feet. As a result of his *Inevitable* installation at the Whitney months earlier, Lanagra had decided to return to an airbrush approach for the next project. With most of the artists now gone, the cannery had been rendered wide open, excepting the broadcast studio. With his microscope lab project occupying the latter half of the warehouse, he utilized most of the I-beams supporting the roof to function as hanging tiers for the ten pages of this new book of canvases he called *Penetration*, a study of the psyche from facial skin through to the brain stem—all with symbolic abstract creatures climbing through and around the maze-like twists and turns of the brain's layers.

As Samara and Theo walked the narrow passages separating each hanging canvas, the skylight ceiling spilled the morning sun through the dust-heavy air.

"Feels like I'm walking through some newly unearthed tombs of history," said Samara.

"This Lanagra is definitely out of the box, isn't he?" said Theo.

"And he completed this in ten weeks? When does he sleep?"

Theo pointed to a dark corner where a tent was pitched. "When he can't raise his arms anymore."

"In a tent?" said Samara.

"He's got a thing about sleeping in confined places. Says it helps him get the most out of the few hours he grudgingly takes periodically."

They turned another corner and peered up toward the top of the canvas. Different abstracted creatures ripped and tore at the jelly-like slice of the brain. "And this is?"

Theo looked down at the child-like scribble identifying the canvas. "He calls it 'Cerebrum's Revenge'."

Samara raised an eyebrow. "What's he got against thought and consciousness?"

"Doesn't appear he has much regard for the co-existence does it?" answered Theo.

She stepped back and held her gaze. "No. But, then again, most of us creative slaves seem to place inordinate credence in the subconscious."

"Yeah, we do visit that playground often, don't we?"

Samara paused. "So, when are we...could we maybe get some air?"

"You mean it's time we actually talk about why I asked you to come?"

Samara took Theo's arm and walked him toward the front. "The tour of what's left was nice, Theo. I mean that. This Lanagra guy is...interesting, but...you're stalling."

"You know me like a book."

"One that gets reread a lot."

Theo cleared his throat as they reached the door. "There are some new chapters I need to talk to you about."

***

As they emerged from the woods, Theo sighed and lit a cigarette. "That's it. That's all the details I know."

Samara continued walking and staring off into the distance as Theo exhaled.

"Thought you quit."

"Bad times make for easy relapses, don't they Doctor?"

Samara nodded. "I guess it could be worse."

"How?" quipped Theo.

"It could be winter already."

Theo nodded toward Echo Cliff. "He said he'd be back in a few days, but he's been there five weeks now, and last Thursday when Jamie told me the basket he lowers for food had a note listing all the shit he wanted, that's what got me going."

"From what you told me, I have to agree. Sounds like he's planning a long stay, and..."

"And?"

"And," continued Samara, "I'm not sure it's a good idea to interrupt that right now."

"Oh, for Christ's sake, Samara. The man's flipped. Derek Turrel, *the* Derek Turrel living in a cave to be with his muse shouldn't be interrupted?"

"You don't know that to be the case. We only know he's asking for more supplies."

"Including crampons? Not much good without some ice to dig into, you know."

"I know. I used to climb with him, remember?"

"And that's why I asked you to come. The fucking rock is inaccessible except up that vertical face."

"Helicopter?"

"We're not about a rescue yet." said Theo. "I just think there's a need for you to find out... need to maybe talk some sense into him."

"And you want me to play spider woman up that wall?"

"He's put up some fixed, whatever you call it...you know."

"Anchors and ropes."

"Yeah. So someone that knows what they're doing can get up there, right?"

"Theo...even if I were agreeing to talk to him, I only mountaineered with him. You're talking technical...rock climbing. I've only been in a class for that."

"How'd you do?"

Samara turned to him. After a few moments, "I kicked ass."

***

As the fishing boat responded to the throttle thrust, Jamie looked over his shoulder at Samara sitting at the stern taping her pant legs tight around the climbing boots. "Lucky for her, Derek's got little feet and she's..."

"Shhhh," said Theo. "Women don't like to hear they've got big feet."

Jamie turned back and peered toward the rock. "He's gonna kill me for this."

"And I'd kill you if you didn't bring us here. Who'd you rather be taken out by?"

"Shit. This is a decent job for the winter you know."

"Not if your client is frozen to death," said Theo.

As they approached the waters where the dinghy was used for the balance of the way to the face, Jamie cut the engines. "Lucky."

"Lucky?" said Samara.

"Wind's out to sea. He probably didn't hear us."

"What's he gonna do if he did?"

Jamie paused, then shrugged. "Not much, I guess, except fire me."

Theo looked at the dinghy. "He's gonna hear when you wind that thing up."

"Not if I row," said Jamie.

"Row," said Samara. "Kinda rough to be rowing in, isn't it?"

"If it gets impossible, we can always flip on the outboard."

"And I'm staying here...alone?" asked Theo as the boat rocked with the wave action.

"You're fine here. Anchor hits at about fifteen meters. You won't go anywhere."

Jamie turned to Samara, who was adjusting her harness and getting used to the spring action of the Jumars. "You sure he didn't leave these behind because they got old and..."

Jamie shook his head. "They're fine. He used them last week. He's always rotating. Moods, he says"

"Moods," repeated Samara. "Sounds like him."

By the time they arrived at the fixed rope, Theo was comfortable with the rolling boat. Knowing Derek might not only fire Jamie, but take issue with his trusted writing friend as well, Theo lifted Jamie's portable phone from its cradle and listened. After a few rings, the familiar voice answered. "Jamie, what the hell you want?" Theo could see the tall man standing at the top of the rock, holding his pneumatic chisel in one hand and talking into his phone with the other.

"Derek, this is Theo."

"Theo? You down there?"

"Yeah."

"What are you doing out here? I told Jamie to tell you and the others that..."

"He did. I'm here because it's been more than a couple of days."

"So?"

"So...I was concerned."

Derek disappeared back from the edge. "So get unconcerned and leave me alone. Okay?"

"I need to tell you something so you don't flip out."

Derek reappeared at the edge. "So what could be your problem?"

"Just don't be surprised with seeing...Look, Derek, you might think me a traitor or something, but...Samara's ascending right now."

"Ascending? What..." Derek moved quickly to the fixed rope belay. "God damn you, Theo."

"I know you're saving your thanks for later, so I'll just buzz off now. Let us know if there's anything more..." The phone went dead.

By the time Jamie pulled the dinghy on board, several minutes had lapsed. "So… that was a lucky break. Nice low tide and no waves," said Jamie as he climbed aboard.

Theo rolled his eyes. "Not the ocean kind of waves, at least."

"What you mean?" said Jamie.

"You expect me to just welcome you with open arms?" shouted Derek.

Samara removed her gloves and harness. "I didn't have any expectations, Derek. You've pretty much proved such anticipations are fruitless. What the hell is this *hibernating on your rock* all about?"

Derek shook his head. "Hey, you can turn around and do your descent now, 'cause there's nothing to talk about." He moved back to where he'd been working and started the pneumatic up again, creating a wall of noise to separate any attempt Samara might make to communicate. She looked about, taking the moment to digest the results of Derek's seeming compulsion. Stepping up to what appeared to be the lower edge of the chin, she reached up and ran her fingers across the stone.

The noise stopped and Derek stepped down to her, putting the tool aside. "It's warmer inside." He moved into the cave and fired up his two-burner butane stove. Samara followed. "You're as crazy as me now", he said. "You know that don't you?"

"Don't flatter yourself. I was crazy before I met you."

As he placed the saucepan on the burner, he reached up to a crack in the overhead stone and retrieved a plastic bag with water. "Condensation is a hell of way to create drinking water, but it works."

"You've done it before," said Samara. "Does it bother you now?"

"It? Look, I know that tone of voice and I don't need any psychobabble, okay? I'm doing fine. You get a nice cup of tea and be on your way. Nice to see you. There."

"There, as in, there Derek's being nice?" said Samara.

"No. There as in nice to see you, and I know you appreciate being appreciated. But that's it. I'm finishing this…whatever it's becoming. Understand?"

"Did you actually think I was here to talk you out of it?"

"I'm gonna ream that little fucker a new one when I get back."

"It's not Theo's fault."

"He called you, didn't he?"

"Only because you're acting irrational and…"

"I said no analyzing. None of that shit, okay?"

"Okay. I'll just be a jealous and possessive woman then. You like it here alone with her?"

Derek took out a tea bag and smirked at the remark. "You're the one, along with that little fucker…can't believe he called…you know damn well what it's all about."

"I know there was a time when…"

"Stop the play acting. A jealous woman, you're not. And possessive? Please. Echo might be possessive, but not you."

"Oh, we are into the advanced phase, aren't we?"

"Your own words. 'A muse is essential for a romantic like you.' You laid that on me years ago when there wasn't any muse, remember?"

"Not that you were aware of. She was in the wings though…waiting."

Derek poured the water into the cup. "Samara…Samara, why can't you just let me do what I need to do right now? Why'd you feel you have to save me?"

She lifted the tea bag up and down. "Is that what I'm doing?"

Derek sat down and began sorting his drill bits and chisels. "That's your MO, remember? That's what you do for a living. Well, there's nothing to save here, because there's nothing threatened or at risk, okay? I'm just finishing."

She took a sip. "Derek, I maybe understand more than you give me credit for."

"What? That I'm working through depression over the loss of the project? Over the loss of a lot of people that depended on me to hold it together? Over causing the death… Anyway. You're wrong. I've dealt with all that. I'm just here completing what I set out to do."

Samara looked to the outside. "And from what I can see, it's probably going to be your greatest work."

Derek looked up. For the first time, he allowed his eyes to remain on her. As she turned back, he looked away.

"Have you heard from Aretha?" asked Derek.

"Once. She asked about you."

"Strange. She's never returned my call."

"She knows nothing she can say is going to change your mind."

"She told you that?"

"She's a bright lady," said Samara.

Derek stood up and walked to the opening. "Hell, you don't need to have a doctors license to know I killed her."

"What if I told you Aretha carries the same guilt?"

Derek turned. "That's absurd. I'm the one Linda was concerned with. I'm the one she thought would bring some kind of peace to her

372

mother if the obstacle was out of the way. She was very clear about that. I intervened and stopped her."

"From killing Stoppard. And that caused you to think you're the reason for her suicide?"

"Now you *are* playing me like I haven't learned a hell of a lot from you. Of course, Doctor! She probably would have never killed the guy, but I'm the excuse for her failing to go the distance. You going to tell me I'm wrong?" He waited. "Not with a straight face you won't."

"It's possible. But neither of us know for sure, do we? For you to carry…"

"For me to carry that burden is the way it's gonna be. Let's drop it." He walked twenty feet to the back of the cave. "I know you're wondering, but it's really quite comfortable. Bivouac equipment works well. Sleeping bag, pad, stove, pan… all the comforts of home."

"Even down to the Yogi Tea."

"You remember that, don't you?"

Samara adjusted her position. "Yosemite, '03."

"'04."

"You sure?"

"You knew me a year before you trusted me, remember?"

"Yeah… Okay. You're right. On top, got the inspiration for the concerto."

Derek moved to her side and sat down. "And made me listen to your horrible whistle… the cellos, you called it."

"They were."

"And the timpani rant you did on the pan." He reached over and lifted the cooking pot, turning it over.

Samara smiled. "Damn thing still has the dents."

"You got excited."

"Yeah. Hand axe made a good mallet," she mused. "Oh, want some." She pushed the cup toward Derek.

His eyes remained on her lips. "I'm thinking about it."

Amidst the rolling of the boat, Theo rubbed his hands together. *Shit, this is only September.* He reached for the telephone and paused. *Checking on her would be prudent, wouldn't it? After all, Derek is… God knows where Derek is.* He looked up toward the top. All was clear. The rope hung secure. No Derek. No Samara. *Must be talking it out.* He glanced over at Jamie, who with his fishing cap tilted down, was catching some serious zzzs. Theo looked once again at the phone. *He might really kill me if….* Slumping on the bench, he too pulled his baseball cap down and attempted sleep.

After a few moments, he mumbled, "How do you do it? I'm ready to throw up and..." lifting his cap and taking one last look at Jamie and the cliffs' edge, he said, "Could be a long afternoon."

CHAPTER 60

The Fall season in Queens, New York, is not exactly the changing of the guards in weather-speak, save the reduction in power bills that retiring air conditioners afford. Falling leaves are scant and far between. Colors? For the most part, nature forgets this metro-scab part of the eastern seaboard and in place of the normally blue sky of summer comes dank skies of gray, foreshadowing the cold and deeper gray of winter.

Those were the meandering thoughts of Pierre as he stared from the Jamaica Café's window out into the rush hour traffic. Tanika tipped her container one more time and moved the dwindling ice cubes around with her straw. Pierre lifted his heavy eyes. "Do you have to do that?"

Tanika stopped. "Sorry. Just thinking. God, Pierre. I don't know what to say." She got up and went to the Coke machine. "You want another cup of coffee or a Coke?"

Pierre shook his head.

Tanika refilled her container and sat back down. "You're sure the demolition notice said November 1st?"

Pierre nodded.

"Well, I don't know what to say."

"You already said that," said Pierre.

She reached across the table and patted his hand. "You worked so hard...spent so much time. I don't want you to get angry, but when you first told me you were going to paint the building, I..."

"You told me I was nuts to create a project out of a condemned building."

"I never used those words, Pierre."

"Yeah, well..." He turned to her. "Samara was going to speak to her friend Turrel, but... nothing. Did you tell her?"

"To contact him?"

"No. About the demolition notice."

"I called this morning. She's out of town." She lowered her voice, feeling his frustration. "I'm sure he'd look at it if he knew. Samara is an artist too, you know. She's seen the pictures you took."

Pierre stood up and strode to the sink with his cup and saucer. "You're right. It was stupid. Who the hell did I think I was? Taking over a four story..."

Tanika moved to the counter. "Pierre! I *know* who you are. You're my boy, and you are a good artist."

"Who, just like the poor bastards up at Gray Cliff, is being squashed by what is called *progress.* What Stoppard, my...Jesus, what my so-called father represents for the whole fucking world to feast on!" He charged toward the entrance door, knocking over a table. "What the hell was I thinking?"

***

"...that maybe it would be seen and appreciated," said Tanika as she adjusted the leather pillow behind her back.

Stoppard pulled the vanity light down closer to the photographs.

"You want me to make another circle of the park," said Siebert as the 59th St exit came into view.

"No, yes. Yes. Another go around." Stoppard turned to Tanika. "This kid is more disturbed than you led me to believe."

Tanika glanced over at the pictures. "What? Something you don't understand?"

Stoppard looked up over the top of his glasses at her. "Please. There's art and there's art. This is the rant of a deranged...hell I don't know. And what's he expecting to do with this...four story nightmare about to be hit with the iron ball?"

"He wants it to be his, I don't know, his audition, his sample. He just wants it seen."

Stoppard shook his head. "Every image of beast and man vomited up, flames, shit, rock and he says this is what lower Manhattan was like in the twenties and thirties? I grew up there. This is..." He fingered through the rest of the photos, stopping on the finger of God ceiling, "Sacrilege. Finger of God touching this...devil thing? You're asking me to get involved with this? The Press gets wind of my involvement with a faggot... They'll destroy me."

"Oh, please, Stoppard. Your dramatics are..." She shook her head. "Even I don't use that word about gays. Who would destroy you for buying a condemned building? Nobody but us knows what's inside. You don't even have to use your name. You can get someone else to buy it."

"I may have taught you enough to run a fucking café, but not enough to advise me on how to run my business affairs."

"Give me the money and I'll buy it," said Tanika.

He continued shuffling through the pictures, idly buying time to think. "Sure. Give you the money to.... What do I look like to you?"

375

Tanika waited a moment. "Like the father of your son. That's what you look like."

Stoppard paused, folded the pictures back into the envelope and adjusted his position. "Well, now that you've finally ridden in a limousine, I suppose you want one of these too."

"Hardly. You know I'm not a boot-licker you can buy off with stuff I don't need."

***

Samara laid her briefcase down and looked at her telephone showing a message total of twenty-six. She picked up the phone and dialed. "Service," came the reply.

"I trust there weren't any emergencies among these twenty six?"

"You would have been paged had there been, Ms. Jennings."

"Good. Three days away usually means hell to pay."

"Not an emergency, but there was," said the operator, "one rather anxious call, or I should say total of...yes, total of five urgent calls. Mister Haweisi."

"Any message?"

"Just to call him."

"Thanks." Samara looked through her appointment book and dialed again. "Pierre, this is Dr. Jennings. Sorry I missed your calls. I'm back, so please get in touch with me. I'm most anxious to see you."

She paused a moment, then looked up a number on her computer and dialed.

***

Tanika rang up the special. "Four-fifty-six. Was everything okay?" she asked the patron counting out some quarters.

"Yes. Fine. Hope you don't mind quarters."

"That's fine," said Tanika. "Just fine."

The patron continued counting slowly, as the phone rang.

"Here, let me help you," offered Tanika. She quickly shuffled the necessary coins and gave him back nineteen cents as the phone continued to ring. "Please come again."

Lifting the cordless, she said, "Jamaican...How can I help you?"

"Tanika, please," said Samara.

"This is Tanika. How can I help you?"

"Oh, Tanika, this is Doctor Jennings."

"Doctor Jennings. How are...is Pierre okay?" Tanika asked as she nodded and smiled to the customer and stepped to the side.

"Well, I think so. I was hoping you could maybe fill me in. I just returned from out of town and he's left me several messages. I tried to reach him, but no answer. Have you seen him lately?"

376

Tanika waved goodbye to the customer and sat down. "He got some bad news and, well, he's going through some bad times right now. The other day, he came to see me and... they're going to demolish the building...the building with the paintings."

As Samara listened to the details of Pierre's meeting with her and the subsequent limo ride Tanika had with Stoppard, she couldn't help but realize, as she had with so many other artist patients, working with creative behaviors was many times more challenging than her schooling prepared her for. As with others, she found herself compelled to solve *their* problems in an effort to stave off the dirge of her own. "And Stoppard just dropped you off?"

Tanika wiped a tear from her eye. "He did say if there was any evidence the boy had talent, he might try and help, but..."

"But?"

"I don't suppose you showed the pictures to Derek?"

"As a matter of fact, I did. I don't think that can be much help right now. He's very involved in finishing this latest project and..."

"What did he say about the pictures?"

"He thought they were interesting, but without seeing the work in person, he didn't have much more to say."

Tanika walked outside the café. "Pierre thinks Derek is some kind of God. He still listens to Simon Greco every night and...he said that the only person he cared about seeing his work was Derek."

Samara sat back in her chair. "I don't know how that would change anything, anyway. You said the demolition was around the corner."

"And Stoppard said if the boy had any talent, he'd consider helping," said Tanika.

"Well, we may have to think of someone else to satisfy Stoppard. Derek's determined to stay on that rock until it's finished."

"Is there any way he could just take off a couple of days and...I'd pay for the trip."

"It's not a matter of money, Tanika. It's...he's stubborn that way...I mean, when he's committed to finishing something...and with the colony on hiatus and the potential of breaking up...". It's the 'I'm not a quitter' thing in him. Someone more persuasive than me would have to...". Samara leaned forward and turned her desk calendar around. "When did you say the demolition would start?"

"November 1st."

Samara circled the date. "That gives us three weeks. Look, I'm going to try something else, okay? I'll let you know. And, if you hear from Pierre, tell him to call me. He's probably needing some help about now."

"Thank you. Oh, thank you, Dr. Jennings."

The backside of Derek's *Rock* resembled an earthquake graveyard, strewn with jagged pieces of granite, as if thrust from Hell. They were sloped gradually some thirty degrees toward the grotto that bridged the peninsula to the isthmus and then the main part of the island, making it impassable—thus the arrival and departure by fishing boat. That's how it looked to Aretha as well, as she peered out the window of Stanton's Cessna banking toward the point and Derek's project. "Just like she said."

"What?" asked Stanton through the headset.

Aretha adjusted her headset and answered. "I hadn't noticed when we flew this before, but Samara is right. The backside is for mules and mountain goats only."

"Got that right," said Stanton.

As the plane banked to circle the point, Aretha picked up her binoculars and peered at the work. "My God...he's making his own Rushmore."

"What?"

"Oh, nothing, Stanton. Can we get a little closer?"

"Yeah, if these winds will cooperate. Damn Atlantic tricks you every time."

He circled one more time, giving Aretha a closer look.

Down below, Derek gazed up at the noise disturbing his otherwise peaceful isolation. He squinted, shook his head, and went back to chiseling some fine details into the earlobe.

"He's sporting a Hemingway," said Aretha, "Don't say '*a what,*' Stanton. That's a beard. A big beard."

Stanton gave an indignant glance and said, "I knew that."

"Well, give him a couple of wing tilts so he doesn't start shooting at us."

"What?" gasped Stanton.

"Levity, dear boy. Levity. Just tilt a couple of hellos, okay?"

The Cessna flew in low, its engines growling for recognition, pulling Derek's attention one last time. Seeing the tilt of the wings, he squinted and thought he saw a woman. Then he squinted again. The woman and the familiar plane. "Well, I'll be..."

The crude airstrip used for infrequent private flights was void of any other aircraft, as Theo pulled up alongside the Cessna in a rented car. Stanton unloaded the overnight bags, as Aretha greeted Theo. "Thanks for picking us up."

"Hey, if Samara took the trouble to talk you into coming up here, least I could do."

"That rock continues to get more formidable."

"Not fit for man or beast. Of course, Derek is neither," said Theo with a sardonic grin as he lifted the bags into the car.

"I didn't know how much to bring. Samara said you told her that Derek could be stubborn as hell about now."

"Stubborn. Yeah. Suppose I did say that. Truth of the matter is he's more likely to couple that with belligerence and plain old anger as well." He started the motor. "Hung up on me yesterday when I tried to call and let him know you were coming."

"You mean he doesn't know?"

"Not unless he's telepathic too."

Aretha nodded. "Oh, boy. This should be good. Samara said when she left him, he told her to stay away until he finished."

"Yeah. That would be him, alright," said Theo. "I've booked your hotel rooms for two nights, just in case he tells us to go fuck ourselves."

Stanton gave a quizzical glance. Aretha patted his knee. "It's just Theo's way of saying Derek might be feeling a bit generous."

Theo chuckled. " 'Generous'. Ha. Good one."

"Well," said Aretha, "This is pretty important. He's seen Pierre's pictures...I assume the same ones Samara sent me?

Theo nodded. "Yeah."

"You've seen them, right?"

"Yeah"

"And?"

"You've got to be crazy to paint up a building as if it were some kind of installation piece. Well, I take it back now when I think about it. Derek just might try to match the craziness by stirring up a media stink once he knows they're trying to bulldoze the place. Getting him to come down away from his chisel and hammer to talk about it... now that's crazy of another kind."

"He's really set on finishing it before the winter, huh?" said Aretha.

"Short of freezing his keister off, he'll do it too. Never known a guy like that. Even when part of the group voted to disband, forget the whole thing, he talked the doubters into going back to the mainland and waiting out the fuel thing. He's got some kind of faith that the fuel prices are going to go down, and the island will prosper again. Finishing Echo rock is just his way of saying giving up completely isn't an option."

"Well, we both know it's more than just the gas prices."

Theo looked over at her. "Don't you love politics?"

"Sure do. If they can work for one purpose, they can work for another."

Theo smiled. "Sounds like you got something up your sleeve."

Aretha laughed. "Find a man's soft spot, and you can get all the favored politicking you want out of it."

"Derek's only soft spot is Samara, maybe his muse, but..."

"And let's not forget Stoppard. Even that kind of human has a soft spot. We'll see. We'll see," said Aretha. "Right, Stanton?"

"What?" grunted Stanton from the back seat, his *half asleep* disposition shining through.

"Beautiful day, don't you think?" answered Aretha, as she rested her gaze through the windshield and out to the ocean.

***

As the ringing continued on the other end, Theo stirred his coffee nervously. "He's probably not going to budge again. He knows Samara, me and Jamie are the only ones with his GPS number, and he's already made it clear..."

"Hello, damn it. This you again Theo?"

Theo shook his head with surprise. "Yeah... yeah, Theo here. How are you?"

"How am I? That's what you bugged me with yesterday and today..."

"Don't hang up, Derek. This is really important."

"What's important is that you know I don't want to be interrupted. Samara knows I don't want to be interrupted, and..."

"But Aretha doesn't know. Here." He quickly handed the phone to Aretha.

"Derek. It's Aretha."

After a pause, "Aretha. Aretha Ballard?"

"You know two Aretha's?"

Derek's voice became the old Derek. "No...No...just a second. Let me...get down...from here..."

Aretha waited as Derek scraped against the rock with his waist belt of iron and picks and moved inside the cave out of the wind. "What a pleasant surprise. How did you get my number?"

"Well, Theo made the call..."

"Oh, yeah. What am I thinking? So...damn...that *was* you in the plane...Stanton's plane, right?"

"Yes...Samara asked me to...there's something I need to talk to you about."

Derek turned aside for a moment. "I tried to talk to you about her before. But..."

"No, Derek. It's not about Linda. That's okay now. Really. It's about...could we talk?"

"Well sure. We are."

"No, I mean...could you come ashore for a little while so..."

Derek stood up. "Aretha...I don't want to be rude, but..."

"Don't tell me to go fuck myself, Derek, please."

Derek, taken aback, blurted out, "Aretha…no…never. What gave you such a thought? I just mean…"

"Derek, an hour with me won't take that much time away from your project. If I could climb that cliff, I'd come up like Samara, but…"

"You sound serious. What's this about?"

Aretha paused a moment. "Maybe it's about a way to get the island back in business."

"I don't get it."

"An hour. Just an hour."

***

Jamie tried to hold the boat steady, but the rough waters were throwing it around like a toy in a hurricane. "Shit," he yelled out to the dinghy. "Can't you paddle faster?"

Derek playfully raised his hand, giving Jamie the bird, and continued battling the waves.

***

Aretha stood at the rail atop the lighthouse. The wind pressed against her cheeks, reminding her how tight the skin of her face used to be. Memories of her youth gazing at what she thought, at that time, was a limitless sky, were now reminders that science had filled in many questions that made "limitless" a relative concept.

The sound of the old iron door at the foot of the spiral stairway brought her breathing to a pause. This man that had made her realize so many new questions about beauty, and death, was trudging his way to the top to perhaps once again set in motion something new and unexplored in her perceptions. She reminded herself that it didn't matter whether they were to talk about him or Pierre, a new expression, or the Echo rock. To Aretha, Derek Turrel could do no wrong, regardless of what or how he expressed himself. She knew a man's man when she saw one. That's one lesson she felt she had learned. She had the schooling of three failed marriages to understand the difference.

The wind had calmed as the door to the platform opened and in stepped what, for Aretha, seemed to her a vision of Hermes. Just as the Greek mythology proclaimed that being in the presence of Hermes was to be in the midst of fluidity, motion, new beginnings, as well as the confusion that inevitably preceded new beginnings, she felt both awestruck and humbled all over again. "Good to see you, Derek."

"And you, Aretha."

They stood for a few moments. "Methinks it be a bit calmer beneath the tower, my lady."

381

Aretha smiled and extended her hand. "Damn straight."

"You like chili pepper, Missy Ballard," screeched Singso from below. Aretha smiled, embarrassed what to say. Derek leaned across the table, "Doesn't matter what you say, she's going to cook the way she wants anyway."

"Oh...sure. Anything you think is good, Singso," shouted Aretha.

"Good," came the cry from below. " Good anything make it better."

They both giggled a moment. Aretha asked, "What is she cooking?"

"Better we don't ask. Just eat it."

"Okay. Okay." Aretha sipped her tea. "Where were we?"

"Whether I thought God ever touched the finger of Satan."

"Right. And?"

Derek sat back. "You know...Aretha...that's what makes us such good friends."

"What? I don't understand."

"Do you realize most of our conversations have been about the hypothetical? Very little talk of...oh, politics, topical stuff, the weather."

"And, that's good?"

He allowed a grin. "We never get bored, do we?"

"True. With there being no answers, only..."

"'Questions.' I know. You taught me that in the hot tub that first night."

"Yes, that first night," Aretha uttered quietly. "Now, about the finger."

"The finger of God, of course. The pictures. Well, you're obviously leading up the inevitable question of how many people would it offend, right?"

Aretha held the cup between her hands, peering over the top at the eyes that wouldn't relent. "It's really the only question that matters, isn't it? Push the wrong buttons in an obsessed and politically correct media, and it's over before it starts."

"You'd know better than I."

"Perhaps," she said. "Perhaps not. In today's art world, you have to turn your head and make a move, and then hope you've turned the right way."

"And you're confident that if enough of that 'right way' attention was brought to it...you believe he's got talent, don't you?" asked Derek.

"I think so. I'm privileged, in a way. I get to *pick* after things are completed. Only an artist, one who is working in the trenches, so to speak, can really tell at this stage whether talent is there. *Works in progress* are not my forte."

"Well," said Derek "Seems my life is nothing *but* a work in progress right now." He shuffled the pictures once again. "Yes…good chance he's got something, but…"

"But?" asked Aretha.

"But, I've only seen pictures."

Aretha smiled. "I know."

"Aretha…You've got that look now. Do you know what happens when momentum is interrupted in an artist's work?"

"I know what it means to be stopped, if that's what you mean. On November 1, it's Pierre's blitzkrieg day in Brooklyn."

"And Samara's got you convinced that if I see it and give it my… my nod, Stoppard will buy the building and save the day?'

"That's what Pierre's mother thinks, not Samara. Stoppard apparently said to her that if someone of *authority* thought he had talent, he'd try and do something."

"Oh, great. You think I'm going to be that authority for him. I'm his worst enemy."

"Precisely. Enemies stay enemies because of distance. History has proven over and over, a head-on confrontation between adversaries determines a victor, and many times, a truce."

"You're thinking crazy. I step into this family squabble and make a worse enemy than before."

"Only if you're dishonest."

Derek held his gaze on her.

"His soft spot. He's a sucker for honesty, because he sees most everything and everyone as the 'Fuckor'…just as he sees himself. If you're truthful in your evaluation, you win. Good talent. Bad talent. Say it like it is, and you win."

Derek thought a moment. "You're not too shabby in assessing people. You know that, don't you?"

"Stoppard is transparent to people like us."

"And the boy could lose. Where do you think that would put him? The graveyards for mortally wounded artists have voracious appetites."

"The risk we take, Derek."

From below came, "You come now! Soup ready! Come now or get cold."

Derek rose. "Saved by the bell." He leaned over the stairwell, "We're on our way, Singso. On our way."

"Not everyone is destined to be worth the effort," said Aretha. "You can't know if you don't look at it…in person." She got up and walked toward the stairway. "For my part, I think that however way you see his talent, you will realize another appointment with Stoppard. You want momentum. It doesn't get any better." Aretha rose. "Not much time necessary. Forty-eight hours, tops. Stanton loves to fly into LaGuardia as well. Says it makes him feel young and daring."

They started down the stairway. "To be young and daring again," said Derek.

"Pierre is," said Aretha. "And I hear some guy in his forties is scaling precipitous cliffs over the Atlantic, as well as tearing mediocrity a new *you know what.*"

Derek didn't laugh. He didn't smile. Aretha didn't even see a grin.

CHAPTER 62

For Stoppard, asking his secretary to send flowers to a business colleague was commonplace. To send flowers to one Tanika Haweisi would only cause questions. So, he decided to ask Siebert to make the purchase and delivery. As Siebert held the car door for him, Stoppard slipped him a small envelope. "Do me a favor. Pick up a couple of dozen red roses, put this envelope with them and run them out to Tanika, okay?"

"Of course, Mister Denning." He looked at his watch, "Should be able to get back here for your luncheon appointment. That's still on, isn't it?"

"Oh, God yes. Editors, even when you own the publisher, can be a pain in the ass, but... yes, noon, sharp."

"Noon sharp it is." He touched the brim of his hat, "You have a great morning now, Mister Denning."

As Stoppard walked toward the entrance to OST, he smiled and thought to himself, *if only you knew.*

As he sipped the last of his coffee, Stoppard smiled once again. The quarterly report would make Wall Street very happy, along with the shareholders. He leaned back in his chair and swiveled to peer out onto the tops of skyscrapers below. Picking up the phone, he said, "Myra, get Sanders to come in here, okay?"

"Right away, Mister Denning."

He glanced at the bottom line once more. His gamble had paid off. Radio advertising revenues were up five percent. Publishing was holding its own, and the foreign markets were booming with three films that OST had written off as losses just two months earlier in the domestic market. Now, what was wrong with TV? News department was fine. After initial high ratings during and upon his return from Sudan, they were set. Original programming on the network was fine, also realizing increased advertising revenues. But cable?

"You're the genius in that area, Sanders. You tell me. Cable is where it's at. Network will always keep the beer drinkers happy, but it's those damn people with *preferences*, everybody is reminding me about. Those are the ones you need to focus on, no?"

"You can't complain about the promotions. We pushed through more guest shots on talk shows than ever before."

"You're not paid to do the *ordinary*, Sanders. Anyone can pick up the phone and get what you got. The subscription base is flat." He thrust the report across the desk. "Remember the shot in the arm we got when Echo looked like they were folding? Remember how you celebrated? Well, they're on what we both hope is a permanent hiatus, but how come we don't have back the turn-coats that went to their side, those *preference* people?"

Sanders crossed his legs and lit a cigarette. "We're not offering what they offered, so how can we expect those subscribers to come to our side?"

Stoppard stood up and stretched. "Echo had it all, remember? They had it all because they respected involvement. Involvement, interactive, making the audiences feel they were part of the process, not just the old-fashioned passive model. You're paid to be the kick-ass imagination provocateur, remember? And get those web designers you glorify to start earning their pay. The web is the portal to everything now. We'll squeak by with this summer quarter report, but this fall/winter...I want more of Echo kind of stuff in the lineup. Let the audience decide endings. Let them choose some options, produce some choices. Understood?"

"Easier said..."

"Than done? I hope not. A good PR man wanting to be creative director...gets it done, so please, spare me the sour pessimism. I know it will cost a lot more to make multiple endings, but we've got a chance to beat them at their own game, God damn it. And one more thing, cell phone broadcast is growing like a weed. Get on it. Our shows should be preparing to compete there, as well."

Sanders started to leave.

"Oh," said Stoppard, "find me another YouTube. We can't be left behind while others get rich, can we?"

"Jesus, why me?"

"Because you want that promotion. And, you're my whipping boy, aren't you?"

"You really piss me off sometimes, Stop."

"Of course. That's why we're still working together. Get the fuck outta here!"

***

Theo, cradling the phone under his chin and packing a few things in his shoulder bag, said, "I'm coming into town this afternoon, Sol. Derek wants me to see something. How about we meet for dinner?"

"Mister Berkowitz, your appointment has arrived," came the announcement from Sol's assistant standing at the door.

"Yeah, okay. I'll be done here in a minute." He turned back to the phone. "Theo, I'd love to see you, but you know my people aren't moving any farther till this fuel thing is better."

"It's not about the fuel, Sol. I really need to talk to you about another matter. We could do drinks if…"

"Okay, Theo. Dinner. I've got to check in on a rehearsal at six, so let's make it seven-thirty. Bintos. Know where that is?"

"Hasn't moved, has it?"

"Same place. Later."

***

The next day's series of phone calls started with Aretha to Samara. Samara to Tanika. Tanika to Pierre, and the final call, Pierre to Samara. He stood in the middle of the third floor, his phone pressed firmly against his ear. "Nervous? Doctor Jennings, you don't understand. This is scary shit. What if he doesn't like it?"

"Pierre, you must have thought of that when you gave me the pictures to show him."

"Yeah. Probably. Yeah. I did. But, I never really thought he'd… Scary shit, mon. How'd you get him to agree?"

"You have to thank one of his patrons, Aretha Ballard. I understand she'll be there too. She's very influential in the art circles."

"Shit."

"And Theo. Derek puts a lot of trust in *Theo's* opinion."

"Shit. And you?"

"Oh, I'll be there too. Wouldn't miss it. This is special, Pierre."

He didn't want to hear those voices right now, voices that told him he wasn't special, and had worked against his self-worth for years. Even after all the hours with Samara, the therapy trips to Switzerland, and the patient understanding of Stan, these were voices that didn't want to go away. "You'll be here in three hours. Shit! I gotta go now." He closed his cell phone and looked around.

386

How would they be able to see everything? Flashlights and makeshift work lights were all he had. "Stan?" he shouted up the stairway. "Stan, wake up." He started running up the stairway, as Stan stumbled out from the fourth floor onto the landing, rubbing his eyes.

"What? What you yellin' about?"

"We need lights."

Stan, grabbing the handrail, lumbered down the first three steps. "What you talkin' about? We got lights."

"No, I mean *more* light. How am I gonna show this to people with flashlights and that cockamamie work-light thing you rigged up with a car battery?"

"You got people comin'?"

"In three hours. We need lights."

Stan shook his head, "And even if we did have lights, what the hell we gonna plug'em into?"

An hour later, as Pierre started lighting the first row of candles, Stan continued to unpack more. "You one crazy Jamaican, Pierre. Burn the fuckin' place down. That's all we need."

"Stop complaining and be thankful we had ourselves some money from the Suit."

"*Had* some money. *Had* is right. After all that paint you bought, these candles wiped us out. You ain't got nothin' now. What the hell we gonna do to live on till next week, fool?"

"Just hope they like it."

By the time Pierre and Stan reached the fourth floor and lit the remaining candles, it was just twenty minutes to zero hour. Stan had placed the last candle on the floor as Pierre rushed to light the last few leading to the corner where they slept. "Throw that tarp over the bed. Don't need them to think where we sleep is part of this," said Pierre.

Stan grabbed the tarp and tossed it over the mattress. Smelling his armpits, he said, "I don't know about you, but damn...gettin' ripe."

"Roll on some of that Mennen shit and give me some too."

As the cab pulled up to the red light at Bushwick and Moore, Derek reached across with two twenty-dollar bills and said, "This is good enough."

The cabbie shrugged as he pulled to the curb. "Works for me."

Derek waved off the change and climbed out. "Enjoy." He opened the back door letting Samara, Aretha and Theo exit. "Just like yesterday," said Theo.

Samara smiled. "The neighborhood?"

"Spent many a night on Bushwick in the old days," said Theo.

As a garbage truck passed, spewing out black diesel smoke, Aretha waved away the exhaust and stepped up on the curb. "Welcome to Brooklyn, everyone."

"It's down this way," said Samara as she raised the note with the scribbled address. Crossing the street four abreast must have given the rappers loitering on the corner some fodder for a new creation, as they immediately fondled their crotches and broke into a rhythmic chant, "*Bitchin' on the arm, on the arm, on the arm, yeah, bitchin' on the arm...*"

As the group moved down the broken sidewalk, Aretha looked back at the rappers and grinned. "They're spontaneous. Got to give them credit for that."

Samara glanced at her watch. "He's not one for promptness, so we're probably shocking the hell out of him being on time."

"You want to go on ahead and..." said Derek.

"No. If I know him, he's watching the street right now, swallowing hard and trying to avoid dry mouth."

Theo looked at the boarded up building on his left. "This it?"

Samara looked at the address again. "Says it's between 103 and 107 with no numbers." She nodded. "Home sweet home. He said to come around to the side entrance, which is..." she turned down the narrow alley separating the building from a sheet metal and chain-link fence with the obligatory razor wire running along the top. The sheet metal *clanged* with the weight of a large dog trying to jump it and savagely barking the kind of welcome no one likes to hear.

"Shit," blurted Theo. "Least they could have done is put a *Beware of Dog* sign somewhere."

Derek chuckled. "Yeah. That would have helped a lot, Theo."

Samara approached the side entrance and looked up at the slats that served as a *keep out* deterrent. It was obvious that Pierre had carefully arranged the nails so they could swing up vertically for entering. As she stepped on the decaying concrete slab that had once been part of the entrance, Derek lifted the slats. "Come on you guys before that dog brings the neighborhood down on us."

Theo and Derek followed Aretha and Samara through the opening. Everyone stopped, all becoming aware of their shortened breath as they peered into the cavernous floor lit by hundreds of candles—flames that flickered life into the painted inferno and smoke that covered the walls and ceiling.

Aretha was the first to let her eyes drop and realize the floor too was painted. Three dimensional hot coals and rubble mixed with remnant pieces of turn of the century paraphernalia. Ashen hand carts, a rocking chair, fruit from a spilled street cart boiling amidst the heat, children in flaming red sweat, men and women with outstretched arms imploring, disintegrating sailing masts flying, falling. And amidst it all, running almost as an interlaced theme, were old currency notes floating through the flames and smoke from the floor and ascending the walls as if being pulled by a vortex at the end of the hall.

"And we thought the fucking dog was scary," murmured Theo.

"Do we just wait?" whispered Aretha.

Clearing her throat, Samara answered. "He said he'd meet us on the fourth floor."

"Means we wage this storm alone, Theo. You sure you're up to it?" said Derek half-joking, half-serious.

A bit dumbstruck, Theo answered. "There are murals and there are murals." He stepped reverently forward.

Watching Theo take the lead rendered Derek cautiously excited, for the look on Theo's face confirmed his own enthusiasm. "And this is only the first floor."

By the time the group had slowly walked the candle-lit open loft area of the second floor—a sort of Guernica of the Roaring Twenties—and started up the stairway to the third, Aretha broke the silence. "This kid is *writing the book* on redemptive encounters of the third kind, don't you think?"

Derek remained silent, carefully examining all the intricate details.

Aretha carried a gentle smile through the four-floor climb.

Theo took the copious notes he was known for.

Samara allowed a tearful emotion rarely seen to come forth.

Hunched in the corner of the fourth floor, atop his tarp-covered bed, sat Pierre, his knees pulled tight under his chin and his eyes remaining fixed on the opening from the hall. Stan skittered in his stocking feet back and forth from entrance to Pierre giving reports of their progress, occasionally relighting a candle that had blown out. "They're taking a long time on the third, Pierre...long time."

Pierre didn't move.

As Derek came upon a depiction of Middle-Eastern men huddled over a table covered with pictures of the World Trade Center, he stopped. Allowing his eyes to roam the room once more, it all came together. Scene after scene brought memories of the latter half of

389

the century and its impact on New York. What had been on the first floor—the beginning of what came to be known as the "melting pot" of immigration—now was like an overflowing pot of incompatible ingredients, a human recipe gone awry. Corporate logos seemed to be disintegrating within the wind and fire. White picket fences were hurling through the smoke and debris like so many rejected projectiles. Everywhere, war-like encounters. Rising from beneath the layers of paint were children and mothers running, crawling, passing through one superimposed country map to another—all seeming to migrate to America—all seeming to seep into the burning infrastructure of Manhattan and over the bridges and congested ethnic caldrons of avenue and street into the smoke-filled block called Moore.

Stan leaned out the opening into the hall, and then rushed back to take up his own gallery seat beside Pierre to hope and pray.

The group came to the wide sprawling space of the fourth floor and stopped. Here, at the largest open area of the building, they stood in awe. Like a surreal ground zero, clusters of candles flickered their illumination upon the Trade Center's broken skeletal structure. The acrid-infused smoke rose up the walls and merged with the broken clouds, surrounding the fingers of God and the bleached bones of evil's favorite icon, Lucifer.

As Theo put his pocket notebook away, he looked to his left. Derek was motionless. To his right, Aretha and Samara stood stoically, save for the grip each had on the other's arm. "Anybody have a cigarette?" Theo barely eked out.

From the shadows, Pierre stepped forward. "I have one."

The group turned as Pierre, appearing as a come-alive-apparition from the flaming walls, stepped into the center of the room, extending his pack of cigarettes.

The hour that followed—as inspiring as it was—was no comparison to the first reaction the group had experienced walking the four floors alone. Pierre's rather timid beginning explanation on the first floor, describing the genesis for the idea, became animated and akin to sheer child-like joy as he finished back on the fourth floor. Theo couldn't write fast enough. Samara couldn't stop dabbing her eyes. Aretha couldn't stop interrupting with the mention of yet another influential art critic she was calling tomorrow, and Derek—remained silent until the end. Then he stepped up to Pierre. "I don't know you, Pierre, but...but I trust I will." He put his arms around the young man and held him tight, whispering in his ear, "Just know, it doesn't get any better than this." As he stepped back, he turned to the group. "We have work to do."

After assuring Pierre that he would do his best to gather support for the saving of the building, Derek walked out with Aretha and Theo. Samara stayed behind a few moments.

"Thank you," said Pierre. "Do you think he *really* likes my work?"

"Likes it? He's on the phone right now canceling his flight. You may not realize it at the moment, Pierre, but you've done the impossible."

"Will it be enough, mon? Enough?"

Samara looked around, reminding herself that saving the building was one thing—getting an audience for the work could be something else. She gave him a hug. "You think you might make your next work a bit more portable?"

The cab ride back to the loft was spent in relative silence. As the girders of the Brooklyn Bridge passed by, Theo found his mind trailing back to his own *down and out* time when the blur of speeding subways gave him similar rushes. In those days, his home was any platform bench he could find, usually downtown where the Port Authority Security was less inclined to hassle. Many a long night was spent trying to sleep, sitting up and writing, and returning to sleep again. Cheap booze and tainted pot was a sure-fire recipe for disappointing self-indulgence, so he didn't expect much from the wanderings of his mind back then. At best, those many scraps of penciled thoughts on life had kept him from jumping on the tracks. He could be grateful for that. Here he was sitting side by side with like-people of neurotic impulses, chaotic lives, and imagination— friends that had to follow their passions, wherever they led. He pulled out his notebook and wrote one word—*tenacity*.

Chapter 62

In another part of Manhattan, tenacity of a different sort was being tested.

"I'll get you the payment," said Sol. "Just don't be so hasty with your willingness to dismiss us as finished." He hung up and stood, peering out the window that overlooked 42nd Street and the resurgence of theatrical commerce in the form of sure-fire escapism. Schubert Alley, it was not. The magic of yesteryear would probably never be replaced. Sol wasn't above nostalgia any more than the next producer who had experienced multiple successes through and after the Golden Era of Broadway. He just felt a bit more proud; given his hits were all straight dramatic plays.

On the streets below, the rising Vegas-style marquees told it all. Animals, magicians and dancers now dominated what had once been the province of Miller, Williams, Becket, and Albee. Gone too were 42nd street's derelicts and smiling tourists gazing through storefront windows of pizza parlors, while flying pizza dough captured their eyes, and smells of bake-ovens and meatball gravy tortured their salivating taste buds. Fortune Tellers had once curled their *come-hither* fingers from behind green and purple neon trimmed windows, ready to make the curious innocents into adamant believers. Gone too was the clashing cacophony of second floor rehearsal studios with their mix of tap dancers, jazz players and vocalists vying for the ears and eyes of the *Sol Berkowitzes* of the world.

The 42nd Street of the past, with all its diversity from street corner preachers to two-dollar sexual encounters, from twenty-five cent peephole movies, to classic cinema from all over the world—that was all gone. Now—between the glitter of enough candy-colored lights to shame the Vegas Strip, and the continued building restoration and remodeling to house more mediocre entertainment—he watched the faces of business men and Amusement Park tourists walking aimlessly amidst the lure of expensive fantasies, impervious to the real effect the splashy block was having on them. They only knew they felt good—for the moment. Sol knew, however, that feeling good only through other people's imagination was the two-dimensional malady of the times, and that the Echo project had met the curse head on. It had to be saved. The satellite costs had to be kept up, even though spring, and the hopeful return to the island, was months away. He couldn't let the allotted satellite space fall into default and go to someone else, especially not to Stoppard Denning who—it was rumored—was willing to pay double for the space.

***

Pin spotlights and carefully lit sculptures filled the loft with appropriate dining ambiance as Derek said, "So, you've been taking a lot of notes in that little black book of yours, Theo."

Theo allowed the swallow of Merlot to take its time massaging his taste buds. "Mmm. Yes, I have, Derek." He smiled with an impish grin and turned to Samara. "When did you switch? You've never been a Cabernet lady."

Lifting the last of the appetizers onto Aretha's plate, Samara smiled. "I knew you were coming."

"You did not," said Theo. "It was just Derek and Aretha till..."

Derek interrupted. "Till I said 'you don't want to miss something that could take me away from the rock' and you came." He pointed his fork at Theo with a *gotcha* wink. "Isn't that how it went, Aretha?"

Aretha, whose dreamy disposition hadn't altered since leaving Moore Street, sipped her wine. "Right you are, if you think you are." Looking at the color of the wine, she smiled. "You're correct, Theo. Excellent." She glanced back at his little book. "And, are we to assume those notes are for a new article regarding one Pierre Haweisi?"

"No, actually. A press release and some thoughts for Sol to work on. Having dinner later with him. This is something worthy of his PT Barnum talents."

Derek raised his glass. "We're not there yet, but let's toast one of the craziest and most talented finds of…oh, I don't know. The decade? Generation? Century?"

The four of them raised their glasses. "You *are* impressed," said Samara catching Derek's eye.

"Not just impressed. Here's to the overwhelming power of the words, '*I must*,' for that was obviously the only justification needed for this blessed nut."

They clinked their glasses and sat back down to eat, drink and plan what to Derek was his biggest challenge to date, and as he reminded all of them repeatedly, "this is what Echo Project is all about…the fostering of accessibility. This is more than the blasting of a rock. More than the creation of a colony. Do any of you realize what we're taking on? The building is falling down. The location, the *installation*, whatever we call it, is *east purgatory* for most art lovers to visit. And the politically correct move on the building department is beyond any of us, not to mention the costs involved."

"But not beyond Stoppard," said Samara quietly.

"Stoppard?" said Derek.

"That's what this is all about," answered Samara. "He's one of a few with the kind of money and political clout that can wade through city hall's red tape. And you've got to convince him to do just that."

"Why me?" said Derek.

"Because Pierre looks up to you. Because he trusts your judgment."

Derek looked to Theo.

Theo looked to Aretha.

Aretha shrugged. "I'm just an innocent passenger."

Derek nodded. "Sure you are."

***

Clauz Bernhardt wasn't your everyday forensic chemist. Long retired from the routine of inspecting and testing works of art about to be auctioned at Krane's—Sotheby's major rival in the world of high-end auctions—he nonetheless enjoyed being called now and again to corroborate the findings of less experienced experts. People with the kind of money necessary to own a master work were often overly cautious in their purchases. Clauz Bernhardt was called to the rescue more often than he wished. He had, after all, his fish to attend to.

Like any well-heeled retiree, his golden years hobby was his passion. As a result of the special requests, however—having unearthed several million dollars worth of forgeries trying to pass off as originals—he had acquired the nickname, *Clout*. Today, Clout was introducing a new Kohaku into his penthouse pond, a one-of-a-kind custom-built hothouse environment high above 1st Ave, overlooking the East River. His first koi had been a Kohaku, and this one, costing him five-thousand dollars, he thought might be his last.

"Owning a Grand Champion is a dream for this old man," he said into the speakerphone. "Excellent body conformation, beautiful pattern of deep scarlet red, razor sharp Kiwa/Sashi and a soft snow white skin...all the right compliments. At just two years old, this bright princess has a big future. So Aretha, sorry. I do go on, don't I? What do I owe this unexpected call to?"

"Oh, nothing. Just thought I'd call and let you tell me about your carp."

"My dear, Koi. Koi."

She chuckled and tipped the hotel room service man. "Couldn't resist. Actually, I'm just in for a special visit."

"With me? Whoa, I'm off marriage, though. You know that. Three is quite enough."

"Touché. No, actually, I need a favor. Need to call upon your clout, Clout."

"Uh, oh. Sounds like I'm going to make some money."

"Well...that's debatable. I'd like to talk to you about helping me with a petition. You have some influence among art experts, and..."

"Well, if I'm not going to make any money..."

"Didn't say you wouldn't, just..."

"I know. It's debatable," Clauz said as he snapped a couple of digital pictures of his new arrival swimming among the other dozen or so Koi. "If there's debatable money, let's at least have some fun. You come up here and I'll take your picture feeding my lovelies."

"Oh, that will be a thrill. In a couple of hours?"

"Dom Perignon is going on ice immediately."

***

The next two weeks passed quicker than anticipated. With Aretha's charm and willingness to pose with his fish—the two bottles of Dom Perignon notwithstanding—Clauz had agreed to help by calling upon favors owed him by some of New York's leading art curators and critics.

Over the phone, Clauz's *favors* didn't like the idea of signing anything. Even after hearing the merits of the installation, coupled with it having been created by a Manhattan house painter from the isle of Jamaica, they were reluctant in subjecting their reputation to such an anomaly. When he convinced them that all he was asking for was a signature on a petition that served to save a work of art worth receiving further exposure, most were willing to receive the mailing of pictures and take a look. They were, after all, just being asked to offer support, not to revue or make a recommendation.

Now of course, the litmus test: *were the pictures sufficiently convincing?* To the group's surprise, several of the critics and one of the well-known curators were sufficiently impressed to want to visit the building in person. The day Justin Q—one of the city's most successful procurers of hard-to-find works of art—walked the candle lit caverns on Moore Street, he not only agreed to sign the petition of support, but wanted first dibs on sponsoring the opening, should it get that far.

Now, armed with the signatures of verifiable and highly regarded names in the art world, Aretha called Tanika with the good news, who in turn made the all important call. Stoppard had flippantly thrown the challenge at Tanika that night in the limo, and had all but forgotten the incident, until Tanika said, "Stoppard, I have a petition with forty-three signatures of New York art critics and gallery and museum curators to save the building."

His compulsive weakness—*say anything to keep her off my back*—had come back to haunt him. Fortunate for her and Pierre, but unfortunate for him, he had been caught with his *big mouth* open. To add insult to injury, she also requested he meet with Derek and discuss the petition. He wasn't, however, going to open his mouth any wider this time than the tip of his Churchill, which by the end of the phone call, was too wet and chewed up to smoke.

CHAPTER 63

The next day, after only a few minutes of niceties that all good politicians exercise before tackling issues, the *word* came back to haunt him. "Let me put it another way. Just as I asked Tanika, Derek, 'who the hell is interested in viewing a *nightmare*?' People have enough of their own, don't you think?"

Remaining seated, I refused to react the way Stoppard was expecting. Remaining focused, and determined to take advantage of the meeting he'd begrudgingly agreed to, I merely said, "Art sees things differently most of the time. *Nightmare?* No. Reaching out? Yes."

Stoppard leaned toward his humidor, lifted a Churchill, and stepped to his picture window view of Manhattan. "You know, the last time we met, we had a pretty interesting talk. We decided we're both stubborn; tried to convince the other he was wrong about everything; and then decided we were both unwilling to give in to the other. That's a good meeting. Now, here you are again, Derek, trying to tell me I'm wrong again, and that Pierre is an artist who's painted a fucking building I should buy...his *condemned* canvas. Right? Well, this is *not* where I give in."

"Why?"

"Why?" Stoppard turned back to me. "Because...look, just because he's the bastard *gay* son of an old acquaintance, doesn't mean I have any obligation, okay?"

"Have it your way. The bastard gay son of Tanika...is reaching out."

"Jesus, what's this 'reaching out' spin of yours?"

"I think if any of us had spent months creating what he's created, we'd want it preserved as well."

"That was just plain stupid what he did. Painting a condemned building. He's in La La Land. What the hell was he thinking, that the world would see his wonderful work and save the building?"

"Who knows, but a rich and powerful friend of his mother did see his 'wonderful work' and was...is in a position to save said building." I slid the petition across the desk.

"What's this?" he asked.

"A petition to stop the demolition."

"Good luck."

"You told Tanika that if some authority confirmed the man had talent, you'd consider helping. Well, that paper is signed by some pretty formidable art people."

"Meaning?"

"Meaning that even though you think it's a 'nightmare,' they have a different opinion."

"That's their prerogative."

"Yes. Their prerogative as authorities in the world of art is to identify and preserve. It's OST's prerogative as the world's most prominent 'provider' of art and entertainment, to consider the *value* in saving it." I pointed at the paper. "They can't all be wrong."

Stoppard blew a smoke ring and leaned back. "Ever hear of 'blackmail'?"

"Never," I said with a half-concealed grin.

His steely eyes gazed at me through another cloud of smoke, and then he leaned down to scrutinize the signatures. "I know any of these people?"

"Possibly. They represent some of the finest taste in art."

"I must know them, then."

"You must."

"This meeting is over," he said without any further fanfare. "I assume I can keep this."

"Sure. Its..."

"...a copy," he said. "Wouldn't expect you to risk my tearing up an original." He leaned over to his intercom. "Myra? Our meeting is finished. Would you show Mister Turrel to the elevator please?"

**

The confusing rage within me made the ride down the forty-eight floors feel like a re-entry experience. I had made my point for Pierre, but...I wanted to kick the side of the elevator...*what happened? I did nothing for the Echo issues. I forfeited the opportunity. How stupid.* The door opened on the main floor.

For no reason I could put my finger on, by the time I'd reached the revolving door to the sidewalk, my mind was processing thoughts of another kind. *What had happened up there was foreign in a way. I was truly with the moment, wasn't I? I was addressing an issue whose essence far exceeded the issue of saving a building...a piece of art. What was really at stake was the relationship of a father and a son, right?* Estrangement had been faced head on and although Stoppard wasn't comfortable with a bastard son—a gay bastard son—he was even less comfortable with me, the messenger, the delivery boy, as he most likely chose to think.

As I walked the busy sidewalks toward the subway, I was barely aware that my shoulders were bumping passersby. I was deeply immersed in the experience that had brought me to a new and different state of mind.

Somehow, I felt I had just discovered the answer.

**

"...I felt different, that's all. Very different. That's why I'm sharing the damn thing with you... why I'm asking. What's it all about?"

Samara had acquired a unique professional personality over all the years she had practiced therapy. It was difficult, even for her oldest patients, to discern at times whether her emotionless silence was a way of exercising patience for important patient data, or whether it was just another way she chose to listen and remember. Today was no exception.

As I paced back and forth in front of the corner window of the loft, she continued to apply lemon oil to the ebony surface of the piano. An occasional verbal response like, "…makes sense," and "okay…" kept me from believing she was treating me with an indifferent familiarity that not only comes with the age of the relationship, but what I supposed was possible with the passing years of professional exchange with the same patient over and over again. God knows, she had listened to my minor and major epiphanies more times than even I wished to remember. It was expected, after all, for artists like Samara and me to experience rushes of exalted revelations with our own "shit," as she preferred to call it. So I asked her, "Is this just another moment of me falling in love with my own 'shit?' Am I mistaking this moment for an answer?"

She paused, stepped back from the piano, tilted her head left to right, and gave a final inspection to her weekly chore. "Could be. Then again, you not pushing personal angst for your arch enemy in the meeting may have allowed some *real* breakthrough."

I was taken aback by the emphasis she placed on *real*. "Meaning?"

She screwed the cap back on the bottle and walked to the sink to wash her hands. "Derek, you gave me a play-by-play call of this visit. There wasn't a moment in that discourse that you didn't suggest to me that you were sincerely concerned with the greater issue…Pierre and Stoppard's alienated relationship. There is the greater question, and perhaps what you refer to as the *answer*."

"What?"

"Why was the Pierre and Stoppard thing capable of keeping you focused, when most likely, your ego was screaming and hollering behind some soundproof wall you put up."

"I'm really that egotistical, aren't I?"

"Echo Life is your effort to balance it all, but…yes, you are that egotistical."

"And so?"

"And so, you may have had a breakthrough. By keeping your eye on a different ball, you may have allowed the greater reward to happen…a revelation about relationships."

"Reward."

"Reward, Derek, is something you've only on rare instances allowed yourself to experience. For you, and that ego of yours, conquering the impossible is what keeps you motivated. Pierre and Stoppard are a worthy exercise consistent with that theory, and it's only a theory, but it also plays into your need to father, as in Echo Life. Only you can determine its validity."

"So that's what it's all about? Conquering the impossible…fathering?"

Samara sat down beside me, took my hand, and said, "We're about to make a transition, Mister Turrel." She leaned into me and pressed her lips ever so gently against mine. As she slowly pulled away, she smiled. "You keep growing. Feels good, doesn't it?"

Our eyes held and for the few moments, I had a mach speed rewind of all the years I'd spent purging and sharing with this woman, this chameleon who could be all things to me at whatever moment presented itself. I nodded. "You know it does."

She slowly nodded her head. "Yes…the reward of growth is reserved primarily for the one experiencing it, but others can sometimes benefit as well. Right now, I'm just looking through the window."

***

After his meeting with Derek, the rest of the day proceeded on a different plane for Stoppard, as well. He cancelled his weekly lunch date with Chico, his tennis partner. Every Thursday was their day, but today, he wasn't up to dining. Instead, he took a walk up and down Central Park South, stopping occasionally to let carriage horses nuzzle his hand for a treat. "How be you, Mister Denning?" asked the carriage driver number twenty-three.

"Doin' okay, Teach. Doin' okay. You having a good day?"

Teach shook his head. "Don't know what it is. This be a good fall, you know. Don't even need a blanket today. So, what's with the tourists?" He gestured to the long line of carriages all waiting to be engaged. "Everybody hurtin' today."

"Well," Stoppard offered, "suppose I just take a quick spin." He stepped up into the carriage as Teach, almost jumping out of his shoes, lunged to offer him a blanket. "You're right, Teach, don't even need a blanket. Tell you what, let's make it over to Lincoln Center and back."

"You got it, Mister Denning."

As Teach pulled out into the slow traffic lane, Stoppard pulled out a Churchill and lit up. He needed something to take the edge off his disposition. From his breast pocket, he pulled the stapled sheets containing the petition signatures. He took out his pen and proceeded checking off the names of those he knew. By the time he finished the two pages, he realized that out of forty-three signatures, he only knew three well enough to call and question. The others were mostly familiar to him, but without any real personal relationship. He puffed on his cigar and looked up at the back of Teach guiding the horse. "Teach, you like art?"

399

"Art?" He burst out laughing. "Real art? You know me well enough to know that answer."

"Yeah. I suppose. Watch much TV?"

"Sure. Doesn't everybody?"

"Hope so, Teach. Hope so."

They both laughed.

"Any good new shows comin' up this month? Fall premiers still goin', ain't they?'

"Sure, Teach. Too many to mention."

"Yeah...I'll be watchin' the box like everybody else. Can't afford to not be up to date, you know. People from all over the world ride this old buggy, and I can't tell you how many ask about TV shows they can go to and be part of the audience, you know? I usually tell'em the talk shows they can get into and then they usually ask what shows I watch, and I tell'em, then I ask what they like, back and forth, you know."

"So, what's your favorite?" asked Stoppard.

Teach looked over his shoulder, then back to the reins. "No disrespect intended, but I really got hooked on that crazy show, Echo Life. They cut back on a lot of the time they were on... somethin' 'bout the fuel prices, I don't know, but, I still watch OST all the time too, you know...but that crazy Greco guy, well...even for a farm boy like me, watchin' those other crazies makin' their paintings sculptures, even the short films, yeah, and especially Greco askin' about their work and stuff. Oh, and I really liked when he got those phone calls from regular people doin' their thing. Man, they could really talk his ear off." He laughed. "I remember this gal once called in, said she was sittin' in her bath tub with the razor all ready to cut her wrists and the radio playin'—you know that show goes on the radio too, don't ya?"

"Yeah. Oh, yeah, Teach."

"Well, she listened, that's what she told him. She listened and got hooked that very night on, 'you are all creative'... that's the theme, kinda, for the show, you know, and she said she climbed out of the tub, went in the living room and turned on the TV and watched the rest of the show while she dripped dry, standin' right there in front of the TV, she said." He laughed. "Said she stood back, saw the wet rug all around where she had been standing and said to herself, 'he's right. We are all creative.'" Teach laughed even louder. "Can you believe, the old bag, least she sounded like an old bag, the old bag said she looked at the pattern of her feet, feet mind ya, and next day got herself some paint and brushes and started paintin' around stuff. You know, anything with a shape. She'd just lay it down on some paper, do some tracin' and paint around it and...she was bein' creative, right? Painted up a whole crap load and sent them into Greco and a few weeks later, he showed 'em on his show. Damn, the old bag painted some pretty nifty stuff. Pretty nifty. Even started stackin' shit, sorry, stuff on each other. Greco called it cold-ag or collage, somethin' like that, collage shadows. That's what he called 'em." He turned around. Stoppard was sitting with his arms folded across his chest and moving the cigar between his lips, left to right, to left, to right.

"Almost called him myself one night, 'bout three in the mornin.' Yup, don't know art, but that show was interesting, 'specially after a couple of brewskies, you know? He was showin' that crazy son of a gun hammerin' rock way the hell up on a cliff over the ocean, you know, crazy guy, but damn, that's gonna be some rock when he's finished...some rock. You know about that show, don't ya?"

"Oh, sure, Teach. Got to keep up with the competition, you know."

"I'll bet."

***

"And you really think he's something more than some amateur trying to get attention?" said Stoppard, lying on his leather couch staring out the window at the afternoon thundershower.

"Is that what you think?" asked Elliot Randolph, one of three art critics that Stoppard knew well enough to call for a first-hand opinion. He expected he'd get an honest answer. He had, after all, given the man a column in his papers for the past five years...a column that, much to both their surprise, had caused as many letters and e-mail responses as the political columnists.

"I'm just a business man. What do I know. You're paid to be an expert," said Stoppard.

Elliot liked his job, and had a reputation of never being bought. "How come you're involved in this?" asked Elliot.

"It's a long story. Is he good or not?"

"Well, if somebody saves that building, he'll probably be famous in no time."

"I didn't ask if he'd be famous; I asked if he's good."

"I don't sign my name to anything I might regret, you know that. When this old friend, Aretha, asked me to help save the building so it could be seen by others, I figured I had nothing to lose."

"I get it, Elliot. I get it. Is he worth saving or is he just a schlock with a gimmick? You saw the pictures."

"I went to the building, Stoppard. I saw the real thing. He's gonna turn the art world on its head, and then flip it on its ass. Good. Very good."

Stoppard rose from the couch. "Jesus, Elliot. You went to that hellhole? That's all I needed to hear. You didn't have to…okay. Thanks." He hung up and went to his bathroom, throwing some cold water on his face and staring into the mirror. His passive face gradually reflected the fear that had been brooding for hours.

Chapter 64

Siebert pulled the limo to a stop on Bushwick. "You sure this is where you want to get off, Mister Denning?"

"Yeah… yeah, Siebert. Need to walk off some of this hooch before I make the visit." As Siebert opened the door, Stoppard reached his leg over the gutter where the combination of a broken bourbon bottle, a used condom and some orange peel infested with ants reminded him once again, anywhere is a long way from Central Park South. "Watch the fuckin' glass when you move the car on around. Jesus."

"Sorry, sir. Didn't see it."

"Not your fault, Siebert." He looked around. "It's everywhere."

As Stoppard tried to pull himself together and wandered toward Moore Street, Siebert gazed over the sidewalk, the storefront, the wire fence. He glanced back in the direction of the corner where Stoppard disappeared. Yellow glare from the street lamp clashed with the spill of pink and green neon from the liquor store, rendering a patrol car, moving slowly toward him, a ghastly mustard and black. The driver and his partner gave Siebert and the limo a look. He quickly decided a step into the liquor store would satisfy their curiosity and save him an explanation.

As he moved up to the fortified enclosure, he cleared his throat. "A… would you have an inexpensive…oh, half a pint of…what do you recommend?"

The clerk removed one earphone, while keeping his body moving to the music, and looked Siebert up and down. "You mean cheap?"

"Well, yes, you see I…"

With a quick turn of his Nike heels, he slid a half pint of Wild up against the two-inch thick glass wall separating them for Siebert to inspect. "You all want to 'kick the chicken' I can tell. Four-sixty-five."

Siebert reached in his pocket for some cash. " 'Kick the chicken?' Quaint."

The clerk gave a burst of laughter as he finger snapped and took the five-dollar bill through the 'mouse hole' for payment. "You all one out-a-place dude. You be careful now with that hunerd proof. Ya hear?"

Siebert tipped his hat, then catching his old-school habit as probably looking even more 'out-a-place,' quickly gave the clerk thumbs up and a big smile. "Have a happy, bro."

The clerk laughed back, "Hey, is there any other way?"

As Siebert ventured back onto the sidewalk, the patrol car was nowhere in sight. He sighed and climbed into the car. With careful restraint, he pulled out onto the road and went a block before turning to make the circle back to the Moore Street building and then wait.

***

"I just wanted to take another look," said Stoppard, as Pierre focused the flashlight on the far wall of the first floor. Stoppard paused. "This is the twenties, right?"

"Toward the end. Back over here..." Pierre swung the light to the far wall. "Here's when the neighborhood was mostly Dutch. Over here, I tried to lay out the collection of neighborhoods, mostly from old towns and villages of the Dutch times...a lot crumbled and over here, the influx of Orthodox Jews, African American, Italian American...even the Hispanic and Chinese American neighborhoods."

Stoppard scanned the two other walls stretching the full expanse of the floor. "How'd you learn all this?"

"Library."

"Library. All this from the library."

"And a lot from Stan. His whole family background is Brooklyn, so..."

"Stan?" said Stoppard, as he feigned a closer look at details to cover his disapproval of the man's mention.

Pierre continued. "He talked, told me stories he'd heard from his grandparents, I made sketches. Did that for a long time."

Stoppard moved to the stairwell. "Well, let's get on with it. Upstairs?"

Pierre hesitated. Having felt their meeting was going better than the last, his mention of Stan had obviously caused Stoppard to break his chain of thought. "Yeah...upstairs there are some chairs."

They climbed the floors to the fourth, the flashlights catching short glimpses of the New York City history ending on the fourth floor with the 9/11 and its aftermath. As they walked toward the makeshift flashlight and battery generated light, Stoppard experienced the familiar chill. As he peered at the burning walls of the city and the overseeing God and Lucifer depiction, he noticed an additional image hovering over both. It looked to him like the intertwining pattern of a giant synapse structure, molecules, atomic structure,

DNA coding mixed into mathematical formulae, with hieroglyphics scattering across the ceiling and down the walls, as if tumbling into an abyss. "This wasn't here before."

"No," said Pierre. "I wasn't finished when you were here last."

"Why above God?"

Pierre looked up. "Seemed right."

"Why the tumbling off into whatever that is."

"An abyss. Just simple decay. Disintegration of all."

"You believe that?"

"Decay? The universe? Beginnings and ends. That's what it's all about. Absolutely."

"So, to you God is just part of the decay?"

"If one believes he is all powerful, then he designed existence to get to where it is. Yeah, he placed himself in the middle."

"Of the decay," said Stoppard incredulously.

"In the middle," said Pierre.

Stoppard tried to walk off his anger by looking at other parts of the mural. He didn't know how to address this man that was his blood. He felt a total stranger to this kind of expression. "You have a strange sense of truth, Pierre."

Pierre stepped up closer and whispered. "Hey, mon, if this is going to get personal, perhaps it's better we talk alone."

Stoppard turned around, his eyes darting from dark corner to dark corner. "Shit. Stan's here?"

From the far corner on the mattress unseen, sat Stan. "I'm always here, unless Pierre says I leave."

Pierre nodded, acknowledging Stoppard's discomfort and motioned. "Stan, why don't you take a walk and pick us up some cigarettes?"

"Sure," replied Stan, as he stood and stepped into the light. "Anything for you. Mister Denning? Coffee, tea, milk?"

The glare from Stoppard was picked up by Stan with a smile. "Oh, come now, Mister Denning. There must be something you'd like. Oh, got it. Me at the door. I'll be gone before you can blink."

"Stan," cautioned Pierre.

"Here." Stan handed Pierre his remaining pack of cigarettes and stepped into the hall. "That ought to hold you for a bit. Ta Ta, you two."

Stan's footsteps disappeared down the stairwell. "'Ta Ta?' Jesus," said Stoppard. "How did that happen?"

"What happen?"

Stoppard waved his finger awkwardly toward Stan's exit and the dark corner.

"Stan?" said Pierre. "We've been over this before."

"No...I mean, when did you...was it always like this?"

"If we're going to get into my sex life, which will ultimately graduate into my belief system, which will most likely give you some answers to questions I'm sure you're here to ask...why don't we sit down."

"Yes. Glad you brought it up. Let's sit down and have a heart to heart," said Stoppard, as if he had been given the keys to the kingdom.

A couple of fold up chairs provided the means of facing each other for the first time. Stoppard was aware that up till now he had avoided eye contact, but once Pierre placed the chairs facing each other, he was given no option. As he instinctively turned the chair to an oblique angle, Pierre reminded him, "You did say 'heart to heart' yes?" Stoppard compromised and moved the chair back half way and sat down, awkwardly crossing and re-crossing his legs, trying to find the right position of power. "I'm here to help. You understand that, don't you?"

"No," answered Pierre hesitantly. "You didn't say what you wanted."

"Well, that's the way I work. This is not easy, you know."

"The talking to your...*me* part, or the *helping* part?"

"Both. We've never talked...really."

"We've never talked...period. You ranted once."

"Okay," said Stoppard. "We've never talked this way."

Pierre gathered himself and said, "Let me say, for my part, I'm glad. I wondered if you would ever get...here...this moment, you know?"

Hearing the sincerity in Pierre's voice, Stoppard paused. "Your mother and I talked about this, getting together and talking...a lot. We had some pretty good fights over it," he said with a chuckle. "She's had a belief about you for a long time."

"About my being sired by you?" Pierre remained still. The sadness of many years without the contact of a father quickly welled up in him.

"She ever tell you about our fights?"

Pierre shook his head. "We seldom talked about you. You were the *friend of the family.*"

Nodding, Stoppard considered a moment. "Guess that's a no-brainer, right?"

Pierre paused another moment, leaned forward arresting Stoppard's eyes from boardroom control to confessional honesty. "I started feeling gay very young. I experimented with boys, then tried girls, then found Stan. I've been with him for several years now. He respects me. I feel the same way for him. I don't think it's going to end, okay?"

Stoppard didn't move. Pierre's coal black eyes—just like his mother's—didn't blink. Not even the trickle of sweat that moved slowly from his armpit down over his ribs was going to disturb the hold Pierre had on the man that was his father. Either he was going to accept things as they were, or this meeting, this first and perhaps final chance, was over.

For the time being, the silence of the room assumed the role of guard, judge and jury.

***

The limo moved quietly around the corner and pulled to the curb in front of the building. Siebert turned the lights and engine off, reclined his seat and tuned up his favorite classical station, WQXR. Satisfied with the string quartet, he tilted his hat, folded his arms and slumped into the corner.

Cigarettes are getting smaller, thought Stan as he opened his pack of Marlboro and lit up. He took another look at the embered stick and nodded to himself. *Yeah. Definitely smaller. Seven dollars. Enough to make you quit.* He counted the coins left in his pocket and slid two of the pacifiers from the box into his shirt pocket. *Fair's fair. He's up there puffin' away and I'm...*He paused and squinted through the spill of the yellowed street lamp. He smiled. *Siebert. Least it won't be boring.* He swaggered up to the window and tapped. "Hey, Siebert, old buddy. Sleepin' on the job?" he chuckled.

Siebert leaned forward and opened the window. "Stan. Well..." He looked up through the windshield, "Guess the meeting's still going, yes?"

"Oh, yeah," said Stan, moving around to the passenger side as Siebert rather reluctantly flipped the door switch. As Stan stepped in, "Don't mind if I do. Mind if I smoke?"

"Yes. Mister Denning prefers the Churchill smell in the car."

"Churchill?"

"Anyway, how are you?"

As he leaned out the door and pinched off the tip of the cigarette, "Damn," he answered. "Better since my ass hit this calf skin."

"Antelope," corrected Siebert.

"No shit? Well, better since I hit this antelope skin." He turned and gazed at the cavernous back seat. "Bet you've heard some good partyin' goin' on back there," as he jabbed Siebert's ribs.

"Mister Denning prefers to ride alone most of the time."

"This 'Mister Denning' sure *prefers* a lot. But...guess you can afford to *prefer* a lot when you're stinkin' rich."

406

"Yes. How's the project coming?"

Walls of Infamy? He paused a moment, his face going lax. "Lot of work, Siebert. Hell of a lot of work."

"You've been helping him, haven't you?"

"I've been there for him, yeah. Help where I can."

"Good friends are not easy to come by."

"Not so hard when you're…" Stan adjusted his seat, allowed the smile to return and reached for the radio dial. "You like classical, do you?"

"Yes. Classical I like."

"Jazz for me…reggae and some jazz, my ears are happy. Pierre likes that Russian dude, Shostakovich, lately." He glanced at his watch. "Hey, it's midnight."

"Yes, unfortunately," said Siebert, pinching the bridge of his nose.

"Ever listen to Simon Greco?"

"Usually, this hour is consumed by sleep," said Siebert.

"Well, mind if I…" he looked to Siebert, who conceded with a nod. Stan punched the digital numbers, finally coming to Echo Life. "You know about this guy, right?"

"I believe Mister Denning has voiced his name from time to time."

"Pierre has a hard…ah, he's got a real thing for this Derek guy…the one who runs to whole thing. Greco's kind of the mouthpiece…you know. You listen a few minutes, and shit, even *you* feel creative."

"Well, until that happens, I'm going to let you listen and I'm going to catch a few more minutes of sleep." He tilted his hat and slumped back into his dozing position.

Like a kid at a three ring circus, Stan leaned forward, resting his chin and elbows on the dash while Simon Greco introduced the night's guest artist, a repeat of an earlier show that year—Lanagra talking as he finished his last installation piece.

The fourth floor seemed bigger to Pierre, or maybe it was that his personal world had just gotten smaller. He felt like a leaf holding onto its branch in a hurricane. Stoppard remained seated, head down, but Pierre, feeling panicked, was now mixing paint, dabbing the back of his hand, comparing it to a shade on the wall, and mixing some more. The frenetic sense of time ebbing away rushed through his hands as he poured a bit, mixed, poured, finally, he said, "There's never enough smoke. Never enough destruction, is there? No sooner do we build, than we tear down, or the crazies will pull another 9/11 on us. What if time runs out, Stoppard? What if?" He

407

looked over at the man hunched over, but there was no reaction. As he turned back,

Stoppard exploded, shouting at the floor, ricocheting his exasperation across the room, never lifting his head. "Fuck, Pierre! Pick the building! Live where you want. I'll take care of your expenses. Paint what you want…Just settle down…for your mother's sake. Just be a little more…."

Pierre waited, but the sentence was never finished, until he said "Sane?" He turned and spoke as a young boy might try to justify his scrawled crayons on the wallpaper of his room. "It was an impulse, this 'fucking building,' as you call it. An impulse that turned into something else. That's all. I'm not nuts." He turned back to his walls and gathered his thoughts. "Why is it you think *settling down*, or painting ocean waves and fruit bowls and…dropping, or forgetting what makes people like us feel alive is the way to go? Insurance for good mental health? That what you think? How the hell you think good mental health works? More trips to Swiss clinics for the depressed?" He started swirling more gray and brown patterns of smoke on the wall. "Well, come next week when the wrecking ball takes down the first wall, I'll be here…I'll be working…they'll have to drag me out."

Stoppard stood up and shouted, bellowing like Citizen Kane in a drunken dream. "And that's just what they'll do. They'll drag your ass out and slam you behind bars. This is against the law, you know? Ever occur to you that breaking the law usually means getting caught? What are you going to do then, take your pencil and paper and draw in a jail cell wall?"

Pierre dropped the brush in the bucket and stood, trying to suppress the rage. "Tell you what, come the deadline, you get OST here early, I'll give them an exclusive. That should get you viewers. 'Jamaican house painter makes building his canvas, only to lose it to the wrecking ball.'"

Stoppard felt equally enraged and equally vying for control. He stepped up to Pierre. "You're hurt. I understand. But…but I'm…I'm who I am and I have a right to ask you to do what I think best."

In a tone barely audible, Pierre sent Stoppard on his way. "Trying to sound like a father doesn't suit you. You're quite a few years too late, Mister Denning."

Pierre lifted his eyes for one last glance as Stoppard disappeared into the hallway, his footsteps and drunken voice slowly dying in the darkness. "I'm who I am, God damn it! Who I am!"

CHAPTER 65

The limo's back door was jerked open, and Stoppard slumped into the seat. Startled, Stan spun around, then leapt out of the car, running to the side entrance. Watching Stan's escape, Stoppard mumbled. "Sorry for taking so long, Siebert."

Straightening his hat, Siebert started the engine. "Quite alright. Stan and the radio passed the time just fine. To your apartment, sir?"

Stoppard, hearing the radio's low volume, leaned forward and adjusted the back seat control higher. "Yes, apartment."

Simon's phone-in caller was finishing her comments. " ...if only we all had that kind of focus and...what is it Simon...losing yourself? Yeah. That man's colors are like...alive. I swear. Some kind of imagination. God, we need more Lanagras to help wake us up, you know?"

"Yes, unfortunately, I know," answered Simon.

***

"So?" asked Stan. "You okay?"

Sitting on the floor and staring at his newly painted smoke swirls, Pierre appeared pensive. "I blew it."

"You blew it? How'd you do that? He said he was going to help."

Pierre stood up, walked to the center of the floor, lay down, and fixed his eyes on the fingers of God and Lucifer. "He wanted to. I just saw things differently."

Stan shook his head. "What else is new?"

"Pardon?"

Stan got up, hesitated, and then walked to the center where he too laid down and joined Pierre staring at the ceiling. "He hated your God and Satan, right?"

"Yeah, I think so. There was more to it than that though. He's...he's more fucked up than either one of us."

Stan smiled. "Yeah. Sure. 'Cept all his fucked-upedness is cushioned by more money than God's got." He chuckled. "Hear that, God? Stoppard's probably got more money than you!"

Unseen by Stan, Pierre didn't let on how hard it was to hold his stare at the ceiling as the tear rolled down his cheek.

All anyone could do now was—hope.

Aretha, feeling that this new focus was a perfect excuse to not return to the Cape and the sadness there, extended her stay indefinitely at the hotel. She sent out thank you notes to all the petition signers, extending her personal appreciation and suggesting they watch the news after the first of November in case they were successful.

***

Samara saw Pierre for two successive days, assuring him that he hadn't screwed up his future—that he had secured his integrity, the most important outcome of this.

***

Returning to the island, Derek and Theo settled in for the wait. Resting only in the early dawn hours, Theo drank gallons of coffee in an effort to write all he could about Pierre's *Walls of Infamy*, going out on his proverbial limb calling it no less a work of art than the Sistine Chapel.

In spite of the cold, Derek ventured back to the rock and kept his phone on his belt while he waited and chiseled smooth an unwanted wrinkle of brow—determined as he was to remain hopeful, not only for Pierre, but for Echo Project's anxieties as well.

***

Pierre spent the next few days pacifying his worry with more detailed smoke and a few historical landmarks thrown into the apocalyptic vision.

Unseen by Pierre at this point, sitting on the roof of 105 Moore Street, peering through the translucent colored skylight, was Echo. A few days of patience were not unusual. Waiting was an everyday pleasure for the lady in scarves.

***

After an eleventh hour rush, and the excessive fees accompanying it, Stoppard's lawyer, Ben Singleton, called him in the limo letting him know the meetings with the appropriate city departments were done and that he had a clean shot to purchase the building. "It will require you to put probably another half million into making sure the damn thing doesn't fall down and passes inspection, but, hey, you're free to spend your money any way you want. You know that."

"Of course I know that. This time, however, I'm transferring the money into your trust account and *you're* going to buy and deed it to The Tanika Foundation which you'll also set up."

"Whoa...Tanika Foundation?" bellowed Ben. "What the hell is that?"

"A new charity you're setting up with Tanika Haweisi as Chair. I'll fax you the necessary details. There's going to be no mention of my name anywhere. Understood?"

"Fine. IRS is going to look hard though."

410

"Let them. My accountant will take care of that. He's always bitchin' about not enough donations and deductions anyway. Just do it and...shred the fax. Okay?" cautioned Stoppard.

"You sober, Stop?" asked Ben.

"Never been so sober. This has got to be done in forty-eight hours to beat that deadline. Happy billing." He replaced the handset and peered out the window. Exercising power always got his libido going. *Driving along Park Avenue mid-day renders the best eye-candy. Sidewalks usually crowded with only spoiled businessmen, spoiled wives and their spoiled dogs, seem to make way for the long legged model types, the just-off-the-plane hungry college-girl types, looking for their first jobs. Then, of course, there are the ever-present A-class hookers, working the early shift.* He nodded at the familiar sight. They were, as always, of one type—high maintenance. He didn't know why, but most days around 3:30, were he out and about, he'd see the promenade of anxious libidos strutting, looking and then strutting some more, which in turn would bring on a rush of *power* tempting him to play an old favorite game...*what would that one cost me?*

Today felt different though. He glanced at the telephone again. He had experienced a great many victories and conquests, but none that felt like this. He wasn't sure it was truly a redemption of guilt, or just the fooling of himself into thinking he was a better human being than people sometimes gave him credit for. What he was sure of, however, was the eerie sense of personal relief being impacted by an insecure corporate feeling he never experienced. "Back to the office?" asked Siebert.

Stoppard paused, collecting thoughts he didn't understand. "Uh...no. Drop me at the apartment."

"Apartment, it is," answered Siebert with a look in the rear view mirror. What he saw wasn't the Stoppard that usually sat just below his vanity light catching up on either The Times or The Wall Street Journal. This was a man gazing out the window with vacuous eyes unfamiliar to Siebert.

Stoppard picked up the phone and dialed. "Tanika...I have some interesting news for you. Have you a minute?"

By the time he walked into his apartment, it was even more apparent. Stoppard was feeling useless, spent, and completely unconnected. He again reviewed the events leading up to this state of mind that even he didn't want to witness, let alone allow anyone else to see who might know him.

Siebert had asked several times before tipping his hat, "Everything alright, Mister Denning? You're sure?" Even followed up by his trademark comment, "You're the boss, Mister Denning."

Being the boss had always been Stoppard's ambition. He had accomplished the near impossible by founding and still maintaining control over OST. He had amassed wealth beyond his wildest expectations, so *why...why...how come I feel this way?*

He shuffled over to the bar. *A good stiff drink. That's all I need. That's all I ever need.* He opened his liquor cabinet and scanned the bottles. He reached toward the back and retrieved a bottle of scotch. Rubbing his hand over the top in a sort of mock polish, he muttered to himself, "Glendronach. You're still the best twelve-year old I know." He closed the cabinet, reached for a crystal glass and set it down with the scotch on the coffee table. For the moment, he felt a bit more like his usual self. Walking to the kitchen to get some ice, he glanced at the wall of photos he proudly exhibited. Presidents, statesmen, movie stars, even the Pope. He puffed up and felt anew. Returning to the coffee table, he filled his glass with ice, and started to open the Glendronach. Without any forethought, he grabbed the phone and dialed. "Tanika? You didn't speak to Pierre yet, did you?"

"He's not answering his phone," she replied, her excitement uncontained.

"Well, don't try again. I'll tell him. I should have never asked you to give him the news. I'll tell him. Let me tell him."

"Okay. Okay. Why the urgency? You don't sound yourself."

"It's better this way. Better."

Tanika paused a moment. "Let me know how it goes, alright?"

"Yes. Yes, of course. Thank you."

Pulling out his cell phone, he looked up Pierre's number and called. No answer. Just as he was about to hang up, Pierre answered. "Yes. What is it?"

"Bad time?" said Stoppard casually.

"And this would be...Stoppard? *The* Stoppard?"

"Yes. This is the 'suit'."

"What's up?"

"Are you busy?" asked Stoppard.

"Always."

"Well, can you un-busy yourself for a celebration?"

"Depends."

"Oh, boy. You want to make this hard for me, don't you?"

"What's the celebration?"

"I've got a vintage bottle of scotch that says you deserve a sip before you hear."

"I ain't movin'. I told you that. So no layin' a house warming, 'let's have a drink to celebrate' shit."

"Siebert will pick you up in thirty minutes," said Stoppard, quickly hanging up. He stared at the phone for what felt like minutes, hoping Pierre wouldn't call back and tell him to get fucked.

It didn't ring.

Chapter 66

Crossing the Brooklyn Bridge, Pierre turned and said, "You sure you don't know what the hell this is about, Siebert?"

"I only know Mister Denning said to pick you up and bring you to his apartment."

"And even if you did know, you want to keep your job so you wouldn't tell me anyway, right?"

Siebert smiled. "That's the way it works. That's the way you keep your job. You're a smart lad."

Pierre turned and looked out the window at the East River. "Rides pretty good up here."

"This is a nice automobile."

Pierre chuckled. "Nice? Shit. Buy a house for this much money."

"And it probably wouldn't need fixing up," Siebert said with a chuckle.

Pierre glanced back at him. "That expensive, huh?"

"Well, I don't know the numbers, but the armor plate pushed it up there."

"This thing is bullet proof?"

"Bomb proof...to a degree."

Pierre became sullen. "Why the overkill, mon? I mean..."

"Mister Denning travels to all parts of the world. Sometimes it's necessary to take the vehicle in countries where things are a bit unsettled."

"He take this to Darfur?"

"No. He hired a few tanks and many mercenaries to keep things safe for him."

Pierre looked around. "Jesus. What a life. Doesn't look armor plated."

"No. It's not the kind of customization you want to advertise. That's why its cost would buy a rather *nice* house."

"Mm."

Siebert looked over at Pierre, who was now quiet. Turning the radio dial, he said, "Would you like some reggae?" The music abruptly became loud and *very* reggae.

Pierre gave Siebert a doubtful look.

"I've grown rather fond of your music lately," said Siebert. "Found the station and got, how do you say, 'hooked?'"

The rest of the drive was without conversation—just movin' and groovin'.

As the elevator rose, Pierre glanced at his shoes several times. Finally, just before the door opened, he leaned over and spit on his finger, rubbing the scuffed toe of his oxford. The mirror in the hall gave him a chance to double-check his uncomfortable appearance. He didn't know whether it was the stress in his expression or the distress of his sport coat, but in either case, he wasn't feeling much like the Pierre Stoppard knew. He questioned his decision to appear this way one last time before pressing the doorbell. "Aw, fuck it," he mumbled and took off the wrinkled tie, opened the collar, and just for good measure, re-scuffed his shoe on the fake statue-ruin that adorned the entrance to the apartment.

The door opened and Stoppard gushed with, "So happy you could come."

Pierre gave a nod to the statue and asked, "Is that Roman or Greek?"

Pleased with the immediate interest, Stoppard said, "Oh, that. Actually, between you and me, it's nothing. I liked it because I knew it would get visitors questioning what great artist had originally done it. It's nothing but a knock-off of something nondescript. Just a conversation maker. Know what I mean?"

"No," said Pierre, "but guess it works for you and your visitors."

"Well, come in. Come in. There are some *real* art pieces inside."

As they made their way down the hall appointed with numbered prints and original oils from the Baroque period, Pierre nodded several times, satisfied that his father had some taste anyway, *or does he have a damn good interior decorator?*

They passed under the three rotunda-designed intersections that split off into different wings of the apartment. Pierre chuckled. "You're really somethin'."

"Oh, this. Just the expected decoration for someone like me. It's not all as sumptuous as it might appear. It actually gets rather boring most of the time. Here..." He gestured to a smaller hallway that led to a rosewood-paneled library.

Books filled the walls, floor to ceiling with a hook-ladder on wheels to access the upper shelves. In the center was a museum quality Persian rug that upstaged a plain antique desk. To the left, two armchairs faced an ornate chess table with oversized pieces depicting feudal Japan. To the right was a brass and glass serving trolley, from which, after offering Pierre a seat on the black pieces side, Stoppard poured cherished amounts of his bottle of Glendronoch into crystal glasses. "Thought this would be a comfortable place to... You did say you liked scotch, didn't you?"

"No," said Pierre. "We never talked about booze."

"But you do...scotch, I mean." He handed Pierre the glass.

"I'm a rum man usually, but...yeah. Scotch on occasion."

Stoppard raised his glass. "Well, 'occasion' it is. Congratulations, Pierre. You and your mother are now the proud owners of a condemned building that houses what certain art aficionados claim is a landmark piece of painting." Stoppard winked, and sipped his fifteen hundred dollar scotch.

Pierre paused a moment, letting the words sink in, and drank his glass straight down in one gulp. In spite of his placid face, there was a suggestion that some tasting might be going on. He then extended his glass. "That...That's worth another shot."

Stoppard smiled and poured. "I thought you'd be pleased. The building department was quite a challenge, you know."

"I meant the scotch. The scotch tastes pretty damn good."

At that precise moment, as Pierre slugged down another shot like it was soda pop, a wave of contempt shot through Stoppard, exiting quickly as he adjusted himself in his chair. He realized now that Pierre wasn't going to make the evening any easier.

"Oh, the building. Thanks," said Pierre.

"You're welcome." Stoppard was rendered nonplus and not enjoying it. He made an involuntary tip of his glass and followed Pierre's lead with a gulp of the balance, quickly pouring another. "So...your mother was happy."

"I'm glad."

"She said I had made her *very* happy."

"I'm sure she meant it."

"And she thought you would be very happy too," followed Stoppard.

"Yes. I am." He looked up at the walls. "You read all these books?"

"Yes. Most of them."

Pierre gave him a sarcastic grin. "C'mon. Zillionaires don't read books. They watch TV."

"I like to read," said Stoppard caustically. Education does that to a person.

Pierre stood up and tilted his head, scanning the spines. "Melville, Faulkner...Miller? You read Henry Miller?"

"You know of him?"

"That fancy school, Mom...you, sent me to, required we know him well."

"And?" Stoppard said cautiously.

"He lived his art."

"That's true. Did you connect?"

Pierre smiled. "House painting is hardly living your art."

"I'm sure, but you did spend a lot of time painting the Brooklyn thing. Wasn't that living your art?"

"Not really. Not until I got pissed enough. Hey, is this gonna be one of those 'let me make it up to you' sessions? 'Cause if it is, I need to leave." He slugged down another gulp, and waited for the answer while holding the glass for another pour.

Stoppard didn't say anything, carefully guarding his expression, in spite of the new kind of emotion he was experiencing—emotion he was unfamiliar with. He finally leaned forward and poured. "I'm not trying to make up anything to you. The past is the past. You've made it clear that the chasm between us is probably permanent. All that's left is the present.

Pierre downed the scotch.

"You may not realize it Pierre, but I could have dealt with that building any way I chose, but I took the route that would be least troublesome, least personal to you. I made it strictly business. Foundations serve many needs for people of my wealth." Stoppard waited a moment for a reaction. There was none. "You and your mother have the building as an asset of your foundation. You may do with it what you wish. I've removed myself from any affiliation. The money used for the purchase is anonymous and I would appreciate you keeping it that way."

Pierre felt trapped by his own arrogance, but didn't know what to do or say at that moment, except "Why not?" He tapped his glass. "I'll have another shot, if that's alright with you."

Stoppard caught himself wanting to say ugly things at that moment, but there were more important words that needed to be said. "Another glass of celebration coming right up." As he poured, he gathered his thoughts. "Pierre, would you mind sharing what you really expect from here on. I mean, what is it you want...for yourself?"

Pierre looked down at his Thrift Store pants and sport coat. "I guess I want something I didn't expect when I climbed into these clothes. Haven't been in a coat since I stopped going to church. Guess I want something..." His eyes wandered to the bookshelves again. "Like a..." He stood up and went to the shelves. He smiled. "Miller and the Bible side by side. That by design?"

"Do you miss church?"

"No. Did you read the Bible?"

"Like any good altar boy, yes. Growing up, there were times when it was unavoidable."

"Here?"

"Here?"

"You grow up here in the city?"

"Mid West in the very beginning, then Brooklyn. Moved around a lot. Mom and Dad were devout Catholics and we always moved as close to a church as we could so she didn't have to walk far for daily mass."

"That strict, huh?"

"Pretty much. Yes."

"So...I guess what I started out painting as a straightforward history of immigration and Brooklyn must have really offended you by the time it reached the finger job on the ceiling."

"Nah. Yah. A little bit. But...hey, what do I really know about art?" Stoppard took a breath and leaned across the chess pieces trying to take a serious moment and use it to—he wasn't sure. "Do you know that I checked out all the names that signed your petition and called a few to see how much that... Aretha woman and Turrel paid them?

Pierre didn't respond.

"Yeah. And you know what they said? I mean all of them...things like 'no one has ever attempted such a landscape' and 'there's something special there,' and one even said 'Michelangelo reincarnated.' Enough to give you a big head, isn't it?"

"Me or you?"

Stoppard paused. The more he suppressed his anger, the more it became contained rage. "You know, you're more unpredictable than my board of directors. You know that? You smile and nod, then bare your teeth and...what is it? Let's stop the dance, okay? I'm telling you I don't understand shit about what you did. I know a signature on a painting means something, like all twelve of those originals in my halls that any museum in the world would give a left nut to own. I know enough about the business of art to know it's as good as investing in gold...maybe better. I know how to turn a business that I started as one local radio station into the largest media conglomerate in the world, and I know how to get rich and stay rich, okay? So don't think I need another big head. My fucking head goes through bursting spells daily. What I *don't* know is shit about you and *your* art, or even worse, how to be a...be a fucking *friend* to you." With that, Stoppard downed his drink. "Excuse me a moment. There's another bottle of this hooch in the other room."

Pierre sat immobile until the dryness of his throat made him swallow, and swallow. Lifting his glass, he swallow what was left... to the last drop.

Chapter 67

By the time the two of them made it to the sidewalk outside Stoppard's building, both men were laughing and arguing which was west and which was east. As their wobbly debate broke into further laughter—giving the doorman a discreet excuse to disappear back into his cubicle—Pierre struggled and found the flask in his pocket. Like a bum that had just scored a lottery ticket, he whispered to Stoppard, "This thing you gave me... is it full?"

Stoppard raised his eyebrow as high as he could to allow his eyes to see. "Just like..." he patted his left coat pocket, panicked and patted his right. Smiling, he lifted his matching flask. "Full just like mine. And it isn't a can, for Christ's sake. Fucker is sterling with gold...inlays." They stumbled off, arm on shoulders, up the street mumbling, "We'll decide this in the...park."

"Won't."

"Will."

"Won't."

"Will."

As they crossed Central Park South, Stoppard raised his flask in the air and shouted, "Teach? Teach?"

The driver of number twenty-three stood up in his carriage and waved back. "That you, Mister Denning?"

Stoppard stumbled up to the horse. "Shhhh. Tell your boss I'm in cognitooooooow"

Pierre wavered up and asked Teach, "You know this guy?"

"Mister Denning? You betcha." He turned to Stoppard who by now was letting the horse lick a new part in his hair. "Mister Denning!" He jumped down and respectfully took Stoppard's arm. "Terrible manners, she has. You like a nice ride in the park?"

Stoppard smiled, ear to ear. "Oh, yes, Teach. A nice ride in the park." Experiencing a sudden mood change, he asked, "Could you help my young friend into the carriage. He's drunk."

Pierre, who was already sitting in the red plastic seat reached down. "I'm up here, old man. Easy on that first step. It's a bitch."

Stoppard looked down at the small step. "I've been riding horses since before you were born."

Pierre pulled him in while Teach pushed. "There you go, Mister Denning. Nice cool ride in the park do you the world of good."

Stoppard slapped his own face and blinked his eyes several times. "We're just getting started, my friend. This is a celebration."

Pierre took another swig from the flask and sat back. "Yeah. A celebration." He leaned over to Stoppard. "What we gonna celebrate now?"

Stoppard turned serious, fingered his chin and said, "I got it. We'll celebrate the bet when I win."

Pierre paused a moment. "The bet? What did we bet?"

"You know. We were gonna settle it in the park."

"Oh, yeah." He stuck the flask back in his pocket and patted it. "Gotta keep my can safe. What bet?"

"Who's the most crea... crea... creative." He shouted to Teach. "Onward, coachman. To the lake. To the lake."

Fifteen minutes later, Teach brought the carriage to a stop. "This is as close as I can get, Mister Denning. You want that I wait?"

"Good idea, Teach. Good idea." With that, Stoppard backed out of the carriage very carefully, Teach jumped down and stood ready, just in case. Pierre slipped out the other side and hid behind a tree.

Stoppard straightened up. "Okay, friend. We go west." He looked to his left and right. "Pierre?" He turned to Teach. "Where's Pierre?"

Teach looked to his left and right, and under the carriage. "He was... Pierre?"

Stoppard joined in. "Pierre?"

Pierre slipped back up into the back seat and after a moment, "Hey you guys. Just gonna leave me here?"

Stoppard looked at Teach who looked at the horse. Central Park quaked with the laughter, until all was quiet again and Pierre climbed down as Teach climbed up into the back seat, pulled his hat down and closed his eyes.

Eleven O'clock rendered the lake quiet, save the two men jousting for laugh positioning as they stumbled onto the lakeside path, staggered backwards, and plopped onto a park bench...still babbling.

Stoppard tilted his flask straight up. "You know, Mister Artiste...we killed a bottle each?"

Pierre trying to hold a straight face said, "Not me. I still gotta drop or two" and lifted his flask, trickling the few drops into his mouth.

"Damn," said Stoppard, "haven't had that much fun killing three thousand dollars of booze... ever."

"What?" said Pierre, sitting straight up.

"Wha?" said Stoppard.

"Three thousand dollars...two bottles, three thousand...dollars?"

Stoppard took a deep breath, and smiled. "And they're the cheap ones. The fives are hidden somewhere." He started to laugh again. "I don't fucking remember where I hid them."

"Damn," said Pierre again.

"What's the matter, my boy? It's just booze."

Pierre became quiet, then burst out, "I could paint half a dozen buildings with three thousand dollars."

"Yes. Yes you probably could. But not have half the fun." He sighed. "Look at that lake. Not a wrinkle on it. Not a whisper of wind."

Both men stared across the lake, each working to keep erect on the bench.

"The *bet*, Pierre."

"I don't know what you're talking about. What bet?"

"Who's the most creative?" reminded Stoppard.

"You're kidding. We don't have any bet."

"Oh, yes. I bet you up stairs."

Pierre turned to him. "Upstairs?"

"So here's how we do it. You okay?"

"Okay? Hell no. You okay?"

Stoppard stood up, got his balance, then cracked his knuckles. "Never been better...or more creative." He turned back to Pierre. "Come let's walk some of this off so we can *take the hill*."

Pierre shrugged and laughed out loud. "Take the hill? Is this some kind of war game we're betting on?"

"Come," said Stoppard. He took Pierre's arm and the two weaved back and forth along the lakeside path. "First off, ever break into something before?" said Stoppard.

"You mean, breaking and entering?" said Pierre. Another burst of laughter. "I wrote the book, remember?"

"And I paid for it." More laughter.

After a brief exchange, sending both of them in boisterous laughter, they stumbled off, each wavering and drunkenly going opposite directions as the path split.

Pierre shouted into the void, "I'm gonna win this bet, old man. Gonna beat your ass."

The windows still alight with nocturnal sleeplessness spilled across the park from Central Park West, South and Fifth Avenue.

On a park bench, Tito lay on his back counting the windows still lit. "Full moon always means more insomniacs, you know?" He glanced down at the twitching tail of the squirrel. He reached over and handed it another walnut. "Who's your daddy, huh?" The squirrel darted away from the bench and up the adjacent tree. Tito smiled and turned back to his counting lit windows. "Don't forget where you got that come winter. No free rides, okay? Homeless get hungry too."

From out of nowhere came Stoppard, whistling as he walked. "Well," he said, "What have we here?"

Tito gave a quick glance and went back to counting his windows, muttering, "Somebody not worth muggin', okay? Just keep your weary ass movin' forward."

"Oh, you read me wrong, friend. Just need to *rest* my weary ass. Mind if I sit down?"

As Stoppard sat, Tito took his stubby pencil and wrote, "84" on his white—well, very dirty white—shirt cuff. "You can sit, but how about downwind. That French stink you're wearing is gonna frighten him away."

"Him?" asked Stoppard.

"My squirrel pal. You can sit. Just hold the questions, okay?"

Stoppard licked his finger, held it to the wind, and moved to the other side of Tito. "That 'French stink' as you call it, is actually a very fine men's cologne. But, you are right. It is from France."

"Mixed with the high priced scotch you've been drinkin', stink like that could scare the rest of them too."

Stoppard nodded and smiled. "Ooo. You *do* have a good nose, you know? And..." He turned around looking to his backside. "If asking questions is out of the question... Oh, that's a good play on words, isn't it? Rhetorical. Just asking myself. Just asking myself."

Tito stopped counting again, jotted down "33" on his cuff and turned. "Look, I don't know what your game is and I don't need to know, but I find it disconcerting at this hour to be sitting next to a well-dressed, disheveled drunk reeking of French cologne who knows the word 'rhetorical' and obviously knows how to use it. Not your common vagrant, you know?"

"Very perceptive. Now, if you can ask questions, or imply that you expect a response from this uncommon 'vagrant,' then I get to ask too, okay?"

Tito smiled, nodded, put his pencil away and shrugged. "Okay? Got me there. Go ahead and ask your twenty questions, then I've got to get back to work."

"Fair enough. But, there is only *one* question, and depending on the answer, you could be sleeping tonight behind one of those windows you're counting. Tell me, are you a quick study?"

***

In another part of the park, Pierre mumbled to himself as he crossed over a hill and dropped down onto the walking path leading to the zoo. *What the hell is he all about, anyway. Shit. I'm so wasted.* He slumped onto a bench and dropped his head into his hands. *Stupidest game I've ever heard. Find me a vagrant to take home. What the hell is that?"* He felt the touch of silk across his neck and jerked up. Dangling from a tree branch above was a long silk-like chiffon scarf. As he tried to reach it, he was sure he heard, "Up behind the monkey cages." Not usually prone to hearing voices, but being giddy and drunk, he followed what he heard.

The high fence surrounding all the cages made it impossible to get very close, but just stumbling around the dry leaves was enough for the family of cotton-topped Tamarin to stick their heads out and take a look and the chimps next door to start screeching. *Great, now I'll have the whole place swarming with security.* As he turned and started stumbling through the leaves, the screeching stopped. The silence stayed. *Oh, boy, I'm more than wasted. I'm..."*

"*G*oing to win this bet." The voice was unseen. He whirled around and looked up, down, across. No one. He walked a few yards toward where he thought the voice had come, but there was nothing. *Finding a homeless person isn't going to be as easy as Stoppard suggested, unless I come to my senses.*

Adjacent to the zoo was the carousel. Fenced in and gated for the night, Pierre proceeded past it without thinking. He stopped. Loud snoring. *Ta Da! A bagwoman! Inside the carousel.* Walking around the fence, he found a gate where the padlock appeared to be open, and entered.

As he tried to walk with balance and alertness, circling the horses, ostriches, swans—and two-seaters for those less inclined— he listened carefully. No snoring. *Damn, I'm hearing all kinds of shit. What the hell did he put in that hooch?*

"Nothing but quality," came the quiet female voice. It was close. He peered over the swan and there she was, huddled under an old worn Navy pea coat: a waifish looking girl/woman, he couldn't decide. *What a find. Dumb luck. Definitely in need of food and bathing, though. All the better.*

Her eyes were unusually bright reflecting the moon as they did through the breached overhead plastic canopy. "You're calm for a girl who's just awakened to a black man peering down at her."

"A stranger of a black man, too," she said without blinking. "Breath of expensive scotch fit for a king. Yes?"

"That too."

She sat up, pulled her coat smartly over her shoulders, and folded her hands. "Doesn't happen often."

"What?"

"A visitor."

"A visitor? Do I look like a visitor?"

She scanned his disheveled appearance. "I guess not. Pervert, maybe."

"Hey, mon, I'm not no pervert, okay?" He climbed up on the bronco and leaned over, allowing his lanky body to relax, crossing his limp arms around the pole, just for good measure. He was still very much aware that his body was fucked up, even if he still had the rules of the bet in his head. "You look like you could use a good meal."

"You look like you could use some coffee."

To Teach, all four looked like they could use a shrink as they walked toward him, arm in arm. Stoppard with Tito… Pierre with "Nobody,"—the name he'd pried from the little waif who gave him a lesson in classic movie history, sighting Terence Hill, the loner cowboy in "My Name Is Nobody," as her *only* true hero and role model.

"Mister Denning," said Teach, tipping his hat once again.

"Mister Teach," said Stoppard as he turned to Tito. "Let me introduce our guests. This is Tito, no last name, and over here, is Nobody, no last name."

Teach smiled his obligatory-*very good sir.*

***

As they reached Stoppard's apartment building, Tito licked his pencil and jotted down one last number. "Added up, six hundred forty-three tonight. Lot of insomnia tonight. A lot."

Stoppard laid a hundred dollar bill in Teach's palm as he shook his head at Tito. "You'll have to explain that further to me, Tito…the purpose and all."

As they climbed down from the carriage, "It's rather complicated. Sure you're up to it?" said Tito.

Stoppard burst out laughing and slapped Tito on the back. "That's what I love about you, Tito."

"What?" said Tito.

"Your sense of humor. You're a very funny man."

"Funny? Six hundred forty-three minds all working to find peace enough to sleep, you find funny? You might lose this bet, you keep thinking like that."

Pierre tilted his head and slowly shook. "Got yourself a good one there."

Turning up her collar, Nobody joined the procession up to the front entrance, where the doorman quickly recognizing Denning, opened the door as he grabbed a surreptitious glance of the *guests*. "Welcome back, Mister Denning."

The cubicle allowed the doorman a longer, unseen stare as the foursome made their way to the elevator. "Wizard of Oz has nothing on that group," he muttered.

Chapter 68

By the time most of the lit windows across the park went dark and the moon had fallen behind the New Jersey horizon in the distance, Tito pulled his gaze back to Stoppard's dining table where all four had spent the last two hours eating, drinking and exploring why people make certain choices.

Stoppard topped everyone's cognac glass and said, "No, no, no. You're not listening. What do you *think*, Tito," asked Stoppard.

"About?"

"Are all choices..." He belched quietly. "... voluntary?"

"As opposed to?"

"Involuntary, obviously."

Tito answered without missing a beat. "Involuntary actions only occur when another person forces our action, or if we are ignorant of important details in actions. Voluntary actions, on the other hand, occur when the originating cause of action, either virtuous or vicious, lies in ourselves. We can thank Aristotle for that."

"Ooo. Do I know how to pick'em. Pierre, your turn."

"My turn for what?"

"Are all choices voluntary?"

Pierre smirked. "I'm supposed to top Aristotle."

Shifting her position, Nobody said, "There's more to it than Aristotle. Got somethin' more important you're chasin', right Mister Denning?"

"And what might that be?" said Stoppard with a smirk that didn't set right with Nobody.

"I don't know, but if I were to guess... you two guys are playin' out generation gaps like a couple of arch rivals, or gladiators. Makes me think me and Tito-man here might be dining in the midst of a weird *involuntary* game. Know what I mean?"

"Of course," said Stoppard, the curve of a suppressed smile seeped through. "We find two homeless people in the park, bring them to a penthouse, let them bath, shave, don some new clothes— that Polo shirt becomes you, by the way—and then engage them in an intellectual debate over right and wrong, poor and rich, *voluntary* versus *involuntary*. Your perception is so noted.

"Now, the courtesy I voluntarily offered, notwithstanding, your *main* purpose is to determine the winner of a bet. You see, I bet my friend here that I was more creative than he and that I would offer him the chance to prove me wrong. It required two strangers and he had free choice of whomever he wanted to partner with, and I the same. The creative challenge?"

Stoppard sat back in his chair, sipped his cognac and leaned on one elbow—exuding calm confidence in his power of persuasion. He reached into his jacket pocket and retrieved four envelopes, one with Nobody written on the face, followed by the $ sign; one with Nobody written on the face, followed by the 0 number; and the other two envelopes identified the same way for Tito. He placed them on the table. "I believe the purpose of creative thinking is for certain people to gather the abstract of ideas and concretize them into coherent understanding, thereby affording other people—those who don't have a chance in hell to organize their confused and impoverished minds—to experience what he or she *wants*. Pierre here, believes in another form of creative thought. He believes his responsibility as an artist, a painter, is to deliver the abstract of ideas to the observer *void* of this concretization theory—and thereby facilitate a *need* for others to concretize on his or her own. He's not alone, of course, for there are *many* starving artists who think they *have it*, but unknowingly don't *get it*."

He smiled confidently at Pierre, then over to his guests. "You see, Pierre follows the 'need' philosophy of a man some would argue is creating mass psychological confusion and doubt among the world's population because he proffers everyone is creative...that all can navigate the unchartered waters of life. Not true. Sails without wind. Compasses without readers. Rafts without paddles. This man, to use your definition as expressed by Aristotle, Tito, is creating an involuntary cultish following of once content people, but who now are slaves to their own ineptness."

"You mean Derek Turrel?" asked Tito softly.

Stoppard grinned ear to ear. "Why yes. You know of his little band of followers?"

"I'm aware of him...and his *growing* band of followers."

Stoppard turned to Nobody. "You?"

"No. Never heard of him."

"Well, I'm sure you're not alone, but...back to the challenge we have here tonight. My guess is that at some point, one of you will step forward and exercise either your *need* or your *want* by choosing one of these envelopes and leaving."

"Which is which?" chimed in Nobody. "Which is the *want* and which is the *need* in this little game of yours?"

Stoppard looked up quizzically. "Everybody *wants* money."

"Doesn't everybody *need* money as well?" asked Tito.

"Now, this is where it gets interesting. According to Mister Turrel, *need* transcends money. To him, 'money comes as a *result* of satisfying the need,' which by his credo, 'is the spirit of man'... I believe that's a quote, actually. I, and the majority of the world, understand creativity comes as a result of satisfying the money needs first. Starving artists, or starving homeless people, can't expect to be very creative if their bellies are empty or they lack a roof over their head. To brainwash people into believing they are all creative—regardless of their economic plight—and that they need to give the majority of their attention to fulfilling *that* desire, well...I rest my case." He sipped more of his cognac.

"But, maybe you shouldn't," said Nobody. "What makes you think just because I'm homeless, there's something missing in me...that I'm racked with want of money and that I can't *imagine*... *create*? Huh? You don't know that. You assume that if you and your boy here pick up a couple of homeless people, you've tapped into the honey pot of obvious answers...that I'm gonna knee-jerk react to your proposition and go for the money and leave, making my black friend here the loser. Well, I have a little different take on things. You see, to me, this penthouse is not freedom. Yeah. You think about that. You've surrounded yourself with all the trappings of success in order to believe it yourself, but really, they're just bars for your cage. You pay a price for success... right? At least in your definition of success."

"In my definition? Well, let's see what success is to you two." He picked up the envelopes. "Dollar sign with your names...thousand dollars in each envelope. Zero sign with your names, cab fare back to your park benches, plus a *fiver* for breakfast. Now, depending on your choice, *voluntary* or *involuntary*—we'll get into that further in a minute—either *need* wins, or *want* wins."

"*Want* being the money envelope, and *need* being the zero envelope?" asked Tito, feigning a struggle to understand.

"Precisely," said Stoppard proudly.

"Whew. Wanted to make sure I got it right. Thank you," said Tito, creating a pause in the conversation one could drive a tank through.

Having explained all he intended to explain, charmingly, Stoppard took on a more serious tone. "Now, this really won't take much longer. The question we were on was voluntary versus involuntary...the creative angle. Tito here offered Aristotle and you, Nobody...I believe you were just thinking it over, correct?"

Nobody leaned onto the dining table and rested her chin on her hands, staring at the envelopes. "And I thought this was just about a shower and a new Polo shirt kind of kinkiness. Look, I believe Tito's got it over me in the intellectual arena. He's a smart dude. Probably harboring a PhD or something under his matted skull. I only made it through a couple of years college. Street smarts? Well, that's where I'm pretty comfortable. I've survived and along the way even *I* have been known to use a metaphor or two, mixed in with the usual oxymorons to make it through the gauntlet one encounters with sidewalk trash, whether they walk 5th Avenue or 9th Avenue. So, here we are..." She straightened up and gazed at Stoppard. "You obviously like the gauntlet variation where one's mind, instead of body, is put through the same test. You either go down the path and take your beating, or you don't, right?"

Stoppard remained expressionless.

She turned to Pierre, who was also quizzically fixed on Stoppard. "Didn't know that was what this was all about, did you?"

"I don't get it," said Pierre cautiously. "Twelve hours ago I was drinkin' fifteen hundred dollar scotch and celebrating...something. My absentee mentor here has cooked up this elaborate game...where the hell is the 'creative angle' in all this?"

"Care to answer that, Tito?" asked Stoppard.

Tito shook his head.

"Nobody?"

"I'm sure you've got the only answer that is acceptable. You made the rules, remember," Nobody replied.

"Precisely. The creative angle is really not an angle. Creativity is direct. It's voluntary, according to Turrel and that Greco show of his that does most of the work, and in its purest sense, is about creatively living without letting pain or discomfort of any kind take control...to manage the ups and downs and to accept that there are no answers, only more questions. Little resolution. Little pause for rest. Just more questions. And...like a water torture, questions can drive you off the deep end...maybe even make you long to get out of the question room."

"The 'question room.' You're a good riddle man, Stoppard," said Nobody. "So, this is the inquisition and you're just getting warmed up. Okay. Voluntary versus involuntary. You're bent on 'creatively' driving me or Tito bonkers in front of your friend here." She looked over at Pierre. "This is really going to be one-sided, 'cause this young guy doesn't strike me as the pushy type. But you, Stoppard Denning, wow, wait till the Rags hear I was having dinner with one of the wealthiest assholes in the world."

"That's not necessary," said Pierre defensively.

"Oh, but it is" she said. "Even Tito here would agree with that, wouldn't you Tito?"

Tito shrugged.

"See, we both agree on that point...voluntarily. So, okay, here's something for you to chew on. See if you can take the heat, Stoppard. Here come the questions from this side of the net! What drove you to this...this game? Do you know? Looks to me like there is one hell of a bunch of entrapment going on?"

"Entrapment," repeated Stoppard. "Explain, my dear."

"I'm not your dear, but here's the explanation. Like I said before, had some mixed schooling. Now, I'm just a street chick, but I know a lot about what turns people into *street* people . One of the great motivators is entrapment. You let your own shit throw a net around you and...voila."

"I don't get it," said Stoppard.

"When you run, Stoppard, it's because the answers caught up with you...the shit. Scared fat cats like you do a lot of running, but few people see it for all the fortification that goes with the job...lackeys, yes men, money, you know what I'm talking about. You also know the best defense for a question, is to ask another question back. It not only provides great escape from your own shit, but usually makes lesser people run too, right along side. Board members, stock holders, customers...all of them. Like a Marathon of bantering Q and Q." She pushed her glass in front of Stoppard. "May I?"

"Planning to stay awhile, are we?" asked Stoppard as he poured the last of the bottle. He rose with a smile to retrieve another from his liquor cabinet.

"I could answer your question with a question, like 'are you conveniently running out of cognac?' But I won't. You deserve just answers. Yes. Yes, I *am* planning to stay awhile."

Stoppard turned to Tito. "And you?"

Tito sighed. "Let the games begin."

"Good," said Stoppard. He uncapped the bottle of Courvoisier and gestured to Tito's glass. "Are you sufficiently…" throwing a wink his way.

Tito put his hand over the top. "I'm sufficiently."

"Pierre?" said Stoppard.

Pierre rose and walked toward the kitchen. "Some coffee."

"Just push the 'brew' button," Stoppard said. "It will make itself. Tito? Coffee?"

Tito smiled and nodded. Stoppard wasn't sure it was a gracious smile or one of contempt. For a wiry little guy who talked philosophy with carriage horses while he fed them, he was overly quiet. Stoppard only knew he wasn't going to let his own grin fade. "Bring an extra cup for Tito here, Pierre." He poured himself another glass. "You obviously chose a rather interesting way to spend your life with that 'mixed schooling,' didn't you Nobody?"

"Education creeps up on some people. I'm a late bloomer. You're obviously a brick and mortar guy...the four to eight year enlistment type. Ivy League, for sure."

"Not bad. And where did you get your formal education?" asked Stoppard as he poured her glass.

"Harvard. Yours?"

"Well, Harvard. Alma mater. You *have* picked a unique way to live. And you, Tito?"

"People, books. Horses. "

As Pierre stepped from the kitchen with two cups, Stoppard chuckled. "You know, Pierre, we did stumble onto a pair, didn't we?" He reached out and pushed the envelopes a few inches toward the center of the table. "Let's play."

Pierre placed his cup down and gave Tito his.

"Now," said Stoppard, "I could try an old-fashioned ploy and begin a strategy of insults. Amazing how carefully executed, it never fails to get a couple of my obstinate board members to huff, puff and shut down. They, of course, don't leave the room, but for all intents and purposes, they're not there. That approach would be lame for two bright losers like you, so…"

"Cute," muttered Tito.

"Oh, you liked that? Very good."

Pierre leaned in. "This is beginning to sound really stupid. Do you know how stupid you sound right now?"

Stoppard raised his eyebrow in feigned indignation. "Moi?"

"Yes, you. I'm going to bring in the coffee. Tell me this is going to get better, 'cause right now…"

"I know…it's stupid," said Stoppard, as he continued to pour cognac, and finger the envelopes.

Pierre returned with the carafe as Stoppard said, "Well, we can't contaminate this table of intellectual prowess with stupidity any longer, can we?" Everyone noticed Stoppard's voice change. It wasn't the pitch, and it wasn't the tempo. The tone. The tone was colorless like the resonance of a hurricane experiencing itself in the eye—the ominous presence of pressure building up.

"We need to talk about the value of this thousand dollars to both of you," continued Stoppard. You're not going to find another 'asshole' like me who will bring you into the privacy of his home, give you full reign of his comforts, including his bathroom, wardrobe, wine, gourmet food, ... and yes, envelopes. This gathering is about many things, most of which we've already touched on, but most importantly, this meeting is about passing the baton."

He turned to Pierre. "What if I was to die tomorrow and you, my formerly estranged friend, Pierre, was to be bequeathed my millions? Daunting thought, yes? Are you creative enough to keep it, or would you squander it? Would you buy lots of paint and mural every flat wall of the city? Would you buy more condemned buildings and paint them as well, just for the fun of the threat? The inevitable wrecking ball threat? Do you like threats, Pierre? Need threatening want. Want threatening need. That's what this little philosophical debate is about, no?" He turned to Tito. "Tito? Nobody? Come on. We all know threats are what make the world go round." His eyes bounced back and forth between his two guests. "Threat of being murdered by some loony in a penthouse?" He turned to Pierre. "Threat of inheriting millions? All fodder for the *voluntary* and *involuntary* way of living." He pushed the envelopes farther to the center. "Your turn, Pierre. I think your partner there is not feeling her best. Are you feeling alright, Nobody?"

Pierre glanced at Nobody, who was not looking well. Her spirited energy abruptly dissipated into a slumped body, appearing very tired and worn. Only her eyes remained unaltered. They hadn't moved from their fix on Stoppard...

"Nobody?" said Pierre. "You okay?"

"I'd really prefer to leave right now, but..."

"Don't worry about me losing the bet," said Pierre.

"You think I'm concerned about you losing the bet? I've been dreaming about the thousand bucks and the space blankets I could buy...the Cliff Bars...the wine...even a gun."

"Gun?" said Pierre.

"Protection in the park, you know. But, then I might be buyin' into 'entrapment'. Freedom might be gone."

"There's no strings attached to your thousand dollars," said Stoppard.

"None that you're 'voluntarily' explaining," she said.

Tito slowly straightened up. "Think she has a point, Mister Denning?"

"Do you?" replied Stoppard.

"Do I think you've scored a first goal, Stoppard? Yes. But while she takes a rest, would you like to go one-on-one with me?" said Tito, as he sat up.

"Is this the 'sleeping giant' part...you've awakened?"

Tito reached in his pocket and pulled out a small pistol. He placed it next to the envelopes as the rest of the room recoiled.

"What the hell is that?" asked Stoppard, his voice returning normal, absent the charm.

"Oh, come on, Mister Denning," said Tito impatiently. "It's a fucking gun."

Stoppard paused. "Well...is the *fucking gun* loaded?"

"Now that is a good question allowing me to answer without running. Get it? Running...questions? What the hell good is a gun that isn't loaded?" he said sarcastically.

"I'm afraid I have to ask you to leave," said Stoppard.

"Why? Because I have a gun? Because I placed it in the middle of the table just like your envelopes? There for anyone to take and use...like your envelopes? Completely voluntary. And...from the need-for-oxygen look on your face, adequately creative."

"Where'd you get that, Tito?" asked Nobody, completely recovered, sitting straight and more than alert.

"A trade several years ago. Bag lady *needed* something I had...a trade."

Pierre took a gulp of coffee. "I don't think that's...the gun. It's not appropriate. The man's right. Best you leave."

"Best I stay," said Tito. "I'm in the middle of a wager. I leave...it screws up the game, right Mister Denning?"

Stoppard's eyes remained locked on Tito's.

"As I understand it, *want* takes the money," said Tito. "*Need* gets a zero envelope. My friend here could use a thousand dollars. She could use that a lot, I'm sure. Make Mister Denning puff up again, all happy proving his point. But, I've not heard what's in this for you, Pierre. Is he going to give you something for helping him play out this little riddle of a parlor game?"

Pierre shook his head, his eyes now fixed on the gun. "It's just a silly proving of a point for him. That's all this is about. Just a silly..." He turned to Stoppard. "It is just a parlor game, right?"

Stoppard didn't move, his eyes now dropped to the gun.

Tito allowed the slightest smirk, then leaned over and turned the gun toward himself. "Amazing what the barrel of a gun staring at you can do," Tito said. "There. That better? Within everyone's reach, but just in case *you* want to check it out, there's no dark tunnel you have to stare into."

Silence.

"We were at the 'one on one' part, Mister Denning," said Tito.

Stoppard cleared his throat. "Quite a shot over the bow."

"Not yet. The gun hasn't been fired," said Tito, smiling.

"I was referring to…"

"Metaphor. I understand," said Tito. He leaned forward, turned the barrel back to Stoppard. "See. It's only *pointed* at you. Unless you pick it up and pull the trigger…it's harmless…just metaphor."

"Why'd you do that?" asked Stoppard, his voice beginning to quiver.

"Do what?"

"Bring the gun…put it on the table?"

"I always travel with my pistol, and putting it on the table? Things were getting rather boring with your trite riddles and twenty-five cent brand of philosophy. You took, by my count," he looked at his watch, "two hours and twenty-eight minutes to explain the rules to your badly conceived game of proving who is the most creative. Where on earth did you come up with such a wordy and flatulent way to entertain yourself? No wonder you found it necessary to break out of your stodgy existence and fuck a black woman." He quickly turned to Pierre. "No offense now, Pierre. Just some *language* to spark up the party. It's obvious, you know. But it's okay. You're not the first father–son fuckup." He turned back to Stoppard. "I am correct in my assumption, am I not?"

Stoppard didn't move.

"The friend bit was cute, but you just didn't seem like the type, you know?"

"I want you to leave now," said Stoppard as he stood up.

"I'm not going anywhere unless you want to try and beat me to the…'metaphor'," answered Tito.

Stoppard twisted his neck to the left and right, hoping beyond hope, it would crack and relieve some of the pressure. "I could call the police."

"Oh, please, Mister Denning. Enough of the melodrama. The gun's just going to stay there on the table…"

Stoppard hesitantly sat back down.

"…until it doesn't."

Stoppard's shoulders went back as if to stand again, but instead, he slid his chair in closer.

Tito laid his arms on the table. "I have longer arms."

Silence, again.

"Now, back to the negro, or colored, or black. For the life of me, I can't figure which word a man of your stature would use. She must have been a pretty good looker, though. Pierre is a fine looking man. Is she high maintenance? I mean, obviously, my guess is Nobody and me are perhaps the only other ones who know you two are related, so you can be honest with us."

Stoppard's stare was without blink, without twitch, without anything but hate.

"So, that's why you work so hard, run so fast? Little lady making you pay for your fling? It was a fling, right?"

"It's none of your business.

"Maybe, but I've got to stay *creative*…take the abstract and concretize it so you understand it and there isn't any guesswork. That's the way you like it, right Mister Denning?"

"It was an indiscreet moment on a vacation."

"Oh. 'Indiscreet.' By Pierre's slight West Indies accent I presume in the islands. Was it her fear of being seen with you, or you with her? Or was it the darkest of darks…the fear of a black child? I guess back then, a man of your stature would have a lot at risk with a scandal. But, hey, I know. I think I know how you handled it. You got creative. You managed to avoid the ramifications of your indiscretion. You created a voluntary action— one that resided within—a voluntary action even Aristotle would have pegged *vicious*. You took away her option of involuntary action and ignored the abstract value of obstacle, crisis, etc. You wrapped it up neatly in a cowardice package of money. I think that is maybe what happened…how *you* got creative. How you fulfilled a *need*, shall we say. Am I right, Mister Denning?"

As all stared at Stoppard, who like a volcano working up to an eruption, took several subtle but deep breaths.

Pierre felt the sweat beading under his nose as memories cascaded through his mind—the lies, the loneliness, the pain of not knowing, just wanting any father to turn to. The boarding schools, the yearly traveling his mother always found money to pay for, the gathering years of hatred. He squeezed his eyes shut. He only wanted to be with Stan right now. He only wanted to be with the only friend he could trust.

"You little piece of shit," growled Stoppard, his voice barely audible. "No one gave you the right to come in here and hurl your insults at…"

Tito jumped to his feet. "They're not insults, you narcissistic parasite. You put yourself on trial here and you've convicted yourself. You can rant and rave…"

"I'll do more than rant!" blurted Stoppard as he lunged for the gun.

Nobody froze in her chair as Stoppard held the pistol in both hands trying to stifle the trembling guilt that now raged through his body.

Pierre lunged at Stoppard, breaking and scattering glasses and coffee cups.

Chapter 69

Samara stood at his side. "It's okay, Pierre, you don't have to..."

Trembling in his chair, Pierre shook his head. "My Dad was going to kill Tito, and before I could grab the gun, he pulled the trigger...once...twice. He tried to kill him many times. Nothing but clicks, one after the other, click, click, click...so many." Pierre dropped his head to his chest.

"Tito leaned in and picked up the two zero envelopes. He looked at me. I nodded. He handed one to Nobody, who looked back at me, then to Stoppard who continued to pull the trigger of the empty revolver. All Tito said was 'One doesn't need bullets if one is creative, motherfucker. Who has lost this wager...voluntarily...huh?' That's what Tito said to my father as he turned and calmly walked with Nobody to the door. He turned back to me and bowed. He bowed to me, Dr. Jennings. Me. I don't know when the hammer of the gun stopped clicking...I just don't know."

"Are you okay now, Pierre?"

"Yes. I think so. I think I'm...is *he* alright? Do you think my father's alright?"

"Let's trust that he is."

"But I just sat there and then somewhere...I don't know, sometime...I got up and left. I opened the door and never looked back. I...left him there...alone."

"Pierre, it's done. It's okay. Your father, for all his shortcomings, is strong-willed. He's going to be alright, too."

"But...we don't know that. We don't know for sure."

***

"And that's how I explained it to Dr. Jennings, Stan." Pierre laid his head down beside his friend and with a last look at the flickering candle light fighting to illuminate the ceiling's painted fingers, he managed a slight smile and blew out the flame.

***

Stoppard awoke with a start. Orientation came slowly as he pushed his body upward. The ache in his shoulders helped remind him he hadn't left the chair for some time. A further reminder, once he was able to focus his eyes, was the three empty bottles of cognac. Jesus, he thought, a bender…and not a cheap one. His eyes drifted to his left and the corner of the table. There lay the gun—in pieces. He could only surmise that he must have taken it apart. *Apart for what?*

He rose. The pain of giants treading on his skull brought tears to his eyes. "Lord, God," he muttered. "Lord, God."

The four massaging showerheads brought some semblance of consciousness back and by the time he managed to dress, he felt sufficiently able to check his phone for messages. He was sure there were many. The date on his watch showed he'd skipped a day. Turning on the TV gave proof as the Sunday football game was going strong…Giants and Eagles. He switched it off, wanting quiet. He walked to the table again. The $ envelopes were still there. He looked toward the front door. His hazy memory placed Pierre there in silhouette as he left. He sat down and once again stared at the gun parts before starting to put it back together.

***

The air was particularly crisp for a mid-fall day. Stoppard took some extra deep breaths as he crossed Central Park South and started walking the sidewalk adjacent to the park's edge. Passing sketch artists on the sidewalk awarding tourists with charcoaled souvenirs was common, but today, the images reminded him over and over of Pierre; the son he couldn't admit to; the son that was *more* than any sketch artist—the son people in-the-know thought had serious talent. He dropped his head. The sidewalk lines passed like so many horizontal *bottom lines*…a comfort zone he knew well, with bank accounts around the world to support his cushion. Right now it felt more like a padded cell. The realization that he had made a fool of himself in front of his son was not what he had planned. Neither had he anticipated the overwhelming sense of cowardice that now accompanied it. *Why can't I admit it's the 21st Century? Gay. Black. We're supposed to be past that.* He was a man of secrets, but like all secret holders, he usually found someone to tell. The loss of control, however, the disgust with which he now saw himself—that would remain a secret unshared.

Coming to the 57th Street entrance into the park, the smell of horse droppings brought his eyes up, and he noticed that Teach's carriage was in the middle of the waiting line for passengers. He walked up, put on a smile, and tried to act like he was just out for a Sunday stroll. "Teach!"

"Mister Denning. How are you today?"

"Well, I'm good, Teach. Very good. Say, you remember the fellow my friend and I picked up in the park Friday?"

"Tito? Sure. All the drivers know Tito."

Surprised, Stoppard blurted out, "Really? How come?"

Teach laughed. "Best damn horse-lover we could ask for. Feeds'em carrots, apples, and once in a while he wanders up with his hat full of oats."

Stoppard paused and looked around. "Seen him today?"

"No…bit early for Tito. Usually at night. He likes the night."

Stoppard nodded and pulled a wrapped box from his shoulder bag. "Well, when you see him, would you give him this and tell him thanks, along with my apologies."

Teach looked down at the small box, wrapped in gold paper. "Yeah…sure. Should see him tonight sometime."

"Great. You have a good day now, Teach. Have a really good day."

"You bet. You too."

The rest of the afternoon's walk gave Stoppard the chance to think about issues he'd never confronted before the weekend. Issues that were long overdue.

***

Mid-November brought unexpected changes and Tanika, for one, wasn't ready for them. She stood in the middle of the fourth floor, helping Pierre and Stan pack the boxes, she asked one more time, "Are you sure you won't come and live with me? There's enough room for you and Stan. You'll have a nice place to sleep and…"

"No, but thanks anyway. It's best I get away from here for a while. Stan's never seen Jamaica, so…. Mom, the notice you got said that the building was going to need a few months to retrofit it to code, so being November and a few months…"

"But you could come here and keep an eye on workers…make sure they don't mess up your murals."

Pierre smiled confidently. "I don't think there's going to be any problem in that area. Your Mister Denning took care of that."

"Pierre…why do you now insist on constantly referring to him as *my* Mister Denning?"

Pierre stood up, books in each hand. He paused a moment, his eyes soaking up the hurt on his mother's face. As he put his arms around her and held her tight, "The notice was very clear. The city's been provided with a staff of guards specially trained for art museum security." He pulled back and kissed her on the forehead. "Hey, if they can look after Picasso, they shouldn't have any trouble with my work." He turned to Stan, at the other end of the floor, who continued to labor at combining half-empty paint cans. "Stan...make sure you secure those lids. I was kinda messy opening them."

"Kinda?" yelled Stan. "You flatter yourself."

Pierre turned back to the boxes and placed his books neatly inside as his telephone rang. "Yeah, this is Pierre."

"This is Derek...Derek Turrel. I'm back in town for a day and I wondered if we could meet...at your building?"

Pierre stood still. "Mr. Turrel. Why...I'm just packing up..."

"Yes...Samara told me you were planning on doing some traveling and that's why I..."

"How soon do you want to meet?" said Pierre, taking his mother's hand.

"Well...you name it."

"Two hours. Okay? Two hours," said Pierre.

"You sure? Don't want to interfere with..."

"Two hours is fine."

"Two hours it is. And, thanks Pierre. Thanks a lot." Click.

Pierre turned to his mother. She smiled and gripped his hand. "You see."

Smiling and beaming back, he said, "See what?"

"You're more special than you believe."

"He just wants to meet."

"From what Samara told me about this man, he doesn't meet with just anybody...one on one."

"He thanked me. Me." He looked around at the mural walls. "God..."

***

Aretha, having decided to stay in New York through the holiday and put some additional distance between her and the loss of Linda, was, like so many tourists arriving for the festive month, catching the sights. This day, she, like so many others, was attending the digital show at the Haydn Planetarium.

Spencer Gooding, an old colleague of hers from the NASA days—who also had the distinction of being one of the worlds foremost astral photographers—had put together the show, combining the world of the brain's own synapse galaxies and that of the universe. The parallels he suggested astounded her as she watched the images on the domed ceiling roll and pitch, morphing in and out of each other, creating a fascinating oneness. She nodded to herself. *If only the world could understand its irony. If only.*

As the lights came up and the applause subsided, she stood up and walked toward the exit, still transformed into his strange universe; a lonely universe that reinforced her own sense of insignificance in the grand scheme of creation.

The walk back to the hotel allowed the reality to sink back in. New York was New York, and as she looked at the buildings reaching skyward, her imagination asked if man would ever realize the infinite possibilities of discovery above them and within. Tomorrow, she would be back at the shore, contemplating the ocean's possibilities once more—perhaps even a fresh glimpse of Linda's journey into her own infinity.

She passed an elderly woman sitting at the bus stop. Both her hands rested on the cane readied in wait for the means of transporting her to where she needed to be. The vacuous eyes and gray matted hair completed the picture—a picture that spoke volumes. *What's left? What's left?* Aretha too had her questions and wondered if she should ever return to the Cape.

***

On another bench, one that provided the perfect view of Manhattan's skyline as well as the solitude of the park lake, sat Theo, dressed in his favorite worn-out overalls, old work shoes and a baseball cap. He didn't like the idea of rushing back into Manhattan on a moment's notice, but Derek insisted. On hearing from Samara that Pierre was leaving town while the building received its repairs, Derek impulsively told Theo to pack an overnight bag and accompany him for a quick trip. "I've got to tell him something before he leaves," he had said.

Now, while Derek made his visit to the building, Theo hunched over and wrote furiously. He was unaware of the momentary entertainment his non-descript humming provided the small twin-girls standing before him. They snickered as they held onto the pram their Nanny was accustomed to pushing through the park daily.

The woman, uniformed in white, stood at the edge of the lake throwing breadcrumbs for the ducks. "Come, children. So hungry today. Come!"

The children snickered once more and dashed for the edge. Throwing crumbs to the ducks didn't appear to be their choice of fun that day, as they continued to turn around and giggle at the man on the bench who now was moving his feet in a sort of tap fashion while he wrote.

Finally, he looked up, muttering, "That's not the word…that's not the…YES! That's it," and he dropped his head again and pinched the stubby pencil into submission, then stabbing his period onto the yellow pad. "When you're right, you're right. Yes. Yes. Yes." After a pause, he changed his humming tune, dropped his head, and began writing once again. This time, however, his wayward attempt to make music arrested the attention of a different kind of audience.

Unnoticed a few yards behind Theo, was a man propped up against a tree amidst a cropping of bushes. With his feet firmly crossed around the support bars of his overstuffed grocery cart, his intention to get a nap was imperiled. He pushed the brim of his old fedora up. "Hey! Tryin' to get a little sleep here."

Theo raised his head, unsure of where the voice came from.

"Yeah? Lullabies not your thing, mister?"

Theo turned around and squinted to see through the bushes. An old red towel on the end of a stick was pushed up from behind the bushes. "Consider it white, I surrender. I'll stay out of your world, okay? You stay away from mine. There's plenty of benches further down." The towel was withdrawn.

Theo paused a moment, then stood up. "Uh...do I know you?"

"I wouldn't think so."

Theo took a step closer. "No, I mean, you sound familiar."

"Look, guy, I'm just gettin' a little late day shut eye here. There're other people you can pester in the park."

Theo stepped up to the bushes and peered over the top. "I know that voice. Just a little more, okay. I know..."

Tito's wiry body bolted up like a target card in a shooting gallery. "Look, you don't know me, and I don't..."

Both men stared at each other. Tito was first to break the silence. "You're not getting any younger."

"Son of a bitch, and you're not getting any older. How do you do it? You've looked sixty-five for...how long's it been...twenty years?"

As they hugged each other, Tito whispered, "Age works for you in the park. Believe it or not, some cops got heart...some of them."

Theo pushed back and gripped Tito by the shoulders. "Always wondered if you were still masquerading as a homeless. You got the letter I sent you a while back, didn't you?"

Tito smiled. "You mean the Echo Life letter? Yeah. Lucky I still have the post office box."

"Why didn't you answer? Hell, we go back a way, you know."

"I needed to stay here."

"In the park?"

"You know the park is just for researchin'"

"Still livin' everything you write, huh?"

"The only way for me. No, I needed to stay at the school. Got a steady guest-lecturer gig at City. Seems my doctorate is trying to keep me alive in spite of my abusin' it. Even got a matchbox pad in Washington Heights now. Best one stays where one feels they have *some* worth, you know?"

"Hell, you'd have tons of worth working with us."

"I listen to the Greco show all the time. You're doing good work. I might have some graduate writers for you if you keep goin' next spring."

"You are up to date. But, next spring is a long way off and those gas prices and...oh, what the hell. How are you? Haven't seen any bestsellers lately. That can only mean you're not writing."

Tito stood back and opened his coat, revealing several notebooks in his pockets. "You think I live like this for the hell of it? No, not writing like I used to, but writing."

"And," said Theo.

"And the words are gathering for the storm, so to speak. Just all up in my head right now. Kind of a writers block. You know?"

"Do I know? And the tape recorder? You're still talking to horses with that thing, gathering *their wisdom*?"

Tito smiled. "You remember that essay, huh? Yeah. What better good could standing horses serve? Every sale of a book gets them buckets of oats, carrots, apples. They're great mirrors, you know. See everything worth seeing. Give 'em some munchies and their eyes confess like a virgin in heat. So...you. The park was never the same when you up and left. Last we talked, you'd just been reborn as you put it. *Jesus Christ Super Star*? Hell of a rebirth experience for an atheist."

Theo shook his head. "You know me. I was then...still am."

"That'll get you to hell fast, you know."

"Good. Don't like long trips." He grabbed Tito and hugged him again. "Damn...can we talk a bit? I can't believe I bumped into you here."

As they sat down, Tito patted Theo on the knee. "There are no accidents, right?"

Theo nodded.

It was sundown when the ducks collected at the corner of the lake, and the popcorn, hot chestnuts, and pretzel carts packed it in and moved their way out of the park. A few couples, grabbing one last moment of romantic escape, stood at lake's edge as the sun dropped behind the trees. Then, they too were gone.

The silence was broken only by the occasional raising of voices behind the bushes as Tito and Theo spent their remaining time together volleying back and forth their thoughts, memories, fears. It was only at the end that Tito shared the experience he had with Stoppard—asking Theo to keep it to himself.

***

Several hours later, Teach stopped Tito as he passed and gave him Stoppard's package as promised. Sitting at the curb, he opened the gold wrapping to discover a silver box with the word Tito engraved on the top in old English type. He turned the box over and inspected the wrapping, finding no note. As he opened the hinged lid, he muttered to the horse, "Good box to carry munchies in, hey?" Inside, he found the gun wrapped in velvet. It had been polished and appeared brand new. Attached to the trigger was a small gift card from Tiffany—"To a creative man who needs no bullets. Stoppard."

After pawning the gun, Tito took up his usual vigil at Central Park South curbside, gathering thoughts for the next essay, while bribing the carriage horses with goodies he'd purchased with the pawnshop proceeds. Teach shook his head. "Probably should have pawned this too, but, what the hell...my Lizzie munchin' oats out of a silver box. Gotta be a first."

Chapter 70

The single candle was all that gave light to the first floor. After several hours of examining every detail of the upper three floors down to the first, Derek, Pierre and Stan were now looking at the flames that depicted the turn of the century transformation of history through and into Pierre's impression of modern day's growth of confusion. Pierre and Stan sat before Derek as he lay back on the floor and peered up. "You know, even the first floor draws us upward. This ceiling with its crumbling chunks of architecture, automobiles, and hordes of books cascading down at us... you've managed to make them all central. These caving in of history...this swirling mass of time in flames and smoke even as its residue falls into some abyss. Do you believe we're really headed in such a direction?"

Pierre shrugged. "Just how I feel inside."

Derek leaned on one elbow. "Stan? You believe we're all being sucked into this vortex Pierre sees as the end?"

Stan straightened up and lit a cigarette. "You know, Mister Turrel..."

"You've addressed me formally long enough. Not necessary."

"Derek..." Stan corrected. "You've let me express myself more than anyone I can remember, 'cept Pierre. Nobody listens to me. But thanks anyway."

"And your answer?"

Stan grinned and glanced at Pierre, who also shared a smile. "You don't give up, do you, Derek?"

"If I do, I'll probably die very quickly."

Stan paused and took a drag. "Yeah. I'm with Pierre. He's right, I think. And, just so you know…if he gave up on me, I'd probably bite the bullet too."

Derek nodded. "And that's why I'm here. Pierre, I had to let you know without a lot of people around that I think you are an artist the world needs…the kind of creator with the kind of imagination that refuses to stop. If Stan here is your connection to that place inside where it happens…then Stan is as important to you as you are to him. That is what motivates all this… us. Love. Do you understand? To stop…giving up…shouldn't be an option for any of us."

He sat up and turned to Pierre. "That story of the penthouse 'game' you told me earlier…the whole 'father' realization and all. That scared hell out of you, didn't it?"

Pierre nodded.

"You know, you didn't give up on this work that had to have had its defeatist days too."

Both Pierre and Stan grinned nervously.

"Sounds like an incomplete thought," said Pierre.

"I didn't come here knowing about the game or the *father* revelation, so I'm not here to preach, but… don't give up on your dad. Yes, pretty bad what he did. But he didn't really do anything other than lose control. Your father is someone that can't accept losing control, and probably won't ever admit he's ever done so. Control is everything to that man. And let's be fair. He earned the control of OST, the largest body of influence the world has ever known. For a man who has nothing else…to face losing that…that's not an option to him."

"That whole night had nothing to do with his bloody empire. It was over my mother. Tito was…I don't know. He knew all the right things to say. He just stripped Stoppard of all the chips he'd gathered. It was like a bad western, you know? Like someone caught cheating at cards." Pierre turned away. "And when all he had was the empty gun in his hand, click, click, click… the winner just got up from the table with what he needed, and left the chips he'd earned. He shuffled out as calmly and unassumingly as he'd entered." He turned back to Derek. "Stoppard didn't even see me. He just kept firing the hammer, and…he didn't even see me."

Derek stood up. "He saw you Pierre. He just couldn't admit it. It's that control I mentioned. Just like he can't really accept he's your father. He'd lost control and he'd lost *you*. That's a moment of truth that makes eye contact hard. Time will heal that. He is your father. Son's without a father don't function the same. And fathers without their son have a tough time too, don't you think?"

"I don't know."

"Time. Time." He turned to Stan and held out his hand. "We'll be seeing each other in the future, I'm sure."

"Thanks. Thanks a lot"

Derek reached over to shake Pierre's hand. With hesitation, Pierre reached up and put his arms lightly around Derek. With the same awareness of the moment, Derek lifted his own arms and gently returned the gesture, holding him like a delicate dandelion whose plumed seeds were about to be released to the wind.

***

As winter approached, Samara continued working on her symphony.

***

The following week Aretha returned to her home by the sea and anticipated long winter nights that would help the continued healing process.

***

With a modest budget, thanks to Tanika, Pierre and Stan headed for Jamaican shores where they hoped to rest and use the time effectively in waiting out the upgrading of the building.

***

Returning to Gray Cliff, Theo locked himself away with renewed vigor to finish his book; and Derek packed up some warmer clothing for the rock to take advantage of the last good week until the winter would force him back to the lighthouse and the long wait for spring. There was a lot to think about. Options had to be thought through. Seeing Pierre's project saved added new hope to Derek's dream. Echo Life had to continue next spring and Gray Cliff had to remain its home. All that remained was figuring out how to make the impossible, possible.

Preparing to leave the lighthouse, Derek looked in the mirror, remembering Samara's pat retort to many *other* impossible challenges, *"So what else is new, Derek? You made a choice, now go take care of business."* He hoisted the backpack and left for the boat.

***

Winter for Stoppard, was always a much-awaited break in his routine. Being confident of his November sweeps ratings keeping him on top, he looked forward to his cruise to the Greek Isles and French Riviera. There was another destination that tugged on his emotions, however. "We'll take a week and check out the Islands of

Maine," he said to his captain, whose only answer was, "The islands of Maine? In November waters?"

***

Stanton lifted the last bag of rock salt onto the pile and counted. "Fifteen. That should do it Bert," he yelled back at the truck.

Bert locked up the tailgate and climbed into his "Truro Hardware" truck and waved. "Just let me know if you run out."

"God help us if I need more. Last winter was enough, aready." He waved back, closed the garage door and stepped into the kitchen. As he started to wash up the lunch dishes, he glanced out the window and saw Aretha across the way up on a ladder oiling her weather vane, a modern sculpture in brass. *Damn fool woman's gonna fall and break that pretty little ass of hers.* He quickly wiped his hands and raced out the door, yelling up the embankment, "Hey, you up there... not a lady's job, damn it." As he trudged up the hill he continued, "Told you last year, your climbin' days are over."

"Don't you be telling me what to do Stanton," she yelled back.

"Damn rights I will. Who else is gonna keep you in line out here, your housekeeper?"

"I'm finished now," she said as Stanton reached the base of the ladder. He looked up. "Now you take it easy comin' down, ya hear?"

As she started to descend, "I swear, Stanton. You are such an old lady."

"Old lady's don't appreciate what I'm appreciating."

Aretha looked over her shoulder. "Honestly, Stanton. Don't you still get Playboy in the mail?"

"Can't afford it."

"Can't afford the subscription cost, or the impact on your old age?"

As she reached the bottom, Stanton whispered, "Ain't nothin' old about me 'cept my hair."

"What hair?" she said.

"That's what I meant. Oh, forget it." He started walking back down the embankment.

"Hey!" Aretha shouted after him. "If you can swallow that pride a little bit, I've got a new pot of veggie stew on the stove."

Without breaking stride, he turned and headed back up. "Hell, woman, pride be damned. You make the best stew anywhere."

She laughed. "Well, are you gonna flex those *young* muscles and help with the ladder?"

"You ready the stew, I'll take care of this."

"Alone?" she said.

"Boy, you don't know when to quit, do you?"

444

"You should know by now that when a guy flirts, women either go shy, or turn into a center-fold. Don't be too long now."

Stanton paused, hoisted the ladder onto his shoulder and shook his head. "I should know when I'm ahead," he muttered and headed for her garage.

There were certain things a man of Stanton's age avoided thinking about. The main one was "center folds." Oh, he wasn't without weakness, so the occasional slip would cause havoc on his budget—which he religiously followed, pension and social security payments being what they were. Such thoughts usually cost him an extra six-pack at the grocery store. What astounded him the most was the freshness that still prevailed, the feelings the pictures could still muster up in him. *He'd looked at them how many years?* They were exciting at times, but there was always the come down, the let down, the disappointment. No one could take the place of Dorothy. But that was long ago.

So, it was with added surprise that he felt aroused while gazing at Aretha preparing some late lunch. It wasn't that she reminded him of Dorothy. After all, Dorothy was in her forties when last he saw her, and Aretha was many years north of that. But something about her up on that ladder had somehow got his attention. "You like high places...really high places?"

Aretha turned from the stove and looked down over the top of her glasses. "What?"

"The ladder? You used to get Bert to come out and winterize that sculpture and the weather vane."

Aretha shrugged and continued stirring the stew. "There comes a time, Stanton, when you realize that you're really not as incapable as you thought."

"But, hell, that's *up there*, you know."

"Hey! Enough. Why are you so interested in my safety on a ladder all of a sudden?"

"Nothing."

"Yeah."

"It's just that a lady like you should take advantage of her golden years and leave work, especially risky work, to others. Enjoy it while you can."

"Worried you're gonna die someday, Stanton?"

"I'm talkin' about...ah, forget it." Stanton squirmed and walked to the fridge. "Mind if I have another brewsky?"

"Only buy'm for you, my darlin'," said Aretha. "You like your veggies somewhat hard, if I remember, right?"

"Oh…yeah," he answered as he helped himself to another Sam Adams.

"You don't forget anything, do you?"

Aretha shrugged again. "Guess it's the curse and the blessing of being independent."

"Is that the same as alone?"

"Oh, I wouldn't say that," she answered with a twinge of pensiveness.

"It must be tough," he said cautiously.

Aretha turned and looked at him a moment, just long enough to see a soft, sincere furrow in his brow. "It's okay, Stanton. Been…an experience."

"It was good to get a break and go to New York, wasn't it?" said Stanton, trying to lighten the moment.

"Going was good. Coming back…not so good. It will take time. Even when she was away at the institution for so long, I didn't really miss her…not the same way. Guess I'm getting old and sentimental, Stanton."

"You don't have to play it down for me. Living alone is expected to bring on longings from time to time."

She took a deep breath and sighed, then chuckled. "Like coppin' a peek?"

Stanton wasn't sure how to react. *Did she mean the ladder? She wouldn't be that crude. Naw.* "Pardon?"

Aretha took a quick taste of the stew, then put the lid on and set the burner to simmer. "Half hour should do it." As she wiped her hands on her apron, she walked to the liquor cabinet. "After a few husbands, Stanton, I think I'm qualified to recognize a sneak peek when it happens."

"That obvious, huh?"

She poured herself a sherry. "How long's it been?"

"What…since I…"

She looked up. "Yeah…since you ogled an old broad."

"Aretha!"

"You only have to worry when you eye up an old *lady*. Broad's are still in for us moderns, yes? Come. Sit down." She curled up on the couch, tucking one leg under the other, allowing an extra portion of hip to upstage her. Stanton, minding his manners, sat at the other end of the couch. "Oh, c'mon Stanton. *You know you want it.*" She giggled. "Terrible phrase isn't it? I wonder who invented that one?"

Stanton swallowed another gulp of beer. "Probably one of those rappers."

"Yeah, a rapper. One of those guys who knows what it's all about."

"Did I say that?"

Aretha smiled, raising her eyebrow. "You like to be teased, don't you?"

Stanton decided to join instead of fight. "Okay. Maybe playin' like a couple of kids has its merits."

"So really, how long's it been? I haven't seen many visitors to your house at night for a long time."

Stanton let go with a laugh, releasing some tension he wasn't comfortable with. "I'm past that."

"Humph. Interesting thought."

"Being past it? Happens."

"I must be in need of help or something, because I haven't gotten bored with men yet."

"Who said anything about bored. I'm havin' a great time."

"Drinking *my* beer and building up an appetite for… *my* stew?" asked Aretha.

Stanton waved his finger at her, shaking his head. "How about a walk on the beach while that simmers."

Aretha glanced out the window. Her mood slipped and went downhill immediately. "I don't think so." She stood up and looked at the shoreline again. "On second thought…yeah. Digging my feet into that cold sand would probably be good for me. Haven't been down there since it happened."

Driftwood is generally a pleasant image for most people. There are those who collect pieces and place them prominently on their mantle or rest them on windowsills. Then there are those like Aretha that find living on the shore presents a virtual nightmare of scattered remnants from far away places that make walking a sandy beach more akin to stepping around and over land mines.

"Dreadful time of the year," said Aretha as she balanced one hand on Stanton's shoulder while slipping her ancient L.L. Bean deck shoes back on. "Can't walk anywhere and feel the real sand between your toes. I've always marveled at how much damn driftwood can accumulate on such a small frontage, you know?" She glanced up at Stanton, then down at his feet. Less inclined to challenge November shores, Stanton had grown accustomed over the years to wearing his own favorite pair of beach walking shoes— old canvas Converse basketball shoes whose uppers had seen much better days some thirty years earlier. "How do those things stay on your feet?" said Aretha with a chuckle. "Must have all of three or four square inches of canvas left."

"Being pigeon toed does have its advantages," smiled Stanton.

"More like 'cheap' has its advantage," laughed Aretha. She took a deep breath and lifting her arm from his shoulder, continued walking through the maze of twisted sticks, seaweed, shells and flotsam. "I don't think even with all my bitching I'd be able to live away from the ocean. You like it here, Stanton?"

"Well, if I don't, must be something twisted upstairs. Been...hell, how long has it been?"

"You moved a year after me. That would make it eighteen...no, seventeen years. Long time neighbor you are."

Stanton took her arm. "Watch yourself...those vines love to trip you up." He guided her around a pile of tangled brown algae.

"No...I like popping the little buggers. Benthic marine algae's little yellow balls are the best. Used...used to pop them with Linda when she was younger."

Stanton gazed out over the low tide. "Kind of late for the vegetation, but the hot summer left the waters warm, I guess."

Aretha nodded toward the horizon. "Not for long. Those are winter clouds blowing in." She broke away and ran up on the higher sands. "C'mon. You're not that old yet. Race you back to the house." *Not exactly a sprint*, thought Stanton as she drove her knees toward the dunes, *but who was he to talk*. He ambled into a modified jog...very modified, pushing his pigeon-toed feet through the sand and yelling after her. "Slow the hell down, Aretha. One of us got to be standing to call 911!"

Dinner was a simple affair. To Stanton, as he sat with his legs propped up on the coffee table, Aretha seemed to have a glow-on as she cut up her favorite salad of sea weed, vegetables, tofu and sprouts, to accompany the stew. She was determined to put him to the test. In spite of his anticipated failing as the enthusiastic guest of Aretha's eccentric tastes in food, he maintained a smile and kept the conversation going with predictions of NBA standouts for the season. Both were avid Celtic fans and many a winter night over the past years had been spent sitting on the edge of her couch, mindlessly munching popcorn and slugging down pints of Sam Adams, as their team fought to regain the dynasty image of the 70's and 80's.

"Did I tell you that you look unreasonably happy," said Stanton. "You only beat me by two minutes, you know."

Aretha looked up from her cutting board. "What? Oh, that. But, those two minutes were golden. You know how long it's been since I tried pushing these old sticks into a dash over those dunes? At least five years. Easy...five or six."

"Well, let's try it again in another five, okay? You're gonna hear my calves screaming sometime around four AM when that liniment wears off."

"Yeah...you need to stay by the open window for a while...you know, let them legs air out."

"Oh, come on. You exaggerate."

She shrugged. "Not really, Stanton. Least the fumes will keep your nose anesthetized when these thousand year old eggs catch your attention."

"Wha?"

"Actually, it's just a name. They're really only about a hundred days old."

Stanton walked up to the counter. "Where?"

"These?" Aretha took the lid off a clay pot. Nestled deep in the soil were two unseen duck eggs. All Stanton could see was rather dark garden soil layered with ash, charcoal, pinewood, and black tea. "They're under all that goop?"

"Hey! A little respect here for the chef. Yeah." Leaning into a witches animation, she whispered in her best Irish lilt, "Just you wait, my handsome one. The fragrance of greenish yolk and no-longer-white whites with the color of blackish amber, hints of yellow, blue, and green hues... the flavor of rich pungent cheese-like, and..." she slid the other parts of her salad over to receive the eggs, "with the compliments of the health laden plate of ..."

Stanton turned and moved to the open window. "Enough. Jesus. And you lured me with that damn stew. Was that to be the appetizer?"

Two hours later, as they both sat in front of the fireplace and listened to the mix of crackling embers and the shallow breakers in the distance, Stanton smiled and said, "You know, it really wasn't all that bad."

"Of course not. You deserve to try new things once in a while, even though my stew always stands the test, eh? You're not ready for mashed carrots and peas yet. And oh, the secret ingredient with those eggs is horse urine. It aids the fermentation process."

Stanton didn't squinch his nose up. He didn't recoil in horror. He didn't run for the bathroom. No, like any old drunk, he just smiled patronizingly and chugged down his third glass of Irish whiskey without taking a breath. As he finished and extended the empty glass to Aretha, she lifted the bottle and poured. "Just a little," he said.

"Absolutely. Just a little. You've got to climb those stairs over there, don't forget."

Stanton turned his weary head toward the staircase and quietly hiccupped. "This your idea of a *subtle* seduction?"

She topped up her sherry glass. "I don't know, Stanton. Call it a precaution at worst. You'd never make it down the embankment to your front door, and I'm not up to carrying you."

"And at best?" he giggled, slipping into his favorite pastime of flirting with her.

"Oh, I don't know. At best…it might be nice to hold hands again with a man…on my bed."

CHAPTER 71

To sweat was normal for me. To be distracted by it was inexcusable, especially this high up.

It had been two days since I scaled the wall and moved back into the cave, taking up my daily routine of chisel and hammer. Today, I needed to make some major modifications, having noticed from the boat that the knot in Echo's scarf rendering was too big. As I climbed across the shoulder, carrying the pneumatic hammer, I flashed back to the first time I scaled the rock and the moment I had made the decision that this would be my canvas for a long time. I couldn't have imagined the stubbornness and control the rock would play in my everyday decisions, or the length of time it would take to get as far as I had progressed. This was proving to be more than a sculpture. It had become what Samara had warned me of many times—an obsession. Since the fuel crisis and the thinning out of artists, I had labored without concern for anything else, until the day Aretha persuaded me to come down just long enough to hear her reason. The experience of meeting Pierre, and the overwhelming impression the man's art had made, left me with questions concerning my own talent. Perhaps that was it, I told myself. Perspiring like it's mid-summer is just my body purging anxieties, or maybe I'm fighting off some bug I picked up.

Whatever it was, I didn't like the low energy I felt or the lack of focus. There was still much to be done before the winter weather would force me off the rock, so with a lunge of my body, I shouldered the hammer, stepped across and wedged myself firmly into the collarbone area. I wiped the sweat from my eyes, lowered my goggles and fired up the hammer.

Within minutes, I had to stop, remove my goggles and again wipe the perspiration from my eyes. *What the hell is this? I never get sick.*

Later that afternoon, a good, but hard fought day's work came to an end, and I weakly made my way down into the cave. Now the heat that had bothered me was turning to chills. "Shit!" I said as I lit my stove and placed some water on to boil. I stepped to the entrance and checked the skies. The dark clouds that had covered the sun late yesterday afternoon were back, this time looking more like a caldron from hell. "Great...just what I need...an early storm," I muttered.

I slipped on an extra sweater and fired up my short wave radio, tuning it to the National Weather Service broadcast for New England. "...Cape Cod to Bar Harbor Maine, winds southwest twenty-two knots, temperatures mid-thirties to mid-forties, precipitation light to heavy rains later tonight. Seas, three to five feet."

"Wonderful," I sighed, checking the water.

"Not really. You let little things get to you," came the voice of Echo.

Without raising an eyebrow, I shrugged. "I got a cold, probably, okay?"

"So, why did you need to create that?"

I looked over my shoulder toward the entrance and saw the familiar strips of color dangling in the wind outside. "And what makes you an authority on cause and effect?"

"Ooo. We're edgy today."

"So. You haven't been around for a while. I've got a lot on my mind."

"Why the invite, then?"

"I didn't invite you."

"Pardon? I only come by invite."

"Yeah, well you misread."

"Hey!"

I switched the stove off and turned. Looking like a court jester, Echo's head appeared upside down at the cave entrance. "Only you can misread. If you want me away...I'm gone."

"Okay. I don't need an explanation of the obvious."

"Good." She cart wheeled down to her feet and walked in. "Like what you've done with the place. Mind if I pull up a rock?"

I nodded, poured my water and began steeping the tea bag. "You know..."

"Yes?"

"You know, we've never really talked about...us."

"What's there to talk about...us? I'm about you, and you're about you, so there's not much to exchange."

I smiled and sipped my tea. "Guess that's a fair assessment. It's just that...why do I need you?"

"Because you *do*, or I wouldn't be around."

"No, I mean why me? Why can't I just do my thing and accept it."

"You do."

"No. If I accepted my work, I wouldn't be needing you."

Echo spread her scarves across her lap and began braiding them. "You've got a cold or some other virus. You're run down. You've seen some art that came from nowhere, from a house painter, no less, and you doubt your own worth again. You usually go to Samara with such problems. Why me now?"

Shrugging, I took another sip. "He is good, you know."

"Yes."

"No, I mean really good. Talent like that..." I looked up from my cup. "So, how come *you* know he's good?"

"You just told me."

"No. Your tone. That's someone who knows. You visit him?"

"And if I said yes?"

"That's...that's okay. Hell, I'm not the only artist that needs a little help now and again."

"He doesn't."

"Thanks a lot. I feel much better now."

"He's young, full of unbridled ideas and enthusiasm, and...he's got the power."

"And I don't?"

"I'm talking about the power that comes from the *need* you talk about. He had the building he knew was going to be torn down and..."

"You have visited him."

"Just listen a minute. The building, his canvas, was going to be destroyed. That makes a man do things he might not otherwise be compelled to do. He thrives on threat, always has. If he's lucky, he always will."

"So? What the hell do we call this island and...and...the bankruptcy threat, and the fuel that..."

"Derek...you're in limbo right now. Hiatus for the show. You let yourself get sick now because you can afford to. You never gave yourself that luxury over the past two years. And... you trust something will save the day by spring, and the colony will be back to normal."

"We don't know that."

"Of course we don't." She held up her braid. "Like it?"

I shook my head. "You're mocking me."

"No. I can't do that."

Shaking my head again, I said, "Okay. Echo 101. I'm mocking myself. We learned all about that way back, didn't we?"

"Lighthouse at Montauk Point, if I remember correctly."

I poured some more hot water in my cup and stood up. "So, what do I do about it?"

"The cold or the block?"

"I'm only thinking about the...it's not a block. I'm still out there doing my work. I still see what I've got to do. There's no block. I'm talking about this...this sense of emptiness outside of the rock."

"Oh. That's a new wrinkle. Thought we were talking about a temporary question of worth because of Pierre."

"So I've stuffed it down before."

"Way down. So, Pierre was just a catalyst, huh?"

"Maybe. I don't know. I mean, you have to have been there and..." I looked up at her. Her smiling face said it all. "You're like playing the tables in Vegas, you know. Just when you think you've got the cards figured out..."

"The changing of the guard gives you a new dealer. Similar."

"So you were there at the building."

"Whether I was or not is irrelevant. I'm here now because you rang your little bell for help."

"Damn, I hate it when you ridicule me."

"You should go easy on yourself."

"Shit." I stepped to the entrance and gazed out at the sun dropping below the black clouds of the horizon. "I'm supposed to be the leader of this war. What the hell good is a guy with self doubts?"

"Not much. You want to tackle it while you're sick, or after?"

I turned. "Rhetorical." I sat down across from her. "Enough of the verbal gymnastics. Will I ever get it back?"

"You're asking about inspiration, as much as your modern day artists hate the word. Most of you prefer words like euphoria and epiphany, the result of altered states, a sense of bliss that convinces you you're good."

"I don't do drugs."

"Not any more."

"That's right. Not any more. So?"

"So, you wonder if Pierre's alleged daily snuffing of kerosene and paint thinner gave him that old long-lost edge you used to have."

"You think he really does that?"

"Irrelevant. What works is what matters. That's what's important here. Feeling empty, worrying about next spring, trying to get your work done before the snows...all that makes you feel a bit alone. For some, drugs make loneliness go away, yes?"

"Aretha said that when she saw Stoppard, he blurted out that for years he'd paid to have Pierre in and out of clinics for the depressed and that they couldn't trace any drugs. Stoppard seems to be the only one convinced that Pierre has an inhalant habit, and Samara reminded him that bagging was usually a kid thing with glue and the like. He's convinced he's right though."

Echo began a new pattern on her braids and said, "And you choose to believe he's right."

"How would I know?"

"You can make a choice without necessarily *knowing*. Just like now. You don't know what's behind your lack of confidence, but you have a choice to either succumb, or kick it in the balls."

I turned, my mouth agape. "You've never talked like that."

Echo held her braiding out in front of her. "But, *you* have. You like this pattern or this?"

I stomped back to my sleeping corner and sat down, wrapping my arms around my knees. "I don't like you right now. Why don't you leave."

"You know," she said looking back and forth at the braided patterns, "you work with what you've got and if you use some imagination, inspiration can always be found...always." She cast the woven scarves toward the entrance. The wind outside pulled the patterns loose.

I looked on as the ballet of color floated and undulated, its colors defying the darkness outside. *A strange reality. Imagination?*

Echo became as one with the ribbons and floated away, her voice merging with the wind. "It's really okay to say it. *Thinking it* is only half the battle."

"Echo? Echo!"

Chapter 72

For a very rich man who lived alone, always being surrounded by people was normal. The exception was being aboard his custom built *Katherine*. It wasn't unusual to depart with but one guest. This year, Stoppard's chauffeur, Siebert, had been asked to join him. Even though the vessel could accommodate up to thirty guests, Captain Ludlow knew, from twelve years commanding various yachts for Stoppard that privacy was of paramount importance. With its staff of sixteen for his yearly winter retreat to the islands, most years had seen no more than three joining him.

"Amazing," said Siebert as he sipped his scotch. He placed it back on the motion-activated tray that floated out from the teak molding above the twelve-person Jacuzzi.

"What?" said Stoppard, leaning his head back and gazing up at a star-filled sky. Even with the rising steam of the jasmine scented whirlpool, the clear and cold night could not be denied.

"Well, sir, you mentioned the boat was staffed with sixteen, but I never see them unless you request their presence with that little remote you carry around your neck."

"Oh, that. Yeah. You're right, I guess." Stoppard took a long puff on his Churchill and slowly allowed the smoke to merge with the steam. "So, you like it so far?"

"What, sir? The boat?"

Stoppard dropped his eyes and looked across at the average man he'd invited for the trip. "The whole thing, Siebert. The ship. The idea of escape. Are you enjoying your escape from me in the car to me on the yacht?"

They both laughed. "Well, sir...you're hardly a person needing escape from."

"Oh, come now, Siebert. All those late nights, early mornings, errands at all hours. Must drive you nuts working the way I demand at times."

"No, sir."

"You know why I asked you to join me this time?"

"No, sir."

Stoppard inched up in the water and took a sip of his scotch. "Pretty good hooch, yes?"

"Good 'hooch,' sir."

"This is a special trip, you know?"

"I gathered, sir. You're not one for cold waters up north."

"You know why we're going to Maine?"

"I did overhear you telling Captain Ludlow you had some quick business in Maine...but that's all I heard."

"I like to understand things, you know? And I respect others who like to understand things. That's why you've been my driver all these years."

"I hope I've pleased you."

"Oh, you've more than pleased me, Siebert. You're what most people dream of being, but few admit it."

"I don't understand. What's that, sir?"

Stoppard paused, then raised up, lifting his scotch glass. "I think you'll discover the answer before this cruise is completed. Shall we try some of Tony's clams? New England waters are the best, you know. Brrr. Not getting any warmer, that's for sure." As he stepped out of the Jacuzzi and wrapped himself in a thick terry cloth caftan bearing the embroidered *Katherine* logo across the breast, he noted the somewhat worn plaid robe Siebert had placed over a deck chair. Tempted to lift and hand it to him, he held back, knowing Siebert didn't like to be waited on, just like *he* used to be. "I like your robe, Siebert."

Siebert nodded, laughed and blushed. "No you don't. That rag is like an old friend. Came over with me from Europe, way back. Hope you don't mind."

"The robe? No. Just know you're welcome to any of the variety of deck robes in your cabin. Comes with the territory."

"Thank you, sir."

"No problem." He took another puff of his cigar and sent a series of smoke rings into the air as he continued to stare at the sky. "Old friends are hard to let go, aren't they?"

Siebert wrapped himself in his robe and smiled as he tied the sash. "This one sure is."

"After you," said Stoppard. Siebert went ahead as Stoppard trailed up to the sundeck door, which being motion activated, slid open, letting out another waft of jasmine scented warmth. "Some indoor comfort is rather welcome now, wouldn't you say?" said Stoppard. "Dinner at nine?"

Siebert crossed to the galley way. "Nine it is, sir." As the sliding door closed behind the *jaunty stride* in plaid, Stoppard looked down at his own custom tailored wrap-around. He too could remember the early days when he didn't even have the *gentleman's version* of a robe. For him, back during the years of Yale and Harvard, a worn t-shirt and boxer shorts was the robe of the day.

As he made his way to the Bridge Deck and his Master Suite, he ruminated over the years at school, through the early law jobs in Manhattan, and the climb through media legal representation to the top rung of the ladder—CEO of OST. As he entered the full-width Master Suite, he looked around at the exquisitely appointed décor in marquetry veneer, sandblasted glass and copper leaf. The suite bathroom featured yet another Jacuzzi, a circular shower, and inlaid floor opening out into the sitting area. The king bed and satellite TV presented on a plasma screen brought back the memories of flying back and forth to Australia for approval sessions while the ship was being built.

Her maiden voyage, captained by Ludlow some two years after the first drawing had been approved, brought the prize across the Pacific, through the Panama Canal and up through Cuban waters to the East Coast and its final berth, The Manhattan Yacht club, where it had become a showpiece for the city and the country. He prided himself in owning a living accommodation that rivaled anything Trump, the Rockefellers or Vanderbilts had ever created. He'd even loaned it to President Clinton for a cruise up the Hudson for a West Point graduation speech. Yes, The Katherine had hosted many a pleasurable escape for not only him, but others. Now, however, escape was not on his mind. Stoppard's focus was on but one action—attack.

***

It had been several months since the group had temporarily cutback on the island mission, and Theo felt long overdue in addressing his correspondence. He'd promised a monthly report e-mailed to everyone covering any and all progress with the fuel and ferry problems, but thus far, there had been nothing to report. This morning, however, that was all changed.

She hadn't been angry like this ever before, at least not since Theo had been on the island. But when Sheila stormed by his cottage window, wearing her Mayor stripes and snorting like a bull ready to take on a herd of heifers, he knew the print-out she held crumpled in her fist wasn't a *welcome hello, how are you*, kind of message. Arnie Rose, her ever-faithful fixit-man, was trailing behind mumbling responses she was in no mood to hear.

"Doesn't matter if you don't have the right tools," bellowed Sheila. "Start boarding up the windows of the merchants who had sense enough to get out when the only threat was fuel. We don't need this kind of storm in November."

Theo got up from his table and opened the door. "What's going on?"

Sheila turned around and pointed a finger at him. "You too. We need everybody with two arms to get this done."

"Get what done?"

"Securin' the island. Coast Guard just sent notice that a 'Disturbance' they call it…a late season hurricane potential is twistin' right into us. Supposed to have continued northeast. Now it's headin' straight north for us. Pick up a hammer and follow Arnie."

The balance of the morning was spent hammering plywood sheets up and down Main Street. The few residents still on the island were uniformly complaining that they should have left with the rest, while Sheila moved like a hurricane herself, making sure all the able-bodied were rounded up and helping. Theo glanced at the sky. It didn't look good. Clouds were growing denser and winds were now noticeable. "How long you think before…"

Sheila paused from checking off her list of stores and homes to board up. "Nobody said it's definitely gonna hit yet. I told the Coast Guard to use the phone next time, as if I sit on my ass watchin' the e-

457

mail all day. So until it gets bad enough, we're probably not gonna know."

Theo pointed to the sky.

"Yeah. I can see. I've got eyes," grumbled Sheila. "So we're gonna get a little rain. So what?"

"So what," said Theo, a bit bewildered. "So why are we pounding all these boards."

Trying to hide her real fear, Sheila dismissed him. "Just keep that hammer movin'. None of us are fortune tellers."

***

Closer to the reality of a storm was Derek, now parka-thick, perched and secured by his harness as the winds buffeted his body. He too glanced over his shoulder and, noticing the darkness of the clouds increasing, turned back and rapidly worked his own hammer and chisel.

***

Some sixty miles to the south, a different scenario had Captain Ludlow and crew alert, but not overly concerned at the moment. "Just keep her north, north east, unless those swells start giving us problems," he said to his First. "I'll be down below. Time to let the boss know we could be in for a rough ride."

With a stride of confidence befitting a man of thirty years experience in waters all over the world, Captain Ludlow made his way down through the Sun Deck to the Salon Deck where he found Stoppard and Siebert oblivious to the changing weather, ensconced in a jaw clenching table hockey game.

"Not this time!" jabbed Siebert.

Stoppard twisted his hip with some body English, "Take that!"

"Oh, that was not nice, sir."

"You bet it was, now..."

"Mister Denning?" interrupted Captain Ludlow. "I just thought you ought to know that we might have some rough seas coming up."

Stoppard quickly nodded, never taking his eyes from the twirling of the battle arms. "Right. Rough. There!" he yelled. "Gotcha on that one, Siebert."

Captain Ludlow smiled and touched the brim of his hat. "I'll keep you posted, sir."

"Right you are, Captain. Carry on," Stoppard volunteered just before, "Game! Game! My Game, Siebert."

"Yes it is, sir." Siebert leaned back and lifted his hands from the rods and massaged his wrists.

"C'mon. One more," said Stoppard. "Can't let me beat you all day."

Siebert, feeling even more relaxed than the previous day on the boat, smiled. "Part of my job."

"Oh, so now it's a mercy loss, eh?" quipped Stoppard. "Think I can't beat you fair and square? Just kidding." He leaned across the table. "I had this built out of the finest Brazilian Rosewood and Ivory available. Balance, surface speed, doesn't get any better. Work with the right equipment and you can't lose, you know?"

"Sounds reasonable, sir. But even on the finest equipment, wrists can go." He held up his arms. "I surrender."

Stoppard grinned. "Okay. You did put up a hard battle."

As they both moved to the lounge chairs and their drinks, Stoppard slapped his leg. "Good to know you've still got some strength, you know?"

Siebert sat and picked up his drink. "Yes, sir."

"I mean legs give out, arthritis…those pesky degenerative diseases, not to mention atrophy."

"Are you talking about old age, sir?"

Stoppard glanced at Siebert and sipped his drink. Putting on the charming, not-a-care-in-the-world look. "Well…not exactly old age. Neither of us have to worry about that for a while."

Siebert raised his finger. "Ah, *you* don't have to worry about that for a while. I hit my fifty eighth next month, you know."

"No, I didn't. You certainly carry it well."

"Well, thank you." He twisted his wrists several times. "Times like this keep me reminded you don't live forever."

"No, you're right there." He looked around at the brushed oak with marquetry inlays, silk curtains and classical furniture, remembering the careful planning it took to accommodate all the details he wanted in his game/entertainment environment. "Helps to be comfortable though, doesn't it?"

Siebert looked up at the surroundings. "Well… of course."

Stoppard, hearing a tone in Siebert's voice, said, "You don't approve of all this, do you Siebert? It's okay. I don't take offense. It's obvious you've lived a different life with different comforts."

Siebert took another sip of his scotch. "You've made my life very comfortable."

"No, I mean before me. You once said you missed the countryside at times. I've never asked you what that meant."

"I was raised on a milk farm, Mister Denning. I don't know what it is, but it never leaves you."

"And that was…"

"A little community two hours drive from London. Pigs, a few sheep and lots of cows. Just enough to keep you busy from sun-up to sun-down."

"And you came here…?"

"When I was fifteen. My father had a chance to work for his brother and with mother nagging him on, he took the job as groundskeeper."

"Groundskeeper? My. You never shared that with me before. From cow farmer to grounds. What kind of grounds?"

"You know…estate."

"So you do know comfort better than I thought."

"I know *of* it more than I know *about* it, if you get what I mean."

"Not quite."

"Well," Siebert went on, "living in a separate apartment above the garages was somewhat removed. We kept pretty much to ourselves, even though he was my uncle."

"What did he do, your uncle?"

"Pretty much of nothing. Old money from his wife's side set him up with very large trusts that his wife drew on and invested…fortunately with success."

"So, above the garage. Did that wet your appetite for cars, driving?"

"I made a pretty good living for a teenager by keeping a couple of layers of wax on his collection of classic cars."

"I seem to remember your application showed two years driving for Smithfield, right?"

"You have a good memory. Yes. A little over two years. He happened to play bridge with my uncle on weekends and caught me polishing the cars. The rest, as they say, is history. I went to work for him, got a uniform, kept his Rolls shiny, drove him to the train station in South Hampton, spent the rest of the days with q-tips, lemon seed oil and…more wax."

Stoppard reached into his humidor and pulled out a Churchill. "Here," he pushed the box toward Siebert. "Have a cigar." As he lit up, his eyes remained on Siebert who chose to just stare at the box. "Go ahead. Don't be hesitant."

Siebert stood up and walked to the windows that wrapped around the room, giving unobstructed views in three directions. "This is most strange."

"What?"

"I don't understand."

"Don't understand what, Siebert?"

"You inviting me. The sharing of all your…hospitality. Most unusual."

"Well, this is day two. You've had forty-eight hours to convince yourself that my intention was *not* to relegate you to some kind of cabin above the engine room, correct?"

"May I ask… what is your intention?"

Stoppard got up and joined him at the windows. "The waves are getting feisty, aren't they? Intention. Well, I'm not sure. Maybe it is to give you a long overdue break from my iron hand. Maybe it's to pamper my ego…having a regular everyday person as guest. Or maybe it is to get your opinion." He shrugged. "Or maybe all of the above."

Siebert chuckled. "My opinion. Why on earth would you want my opinion?"

"Not sure, except you're going to witness some rather unexpected events and I might react in ways you're not accustomed to. Not like looking through the limo's rear view mirror."

Siebert paused a moment, then cupped his hands and leaned them against the window, peering out at the ocean below. "Unexpected events? Like some rough waters?"

Stoppard nodded toward the window. "Oh, that. Forget about the weather. Ludlow's job. No, I'm probably going to drink more than I should; smoke more than I should; and get more comfortable than I should. But, whatever comes of all that…you're going to be there to get me to my proper destination, I'm sure. Just like you do in the city."

Siebert shook his head. "With all due respect, sir, you certainly can confuse a person when you want to."

"Yes. You're right about that. I confuse myself at times as well. A lot of the time lately." Stoppard moved from the window. "Well, I'm…" He lifted the remote hanging around his neck. "I'm going to get us some oysters on the half shell, some ice cold Grey Goose, and we're going to…"

They both felt the ship listing to one side, just enough to make them aware they needed to balance. "Now that's a first," said Stoppard.

Siebert grinned. "You mean *The Katherine* is never affected by rough seas?"

"Of course not. I paid to have her engineered for anything…" He peered out the windows again. "Anything."

The captain's bridge was quiet, save for the nervous whistling Captain Ludlow chose to engage in as he checked his charts. Nolan Bathgate, The First Mate, checked the radar and several computer screen readouts. He jotted down some notes and quickly handed them to the captain. "It's still ahead of us, but her tail is getting edgy. Might even justify a Dramamine."

Ludlow scanned the notes, stepped to the radar to double check, and then donned his captain's hat and left the bridge. "Hope the boss's got a big bottle of them pills. Alert the crew."

CHAPTER 73

Theo was on his fifth Band-Aid. The fleshy part of his hand was raw. He figured he had nailed fifteen of the four by eight foot slabs of plywood, and now he was paying the price. His thumb and two fingers were hurting, but not like the palm of his hand. Finishing the bandaging, he looked at it thinking it was going to be a couple of days of clumsy writing. That's for sure. Looking out the window of his cottage, he shook his head, threw on his coat and exited into the night wind, now feeling like twenty below. He imagined Derek getting a real taste of cave living now. He smiled and turned down the path toward the cannery.

Lanagra huddled comfortably in his corner, feet facing an electric heat fan and gloved hands holding an e-mail printout of an article. Just as he smiled at finishing, Theo strode in bellowing, "Better board up your skylight, Lan. Think you're immune?"

Lanagra stood up and passed the article to Theo. "This kid's work you saw...got some attention in a Stoppard paper no less and he's not even showing yet. Is he really as good as Randolph says?"

Theo glanced at the article. "If the art critic for the Tribune writes about him months before a showing, yeah." He handed the article back to Lanagra. "He's good. He works on anything that will hold paint...ideas *you* get commissioned to put on those monster canvases of yours."

Lanagra pointed to the end of the article. "Says the building's *retro-fit* will be finished by February, weather permitting."

"Speaking of which," said Theo, peering at the overhead skylight. "You really think that's safe?"

"I went out and climbed up there this afternoon. With all that imbedded chicken wire, that glass would have to work awful hard to shatter. Besides, don't see what all the fuss is about. Radio says the storm's way east of us."

"Turning west. Better listen to the latest," said Theo as he turned to leave. "If it gets too cold in here, you know the invitation is always open. Couch is always empty."

Lanagra looked up at his latest giant canvas. "Thanks, but you know I get claustrophobic."

Theo grinned and shook his head. "Yeah, you've reminded me often enough. Just take care of that neurosis and stay low to the ground for twenty-four. Let this thing blow over before you get up on that scaffold again."

"Yes, Daddy. No problem."

"Got enough food?"

"Yes, Daddy."

Theo opened the door. The wind had picked up. He glanced one last time over his shoulder, turned up his collar and left.

***

"More popcorn?" shouted Aretha from the kitchen.

Stanton's eyes remained fixed on the TV as his hand dipped unconsciously into the bowl and lifted another mouthful. "Ronald says it's holding course out to sea."

"Well, if that old coot of a weatherman says it holding course, must be heading back to hit us broadside. Popcorn?" repeated Aretha a bit impatient.

"Oh…" He glanced into the bowl. "No… No, I'm fine. Enough here to roto-root us both."

Aretha sauntered back into the living room, catching a glance at the weather map on the screen. "With all the popcorn you eat, you must have the colon of a baby." She pointed at the map. "See…he says right on course and the map itself says it's veered five degrees in the last hour."

Stanton looked up at her. "Damn, woman. Five degrees isn't exactly a turn-around."

"You might know a lot about flying above the clouds, but I think I've gotcha when it comes to reading winds down here. We don't get the kind of driftwood we saw on the beach this morning and yesterday this time of year 'less it comes from a hell of a long way off." She handed him his cup of hot chocolate. "Don't be grabbing it now. Still hot."

"Thanks, my love," and he threw her a kiss and patted the cushion next to him. "Come on down here and let's watch some old black and white while that hurricane makes its way toward us."

Aretha sat. "Don't be making jokes, Stanton. We've not had one for a long time."

He threw his arm around her. "Well, I'm going to go along with Ronald and enjoy my popcorn, hot chocolate and a little neckin', okay?"

Aretha smiled, leaned her head on his shoulder, picked up the remote and switched the channel. "*Tonight, Turner Classics is proud to bring you Key Largo. Set in the Florida Keys during a tropical storm…*"

463

"Sure know how to pick-em, don't we?" quipped Aretha.

***

I looked closely at the dipstick for the generator. *Enough fuel there for another ten hours of drilling, or... got to be plenty enough for heating too. Damned if I'm gonna freeze to death in a cave.* Screwing the cap back on, I looked across at my Coleman heater, pulled it closer to the sleeping area and plugged it into the generator. I walked back a few yards and leaning over, shook up the down in my sleeping bag. Even though it was an easy thirty-five degrees inside, outside I could hear the winds picking up, letting me know the next few hours could create one hell of a wind chill factor. I stood, lifted the generator closer to the cave entrance and dragged the heater back closer to my bag. *Well, might as well get used to the noise.* I pulled the starter cord, sending the motor into its usual spasms before settling down to an angry chant-like drone. As I slipped into the bag, I watched the circular wires of the heater turn bright orange. Flipping on the short wave radio, I turned the dial to the coast guard weather, catching the tail end... *"Winds north north east up to 30 knots along the coastal areas, 20 knots inland. Temperature 35 degrees Fahrenheit, wind chill at 22."*

"Nice and cozy," I mumbled as I turned the dial, drifting in and out of poorly receiving music broadcasts.

A station came in clearer and much to my surprise, was playing Samara's concerto. I was aware of the latest recording by the Boston Symphony being released soon, but was surprised to hear it...especially this night when memories were about all I had to ward off the anxiety of the anticipated havoc outside. My mind started to relax as I laid back and let the music remind me of warmer nights in the loft I'd grown to love, not only for its workspace, but for the comfort of being with the only woman that truly understood me. I closed my eyes wondering as always, how much of her understanding was professional conviction, and how much personal. *Did she really support me in this—the wildest of wild adventures I had ever undertaken? Was she patronizing me or did she actually believe, as I did, that there are some things in life that can't be explained in normal everyday language...like subjecting oneself to sub freezing temperatures in a cave for the sake of an obsession to immortalize one's muse?*

The grind of the generator became dimmer and dimmer as I allowed the strains of the concerto to fill my mind with memories of holding Samara in my arms. For tonight, however, I'd have to be content with *spooning* the canvas water bag that now occupied the

464

embrace of my arms. *At least I'll not have to chip away ice chunks for tea in the morning.*

"Sometimes… I really miss you, Samara...really miss you," I murmured.

***

Throughout New England and the coastline, various radio broadcasts served to only confuse many listeners.

> *"A late season tropical storm watch had been issued for Eastern Cape Cod and parts of Maine, but was discontinued early Friday as the storm moved northeast. Temperatures remain sub-normal with the highs in the low thirties, some parts of the coast line below freezing."*

> *"At 5 a.m. Friday, EDT, the storm had maximum sustained winds of about 50 mph, and was about 35 miles northeast of Kennebunkport. It was expected to weaken over the next 24 hours and lose tropical characteristics by Saturday morning."*

> *"Moving at about 21 mph, it was expected to increase in speed Friday. The center of Sandra was expected to be near or over Nova Scotia late Friday or early Saturday."*

> *"The Coast Guard was monitoring about 50 commercial fishing vessels still on the New England waters near the storm's path late Friday night, but had no reports of vessels in trouble, said Chief Petty Officer Scott Michael."*

Alarm clocks had years before progressed away from the jolt of a bell or buzzer, sending one's body into spasms of rejection. Modern day means of awakening had progressed to gentle CD music to room-filling sound. If one preferred, one could even pick an environment sound like the early morning sounds of Lake Erie, or the gentle winds of a desert. The idea for the 21st century alarm clock was to give the sleeping body a chance to ease into the turmoil that lurked outside the bedroom door, be it domestic chaos or city traffic. And little bedside machines were plentiful, from a simple, no frills low volume radio station wake-up call to the more elaborate multiple choice models which included buzzer, bell, your own recorded

465

voice—or of some significant other—whispering in your ear that it was *time to open your eyes.*

No one yet, however, had thought of the wake-up sound that could ease a noisy hangover, the kind of hangover that bangs on your head like an out-of-tune kettle drum as you open one eye; or the type that maintains the 60db screeching, like a ton of scrap metal being dragged across an iron floor. No, an alarm for drinking heavily during the wavy action of a tropical storm gone astray far too far north for any sane Easterner to tolerate in November, mixed with a half-bottle of Dramamine, was not on the drawing boards just yet. Not even in the think tanks of Sharper Image, had such an idea been conceived. Waking with this kind of luggage was still the exclusive province of the stupid—and oh how stupid Stoppard Denning felt this morning as he rolled his bursting head over and painfully opened both eyes to the gentle shaking of the cabin boy. "You asked to be awakened at nine, Mister Denning."

Stoppard fluttered his eyelids that hung like waterlogged cardboard. "Oh, God. Nine. Yes. Thank you."

The cabin boy bowed and exited, leaving behind the tray of Stoppard's usual glass of orange juice and carafe of coffee.

Even touching his eyelids hurt, but he managed to rub the residue from his lashes well enough to see the closed drapes were filtering sunlight. "Sunlight," he muttered and walked to the window, pulling the drapes. The sea was dead calm. He reached over and grabbed the glass of orange juice, picking up the ships phone with the other hand. "Ludlow? Where the hell is the storm? Where?" He leaned closer to the window, craning his neck to see further forward. "I don't see anything...yeah...you're kidding...all that for nothing? Well, it was enough cork bobbing to last me a lifetime, thank you very much." He hung up, pressed his temples and like any good and honest alcoholic muttered, "I'm never taking another drink."

Topside, Siebert stood on deck, his hands grasping the railing. He pressed his face to the rush of cold air biting his cheeks and making him appreciate his down jacket. In the distance, he could see a stretch of rock mass, small as it was, protruding from the water like a hidden secret from the chapters of a fantasy novel. Even from this distance, if there was any habitation, the gray granite pitted against the clear blue sky suggested a sense of cold that only the heartiest could endure this time of year.

On the bridge, Captain Ludlow saw it as the end of a night he hoped would not repeat itself for a long time. "Hold due north, Nolan. Make it about an hour away."

"Thank God," said Nolan. "This is one shore leave I'm gonna spend in bed."

"You did well, old buddy. Real well. Could have been a lot worse."

"Mother Nature isn't that much a bitch, now is she?" said Nolan.

"I guess we'll find out if another one of these is lurking down in the warm waters of Florida or Bermuda."

The Katherine cut through the waters of lower Maine, as several fishing boats in the distance crossed her bow heading to port with their early morning catch.

***

The early sunshine was a welcome to the island as well. Sheila had gotten a head start on removing the plywood on Main Street, dragging Arnie Rose along with his Cushman and flat trailer in tow to take the boards back to the village warehouse. For the mayor, it was hopefully the last false alarm for the season.

Theo, unable to sleep with the high winds, continued to sit at his table putting notes together on his latest chapter.

Lanagra, as usual, was up on his scaffold taking advantage of the morning light. Not caring for the mid-day rays coming directly down through the skylight, early rising had become a habit, even after nights of little sleep. This morning was particularly laden with low energy, and as with Theo, Lanagra too had lain awake staring up through the skylight, listening to the noisy threat that never materialized.

So, although most on the island were heaving a sigh of relief, on the remote point of Gray Cliff, Echo rock was crusted with two inches of ice and the twenty-eight degree wind chill factor was not making the slippery effort of removal any easier.

As I paused to catch my breath, I peeled back the fingers of my gloves and shoved the numbed digits into my mouth. Realizing some momentary relief from the cold, I impatiently slid my warmed fingers back into the gloves, cinched up the harness, and looked above at the anchored belay disappearing over Echo's hairline. I pushed off, arcing the traverse to my left once again, hoping to get a better foothold on the frozen rock. Not expecting this kind of severe weather, I'd left my crampons back at the lighthouse. Now, with nothing more than my hiking boots, feeling *secure* two hundred feet up an iced wall of granite was more of an act of faith, than logic. I wedged my feet and once again began chipping the ice away with my axe.

The *eyes*—because they had to be appreciated from hundreds of yards away and from below—were the most difficult part of the work and each time I saw Echo, I found my previous effort lacking in the capture of their mystery, especially after the last encounter. This one, with all my insecurities and doubts rising to the surface, had been my most brazen to date. For the first time, I realized when threatened, her eyes were capable of recoiling into a cocked and ready position to fight back. I had pondered those last few moments with her many times in the last few hours. *Why had I asked her to leave...really?* It wasn't that I didn't like her. What an absurd thing to say. She was my muse, for God's sake. *Why had I perceived her reaction as a defense? Muses didn't need to defend themselves. Did they?* I knew she never showed up arbitrarily, and I knew she called the shots when we were together. *So why, after all this time, had I challenged her so that she was made to defend herself. This all giving, all inspiring entity I so depended on, had been made to fend off aggression...my aggression? Even in reviewing my memories of wildest anger, I couldn't figure it out. Why? Why had I pursued such a losing argument over the justification of my insecurity?* There was no reason for me to lose confidence in my own talent after seeing a young artist with surprising originality. I may not be Michelangelo, but I too had been showered with accolades for my original vision...and many times.

I shook off the daydreaming and tried to refocus. Hanging before the challenge of my life, I chipped away at the twisted strands of frozen icicles curling over the heavy eyelid like the shattered edges of a surreal cornice. As the clearing continued, I began to feel inept again. There, staring back at me was the ten-foot wide socket of defiance. A sense of impotence rushed through me. I slammed my ice axe into the center of the iris. The granite accommodated and bounced the blade back, narrowly missing my own eye. "Shit!" I yelled out. "Dumb shit!" Granite didn't like to be played with. Years of searching and taking just the right stone from the various quarries of my past had taught me that. Only when the pneumatic was in my hand would the rock take me seriously.

The wind picked up and sent a chill through me. I reluctantly paused to rest, dropping my arms. *This is no time to lose it.* I thought back at how the making of the Ode had taken its toll on my fortitude, how during the polishing process I had reached a point of such frustration, I had screamed obscenities and threatened it with a fifteen pound hammer. I shook my head with disdain...*threatening a piece of marble as if it was real.*

Remembering my vow to never repeat such behavior, I glanced over my shoulder again as the wind buffeted my half-frozen body. Losing my capacity to endure hardship or inconvenience—especially two hundred feet above an icy ocean—was not an option. I peered at the water. To my eyes, it was so cold. Everything appeared to be in slow motion. *Scary.* I looked out to sea, the largest blank canvas on the planet. Lifting my ice axe, I shifted my gaze to the convex arc of the iris. I remembered Echo's words, "...if you have some imagination, inspiration can always be found."

At that moment, I felt I knew the common thread connecting Pierre and me...what Pierre had, and I almost gave up...the ability to summon innocence and brazen courage when all else failed. And here I was, pushing that belief on a smidgen corner of my biggest of bigs.

My eyes darted back and forth across the rock before me while I gave my fingers another mouth-warming. With renewed energy, I leaned forward and with a broad arc of my axe, gouged a new line of direction for the iris. "What do you see when you look back at the village, Echo? What do you see?"

The wind gusted. I braced myself and repositioned my feet as I strained to hear Echo's reply, but nothing came. "What do you see, God damn it! You going to abandon me while I'm stranded on this frigid fucking rock?"

I gazed long the distant and jagged outcrops leading back to the docks and lighthouse, impervious to the biting wind whipping my body. I held my breath to hear her, but there was no voice, only the distant sound of a large ship's air horn announcing its approach to the harbor.

Chapter 74

"Now who in hell is that?" said Jamie, standing on the pier and eyeing The Katherine far off shore as she turned north toward Gray Cliff's jetty.

"Must have blown off course or somethin'" answered Arnie as he surveyed the light boats that had blown from their moorings onto the pier.

Jamie shook his head and untied his boat. "Hope he's not expecting a rousing welcome." He looked at the damaged gunwale. "Hull seems to have weathered it okay. Damn, lucky we secured those spring lines. Could've ended up on the pier like those."

Jamie surveyed the other small fishing vessels. "Better check and make fast to those piles too."

"Damn lucky. Slippery mothers with all that ice," said Arnie as he attempted to cinch up the loose knots.

***

On board The Katherine, Captain Ludlow watched from the bridge, shaking his head.

Siebert watched from the warmth of his stateroom port. He too had a questioning look.

Stoppard, the focus of their attention, was sitting on the sundeck, bundled in down jacket and hood, his legs covered in a llama hair blanket, his gloved hands holding a prized possession—high-powered military binoculars. These weren't just ordinary glasses, however. Given to him by the general in charge of distributing food and medicine in Sudan, they were usually reserved for those surviving far behind enemy lines—far out to sea, as it were. He once again marveled at their ability to magnify one hundred forty times. Even at over a thousand yards out to sea, he could see the details of an unfinished form that looked like a face with a scarf sweeping upward above the plateau. The chin jutted out in defiance. The rough formed mouth whose lips were slightly parted seemed about to speak. The nose reminded him of...he couldn't put his finger on it. Then, as he tilted up to the heavy eyelids, it came to him. Here was an image of strength and power not unlike that of the historical Queen to Rameses II, Nefertiti. He remembered his trip to Berlin several years before and viewing the statue of the famous Queen in the Bode Museum.

He had to adjust the focus and blink a couple of times for there, two hundred feet above the jagged buttress and ocean waves, was the belayed Derek, swinging from side to side, eye to eye, carving lines around the iced iris with his axe. "Truly a nut case," muttered Stoppard. "Truly...something else."

He lowered the binoculars to his lap and reached across for his thermal coffee mug. Sipping, he studied with his naked eye the man who appeared like a tiny spider, arcing back and forth, wielding his cutting tool into web-like sketching swaths in preparation for the larger task of carving out hundreds of pounds of rock.

Stoppard thought back at his first meeting with this man who tried to save him from being murdered—this man who Pierre respected like a God. *What was it all about? This was a man who seemed able to attract millions to an idea that didn't put food on any tables; roofs over any heads, or clothes on any backs?* What the hell was this proffered belief that everyone was creative, that what Echo Life advocated could give all who believed the key to real happiness, a return to unbridled imagination, a quality of well-being left behind in childhood. A sense of "worth" Simon's broadcasts reinforced night after night. "A quality that could be used to overcome any obstacle" Simon had said so many times. What he suggested was costing OST millions.

Stoppard Denning had built an empire accommodating a passive world. TV couch potatoes, together with pulp fiction, plus dumb and dumber movies, had made his stockholders wealthy. He had been right enough of the time to reign unchallenged for almost two decades. And why not? He, his staff, and the thousands of working artists he employed knew what the people wanted and they labored tirelessly to satisfy.

Still, he let his eyes wander across the deck to the bridge, a tower of electronic navigation tools that could guide him to any part of the planet he wished to visit. *Who could challenge that as being anything but the quintessential freedom experience? Derek had offered his idea of freedom in the form of some cockamamie self-realized creative will. To get what? What's his game, really?*

Staring blankly, he once again flashed on Pierre, his self-realized son, laboring months in a four-story labyrinth of desolation and crumbling reality to express his creative will, knowing it had no guarantee of ever being seen. *Why would anyone commit to such a gamble?*

He looked back at the cliffs in the distance and pulled the binoculars to his eyes once again. The spider image was gone. There was no Derek. He leaned forward, tilting his binoculars down the cliff to the ocean's edge. To the left. To the right. No Derek. For the moment, he consoled himself that Derek was safe. He hadn't traveled through a freezing Atlantic storm to be cheated out of once again confronting the man who was becoming more of a father to his son than he was.

***

As The Katherine made its way past the jetty toward the pier, Jamie and Arnie sat in the small cabin of the fishing boat and watched in awe. Except for ferryboats, nothing this large had ever chosen to dock at Gray Cliff. "Definitely off course," said Jamie.

"Definitely," chimed in Arnie. "Jesus, will it even fit?"

"Good thing the ferry service is closed for the day. It'll fit just fine along their landing area."

"Gonna say hi?" asked Arnie.

"You mean be hospitable? Sure. Why not?"

Jamie stepped up on the pier and walked the short distance to the ferry docking area, as the deck of The Katherine came alive with French sailor suits, every man a study in perfection, going about their business of docking the two-hundred-thirty-eight foot yacht with the precision of a lunar landing. As the mooring was secured, the First Mate lowered the gangway, and after securing it to the pier, stood at attention as Stoppard Denning proceeded down the narrow walkway to the dock. Wearing a windjammer jacket over a down vest, New York Yankees ball cap, and carrying a small valise, he fully looked the part to Jamie. "Good morning, sir. Quite an entrance. Might I be of assistance?"

471

Stoppard looked Jamie's scrawny physique over, noting the frayed jacket sleeves and collar. "Well, thank you. Just a short stop. On our way to The Greek Isles."

"Well, long way to go."

"Yes," smiled Stoppard. "You wouldn't happen to know Derek Turrel, would you?"

Jamie paused a moment, thinking this was probably some rich patron of the arts come to buy something. "Well, yes. Matter of fact I do."

"Good. I came to speak with him. Where might I find him?"

Jamie grinned. "You ain't gonna find him, mister. He's in a cave and he's not coming out for a while."

"Cave?" said Stoppard incredulously. "You mean a real cave?"

"Think so. Big hole with rocks all around. That's a cave, right?"

"So that was him on the cliff back at the tip of the island?"

"If you saw a guy roped up, bangin' hell out of rock, probably was."

"Yeah," laughed Stoppard. "Definitely banging hell out of rock. So, he stays out there...in a cave?"

"Yes, sir."

Stoppard sighed. "So wanted to meet him, but... oh, well, perhaps you could help. Would there be someone I might talk to about the Echo Project?"

Jamie cast a glance out to the yacht. "You interested in buying something, it's gonna be next spring before most everybody's back."

"Oh," said Stoppard. "I'm really just interested in getting to know more about the artists right now. You see, I'm on my way to The Greek Isles, and... "

"Mister, the only person that can tell you with much about Echo Project besides Derek is Theo. He assists him."

"Oh, yes. That must be Theodore Donnaly. Know of him. Very good. Where might I find *him*?"

Jamie looked at his watch. "At the café 'bout now. Likes a late breakfast."

"Thanks. And the café?"

"Oh," said Jamie turning toward the village. "Just past the end of the pier, make a right, then at your first corner, that's Crab Street, hang a left to Main Street. Two doors to your right, that's Ziggy's Café."

"I'll bet he serves the best coffee in town, too. Right?" Stoppard nodded and smiled as he dug into his pocket and handed Jamie a ten-dollar bill.

"Well, Ziggy has the *only* coffee that... Oh, you don't need to do that..."

"But I want to. One gracious gesture deserves another, right? You buy yourself a nice lunch. Now..." He turned, "down past the end... " .

Jamie smiled, then... "Thank you Mister... oh, I didn't even get your name."

"Stoppard. Stoppard Denning." With that, he strolled toward the end, but stopped short and turned. "Oh, by the way, if you hear from Mr. Turrel, tell him I dropped by." He turned and continued toward the café.

Jamie stood motionless. *Oh, my God! That's the creep Derek said was....* He turned and moved quickly toward his boat. "Arnie? Arnie?"

Arnie stuck his head out from the engine compartment. "Yeah. Yeah. What's all the excitement?"

"How's the engine?"

"Storm didn't hurt her any."

"Get her gassed up. We've got an errand to run."

Arnie did a double take. "Jamie...it's colder than..."

"...just get her gassed."

***

With the phone tucked under his chin, Theo pulled his socks on as he finished his conversation. "Well, don't push it, for God sake. You always said ice climbing wasn't your forte... Supplies? Probably in a couple of days. You got enough of everything till then? I'll send some extra fuel as well, 'case Mother Nature decides to keep you busy again. Yeah, yeah, yeah... I won't forget it. You want the creamy or crunchy?"

***

It had been a long time since Stoppard had strolled the streets of a small village, let alone an island village in freezing temperatures. He noted the lazy look, as expected. Some of the stores were still boarded up for the storm, while owners were putting others back to normal. As he proceeded to the café, he noticed a small grocery store, a hardware and drug store were open for business, but the rest of the assorted tourist type shops were closed for the winter. Pushing the door open, he looked up at the tiny bell announcing his entrance and proceeded to the counter where the waiter/cook, Ziggy he presumed, scurried to wipe down the top. Sporting a Danish fisherman's cap, apron, denim shirt and khakis, Ziggy's short, squat body was all business... tourist business he hoped. "Morning to ya," he said with all the enthusiasm of a door-to-door salesman. "And a cold one it be. What can I git cha?"

Stoppard glanced around at the empty café and slid onto a counter stool. "Well, I'm really looking for a fella named Theo?"

473

"Theo it be. But he's not popped in yet. Coffee? Best in…"

"Town. So I hear. Sure. Cream and sugar."

Ziggy leaned on the counter. "Sorry, but Beth, that's our resident dairy lady, she's not brought in the cream yet. Probably had some trouble with frozen udders, you know?" He laughed. "Will milk do?"

"Sure. Milk will be fine. You really did have yourself a cold one here, didn't you?"

"Doesn't happen often this late or early, dependin' how you look at it, but boy, we're just lucky it didn't swing in full blown, you know?"

"Yes. I can appreciate."

"Say…ferry hasn't come in yet. You fly…I mean, haven't seen you around before."

"No. Just arrived this morning."

Ziggy slid the coffee across the counter. "Wow. Must have been one bumpy flight, eh?"

"Well, no. I came in by boat. But, it was a bumpy ride. Yes, very bumpy."

"A boat? Well now…" Ziggy walked around and sat down next to him, whipping out his wallet and opening it to a plastic envelope showing his card: Model Makers of New England – Ziggy Wolchetz - President. "I've been known to sail a boat or two myself." He chuckled. "Not a big one of course, least not big enough to sail the coast, but…" He shoved his wallet back in his pocket, "Won first prize last year for a thirty-seven inch schooner—the famous Schooner America. The one that started it all!! Built in 1851 to race for the 100 Guinea Cup in Cowes, England… took me two years to build. Two years. Your boat big?"

"Pretty good size. You think Theo will be here soon?"

"Ah, sure. He's gotta have his coffee. Pretty good size, eh. Sixty, seventy footer?"

"It's actually a bit bigger."

"Bet it's got some kind of engine…or two." He laughed. "More coffee?"

"No. I'm still fine."

"Good." Ziggy waited, then said, "So, c'mon. Two?"

"I'm not much into the technical side," said Stoppard, wanting to remain his charming and arrogant self—a quality that had always gotten him what he wanted, "but the captain says the two twin CAT thirty-five sixteens with their twenty-three hundred horsepower engines are the most reliable he's skippered in his twenty years of piloting owners like me around. They push the two hundred thirty-eight foot hull around pretty well." He turned toward the door as the tinkling of the bell said there was another customer. Ziggy didn't hear the bell for a moment, however, concentrating as he was on lifting his lower jaw back to its rightful position. "Holy Mother of God! That's not a boat, that's a… a…"

"Yacht?" said Stoppard, patting Ziggy's hand. "Just a perk. Nothing more. I'd love to see your schooner. You…" He looked around, noticing the slight man with a notepad take a seat in a booth and pull out his pencil. "You display it here?"

"Two hundred thirty-eight feet. Nothing that size ever been on our docks," said Ziggy, mesmerized as he stepped around the counter and picked up a cup and the coffee pot.

Stoppard repeated, "You display it here?"

Ziggy let out a nervous laugh as he passed Stoppard, making his way to the booth. "No. My little boat is home on the mantle piece."

"Hey," Stoppard said, as he put his arm out and brushed Ziggy's arm. "I used to make models myself. Sorry it's not here."

Ziggy turned, his face reflecting the surprise. "Really? I mean…" He continued toward Theo, then looked back. "I could…oh, hey, what's the matter with me? This is Theo, the guy you're looking for." He started to pour. "Theo, this is…a man wanting to talk with you."

Theo looked up as Stoppard turned toward him, stepped down from the stool and approached with his hand held out. "Stoppard Denning, Theo. Pleased to meet you."

Theo hesitated with surprise, then lifted his right hand and taking the pencil with his left said, "Well…and what do I owe this visit to, Mister Denning?"

"May I?" said Stoppard, gesturing toward the bench.

Theo nodded cautiously. "You've come a long way. Sure."

Stoppard sat down as Ziggy rushed back behind the counter, picked up a fresh cup and returned.

"It's really not all that far. Charming island you've got here."

Ziggy poured Stoppard a fresh cup and gestured to the creamer. "That's got the milk, you know…"

Stoppard looked up. "No problem. Thank you Ziggy."

Ziggy paused. "You know, if you're gonna be here awhile, I could…. Are you sure you'd like to see it?"

"I'll be here for a little while, if Theo can spare me some time."

Theo shrugged. "Sure…bring it on in."

Ziggy rushed back to the counter and placed the coffee pot back on the warmer, whipped off his apron and dashed for the entrance. "Anybody come in…tell 'em I've gone fishin." He laughed and shot out the door.

"Nice man," said Stoppard, watching Ziggy disappear down the road, leaving him and Theo alone. "Trusting soul as well."

Theo leaned back and put his pencil and tablet down. "He never locks the place during the off-season. Not enough people on the island to create any crime."

"Sounds exemplar."

"Good word for it. Stealing seems the way of the world now days."

Stoppard lifted his coffee cup. "So true. Hard to find honest people."

"Very," answered Theo. "So, you wanted to see me."

"Yes. Well, actually, I cruised up here to see Derek and take a look for myself."

"Look for yourself?"

Stoppard sipped and nodded. "Yes. Your Simon Greco manages to keep the world up to date on your moderate hiatus and Derek staying behind to keep things...together?"

"Together. Yeah. There's a few of us waiting it out."

"You're the journalist Theodor Donnaly, aren't you?"

Theo smiled. "C'mon, Stoppard. You know damn well who I am. You also know everything there is to know about me, Derek, and all the rest of the artists waiting out the...problem."

"Ah, yes. The problem. How do you see it?"

"Just a problem. We'll solve it."

"My. You are confident. I understand the high price of fuel and its impact on the ferry service almost pushed the island under, yes?"

"Almost, yes. Almost."

"You're hopeful then?"

"That the scum bag union calling all the shots with the fuel drivers will soften? Hell no. The union, the drivers, the ferry companies...all the same."

"I don't understand," said Stoppard.

"Look, Stoppard, if you came here to see Derek and 'take a look' for yourself, you've had your look, and Derek isn't around, so..." Theo started to leave, picking up his notebook and pencil.

Stoppard reached across and grabbed his hand. "Jesus. Settle down. I'm not here to make any trouble."

"You figure you've made all you can stomach? Is that it?"

"Look, we're competitors, but that's healthy. That's the American dream."

"That's your dream."

"And lots of others. Please, just hear me out."

Theo sat back down. "Fine. Till Ziggy gets back."

"Till Ziggy gets back," repeated Stoppard. He took a deep breath and crossed his hands in front of him. "I listen to Greco just about every night. I'm aware of Echo Life and its dreams. And I can now say I've seen Derek's big dream…the cliff he's carving into what looks like a face of someone…a woman…an ancient woman."

Theo nodded. "I'm listening."

"Any idea who it is?"

"Yes."

Stoppard waited. "Personal?"

"Personal."

"Fair enough. It's…it's quite an undertaking."

"As all of Echo Life is."

"By the way, where did you get the name, Echo Life?"

Theo sat stoic.

"Personal," said Stoppard. "I guess I've got to accept you folks got a lot of personal secrets."

"Yes."

"Well, I won't pry. Mister Donnaly, I understand from the papers and TV that a building somewhere in Brooklyn was recently purchased and kept from being demolished because some new artist, Pierre Haweisi, I believe, has painted the inside of the building like a giant mural."

"Stoppard…"

"Please, let me finish. That painter, Pierre Haweisi, has been quoted as saying he was… influenced by Derek."

"And your point is?"

"I don't have a point, Mister Donnaly, except…" Stoppard lowered his voice to the smooth, silky level he was notorious in using at board meetings for the kill—a tone known as the *velvet buzz saw*. "…I'm here on a friendly visit to know and understand my competition better. This Pierre is known to a friend of mine, and she is a bit concerned about his relationship with Derek."

Theo leaned forward. "Derek's straight, Stoppard, if that's what you mean. Pierre's got a lover, Stan. I'm sure you're aware of that. Your lady friend is probably Tanika Haweisi, Pierre's mother, who to my knowledge, hasn't got any problem with Derek. And…" he leaned back, "and as I'm sure you're wondering, I am speaking to you this way because I've got nothing to lose from you, unlike so many others, and I don't like your bullshit. I still don't know why you're here, really, but you can spare yourself and me your drawn out strategy or negotiating ploy…"

Stoppard raised his hand like a traffic cop. "Forgive me." He rose and carrying both their cups, walked to the back of the counter and refilled them. "I can see you're far too bright to tolerate such goings on. I do get spoiled with my company's allegiance, you know." As he walked back, "They're such kiss-ups." He nodded as he sat down with the cups. "And…you're right. You have nothing to lose, unlike them. So…you're right about the woman. Tanika is an old friend I'm trying to help. Her son Pierre has a history of…problems. She mentioned Pierre's adulation of Derek to me, and I said I'd met him, and she asked if I could intervene and well… Derek is straight, you say, but Pierre is obsessed with him. Okay? There. No bullshit. I've said it."

Theo tilted his head and chuckled. "This sounds like a bad soap opera. You're better than that…or is it the gay thing that's got you so rattled? You're talking like a wronged father or something. This woman must mean a lot to you to go through this. Can I get you some water?"

"You sound just like your old editorials… straight for the jugular vein. Sarcasm isn't going to work for us either, is it?"

"Great. That's three against me, one against you. If strategy, negotiating power, and plain old fashioned bullshit countered by sarcasm is not working…please…just spit it out. What do you want?"

"I…" started Stoppard as the front door sprung open, and in walked Ziggy, proudly displaying his thirty-seven inch, three-mast schooner. He took it to the counter, pushed aside the sugar, salt, pepper shakers, napkin holder and ketchup and gently placed it down.

"Here it is, Mister Denning. All twenty-four months and two days of her. From scratch I made that. No kit for me. No sir. Can't be the president and cheat."

Stoppard rose. "Excuse me Theo." He stepped to the counter and studied the stitched sails, hand-planked wood, enameled black painted hull, and gold trailing boards. The details were exceptional. "No you can't, Ziggy. That's a fine piece of work. Fine. What would you take for it?"

Ziggy smiled. "Oh, it's not for sale, Mister Denning. Not many things in life *don't* have a price tag, but this…no. See those rope ties? Enough to set ya blind. And lookee up here." He pointed to the distressed work he had done on the sails. "Sails don't stay pretty that long, ya know. Had to make them real. Number two sand paper. Real gentle had to be. Real gentle."

"Sure you wouldn't like to make some money on her?"

"Thank ya, sir, but no. Thank you a lot. Nobody ever offered to buy her, but I couldn't."

"You know I could pay you enough to close this shop and make boats the rest of your life."

Ziggy paused.

"Leave him alone, Stoppard," said Theo. "My God. The man has some pride."

Stoppard nodded. "You're right. I'm sorry, Ziggy." He patted him on the back. "Easy to get carried away when something this beautiful is in front of you. But, thank you for showing it to me." Stoppard walked back to the table and sat.

"Believe it or not, Stoppard, there's a lot of people just like Ziggy there."

"You mean who can't be bought?"

"That's one way of putting it."

"Everybody has a price, Theo. Sometimes it isn't money, though."

"Now that...could be argued, but...best thing you've suggested so far."

"Right. Could I suggest something else? How about you showing me the cannery Greco is always talking about."

"Trying to make the trip worthwhile?" Theo rose and gathered up his tablet and pencil. "Show and tell is fine with me. I show... you tell me why you're really here."

"I've already told you."

As they started to leave, Stoppard surreptitiously slipped a hundred dollar tip under his cup.

Ziggy scurried to open the door. The little bell jingled.

Stoppard made a last effort, "You ever decide to sell that Ziggy..."

"You've been real kind, sir," said Ziggy. "Thanks for your kind words."

***

As Derek stood on the ledge looking down at Jamie's fishing boat, 'kind words' were not being spoken into his walkie-talkie. "You come all the way out here, wasting fuel, to tell me Stoppard Denning is in town snooping around," shouted Derek into his walkie-talkie. "I watched his floating palace cruise in. Think I don't know that vessel?"

"Hell, I didn't," said Jamie with chattering teeth, as he huddled in the corner of the cabin. "Just thought you would want to know."

"Next time use the cell phone. A lot cheaper."

"You never answer it, damn it."

"I'm working."

"That's what I mean...shit. Okay. False alarm. My fault. Five lashings. I'll still come out with the provisions tomorrow. You can subtract the fuel for today from my pay."

"Only if you stay around whining and bothering me. Now git! And, oh, if you see Mister Denning back at the docks, give him a message."

"Oh, so now the trip was worth while?"

"Just tell him this exactly, okay?
"Okay."
"Tell him…Oh, fuck it."

Chapter 75

Theo and Stoppard walked along the sparsely populated Main Street, Theo catching a wave now and again from merchants still working to remove the storm coverings.

"So…" said Theo, "you came all the way up here to this forsaken island to do what?"

Stoppard smiled. "You are persistent."

"Aren't all journalists?"

Stoppard nodded. "Yes. Right you are. Truth is, Mister Donnaly, I don't know…really."

"We're going down that path again?"

"I'm being honest with you. I could give the obvious answer that I cruised up here to just see what all the fuss over Derek's cliff project was all about. Or I could say I came up to threaten the man. Or I could say I came up because it was necessary to understand more. I could give you any one of those answers or all of them, and I would be guessing because I'm not sure."

Theo glanced up from the street to grab a quick look at the man he didn't trust, but who was professing honesty. They walked a few more yards. "Only a few dozen residents left on this island, you know," said Theo. "Most of them packed it in at the end of summer, vowing to find another way to make a living. That was a pretty big move for most of them."

"I can imagine."

"Can you, Stoppard? Do you actually think you have anything in common with these simple fisherman and shop keepers?"

"Perhaps. I just got back from Darfur, you know. A lot of simple people there, too."

"And you found identity with their plight?"

"A bit different than Gray Cliff, but yeah. There was something. I wasn't always rich, you know. I know humble beginnings."

"But do you know humble endings?"

Stoppard looked at Theo, not sure what to say. "How much farther is the cannery?"

Theo shook his head. "Coming up past those trees."

The two walked the last fifty yards in silence. Theo was convinced that getting an answer why Stoppard had traveled there was futile. As they reached the front door to the cannery, Stoppard rubbed his hands. "We're here, I presume. Thank God. Doesn't want to warm up, does it?"

"It could be just as cold inside. Lanagra doesn't believe in heat."

"Lanagra," Stoppard repeated. "He's the guy Greco keeps talking about."

"He's a pretty good conversation piece," said Theo, as he opened the door.

Inside, the morning sun coming through the skylight cut accents across the barren floor. At the far end, hanging from the forty foot I-beams, hung several Lanagra-sized canvases. On one, there was only a sketch showing the beginnings of an underwater world. On another, painted washes starting at the top as light blue graduating to the bottom in coal black. The third, upstaged by a scaffold, depicted a huge pile of scrap metal, parts of boats, life vests, and other remnants of ocean flotsam and jetsam mixed with pieces of land objects, all the way from crumbled buildings to smashed cars and broken air craft. The pile pyramided up from the bottom, surrounded by the swirls of a whirlpool widening toward the top, exposing a bright star-lit sky. "Don't slam the damn door. Don't need any more drafts to destabilize these monsters," bellowed Lanagra, as he reached from the top rung of the scaffold to paint the stars with an unwieldy broad paintbrush attached to the end of a broomstick.

"Damn," whispered Stoppard, "he really doesn't believe in heat, does he?"

"Makes him sleep too much, he complains," answered Theo. "Hey, Lan? Looks like you never came down."

Lanagra peeked down over his shoulder at the two men approaching him, then went right back to his painting. "Why come down when you can paint? Who's the stranger? You know I don't like *sniffers*."

Theo looked up through the scaffolding. "No problem. He's just a billionaire trying to spend his money."

Lanagra paused a moment without looking down, then continued. "Not selling."

Stoppard chuckled. "What's with this town?"

Theo shrugged. "What can I say? Some people think for themselves. Must be the fear, don't you think?"

"Fear? Fear of what?"

"Fear of being ripped off. Hey, Lan, you afraid of being ripped off...you know, your paintings?"

"Not selling. What the hell would I do with money anyway?"

"See," quipped Theo. "And you thought Ziggy was stubborn. You seen enough?"

Stoppard looked up. "Mister Lanagra thinks big...just like Pierre."

"Well, yes on the big, but unlike Pierre, he only paints on commission...a waiting list of museums."

"Nice work, Mister Lanagra!" Stoppard shouted up. Lanagra didn't acknowledge. "So...care to show me more?"

Theo grinned. "This is it. Most everyone else is back on the mainland... waiting out the winter."

Stoppard gazed at the open floor space. "Must have been teeming once."

"And it will again. That ferry nonsense can't last forever."

"Seems to have done its damage here, though."

"Don't get your hopes up, Stoppard. Sooner or later gas prices will stabilize regardless of the profiteers. Public will put up with just so much." Theo led him over to a side door. "Over here... I'm sure you're interested in this."

As they walked, Stoppard asked, "So you think the island will return to normal next summer?"

"Next spring. Spring break is always good for tourism, and tourism's good for Echo Life."

Stoppard laughed as they continued up to the side door. Theo took out a set of keys and opened the unmarked door. "Maybe this is why you came here," said Theo.

Stoppard peered through the door to see a state of the art small digital broadcasting studio, complete with three cameras on dollies, editing facilities and a wall of satellite up-link equipment. "My, my. So this is where it all happened."

"*Happens*. Yes. Your competition."

"Amazing isn't it? Digital lets anyone become a broadcaster."

"But only a few with interactive *creative* content."

"You know, Theo, not everyone thinks your way."

"You're right...not yet. Would you like to see the dishes? They're just out back."

"No. That's...fine. I'm sure you've got something to link up with."

"Actually, we have three Intra-Probe four one-thirty dishes that were going your way...your Atlanta station, I think. But we managed to get our order in with a little premium payment and... well, I believe you got yours a few months later, if I recall. They are the best money can buy, as I'm sure you're aware."

Stoppard's grinding teeth betrayed his stoic face.

"You can't win them all, can you Stoppard?

With as casual a turn as he could muster, Stoppard nonchalantly walked back out into the open space as Theo locked the door.

"If the island's tourism can stay viable next summer, you *might* have something to broadcast," said Stoppard. "I'd be kind of afraid of that."

"The person fucking around with the teamsters is the one that needs to be afraid."

"You really believe someone is influencing the union and its fuel drivers? Sounds a bit farfetched to me. The whole world is suffering the effects of the oil prices, not just your little island here."

"All the world except the other four major tourist islands off Maine. They didn't seem to have any problems last summer getting ferry service."

"Well…I'm just a media guy. Don't know about such things."

"Except what you read in the papers."

"Except what I read in the papers." Stoppard glanced at his watch. "Well, I best be getting on. The Captain is persnickety about timetables, and I assured him I'd be back for cast off by noon. Shall we?"

The mood of the walk back to the pier was unexpected for both. Stoppard puffed away on one of his Churchills and found himself overly interested in the book Theo mentioned he was writing, even offering to publish it, sight unseen. "Don't know why you resist," said Stoppard. "No one has the reach our publishing company has. You might find it somewhat difficult to cultivate another publisher for such an obscure manuscript."

"For you, it might seem obscure, but I think there are a lot more innocent converts to the idea than you might think."

"Theo, mysticism is a hard sell now days."

"And yet, there are those who would argue that the presence of a muse in everyone's life is no less possible than the theory that God exists within us."

"And you think that's an easy sell?"

Theo shrugged. "No harder than say… Neal Walsch's 'Conversations with God'."

Stoppard took a long puff on his cigar. "And to think we had a chance to publish that."

As they rounded the corner onto the pier, Stoppard noticed a man leaning against the gangway. As they came closer, both Theo and Stoppard recognized it was Derek.

"Well, coincidence or not, I know one man happy to see you," said Theo.

Derek, still dressed in his climbing gear, nodded.

"Let's hope the *happy* one makes this frigid trip worth while," said Stoppard.

Derek extended his hand. "Mister Denning. Understand you wanted to see me."

Stoppard pasted on his most business-like smile and shook hands. "Yes. After hearing from Jamie that you were indisposed—on the rock, as it were—he recommended I talk with Mister Donnaly."

"And?" asked Derek.

"He was most helpful, but now that you're here, let's go aboard and talk a bit." He looked at his watch. "Actually, lunch should be about ready. Please join us, Mister Donnaly."

"Thanks, but I've got some work to do. Have a safe trip back."

As Stoppard led the way up the gangway, Theo smiled and grabbed Derek's sleeve, whispering, "Be careful. He's kept me on an icy slope all morning."

Derek grinned. "Kinda used to that, Theo." He held his gaze on Stoppard's back a moment, then proceeded up the gangway.

CHAPTER 76

Two stewards in French sailor suits stood at attention atop the gangway as Stoppard and Derek passed and continued the length of the boat to the main salon. Stoppard made small talk, prompting Derek to nod occasionally as he marveled at the "spare no cost" appointments and engineering of the vessel. Everything was precise and organized befitting the luxury living it accommodated. Deck hands polished the brass and wood, stewards scurried to open doors, and even the whiff of lunch cooking in the galley seemed orchestrated to perfection, including a duet of grilled garlic and shrimp aromas forming the unmistakable scent of scampi. Coming from days of cave food, his jaws involuntarily ached and he had to swallow several times to keep the telltale juices from escaping. At that moment, his only thought was whatever kind of "slope" Stoppard had planned, it would be worth it.

"Nice boat," said Derek as they approached the main salon. "Boat. Yes." said Stoppard, winking. "This is the kind of ship you can have when you give the people what they *want*."

As the doors were opened by two Filipino cabin boys, it was apparent to Derek that Stoppard was beginning his taunting routine, a business habit that had been written about by both the Wall Street Journal and The National Enquirer. "You're right there, Stoppard. Doubtless, there are few who *need* this."

"Ah, but it *is* a need, Derek." He gestured for him to sit down. Derek took a quick glance around as he sat, noting the concert grand Steinway; the brushed oak, rose wood and ebony counter and floor inlays; the silk curtains; and the museum quality antique furniture mixed with the ultra-modern feather-filled leather he was sinking into.

"You can't imagine," continued Stoppard, "the amount of business I've done in this very space. The ship has a magical persuasive power." He scrunched his shoulders up as if reacting to a chill. "Don't you feel it?"

"I should probably be trying to avoid it," said Derek.

"Oh, come now, Derek. This is just a friendly visit. Truly. I'm on vacation, you know."

"In Maine...last week in November?"

"Well, I couldn't wait another minute to see what all the talk was about. Seeing you swinging about on the rock this morning was something, you know?"

"So you took a vacation to come and see my rock?"

"Well, I'd be lying if I said you were the sole focus of my vacation. Actually, I wanted to get it out of the way so I could really relax. I'm on my way to the Greek Isles."

"Greek Isles. And my work is...keeping you from relaxing. Hard to believe."

"Oh, it's not your work. It's *you*," said Stoppard, as he lifted a small remote control dangling from a fine gold chain beneath his collar and pushed one of its keys. "I'm sure we could both enjoy a drink. What do you prefer?"

Derek had little time to think as the door opened and in glided another steward. This one French, hair pulled back in a ponytail, and looking like he was poured into his perfectly tailored white suit. His custom white spats with the *Katherine* logo embroidered on each side of the ankles were matched in uniqueness only by his raw silk brocade tie and *Katherine* stickpin. "Yes, Monsieur."

"Good afternoon, Armand. Derek?" said Stoppard again.

"Oh... yes... some... wine. That would be fine."

"White or red," asked Stoppard.

"Red, thank you."

"Cabernet Sauvignon? Bordeaux? Merlot? Whatever you *want*. We have it all."

Derek smiled. "Whatever I 'want.' Okay. I might as well get used to it. Do you have an '82 LaFite Rothchild?"

The steward let his eyes dart ever so quickly to the lips that had just uttered the words, then back to his pad and pencil.

Stoppard grinned ear to ear. "Well, you old kidder you. Know your wine, don't you? One of my favorites, as well." He looked up at

Armand. "You know, Armand, we may be a bit low. Check the cellar and if we are, order another couple of cases. We can pick them up in The Vineyard on our way down the coast, I'm sure."

"Very good, Monsieur."

As Armand left the salon, Derek sat back, a subtle grin enveloping his face. "That was a joke, Stoppard. That shit is a grand a bottle."

Stoppard reached into his humidor and retrieved a Churchill. "Actually, it went up this fall. Best I could find was eleven and change. So, tell me...oh, would you care for one?"

Derek waived him off. "No. Gotta save those taste buds for the..."

"*Joke*. Right?"

Derek hesitantly chuckled.

"So, how does a man with obvious taste, education, even the heart to save his enemy from some murderous...somebody...how does one like that make such an impression on the *nobodies*?"

"Nobodies? I don't understand."

Stoppard eyed Derek as he prepared his cigar, lit up, and blew a perfect ring into the air. "A man who prefers to live in a cave, a cold cave at that...hang from a cliff a couple hundred feet above the ocean...carve out some eyes, nose, mouth etc., while freezing his balls off, well...what do you think makes people admire that...the nobodies you seem to appeal to?"

"The nobodies, again. You must mean the subscription base we garnered this past year, yes?"

"You are perceptive."

"So, let me understand this. Boy, you don't waste any time, do you? Echo Life's subscribers are 'nobodies,' but OST's monopoly in the media is comprised of...what? The elite?"

"We don't need to revisit that again. We covered our business differences thoroughly on our last visit. I'm talking about the artists. The people you have convinced that they're creative."

"The *nobody* artists?"

"Oh, I give you the *big shots* you've managed to bring in. Actually, you've got quite a good mix in your 'A List.' Even got a couple of bands from my label."

"No," said Derek with feigned surprise.

"And people like Lanagra. Impressive. Even Greco's no slouch for a talk show host. Yeah, he's creative. He pulls in some decent numbers, too. But...beginners, real beginners, nobodies...like Pierre."

"So that's what this is about. You've got a problem with his interest in Echo Life."

"No…his interest in you."

At that moment, Armand knocked.

"Come in Armand."

Armand entered and proceeded to prepare the wine.

"Pierre told you that?" asked Derek.

"C'mon. It's common knowledge. Greco interviewed him before he left for Jamaica. He couldn't stop talking about his adulation for Echo Life and you." Stoppard, feeling he was getting ahead of himself, used the moment to taste the wine. He nodded, and stifling his anger, continued. "Let me ask you, Derek…enjoy your wine…let me ask you a question. Is this kid just a fluke, or is he the real thing? No bullshit now. Is he?"

Derek savored the swallow of wine. "There is a difference."

"Yeah. Funny what a few years and a thousand bucks can do for a bottle." He waved Armand off. "About Pierre, Derek."

Derek leaned forward holding up the bottle. "Think of the thousand bucks in this. We both agree, it's the *real thing*. That building is a first, you know. There's nothing anywhere that says art has to fit into museums and galleries. In my judgment, the half million investment is just as likely to realize unique rewards as this bottle. Pierre will age well too, if he's cared for."

"Meaning?"

Derek eyed Stoppard who was now nervously fingering his cigar. "Can I be perfectly frank with you?"

"I guess we're past the introductions, aren't we?"

"I mention caring for the guy, and you…you get uncomfortable. I think you're scared to death of something, but damned if I know what," said Derek carefully. "I wasn't using the word to hint that you should be some kind of mentor and sponsor, you know. You care to respond?"

"That's frank, alright." Stoppard rose and walked to the windows. "What *did* you mean then?"

Derek paused just a moment. "You were instrumental in getting the building saved. That's a given. I'm sure Pierre is aware of your influence, and everyone is grateful for your help. That took *some kind* of caring, I think. Probably some courage as well."

"His mother's an old acquaintance. Good woman. She asked for help. I did what I could. That's what wealthy people do sometimes. You know…the Darfur thing and all."

"Understood," said Derek. "There are those who see your Darfur operation as a means to lift your ratings…"

"Pardon…"

"But, I see it as more than that. Like your gesture with Pierre. As a wealthy man, you have to think wisely, spend wisely, and watch that your heart doesn't get in the way sometimes. I can only assume with all your money...well, there's a price for everything, isn't there? Including being very, very rich."

"Yes. I'm afraid you've got that right, my friend. 'Price for everything.'" Stoppard took a deep breath and checked his watch. "So, we're off to a flying start. We haven't killed each other yet, so we might as well enjoy some lunch and after our bellies are full, see if we want to go back into the arena. Okay with you?"

"And if it's not?"

"Good." Stoppard took Derek by the shoulder as they walked out. His voice was melancholy, almost apologetic. "There's nothing like the strategy of battle, you know? Ever read Sun Tzu's *Art of War*?"

As they entered the innovative dining room—capable of seating forty for formal dinners—the featured classical furniture in an art deco ambience, complete with recessed ceiling and a teak floor, suggested once again that Stoppard was a man of indulgences, albeit tasteful. The glass partition walls, incorporating fiber optic lighting, created a cozy bar area with more deep sofas. A steward led the pair to the far end where a breakfast area, with seating for four to ten guests, was prepared for the lunch. Seated on the sofa was Siebert.

"Oh, Siebert, so glad you could join us. Siebert, Derek. Derek, Siebert."

Siebert rose and extended his hand. "Pleased to meet you, Mister Turrel."

Stoppard grinned. "Even on the high seas, you have respectful fans, Derek."

Derek smiled, a bit embarrassed and shook Siebert's hand. "Pleased to meet you as well. Just call me Derek."

The steward pulled out a chair for Derek, then Siebert, and finally the head of the table for Stoppard. He then stood to attention and asked, "Would you care for some wine with lunch, Mister Denning?"

"Absolutely. Derek? Oh, we know your preference." He laughed. "Siebert? The old standby?"

Siebert sat properly and nodded with a smile. "That would be delightful, Mister Denning."

"Juno, we'll have another bottle of the '82 LaFite Rothchild, and a bottle of the '98 Hirsch, 'Gaisberg' Riesling. Make that two. You really have to try the Riesling with the scampi, Derek."

"And if I say no?"

"Excellent." Stoppard nodded to the steward, and he was off. "So, Derek, Siebert is an old friend and employee. He agreed to join me for this trip, seeing that I've not given him a 'real' vacation in how many years, Siebert?"

"Fifteen, sir. I mean, I've been in your employment for fifteen years, but I've always had the winter time off while you cruised."

"Fifteen," Stoppard repeated. "My God. Time, time, time."

Derek nodded. "What position do you hold with Mister Denning, Siebert?"

"Chauffeur, sir. I'm his driver."

Derek nodded again. "Well, this must be a real treat then."

"Oh, very much so. Rather hard to get used to. All this comfort."

"Yes. Comfort can be difficult sometimes, can't it Stoppard?"

"Interesting question. Why do you ask?"

Derek realized he may have been overzealous and opened up a door he wasn't prepared to walk through, but he had nowhere else to go now. "Well, I'm sure you've had other guests onboard that found the surroundings a bit difficult to get used to. That might make you a bit uncomfortable as well, yes?"

"Not really."

"Oh."

"You see, Derek, not everyone thinks like a cave dweller. For Siebert, he knows me. He's just getting used to all this. I'm perfectly comfortable with that. For you...this is perhaps...I don't know...you tell me. Maybe you'd be unwilling to get used to this, were it available to you."

"You mean if I owned this?"

"No. It's not about ownership. If I invited you to cruise with me for three months...would you come along?"

Derek smiled. "Okay. You're probably right. This is a bit..."

Stoppard rolled his hand. "And? Come on. Finish your thought."

"I live comfortably and..."

"In a cave?" quipped Stoppard.

"Even there, given what it is...a project really. I...well, my home in Manhattan is very comfortable. This is beyond comfort to me."

"And that makes *you*...uncomfortable?"

"We are having a fun play on words, aren't we?"

Stoppard repeated. "Uncomfortable?"

"No. I'm fine with it, actually."

"Fine with it? Bullshit," said Stoppard with a chuckle and an air of charming dismissal. He looked up as the steward entered with the wine. "Well...a few more glasses of your LaFite and you'll be even more 'fine,' won't you?"

At that moment, all Derek could think of was how arrogant and rude Stoppard was capable of being, without even knowing it. Derek imagined this was just another day at the office for the rich man. Holding court, whether atop the OST building in a boardroom, or in the dining room of The Katherine, it didn't make any difference. Stoppard believed money and power could satisfy any and all his kind of needs. Derek wondered, however, about something else.

"So, Siebert, this is this your first cruise?"

"Yes. Very exciting."

"And the Greek Isles. Have you ever seen them before?"

"No. I did have occasion to visit Athens many years ago, but no. The Greek Isles will be a first for me."

Derek turned to Stoppard. "And you?"

"Every other year I make this little thirteen day trip."

"My. Thirteen days on the water. Long trip," said Derek.

"You've not been, I presume?"

"You presume right. No. It's on my list, though."

"I would assume a famous sculptor like you would have visited the region countless times."

"Countless. Well... there's much art to appreciate in Greece, but I just haven't made it yet."

Derek felt saved by the bell as the door opened and in strode three stewards pushing various carts of food. The aroma of the scampi once again aroused his juices, and he relaxed, knowing the next few minutes, at least, would be filled with eating. What he didn't expect was the additional two hours that Stoppard hosted with not only the scampi, but more wine, cherries jubilee, more wine with cheese and finally, cordials of cognac to really top off the indulgence that was going to cost him a hangover and a day's loss of work. He finally looked at the time and laughed out loud. "What was that you said earlier...'back into the arena'?"

Stoppard was feeling no pain either. "Oh, hell, lets just throw ourselves to the lions and forget about it." He laughed.

Derek laughed.

Siebert snorted, only slightly disturbed from his napping on the couch, and turned over.

Derek looked over at Siebert and smiled. "He must mean a lot to you."

"What, Siebert?" said Stoppard as he poured another cordial of cognac. "The best. He's the best."

Derek used the moment to ask a question he had been holding back. "Can I ask you a personal question?"

"You mean we haven't been personal yet?" said Stoppard with another laugh.

"You pick your friends rather carefully, don't you?"

"Why do you ask?"

"This boat, uh, ship, is quite a carrot."

"Carrot…meaning why did I bring Siebert when I could have a broad on this trip if I wanted?"

"Well, that's putting in bluntly."

"Only way to be, Derek. Only way to be. Sure. A broad, lady, would be alright." He leaned forward and laughingly whispered, "God knows this thing is big enough I could lose her if I wanted."

"Yeah. True enough," said Derek.

Stoppard, now feeling the full effects of an afternoon of heavy drinking, nodded and shook his head simultaneously. "Damn straight." He laughed. "Damned straight… good phrase for a stiff like me, don't you think?"

Derek nodded.

"Broads are broads, bitches, whatever the trendy word is today. Hell, once I get to the isles…" He snapped his fingers. "…not a problem." He burst out laughing again. "Except in Mikonos. Wrong kind of bitches there."

"You mean…?"

"Gays. Jesus, Derek, do you know that island is…is…makes Fire Island look like a sandbox. Fruitcakes are everywhere."

"That bother you?"

Stoppard lifted his heavy eyelids and went grim for a moment, then pasted on his smile. "Why should it bother me? Just said there weren't any women there."

"Got to be some. You think that the entire island is gay?"

"Rhetorical question. You know enough about the world." He pointed his finger at Derek and said, "Tryin' to jerk my chain. I hate that kind of question, you know."

Derek tried to lighten the moment. "I wasn't trying to…"

"Hell you weren't." Stoppard went serious again and stared at him. "Mind if I ask *you* a personal question?

Derek shrugged.

"Why the hell does Pierre take to you…really?"

Derek was surprised at the question coming out of the blue and shrugged again. "Where did that come from?"

"You think I don't know why you're hanging on the Mikonos 'gay' thing?"

"Hanging on?"

"Pierre…you bi?"

"Whoa. What's that supposed to mean?"

"Just one artist to another? Is that what you want me to believe?"

"I'm really not following you, Stoppard. Maybe I'd better go." As Derek started to rise…

"Sit the hell down. We're not finished yet."

"Fine. This must be where we're supposed to kill each other."

"He doesn't just look up to you, he fucking worships you. How come?"

"Look, Stoppard, I don't know where you're taking this, but Pierre is just another artist interested in what Echo Life is doing and…"

"He told his mother to get pictures of the walls to you, didn't he?"

"There were pictures I saw. Yes."

"He also told her that if *you* thought it was good, maybe *you* would help save the building, right?"

Derek adjusted his seat, feeling the muscles in his neck tighten as he tried to ward off the anger that was building. "After we saw the work, my friend Aretha did the leg work."

"You mean, she's the one that got all the signatures?"

"Mostly. Yeah."

"After you fell all over yourself in praises to the kid, right?"

"Kid? He seems grown up to me."

"I have a right to call him kid, or…any other God Damn name I want. I have that right. I've paid for that right."

"Boy, you've had a few too many."

"I'm just beginning. It's only mid-afternoon. Are *you* like him?"

The anger boiling over, Derek got up and started to leave.

"I asked you a question!"

Derek stopped at the door and turned around. Stoppard sat slouched in his chair, dangling his little remote control on his finger. "Nobody leaves my presence unless I want them to."

Derek turned back to the door and tried the handle. Locked. Seething, he gathered his composure and turned back. "The question again, please."

"Are you like him?"

"If you mean gay, no."

"Do you approve?"

"Stoppard…Jesus, this is the 21st, you know. Is that what this trip to Maine is all about? What's the problem with you? What does it matter if I or you or anybody else approves. It is what it is. I don't give a rat's ass about his sexual preference, and for the life of me, can't figure out why you're so hung up on it. He's just…"

"He's *my* son, not yours, that's the fuck why! Not yours. You understand?" Shocked by his declaration, Stoppard turned his head and peered at the floor. "That wasn't planned." He looked away toward the windows. "You're the only other person of consequence, besides his mother, that knows the connection to me, and you God damn well forget you know. Understood?"

Derek heard the latch unlock as Stoppard raised the remote, still staring toward the windows. "This is private. One word, and you'll have more than a fuel problem to cope with. Clear?"

"Clear. Very clear," said Derek.

"Then get the fuck out of here."

Derek paused a moment to take in the disturbed image of Stoppard standing with his back to him, shoulders rounded, Churchill dangling toward the floor, head slumped to his chest.

"Just so we're clear... telling you about my son's sickness is not why I came here. Remember that. NOW, OUT!" bellowed Stoppard.

Some time later, Siebert rolled over, opened his eyes, and saw Stoppard slumped over the table passed out. He rose and shuffled over to his side, shaking his shoulder. "Mr Denning? Mister Denning? You okay?"

Stoppard turned his head over and slumped again, muttering a slobbery, "He's tryin'... to... fuck me... tryin' to... he's not his father..."

"Who, Mister Denning?"

Stoppard fell into a deep sleep and awoke around midnight—in his Master Suite. On his nightstand rested an e-mail:

> *Stoppard,*
>
> *Through Sunday Nov. 27, with 25 nights of the 28-night sweep period measured, November 2006 sweep averages in adults 18-49 are: CBS (4.4/12), OST (4.4/11) ABC (4.3/11), Fox and NBC (3.2/8), UPN and WB (1.5/4). In total viewers, the 25-night November sweep averages are CBS (14.6 million), OST (14.1 million) ABC (11.4 million), NBC (9.2 million), Fox (7.6 million), UPN (3.7 million) and WB (3.5 million).*
>
> *OST DSL Modem customers gain of 370,000 to 6,422,129*
>
> *SBC Modem customers gain of 360,000 to 5,968,000*
>
> *Seville Modem customers (Echo Life carrier) gain of 123,446 to 4,123,007 (up 23% from last quarter)*

OST CABLE Modem customers gain of 204,336 to 5,124,550

COMCAST CABLE Modem customers gain of 297,000 to 7,705,000

SATELL-COM CABLE Modem customers (Echo Life carrier) gain of 97,445 to 2,745,000 (up 31% from last quarter)

This is not good. Please call– urgent.

Adam Sanders

CHAPTER 77

"...and my presidency didn't mean diddly squat before, so why should I think *this* is going to help it?" asked Terrence Kensington, as he stared out the window at Manhattan from OST's executive dining room..

Adam pushed the type written page closer to Terrence, then smoothed the linen napkin across his lap and carefully scooped up a spoonful of his Vichyssoise. "Because I know if *I* suggested it to him, he'd give me a pat on the back and most likely ask me to join him on the Riviera for a month. Coming from you, well, that might insure your job another quarter and spare me having to find your replacement. Besides, he's going to insist I get the fucking network ratings turned back around. He's not going to be too happy dropping to second, you know."

Terrence snapped up the paper and paused, glancing again out the window at the crystal clear November sky. OST's Executive Dining Room was like everything else "executive" at OST... dripping with expense. Stoppard liked the idea that even when his quarterly reports were short of his and the other stockholders' expectations, he could always dip into his personal accounts and spend whatever he wished on whatever he wanted. The luxurious dining room, notwithstanding, his pride and joy on this private corner of the top floor were the three high-powered telescopes mounted on the balcony. They could accommodate the prurient, as well as the scientific interests of his staff during the day or night. Terrence could only stare at the telescopes and dream. Reality was not preferred at that moment. He read the paper again. "And you think this will pacify him?"

"He likes a good battle when he knows he can win. And in this case, hey, Echo Life will be given the old 'offer they can't turn down.'"

"It's got to be more complicated than just offering, Jesus, that's a lot of money, eighty million?"

"Everything's relative. Eighty to help insure OST's return to number one? We've got two months 'til the February sweeps. With both Echo's contracts coming up for renewal and the pressures they've got comin' up around the bend… Echo Life will piss and moan, but ultimately, welcome a chance to stay alive. Plenty of time to un-complicate it."

"What if he doesn't want to?"

"Who? Stoppard or Turrel?"

"Stoppard. There's no love lost there, you know."

"Stoppard's a whore," said Adam sarcastically. "He'll do whatever he has to do to win. You know that." Adam winked. "And in this case, *you're* the quarterback suggesting the Hail Mary. As far as the math is concerned, Boswell worked all weekend crunching the numbers to what he knows will satisfy Stoppard. It's all…"

"I know. Relative." Terrence shook his head. "Assume he buys into it, why me? Why would you want to give up a month of pampering on the yacht?"

"A month of hell. Traveling with him is like being a poodle on a leash. You're under his command 24/7 except to shit, shower, and shave. Once was enough."

"I don't know. He could have done this himself months ago."

Adam leaned across the table. "He thought that fuel thing would keep Echo Life in its place. He was wrong. This way, he doesn't have to talk about it."

"Okay. Let's say he goes for it, he's going to want full control like everything else, and Turrel doesn't strike me as someone that would bow down."

Adam nodded toward his plate. "Squab's excellent today. You ought to try some. He dabbed the corners of his mouth with the napkin. "You're missing the point. You and I both know that even with the oil prices down today, nobody trusts they'll stay there. Stabilization of the gas prices isn't going to happen…not long term, anyway. The Iraq war is a mess, with no answer in sight. Gray Cliff will never be back to full operation without the ferry service running normal, and the ferry service won't be a service without the fuel costs staying down. Union won't allow it."

"If this fuel thing's such a sure bet, how come his subscription went up, what…" he looked at the paper again, "twenty-three and thirty-one percent this past quarter and they weren't even operating up to normal? Just the Net and that Simon broadcast with a couple of artists?"

Adam leaned across the table. "That's what this is about. You can call it a fluke happenstance and risk it won't happen again, or…" He nodded at the paper. "You can make sure it continues to happen…our way. Look, we're paid to come up with solutions, remember? When's the last time he gave either one of us time to explain our proposed remedy for anything? Never. He hates wasting time hearing explanations. 'Tell me the solution, God damn it!' Voila. Enter, Terrence Kensington with the save of the year."

"Maybe we're jumping to conclusions. Maybe Echo Life was only a tiny piece of the subscription increase. Satell-Com and Seville both have other programming."

Adam sipped his wine. "I've already checked. Echo Life was responsible for ninety percent and eighty-three, respectively. You do the math. To use your phrase, Satell-Com and Seville don't have 'diddly squat' subscription pull except for Echo Life. Those two losers lucked out with a dark horse to carry their ass." He reached over and patted Terrence's hand. "Now it's your turn to grab the reins. You up to it?"

It didn't take much of a leap of faith for Adam to expect a call waiting on his return from lunch. He quickly phoned, getting a bad connection on the first satellite call, but lucking out on the second. He let Stoppard rant and rave about his staff falling asleep at the wheel and letting OST slip to second in the network ratings, followed by a tongue lashing over the cable and broadband numbers. Once Adam had a moment to get a word in, he quickly outlined how the network problems would right themselves, sighting the astronomical numbers for their Monday through Thursday reality show SO YOU WANT TO BE AN EVANGELIST that Adam had promoted so the viewing audience not only picked their favorite preacher-in-the-making—whose grand prize was his own TV show—but also participated in a lotto drawing that guaranteed the lucky ticket a hundred thousand a year for ten years as an employee of OST. At least that pleased Stoppard… especially since it was opposite The Apprentice. Viewers were salivating for the hundred thousand a year, even though once on board, Stoppard would have him or her licking stamps in the mailroom. After Adam convinced him that he had the network thing under control, he immediately launched into prepping him for the Terrence call that was coming at him momentarily.

"What excuse is that piece of drek gonna give me now?" bellowed Stoppard. "God damn. Seven years. Contracts like his are gonna be the death of me."

"His attorney works for you now, so relax. You do have a way, you know."

"Damn right, I do. Can't beat'em, buy'em. Little bastard."

"Precisely. Let me transfer this over to Terrence. I think he's really got a good idea."

Adams pressed the hold button and wiped his forehead. For a man who had a sweating problem of late, it always amazed him how much punishment his body could take with Stoppard's tirades before breaking a sweat. Must be the Qi Gong classes, he thought. He punched in Terrence's private line and listened as it connected.

"Stoppard, how's the weather?"

"Terrence... the weather is as you might imagine, Novemberish up north. Now, what the hell you doing about these numbers Adam sent me?"

It was five minutes later when Adam dabbed his forehead again as he heard Stoppard scream, "Eighty Million? What, are you out of your fucking mind?"

***

In another office, one less saturated with sweat, Samara listened intently to the voice she'd grown to expect would always be soft spoken and withdrawn. Not today.

"...and yes, I may never come back," Pierre said with a laugh.

"Well," said Samara, "your fans might not be too pleased."

"Oh, but this...this is so...different than I remember it. It's been eight years, you know."

"It's got to be a big change from a condemned building."

Pierre's voice went sullen. "Jamaica has its own kind of crumbling homes." With an upsurge of energy, Pierre continued. "But the sky, the water, the coconuts...ah, I have to send you coconuts. They're like nowhere else."

"I'd love one. Now..." she looked at her clock. "I've got another patient waiting so let's talk again toward the end of the week."

"Yes. Yes. This is really good for me, yes?"

"Pierre, if you could remain this excited forever, I might even say never come back."

"But...I can't, can I? I mean, staying this happy never lasts, does it?"

"That's not what I meant. I'm sorry to not have more time right now, but we'll talk further...you call me Friday, okay?"

"Yes. Friday. Goodbye, Doctor."

"Goodbye, Pierre."

Samara hung up the phone slowly, her thoughts remaining focused on the voice that could change so rapidly, so impetuously. *Was it because of the happy tourists mixed with the poverty, drugs and crime in Kingston? Was he going to be alright?* But now it was time to put her attention toward the waiting room where an unexpected friend awaited.

She opened the door to the reception area, and Tina rose. She wiped her eyes, apparently having been weeping for some time. "Tina, so good to see you. Such a surprise when you called…"

As Tina reached the door, she threw her arms around Samara and wept uncontrollably. "Tina, hey, it's Okay. It's okay."

They walked into the office and Samara poured her some water. "Just relax and drink some water."

"I'm so fucked up, Sam. So fucked up."

"Just drink a bit and tell me. It's okay."

But within twenty minutes, Samara knew things were not okay. Tina poured her heart out and maliciously berated herself for the sudden end of her relationship with Leonard. Samara, trying to ride the fine line of balance between personal and professional advice she had only used with Derek, found herself returning to the compassionate feeling she had experienced the first night she'd met Tina.

"You slipped, Tina. That's all. You slipped, had an accident, and it's going to take a while to heal."

"I didn't want to do it, but…I only have a high school diploma. I can't make that kind of money with my education."

"You slipped, Tina."

Tina shot up out of her seat. "Bein' a whore is more than a slip. I didn't just have an affair. I just didn't play around at some office Christmas party. I fucked again for a living. I fucked until I couldn't sit down, and I brought home the money, and I bought the fucking pain killers, and he took the fucking pain killers, and…" Once again, Tina dropped onto the couch sobbing hysterically.

"Tina?" Samara sat down beside her and took her hand. "I'm not making a joke, but can you accept the fact that you're probably a good hooker…maybe one of the best?"

"Great accomplishment. Married…was married…to a classical musician, and the best I can represent to my husband is that I'm a good, no, 'one of the best' hookers in the city? Do they give awards for that?"

"How rough did it get at home before you 'slipped'?"

"He tried…he tried so hard, but…he still couldn't make the sounds he knew he was capable of making. It drove him into so much depression. He lived with it last year. He could still perform satisfactorily for everyone but him. He was still recording, still getting 'side-men' calls, was working the jazz and the classic studios and then he started getting weaker. The doctor said his muscles were just atrophying and that he could overcome it with exercise. We got weights and he worked so damn hard. After a couple of months, he wasn't improving much, so he bought a special-made apparatus attached to his wheelchair that held his trumpet for him when he was home practicing. He'd never take it to sessions. Too much pride, and two months ago, he dropped his horn twice in a recording session, and word passed like a brush fire. 'Leonard's losing it.' No more sessions. Bills piled up." She looked up at Samara, tears streaming down her face. "I'm so ashamed."

"He knows you did it for him, doesn't he?" asked Samara.

"When he found out, I mean, the phone stopped ringing from bill collectors and he got even more nervous, thinking they were preparing to sue him, so he called a couple to arrange for payments, and found out I'd paid the bills in whole. I just couldn't lie. I should have, but..."

"He'd have learned of it somehow. Tina, it isn't the end of your life. This can be dealt with."

"Yesterday, he told me to never come back."

"You understand his pride was devastated, don't you?"

"Of course."

"That will take time, but we can work together and try to solve both your weakness and his."

"He doesn't have..."

"Oh, yes he does. We all do. He's no different. Were that weakness a strength, this would have never happened. Same goes for you."

"I'm really not a whore...not any more."

"*I* believe that, Tina. Do you, or are you just *trying* to convince yourself? You're the one that has to believe it and that's what we'll work on, okay?" Samara stood and walked to her appointment book. "How's next Monday at three?"

Tina shook her head. "I just had to unload on someone...I can't afford weekly..."

"This is not going to cost you anything now. If and when you're both on your feet again, we can talk about paying. Now..."

She walked back to Tina who rose and nervously wiped her hands on her dress. "I can't."

"You can and you will. Remember, we're friends first. The fact I can maybe help professionally is my way of reminding you...I *am* your friend." She guided her to the door. "Do you have a place to stay?"

"Yes. My brother has an extra bed."

"Your brother. You never mentioned you had a brother before."

"He was in prison at the time. Yeah. Us Fosters have a habit of fucking things up."

Samara opened the door. "You call me anytime, day or night, you hear?"

"Yes. I can't thank you enough."

"Just letting me help is all the thanks I want or need. You're a golden lady, Tina. We just have to polish you back up. Monday." They embraced and Tina left.

Samara returned to her office and slumped in her chair. She opened her drawer and took out a double picture frame. Opening it, she placed it on her desk. One side showed Derek with his arm around the Ode. The other side showed his arm around Samara. As she stared at it, tears came to her eyes. It was an hour later, after the sun had gone down, that she took her eyes from the picture and returned the frame to her desk drawer.

Chapter 78

November was rapidly showing signs that Christmas was imminent. Truckloads of spruce and evergreen trees crowded the highways in preparation for the holiday season. Bags of salt, piles of logs, barren trees and lawn bags full of leaves, all served to remind the east coast that winter was knocking on the door.

Samara used the cold drafts of the loft to spur her on in completing the symphony. For reasons not even her professional experience could help figure out, she looked forward to Tina's weekly visits like no other patient she had ever had.

Theo used the comfort of a fireplace to write extra hours at night, while other fireplaces, such as Stanton's wall-sized hearth, served as a constant lure in getting Aretha to spend more time with him — a game of sorts both relished.

Yes, for most everyone in Derek's circle, winter was a time to reflect and contemplate the past year and dream about the future. For Derek, however, thoughts ran differently. He was immersed in that place of intense imagination Samara had spent years convincing him was the place he belonged. For him, it was the moment, and the moment *only* that mattered. No past. No future. These were the thoughts he pictured in his mind as he continued to be committed to finishing what he set out to do. And what he was determined to finish right now was Echo's scarves trailing up and over the plateau of granite. He was convinced that the completion would supply him with the necessary patience he needed to survive the wait for spring. The biting cold seemed a small price to pay as he worked well into each frigid night of his last week on the rock. Wearing a miner's lamp, parka and balaclava, he chipped away at the rock until numbed fingers would force him to retire into the cave and another short night of restless sleep, always allowing the murmuring of one word Samara had ingrained into his soul—patience.

***

Stoppard, having turned down what he thought was too risky an idea from Kensington in trying to *buy* Derek, stopped at Martha's Vineyard to pick up his case of wine, and set sail for the Greek Isles, determined to think of a better way to stop the steady upward trend of Echo Life. He would stay focused to live down the November numbers that left him both angry and completely surprised; live down the wait for the February sweeps; live down the anxiety that always accompanied the year-end over all figures for OST; even live down the loneliness of the next couple of months in spite of Siebert's effort to the contrary—going so far as to every night clumsily let Stoppard win the majority of table hockey games. All seemed doable, except the unexpected gloom the OST figures put of the voyage.

Siebert tried to read for most of the crossing, while Stoppard waited for the sunny days to try to think through his problems, lounging atop the fifty-foot sun deck bundled in cashmere and down. But in spite of his efforts, he found little reward. His focusing ability was a shambles. Business thoughts were constantly interrupted by confused feelings over his son. To Stoppard, Pierre's worship of Echo Life and Derek, his relationship with Stan, and the little he really about his son was more than he could handle at times. He wasn't used to feeling guilty over anything. He kept reminding himself that he was Stoppard Denning and the young man he helped was accustomed to just being Pierre Haweisi. There was no reason to try and change things. Pierre had survived years of depression and reasonable economic comfort thanks to Stoppard's help. He was even surviving being an artist. At his age, he didn't need a bigoted absentee father showing up and sticking his nose into a life he knew so little of.

Those were the thoughts of the lone image sitting in a deck chair. As seen by the captain from the bridge, Stoppard Denning represented the quintessential symbol of loneliness that wealth and power was paradoxically capable of delivering. To those in the know, this was one of the richest and most widely known men in the world, the man who just happened to also be the phantom father of one of the least known artists in the world.

***

The temperature along the beach was eighty-five degrees, making the turquoise waters perfect for the sun worshipers and surfers. Rainbow fish swam with the Jamaican natives, and tourists snapped pictures and pitched fifty-cent pieces to the divers. Hawkers sold their shell and beadwork up and down the shoreline, while in the distance, the cacophony of motor scooters remained a constant reminder that this was the Caribbean.

"Whoa!" yelled Stan above the whine of the motor as Pierre— gripping the handles and slumping forward like a competitor— bellowed back over his shoulder, "Only a few more blocks, mon."

The western shores of Kingston harbor disappeared behind the rented Vespa as it whisked the two of them around some sharp curves, ending up at the Sea Crest Oceanfront Resort. As a teenager, Pierre had been a busboy at the resort and longed to show his friend how he'd spent one of his summers.

Pierre pulled the scooter up at the front and jumped off, pulling Stan's shirt to follow. "You gotta meet Azura, mon. She got skin like...oh...and smart? She taught me French that summer." As Stan followed, Pierre strode into the lobby and up to the Porter Station. "Hey, mon, you work here long?" he asked of the tall, muscular man in starched whites behind the counter.

"Uh..." The man looked the two of them over. With Stan wearing camouflage shorts, a 'War Bites' t-shirt with a sporty red beret and Pierre's paint-splattered cut-off bib overalls, they had the porter's attention. "I've been here awhile. Why?"

Pierre held out his hand. "Well, I'm just visiting, but back in the 90's I worked here one summer and there was this girl, Azura, which I was wondering..."

"Azura? Don't work here no more."

"Oh. You know where I might find her?"

"Last I heard she was on the streets again."

Pierre shook his head. "On the streets? I don't understand."

"You obviously didn't hear. Was all over the island. She worked her way up to assistant night manager, got knocked up, got fired, had one, I don't know, maybe two kids, then one day her picture pops up in the paper. Spent year and a half in England prison for packin'."

"Packin'?" asked Pierre.

"Mule. Sucked up a shit load of cocaine. Got caught at customs in Heathrow. Busted her ass real good. Got out first of the year, but nobody here see her after she came back. Damn, even after two kids, she was a looker, you know?"

"Jesus," said Pierre. "And you say she's on the streets?"

"Just a guess. You know. That's how most of them end up after they serve time and come back here. Can't get jobs. Don't know why so many girls do it, but *packin'* is like an epidemic here."

A guest stepped up to the counter. "Got a load outside."

"Right away, sir." As he stepped around the counter...

"Wouldn't she be with her kids now?" asked Pierre.

"Husband takes care of them. He was on TV last year. Sad. Got to go."

Pierre shuffled toward the exit with Stan. "A mule? She was so damned bright. Played the piccolo like an angel."

"Piccolo. And 'a looker' too," said Stan a bit sarcastically. "What do you expect?"

Pierre turned. "Christ, Stan. You think all women are garbage. She was like a sister to me."

"Okay. Okay. So what else you want to show me here?"

Pierre looked around. "They've changed it a lot." He walked to the hallway leading to the beach. "You want to see the beach?"

"A beach? Wow!"

"Oh, fuck you, mon," said Pierre as he strode back toward the entrance, again catching the eyes of the guests mingling about. Stan followed, turning to the guests and saying, "Just on the rag. He'll be fine."

The ride back to their hotel was slow and somewhat precarious as locals zoomed by in small cars and scooters, crowding the less experienced Pierre to the side. "You're drivin' like a tourist, for God sake. Gonna get us killed," yelled Stan.

With that, Pierre slowed down even further.

At the bed and breakfast, Pierre moped around the room, flipped the TV on and off, glanced out the window onto the street, and smoked incessantly while Stan tried to get the tired air conditioner to belch out more cold, tapping it, hitting it, and finally lifting his foot and giving it a kick. "My God, Stan. Give it up."

"It's hot, God damn it."

Pierre shook his head. "We're in a free room. That's the temperature that comes with it."

"Very funny." He slapped it one last time, reached in his pocket and pulled out his wallet. "I got a couple of bucks. Buy you a beer."

"Stan, put it away. We'll let Mom's money from Stoppard buy us a couple."

"With that roll, we could have stayed in a real hotel."

"That 'roll' is money Mom could have used with the business."

503

"Yeah, but the rich guy gave it to her to give to us, so we could…"

"Last. Just so we could *last* the winter. Lucky for us, Mom's old friend still runs this place, so we got extra lucky."

"Yeah…that's a good word for it. Place. Sure as hell isn't a hotel."

"You bitch a lot, you know that?"

"Yeah. I know that."

Pierre shook his head. "C'mon. Maybe we can splurge on a rum and coke."

"Now, you're talkin'. Been here what, eight, nine days and haven't even tried the national pastime in a glass."

Pirate's Cove, although short on originality, was nonetheless a cool stop to beat the heat. Decorated with fishnets, shells and an occasional anchor here and there, the five o'clock Happy Hour crowd of locals elbowed their way through the hanging décor and occasional open treasure chest of polished rocks and glass to the bar for the two-for-one drinks. Unlike New York, the Happy Hour was just that—one hour. Apparently, the Jamaican rum didn't need extra time to convince people they were happy. For Stan, this was like dropping into heaven. Still feeling a bit depressed, Pierre wanted to go easy and ordered a beer. Stan, taking up the slack, got the bartender's attention and pointed shamelessly at Pierre as he ordered a pair of twofer-shots.

They stood, elbow to elbow, with the rest of the bar as Stan quickly downed his first shot of rum, then grabbing an unused glass from the bar, poured the other three, and ordered a coke. "Wasn't this crowded yesterday when we passed by," shouted Stan.

"Wasn't this hot, either."

"Yeah. Good point." Stan looked around at the crowd. "Pretty *straight*."

"Yeah. *Straight*," answered Pierre.

Stan gave him a look. "What's bothering you now?"

"Just thinking, Stan. Just thinking."

"That usually means we're about to fight."

Pierre put his arm around Stan's shoulder. "Over a girl?"

"Oh…that kind of thinking. Azura?"

"Azura. Yeah."

"Why you so concerned?" asked Stan.

"Well, not because I'm madly in love with her, so relax. I already told you…she was like a sister."

"It was a long time ago, I know," said Stan.

"Yeah." Pierre noticed a trio of girls huddled at a table. "She'd be about their age now."

Stan did a double take as Pierre walked over to the table and asked, "Excuse me ladies, but you wouldn't happen to know another lady named Azura, would you? Azura Samuels?"

The three girls looked at Pierre, eyed his clothing, and giggled. One asked, "You don't mean *the* Azura Samuels that mules for a living?"

"You know her?"

"Everybody in Kingston knows *of* her. Her story won't go away. On TV least once a month. Her old man with the four kids is trying to get it taken off the air, but the station fights him. Papers love it. You're not from around here, are you?"

"No. Not now. I worked with her a few years ago. Tryin' to find her."

"Good luck," said the girl. "Probably on 5th Street after nine." All the girls laughed.

"What's on 5th Street?"

"Work for her kind." The girls turned away and Pierre walked back to Stan.

"You about finished with that?" said Pierre.

"Hell," said Stan, "I'm just gettin' started."

"Well, unless you want to drink by yourself, I'm on my way to 5th Street."

"5th Street? What the hell's there?"

"Girls working. Probably some stealthy boys too for you to ogle. Just don't get caught."

"Humph," sounded Stan. "I can only imagine what jail time for gays in Jamaica must be like." Stan looked at his watch. "Damn…it's early."

"I want to look around before it gets busy. C'mon."

Stan looked at his glass. "No thank you. You go ahead. I'll hang out here."

Pierre sighed. "I'm not gonna drag your ass through the streets later, so go easy on the stuff, okay"

Stan shrugged. "Can't get arrested for having a couple of drinks"

"Yeah. A couple."

"Spare a few bucks?"

"You got a pocket full of cash, mon. Just don't spend it all, okay?" Pierre waved and walked through the crowd and onto the sultry street. He paused a moment as a low-rider Buick cruised around the corner and pulled to a crawl. As the reggae blared from the over-kill speakers, the occupants gave him a hard look. Pierre began walking, feigning some window-shopping as he focused on the car's reflection. *Just what I need...gang bangers looking for some fun.*

Finally, the car picked up speed and rounded the corner, but not until a clear message had been bellowed over the music. "You might want to put that earring on the other ear, faggot!"

CHAPTER 79

Tourists still cluttered the sidewalks, their faces pressed against windows, peering at typical island goods. There were stores with the expected, and stores with something other than souvenirs and beach attire. Pierre's offbeat cut-off bib overauls topped off by his Rastafarian hairstyle allowed him to blend into the island's middle class look without drawing too much attention. That's how he preferred it. What he didn't need was what Stan thrived on—attention from boys. It had always bothered Pierre that there was this flaw in their relationship, but given there had never been any serious repercussions—no cheating to his knowledge—he chose to chalk it up as one of the lesser things to worry about. Stan's old cocaine habit was far more threatening. He'd been clean for a year, and Pierre was determined to not do anything that might tempt him back—like making him think Azura was anything but an old friend.

As he rounded the corner onto an unpaved narrow street of storefronts and dilapidated homes, some just a step above a shack, he noticed the smells change. The stench of garbage waiting to be picked up mixed with the ever-present humid air of cooked and raw fish made his gait quicken for the next few blocks. As the sun was setting, ancient mercury-vapor street lamps came alive with their purple cast of illumination, making the already heavy reminder of squalor conditions even worse. Natives—mixed with a few tourists braving the offbeat paths of Kingston—shuffled along, as the visitors clutched their cameras and handbags, probably wondering why they had ventured into such precarious surroundings.

As Pierre reached his destination, a long street fronting numerous houses with long balconies—like transplanted Basin Street landmarks from New Orleans—his eyes took in the visitors that were visibly eyeing the architecture, but for different reasons. This was the *red light* district, and one that still looked no different than when he left. Pimps, some in flashy rayon flowered shirts and white Panama hats, and others, attempting to attract a different type of lady, wearing the more typical American look—wild bright colored tailored linen suits, silk shirts open to the navel, topped off with strands of gold chains, and the fancy white patent leather shoes. They strolled conspicuously from building to building.

No, 5th Street hadn't changed.

He walked up and said "Hi," to one of the girls coyly swinging around a balcony support pillar as if she were about to do a strip dance.

She stopped abruptly and squinted at him. "Twenty-five dollars before nine," and went back to swinging off the beam, her chiffon-like dress barely covering her smooth, caramel plump calling-card-hips and forty-eight rack.

Pierre sat down on the stoop and leaned on his knees, looking like a resident scanning the daily street action. She stopped. "Hey, you buyin' or not? This is my spot. No popsicles allowed. Find your own corner."

"No...I'm not workin'. Just tryin' to find a friend, lady."

"Don't you be playin' with me, pig man. You wanna' check me out, I got papers and clean health certs right here." She leaned down for her purse. "Wanna bust somebody, go..."

"I'm not a cop and I'm not lookin' to get any action, okay." He reached in his pocket and took out a twenty-dollar bill. "But I could use some help."

"What kind of help?" she said eyeing the twenty.

"I'm just looking for a girl."

"Aren't you all, honey."

"Azura Samuels. Know her?"

"Shiiit," she mumbled, looking at the twenty again. "You got any more of those?"

"Maybe."

"Maybe? Well, 'maybe' I know her."

"We gonna play cat and mouse?"

She held out her hand. "Look, I don't need no trollin' time. I could be pullin' in a fish, you know?"

Pierre gave her the twenty. She kept her hand there. He laid another twenty on top. She put the money in her purse and spotting a couple of preppies timidly walking down the middle of the street, slowly worked the column like a python eyeing the prey. "Best be lookin' down the street... green house with the purple balcony. Bit late for her, though. She likes to get it over with early." Holding the column, she leaned out over the steps toward the two men. "Twofers my specialty, sweet cheeks. Thirty-five gets you both an intro to Momma Teresa's heaven."

Pierre stepped off the porch and passed the curious guys who paused and studied the outdoor pole dance. As he walked down the street, more ladies presented themselves, some from the balconies, others on porches, and the more aggressive ones, walking alongside. By the time he'd shaken his head several times, he reached the purple porch where not one or two ladies sat, but six, all looking like they'd already worked a very long night. Most were able to make an attempt at being sexy, but a couple were thankful they could just move, their heavy eyelids and track marks telling it all. "Hi, ladies," Pierre said with a big Jamaican smile. "Any of you *fine lathers* know Azura? Told I could find her here."

The idea that "girls stick together" had to be a foreign thought to this group on 5th Street. Rather than leaning toward the side of caution, everyone had a gesture and or a turncoat word or two. "Finally a cop when you want one," chortled one while pointing to the backside of the house.

"In the back."

"Take the psychotic hose-beast away."

"You want a nickel trick, she's your bitch."

"Just keep your undercover ass away from the rest of us."

Pierre, maintaining his smile, nodded. "Well, you ladies have a nice night now. I'll let the boys at the station know how cooperative you were."

More chimed in with, "You do that."

"Tell them to roust down the block for a change."

"My lord, not even the tourists dress that ridiculous. Polly there got some straight grain that'll take off those paint stains, you know."

All laughed as Pierre walked around to the backside of the two-story railrcar shaped house of pleasure. Sitting on the back stoop were two girls in their teens grappling for the hand held video game.

"Is to."

"Is not."

"You had it ten minutes now. My turn. My turn."

As they rolled off the stoop onto the dirt path, Pierre stepped up and tried to separate them. "Hey, you roll around like this, that game isn't going to be able to be played. Girls! Girls!"

"Mind you business, mon."

"Yeah. Fuck off."

And they were back to rolling across the dirt, pulling each other's hair and giving each other hearty whacks.

"That's enough," said Pierre finally pulling them apart. "Gonna hurt yourselves." Holding each at bay, they continued flailing their arms. One girl broke away, still clutching the game tightly as she ran down the alley, her friend in hot pursuit. "My turn, God damn it! My turn."

Pierre focused back on the house and looked up the back staircase. Leaning limp-armed out over the balcony was a girl whose condition suggested trouble—real trouble. The spittle continued to drip from her mouth as she slurred, "Just kids havin' a go at it. Just kids." She failed another *hurl* to her left, realizing only the pathetic sound of lungs at their limit, forcing but a tired spew of bile. As she tried to wipe her mouth, her wandering hand found only an ear and forehead.

Pierre called out, "Wouldn't know where I could find Azura, would you?"

The girl pulled herself back to the railing, and in an effort to move the paralyzed flesh around her mouth, mumbled, "You got a super size for Azzy, huh?"

Pierre squinted toward the girl, not believing this could be the one he once thought an angel. "Azura?"

Once again, the girl tried to push out some words, "She don't live here no more. Just Azzy!"

"That wouldn't be the Azzy that plays the piccolo, would it?" Pierre said with a forced smile.

The girl craned her neck and looked down. From inside the house, the bellowing roar of a customer startled her into a quick stumbling descent of the stairway.

Behind her in the room roiled the customer. "Hey, what the fuck? Jesus, I didn't pay for...oh, Christ...whew! This place reeks way too much of puke, bitch. Gimme my money back you!"

Pierre lunged toward the bottom of the stairway as Azura staggered into his arms and collapsed.

On the front porch, heads turned toward the top floor as the customer stomped down the front stairway and out the door. He turned toward the rear of the house and threw a finger back at the porch where the 'ladies' all joined in with a chorus of cursing the one known as Azzy. "Fuckin' whore."

"Fuckin' up our rooms again."

"Ain't my turn. Don't you be lookin' at me, Brandy."

"I wiped up her shit yesterday."

"Well, I ain't movin' my fat ass to clean her up," grunted another.

"You *can't* move your fat ass 'less you got a guy's pole up your front workin' it over."

With that, the hefty lady in lavender, pushed back her curly-locks, repositioned some hairpins, and sprung up like a waking hippo, waddling aggressively toward the smart mouthed lady now running inside. "Okay. Okay. So you can move that whale meat. I'm goin'. I'm goin'."

The man's anger peaked as he stopped, looked both ways and kicked the dirt. "God damn your crazy ass. Where are you?"

***

The darkness of back alleys provided privacy as Pierre struggled to keep Azura walking toward his bed and breakfast house. In one hand he tried to keep the coffee from spilling. With the other, he held her arm tightly around his neck. As they hobbled through the narrow passages, he continued making her talk. "Got to work this off, Azura. Keep taking deep breaths. C'mon now."

By the time he had reached his room and laid her limp body down on the bed, he was exhausted. But his night had just begun. "I've got to go and find Stan now, Azura. You rest. I'll be back real soon. You just relax." He grabbed a towel and quickly filled a bowl with water. "If you feel hot, just use this. If you feel like a shower, it's just through that door. Okay? Azura, do you hear me?"

She nodded and fell backward onto the pillow. Pierre stood a moment, muttering to himself... "Don't know what you're on, but it's nasty shit, mon."

Reaching the bar a little past ten, Pierre wondered before entering if he would find *another* half-alive body. He pushed open the door and gazed at a swirling array of natives and tourists dancing elbow-to-elbow in what was supposed to be a two hundred maximum occupancy, easily exceeded by that many again. Reggae music numbed the senses as he maneuvered his way to the end of the bar where he'd left Stan three hours earlier. Surprisingly, he was still there—sort of. Stan sat atop his bar stool, propped up by a girl on either side, laughing and helping him finish off the remains of a fourth bottle of rum. Before him on the bar top was a triangular wall of stacked shot glasses waiting to be toppled so he could part with another couple of fifties to pay for them. *That had to cost a few hundred we don't have to waste. Shit!*

As Stan focused on the wavy look of his friend approaching, he smiled ear to ear. "Girls, this here is my...my bro. My real bro. Aren't ya, bro?" He gestured toward the wall of glasses. "Look at that. A first, bro. A first."

Pierre looked at the girls holding each arm. "Yes it is. My, my. Yes it is. Hi, girls. Hi Stan."

Stan put on an impish grin and grimaced at the glasses as if to say, *don't you fall on me.*

"Guess this night was not meant for pleasure," said Pierre as he politely dismissed the girls with a flick of his hands, and hoisted Stan over his shoulders in a fireman's carry, wondering how in hell he made it work.

"Hey, little bro," stammered Stan, "Aren't ya proud? Just like you. I don't hate girls." His drunken laughter was tinged with his real feelings toward women.

Pierre put a fireman's carry on him. "No, you don't hate girls if they give you an audience. C'mon, *big* bro. Gotta get you to bed."

"Is this...carrying shit really necessary," said Stan as his body got progressively heavier with every breath.

By the time Pierre dropped the unconscious Stan on the bed, he too muttered, "Was this really necessary?"

In return, Stan's mangled reply, "I love you" fluttered across the sheets as he unknowingly flung his arm across the shoulders of an equally unconscious Azura.

As he eyed the unlikely couple on the bed, Pierre staggered exhaustively backward into the easy chair, muttering his last words for the night as well. "This should be interesting in the morning."

Chapter 80

Getting away is famous for having various meanings. It had been almost two weeks since Derek, Stoppard, and Pierre had begun their *getting away* effort. For Derek, it was being able to pack it in for the winter and leave the cave, nursing his ever-sore muscles in front of a fire while catching up on his reading. He anticipated the long, uninterrupted daydreaming of Samara, and enjoying sunsets from the lighthouse. It was a time to contemplate how well he'd manage the down time and its accompanying anxiety.

For Pierre, the first few days of being in Jamaica had been all nostalgia. But, as he was about to find out, even memories can twist one's sense of control when they come back as remembrances best forgotten.

For Stoppard, it was the relief of reaching dry land for a change. The Katherine dropped anchor in the port of Lisbon harbor, the journey's halfway point. Customs inspectors came aboard, satisfied themselves, and allowed the ship to dock for the twenty-four hours of re-supplying and maintenance. The stop was a welcome relief for the sea-weary legs of Siebert, as well. Even with all the luxuries, nine days had taken its toll. The early morning sunrise reflected off the calm wake, as the ship pulled anchor and slowly maneuvered through the sleepy harbor. Like children being dropped off for summer camp rather than sophisticated travelers, Stoppard and Siebert excitedly watched the mooring area get closer and closer.

Donning their windbreakers and sneakers, they disembarked and jauntily strode the streets where proprietors of small shops and bistros swept their walks, raised their Cinzano umbrellas, and with cheerful greetings, welcomed both native and tourist alike.

Stopping at a sidewalk café, Stoppard said, "Well, some Portuguese coffee should help get our legs working again, eh Siebert?"

Siebert sat across from Stoppard, nodding. He rubbed his hands together, enjoying the brisk temperature while taking deep breaths. "Yes, sir. Yes, sir."

Quizzically, Stoppard tilted his head and smiled. "You really like that smell?"

Siebert took another deep breath. "Fresh fish. Reminds me of holiday in England as a boy. Always went to the sea shore and hoped for sunshine."

Stoppard looked up. "Well, don't have to hope here. Not a cloud."

The waiter, a slim, effete man in his forties, wearing a white apron and the obligatory towel over his arm, approached. "Bom dia. Good morning. Coffee?"

Stoppard sat up and took the menu. "Obrigado...very strong...two Bica Curto, and let's see...you speak English, yes?"

The waiter nodded graciously. "Whenever I get the chance."

"Good." As he scanned the menu, he kept glancing up at Siebert who was still inhaling deeply. "I'll have two croissants and my friend...he'd love some mackerel with sour cream and anchovies."

"What?" Siebert turned abruptly to Stoppard.

"Just thought you'd like to satiate that nose of yours."

They laughed, changed the order to an additional croissant and jelly, and continued to take in the local color. Merchants continued to open their stores; delivery bikes dropped off baskets of flowers and bread; and the occasional twenties-something met their motor rides into the city. A child ran out of her second story apartment with book-straps securely wrapped around the day's schoolwork. All were part of an early December sunrise on the lower docks of Lisbon.

"You know, Siebert, people are the same no matter where you go."

Siebert glanced at Stoppard and then followed his gaze out to the street where a middle-aged lady maneuvered her bicycle around the broken cobblestone, avoiding the worst bumps to prevent her two bottles of milk and baguette from leaping out of the basket. "Meaning, nothing is easy?"

"Mmm. Hadn't thought of it quite that way, but... yeah. Think she'll make it home?"

"Hearty."

"Pardon?" said Stoppard.

512

"Sure. She's hearty and look at that determined look on her face."

"Like the merchant over there." Stoppard nodded across the street. "The one painting his sign. Could use some help though, couldn't he?"

Siebert smiled. "He's fine. Got the bucket between his legs, one hand to paint the sign, and one hand to break his fall."

"Like I said, could use some help," said Stoppard.

They both chuckled. "This is good for you, isn't it?" continued Stoppard.

"Traveling? Not complaining, sir."

"You know Siebert, for the rest of the trip, let's just make it Stop, okay? You know that's what my friends call me…Stop."

Siebert looked over. "Stop. Okay. Stop it is." After a pause, "Just want you to know, I'm enjoying this trip as much as you."

"Nice to help…I mean, *glad* I could make this special for you."

"You're early today," said Siebert.

"Early?"

Siebert smiled. "You usually reserve your happy words for later in the day."

Stoppard patted his arm. "You're right. That's a bad habit of mine. Good words. Happy thoughts in the morning… that's how I feel now. And…"

The waiter stepped up with tray of food and drink. "Your croissants and Bica Curto, sir."

"Obrigado." He looked over at Siebert. "Ever had Portuguese coffee, Siebert?"

"No, sir…I mean, Stop. Haven't had Portuguese coffee."

"Well, forget all you think you know about coffee. Brazilian and Angolan beans usually make up the brew that's rumored could grow hair on a billiard ball."

The waiter leaned in. "But our coffee, sir, is smooth as velvet on the end of a hammer."

Stoppard laughed. "Now where'd you learn that little bit?"

"From sailors I've served here late at night after they spent the earlier hours on 'Bar Row'."

"And where might 'Bar Row' be?"

"Two blocks east of here."

"Fun?"

The waiter winked. "Depends on your preference."

Stoppard innocently smiled back. "Preference?"

"You know…orientation… *preference*," his voice now filtered by the sound of *his* obvious *preference*.

Stoppard felt uncomfortable. "Sure. Absolutely." He nodded. "Obrigado."

As the waiter sashayed away, Stoppard tried to cover his embarrassment with a noisy slurp of coffee and a carefree glance to the street once again.

Siebert watched as Stoppard continued holding his gaze to the street; the pain of a reality Stoppard would prefer to never be reminded of had once again been brought to the surface.

From all the years of listening and viewing the man through a rear view mirror, Siebert knew him well enough to know this was a new emotion that could not be covered very well. The man sitting across from him had everything most people can only dream about, but something he didn't have—something wealth couldn't buy—was that certain kind of understanding and compassion reserved for a loved one, a family member. "He made it."

Stoppard blinked his eyes, forcing a smile. "Pardon."

Nodding across the street, Siebert said quietly, "The shop keeper. I think he's got a system. The sign is almost finished."

Stoppard moved his eyes to the man atop the ladder. "Like you said, 'nothing is easy'."

"Not without determination," followed Siebert.

"Not without determination," parroted Stoppard.

The rest of the day, the two men wandered the streets of Lisbon, finding the hills a challenge for their legs, but rewarding as they reached the crests and took in one view after another of the city whose history dated back to the occupation by the Romans in 205 B.C., according to Siebert, as he continued, "... through the conquering by the Moors in 714, and into the King Alfonso 1 era, where with the help of the Crusaders, drove out the Moors in 1147. Today it is one of the most important ports in the world."

"You're full of surprises, aren't you, Siebert?"

"I had a crush on my history teacher. Only 'A' I ever got."

They both chuckled and continued their day of sight seeing.

By nightfall, both men had not only lost their sea legs, but felt like they'd lost their land legs as well. Finding another quaint sidewalk café surrounded by ancient architecture, they dropped their weary bodies down and ordered beer.

Siebert removed his sneakers and began massaging his feet. "New York walking is supposed to toughen up the legs they say, but..."

Stoppard held up his hands in surrender. "Hills are another thing, my friend. I'm for a cab back to the ship."

"You'll get no argument from me," answered Siebert.

The two men drank their beer, then another, then another as they enjoyed the street performers and mimes weaving their magic spell over the crowd. Children and adults all watched in awe as the cobblestone stage—whose backdrop was an ancient medieval church complete with gargoyles maintaining their shadowed watch over the square—grew darker, accommodating the portable black-light that illuminated the glow-in-the-dark makeup on the performers portraying a mythical death ritual. Their costumes of shredded rags only added to the bizarre image of celebration.

"Weird entertainment," said Stoppard.

Siebert didn't respond immediately, his eyes fixed on the lute, mandolin and drum players accompanying the performances. Faces of the mimes moved in and out of the shadows, around the tables, then back out to the square to join the dancers who moved around the center fountain like medieval warriors, lifting their knees and bowing their heads as some ancient come-to-life lepers.

"Can I buy you another beer?" asked Siebert in hushed tones.

"How about a Bloody Mary?" answered Stoppard.

The cab ride back to the docks was bumpy even to the anesthetized passengers whose painted faces kept the driver humorously glancing back often...just in case. After a particularly hard bump, Siebert woke up and lifted his heavy eyelids to see Stoppard glowing in the dark. He burst out laughing, shaking the painted face.

"Stoppard? Stop? When'd you get so pretty?"

Stoppard woke with a start, jerked upright disoriented, then sighting Siebert...added to the laughter. "Holy shit! What happened to your face?"

They both struggled to lean forward and glance in the driver's rear view mirror. The drunken pair had somehow been painted up like the mimes with war-like stripes across their foreheads, circles on their cheeks, and multi-colored rings around their eyes, making for a laughable, if not scary sight for the driver.

"You two had a good time, no?"

Siebert slumped back into the seat. "Good time, yes," he mumbled amidst his giggling.

Stoppard tried to sit back in a more gentlemanly manner, only to miss the seat and land on the floor. Both burst out laughing, as he pulled himself into the seat. "Oh, boy... we must have drunk that café dry, eh driver?"

"Not in Lisbon, sir. We never run out of booze," and he joined in the laughter.

"We look like shit, eh?" asked Stoppard.

"I've seen worse," laughed the driver. "But not still breathing." More laughter.

As the cab dodged other late night drunks and made its way through the winding streets, Stoppard tried to search for a cigar. He went from one pocket to the other, his hands not going where he wanted them to, prompting Siebert to laugh more. "Did somebody roll us? My cigars are gone."

"Your...your cigars are..." Siebert raised his finger. "You made sacrifices to the what-ever gods back there. You...filled them...full of toothpicks...looked like voodoo dolls."

A different comical expression enveloped Stoppard's face, one of disbelief. "My Churchills? My...toothpicks?" He kept patting his pockets.

"Your Churchills," answered Siebert. "Last time I saw them...they were burning like crosses at a *Clan* hanging." With that, the driver burst out laughing.

"Gotta have a cigar, damn it. Gotta have a smoke," slurred Stoppard.

"I know a late-night bar that'll have cigars. Got a couple bucks?" said the driver.

Stoppard pulled out his money clip. "They take U.S. green or just Euros?"

"Easier with Euros," answered the driver as they hit another hole in the road, sending Stoppard sliding back onto the floor. "Shit... "

"Sorry," said the driver. "You said 'fast' when I picked you up, so I'm..."

"Forget what I said," roared Stoppard as he passed a hundred dollar bill over the seat. "You think *that* will make it easy for whoever to sell me a cigar?"

The driver laughed. "You two go in together, they'll probably give you a box of them...no charge. *Night of the Dead* celebrations give prizes for that kind of look."

"'Night of the Dead?' What the hell's that?" asked both Stoppard and Siebert almost in unison.

"You didn't know... you didn't know that's what your paint job was all about?"

"Hell... I didn't even know... we got painted," stammered Siebert, bringing the laughter to tears.

***

Heavy Metal music and cigarette smoke wafted heavily past them as Stoppard and Siebert opened the door to the club and entered. The noise was deafening in the strobe flashing, black-lit dance bar the driver called "The Dungeon." There were sweaty bare-chested men rubbing past them as they made their way to the bar. "Jesus..." shouted Stoppard. "What the hell is this place?"

"Looks like it's a gay bar," shouted Siebert, obviously enjoying the sights.

"What?" hollered Stoppard.

"Gay, a Gay bar."

Stoppard blinked rapidly, looked to his right, his left, and convinced he had heard right, bolted for the bar, slamming down a hundred. "Cigars...you got cigars the cabbie said."

The bartender, a muscle bound titan, himself painted up like the Hulk, grinned. "Cigars?" He winked. "With that, you can get a Havana."

Stoppard, always able to get sober quick when negotiations were at stake, winked back. "With that I can get two. One for me and one for my bitch, right?"

Siebert eyes widened. The bartender's grin broadened as he passed the box, allowing Stoppard to extract two Havanas. He quickly passed them under his nose, and then whipped out another bill—this time examining it closely to make sure it was a twenty, and slipped it under the ashtray. "For you to buy some more steroids."

"I thank you, sir. And..." the bartender picked up the twenty, then flashed his bicep at Stoppard, flexing a tattoo of an ass moving in and out. "My buddy thanks you too."

Back in the cab, the two lit up and quietly glided the aromatic gold into the air. Neither spoke. The driver smiled. "Glad I could help."

"Yeah," said Stoppard soberly. "Glad you could help." He turned toward the window and gazed out at the semi-darkness, occasionally broken by the light of a street lamp circling a couple walking arm in arm. As they got closer to the docks, the frequent red spill flooding down on the street from second story windows occasionally revealed shadows of half naked occupants sweating their way toward the sunrise that was but an hour away.

As the cab turned the corner and headed for the pearl-gray ship lounging in the purple hue of pre-dawn, Stoppard wiped the paint-tinged tears from his cheeks and drew heavily on the Havana.

CHAPTER 81

That same moment, some forty-four hundred miles away, cigarette smoke rose across another window. Darkness of an unexpected kind invaded the small room where Pierre sat calmly sipping coffee and lighting another cigarette. Stan and Azura were still lying on the bed, one sprawled across the foot and the other crunched fetal at the head. Both continued to sleep heavily. Pierre looked at his watch once again. Midnight. *Into their eighteenth hour.*

For Pierre, sleep had come in spurts the past day, leaving him exhausted. He adjusted his seat, took another drag and peered out the open window toward the opposite building. The blue-gray flickering of TV and sounds of horses, music and six-gun firing told him that someone besides himself could still get off on westerns. His TV watching had been minimal for years, but of late, he had tried to watch Greco whenever he could. Now as his mind struggled to stay awake, he wondered what Simon would be talking about tonight. Would he someday be talking about his building, *his* art? His thoughts wandered to the construction and the trust he had to maintain that Stoppard's assurances of three full-time guards continually monitoring the construction would more than insure its safety. He wanted to believe. He glanced back over at the bed and remembered the assurance he had given his mother that all would be fine, that he needed to get away and that some rest would be the best thing for him right now. Everything *wasn't* fine though. Getting away to this surprise was the last thing he really needed. And he sure as hell wasn't getting any rest.

Stan bolted up, shook his head, blinked several times, and said, "Jesus…where am I?"

"Try your room," said Pierre. "How's your head?"

Stan took a quick glance to his left, blinked again and flung himself out of bed. "Who the hell's that?"

"Azura. You both had some difficulties a couple of days ago."

Stan did a double take of his bed partner, then to Pierre. "Two days ago?"

"Well, actually a little short, going by twenty four hours. You've had an eighteen hour snooze though."

"And her?" asked Stan. "Why she in our bed?"

"Already told you. Just a bad night." Pierre started for the door. "Some breakfast?"

Stan, still gathering his wits about him, turned, looked at his body, clad only in his skivvies, and again asked, "Her. This is the girl friend, right?"

Pierre nodded and smiled. "Stan, you big dummy, I worked with her…like a sister. Remember?"

Stan looked for his pants and slipped them on. "This is wrong. Just wrong. You schtoop her? Huh?"

Pierre took his hand off the doorknob and turned. "You know, for a guy who was only drunk *out of his mind*, you're acting more like a mental case."

Stan yanked the pants up, tightened the belt, grabbed his hat and made for the door. "No, man. You're the one with the screws fucked up, remember? I'm getting me some coffee."

Pierre gave a quick, but concerned glance to Azura. Satisfied, he called out to Stan, "I'm joining you."

"No, you're not," said Stan.

Stan shot out the door. Pierre quickly wrote a note on some scratch paper and laid it on the bed.

As he left the room, the slam of the door brought Azura to a turn on her other side, then back to sleep.

The café wasn't much to look at. A neon sign spewed a purple haze over a few weathered tables and chairs beneath an awning that had seen much better days. In the corner were the remnants of a palm tree that appeared like a survivor of many hurricanes. The waiter seemed more inclined to sleep on his corner chair than wait tables.

Pierre sipped his coffee, glancing from the barely lit street and its foot and auto traffic to Stan, who sat rigid, occasionally gulping his coffee. After several moments of silence, "How do you feel?"

"Fuck you."

"Good. You're back to normal," said Pierre.

"How could you?" growled Stan between clenched teeth.

Pierre rolled his head. "Oh, come on, Stan. My God. She's just a girl in our bed."

Stan gave him a quick dirty look, and returned to gulping his coffee. He raised his hand. "Waiter...more coffee."

The waiter, leaning back in his chair, his hands resting on his potbelly, squinted, and disappeared to the kitchen.

"Why is it that when it comes to *my* feelings...they don't exist for you?" grumbled Stan.

"Not true. When did I ever ignore your feelings?" answered Pierre.

"You want to start at the beginning or the end?"

Pierre shook his head. "Whatever."

Stan leaned across the table. "In the beginning, you had me move out of my comfortable Village pad and move into the Bronx. Did you ever ask me if I *wanted* to move...to just...move like *that*? No. You just said, 'we got to lower *our* rent.' That's all. Just 'lower *our* rent.' I was doing fine before you, you know. You move in, you...you...ah, fuck it."

"And the end," said Pierre sarcastically.

"You drag me down here to…. Did you even ask me if I wanted to meet Azura? What the hell do I care if…"

Pierre stood up. "Fuck me? Fuck you." And stormed up the street.

"Hey!" yelled Stan. "I didn't bring my wallet, God damn it!"

"You don't need me. You'll figure something out," yelled Pierre over his shoulder as he shoved his hands in his pockets and merged into the middle of the night.

The waiter reappeared, carrying the coffee pot. Stan held his hand over the cup. "I ain't got no money." The waiter looked at Stan's distraught face and sighed. "You pay me tomorrow?"

Stan looked up, surprised. "Tomorrow? Yeah, I just left me wallet behind and…"

"Tomorrow fine." He gestured to the other cup where Pierre had been sitting. "Your friend? You pay for him?"

"Fuck no! Yeah. Shit… tomorrow."

The waiter poured and smiled. "You know old song, 'Don't Worry, Be Happy'?"

Stan thought a moment. "That black dude…Bobby…what's his name?"

"McFerrin. Bobby McFerrin. He know all about it. So…don't worry. Be happy…you pay tomorrow."

Stan, not quite sure how to react to his little waiter-philosopher said, "Carry me for a donut?"

The waiter stood for a moment, waving his finger at Stan. "You from the states. I can tell. New York, too, right?"

"Right. How'd you know that?"

"Me too. Long time ago. You pay tomorrow or neither of us be very happy, yes?"

"Yes. Thank you."

As the waiter walked back toward the kitchen, Stan yelled after him. "What part of New York you from?"

"South Bronx…" He lifted his shirtsleeve and flashed a tattoo. "Savage Skulls. Know us?"

Stan nodded, forcing a smile. "Retired, huh?"

The waiter didn't change his stoic smile, only now, he added some steely eyes. "Tomorrow. Noon. Okay?"

Stan, trying to be casual and fearful he might wet himself, nodded.

The waiter acknowledged. "Be a nice man now and don't forget the tip."

"Absolutely. No problem. Good tip, too. Yeah, man. Good…*Great* tip. Yeah."

As the waiter disappeared into the kitchen area, Stan cracked his neck and then his knuckles. As his trembling hand lifted the coffee cup, *and he leaves me with a fucking Savage Skull. Fuck!*

As Pierre reached the top of the stairway, he heard commotion coming from his room. Swinging the door open, he was faced with a wild-eyed Azura trashing the room, throwing things out of the drawers with one hand as she held tightly to the Sony boom box under her arm. "Hey!" shouted Pierre.

Azura made a leap for the window, but realizing she was two floors up, thought twice. She turned back into the room, now holding the boom box like an oversized ball bat. "Just stay the fuck away, and nobody gets hurt."
Pierre held his position at the door. "Shit, Azura. It's me, Pierre...bus boy, summer of ninety-eight. The Sea Crest."

"Okay. Nice to see ya, again, dude, but I got other things on my mind," snapped Azura as she raised the boom box like a war club "Now get outta my way 'fore this does some damage."

"Then what would you have to buy junk with?" said Pierre. "I've got money. Let's sit down and..."

"Don't need no handout. Get outta the way. I mean it."

Pierre stepped to the side. As she passed, he said, "Doesn't work."

Azura stopped, looked at the machine, then him. "What do you mean, 'doesn't work'?"

"Stopped two days ago. Haven't had time to fix it." He lifted his wallet. "Let's talk."

Azura threw the boom box at the bed and burst down the stairway, running into Mister Grooder, Pierre's three hundred pound neighbor, who was pulling himself up the narrow stairway after completing his bus-driving shift. "Shit!" Yelled Azura, seeing next to no room to pass.

As she tried to turn sideways and squeeze by, Mister Grooder raised his sweating head. "Whew! You got to be kidding."

Azura, seeing there was no way to pass, blurted out, "Shit, fuck, piss."

Mister Grooder's eyes shot open like two high beams. "Say again. ma'am, "

Azura looked back up at Pierre, then Mister Grooder. Resigned, she trudged back up the stairway to the landing and waited.

"Just give me a minute, ma'am," said Mister Grooder apologetically as he made his way up the stairway.

Pierre calmly took a couple of steps toward Azura. "In case you've forgotten, I did work with you and I just wanted to look you up and thank you."

Azura shot a glance over her shoulder as she said, "C'mon, lard-ass. Move it."

"Doesn't sound like you," said Pierre.

"Yeah, well, doesn't sound like you either, whoever you are."

"You don't remember me."

Mister Grooder pulled himself up onto the landing, wiped his face with his shirt, and bowed. "Sorry to have delayed your departure."

Azura shot down the stairway, followed by Pierre.

As the two walked rapidly down the street, Pierre kept an arms-length distance. "Look, Azura, I did work with you that summer. You had tables six through eleven and I was always trying to find more dishes to bus."

Azura stopped and turned. Squinting once again, she took a long look. "Shit. Bean. Didn't I nick name you 'Bean'?"

Pierre took an extra step to her side as he banged the side of his head. "Yeah. Yeah. String Bean."

Azura nodded, turned and continued walking. "So, now we've got that straightened out, I gotta do some business, okay."

"You liked my drawings, remember? I hated them, and you liked them."

"Kinda."

"Kinda what?"

"I kinda remember. Damn you ask too many questions."

"Sorry. Just wanted to thank you. About the drawings and all. I played around with drawing some more, and well, I think I might be getting better."

"Good for you."

"No, I mean, I did some work and I might be able to make a couple of bucks, you know?"

"Couple of bucks? Yeah, I know about that."

Pierre pulled out his wallet again and lifted three ten-dollar bills. "Here, let me be your trick for an hour."

Azura slowed down and glanced over at his extended hand holding the money. "I get more than that an hour."

"Okay. I'm sure you're worth it, but that's all I can afford. One hour...in a café."

"I don't do kinky."

"We talk. Just talk."

She grabbed the money, slipped it under her dress, and pointed. "Around the corner down there."

Stan opened his drawer and grabbed his money clip, checking to see if he still had forty dollars. *Damn, our money must be almost gone.* As he started to leave the room, he paused at the door, turned and stepped to the bed, pulled back the cover and examined the sheets for any tell tale stains. Satisfied, he carefully remade the bed and fluffed the pillows. He looked around the room one last time and seeing some dirty clothes on the floor, picked them up and threw them in the closet. Drawing his hand across Pierre's side table, he looked for dust, then wiped the ashtray and placed it neatly beside the reading lamp. As a last touch, he put the window shade at the half-way point, just the way Pierre liked it.

The clerk stood patiently holding the open box waiting for Stan to make up his mind. "Maybe some peanut brittle, or the chocolate covered orange slices. They're big with the tourists."

Stan leaned down, peered intently at the various chocolates and chocolate covered nuts, fruit and pretzels. "The banana. That's half coated. Got one all chocolate?"

The clerk smiled. "Not 'til later. All out right now."

"Okay. The banana and two covered strawberries. The big ones."

"The banana or berries?"

"Both. Both big."

"Both big. For sure." He lifted the banana and strawberries into the box.

"Hey, don't just put them in any old way," complained Stan. "You know, scrunch up some paper so they don't roll around. And banana on top, berries on the bottom. He's an artist, you know."

The clerk did as he was told. "Up or down?"

"What?"

"Up or down. The banana."

Stan looked in the box. "Up. No, down. Don't want to look too forgiving."

The clerk fought back a smile and closed the lid. Stan gave him five dollars. "Keep the change. Buy yourself something."

As Stan left the chocolate store, the clerk rang up the sale. "Four dollars eighty-eight cents."

The café tabletop was strewn with napkins; all with various sketches from Pierre's building murals. "And this one..." He pointed to the knife sharpening handcart. "This one is still there, off Houston. Four generations of Polish immigrants have made their living runing it."

The waiter stepped up. "How's that coffee?"

"Cold," said Azura.

"Well, we can fix that. I'll get you a fresh cup. And you, sir?"

"I'm fine." As the waiter stepped away, Pierre started to crumple the napkins.

Azura reached over and caught his hand. "Don't. Can I keep them?"

Pierre chuckled. "They're just napkins."

"I know, but, well, probably never be able to afford one of your works, so..."

"Sure," said Pierre. "If you're sure you want them."

"You think I'm faking it?"

"Didn't say that."

"I only fake orgasms." She folded them neatly and placed then to the side. "So... aren't you gonna ask me how I got all fucked up?"

"I figured if you wanted to tell me, you would. Otherwise, I'm alright just seeing you and thanking you."

"Thanks accepted." She smiled to herself and turned away. As sadness crept back into her face, she said, "Another guy once said I was a 'good whore'."

"I never said..."

"No, but that's how it is. Good whore. Bad whore. Some kind of whore. Doesn't matter most of the time."

"What about your kids?"

"Know about that too, huh?"

"TV has a habit of informing the neighbors. I did some snoopin'."

"Yeah. I wasn't even back and the whole island knew England was letting 'little Miss Pretty' out of prison. You know that's what they used to call me?"

"Really?"

"Yeah. Long time ago. *Long* time ago."

"When'd you see the kids last?"

"Couple weeks. I give my guy money to watch them, you know."

"Your husband?"

"My boyfriend. Kids think he's there father, but he's just a nice guy, except when he's not. Pretty unpredictable. Thinks that 'Little Miss Pretty' will be pretty again, test clean, move back in and play Suzy Homemaker."

"And?"

She flashed her arms at him. "With a road map like that? Join the dots and you see an interesting circle. I ain't never gonna be clean."

"Those are scars. I don't see any fresh."

"Of course not. They'd haul my ass into jail, and London's shit-hole cells are *four star* compared to Kingston."

"So?"

"So, I got me a good doctor. Corrupt as hell, but good with sellin' stuff that's good at foolin' blood tests. Long as you pay him."

Pierre looked away, not knowing what to say or do next.

"So, what else you want to know?" She looked at the sun. "Looks to me like you still got a few minutes on the meter."

"Whatever you want to tell me, Azura. Sounds like there's more."

She got up. "C'mon. Nothin' to tell, but I'll show you somethin'."

Ten minutes of walking brought them to a run down street paralleling the docks reserved for the local small fishermen. Anchored rickety boats bobbed with the inlet tide, their paint visibly peeling and dropping into the water.

On the other side of a potholed street were the shacks made of discarded pieces of sheet metal combined with broken sections of fiberglass fence and roof remnants, along with miscellaneous scraps of wood and cardboard. What made the street different from the cliché poverty photos National Geographic was famous for, however, was the lack of any visible life. For all intents and purposes, this was just an abandoned street. "Strange street," said Pierre.

"What, the lack of people?"

"Yeah. Kinda."

"Slums are low profile to Kingston. There are probably thirty or forty families along here. You can't see them, but they can see you."

"I don't understand."

"They get protection to stay out of sight."

"Protection?"

She nodded and pointed to the far end of the street. "Around that corner down there, probably ten or fifteen 'Dream Boats.' That's what certain people call them."

"I probably shouldn't ask..."

"But you will. This is Eel turf. Gang turf. Drugs, sex. Dream Boats are pleasure boxes, opium dens, rooms, safe havens for those that like to dream a lot, if you know what I mean. Around the corner out of sight. Blends right in with the neighborhood. A quiet little forgotten slum. That's the way the gang and city politicians on the take want it."

"I didn't hear that."

"Course not, or I wouldn't have told you. C'mon. Wanna see my kids?"

Pierre stood a moment, staring at the patchwork housing.

She smiled for the first time. "You get used to it, Pierre. Number seventeen. Wanna say hi?"

As she pushed aside the sheet metal door and led Pierre into the twelve by twelve room, two small children rushed in from the back. "Mommy. Mommy."

Azura swept one up in each arm. "How's my angels?"

Amidst the old linoleum covered earth stood two beds, a dresser, table and four chairs. Even in this impoverished living space, the wide eyed, beautiful children did indeed seem like two angels.

"We fine. Who that?"

"A friend of mommy's. Where's your brothers and Luke?"

"Cleanin' fish," said the smaller of the two. Both looked with suspicion at Pierre who smiled back, noting that both were clean and wearing fairly decent clothes.

Azura put them down and stepped through an opening into the back area. "Luke? It's me."

From behind the sheet metal, Pierre heard, "What the hell you doin' here. Every other Tuesday. Want to lose them completely?"

"Nobody saw me come in. Want you to meet an old friend. Come here. Meet Pierre."

Azura stepped back into the room and waited. The man called Luke stepped through the opening, an eight-year-old boy under his right arm and a six- year-old under his left. All three were wearing fish stained clothing, knives in their hands, and no smile. None whatsoever. "Told you not to bring your johns around here, remember?"

"I'd never... Pierre's from New York. We worked together at the Sea Crest many years ago."

"Fine," said Luke, ushering the boys into the back again. "Pleased to meet ya. Got dinner to clean." He turned back to Azura. "And you, Little Miss Pretty, better get your ass out of the neighborhood."

"Just leaving. Bye boys. Miss you." She picked up the two little girls, hugged and kissed them. "Mommy see you soon. Be good. Listen to Luke, okay?"

Once outside, Pierre turned to her. "That had to be the shortest 'hello, pleased to meet you' I've ever experienced, not to mention hardly a visit for your kids."

"I can't visit except every other Tuesday. Court order. Three more months' probation. Then if that doctor's right and I seem clean..."

Pierre turned back and walked along the fence-like façade that represented a hundred yards of living space for Kingston's poorest. "How do you live like this?"

"More questions?"

"Sorry."

After a few steps, Azura said, "It's the best we can afford right now. Eels keep the street safe, and... things will get better. Things will get better."

They walked to the end of the street where Pierre turned and looked back. His gaze drifted from the facades of all the shacks to the harbor. In the distance, a cruise ship made it's way toward the other end of the inlet for docking. "Do the big ships ever come close to here?"

"No. They used to, but not anymore since it got so run down. Bad for tourist business. Why do you ask?"

"Just thinking," said Pierre. "Just thinking."

Walking many blocks, Pierre escorted Azura to the small one-room apartment her pimp provided. Feeling sad and very uncomfortable, their goodbye was short. The walk back to the B and B reminded him of how hot and muggy Kingston could be. By the time he started up the stairway, he was drenched. As luck would have it, Mister Grooder was making his way down the stairway. Pierre politely stepped back onto the entrance floor as the gentle giant passed. "Thank you, Pierre. You have a nice day now."

"Hope to, Mister Grooder." He trudged back up the stairway, starting to unbutton his shirt even before taking out his keys. As he inserted the key, he realized it was open. "Stan?" He pushed the door open to see Stan sitting in the easy chair, smoking a pipe. "Pipe? Since when?"

Stan smiled. "Just thought I'd try one. Does it fit me?"

"Back in the '50's maybe, but... no. Smells good though."

Stan got up and put the pipe down in the ashtray. "So look, I'm sorry...for all the..."

"Not necessary, Stan." Pierre pulled his shirt off, "I'm bushed. Long couple of nights, you know?"

"I know. Sorry."

Pierre shook his head and smiled. "Forget it. You may have to haul my ass up those stairs some night too."

Stan stepped up and hugged him. "Hey, I'm a sweaty mess. Gotta shower."

"Thanks. Just thanks," said Stan as he released him. "Think I'll read a bit."

As Pierre opened the dresser drawer for some underwear, he noticed the gift box on top next to a bottle of wine. "What's this?"

"What?" said Stan with a feigned surprise.

"This. Box. Wine."

"Oh. That. Just a little something. You have your shower first."

Pierre picked up the box and examined it. "Smells like chocolate."

"Really?" said Stan. "That's strange."

Pierre grinned. "Playing up to my weakness?"

"All the time. Get your shower."

Catching an early night left Pierre waking up long before sunrise. Stan, like the child he could sometimes be, was curled up on the other side of the bed, a pillow tucked securely between his legs, a peaceful expression on his face that still bore the remnants of the chocolate feast hours before. Pierre moved to the window where he sat at the table and lit a cigarette. The temperature had dropped and the distant sound of early tropical birds put a smile on his face. After a few moments, he got up and took some paper and a pencil from the dresser drawer and sat back down. Drawing a straight line from the lower corner to the upper far corner, he then drew in a few irregular vertical lines. He stopped and leaned back. Blowing a smoke ring into the air, he closed his eyes and quietly hummed the theme song from Simon Greco's show.

CHAPTER 82

Although Echo Life was in a holding pattern, during the winter months Sol Berkowitz was determined to keep his investors temporarily happy with Simon Greco's audience numbers—happy enough, at least, to maintain the payments for the satellite space and to pay for the live Echo Life radio and TV broadcasts of reruns, and Web updates. As Stoppard Denning had realized the hard way, network numbers may have been the holy grail in the past, but in the Twenty-First Century, cable and Internet broadcasts were whittling away at the sacred Nielson ratings, while exponentially creating a new paradigm of audience preferences. As Christmas neared, advertisers beefed up their retail ads; TV network programming departments scrambled and debated mid-season replacements; and Greco continued luring creative spirits—some just listening, while others shared their creative ideas by way of e-mails, mail, photos and recordings. The fan mail department had to hire three more assistants (island residents) to handle the overload.

Like every other night lately, Greco found himself deluged over the air with variations on the same question: *"when are you going to produce new original material for the web and TV broadcasts again?"*

"Hopefully, never," said Stoppard as he turned the volume down on his satellite radio reception and turned to Siebert. "That guy is like stink on you-know-what, you know?"

Siebert turned in his chair and studied the board. "Were you aware your Queen was vulnerable?"

Stoppard leaned forward. "Damn." Smiling, he leaned back. "You going to do that to me again?"

"Probably. I need a little glory too. You'll create my daily depression soon enough with that hockey hand of yours."

"Gotta win at something on this trip, eh?" Stoppard said with a smile as he looked at his watch. "Eleven. Time for lunch soon. Finish this before or after?"

Siebert answered with a move of his Knight that toppled Stoppard's Queen. "To concede would give us time for another before lunch."

Stoppard took a deep breath and leaned back, picking up his cigar, relighting, and studying the board.

Siebert picked up the December issue of *Air and Sea Satellite TV*. "Thursday. Your favorite re-runs are on tonight."

Stoppard took a puff on his cigar. "I could say, 'not funny, Siebert' but that would be disingenuous. As long as Simon stays in re-runs, I can enjoy watching and studying. After all, to beat your enemy, you must be able to think like him, yes?"

Siebert put the magazine down. "In chess, yes. With Simon Greco, I don't know."

Stoppard advanced his Rook. "I know you won't offer your thoughts without my asking, so, tell me. Tell me why in chess and not with Greco."

"Respectfully, just an observation, Stop, but you're who you are because you have a different model of the world than the Grecos and the Turrels. It might be very difficult, if not impossible to think like them. Chess has common rules based on a common model."

"Different ideologies is what battle's all about," said Stoppard, his voice crisp and sharp like a sabre catching the sunlight. "You think Patton found it comfortable to think like Rommel, or Hitler, for that matter? I think not. But that's how he won his campaigns. He had to climb inside their heads. And let's not forget, with every victory, there must be a preliminary sense of defeat."

"I'm afraid I don't understand."

"Well, Siebert, perhaps that's why I'm who I am and you are who you are."

"Mmm." Siebert moved his Bishop and called out "Check. Pardon, me. Check Mate."

Stoppard shook his head, the cigar receiving a permanent dent between his fingers. "How the hell...I couldn't have missed that."

"Just a distraction of thought, perhaps. You merely lost a skirmish, however. You've not lost the war. I believe you're only three up on me now, though."

"Yes. Three. Siebert, you're scary sometimes. You know that, don't you?"

"Scary, sir?"

"Ah, you slipped."

"Sorry. *Stop*. My apologies."

"You understand more than you let on. A lot of the time."

"I don't mean to. I apologize if that makes you uncomfortable."

"No, no," said Stoppard as he started to rearrange the pieces on the board. "Not uncomfortable at all. I like it. Maybe I subconsciously saw that in you a long time ago. Maybe that's why I asked you join me on this voyage."

Siebert watched as Stoppard's fingers moved the pieces into perfect symmetrical position. "I noticed you have Sun Tzu's *The Art of War* in the library. Are you familiar with the quote, *'It is only one who is thoroughly acquainted with the evils of war that can thoroughly understand the profitable way of carrying it on.?'*"

"Interesting you should ask," said Stoppard. "Does that explain the last game?"

"You mean the *win*?" said Siebert with a self-effacing grin.

Stoppard waved his finger at Siebert and smiled back. "Touché."

***

"What the hell is this?" asked Theo, standing at the top of the lighthouse stairwell.

Derek, sitting in his underwear, dabbed the rag into the paste and continued polishing his crampons. "I'm hunkered down, as they say, Theo. That's all. Hunkered down." Derek's scruffy beard and hair were understandably overgrown, island life being what it was in the winter.

"You're a mess," said Theo.

Derek looked up at Theo lingering in his old heavy coat "Yeah, and I suppose you look like a GQ cover?"

"I'm not talking about your appearance. You've been back from the rock for three weeks and you haven't wanted to see anybody. Not even me."

"You're here, aren't you?"

"After threatening Singso to let me in for the umpteenth time."

"Yeah, well, I'll have to ream her out for giving in."

"Jesus, Derek. What's with you? Thought I was a partner of sorts."

"You are. Just want to be alone right now."

"Locked away in your tower, trying to polish the stainless steel away on your equipment?"

"I've got more paste in the cupboard."

"This is not a joke. You've never been like this. Talk to me."

"Nothing to talk about, yet."

"Yet? Do I get a clue?"

"Not yet."

Theo stood up. "You're back from that cave, but you act like you're still there."

"Maybe I am."

"Maybe you're psychotic too."

"Maybe."

"You don't mind if I take my coat off do you? Hot as hell in here."

"I like it hot. Still thawing from the cave." He looked up. "Don't be getting too comfortable now. I said I wanted to be..."

"Alone. I know. Here, I brought you some of Gretchen's gingerbread." He lifted a brown bag from his coat pocket. "Storefront window is full of this stuff. You'd think she was baking for the summer tourist trade. Little bakery is a godsend though. Her croissants are my first thought when I wake up." Theo laid it down on the table next to the array of axes, carving tools, hammers and climbing gear.

Derek nodded and dabbed some more paste.

Theo sniffed. "What is that stuff?"

"Polish."

"I gathered that. What's the stink?"

"Got some acetone to cut the grease stains. Pneumatic spews all over the place."

"Oh," said Theo as he surreptitiously made his way to the stairway. "Singso? Could you rustle up some coffee?"

Derek's head jerked up. "Hey, I said I wanted to be alone."

"You drink coffee, don't you?"

"That's beside the point."

"Can't eat gingerbread without coffee."

Singso yelled hesitantly from down below. "Is okay with Mis'er Turrel?"

"She's scared to death of you," whispered Theo.

"Should be, letting you in." Derek put down the rag and stomped to the stairwell. "Okay with Mister Turrel. Bring up some cream too. Mister Donnaly likes his cream."

"More like it," said Theo.

Derek shook his head as he returned to the table. "Don't think that's an invitation to stay. Drink your coffee and let me have my peace."

"Fine with me." Theo looked over at the CD player. "Mind if I put on some music?"

"Oh, boy. Now you're really settling in. Why don't you just say what you've got to say."

"While I drink my coffee."

"While you drink your coffee. Fine."

Theo walked to the stack of CD's and started thumbing through them. "I know you like Wagner."

"Not today."

"Okay. How about... oh, here's a good one."

Derek put the crampons down and picked up a chisel as the CD started playing—Samara's Trumpet Concerto. Theo turned. "Good choice?"

Derek lifted his eyes and stared out the lighthouse window a moment. "You hear from her?"

"I was about to ask you the same thing," Theo said casually.

Derek picked up the chisel again and started polishing. "Should have stayed in the cave."

"Pardon?"

"Nothing."

"When did you speak to her last?"

"Just before we left New York."

"New York?"

"She wasn't very pleased I was staying here for the winter."

"Whoa. I'd have never thought," said Theo sarcastically.

Derek gave Theo a dirty look then went back to the polishing. "As if you know a fucking thing about relationships."

"Well, I know enough."

Singso yelled coming up the stairway, "Singso bring coffee. Put on pants."

"Shit," said Derek, quickly grabbing a pair of trousers. "She gets so offended at my bare legs."

Theo looked at his legs. "Understandable."

"Shut up."

Singso stepped up on the landing and placed the coffee tray on the table.

"Thank you, Singso."

"You're welcome." As she turned to go, she said, "No nice to have zipper down, Mis'er Turrel."

"Shit. I mean, sorry, Singso. My mistake," he muttered zipping up.

"Yes," said Singso as she descended the stairway. "Your mistake."

"Pain in the ass, but she's the best cook you could ask for," grumbled Derek as he poured coffee in the bigger of the two mugs.

"I believe that's my cup," said Theo.

"Not today. You drink from smaller one this time and you'll be out of here a hell of a lot sooner."

"That's what I mean."

"Yes? What do you mean?" said Derek, taking a sip and breaking off a piece of gingerbread.

"I know enough about relationships to know Neil Simon's famous quote was right: 'It's harder for me to watch what you're doing, than it is for you to do what I'm watching.'"

Derek didn't say anything as he continued polishing, but after a few moments, "It's that obvious, huh?"

Theo nodded. "Yeah. And you're right about my relationships. Been a long time."

"I'm sorry."

Theo waved him off. "Forget it. Just is what it is, but you? That's another thing. You two are special. Never seen two people so perfectly suited with their craziness."

Finally, Derek broke a smile. "And one of the crazies is a shrink."

"And one of the crazies is a shrink," Theo repeated. "You miss her, don't you?"

"You putting on that music doesn't help."

"Why don't you go back for the winter? Whatever you need to do, you can just as well do it there."

"I need to think."

"About?"

"Echo Life is hanging by a thread."

"And?"

"I need to think about it. Alone."

"She lets you be as much alone as you want. A blind man could see that."

Derek started to object.

"You're polishing those tools like they were children. The other tools you baby are back in the loft. The ones you made everything with 'til Gray Cliff. Remember? I'm sure they'd appreciate being picked up again."

"Talking nuts now."

"Well, never lied to you before about my mental condition. Why start now?"

"So you have an opinion. Fine. I've heard it." He looked down at the gingerbread. "You gonna eat some of that so you can go?"

Theo took a gulp of coffee, grabbed a piece and started putting on his coat. "Just leaving. Remember, even if you don't lift a tool, *she'd* appreciate you being there."

"How the hell you figure that? She all but said get fucked when I said I was staying here for the winter."

"She's got a symphony to finish. If my memory serves me correctly, her last work, that concerto you're listening to, was created while you chipped away marble on the other side of the loft. Her interview with the Times even quoted her saying an unnamed artist was her inspiration. That wouldn't have been you, would it?"

As Theo reached the stairwell, he turned. "Some people go for it all, and some just go for what they need, right? Seems I heard a variation on that credo somewhere." As he descended the stairwell, his voice drifted back up, merging with the music. "Deprive yourself of what you need and what do you end up with, Derek?"

Chapter 83

The bright lights of a holiday-decorated NBC Plaza reflected off the ice rink, keeping Samara's attention as she waited at a table inside the restaurant overlooking the skaters. It had been a long time since she had donned blades and attempted to make it around a rink, but this was a special occasion. She looked up at the restaurant entrance several times over the next fifteen minutes, but always returned for another sip of her tea. Finally, Tina appeared and made her way to the table. Unlike the meeting several weeks earlier, Tina was smiling and happy.

"I'm so sorry," said Tina. "Last minute shoppers kept me wrapping for twenty minutes." She leaned down and exchanged a hug with Samara, then sat down.

"No problem. Gave me plenty of time to realize what a coward I am. That ice looks hard."

Tina reached across the table and patted her hand. "Oh, you'll do just fine. Just like a bicycle. You'll remember everything."

"Let's hope. You look wonderful. Job agrees with you."

"Well, let's just say, I agree with the job. Lucky to get it, even if wrapping Holiday gifts is a drag on the feet."

"Your feet hurt? We don't have to skate, you know."

"Oh, not going to get out of it that easy. My feet will come alive once those skates hit the ice."

"Well, how about a little food first?"

"And some wine. And that part's on me."

"No, no, no. This is my treat."

"Please. Least I can do. It's not cutting into my regular pay. Worked some *special-time* at the store."

"If you insist. Now, tell me all about the job."

For the next hour, Tina outlined every kind of wrapping challenge imaginable. Putting paper around toys that in many cases weren't boxed left imagination at risk, especially at FAO Schwarz. By the time they had eaten their salads, and had two glasses of wine, Tina was down to the last story.

"Now you have to picture this, Sam. I hear this cursing and grumbling coming from a very old lady way at the back of the line. She obviously was determined to get her way. I peeked over the top of the counter—you know how wrapping stations are always with the high counters—well I look over the top and two of Schwarz's finest— that's stock boys—were holding up this six foot robot, while the little old lady—and she was in white tennis shoes, I swear—flashed orders like a Drill Sergeant. The poor guys were trying to move Zergon the Robot along the waiting line while they loaded him up with three different sized batteries. She was dead set on getting Zergon wrapped with its computer program set to deliver the words, 'Merry Christmas Billy Bob'—I'm not kidding—Billy Bob, and she wanted the message to pop when the wrapping was removed. You know, the big, 'Merry Christmas Billy Bob,' as the paper was ripped away. And, she had one of those little old lady purses, you know, the kind that's gripped with the one thing in mind, 'someone is going to try and mug me.' The two guys didn't know whether to keep their eye on the battery case, or watch out for grandma's swinging right arm.

"Well, by the time she reached the counter, luck would have it, I'm the one. I think the other four girls purposely slowed down just so I'd get the *big* job. And I mean *big*. I'd thrown this green and red stretchy shit, oops, sorry, paper, actually, plastic, around giraffes, a pony, even a half-sized Hummer in bright yellow, you know, but nothing this awkward. Damn arms had a Schwarzenegger-like weapon in each; the knee caps had rocket launchers bulging to let free; the head-piece, like a helmet from hell, had an array of laser weapons protruding…it was a nightmare waiting to happen.

'Hello, there, Hottie,' says the be-speckled granny, holding her one hand over the trip mechanism for the *message*, and the other still gripping her own weapon, the purse. 'Whadda ya think?'

'What do I think,' I say.

'Yeah. Gotta get this into a cab. What do you recommend?'

'A big cab?' I say with all due respect.

"She breaks out laughing, almost forgetting to hold the message lever in place, while the two stock boys stand ready to collapse from the pressure of not wanting to reset the program again. It would have been really funny were I not the one on the hot seat right now. So I try. 'Ma'am, I… how would you like it wrapped?'

'Any way you can, honey. My arm's gettin' tired.'

'Oh, shit," says one of the boys as he steps forward to maybe hold the lever.

'Hey,' she says, 'Back off. Us girls got this in control.'

"At this point, I'm at the stand maneuvering the big six foot roll of colored plastic to the entrance and motioning the boys to push Zergon up for wrapping. First thing I do is look at her hand, and ask, 'How we going to do this?'

"She looks at me kinda quizzically, you know, then she grabs the plastic, puts it over her hand, pulls it out, now she's holding the plastic against the lever with the other hand, and she says, 'Get the *mummifying* started, Hottie, and I'll hold her together as long as I can. Okay?' Now the rest of the girls are trying to keep from laughing; the boys are turning their backs to us so they can let off some suppressed laughter; and I'm supposed to keep a straight face. So, I start rushing around the robot with the plastic, moving in and out of granny while she keeps saying, 'I'm losin' it. I'm losin' it. Hurry up. Hurry up.' I'm feeling like some kind of animated machine, up, down, around. Finally, the mess is finished. She stands back and says. 'Kinda ugly, ain't it?'

'Ma'am,' I say, 'I don't think we're going to get it any better. How about a big ribbon?'

"She likes that idea and scurries around the counter to pick one of the foot wide ribbons specially made for 'big' packages. We do another round of wrapping the ribbon and she's smiling so hard, she has to wipe tears from her eyes. 'Beautiful,' she says. Samara, it was the ugliest wrapping I'd ever done, but you know what?"

Samara, having enjoyed the story, shook her head and smiled. "What?"

Tina pulled a hundred dollar bill from her purse. "This was my 'special time at the store' I told you about. I usually only see one of these after a late night, you know."

"She gave you that?"

"And the boys each got a twenty."

"How did she get it in a cab?" Samara asked.

"Story at eleven?" said Tina laughing. "Last I heard from the guys, she hailed a horse and carriage and took off down 5th Avenue with Zergon strapped next to the driver."

Night skating at the NBC Plaza rink is special, especially as holiday time approaches. With music enhancing the experience, skaters seem to glide about the ice as if living out a modern Norman Rockwell painting. For Tina and Samara, it was further enriched by the exhilarated feeling that *anything was possible*. For Tina, healing was happening. She had a job. She had counseling. She had a friend. For Samara, the reward of helping someone get through their pain was always a cherished experience. "I owe you a lot," said Tina as they held hands and moved through a turn.

"It's mutual, Tina. I've never told you, but you are the only patient I've ever befriended, besides Derek, and it's very much against the rules."

"Ooh. You mean you think for yourself?"

"Shhhh!" said Samara.

Tina gripped her hand tighter. "Thanks, again."

Both lifted their faces into the cold night, feeling the other's thoughts. Both were thinking of the loneliness that would invade their bedrooms tonight. Both knew the pain of absence was unavoidable, but it didn't lessen the struggle to keep the tears in check. Neither bothered to clear the subtle emotions wending down their cheeks.   The commonality of missing their men was mutual, and unavoidable.

***

Just as *getting away* has different meanings to different people, so too does the term *holiday season* deliver a like mix of differences. History repeats itself here as well. For some, Thanksgiving through New Years Day represents family, friends, and gratitude for just being alive. Others, having waited the whole year for the Day-After Thanksgiving sales, prepared to drain their bank accounts in anticipation of smiles and thank-you sentiments for giving just the right gift. There are some who are satisfied with just the sounds and sights, spending hours walking the city streets ablaze with multicolored lights, while loud speakers proclaim the various musical reasons for all the commotion. Over-spending dominates the holiday postmortem, and of course, there are always those who see the holiday as a self-destructive test, resulting in suicide for some.

From Theo's perspective—writing what he hoped to be the surprise guidebook of the decade—holiday season was a time for reflection. Limited to a room, fireplace, table, chair, and bed, there were moments in November when he thought he was living the life of Van Gogh, seeing what others couldn't see, feeling his life's experience as a heavy burden. Theo ruminated on the idea that his motorized miniature Christmas tree would soon be unpacked and set up, performing it usual magic; nudging him closer and closer to

537

understanding why the world of an artist was so compelling and yet so isolating.

***

Pierre, Stan, and Azura discovered life was too short to be wallowing in petty differences and found themselves playing out a contemporary version of Jules and Jim, running about Jamaica—the Vespa barely able to move with the three taxing the suspension with not only weight, but the rhythms of Reggae—and in general, finding tolerance a new kind of reward to add to their holiday memories.

***

As the distance from home lengthened with Stoppard's arrival in the islands, e-mails, telephone calls, and web streamed OST shows for the February sweeps, dominated the time he otherwise would have spent on the islands with Siebert. As it turned out, Siebert became the wandering off-season tourist while Stoppard became the wondering prime-season media executive aboard his boat, ensconced in his media room. His all consuming thought became: *Am I going to survive the Nielsens this time?* The tension of each day took its toll on the nerves and liver of the man, who for the first time in his career, felt pressure he couldn't control. Empty Greek wine and ouzo bottles filled the refuse containers of The Katherine more than once, and tensions began to rise between him and Siebert, his only trusted friend at the moment.

Immersing herself into the third movement helped Samara avoid the cheerfully lit streets and buildings of Manhattan... a sensation to be avoided. Within the loft, a few simple white miniature bulbs coiled about the pillars, giving just enough acknowledgment of the holiday to satisfy anyone who visited—mainly Tina. With her job satisfying her meager needs—even affording with the overtime enough extra to deposit helpful amounts into Leonard's personal account—having dinner and wine with Samara once or twice a week was all she needed. For the lady who had just a few short weeks earlier been on the verge of mental collapse, reaching the holiday period with healing well in progress was a milestone.

Aretha and Stanton hadn't been seen leaving their love nest for weeks.

Hoping for the best on Gray Cliff come spring, the Echo Life artists continued their passions, allowing little time for festive risk—instead, living in various parts of New York, Jersey and a few minor locales westward, never losing their edge, disallowing sludge and flab to gather around their creative energies.

For Derek, however, neither work nor holiday acquiescence soothed his longings for Samara. Time, ambition, and neurosis, all had taken their toll. He felt *too much* alone. He saw much of the same malady taking over Theo. Coercing the little man with a pencil and pad to pack up and join him for a change of scenery wasn't easy, but after threatening to leave him alone on the island with Sheila as possibly his only source of company, Theo packed his meager belongings. They were going to spend the balance of the winter in Manhattan, and they were going to start with a surprise New Year's Eve visit to Samara. Catching the once-a-day ferry, they made the airport barely in time for the afternoon flight to LaGuardia.

As the plane circled the airport and pointed south, they both peered out the window at the Maine coastline and the distant island of Gray Cliff. On their laps were the latest edition of The Times and The Wall Street Journal. Both with the same headlines. INTELLIGENCE SUGGESTING INSURGENTS PLAN TO SABOTAGE THE WORLD'S OIL FIELDS, THREATENS TO DRIVE OPEC OIL TO ONE HUNDRED DOLLARS A BARREL BY SPRING. They both felt a chill—the chill of fear that there might not be a reason to return.

CHAPTER 84

Derek couldn't put his finger on what it was about Lower Manhattan that still drew his sense of mystery and surprise. What he was sure of, as the cab turned the last corner before his loft, was that he couldn't remember ever surprising someone on New Year's Eve with his presence, let alone with another friend in tow. Theo's steady gaze out the window all the way from LaGuardia told Derek that a part of Theo had missed the city as well.

"How long's it been snowing?" Derek asked the cabbie.

"Last couple of days."

"Gonna put a damper on Times Square tonight, I bet."

The cabbie smiled. "You're not from New York, are you?"

"Why do you ask?"

"Nothing squelches New Year's Eve in Times Square."

"No, I guess you're right. Never saw it this cold though."

"Ah, just a few degrees worse than last year. Makes for good cognac sales, you know?"

"Oh, that reminds me. Could you pull over at the liquor store. It's just beyond the address I gave you."

"Not a problem."

Derek felt Theo's hand slap a bill in his. "Cognac. Sounds good. Get me a bottle."

"Wanting to sleep through the Rose Bowl, eh?"

"Hopefully," said Theo. "You're not going to be all noisy, are you?"

"Damn, Theo, if I didn't know you… remember, she hasn't spoken to me since the last trip here. She's liable to throw us both out."

Theo shook his head. "It's your pad, and you think she's gonna throw you out of your own home?"

"I should have been the male, you know. Called *her*. She likes that."

"Trust me. Assuming she's home tonight, she's maybe gonna throw me out, but not you," said Theo.

"You're sleeping in the guest room. No argument."

"Maybe tonight, but tomorrow…"

"You're not going anywhere. Waste of money to put up somewhere else."

"We'll see."

"We'll not see. Oh, cabbie, right there… the corner store."

The cab pulled over and Derek rushed through the flurries to purchase some champagne and cognac. Theo continued his gaze out the window. Remembrances of New Years past brought images of his one main relationship, especially that Christmas, nineteen ninety-two. *Cylia was small like Theo. They'd met at a benefit for the homeless in Battery Park. He was covering the story for two foreign publications, and she was serving food.*

"Go easy on the potatoes, Miss. Got to watch the belt, you know."

Cylia had only smiled and said, "Theodore Donnaly hardly needs to watch his waist line."

"You know me?"

"I read. Your Press Pass is kinda out there, you know."

"They are kinda gaudy, aren't they?"

"They get you to where you need to go, though, right. Dressing?"

"Oh, yeah. Some of that spinach too. Little extra, actually."

"Popeye man, eh?"

"Well, my mother always said, 'eat…"

"… 'your spinach.' Mine too. You from New York? Gravy?"

"Yeah… Yeah to both."

"Me too. Crazy way to live, isn't it?"

"New York. Not really. You still have a smile, so it's not done its dirty deed on you yet."

"It's all an act. Here you go." She handed him the plate.

"Thanks. Isn't it all?"

"Pardon?"

"It's all an act."

"Just my smile. Doesn't fit. You have a good night." She turned to the next man in line. *"What can I whip up for you, big guy?"* Theo turned to see a police officer who looked like the Hulk. He made a note to never stand next to such a height ever again when romancing. Three months later, just a heartbeat away from asking her to marry him, she blew her brains out.

"Damn, cold out there," said Derek as he lunged into the cab.

"Colder in here," mumbled Theo.

"What?"

"Nothing. So, what did my twenty get me?"

"Not the best, not the worst." Derek pulled out a bottle of Remy Martin Cognac.

"Remy?"

"Interesting what twenty bucks buys nowadays. Oh..." He reached in his pocket and pulled out a box of Bayer. "You did have a buck thirty in change so I got these. Just in case."

Theo took the bottle, looked again at the label, and twisted the brown bag tight. "Aged in pine wood."

"Hey, like I said."

"Twenty bucks is twenty. I know."

As the cab pulled up to the loft, Derek drew one of three other bottles from the bag. "Got you a Dom to start with. Maybe you'll pass out early and not have to suffer the Remy."

Theo smiled. "Thanks. Dom is good."

"Humph," blurted Derek. "Dom is damn good. Hope we don't have to drink alone." He peered up to the windows of the loft as he paid the driver.

"Thanks," said the cabbie.

Derek, temporarily lost in anticipation, caught himself. "Oh. Sorry." He slipped the cabbie another twenty. "Happy New Year."

"Same," said the driver.

The two men stood on the sidewalk a few moments, their head turned up to the top floor. "See anything?" asked Theo.

"Nothing."

"Well, might as well get the bad news now and have more time to drink this party away."

They stepped up to the door. Derek unlocked the two tumblers, and they walked in. The foyer—as Derek liked to refer to the non-descript old brick enclosure —was decorated with the usual New Year's stuff. The freight elevator had a bit more imagination. One of the artists in the building had created a collage of odd shapes in the traditional holiday colors; the other side in newspaper clips from many years of *New York's Neediest* stories.

"Wrote one of those once," said Theo.

"Really. Good story?"

"Sad, like all of them. But, guess it helps wake up some people. Holidays are like letting out the asylum for a couple of weeks. Anyway…"

The elevator stopped and they stepped out and took the few steps to the loft entrance. They stood there a few moments. "So?" said Theo. "You going to open it?"

"I think I should ring."

"You think you should ring." He stepped forward and pressed his cheek to the door. "Hey, Samara! You there? Derek thinks he should ring!" He stepped back, standing a little further away just in case Derek decided to punch him out. "It was necessary."

"It was not neces…"

The door flew open. Samara stood there for just a moment. Derek thought it was only a moment. Theo told him later it was a millisecond. "Oh, my God!" she blurted out and threw her arms around him, kissing both cheeks, repeatedly. She then grabbed Theo, and kissed him on both cheeks. She calmed momentarily and turned back to Derek, saying, "Turn away, Theo."

Theo obliged and waited… waited… and finally, turned. They were gone. He peered inside and they were leaning against the wall, or maybe better to say, she had him pinned against the wall. As the barely audible Spanish guitar music played, she maintained a lock on Derek's lips that Theo figured would hurt for a month. As he tried to act casual and enter, close the door quietly, he was startled by, "Hi Theo."

He whipped around and there in the shadows across the room was what he thought… "Tina?"

***

In another part of the city, several men gathered around a fire to celebrate the New Year. A few had begun drinking much earlier. One man, Detroit, stared into space, a celebratory toast was the last thing on his mind. Holding an M82 rifle magazine in his right hand, he involuntarily brought it up and tapped his Desert Storm helmet every few seconds. Over and over again.

The fire rose from the oil barrel, illuminating the undercarriage of the Manhattan Bridge with dancing shadows and flickering colors as another man wandered into the circle. "Here you go fellas," and he opened his coat, where several bottles of cheap whiskey, rum and gin were dragging the hemline down to his ankles.

"How'd you score all this, Tito?"

"Gimme the gin. The gin is mine," said one.

"What kind of whiskey? What kind of whiskey?" shouted another.

"Hey, you guys. Take it easy. Leave some for the guests."

"Who's comin', Tito? Who's comin'?"

"The usual. No surprises," said Tito.

"Tony?"

"Yeah."

"Sam?"

"Yeah. And Larry and Teach, and..."

"Oh, not Teach," said Ohio.

"Fuckin' stuffed shirt," chimed in California.

"Look, Ohio," countered Tito. "You and California there are just going to have to get used to the Englishman. He's been honoring us with his visit for three years and I'm not about to ask him to stop. He's a good driver and good horseman. And he always brings cream puffs from his sister's bakery, so shut up. Now, let's clean this dump up a little bit. It's only eighteen degrees and you guys are standing around like it's cold. C'mon. Move your ass, Utah. This ain't a union shop. C'mon."

The group grumbled their way around, grabbing old tires, a car seat, some apple crates and an old bean bag. Tito arranged them around the fire, grabbed some more scrap wood and stoked the flame.

As the magic hour of midnight drew near, the group was carefully rationing their swigs, and Tito maintained the job of liquor cop.

"What time is it, Tito?"

"Eleven-thirty."

"Where are they," shouted California, showing his anxiety for midnight to arrive. In one hand, he held a small firecracker tight. In the other, a long match, the kind used for lighting a fireplace.

Tito grinned. "They'll be here. How long you been hording that match, California?"

"Fourth. Fourth of July."

"Damn. That's a long stick."

"Not a stick. It's a fucking match, stupid."

"Okay, California. A match. Sorry." He looked a few yards away where Detroit continued his staring vigil, tapping his helmet with the rifle clip and now focused toward downtown where the Twin Towers once stood. Tito walked over and put his hand on his shoulder. "Excited?"

The man nodded. Tito reached over and pulled a pigeon feather from his beard. "You look real good tonight, Detroit. Real good."

Detroit nodded, his stare unchanged.

"You warm enough? The fire's right over there."

Another nod.

"Okay." As Tito started to walk away, Detroit mumbled, "Ya gonna read to us tonight?"

Tito turned back. "You bet, Detroit. There's a new war in the Middle East, and Texas still can't keep the border secure. You like those kind of stories, don't you?"

"Favorite," he mumbled, and tapped his helmet with the magazine again.

Tito paused a moment, turned his collar up, nodded and turned back to the excited group. "Hey you guys, save some celebration for the gong. Utah, you got the gong set up?"

"All set."

Ohio ran to the side. "Hey... God damn it. I hear'm"

Everybody stopped in their tracks, ears tuned to the north. Nobody took a breath, then, the telltale battery operated lanterns atop each carriage came into view around the corner with the accompanying *clippity-clop, clippity-clop* of the horses. Back lit by the city, the riders' silhouettes came into view as the steaming hot breath of the steeds proudly led the way. "Fit for a king's palace," said Ohio. He started running toward the caravan, yelling, "Over here! Over here!"

Tito greeted Teach and the other carriage men. After getting everyone situated and paper cups topped off, they toasted in the New Year, and then Tito sat down, pulled out newspaper clippings and started organizing the *history read of 2006*, a Manhattan Bridge New Year's ritual for the past ten years. This was a time when Tito gathered his thoughts on where the world was coming from and going, if anywhere. It was a time when his homeless friends and the carriage drivers would hotly debate the direction that the following year would take. But this year seemed different. Not even Tito with all his worldly understanding knew what unexpected conclusions would arise from the past year's insanity. It had, after all, been a year when both Iran and Korea threatened the world with nuclear power and weapons; Iraq had continued its four year tribal tradition of blood letting; Afghanistan had maintained the status quo; Bin Laden remained the phantom of the mountains; and Israel and Lebanon perpetuated their decades old land fight with a thirty day war that left many more civilians than military dead. He especially found the thwarted airline bombings out of Heathrow disturbing.

The *in your face wars* notwithstanding, for Tito, arresting twenty-one major players in the plot was only another reminder of how few in number it could take to bring the world to its knees. As he

544

prepared to start his pre-midnight read, he raised his eyes in thought, catching sight of the oil barrel holding firm the fire's ten-foot-high flames. His all-encompassing question was: *would there be another year to gather beneath the bridge, or did 2006 portend a rapidly approaching ashes to ashes, dust to dust state of existence?* He looked around at the homeless enjoying the camaraderie of the carriage drivers and thought of the world's college graduates who would soon perpetuate all the wrongs in the world, some knowingly, others ignorantly, but all threatening the basic simplicity and innocence before him. *Where had it all gone?*

Chapter 85

Flames of another sort rose delicately from candles casting just enough light to maintain a sense of romance, albeit tenuous. For Samara, the surprise visit from Derek was only an interlude, a much needed break for both of them, but one that in her heart she knew was temporary, at best. Nevertheless, she was determined to fully enjoy however long it could last. She had been here before. She had convinced him to be forthwith and determined with the love of his art, and she had taught herself to accept the agony and isolation that accompanied such a love. At least, so she thought.

Tonight's surprise visit had caught her totally off guard. Feeling like a school girl, her emotions gushing forth unguarded, she dropped all her pre-programmed plans and thoughts for a celebration with Tina, including all her carefully designed defenses for lonely nights and the rationalizations associated with the masochistic torture of being in love with an artist. Most importantly, she was willingly setting herself up for the inevitable pain of his leaving. The only question was when. These were the ruminations swirling through her mind as she watched him carefully remove the cork from the second bottle of champagne and refill her flute. Midnight had come and gone with the traditional embraces, and now as one o'clock approached, they waited for Tina and Theo to return with more champagne. Samara posed the question. "Why did you do this?"

"Why did I do what?"

"Come so unexpectedly"

"Are you afraid of surprises?" and he raised his glass for a toast. "Here's to never avoiding surprises."

She raised her glass and paused. "I don't know if I want to toast that. Could be painful as hell later."

He gently took the hand holding the flute and guided it to a quiet *clink.* "You know how scared I was tonight?"

"Scared? You don't seem scared to me."

Feigning a bad commercial, he said, "Without the protection of my triple-the-hours underarm deodorant, I could have never knocked on her door. Remember, TTH Deodorant is made for scared-i-cats... just like you."

Samara lifted his arm. "Really?"

Derek crossed his heart.

"Don't believe you."

"Ask Theo," said Derek. "He thought it was stupid to not just take my key and let myself in."

"So, why didn't you? It's your loft."

Derek paused. "It used to be *our* loft. Why do you say that?"

She smiled and leaned across kissing him on the cheek before walking to the window. She looked below to the street. "Think they decided to leave us here?"

"You haven't answered the question."

Samara turned and walked back to the couch. "Maybe just a woman's way of protecting herself."

"Oh, c'mon, Samara. Since when did you start feeling you needed to protect yourself? Have you forgotten it was me that insisted you move in?"

"It's still your loft and you could ask me to leave anytime."

"Jesus, where's all this coming from. It's New Year's Eve. I've traveled all the way from the island to just be with you. Does that sound like someone ready to ask you to leave. I don't get you." He rose and walked to the stereo. "Feel like some Bartok?"

"Bartok?" she asked incredulously.

"Just to accompany your morbid mood."

"Who said anything morbid?"

"Maybe some Shostakovich while we pick our weapons."

As he thumbed through the CD's, Samara came up from behind and wrapped her arms around him. "I'm sorry. I'm acting like an insecure child. Put on some Botti trumpet."

"So, just because you're a shrink, insecurity is ruled out?" said Derek, as he placed the CD in the tray and "My Romance" filled the room.

As he crossed his arms over hers, she slid around and faced him, holding her fix on his eyes for several moments. "I missed you."

"I was wondering if you did."

"All the time."

"You're still not jealous over Echo, are you?"

"Of course."

"Of course?"

"Of course."

He nodded. "Guess that's settled."

"It's not easy to share you, even with a… even with Echo."

"Go ahead and say it. With an Enigma. You said it before. It's okay. I can handle being a nut. Got a shrink in the family to take care of me."

Samara took his hand and walked him to the far corner where their bed stood. "Are you relaxed?" she asked.

Derek chuckled. "Am I relaxed?" He gestured toward the front door. "The extra champagne will be here any minute."

"Theo's a big boy, and Tina's a *very* big girl."

"Of course he is, they are," said Derek as she sat him down on the bed.

"And they won't mind the fact that you and I are retired to the bedroom to have a heart to heart," offered Samara.

"Heart to heart. We're going to have a heart to heart now?"

"You always express yourself best when staring up at your monster mobile."

"Why do you insist on calling it a monster?"

"Because you insist on calling it 'Family'."

"It's sentimental."

"It's a monster."

"It's…" He looked up at the iron and marble apparition he had affectionately named when the world around him seemed overwhelming.

"Look at it. Jesus. Derek. It was a long haul just getting used to sleeping under a half ton of marble. Let me call it a monster, okay?"

"It's… let's just leave it at that."

"Good." She pushed him over and lay beside him.

Derek took another sip of champagne, placed the flute on the bedside table, and crossed his hands over his chest, a favorite position in preparing for 'heart to heart' talks.

She glanced at his position and smiled. "C'mon. You know how crossed-hands remind me of death."

"Death? Ah, what if that's why I do it? My Family…your monster. Both right above us. Death. Interesting."

"You never expressed it like that," said Samara, her voice turning serious.

"Nope."

"All the times I told you it bothered me, you never said a word." She uncrossed his hands and placed them to his side. She laid back and looked up at the carved boulder suspended by iron cables. "Your crossed hands…not a sign you don't trust the cables, is it?"

"Not as long as the inspectors give it the high five every year. C'mon. The meter's running. You wanted a heart-to-heart, remember?"

At that moment, the front door flew open and Theo and Tina stumbled in. "Happy New Year," bellowed Theo, followed by drunken laughter.

"And may all your dreams come true," giggled Tina.

Samara sat up. "So much for *our* talking. Sounds like they made a stop at..."

"Hey you two. Hiding in the bedroom again?" Theo laughed as he made his way to the kitchen, bumping into the table and couch. The sound of a serious 'plop' on the couch signaled Tina hadn't made it that far.

Derek rolled out and stood up, grinning back at Samara. "Trying to tell me you think they made a stop at Stefano's?"

Samara stood up, straightened her dress and said, "Could be wrong."

"But you're not." He walked toward the other side of the loft. "Hey, Theo! Feeling pretty good, are you?"

Theo squinted and tried to unwind the wire covering of the cork. "You'd think they never wanted you to drink this stuff."

Derek stepped up. "Need some help?"

"Nope. Anytime I get the chance to open some Dom, don't need any help."

And so for the next hour, the topic of conversation was the virtue of real cork versus the synthetics now in vogue for wine and champagne, complete with the ethereal ramifications of fake cork. Once the two new bottles were nearly empty, as if on cue, Theo passed out, his head comfortably landing on the lap of Tina, who had never fully recovered from her 'plop.'

Samara and Derek weaved their way back to the bed amid the continued sounds of Chris Botti's trumpet and allowed their remaining swallows of champagne to administer the final knockout punch. As they both lay with hands crossed, staring above them with eyelids holding desperately onto consciousness, Derek mumbled, "What was the 'heart to heart' supposed to tell me?"

"That I love you."

"Nice."

"Yeah."

***

As carriage drivers and the homeless rag soldiers, enjoined at the shoulders by hands that had known survival perhaps like few others circled the sparking embers of the oil can, Tito to the music of

Zorba, stomped the joyous dance on the weathered ground with arms outstretched. Horses held their position on the circle, nostrils spewing the vaporous excitement of something they didn't understand, but attentive to. As Tito's friends crossed their legs, kicked high and wailed their defiance at the bridge's super-structure above them, he sang out, "Where shall the new year take us, my friends? Where shall it take us?"

Among the hysteria that only a joyful release once a year might claim came the utterances of "Love!" "Peace!" "A few more dollars in the bank!" followed by raucous laughter and spirited chanting of years past in unison, "Imagine, imagine, imagine.!"

For Tito, all he really had to offer his friends of the night was that which no one could take away from him, or them—that which frightened many, but made this group's existence tolerable—*the adventure of imagination.* Tito was their leader—a man of the night on a park bench—a man of the day in a lecture hall.

Many readers of his bestsellers and regular newspaper stories asked, "What drives such a man? What binds such a man to the likes of such inordinate friends? Defiance? Stubbornness? Determination?" For Tito, *labels, classification and acceptance* were words that bore little meaning. For him, the quest for understanding was all that was important, regardless of the struggle. Remaining alone and independent was all that mattered to him, excepting nights like this.

As Tito—the little man who was an outcast to many, a friend to few, and an inspiration to most of his varied students—continued dancing and expounding "headlines of the year," his voice painted a sad and poetic world capable of hope as well as despair, choice or subservience, love or hate.

He slowly brought his presentation to a halt. Walking the circle, he thanked everyone for coming, giving each of his friends personal encouragement for what lay ahead. As the cheap wine and bathtub hooch continued to be poured down the gullets of the proud, the stubborn, and at times, the profane, Tito pulled from the seams of his coat handfuls of oats to feed the steeds. He smiled gently into the cold night as he continued making sure everyone was instilled with hope for how they could exist another year on the streets of New York.

As dawn approached on that first day of the new year, frigid whispers of homeless huddled beneath the bridge under cardboard and worn blankets drifted upward into the ever-present noise of overhead traffic rumbling to and from Manhattan. *Just another day*, thought Tito as he trudged away, jotting notes on his cuff.

He stepped aboard an uptown subway to Washington Heights, and noticed the overhead advertisement promoting February Sweeps Week on OST:

Don't miss the Special Finalist's Week of *So You Want To Be An Evangelist*.
America's Biggest Surprise Hit Of The New Season.

He shook his head. *Just another day.*

CHAPTER 86

The streets of Mykonos—better described by tourists as "sidewalks"—allow both foot and small golf cart sized vehicles to move about *carefully*. With doorways to shops, apartments and hotels opening directly onto the cobblestone walkways, moving about as a pedestrian can be a risk. Stoppard strode along gingerly, his New York Yankees hat, brightly colored shirt, cargo shorts and sneakers allowing him to blend in with the meager tourists this time of year. The fact that a winter cruise ship had just docked for the morning, made the atmosphere a bit more challenging as passengers moved quickly from shop to shop—many being closed for the off season—spending as much as they could as fast as they could. By noon, his leisure stroll in and out of the narrow alleys met head on with the tourist frenzy, and he decided to wander over to the old amphitheater to rest and drink a beer. Much as he hated to admit it, the harbored guilt over tensions rising between him and Siebert— compounded by vanity preventing him from admitting the *sweeps* threat was making him crazy—forced him inward, a place he didn't like at times. This was one such time.

As he walked into the stage area, he was surprised to see a young Greek holding a tattered book, sitting on one of the stones used for décor and/or stage pieces while rehearsing a Hamlet soliloquy. Unseen by the young man, Stoppard slipped into one of the rows of stone seats and watched. With the humdrum of the village life behind him and only the words of the great Bard filling the quiet space, he found himself remembering his own teen days as an aspiring actor. Not many knew this about him, and he preferred it that way.

He smiled as he listened to the boy stumble through the eloquence of the master, and recalled his own experience auditioning at his high school in Brooklyn for the role of a brilliant child prodigy in mathematics. On the day of auditions, he stopped at his father's bar, picked up the two dollars he needed to get his suit out of the cleaners, and rushed home to change. Arriving at the audition fifteen minutes late was bad enough, but when he saw the other boys trying out for the part were wearing jeans and t-shirts, he felt even more embarrassed. As he read for the part—the other boys all sitting in the back of the auditorium, hidden by the shadows, with only their snide snickering heard—Stoppard had the beginning of his worst experience in humiliation. It would stick with him the rest of his life. He had gone into the casting feeling confident, his straight A grades for five years running in mathematics made him think he was a natural for the part of an intelligent son. But, knowing something about what made a character tick was only the beginning of getting the part. He read with a stilted delivery. The boy was supposed to have a casual attitude toward his genius. Stoppard saw him as a straight, by-the-book academic. When it came time to read with a girl, he froze completely. Girls and casual attitudes were out of his realm of experience. He was by today's standards, a "nerd." For Stoppard, a good time was more akin to SAT finals. Books, chess, and classical music occupied any down time he had from studies, and he'd only had but two dates up to that point, both proving disastrous.

After the audition, he yanked off his tie and sulked off to the bus stop. While waiting, one of the girls from the auditions walked up and sat.

"Which one you ride?" she asked.

"Number twenty three."

"Me too. Where do you get off?"

"Bushwick and Graham."

"I'm Bushwick and Graham too. Never seen you before on the bus."

"Me neither. I mean, haven't seen you either."

The girl stood up as the bus approached, stepped on, paid her fare, and stepped to the back where there were several empty seats. She sat down as Stoppard paid and walked down the aisle. He sat across the aisle. She patted the seat next to hers. Stoppard felt nervous and hesitated. She patted again. He moved over to the seat next to her.

Katherine Thompson was an attractive girl and therefore Stoppard couldn't figure out why she was flirting with him. He was, after all, the subject of many a joke at school because he scored high on everything and disappeared whenever there was a social event. Even though he excelled in math and science, his pariah status didn't even afford the opportunity to turn down dummies and cheats willing to pay for answers to tests. Even they passed him up, just like the girls.

"You going to the prom?" Katherine asked.

"What?"

"The prom. You have a date?"

"I... when is it?"

She giggled. "You don't know when the prom is?"

"I've been busy."

She patted his hand that rested on his knee. "You should never be *that* busy."

Stoppard wanted to take his hand away, but he knew that would signal he was fearful or didn't like her. He was afraid to admit it, but that bus ride home was one he didn't want to see end.

As he sat at his desk that night studying, his eye kept wandering to the telephone. She had given him her number before they got off the bus, because the one thing they had in common was that they both loved chess, and she didn't hesitate telling him she hoped he'd call sometime. Although he didn't call that night, and he didn't ask her to the prom, six months later, the nerd from math class and the girl who got the lead in the play were going steady. Six months after that, they were studying for their SATs together and listing the colleges they were both interested in going to.

Less than six months later, Katherine Thompson moved to Europe when her father was reassigned in his work. He never saw her again.

Stoppard smiled to himself as the boy in the arena stood, and in the midst of his soliloquy, turned and spotted him. The boy felt so embarrassed, he started to run out. Stoppard stood up and told the boy he was doing so well. "Please," he said. "Finish it. I was getting into it. Please."

The boy, sensing the sincerity, continued, and Stoppard listened to the terrible performance for another hour, all the while, revisiting the days and months that had been his last serious experience with a female. From that point on, he had become a one-night-stand man. No attachments. No commitments. No violating the sanctity represented with his most precious possession, The Katherine memory.

***

Theatre of another sort was not without its own problems. Nathan Wollzak jerked open the frozen door of his trailer and quickly blew into his cupped hands. The fifteen-degree temperature, coupled with the twenty miles per hour wind, made for an uncomfortable trip to his Long Island City storage lot for the big rig.

Looking inside, he shuffled through the costumes and props, finally stopping at a file cabinet. He fingered through the folders and pulled one labeled *The Simon Greco Show - Echo Life Phone/Mailing List.*

***

In another part of town, Sol Berkowitz pushed forth his tempting ploy, and worked tirelessly to pull the necessary financing together to pay for some special TV, radio and Web broadcasting.

***

From behind a glass door carrying the sign, "Temporary Office Space for Lease," busy actors sat at rickety card tables and stacked boxes, some manning phones, others on laptops, all addressing a copy of the *Echo Life Phone/Mailing List.* Either through the e-mail or phone, the message was clear; David was taking on Goliath and Echo Life would be giving the behemoth of the media world a major run for its money. The sound of phone messages filled the room, mixed with the cacophony of keyboard transmission of e-mails.

"This is a message for Lawrence Wiley: This is Echo Life calling to alert you to a special night on..."

"... Wednesday, February twenty-first..."

"... Echo Life will be broadcasting a Sweeps Special via Web..."

"... and our cable channel. Please note ..."

"...your calendar for that night 7PM to 7AM."

"...Artists from around the world will be on..."

"... interactive mode to answer your questions and to..."

"... interact with your own work for those who wish to feed their video into the web."

The following weeks proved that not only was the colony of charter members still intact, in spite of the partial hiatus from the island, but subscribers were forming blogs and discussion groups on Facebook and other social networking sites all over the web. Subscribers were alerting others to the benefits of Echo Life as an alternative use of their surfing time.

Berkowitz e-mailed database results to all his investors.

Derek enjoyed a mini-celebration each night after the day's results and more than once thanked Theo for making the original suggestion on New Year's Day.

Stoppard spent more time on the ship, exchanging e-mails and phone calls with his office, than on the islands. This was not how he had anticipated his vacation.

Word reached Pierre as well. Tanika, in keeping him aware of the progress on the building, slipped in the developing news that had now become part of nightly entertainment shows as well as *regular* news updates on various network programs; even catching the attention of C-Span's Books and Authors show. It seemed that media, as usual, liked a new and fresh attention-grabber story relating to the frenzy of effort on the part of the networks and cable companies during *sweeps*. The angle this year was the Echo story and its daily growing numbers now flashing on a Times Square digital billboard, showing minute-by-minute subscriber increases. Echo Life was the darling of the air and cable waves. *Goliath* watched as *David* became bigger and bigger.

***

Sol sat across from Theo and Derek, slowly turning the decorative umbrella in his pink drink. "These things could kill ya, you know."

"Just don't eat the Marciano cherry," whispered Theo, smiling.

Derek gave Theo a look. "You have a *habit* of interrupting, you know! Sol? Please continue."

"Had to be said. What do you call this drink again?"

"Pink Thing," answered Theo.

"Very original."

"Basic."

"Neighborhood Chinese," chimed in Derek, "Now, as we were discussing, we need more digital storage and satellite time. You yourself said you doubted we'd make it for a week. Now you're getting thousands of terabytes upon terabytes of video material you've no place to store, and..."

"There's only so much money, Derek. You want a twelve-hour broadcast. Satellite time isn't cheap, even with the ginormous discounts we've been getting."

"Just another problem. How do we solve it?"

"How do we solve it? Money. Plain and simple."

"How much?" asked Theo.

Sol paused a moment. "If this rate of submission keeps pouring in, I'd say another hundred."

"As in thousand?" asked Theo.

Sol gave him an *obviously* look.

"And the investors?" said Derek.

"They drew the line last week. No more."

"What if we stopped the Times Square billboard."

"Can't."

"Contract?"

"Could cancel on that, but don't even suggest it to the investors. That stupid sign is bragging rights to too many of them. Half are my *Angels,* you know. They find their way into the Broadway area weekly. They love being part of that sign. The theatre marquees are like after dinner mints compared to that sign. Not an option."

"Aren't the subscriptions big enough?" asked Theo.

"They're taking care of this frenzy of expenses past two weeks. That's all."

Derek pondered and took another bite of his fried rice.

"Isn't that stuff cold?" grimaced Sol.

"So?" said Derek.

Sol shook his head. "I hope for both our sakes this crazy idea of yours works so we can eat hot meals, in hot places, you know?"

"Talk to Theo. His idea."

Theo held up his hand. "I heard you. I heard you. We only have ten days to worry."

"I'm worrying right now," said Sol. "Hundred grand at this late date is going to be tough."

"That's why you're a producer, remember?" said Derek between bites.

"Could always rob a bank," quipped Theo.

"Brilliant, Theo. Absolutely brilliant," said Derek.

"Or..." Sol appeared suddenly wired.

"You didn't eat that cherry, did you Sol?" said Theo with a grin.

"Would you bend to have a sponsor," said Sol, gripped with excitement.

"You know that's not an..."

"Don't say it, Derek. Maybe now it's the only option we've got."

"No."

"What if we just book-ended the night with an institutional kind of uninterrupted twelve hours 'brought to you by,' bla, bla, bla. You know, Public Television style."

"Who the hell would pay a hundred thousand for that?"

"Somebody who hates OST more than me," said Sol. He jumped up. "Order me another one of those *pink things*. I gotta make a call."

CHAPTER 87

Pierre walked the red light district for days. Still no Azura. After the initial few days of what appeared to be a more relaxed woman, her abrupt disappearance was both a disappointment and a worry. She was continually concerned about money, and that probably meant she was working the streets again. Between his concern for *her* and worry over Stan's understanding of love all of a sudden bound up in adolescent possession and jealousy, Pierre found

Kingston less and less fulfilling. He was, after all, there for the sole purpose of relaxing and waiting out the building renovation.

As Pierre and Stan sat at a sidewalk café and stared blankly at the tourists wandering aimlessly between one curio shop to the next, Stan pulled restlessly at his humidity soaked shirt and eyed Pierre's half-full glass of warm beer. "You gonna drink that?"

"Probably," said Pierre as he watched a middle-aged husband and wife stagger out of a tourist shirt shop, both giggling about their classless t-shirts of palm trees and ocean in glorious souvenir colors. "Now, that's ugly, mon."

Stan, undaunted, asked again. "You sure you're gonna drink that? I know how you hate warm beer."

"And how you love it. Okay, here." He pushed the beer across to Stan and continued to watch the couple—obviously a pair of enthusiastic early drinkers—bump into other tourists, all the while bellowing about their coup. "These things would have cost us twice...twice as much...how much did we pay?"

The wife patted him on his sunburned pate. "Not so much we can't continue celebrating with another pitcher of Sangria. Okay, cheeky boo?"

"What are we celebrating?"

"Sunday, stupid."

"Oh. Okay."

Pierre lit a cigarette and listened to Stan urge out a succession of annoying belches. "Do you have to do that?" complained Pierre.

"Just a natural progression of nature, ol' buddy."

"You know, Stan..." Pierre stood up. "You're getting on my nerves."

Stan's expression immediately changed. "Hey...I'm sorry. Just having some fun."

"Well, try something different. Let's take a walk."

Stan shook his head sheepishly. "Another walk? You sure? It's hot. You just get depressed with walks."

"Only in the red light area. Let's try the docks."

***

Luke propped the broom up in the corner and stepped outside the shack to empty the dustpan. He watched as a moped sped by. Hanging from the driver's shoulder was the all too familiar *special delivery* bag that residents along *shack row* knew was a drug delivery satchel. The scooter made its way to the end of the street and turned into the neighborhood where the resident gang turf began.

Trafficking to and from the neighborhood was common knowledge among the police and politicians, but corrupt economics dictated silence by all—including Luke. Having to see Azura suffer her habit drove him to the brink of informant many times. He was always stopped by his own rationale—who could he tell it to that wasn't on the take? Each temptation was tempered by the realization that he would also be blowing the whistle on Azura, and that would send him back into his role as Mister Mom for the children.

A piece of scrap tin screwed to the wall of boards and fiberglass roofing carried the calendar that he marked off each day. He was now down to just eighty-four days until Azura would be up before the parole board. Just eighty-four days to get her clean.

"Daddy," yelled Banya. "Can we have papaya today?"

Luke hugged her shoulder. "This week-end. I promise. I'll sell some of my catch on Saturday."

Banya jumped with joy. "Oh, goodie. Papaya!"

"Now go help your brothers lay out the bones. Go on now," he said while gently pushing her toward the backyard.

Luke checked the room. The floor was swept; beds were made; Banya and LeeLee's mirror was polished; and Frankel and Ned's hockey sticks were hanging properly on the wall. It was time for his mid-day tea.

In the back yard, the four children worked silently sorting sun-dried fish bones and various other bone remnants from sea creatures. Lining the junk-tin walls of their twelve by twelve back yard were pieces of weathered plywood, each with a collage in progress using fish skeletons and beaded vertebrae from larger catches. A small pushcart stood in the corner with several finished works standing on edge, their five-dollar price tag marked plainly on affixed pieces of paper.

On another stretch of shore, some half-mile away, Pierre and Stan stood before a stretched out pile of hurricane thrashed boats of all sizes. Fifty yards away, what was left of a pier stood mostly submerged. "Damn. Now that's some mess," said Stan as he walked closer to the boats. "Hurricane do all this?"

"September, 2004, I suspect. Ivan. Did a lot of damage."

"Why don't they clean it up?"

"We're on the fishing side of the island. Only the poor live here. Opposite shore of this cove is where Azura lives." He turned around, and like Azura's neighborhood, wall-to-wall shacks lined the street stretching two or three blocks toward the city.

"And?" said Stan.

"And what?"

"You're staring at this mess like it's something sacred. You've got that look in your eye."

Pierre reached in his pocket, retrieving a folded piece of paper and a pencil. "What kind of look would that be?" He squatted down and began hurriedly sketching the surroundings.

Stan shook his head. "That same kind of look when we walked into your condemned building. We're not gettin' *that look* again, are we?"

"We? Hardly. I might be thinking something, but you don't need to use 'we.'"

Stan peeked at the sketch. Pierre had spread the boats out in a more or less straight line bordering the shore. Stan looked out at the boats piled on each other. "Must be ten or twenty of them."

"More like twenty or thirty."

Stan looked back at the sketch. "What are you thinking?"

"Just a day dream."

***

On the *luxury hotel* side of the island, just off shore, a small yacht rolled gently with the tide, as its mooring line tugged at the anchor. On the bow, the brass word, *Cha-Cha* reflected the calm waters. A dinghy stood idling in the water. Its black helmsperson with a shaven head proudly displaying a swastika tattoo, held the outboard motor at the ready, his flexed biceps covered in snake art glistening with sweat. From above, two more shaved heads emerged from the cabin…both naked. Behind them, Azura, her dress ripped, staggered and held onto one of them. Both her cheeks displayed fresh bruises. "Hun…hundred," she mumbled, her eyes and tongue desperate to function properly.

"Do I look like I've got money?" laughed the larger of the two naked men. He turned to the other man. "Do I look like I got money, nigga?"

"Maybe up your ass, mon" laughed the other.

The first man leaned over and parted his cheeks. "Take a look 'pretty one.' See any money there?"

Azura wavered, but held on to the other man. "You said…a…hun…hundred"

The second man rose back up laughing. "That was before you slammed Pappy's best horse between those beautiful toes of yours every night you be our guest."

Both laughed.

Azura tried to straighten up and took a limp swing at him. "You gave me that."

Pappy grabbed her by the throat; his eyes bulged like rivets of fire. "Don't give nothin', bitch." He pushed her to the other man and nodded. "Set her down gently, Beebee. Don't want to mess up that beautiful ass of hers."

Beebee lifted her over the edge to the outstretched arms of the Neanderthal captain of the dinghy and dropped her.

"Thanks for the week, Az. Looking forward to the next time," yelled Pappy above the screech of the outboard as it pointed toward the pier in the distance. Sprawled and passed out, spread-eagle in the bottom of the boat, Azura never knew when the boat stopped midway, and she was once again propped up and raped.

***

Later that night, while Stan remained in deep sleep, a knock at the door awakened Pierre to a woman he'd never seen before. In her hand, a simple note, written in broken child-like letters. "Please help me. Azura." He stuffed the bloodstained note into his pants as he quickly dressed and followed the woman into the night—expecting the worst.

***

One of Sol's least favorite ways to spend an evening was courtside at a Knicks game. Not that he had anything against the Knicks, or basketball in general, but as a producer, there were better places to rack up points with an investor—unless his name was Nate John. He didn't know which he hated most, sitting through a basketball game, or introducing his high school classmate to uninformed sophisticates. Nate John certainly wasn't a name from royalty, nor was it the most sophisticated name on the Forbes list, but for those few in the know, Nate John was one of the youngest self-made billionaires in the country. And, he owed it all to the collapse of the dotcom industry in the fall of 2001.

Starting a dotcom company, just when everyone was tanking, proved to be one of those ideas that found the right place at the right time. As hundreds of start-up companies scrambled to sell off inventories of computers and software, Nate John offered to take the new equipment off their hands in bulk at reasonable prices, thus saving many companies the aggravation and lengthy task of selling everything at auction or piece-meal. His inventive contracts to rent substantial numbers of computers to foreign-based entrepreneurs trying to get in on the beginning of the *outsourcing* industry proved to be a bonanza.

From there, he graduated into the more lucrative chip industry and now enjoyed all the luxuries afforded the rich, including three-season boxes for the Knicks games. The only regret—or perhaps grudge—he held against OST was their cancelling, or "screwing" as he called it. After spending over a year negotiating and exchanging non-disclosure documents, The John Company was to supply an integral memory component for OST computers around the world. Then a dispute over patent and intellectual property rights started to be debated by the lawyers, who continued getting rich over what was already a fourteen-month battle.

As the Knicks scored again, Nate shot up out of his posh kidskin covered lounge chair and high-fived the other four guests in the box, turning to Sol with, "How much did you say?"

Sol, who hated doing business in the presence of strangers, whispered, "Hundred twenty-five...just to be sure."

Nate patted him on the leg and blurted out, "You don't have to be shy about a hundred twenty-five thousand dollars. It's just money." He turned back to the sixty-inch plasma screen and craned his neck from screen to live action below with, "Fucking refs. Fucking refs!" He stood up. "Shit! I need a drink."

Sol casually pointed to the two scotches he hadn't touched. "You have a couple."

"Oh, damn. So I do." He took a quick gulp, grabbed his gullet and feigned a struggle to get it down, bringing laughs from the other guests, and turned back to Sol. "I lost on your last two shows. That why you haven't been back to see me?

Sol smiled sheepishly and nodded. "Broadway is fickle."

"Tell me about it. What's my chances of making any profit on this deal?"

"Zero and none, probably."

"And what's my chances of fucking Stoppard?"

"His bank account, very little. His ego, probably a lot."

"Where do I sign?"

***

The electrician pulled his flashlight from between the ancient walls of Pierre's building and began inspecting another part of the 2nd floor wall with his scanner, the digital read-out showing nothing but zeros. "Not here, Pete," he yelled back across the room.

"Well, keep on lookin' 'cause ain't no way we're gonna break the wall to find it," said Pete, a foreman specially chosen for the job. He adjusted his hard hat and walked with the building inspector to the other side where recessed ceiling lamps poured museum quality light across the depiction of the immigrants lined up on Ellis Island, circa 1900.

The inspector craned his neck backwards, and made a couple of notes. "Same wattage?"

"Yeah. Same on all of them."

The inspector made another note. "You know, until this is corrected, I'm gonna have to hold back signing off."

Pete wiped his sweaty hands on his pants. "I know. Just doin' your job." He kicked a piece of scrap wood. "Wouldn't be so bad if we could touch these Goddamn walls. Shit. Whoever heard of making a painting out of a condemned building in the first place?"

The inspector ripped off a carbon of his report and handed it to Pete as he closed the report book. "Welcome to New York. I wouldn't complain too hard, though. From what I read down at the Buildings Offices, you got enough pay on this contract to put up a building of your own. Have a nice day."

Pete wandered back over to the electrician. "Gotta find that fucking box, Sam. Blueprint says it's in one of these walls."

"God knows how many unlicensed renovations might have been done. That blueprint could be useless."

"Hey, it's tradition, Pete. What are ya gonna do when over the years building department looks the other way for a few bucks under the table?"

Sam continued to scan. "Even if we find it, how we gonna access? Divine intervention?"

"Got no time for jokes, Sam. We got three weeks to finish this piece of shit. You got anymore of that Tylenol stuff?"

Chapter 88

February sweeps were around the corner. Stoppard had spent the better part of the past two weeks barricaded in his suite viewing programs for the all-critical week. He was down to his last DVD and he knew it was the most important. SO YOU WANT TO BE AN EVANGELIST held the key to the whole week. He was confident he was presenting the best show of the year plus several repeats throughout the week for the "Evangelist junkies" as he called them. He knew America was still basically right wing when it came to viewing habits. Polls had proved that. While his competitors were sure their titillation shows would swing the balance their way, Stoppard held that he had known the taste of the people for the past fifteen years, and he wasn't about to challenge a good thing. The cliché, "If it ain't broke, don't fix it" still held true for network television. His line up—given the modifications he had ordered—was primed and ready. February sweeps were his. He brought the Evangelist on screen and turned to Siebert. "This is the Thursday show. We're going to run a new season's highlights on Friday, plus the repeats, so this is the big one."

The screen filled with the show's opening montage of worshipers from every denomination entering their various places of worship.

This montage was followed by a Voice-Over, proffering the virtues of charity work by various ministries, which then dissolved into the giant stage where the amphitheater setting was filled to capacity with the audience—hooting and hollering as if an ancient gladiator battle was about to take place. The stone-carved lectern in the middle of the arena suggested nothing short of a Greek oratory, as the host came in from one side, and the hostess from the other—both wearing tasteful, quasi-modern togas. SO YOU WANT BE AN EVANGELIST? They both bellowed into the microphones. The crowd yelled back, YES! The show was on. For Stoppard, the question of whether the gimmick would ever burn out began to taunt him. As he watched his hit show, there was a moment, ever so short, when he saw his reflection on the face of the screen. *This is what I'm all about. Give 'em what they want?*

The Greek Isles are hypnotic, especially in the off-season when the landscape and people can be seen unencumbered by the frenzy to please tourists. Yes, some of the flowers aren't changed mid-day, as in the summer; yes much of the charm of quaint fishing boats bobbing on the shoreline isn't apparent—their famous Mediterranean blue colors soaking up the hot Aegean sun absent—but the calm following the exodus of shop owners off spending their hard earned tourist money in some other corner of the world, left the island tranquil and different, just the way Siebert liked it.

As he strolled the alleys—a habit he had created in a few short weeks, given the tension on the boat—he came upon a shop that had always been closed. Today, however, the front door was wide open and the owner was inside sorting photographs. Located at the far end of the village shops, the little studio overlooked the bay and was the perfect setting for sunsets, often resulting in framed photo sales. Tourists would pass the photographs of previous sunsets and pull out their plastic and hard cash, giving into the impulse to please their romantic interest. "Hello?" said Siebert.

The man, dressed in gypsy-like peasant attire, rose up from his kneeling position and extended his hand. He seemed genuinely pleased to see an English-speaking stroller. "Good afternoon. What can I help you with?"

"Oh, nothing, really. Just having my daily walk. Hadn't seen your shop open before. *Are* you open?"

"Well, no, not really. Just taking inventory. I have another store in Hawaii that I run during the winter. Just needed some additional inventory. Strange how warm skies and water appear the same to a lot of people. You'd be amazed at how well Greek Isle photos sell in

Hawaii. You sure I can't help you? I'd be happy to sell you a photo, you know."

Siebert smiled. "Perhaps. You just continue. I'll take a few minutes to look around, if you don't mind."

"Never turn away a browser, my father used to always say. Make yourself at home. Oh, by the way, my name's Arnold," as he extended his hand.

Shaking, he said, "Thank you. Siebert."

"Don't be shy now. Got a lot of pictures here," urged Arnold, as he went back to sorting.

Siebert walked the tight aisles, thumbing through the matted photos, and listening to the opera music playing softly in the background. "You like opera?"

"Second passion, next to photography. You?"

"I really don't know much about it, but find myself always listening when its played. My boss likes it."

"Here on vacation?"

"Yes."

"Most people come in the summer, of course, but winter in the islands can be quite surprising."

"I've noticed. Different, not seeing a tourist location flooded with traffic."

"How long have you been here?"

"Couple of weeks now. Looking to sail in a couple of days for Santorini, and then on to the Riviera."

"Whoa. Out of my league."

"Mine too. I'm a guest."

"Need a photographer?"

Siebert chuckled. "No. Don't think so. He gets quite enough photos taken of him in America."

"My apologies. It's obvious that the kind of people who can sail from the states to here and on up to the Riviera are probably public enough."

"That might be an understatement."

"Okay. You've piqued the curiosity of an old die-hard photojournalist. Somebody I might know?"

"Perhaps."

"But, you're sworn to secrecy, right? Privacy, and all that."

"Oh, it's not that bad." He smiled. "I'm sure you understand privacy, yes?"

"Absolutely," said Arnold, crossing his heart.

"Stoppard Denning," said Siebert.

Arnold stopped his inventory counting and raised his head. "There's only one Stoppard Denning."

"True."

"My god. I actually did a piece on him many years ago before I packed it in and moved here."

"You're kidding, of course."

"Not at all. Ninety...ninety-one...just at the time of his purchase of the publishing and recording companies. My God. He may have never read it. It was for a foreign publication." Arnold turned quickly to the rear of his shop. "I actually believe it's still...hold a minute." He scrambled to the rear, and after a few moments of file cabinets being opened and shut, reappeared with a magazine in his hand. "God. Can't believe it. Stoppard Denning here on the island." He pointed at the date. "September 23, 1992. Not far off."

Siebert smiled once again and looked at the cover photo of Stoppard. "Been a few years. He's still as handsome, but that hair line is receding."

Arnold laughed. "Something we can't control very easily without Photoshop, eh?"

Siebert stopped his thumbing through prints and pulled one out. "This is extraordinary."

Arnold leaned over. "Oh, you've picked a new one. Took that last week during a wicked storm. Like a tempest, it was. Rare to see a seagull around here, you know. In the summer, some. But winter. They're usually long gone further south. That one held onto the edge of the boat, feathers blown back the wrong way, pieces of rubble blowing all around her, then...look up here. See this crazy W, kind of a double-wedge in the sky? Can't figure that out. Almost looks like a flock in formation, doesn't it?"

Siebert pulled the picture closer. "Yes. Yes, it does."

By late afternoon, Stoppard was exhausted from watching alternate endings to shows and especially the alternate endings to *Evangelist*. His speakerphone conversation to Terrence Kensington said it all.

"...and I don't care who decided. I'm not in the mood to fire anyone, so just tell me. You or that..."

"Sanders," said Terrance from the other end.

"What? Mister Sanders?"

"It was a consensus of both of us, actually."

"Okay. I get it. *Both* of you thought seeing this *bimbette*-winner's speech praising the world including Allah was PC?"

"You don't want the Muslin community all over us, do you? And Stoppard, she's hardly a bimbette. She's Pastor Latisha from Tennessee."

"Yeah. How in hell did she win with a title like that? Don't tell me. Tits and ass. Like I said, I know a bimbette when I see it. Now, you edited four other versions. Why this one with the heavy Muslim reference that will have everyone, including the radicals, making a lot of noise?"

"It's a good *cashing in.*"

"Cashing in, my ass. It sucks. Dump it. I give enough to the Islamic Faith to do all the pacifying we need. Use the one with the general thanks...the version with the cursory praises to Muslims, Jews, Protestants, and Catholics will do fine, thank you very much. You can throw in a crawl at the end thanking all religions. Just make sure you don't miss any important ones. And for God's sake, show the losers doing something besides lifting their arms praising God. Not even hard-core *religious righters* are gonna buy that. A little sadness and regret goes a long way in a stupid contest, you know? This is a reality show, remember? Show some."

He turned off the speakerphone and grabbed his glass. Empty, he filled it to the top with scotch and switched the TV over to a satellite channel more to his liking—The Colbert Report. *Now, there's a show that's got the pulse of the nation thumping. Why can't my guys come up with one like that? Talk about giving them what they want.*

"Stop?" said Siebert, poking his head through the door of the game room. "May I come in?"

Stoppard leaned back from the snooker table and stretched his back. "Why not? Can't beat the table anyway. Got to get those cushions redone. What's up? Have a good walk?" He looked at his watch. "My. Must have been. It's five."

Siebert stepped in. "Actually, I had a most delightful walk. I ran into someone I thought you might enjoy meeting."

Stoppard craned his neck, but no one was behind Siebert.

"No, he's in the reading room. I thought it best to check first. You've been rather private lately."

Stoppard laid his cue down and said, "Christ, if *you* think he's someone I should meet, I'm sure I should. You know how I hate strangers."

"Well, once you meet him, I don't think he'll feel like a stranger. I'll bring him up."

"Let's meet on the sun deck. Looks to be a great sunset, and you know how I like my drink with a sunset. Uh, Siebert, sorry for all the...well...I can be ornery at times. Has nothing to do with you. Just wanted you to know. "

"Duly noted, sir…Stop. Sorry. Sun deck it is. Meet you there."
Siebert stepped out and closed the door.

Stoppard, feeling no pain, opened his eyes wide and looked at
the snooker table again. The black was all that was left. Hugging
the cushion in the corner, it was a sure scratch shot, unless—

He picked up the cue, chalked, aimed, took a deep breath, let it
out slowly, then—leaned back up. He glared at his hands as they
shook. "Nonsense." He said it again. "You hear me, nonsense."
Still shaking, he leaned down. "Fucking sweeps!" The English spun
the ball off the far cushion, sent it to the opposite, straightened out
and slowly, like a putt on the 18th hole for the championship, rolled
back up, kissed the black, and sent it into the pocket. He stared a
moment or two, stepped to the rack, replaced his cue, and looked
once more at the table, then at his hands. They trembled a moment,
then stopped. His face relaxed. He picked up his glass, then on
second thought, placed it back on the table. *Siebert has a guest.*
Hosting time. Wine perhaps.

Siebert made the preliminary introduction, pointing out the fact
that Arnold had done a story on Stoppard and was a part-time expat
enjoying the simple life of just taking the photos he wanted.

Within an hour, following sunset and some fine wine, Stoppard
and Arnold were laughing together and fingering through the dozen
or so *collector's* LPs. "Siebert thought you might like to hear some of
these old LPs, so I brought them along."

"Well, Siebert never does anything arbitrarily, so there must be a
reason."

With half the crew ashore for a free night, including the stewards,
Siebert was doing the pouring of their third dusty bottle of vintage red
when he heard Stoppard exclaim, "Oh, my God!" He looked at
Siebert, then lifted a dog-eared cover from the stack. "My father
used to have this. I can't believe it. Jussi Bjorling. The 1938
recording of La Boheme. Metropolitan, wasn't it?"

"You know your opera."

"My father knew his opera. But this man…this voice. May I play
it? I mean, can you put it on the turntable?" Stoppard almost fell
over himself moving to the adjoining indoor recreation and screening
suite. A press of a button, and teak wood cabinet doors
automatically opened and displayed to Arnold a state of the art array
of sound equipment, plus an old turntable.

"This…this is really something," said Arnold as he carefully
placed the LP on the turntable.

"You don't mind if I copy it onto a CD, do you?" asked Stoppard.

"Be my guest. Such a wonderful array of equipment."

"Just show. It's the speakers that count," said Stoppard.

Arnold looked around. "Hidden?"

"The speakers?" Stoppard just smiled and gestured open arms. "Anywhere and everywhere on the ship." The needle dropped and Bjorling's voice filled the boat, the shoreline and probably half of Mikonos with *Che Gelida Manina.* The men all sat down on plush deck chairs, drank their wine and smoked Churchills, as the remaining purple hazed skies darkened, and the tenor with the golden voice filled the waning hours with sounds that brought memories Stoppard hadn't visited in a long time.

It wasn't until they sat down and waited for dinner to be served that Arnold took from his satchel a gift-wrapped photo and placed it on Stoppard's plate. "Siebert was insistent on buying this for you, but I refused any money. With all the souvenir shops closed, this will at least give you something to remember the trip by and serve as a token of my appreciation for the visit."

"Well, thank you. You as well, Siebert. Trying to bat a thousand for the day?"

Siebert nodded toward the gift. Stoppard pulled the wrapping away and held his gaze for a long time on the gull. "Interesting picture."

"You like it? asked Arnold.

"Little bastard looks determined."

Arnold leaned over and took another look. "Yes. You were here as well, I believe, during that stormy period last week?"

"Yeah. Yeah, we were here."

"What do you think of this thing up here?" He pointed to the double-wedge shape in the sky. "Couldn't figure that out. Just a lucky moment, I guess. Almost looks like a flock of birds, but...can't really tell. Don't see many birds, and especially seagulls 'round here in the winter, you know. Never around during storms like that one. What got me was, if they were birds, how the hell could they manage to hold that formation with those winds. Freaky, you know? Your friend Siebert has a special eye for the unusual."

Stoppard glanced at Siebert. "Yeah. Unusual. Freaky. Ever see anything like that, Siebert?"

"Only once sir. But there weren't any winds."

"Yeah. No winds. Just freaky gulls in a double wedge like that," said Stoppard. He laid the picture aside. "Well, at least this time, they didn't shit on the boat. Remember the car that day?"

Siebert nodded. "Guess they know now you don't do it on the boss, right?"

"Got that right," Stoppard said with determination.

After a moment of silence, Arnold smiled and shrugged.

The meal arrived.

CHAPTER 89

It had been over twelve hours since Pierre was awakened with the note. Now, still sitting in the chair beside her bed, he held Azura's hand as she continued to sleep off the drugs and ordeal. He pondered as he stared at the small photos of her children pinned to the wall of her tiny room. *What's wrong with the world?* Here was the broken spirit of a beautiful soul. Here was a mother who dearly loved her children, who had made a wrong turn and was faced with losing them. Her swollen and cut face was a testimony to the out-of-control greed and violence that was everywhere. It was times like these, the thinking times, that Pierre also pondered the *inordinate* feelings he carried around.

It was different dealing with the regular emotions of feeling compassion and love for someone like Azura. Wanting to be open and visible with his love for Stan, well, that was fraught with many problems. New York allowed him to be more open, but he was in Jamaica, where there was no tolerance for even a hint of being gay. He didn't know it had gotten so bad, and he knew Stan was suffering not only from jealousy over Azura, but just having to watch himself carefully for fear of being *outted*. The two of them didn't dare make any kind of physical contact with each other in public, no expression of affection, not even a little horseplay, which was so much a part of their personalities. He thought back to their near-death experience.

He had been painting a large floor in a renovated office building when Stan walked in with a delivery of paint. Stan, the muscular guy who could heft three five-gallon cans of paint on each arm, walk four flights of stairs, and deliver it with a smile said, "Hi. Paint delivery."

He placed the cans down carefully and whipped out an invoice. "Gotta sign here."

Pierre took the paper, and just as he finished—that's when it happened. The floor and walls shook and the next thing they knew, they were falling through to the next floor. The good part, he remembered, was landing on stacks of fiberglass insulation. The bad part was the upper floor also landing on the same fiberglass and pinning the two of them. He remembered blacking out as he hit the padding and waking several minutes later with his head in Stan's lap. Buried in the rubble, with only the twisted remains of two metal desks forming a protective covering as well as holding the rest of the debris away, Pierre found himself being rocked by this stranger who was covered in blood and dust and missing half his skull. In spite of his injuries, and delirious with shock, Stan kept rocking, "Gonna be alright, Momma. Gonna be alright, Momma." Over and over again he repeated it like a mantra.

About the same time Pierre realized his left arm must be broken and his legs were pinned, voices could be heard somewhere beyond the darkness of what Pierre thought was the end. "Hey," screamed the panic voice, "Anybody in here. Hello! Anybody hurt?"

Stan kept on rocking; stroking Pierre's head and starting to pray short sentences in between the mantra. "Bless me father, for I have sinned... Gonna be alright Momma... gonna be alright." Somewhere in there, he remembered Stan stopping the chanting and looking down at him. "Gonna be alright."

Like Pierre told shrink after shrink, "I don't know why, 'cause I love my mother very much, but at that moment I felt loved like never before, and I never want to lose it." No amount of therapy was successful in talking him out of it. That was years ago.

He let his heavy eyelids look down at the sleeping hand he was holding. He knew what it was like to be loved when all hope seemed to be gone. It was a good feeling to be reliving the experience again. He closed his eyes and grabbed some much-needed sleep.

Some time later, he woke and looked at Azura as she coughed and turned. Gradually, her eyes opened. She slowly and painfully rolled her shoulders toward the wall, then toward him. Her eyes welled up. "Gonna be alright. Gonna be alright," said Pierre.

Even the act of sipping soup was difficult for her, as the swelling hadn't gone down from the roughing up. Her eyes were still telltale with the effects of heroin, but she was trying—trying very hard. "Want some water?" asked Pierre.

"Thith is fane," she answered, as if her lips were numb and unresponsive. She gripped his hand, and he knew she was feeling stronger. The question was would she be strong enough to continue living with what had just happened to her.

***

"That's the choice we have to make, Stan. Plain and simple. I'm not going to just up and leave her like this...alone in her coffin-like room." Pierre stepped away from the mirror and wiped the shaving cream from his chin.

"What's wrong with her old man? What the hell's he doing to take care of her?" asked Stan as he got up and walked to the window looking out onto the street below.

"I haven't gotten that far yet."

Stan whipped around. "What do you mean you haven't got that far?"

"She's scared of something. Not sure if it's him or what?"

"Scared?"

"Yeah, you remember what that's like don't you? 'Everything gonna be alright, Mamma'."

Stan looked away and sat. "Well, *three* of us in this hotel room sure as hell isn't the answer."

"I'll have to stay at her room then. She can't even feed herself yet."

"Fuck it," said Stan.

Pierre buttoned his shirt and grabbed his keys and shaving kit. "Okay. Fuck it. Got to do what's right, Stan." He calmly opened the door and left, shutting it quietly.

Stan kicked the bed, kicked the dresser, then shot out the door. "Pierre?" he yelled down the stairwell. "Pierre, you can bring her here."

He didn't hear any answer, and as he returned to the room, Mister Grooder opened his door. "Having a nice day, Mister Stan?"

Stan shook his head. "Not a good question."

***

Traditionally, January in New York brings on inordinate anxieties and depressions like no other month. For Samara, it was pretty much as it had been. Getting closer to finishing the symphony, however, brought on more time pressure. She was grateful for the few patients that took extended Christmas vacations, allowing the extra hours to be spent at the piano. She arrived home on Tuesday after a short day of sessions to find Derek dangling from the top of the loft by his harness with a plumbers wrench. "Hello. Anything I can help with?" she quipped.

Derek looked down and laughed. "Yeah. Would you mind *spotting* me on this... just in case it breaks loose?"

"Very funny." She walked to her closet and started changing into comfortable clothes. "What are you doing up there?"

"Haven't checked these cables since the last building inspection. Close to a year now. Can't be too careful, you know."

Samara looked at the bed, the rock, the cables holding it and Derek. "You have a point. So, I'm in the mood for Greek tonight. Okay with you?"

"Long as you shower."

"You're disgusting. You know that, don't you?"

"Couldn't resist. You have to be a little off-color once in a while to test the water."

Samara stepped back over the bed and looked up. "Testing, are we?"

"You know a man needs to get laid when he starts tinkering around the house, honey."

"Oh, listen to Mister Domestic."

"Don't change the subject."

"You tinker. I'll work the piano. You pick up the food. I'll prepare dessert."

Derek looked down from his hang. "Dessert? You playin' with me?"

"You playin' with me?"

Derek smiled. "Nope. Deal. Hey, could you turn that light up this way?"

Samara turned the floor lamp toward his perch. "Do me a favor. As you walk the beams back to civilization, would you give them a dusting, as long as you're in the 'tinkering' mood."

"Taking advantage of me now?"

"Later."

She walked to the piano, lifted a page of manuscript and began rewriting a section of the 2nd movement. Derek locked the wrench onto the two-inch nuts and gave each one a secure twist. They didn't budge.

Following dinner, it was hours before Samara put down her pen. She took one last look at her night's work and loudly sighed. "God! Is it really worth it?"

From the other side of the loft, she heard Derek. "I've been asking myself that question, too."

Surprised, she turned and peered into the darkness. "You still up?"

"Yeah. Me, myself, and I are still up."

Samara walked over to the sitting area and found Derek lying on the couch, staring up at the ceiling. She glanced up. "You were so quiet."

"He's going to do whatever he needs to do."

"He?" asked Samara.

"Stoppard."

"You were in such a good mood earlier. Is it coffee time?"

"Only if you're willing to battle my demons with me."

She walked to the kitchen. "Demons are part of our landscape aren't they?"

"Should have been squashed by now."

"Takes time."

"We've had time," grumbled Derek.

She put the kettle on and prepared the coffee-press. "We? This is still about Stoppard, isn't it?"

"About everything."

She walked back to the couch while the water heated up. There on the coffee table she noticed a small mound of clay molded into an abstract. Derek had begun his preliminary process for a new work. She sat down in the lounge chair opposite his prone body. His eyes were still fixed on the ceiling. "You haven't made *me* one of your demons, have you?"

"Insecurity doesn't fit you."

She nodded. "Just checking."

"Have you spoken to Pierre lately?"

"Pierre? Funny you ask. He called me today from Jamaica."

"Is he alright?" Derek asked.

"He's having some problems, but he'll be alright."

"Does he know the renovation is behind?"

"I didn't even know. Where'd you hear that?"

"His mother called here today looking for you. I gave her your office number."

"I didn't get a call."

"When she asked who was speaking, I told her, and she unloaded about the wiring being so fouled up they didn't know if they could bring it up to code without tearing down Pierre's walls."

Samara pondered a moment. "Pierre's got enough on his mind. Hope she doesn't call him."

"I asked her not to."

"Good. That's not what he needs right now."

"*His* problems...I don't suppose you can talk about them."

Samara rose as the teakettle began to whistle. "You know the rules."

"Yes. Yes I do." He sat up, looked at the sculpture, downed the remaining swallow of Jack in his glass, and slumped back. "Make it strong."

"Gonna be a long one, eh?"

"Hope so. Demons love the *dream state* 'bout as much as I hate it."

"You still have to sleep."

She returned with a tray of cups and a carafe of coffee. "I understand they hate Turkish coffee."

"Oh, Christ. So do I. You didn't..." said Derek.

"We'll try and fool them. Pressed triple Espressos should send them away."

Derek broke a half smile. "And the Gargoyles they rode in on."

"Them too." She poured. "I'm sorry you're... whatever it is."

"You know what it is. Echo Life is holding on by a thread and Stoppard knows that for sure."

" Of course. He's known for a long time," said Samara.

"And he knows we can hold on for just so long."

"And he can hold on forever. Is that what's got you depressed?"

He sipped the coffee. "Damn. Hair-on-your-tongue time."

"Want some cream?"

"No. Just play witch doctor and drip a ring around us. Sure to send them running."

"Maybe I should send a gift carafe to Stoppard."

"He runs from nothing."

"He does have that reputation, doesn't he?"

"So, I've got this Echo Life thing, the Stoppard thing, and this being patient for the spring thing so I can finish the *rock. And, there's us.*"

"We'll survive."

"I don't just want to 'survive.' Been doing that most of my life."

"We're fine. Let's talk about the *other* things."

He sipped his coffee again, keeping his eyes fixed on hers. " 'Is it worth it?' Why did you mumble that a few minutes ago?"

Samara paused. "Lot of work, a symphony. You?"

"Me?"

"You uttered pretty much the same, remember?"

"Yeah. I did. I don't know. Life was a lot easier when it was just me, my sculpture and you."

Samara poured another cup of coffee. "Yet, an easier life doesn't always guarantee rewards, does it?"

Derek reached out with his cup. As she topped his up, he said, "How do you do it?"

"Do what?"

"Keep yourself sane?"

"Deal with enough of the troubled, and you kind of build an immunity." She laughed. "That's a bad joke. My apologies."

"You sit at that piano for hours and sometimes I only hear one or two notes being worked. Oh, maybe half dozen, but it's so far removed from what I hear in a concert hall. That would drive me nuts. Working that way, I mean."

"You do the same, Derek. Pierre, Lanagra, Nathan, Hensky, all of them. I watched you chisel and polish the Ode inch by inch for over a year. Remember? That's what kept you sane. Reworking the details to arrive at the essence. It's the same for me. Note by note. Interestingly, we're drawn to people for inspiration. And conversely, those same people unknowingly drive us back into isolation to work the inspiration out. Just an artist's plight, maybe."

"Maybe. If people are so important to us, why do we retreat into our isolated space?"

"You just heard the answer to that. Incidentally, I learned all about isolated inspiration from watching you."

"Me? I'm the one with the diseased head."

"Whoever said you had a diseased head?"

"Pathological. That's what you said."

"Only in the context of describing your obsessive nature for perfection and getting to the root of everything...the essence. You're not, nor have you ever been, 'diseased.' I don't choose to live with a diseased mind."

"Splitting hairs again, is that it? The fine line separating me from the really troubled?"

"The fine line separating neurotics from psychotics is a better way to say it," said Samara with a professional tinge to her voice.

"And by which definition have I lost contact with reality? Echo is hardly real, you know."

"We're back to you, again. Thought you wanted out from that."

"So I'm back. So I'm back," the frustration obvious in his voice.

"And trying to be impossible again. Look, Echo is a label you gave a part of your imagination that was uncomfortable. By giving it a name, you lifted it from the abstract and concretized it into a narrative. Narratives are always easier to live with. I know. I do it myself. My sound—thing, well, it existed a long time before I gave it a label. And now, the name is indispensable." She smiled and seemed totally at ease.

"Common sense? You trying to bring me to..."

"Yes," she said, taking his hand and placing it on her face. "Common sense dictates I'm here for you. Always have been. We're just regular people with a bigger itch than most. Tired?"

"I don't know."

"I'll bet I can get you there."

Derek smiled. "You're something else."

"For you."

He stood and lifted her into his arms. She nestled her head against his neck as he carried her to their bed. He laid her down and she whispered, "Take your time. I don't have any patients till noon."

"You may have to cancel that first one...or two."

As he kissed her, she looked up at *The Family* and whispered, "Call me crazy, but I love you." She moved her gaze to Derek. "*All* of you."

He opened his eyes, and after a few moments, she returned her focus to the marble creation above. Gently lifting her blouse, he laid his head on her breasts. "Thank you," he uttered quietly.

She wrapped her arms tighter around his shoulders as his hand found its way to her thigh. "You know what that does to me," she whispered back.

"Yes."

Their whispers became absorbed into sounds of breath dancing across the exploration of yet another layer of their synergy, another venture into the innocence of renewed discovery.

It was some time later when both became aware their naked bodies were ready to pass into another dimension. It had been a long time since either had been willing to let go of everything and just be completely in the moment. With both libido and heart satiated, neither wished to concede to the reality that dawn would bring. Derek gazed at his sleeping lover as his weary body betrayed him once more. Mind demons of the night wanted back in. He squeezed his heavy eyelids shut. For how long, he didn't know, but for the time being, there was only blackness... that place he called his *safe room*.

CHAPTER 90

At the shoreline of hurricane-ravaged boats and other debris, Pierre sat on the stack of old tires and he laid down a rainbow of colors to the sketch on his pad. "With my own money, Azura," said Pierre, as he tried to reason with her while she paced back and forth. Stan stood a few yards away, still aloof, pitching rocks into the surf as Pierre continued. "All I need is a meeting with one or two hotels. The rest will want in if it works."

"The city has to approve it," said Azura.

"Why wouldn't they? It saves them the clean up costs— something they're probably never going to do anyway—and gives them some taxes. Making a work of art out of a salvage pile of hurricane wreckage is a lot cheaper for them than eventually having to haul it all away."

Azura continued pacing, looking at the pile of crushed boats from Ivan that littered the shore for several hundred yards.

He laid his pad and colored pencils down and stood up. "Azura, look, I'm not going to be the only one worrying about your children. Do you understand? If you want me to forget it, I will. But, you just tell me how you're going to show that parole board you're clean and able to support the children. They're going to ask about a job. Go on, tell me."

"Luke is doing a good job."

"Oh, and loving it. Right? What do you do if he all of a sudden gets fed up and leaves?"

Azura said nothing.

"Azura, you get yourself to that clinic and dry out, I'll get you a living started. Aside from beaches and resorts, this island of Jamaica isn't exactly a sightseer's delight, you know. Hotel owners will flip being able to offer their guests a trip to... what should we call it? *Works of the Sea*? How about, *Ivan's Wrath*, or... "

A familiar motorscooter cruised by and left Azura's neighborhood, the driver's shoulder bag containing what they both knew was another drug delivery going somewhere.

"But what if it doesn't work? Then you've worked for nothing," said Azura.

"Hey, Stan and I need something to do. Okay? Waiting for the New York renovation is driving us both crazy." He took her by the shoulders. "Azura, I've only got a few weeks left here. You did something for me a long time ago, let me try and repay you. If it doesn't pull the tourists, well, nothing lost except some paint. I can afford that big loss. Please."

"Do you really think tourists will come to see painted garbage?"

"Painted debris. There is a difference."

"I think you're crazy sometimes."

"Get in line. I've got a whole string of doctors that agree."

***

A politician in Kingston thinks different than most politicians around the world. He's got a constituency that is *dead* poor. He's got gang warfare that has catapulted his city into the unenviable position of having a homicide rate ten times that of the United States. Extortion runs rampant with the gangs with shopkeepers cowering at the very mention of *protection*. He's got all the tourists and their money going to resorts on Montego Bay. He can only hope the local fishing is good enough to keep the residents fed and off his welfare list.

The 'He' in this case was Mister William Jones, Deputy Assistant Minister of Tourism for Jamaica. After hearing Pierre's idea, he welcomed him with open arms, falling all over himself trying to be helpful.

"What you have to offer may not take the place of souvenir packages of Blue Mountain coffee, but at worst, it will be a diversion for cloudy days," said Mister Jones. "How can we help?"

Pierre, who had arrived with apprehension and fear of rejection, was caught completely off guard. "Well, I guess...do I need a permit?"

"No problem. Any thing else?"

"Gangs."

"Yes. What about them?"

"What do you think?"

Mister Jones demeanor changed immediately. " We don't like to talk about that problem. You understand."

"But, I know they like to horde their turf and, well, I might be on someone's turf."

"I can supply you with an officer while you paint," he said coolly and matter-of-fact. "The shore belongs to the city."

"The city."

"Yes."

Pierre was feeling the awkwardness more than he wanted. "I don't mean to be a bother, but if I go to the hotels and try to get them to participate…"

"What do you mean, participate?"

"Well, in order for his to be of value, there's a need for some tourisism."

"No worry. I will make sure buses run daily to the site…assuming you perform up to your standard." His face lit up in a patronizing smile. "I did read all about you on the web, you know. You're quite the anticipation in New York. When does your building become ready?"

"Oh, thank you for asking. Was supposed to be in three weeks, but there's some wiring problems that will delay it a bit longer."

"Well, with the clock ticking, you'd better get started on the project, then. Any more questions?"

By the time Pierre had put the final touches on the colors, his drawings of the boat wreckage looked more like a Picasso rendering of a centipede than a blueprint for the next two weeks of work. Running off color copies at the tourist offices, he was ready to begin. Stan purchased 175 gallons of paint and over 200 brushes, buckets, rags and stir sticks. Needless to say, the owner of the paint store was ecstatic. After loading up the delivery truck he'd hired, Stan chuckled as the owner put a sign in the window, "gone fishing."

Back at the site, Azura brought several of her neighbors to help, promising to give them jobs when the project opened to the public. In preparation for the painting, Pierre walked the site one last time, pulling on any precarious looking pieces and making sure there weren't any obvious accidents waiting to happen.

Three days into the project, Pierre noticed questionable cars pass, their occupants huddled low in their seats with eyes that could cut through steel. The officer stood firm at the head of the street.

Within a week, the cars increased, double. Some of Azura's helpers having noticed the cruising routine, obviously became frightened and feigned heat, flu, monthly cramps, anything to excuse them from the completion of the project. With the loss of painters, Stan, Azura and Pierre had to do twice the work in half the time. The police officer maintained his watch.

By the end of the second week, after working fourteen-hour days, the major part of the project was all but completed. All that was left were the final touches that only Pierre could complete. As the three finished the last day of the week's work, they sat down for their customary beer and cigarette, inviting the officer over to share an end-of-the-day cold one. As they laughed and felt relieved they were all but finished, one of the familiar low riders cruised by. They didn't take too much notice, although, the officer stopped laughing abruptly and stood up. The car stopped at the end of the block, turned around, and slowly cruised back. It stopped across the street in front of them.

"Hey, mon. C'mere," said a raspy voice from the darkened car.

The police officer pointed to himself.

"Both of you. The brother mon in the dread locks. Him too. He boss mon, yes?"

The officer looked at Pierre and motioned they should do as they're told.

"Don't go, Pierre. Don't go. I know them. Don't go," whispered Azura.

"It's okay," said Pierre. "They're not going to do anything with the cop here."

"You don't know Kingston. Don't go."

Pierre patted her shoulder, rose and walked over with the officer.

Azura and Stan stood nervously smoking and drinking their beers. After about three minutes, the officer and Pierre returned as the car drove off.

"What did they say?" asked Stan.

Pierre looked at Azura. "You just got a partner. A Mister Yenni. I'm sorry."

"I knew it," she huffed. "Bastards."

"50% during the week. 60% on the weekends."

"Tell me that doesn't mean what I think it means," said Azura.

"You're probably thinking right. They claim this is their turf. As long as it makes them money, you can stay and they'll protect you from the other gangs—for a piece of the action."

Azura and Stan both looked to the officer. "Can they do that?"

"Miss, you know they can," said the officer.

"So much for working on city property," said Stan. "Mother fuckers."

Pierre started cleaning up. "It is what it is, Stan. At least they didn't graffiti the work."

The officer's eyes remained fixed on the stretch of debris that now bore the bright color mix of a cubist installation. "I will stay here tonight."

Pierre turned. "Why?"

The officer nodded. "I am tired. It is a long walk to my house." He smiled and sauntered over to the cornerstone fishing wreck, its main cabin still intact. As the officer disappeared into the cabin, Pierre hoped this wouldn't be the beginning of a nightly vigil.

The three cleaned up the site, and prepared to leave. They looked up and down the street. All was calm.

It was a long, silent walk home that night.

The next week was surprisingly without incident. Pierre's assigned police officer, Paul Kingly, wasn't getting much sleep, but at least his pride was well nourished. This was something special for a police officer to be involved in, he explained to Pierre, and as such, insisted on holding vigil each night for the following two weeks while the project's detail-painting was in progress. Pierre, in turn, insisted that the man go home and sleep during the day, as there really wasn't any need for security during daylight. The arrangement proved workable for both, and on day twenty, the detailed portion of the painting was finished. True to the drawings, it did indeed look like a centipede with a feeling of Dalí meets Picasso on a seashore.

With nothing more than cruise-by cars to concern themselves with, Paul took the day off. At 5 p.m., he returned, his face aglow with excitement. "Mister Pierre, my captain said I could stay on. I met with him today, and he said I could stay on as night watchman. I am so happy."

"Excellent," said Pierre. "We do have to get you a better chair to sit on, though."

"Old chair is fine."

"No, we'll find you something more comfortable. Don't you concern yourself."

With flyers delivered the previous week to hotels, and the Minister of Tourism putting in the good word, buses started arriving not just on the cloudy days, but everyday. Within two weeks, Azura had other neighbors of hers offering to set up small stalls on the peripheral ends of the work to sell drinks and sandwiches. That same week, word came that the newspaper coverage had spurred the interest of schools, and now school buses were bringing children to see the colorful work on the beach Pierre had finally named, "Ivan-Scape."

Pierre enjoyed seeing his work appreciated, even though he was in the midst of more anxiety over the renovations in Brooklyn. Tanika had informed him of an additional month needed to complete, so with the extra money she had sent him, he now waited out the delay, hopeful his "Ivan-Scape" would continue to enjoy success.

Chapter 91

It was February sweeps. From opposite sides of the world, Stoppard and Derek, along with the OST executives and Echo Life's members, read the daily results off the web. Of special concern was Thursday of the first week. When all was said and done, only on Thursday did OST's viewership suffer additional erosion as Echo Life's numbers went up, largely due to the draw Simon's weekly review and special "New Artist Video" created. Derek and Stoppard sensed a race to the finish line, so both men spent the following week analyzing numbers and determining the appropriate next move. Strategizing from his loft, Derek was cautiously optimistic. Stoppard, enjoying the Riviera life, remained concerned, but confident.

From The Katherine's sundeck, overlooking the picturesque harbor of Monaco, Stoppard found it hard to get too upset as he conferred with Kensington by phone. "So, we've both spent the past week going over the numbers, and they're not really that surprising," said Stoppard, as he continued his rationalization. "We knew our biggest audiences weren't included, so we'll just beef up the promotions and go for the full 210 markets end of February. Turrel realized some surprises on his Thursday night push, but that was in the urban centers. Plenty of city crazies there to wallow in his shit. The bigger numbers of the Deep South and Midwest—that's where OST's home churned butter is appreciated. And by the way, use ending #3 on *Evangelist* for the next week. All that gushy shit will push the buttons of most every market in the 3rd week. You got all that?"

"You got all that, Lenora?" parroted Kensington to his secretary.

"Writing as fast as I can, Mister Kensington."

"She got it, Stoppard. Now, can I ask you something?"

"Long as it's quick. Got lunch waiting and you know how impatient live lobsters can be." He laughed at his own joke while Kensington asked Lenora to leave the office. As the door shut—

"Stoppard, I don't want to spoil your vacation, but with sweeps goin', well, you've got to know that according to my sources, there's no less than six international newspapers and tabloids working an "in progress" story around the kid with the building in Brooklyn that Echo Life is pushing like hell on their broadcasts. You know, that Pierre guy."

"Yeah. I know about him. That building is old news."

"Yeah, well, the kid's stayin' alive. He's down in Jamaica and he has this crazy crashed-up boats project that's got today's AP wires hot as hell. Rumor is UNICEF's even talking to him about doing other projects in third world countries to help raise money. And get this, Sesame Street, you know, Grover and all, PBS says they want this Pierre guy for a special. Garbage seems to be 'in' again."

"Whoa. You're going too fast for me. What fuckin' crashed-boat thing you talking about?"

For the next twenty minutes, Kensington explained what was going on with Pierre and *Ivan-Scape,* emphasizing his concern that Echo Life would pick up on the action and exploit it to the hilt just like the building project. "You watch Greco still, right?"

"Been missing him on purpose lately."

"Well, I'd watch him *on purpose* over the next couple of weeks. Last night his 'you are all creative' slogan got cell phone calls and e-mails from places that barely know how to make paint, let alone throw it on something. Greco's been all over that building for weeks—cell phone videos, stills, even broadcast quality footage from somebody—and he's definitely going to promote this kid more because of this boat thing. Stoppard, this is the kind of oddball shit that draws curious audiences to that quirky Echo Life image like nothing else...curiosity that equates to numbers is not what we want right now. They've got the final weeks of sweeps to make a whole hell of lot of trouble."

"Okay. I hear you. Gotta go."

Stoppard hung up and pondered a moment, then wandered back to the aft of the boat where two white clad chefs stood over a boiling pot of water. Next to them was a small aquarium-like tank with lobsters lumbering through their last moments, unaware of their fate. "Boil the little fuckers," barked Stoppard as he sat next to Siebert, who was munching on a cracker with pâté and sipping champagne. "Not a good call, I gather."

Stoppard turned his attention from the boiling water as the lobsters were dropped. "How'd you guess?"

***

Derek sat with Theo and Sol, as the two of them wolfed down their corned beef and pastrami sandwiches. *"The Stage Door,"* said

Sol as he navigated his mouthful, "doesn't have as many customers anymore—too many fast foods, you know—but these sandwiches are still the monsters they've always been."

Theo wiped the mustard off his mouth. "You can say that again."

"Guys, I've got another appointment in twenty minutes, so let me say my piece and you two can finish those mountainous plates." He laid out some 3 X 5 photos. "Speaking to Pierre last night and getting these digital photos over the web says just one thing: we can benefit from each other. I want to make sure Greco does a piece nightly on this *Ivan-Scape*. That's for you to follow up on, Theo."

Theo nodded toward the pictures. "Good color."

Derek leaned in. "And Sol, you make sure all the investors get a copy of the pictures and whatever else might get put on the tube or radio or newspapers on this genius. God, this is so great for him. Word is he even has Sesame Street people talking to him about a Special. UNICEF's begging him to work with them as well. Take this idea to other poor countries and help them raise money..." He shook his head and smiled. "Not even Stoppard's money could buy this kind of awareness."

"Called publicity, Derek. The hard crass word is publicity," said Sol as he dipped in the jar for another pickle. "You know he's not used to this."

"I don't understand."

Sol chomped down on his pickle, pushed his plate away and leaned across the table. "Derek, Pierre has done a nice thing for that ugly part of town down there. You ever been to that dung heap? But, the place could start crawlin' with cameras and journalists from all over. Paparazzi will eat him alive. Aren't you worried what all this exposure will do? He's not even had his opening yet."

Derek picked up his photos and rose. "He'll do fine. Guy's got his head tacked on." As Derek left the table, Sol muttered to Theo, "For now."

***

As prophecy would have it, the short stretch of beach separating harbor waters from several blocks of poor residents thrived as the "Ivan-Scape" project brought busloads of tourists and schoolchildren to see the painted piles of rubble that one newspaper called "a rainbow from the storm."

It was February 16th, and after being open for business just ten days, Pierre was still giving guided tours along the stretch, answering questions about how he came up with the idea, his choice of colors and why he had left some parts in their rusted state. Azura and her neighborhood helpers continued selling tickets for $2.00; others sold drinks and sandwiches at the modest stalls dominating both ends of

582

the street. Officer Paul Kingly arrived for his night watch job an hour early each night so he could stride proudly up and down the street, tipping his hat and smiling to all, his boots always appearing as if they'd just been shined.

Friday's sundown came, and right on time, the old car with the shiny chrome wheels, carrying the daily pick up man, showed up at 9 PM sharp to collect the *partner's* take. As the teenager with the pure white baseball cap stood in front of Azura and counted the cash he had been given, Stan came up to Pierre and asked him to look at something. They walked halfway down the project and Stan led him up to a boat precariously teetering atop another. "How'd that happen?" asked Pierre.

"Must have been the winds last night. I think we better secure it so nobody gets hurt. Tomorrow's our biggest day, Pierre, and you know how they love to get up close and touch everything."

Pierre inspected it closer. "Yeah. Damn, I wanted to treat you guys to some shrimp tonight. Tell you what, you take Azura to Chi Chi's and I'll meet you there soon as I can. Kingly and I can secure this."

"You sure you don't need more help?"

"Nah. You take care of Azura. We'll get some boards from out back and wedge it. It'll be fine. Shouldn't take us but an hour. I'll see you there." Pierre turned up the street and yelled, "Hey, Kingly! Give me a hand, will ya?"

Stan leisurely walked the half-mile to Chi Chi's with Azura, entertaining her with jokes she barely understood, but enjoyed because of Stan's enthusiasm. "Then there's the one about the drunk who…"

Laughing to the point of tears over the last one, Azura held up her hand. "No, no. Not another one. We're here and I've got to calm my stomach down."

They went inside and Stan ordered them beers and peanuts while they waited.

Nightfall came quickly as clouds brought the remaining rays of the day to an abrupt ending earlier than usual. Pierre and Kingly hurried their pace, using two flashlights and lugging boards from the far end to right the boat. "How many we stuffed in there, already?" panted Kingly.

"More than I thought we'd need, that's for sure. Your fine sand doesn't like weight very much," said Pierre as he laid another stack of boards down and flashed his light into the crevice. "Shouldn't take many more. You hold this end up again, and…"

"Hey, friend, you look like you could use some help," came a voice in the darkness.

Pierre jumped, dropping the boards. "Damn. You scared me." He squinted. Silence. "Hello?" he said.

Kingly laid his stack down carefully and leaned back up. "Hello?"

"Hello, to you." came the unseen voice. "We offer our services."

Pierre and Kingly peered into the moonless night, seeing nothing. "I think we're fine. But thanks, anyway," said Pierre.

Without warning, there were half a dozen teenagers surrounding them, each looking more violent than the next. Shaved heads and facial tattoos dominated what little could be seen. Another man, much older, beard, and red cowboy hat, stepped into the circle. His chiseled face carried a lizard tattoo from his chin to his left ear. "I think we need to help you."

"No. We're fine. Really."

"You know who I am?"

"No," said Pierre, his voice beginning to show a quiver.

"He's Turk. Leader of STZ, down the beach in Azura's neighborhood," said Kingly.

"Very good, mon. You read your bulletin board down at the station, don't you?"

Kingly didn't answer.

"Don't you!" demanded Turk.

"Yes. Yes, Mister Turk."

"So you know why I'm here then, don't you?"

"No. Yes. I mean, not sure," said Kingly, his right hand inching it's way up to his holster.

"Uh, ah. Not a good idea."

Kingly relaxed his hand.

"Not very friendly to someone that wants to help you."

"Okay. Okay," said Pierre. "We're fine with you helping. We just need to get these boards..."

Turk laughed. "No, mon. Not that. Help you touch up."

"Touch up? I don't understand," said Pierre.

From behind and all around, Pierre heard the familiar sound of spray cans being shaken. "This is not good," mumbled Pierre.

"Oh, come now, Mister Haweisi. The one and only big man Haweisi doesn't like a little help touching up the rough edges of his FUCKING MONEY MACHINE!"

Turk took a step forward and planted his heel in the ground, his nose all but touching Pierre's, his voice back to its studied lethal charm. "Now, we want you to supervise, you understand. We're not here to cause any trouble, it's just after a long day, 'touchin' up' can be tiring, you know?"

"Please?" said Pierre, his voice now trembling.

Kingly took a step forward, "Hey, Mister Turk, why don't…"

BLAM! BLAM!

Kingly jettisoned back several yards, his stomach all but scattered about the sand.

"Oh, my God!" gasped Pierre as he started to run to his side, only to be held back by a hand with the grip of steel about his shoulder. His eyes slowly dropped to the muzzle of a very large gun now pointed at him. "Please. Oh, please."

The grip on his shoulder turned him toward the front of the project. "No worry, Mister Haweisi. I know you want us to help you now, right?"

"Yes," came the word he hoped might save him as Turk guided him around to the front. The sudden headlights of half a dozen cars lit up the expanse of art.

"See what you could have had if you partnered with the right people… night lights. Night tours. Even more money. But, no. You had to take the first offer made to you. Haven't you learned in America to not take the first offer? Always negotiate, Mister Haweisi. Always. Now, let's start over here, 'cause I've been told you messed up and used the wrong color. Right over here." He nudged Pierre with the gun and they stepped to the hull of a boat that Pierre had painted a deep charcoal. "You see," said Turk, "with this…" He motioned with his head and a teen boy with two spray cans rushed up. With a flick of his wrists, he laid down the gang's letters and numbers, "SKZ" and "999" in gold and purple.

"Hey, you know those are the colors of the Lakers? Don't ya?" said Turk.

"Yes," said Pierre as he fought back the tears that wanted to rush out.

"Well, they be ours too. We keep good company, hey Lil' Killa?"

The teen with the spray cans smiled, showing three teeth missing.

Turk pushed Pierre. "Now, you and me gonna walk back over here to mid-court, sit about where Mister Nicholson sits every week, with his dark shades and his fifty dollar cigars, and enjoy the show…Oh, excuse me, the 'touchup.' C-Dog there is gonna help him."

As another gang member swaggered up to the brightly colored work, Turk motioned and two fold up chairs were placed in front of one of the car's headlights. He then motioned for Pierre to sit down. By this point, the boys were rapidly placing their gang logo on every flat surface they could find. From one of the cars came the rumbling bass of a rap recording. "You know Aki Nawaz? He's the best, mon.

They ban his music on the radio, you know. Say he 'glamorizes' terror. You think he's glamorizin' terror, Mister Haweisi?"

Pierre shook his head. "No."

"Neither do I. Just don't understand people sometime." Turk pointed his gun. "Oh, look at that. Look at that. C-Dog's got inspired. He's puttin' your initials up there with his." Turk elbowed Pierre. "He likes you."

Impulse took over and Pierre lunged forward, running as fast as he could toward C-Dog. A shot rang out, kicking up the sand in front of Pierre. He hesitated only for a split second, and was off again. Two other gang members tackled him and pressed his throat to the ground with a chain. Pierre looked up into the eyes of what he imagined was his end, but nothing happened for several seconds. The horrific lyrics of the music continued and after a few moments, Turk stepped up into his vision. "Now, you shouldn't have done that, you know. Mister Nicholson never run out and mess with the players like that. Now, you obviously want to watch the rest up close, so..." he snapped his fingers and Pierre was taken by the arms and walked to the center of the work. "Please, Turk..."

"Mister Turk, to you."

"Mister Turk. What do you want?"

As Pierre was laid up against the hull of a boat, Turk walked up and stared in his eyes. "You think this is your territory? You think 'cause you're black you can just wander around and do what the fuck you want, mon?"

"No. I never..."

Turk snapped his fingers again and Pierre's arms were pulled up and to the side. Turk slowly shoved the gun into Pierre's mouth. Pierre's eyes flooded and he tried to shake his head, but it was no use. The gun was pressed hard and he was beginning to choke. Turk's eyes narrowed. "You should have negotiated."

Without warning, Pierre's eyes were blasted with a spray of purple paint. His mouth shot open, his screams were lost in the blast of the music, as he struggled in vain to free his arms. The screams grew louder.

"Ah, for Christ's sake. He's fuckin' up the music," growled Turk. One of the boys jumped forward and stuffed a do-rag in Pierre's mouth, while the other boys pulled his arms back further and secured them to the boat with rope. With another spray across his eyes, this time gold, the muffled primal screams caused the boys to cringe. Within moments, defenseless to the pain, his body slumped as he lost consciousness. With his head hanging limply to his chest, one of the boys asked, "Aren't you gonna do him?"

"Why?" sneered Turk. "He ain't never gonna be able to identify us. Makes a better point this way. C'mon. Finish up here and let's get us some *stuff.*"

The headlights beamed in on the graffiti covered surfaces of what was now just another scourge of defiance. Like a feeding frenzy, five more boys ran up with spray cans and swirled and splotched their initials and numbers everywhere. Turk walked back to his car and another boy opened the passenger door. He climbed in and sat down. As the music pounded the air, he gazed out at the surreal scene of art and violence. "Now, you guys don't own this no more, you understand. You aren't gonna collect nothing no more. You understand?" Turk slowly turned around and looked in the back seat at the tied and gagged man nodding with out let up, as his panicked eyes opened wider and wider. "Oh, stop that nodding. You look like an idiot, mon." Turk leaned over and adjusted the man's pure white baseball cap. "You wear your hat funny too, you know." He turned the hat side ways, so the spray painted SKZ was at the front, and 999 was at the back. "Walk proud, mother fucker. Walk proud." Turk turned back, nodded and the back door was flung open, the partner-man was pulled out and pushed into the headlights. As he tried to run, the other boys grabbed and beat him mercilessly, then stood him up and pointed him once again toward Ivan-Scape.

"Walk proud, mother fucker. Walk *really* proud," Turk repeated. The teens walked the gagged boy up to where Pierre still hung limp from the ropes, his entire body now a mere continuation of swirled graffiti running left to right across the hull of the boat.

Turk slumped down in his seat, lowered his cowboy hat down over his eyes and turned up the music.

BLAM! BLAM!

CHAPTER 63

As if the close-knit world around him had chosen to move in silence, the news of Pierre's ordeal left everyone speechless.

Stan and Azura sat limply in the waiting room of the local hospital.

Tanika sat expressionless in a corner of the café staring at the drawn shades and off-kilter CLOSED sign.

Derek and Samara slumped on the couch without emotion as they watched TV coverage.

Simon Greco, his show cancelled for the night, sat in his apartment drinking himself into a stupor.

Stoppard Denning, now halfway across the Atlantic aboard a chartered jet, sat with his head buried against the window, letting the pillow soak up the tears that uncontrollably flooded down his reflected image—an image unfamiliar to the man of iron will.

Under sedation in his hospital bed, Pierre's only thought, as he held his hands against his bandaged eyes was, *where are all these wonderful colors coming from?*

***

The Jamaican airport is not a LaGuardia or a Kennedy where private jets are seen as frequently as jumbo carriers. So, when a custom painted OST Cessna Citation jet came in for a landing, heads turned—especially the news photographers and TV crews who, with advance notice over the wires that Stoppard Denning was somehow involved with Pierre's family, planted themselves dead center tarmac. At twenty million, without the paint job, Stoppard's private penthouse in the sky guaranteed to not only accommodate his son's return flight to New York, but all of his closest friends as well.

As the silver and gold feat of engineering taxied to the tarmac, Stoppard stood up and addressed his guests. "Derek, I think he would appreciate hearing your voice first." He turned to Tanika. "You understand, don't you?"

Tanika patted Stoppard's hand. "Of course."

Derek looked to Samara. "If *you* think it right, of course," answered Derek. She nodded.

Stoppard turned to Samara. "You truly agree, don't you? I mean, you being the professional and all."

"I agree," said Samara. "Not to lessen the value of parental love here, but given the circumstances, it would probably mean a great deal to know Derek is here supporting him—yes."

"Theo," said Stoppard, "I know we've only exchanged a few words, but Derek confirmed you were pretty fundamental to Echo Life, and well...we all know Pierre's opinion of the project. That's why I asked you along. I hope that book of yours might have a bit about Pierre, so...well, I hope this is something you can use."

Theo nodded.

Stoppard turned back to Tanika. "You okay?"

Clutching the bouquet of roses firmly, she nodded, and with her free hand wiped her eyes that had been red since takeoff. "Sure."

***

The drive to the hospital was silent. Stoppard, having arranged a limousine for the journey, sat with a glass of scotch in one hand, and Tanika's hand in the other. Derek, Samara and Theo sat separated, each with an empty gaze out the windows.

***

"Pierre?" The nurse gently shook his shoulder. "Pierre?" He turned over. "Yes. Sorry. I was sleeping. Is that Polly?"

"The one and only. You comfortable?"

"Yes." He pressed his hands against the sheets. "All the comforts of home. Thank you."

"You know, you have some visitors arriving."

"Yes. My friend Stan said they'd be here today. It's still day, isn't it?"

"Little after four."

"Good. Well, guess it's touchy-feely time, right?"

"You got one hell of a sense of humor, you know that?"

"Better than not having anything at all." He patted her hand. "Oh, how about another one of those shots before they get here."

"Depends. You know you're limited to one every four hours."

"Last one was when?"

"12:30."

"Well, try and bend the rules if they get here before 4:30, okay. I'm sure they didn't come all this way to hear me moan and groan, right?"

"Right."

"How's the pasties?"

She chuckled and leaned down to check the gauze dressings on his eyes. "Don't think they're goin' anywhere."

"Oh, my glasses. Where are those Paparazzi specials?"

Polly lifted the super large dark glasses from the bed-stand. "Biggest damn glasses I ever see."

As he put them on, he said, "Trust Stan to find the unusual. There. How do I look?"

"Like a fly's head under a microscope."

"Perfect. Don't want to scare them with these bandages."

Polly shook her head and smiled as she double-checked the bouquets of flowers he had received, and left.

The relaxed expression around Pierre's lips quickly faded as his cheeks ballooned out with the grinding of his teeth.

***

Stan and Azura sat patiently sipping their espressos at the coffee shop opposite the MoBay Hope Medical Center and watched the sailboats on Montego Bay. Neither had slept much in the three days since the tragedy, but their energy was high in anticipation of Pierre's mother arriving. Calling and letting her know what had happened had been the hardest thing Stan could remember. He remembered there was a moment of silence, and then the whimpering like a child, escalating to wails of primal purging unlike anything he had ever heard. Amidst the horror she had just heard, she asked for his telephone number, thanked him and hung up. Within a few hours, he heard from Mister Denning, who after hearing details from Tanika, told Stan he was flying home from the Riviera and would fly Pierre's mother down on his private jet. He asked that Stan tell Pierre not to worry. He would arrange the best care money could buy.

Now, waiting for the arrival, Stan fidgeted with his napkin and lit his last cigarette, crushing the package and walking to the counter for another pack. Azura, still consumed by shock, remained lethargic and tentative.

Once the limousine arrived, Stan and Azura joined in the quiet introductions and handshakes. Then, the group made the walk into the hospital and up to the top floor, where Stoppard had arranged the largest room in the hospital for Pierre.

Pierre, sitting up in bed, listened for the door to open. The pain in his eyes was starting to reoccur. He hoped it was close to 4:30 as he turned to hear the sound of several tropical birds fluttering about outside on the windowsill. Nervous, he flipped on the TV, only to hear a local interview with a drug enforcement official running for Parliament rattling off crime statistics for the year. As the number of homicides, robberies, domestic violence and drug arrests were touted as the worst in Jamaican history, and how he was going to change it all, Pierre turned to another station, thinking, as he had since regaining consciousness days earlier, *why did this happen to me?*

Finally, the door squeaked open. "Polly?" asked Pierre.

"Will I do?" answered Derek.

"Derek?"

"And your mother, Stan, Azura, Dr. Jennings, Theo and Mister Denning, who got us all here."

"He reached out with both hands. "Stoppard? You arranged all this for me?" Tears seeped out the corners of the bandages.

Everyone had to stop and try to hold their breath for fear of losing their composure—especially Stoppard. He walked to Pierre's outstretched arm and took his hand. "They treating you okay?"

"Yes. Yes." He gripped Stoppard with both hands now. "Thank you for all this. The doctor told me you..."

"Shh," he uttered softly. "I just want you comfortable until we can get you back state-side and best-of-the-best."

Pierre nodded and reached out again. "Mom?"

Stepping forward and sitting on the bed next to him, Tanika said, "Yes, dear. I'm here. Brought you some flowers." He touched the rose buds one at a time. "They're beautiful. Very beautiful. Thank you." He turned to the center of the room. "Thank you all for coming. This wasn't expected. Wasn't expected at all." He turned in the direction of the door. "Stan?"

"Yeah, I'm here, buddy."

"Good. Wouldn't be a party without you."

Everyone nervously chuckled.

"Now," followed Pierre, "I'm due for some fun juice—that's morphine for the stiffs in the room—so give me a minute while I roust up Polly and get this soiree started."

As they left the room on Polly's entrance, Pierre grimaced and lifted his glasses. "I didn't scare them, did I?" The clear liquid seeping out the corners of the bandages brought tears to Polly's eyes as well. "No. I think you did good. Keep up that kind of acting, you might have a new career ahead of you." He slipped the glasses back on and leaned his head forward in mock housefly fashion. "I understand there isn't much casting for a fly under a microscope."

"Shut up, you, and turn over. I got an extra long needle this time."

He smiled. "Wonderful." A sudden shot of pain brought his shaky hand up to his temple. "Damn. Hurts. Bring it on."

***

After a long visit, the group left the hospital for the night, Tanika and Stoppard were told by the doctor that blinding of this kind takes its major pain toll in the first few days. The doctor said it should subside before the flight to New York and the continued care of a specialist. Stoppard was encouraged and per the doctor's recommendation, arranged for the transporting after another two days.

That night, as they all had dinner at the Montego Bay resort, Tanika continued to lament the tragedy while Stoppard. Determined to realize some justice, Stoppard kept his cell phone humming with calls to his attorney, the local police authorities, even the State Department. It wasn't in his nature to take what had happened lying down. He wanted blood. He was told by all, however, to stay calm or he risked stirring up more gang trouble. Racked with frustration, he did what he usually did when not getting what he wanted—spent money.

No one felt very resort-friendly so, following a lavish dinner, where plates were left half eaten, everyone retired to their suites— their bodies for the most part exhausted from the traveling and tension of the experience.

Stoppard asked if Stan and Azura would stay a bit longer before the limo was due to return them to their apartments. They agreed and Stoppard proceeded to ask many questions pertaining to the *Ivan-Scape.*

"Stan, I know we haven't been on the best of terms before, but I'm trying to put that all behind us now—I hope. Just to be perfectly honest, I'm still adjusting to… you know."

Stan nodded.

"But, I know how much you and Azura said the Ivan project meant to him, so let's just talk a minute about it, okay?"

"Sure," said Stan.

Azura nodded. "So what do you want to know?"

Stoppard leaned forward. "I don't intend on getting anybody killed, you understand. Enough people down here and in New York have told me to mind my own business, but I just want to know, for my own sake, who did this?"

"Mister Denning, " said Azura. "You know who I am, don't you?"

"Just a friend of Pierre's"

"I used to work at night."

"Yes. So?"

"I'm wasn't a convenience store employee."

"Oh. That kind of night work."

"Yes. Down here in Kingston, 'that kind of night work' is run and controlled by the gangs. I know them. They know me. If I tell you anything about who's responsible, I maybe don't live."

Stoppard paused a moment, taking in the seriousness of her expression. "I think I understand."

"Good. I want to do anything I can to help Pierre recover, but I can't help with any revenge. You understand."

Stoppard nodded. "I understand the project was making you a living, so I'm a little confused, given you had to used to a hell of lot more money with your night…"

"Work?. A hooker makes good money at night, Mister Denning. But that guarantees one doesn't stay clean, or get to see their kids very often."

"Got it. So, this 'day job' was an effort to change—jobs?"

"That's what Pierre was trying to do for me, yes."

"And you were okay with that? Can't imagine two dollar tickets, with half or more of the take going to some gang, much of a living."

She stayed silent.

Stoppard continued. "The police told me about what they knew—you know—about the arrangement and why the rival gang must have done the…"

"Mister Denning. I have four kids. I'm on parole. I'm a junkie and a hooker. The day job, and me getting clean, means I see my kids more than once every week. That's why Pierre was doing this. I did him a favor once. This project and my participation was his way of returning the favor. He insisted."

Stoppard nodded, taken aback. Thank you. I think I understand." He turned to Stan. "Stan, *can*, or *should* this *Ivan-Scape* be repainted?"

"Same thing could happen again, right Azura?"

Azura nodded.

Stoppard turned in his chair, fingered a Churchill from his leather case, lit up and said, "But if we could make it so it didn't happen again…I mean, nobody gets hurt 'cause there's nothing to be gained by hurting anybody. But let's just say we could protect the project. Would it be doable—the repainting?"

"Wherever money's being made in Kingston, there's always the possibility of somebody getting hurt. That's just the way it is. Gangs and paid off politicians run this town."

"But…if there wasn't any money changing hands…if there wasn't any admission price, why would anybody get hurt?"

Azura paused. "Only way that could work would be to give the project to both gangs that claim that particular piece of city property is their turf. Crazy, but that's what they battle over."

"So, they'd kill each other."

Azura giggled embarrassingly. "Could happen."

"Not a very good solution," said Stoppard.

"People like these animals," said Azura, "where money and power is all it's about, ain't nothin' they'd shy away from doing to protect their cash flow."

"So, how much is that cash flow? How much were you taking in?"

"Six to eight hundred a day," said Stan. "Right, Azura?"

"Actually, with the food sales, more like a thousand."

Stoppard took a long drag on his cigar. "So, Pierre is blind over a fucking thousand a day?"

"The gang got sixty percent. The rest was mine, less the payments to the workers."

"And that was to get you clean and keep you working days and getting your kids back," said Stoppard.

"Yeah. That's how it was working."

Stoppard leaned forward. "You can get a meeting with the heads of the gangs?"

"What, you crazy?"

"Okay. Separately. Possible?"

"A meeting with who?" asked Azura.

"Me."

Stan did a double take. "You? You're going to meet with the guy who ordered Pierre to be blinded?"

"Yeah."

Stan's look of disbelief didn't alter one wrinkle on Stoppard's face. "And we're supposed to think he'll meet you, or that you won't come packin' to kill him?"

"Right."

"You are crazy."

"Like a fox. I don't have to worry about money. I want to get *Ivan-Scape* back up. I want to help Pierre's reason for doing it all. That's the least a...well you know. That's the least I can do."

"Do?" said Azura.

"Get the meeting. I'll make them a 'Godfather' offer."

Stan started to laugh, then stopped. "An offer they can't turn down?"

"I think I could take care of your extortionist-partner's take on a year's admissions and food sales fairly easily. They just have to stay away."

"Doubled, " said Azura. "We're now talking *two* gangs fighting, remember?

"And don't forget the politicians skimmin' off the top," reminded Stan.

"Two gangs, three or more partners," said Stoppard. "Gets complicated, doesn't it?"

"More than you think," said Azura. "May I suggest something?"

"Sure," said Stoppard.

"You're setting yourself up for *real* extortion. These people smell money oceans away. The minute they know who they're dealing with, and I'm sure they already know you're here; your pockets are going to be fleeced over and over. They'll never stop. My suggestion is if I go to them with a pile of cash, and say I had a good month," she laughed. "Just kidding. The real deal...I tell them the family has a friend who wants to see the project go forward without any more violence. I tell them he wants to make a year's payment to insure peace, etcetera. I think it could work."

Stoppard turned to Stan. "Not that you know these people, but, what do you think?"

Stan thought a moment. "Now that she mentions it, she's probably right. You stay out of it... directly."

"So you think she could persuade them?"

"No," said Stan. My guess that "family" story would fall flat. Like you said, they're aware Stoppard Denning is here and they'll automatically think any chunk of money is his, and then the extortion sets in and...no. Stan turned to Azura. "Just a thought. Azura, you said politicians run these gangs."

"Don't run them, but let's just say without them, the gangs would probably destroy each other very quickly and politicians would be a lot poorer. It's in the best interest of their bank accounts that gangs not kill each other and stay healthy to do their dirty work. Pierre's *Ivan-Scape* was just a pride and vanity thing to the big shots. What really rakes in the money for both gangs and politicians is drugs and prostitution."

"Pride and vanity are incredible narcotics. I have a little bit of experience with that...know how to play that game," said Stoppard. "Can you talk to the right people to get me a meeting with one of the politicians on the take?"

"I used to fuck the tourism guy who pulls all the strings. Probably could be arranged."

"Pardon," said Stoppard.

"Sorry, Mister Denning. Street talk slips sometimes. But, I *could* get you a meeting with the guy. He still calls me, even though he knows I'm tryin' to go straight now."

"He sounds like a competitor. Paying off a couple of gangs might be easier," Stoppard said with a laugh. "Politicians are pros at extortion, only they call it 'lobbying.' Set it up."

Azura nodded. "I hope we're not starting something you can't finish."

"Money is an easy closer. Let's hope somebody's pride doesn't get in the way," said Stoppard.

"That would mean a lot to Pierre...knowing the project was still up."

"That's twelve hundred a day split between the two gangs, and four hundred a day for you and your workers. That's... four, one, two, seven... given six month of off-season, I figure yearly... approximately two hundred for them, seventy-three for you... round figures. Only, you don't charge admission. That's figured in your seventy-three. Admission free. You let your stall people sell their snacks and drinks. They keep their earnings."

Azura looked suspiciously at Stoppard. "You that rich?"

Stoppard nodded, his face a bit flushed. "Afraid I am."

After a moment, Azura slowly shook her head. "I can't take the money. Sorry. Hand outs are not me."

"Consider it a *finder's fee* which is standard in financing deal. That's all this is. You found a financier, and that's your *finder's fee*. Please. That's all it is, actually. We're just putting together the financing to insure Pierre's project stays up. You just have to get me that meeting."

Chapter 93

The next day, once William Jones knew he was meeting with Stoppard Denning, cloaked his favored persona as *Deputy Assistant Minister of Tourism* in a veil of full cooperation. With all the aplomb accorded a firm political handshake, Jones gushed with, "Getting one of our most surprising tourist attractions operational again is important to the community. Such a shame about Mister Haweisi."

Those being the first words out of Jones' mouth, Stoppard found it hard to smile, but forced a cordial "Yes. A very talented man to lose his sight in such a disgraceful way. By the way, he sends his appreciation for the flowers. He said they felt and smelled very nice."

"Well, least we could do for such an unfortunate accident."

"Yes. Unfortunate accident. Now, as you were informed by Miss Azura, I'm prepared to arrange for a bank transfer each month to an account of your choosing to keep Ivan-Scape running without incident once it's repainted."

Jones slipped a folded piece of paper across the desk with all the charm of a python about to be fed a large goose. "I believe it best to use this account. I fund many of the cities projects through here."

Stoppard opened the paper and recognized the offshore bank name. "The account is a charitable fund of course."

"Of course," said Jones with a smile.

Stoppard refolded and placed it into his breast pocket, sliding his own letter of instructions across the desk.

"Do you mind if I smoke?" asked Stoppard.

"No, of course not," said Jones, as he opened the two page document. His face straightened into a momentary business frown at reading the top few lines. "This figure, forty two hundred—I was expecting double this."

"Mmm. Double, eh?" said Stoppard, leaning forward, taking the paper, and quickly jotting down another figure. He then slid it back.

Jones hesitated, then smiled, noticing the sum of forty-two hundred dollars, per month, crossed out and replaced with sixty-two hundred dollars, along with Stoppards initials.

"That is double where I come from," said Stoppard with a puff of smoke engulfing Jones.

"It's just… there are always administrative costs, you know."

"Yes. I know." Stoppard pointed at the paper. "Don't forget to initial that little 'administrative cost' figure."

"Oh, yes. Of course." Jones said with a studied smile.

Stoppard pulled out a duplicate copy from his jacket and changed the figure, initialed it, and slid it across to Jones. "I thought it important to make sure the number was consistent with the seasonal ebbs and tides, the off-season, versus high season, yes?"

Jones nodded weakly, initialed Stoppard's copy and then read on. "It says here that should there be any further violence or 'desecration of the site' you will hold me responsible and all funds will cease until it is 'remedied'?"

Stoppard blew a smoke ring and carefully rolled his Churchill between his fingers.

"'Remedied' as in brought back to normal. And, should any harm come to Azura, her family, her boy friend, or any of her workers, you will also be held responsible."

"Mister Denning, I can't be responsible for what might happen down there. That's a rough part of town."

"That's why it's a feather in your cap to be doing something to clean it up. And, Mister Jones, let's not forget…" He pointed to the last paragraph at the bottom of the paper. "You will provide sufficient armed police officers 24/7 at the site as insurance that your deposits are made in a timely manner. I'm sure you can handle it. And oh, be fair with your sharing of the administrative costs, eh? I had a copy of the arrangement delivered to your other two *administrative* partners. Wouldn't want certain people to feel left out or shortchanged with all this violence that going around like a common cold.

"Two? I don't have two *administrative* partners."

"I believe you do. Mister Turk and Mister Yenni. Unlike my esteemed president in the USA, I *do* believe in talking with my enemies. Letting everyone involved think they know what the other person is doing, is such good insurance, yes? Insidentaly, they say only good things about you, Mister Jones. Stoppard waited. "Your signature, Mister Jones."

Jones reluctantly signed, double checked he'd initialed all the right places and slid the document back to Stoppard. So, we'll arrange to have the repainting completed in the next couple of weeks, and you can alert the hotels, etcetera. It's been a pleasure to

597

make this donation. I'm sure the island will appreciate your gesture of goodwill as well. Goodbye, Mister Jones. Oh, don't bother. I'll let myself out."

Stoppard stopped at the door and turned around. "By the way, that police protection is noted to take place during the painting as well. My foreman, Stan, Pierre's dear friend, well, he might be perceived unfairly, given the sexual preference laws here in Jamaica. But we'll keep that secret just between us men, right?"

Mister Jones remained standing behind his desk, his face allowing little expression.

"I know," said Stoppard as he opened the door. "I reacted the same way first time I heard about them. You'll get over it. And, you'll fucking work with it. Good day."

For Jones, the door's closing was more akin to the sound of a cell door being shut.

***

Stoppard's next stop was the doctor's office. The physician in charge of Pierre's eyes was an elderly black whose white hair framed an intelligent face that naturally complimented his reputation as the island's *best* doctor. "I wish I could have done more, but I'm not a specialist," said Doctor Raymond.

Stoppard continued writing out the check. "You did all you could. Even the specialists I spoke with in New York said there wasn't much that could be done other than keep him sedated and let what healing could take place do so. I appreciate your effort and skill, Doctor." He ripped off the check and handed it to him. "I've included a little something extra for the hospital as a token of my deepest appreciation."

Dr. Raymond calmly looked at the check. "Hardly a token, Mister Denning. This is not necessary."

"I understand. But, well, he's a special talent. Your quick action may turn out to be the key to his getting back some partial sight in time. You enjoy. Now, we'll be taking him to the plane around eight tomorrow morning, if that's agreeable."

"His pain has subsided slightly, so I think he should be fine for the flight time. Your Dr. Jennings is perfectly capable of administering the pain killers as needed. She understands the handling of such things."

Stoppard stood up and shook hands. "Again, many thanks to you and your staff."

"Just wish I could have done more. I've been hearing about him on the radio. He's quite the talent according to Simon Greco. Do you know of his show?"

"Yes. Yes, I do. Well, got to run."

Pierre's pillows propped him up, as Stan sat on the bed's edge holding his hand. Having just been given a shot, Pierre's speech labored under the influence.

Stan gripped his hand. "You can believe what you want, Pierre, whatever you want, but I choose to believe the best. Stoppard said the eye specialist he's got you going to is the best the country. If anyone can help you, it's him."

Pierre's eyes were again covered by the dark glasses. He smiled and rocked his head side to side. "You are the sunshine of my life, yeaaahhh—think I could make it as a..."

"No, God damn it. You're gonna see again. Stop thinking that way."

"Stan, you always were prone to romancing life away. But...not now. Not with this."

"I don't want to talk about it. I'm going to paint Ivan back up the same way you left it, and you're going to get back to New York where they can start to work on you seeing again."

A silence took over the room. Pierre sat with the reality of being blind; Stan with the romantic idea that with enough money, anything could be fixed.

"Stan? Why do you think he did it?"

"Who, Turk? 'Cause he's..."

"No, Dad. Stoppard. Dad. God, that's so hard to say sometimes."

Stan looked out the window toward Montego Bay where boats, water skiers, Para-sailors, all were enjoying the late day temperatures. "Good question. I don't know. Guilt, probably. Maybe regret?"

"Over what. Not ever treating me like he's my dad? If that's what you mean, forget it."

"Bothers you, doesn't it?"

"What, that my mother and I have had our lives supplemented by this guy who refuses to accept a black for a son."

"Whoa. Not like you to play the race card."

"What? You think that doesn't have anything to do with it? Pierre continued, but without rancor. Just sadness. "How about a nigger-fag son?"

"I think he might be beyond that now."

"Why? Because he probably heard my mother sounding like she was dying over me? Because the son-of-a-bitch now is footing the bill for a *blind* painter, instead of a nigger fag son—painter? At least before, he always had the option to admit he was the father of an artist who could see. What the hell does the fucker expect to gain from this?"

"Don't let the anger get hold of you now, Pierre. I think he's really trying." Stan stood up and walked to a table where a water pitcher and glasses sat.

"Where you going, Stan?"

"Just getting us some water, okay?"

"Thought you were leaving."

Stan carried the glasses of water back to the bed and looked down at Pierre. "You thirsty?"

"Always. This morphine leaves you dry as a bone and constipated as hell." Stan put the glass in his hand.

"What you laughing about?" said Pierre.

"You forgot *temperamental*." He cleared his throat. "So, what does he expect to gain from this?

"Yeah. How many times we going to repeat that little phrase, eh? Tell me."

"Don't have a clue." Stan took a swallow of water. "A guy who won't really admit to being a father, well, let's just say we should both be glad he's rich, 'cause right now, that's the only *worth* he's willing and ready to give, you know what I mean?"

"Maybe." Pierre slowly drank the water, trying to force back down his throat the pain that was trying to erupt.

"Maybe?" asked Stan.

"Yeah." His brow twisted with furrowed lines of pain. He gently placed two fingers on his temple. "Just thinkin' out loud. Forget it," answered Pierre.

Chapter 94

February came and went. Stan supervised the repainting of Ivan Scape and returned to New York. Pierre hesitantly accepted the medical attention in Manhattan and opted to stay at his mother's apartment in spite of Stoppard's willingness to put both him and Stan up in a Manhattan apartment. His decision left Stoppard with a blow to his ego. He was slowly becoming accustomed to Pierre's stubborn ways. In spite of conversations with himself in front of the mirror, and at times long talks with Siebert from the back seat of the limo, having someone turn away from his generosity was unprecedented. After all, he was Stoppard Denning. *No one in their right mind turns down help, especially if they're blind,* was a thought he couldn't shake.

600

The major market sweeps came and went with much the same numbers and percentages as in the earlier first week's ratings. The difference being that over two hundred additional markets had been tested, compared to November's sweeps. There was no denying the fact that Echo Life wasn't just a freak chance in programming that got lucky. Pressures from board members, coupled with the Pierre situation, combined to make February a month Stoppard wanted to forget.

By March—and after numerous eye specialists concurred that Pierre would never see again—Stoppard became even more insistent that Pierre and Stan take up residence in Manhattan. But, even after offering to provide anything Pierre wanted: a loft, a penthouse, even trying to ease the pressure of deciding by offering to let him stay on The Katherine—which was once again docked at the Hudson River Yacht Club—Pierre declined, saying he wasn't going to be a charity case any further. Each of the men, being frustrated with the other, decided that a little time away from one another's presence would be good.

Pierre was overwhelmed with the opening of his renovated building and the immediate success the creative phenomenon realized. After the New York newspapers crowned him the "...the Michelangelo of the 21st century..." radio and TV interviews followed. Following a week of celebrity pressures, Pierre asked Stan to graciously turn down any more publicity and live appearances, sighting rest and rehabilitation as the reasons. Global media had to satisfy themselves with earlier video taped interviews and appearances, creating an even greater myth around the now blind artist. For Pierre, the feeling of accomplishment was bitter sweet. Many a night he cried himself to sleep with the joy of knowing there was more to accomplish. Outweighing the sadness of being blind was his tenacity wanting to believe he could see with his hands, and work with his heart. Dreams of the impossible carried him through the darkness of night into the light of his imagination once more.

***

Stoppard concentrated on the fall season, with his executives planning out both TV and publishing, and spending even more time with the accelerated popularity of Inter-Active Media—an area of consumerism Echo Life now led. For OST to not have a prime market share of the new media was unacceptable in Stoppard's mind. He determined something radical had to be done to change things, and it had to be done soon.

***

In early April, Derek offered Pierre and Stan an opportunity to spend some time on Gray Cliff Island and make some money as well. Theo was still in Manhattan finishing his book, but there were hours and hours of tapes he'd recorded that needed transcribing. *Would Pierre be up for the job?* Knowing he could type, Derek thought it a good opportunity for him to get his mind off the events of the past few months and have a new environment to explore and keep him busy.

As oil prices were beginning to drop, which meant there might be some hope for the future of Echo Life on the island, Derek explained that it would be another month before any hard decision could be made. Until then, there were several cottages vacant. Pierre could take his pick.

Pierre felt somewhat guilty in distancing himself from Stoppard, but he had mixed feelings and didn't want any added pressure to acquiesce to his control. He gave it a lot of thought and asked Derek if he would be willing to keep their whereabouts quiet so they wouldn't be bothered with any more pressure from Stoppard or the press. Derek agreed, but voiced his discomfort in having to lie about their whereabouts, if asked, especially given his own mixed feelings about Stoppard the business rival and Stoppard the generous caretaker of Pierre's recent plight.

"I will honor your privacy, however, let's hope your confused feelings over Stoppard settle soon," had been Derek's last words before Pierre and Stan agreed to move into a small cottage on the edge of the pine forest leading to the rock, and immersed themselves in the transcribing work.

***

With the warm weather maintaining itself, Derek labored long hours to finish the Echo rock. There were moments of depression, as he would allow his mind to visualize the island deserted, should the oil become a crisis again, but with the kind of determination he was known for, he molded the final lines and crevasses of Echo's scarves, and on April 24th, he put down his chisels and gloves, sunk into a fold of the scarf, pulled out a mini-bottle of champagne he had been saving, and toasted himself and Echo. It was a private moment of elation for the man who, up till now, wasn't sure he could finish the dedication to his muse, but now that it was finished—"Thank you Echo," he whispered to himself. "There are few places I'd rather be right now than right here...this is comfort beyond words, Echo. The embrace of the colors and movement you so carefully shrouded me with these past years...well, I thank you." He raised his bottle and drank slowly. For the next few moments, the moisture in his eyes blended the clouds into what felt like the liquid ripples of a rebirthing...a sense of worthiness he hadn't felt in a long time. He lay there a long time.

It was sunset when the familiar bellow of Jamie's bullhorn broke him out of his reverie. "Let's get it goin'," yelled Jamie. "Damn waters are wantin' my hide again."

Derek pulled himself up, gathered his tools and wound his way down to the cave. After placing everything inside, he looked one last time at the carved eyes of Echo, now heavily shadowed by the low sunlight. A gust of wind swept up his backside, hovered about his head, and then dissipated into the air. "Thank you," he said. "Thank you."

***

By late April, Pierre's disappearance was not only upsetting to the media hounds, but to Stoppard as well. Tanika, having also been sworn to secrecy by Pierre, kept the truth back, even after many calls from Stoppard questioning her. His additional calls to Derek proved equally fruitless. Stoppard blamed himself for the disappearance. He sank into depression and a strange kind of paranoia he couldn't shake—a crazy kind of guilt giving him thoughts that his vast wealth and accompanying power might be proving to be his worst enemy.

***

"What's it all about, Tito?" said Stoppard. "What's it all about?" Sitting at his dining table with the little man of the park was an idea that only an hour before was non-existent. Writing numerous checks in the past week to various charities around the world had not alleviated his troubled sense of worth. During an exasperated brisk walk in the park, he had come upon Tito sitting on his bench observing the passersby and as usual, taking notes.

Now, high above the park, Tito sat quietly, not sure it was time to tell Stoppard *what it was all about*.

Impatient, Stoppard gave a glance to Siebert, who remained stoic in the corner, gazing out the window, obviously asked by Stoppard to be there to listen and listen only.

"It's not about what you think," answered Tito.

"I knew that was coming."

"Why'd you ask, then?"

"I mean, you're too smart to *give* answers. You're all about discovery for one's self, making us discover *our own answers*. I saw that in you the last time you were sitting in that chair, and it's prevalent throughout your books."

"You read my books?"

"Of course not. Who's got time to sit with a book? I had my readers do what they get paid for. They gave you some good reviews, by the way." His face sank and, like a child asking why he can't fly, Stoppard leaned forward, "Why would he just up and leave? Disappear?"

603

"I'm afraid neither one of us may have that answer. Maybe a guess."

Stoppard waited a few moments, then asked, "And the guess might be?"

Tito could be stubborn with his principles, and he wasn't about to make an exception. He too waited and held his blank look.

"I'm asking you, God damn it. Break your fucking rule, just once. Why the hell you think you're here? I've tried to come up with an answer for where he is and failed."

"You don't need my *guess*. Just let the truth out."

"Truth? I'm not lying about anything."

"You don't have to be lying to not be living the truth."

Stoppard paused a long moment. "How long does he think he can just run off with Stan and survive? What's he going to use for money?"

"He didn't strike me as stupid. I'm sure he thought about that before he went wherever he went. And lest you forget, money to him is much different than money to you or me for that matter." Tito wet his fingers and rolled the loose thread holding his coat button barely in place.

"Oh, come on," exclaimed Stoppard. "Even *he* has to eat and have shelter. It's been almost a month now. His mother's going crazy over the doctors insisting he needs his medication. At two hundred a bottle, what the hell's he going to do?"

"Medication for what?"

"For the pain."

"Maybe he feels he can live without the medication."

"I asked the doctor the same thing."

"And?"

"He said picture a cold ice pick in your eyes. Even if he were super-fucking-human, where would he go?"

"What if he's found a place...inside...his own space, where the pain doesn't register?"

"Oh, Christ. That's horseshit New Age crap. You're impossible."

"Maybe. But people like that do exist. So...what if he is gone?"

"He is gone."

"I mean—gone."

"You mean dead?"

"I mean gone. Alive, but never to return."

"Why the hell would he do that? He's a fucking celebrity. He's got the world at his feet."

"You're serious, aren't you."

"Of course. It was a terrible thing that happened to him, but the public loves him even more because of it. He doesn't have to worry

604

about *becoming* an artist. He has immortalized himself with that building. You know the police have to run barricades daily for the line? Did you know that?"

"Yes. I *do* read. A lot, actually."

Stoppard continued, "And his *Ivan-Scape* by last reports has been covered by every major news agency in the world. God damn it. He was right in the middle of negotiations for a special on him. Those assholes at CBS were wining and dining him and…he wouldn't even speak to me about a show on his work. God damn it. Who the hell paid for everything? Who has been behind him all along?"

"Not you."

"That's unfair. You know what I did."

"Yes. You were very concerned and you were portrayed by all the news reports as a sort of philanthropist for the arts. But we both know that's not where you were coming from."

Stoppard turned to Siebert. "You believe this? This guy from a fuckin' park bench is telling me…"

Tito rose and started walking to the door.

"No, no, no. I'm sorry. I didn't mean that."

Tito turned. "You're the one dragged me up here. I was doing just fine with my horses, pigeons, *and* park bench, remember?"

"Yes. Yes. Please, sit down. I apologize." He turned to Siebert again. "Do you believe this is me acting like a scared rabbit? Me?"

"Pardon my commenting, sir, but you are human—just like Tito and me."

"Yes. Yes, I am. Please come back and sit down, Tito. Siebert, pour him something. What would you like? I've got everything." Without waiting for the answer, Stoppard stepped to the window. "Yes. Everything. I'm disturbed over all this, Tito. I think I miss him. I don't deserve this." He turned back and slumped into his chair. Tito sat back down. Siebert stood at the liquor cabinet. "Your usual, sir?"

"No. Open a bottle of wine. I'm sure everyone is thirsty. You're thirsty, aren't you Tito? Of course. The good stuff, Siebert. Dust off the good stuff." After a few moments, he raised his head with a start. "Hey, what did you mean 'that's not where you were coming from?' You think I had some ulterior motive in helping him? Huh?"

Both Tito and Stoppard's eyes locked on each other. "Speak the truth, Stoppard. It's nothing but the truth," Tito said quietly. "Remember from your studies: *Veritas vos liberabit?*"

"Yeah. Yeah. *The truth shall set you free.* Quid est veritas?"

"What is truth? A question only you can answer…for you."

Chapter 95

"I think it's better *you* commission him," said Derek over the phone. "You're a patron of the arts. From you it will be more legitimate. I'd run the risk of appearing like his father, giving him a handout."

Aretha leaned back from the speakerphone on her desk and peered out the window at the long grass now moving gracefully with the afternoon breezes behind the Ode. "But that's your money. It's *hard earned* money, Derek.

"An investment windfall here and there deserves to become another investment. That's always been my philosophy with stocks, so why should I change now. And I choose to spend it on this investment. He needs to have something that pushes him. He thinks his artistic days are gone, but...you weren't there. That first day when I took him to the rock—to see Pierre hanging in my harness, touching every foot of Echo's face, to defy the heights and fully trust my belay...and then to talk as he did about what he felt with his hands. That man will sculpt, Aretha. I know it. He just needs to feel there's someone confident in his ability...someone with expectations of him."

"And that someone can't be you?"

"No. I've already explained. Please. Just do this one favor for me. You always said you wanted a work of art surrounding your house. What better way than a sculpted wall? Forget it would be coming from a blind artist. You do the commissioning. I know he'll get into it. He just needs a little time to get used to the idea."

"What if he doesn't want that? I mean, have you asked him what *he* wants to do?"

"Yes. He told me he wants to be with his memories of light and color, and...he wants to be alone with Stan. "

"Why would he take to sculpture, Derek? You're assuming a lot."

"Like I said. You weren't there. He even described the color of Echo's eyes."

"I don't understand."

"I didn't either at the time. His hands touched and moved around the eyes and he described the green and blue mix of her eyes. He's special, Aretha. I can sculpt, but he's special. If he has the tools—and I can advise him on that—with tools and some time, I feel strongly he'll discover sculpturing can be created even with his blind eyes. He only has to be around the stone."

"And where would that be?"

"We should send him and Stan to Greece," replied Derek without any hesitation.

"Greece?"

"Kavala in the North. Let him pick the slabs for shipping back to your house. We'll find them an apartment in Truro and let Pierre just be there with the stone—until it's finished."

"Not exactly a summer project."

"No, more like several years."

"Several?"

"A year?"

***

With the mist rising from the Atlantic, making everything around him moist, Pierre leaned against the old pine tree, his cheek and ear pressed firmly into the bark. "Do you hear anything?"

From the other side of the tree, Stan pressed his ear to the bark and looked up at its forty-foot top. "I'm trying, Pierre. Kind of…like a seashell. You know, the kind you're supposed to hear sounds from."

"Yes. But do you hear anything besides that?"

"No. Am I supposed to?"

Pierre pulled his face away, and placed his hands on the tree, slowly exploring the channels of raised bark. "I don't know. Maybe it's just my imagination, but I hear more than air passing through. It's somewhat musical, you know. I mean, there's pitch and tempo. Even harmonies if you press your ear to the right place."

Stan stepped around the ancient tree and smiled as he looked at the peaceful expression on Pierre's face. With the bandages gone and only dark glasses covering his eyes, Stan felt his partner was at least back to a semblance of the old Pierre. "This island is good for you. You look so at ease right now. How's the pain?"

"Gone."

"But yesterday…"

"Gone," repeated Pierre.

"Hard to believe."

Pierre just smiled and leaned his face into the mist. "Of course there's a little pain still, you dummy, but I don't allow it much room in my brain anymore, okay?"

Stan peered through the pines at the bright blue sky and ocean. "God, I wish you could experience this."

"What?" said Pierre.

Stan gently wiped the mist from Pierre's forehead. "The forest and the ocean."

"I can smell it. Tell me what it looks like."

"These trees have seen a lot of weather, just like the rest of Gray Cliff. The mist rising up from the cliffs has put sheen on everything,

607

you know? Rocks, pine cones, limbs, the pine needles...even the moss. They're just plain wet. Nice. Pretty."

Pierre, lifting a long walking stick he'd carved the first day on the island, felt his way back onto the path. "Come. Time we talked."

Stan followed. "What do you mean?"

"Let's go to the edge."

"Be careful. Everything is slippery right now."

Pierre took his arm and the two made their way through the worn tourist path that snaked its way along the long, rugged plateau leading to the beginning of *Echo Rock*. "You want to go to the end, or..."

Pierre interrupted him. "The end. The path's completed, isn't it?"

Stan nodded. "Yeah. All mile and a half of it."

"Thought so," said Pierre. "I could hear them while I was typing Theo's tapes. Sounded like everything from rakes to jack hammers."

"And a back-hoe in one spot. Derek's fifty grand gift to the mayor sure put a lot of hungry islanders and fishermen to work. Here, watch your step, coming out onto the rocky part." Stan guided him out of the cluster of pines onto the barren stone and grass where summer flowers were beginning to bloom. The mist became thicker as they approached the end. "Steps," said Stan as they reached the stone cut stairwell leading down, and then back up to a view point of the actual work of *Echo* and the cave.

The façade of the Echo rock and cave being inaccessible, save a climb from the ocean floor, a large Plexiglas enclosed view box showed a series of close up photos of Echo's details as well as the cave's interior where Derek had lived during the many months of finishing the project. The photos showed what it had been like to sculpt and live away from everyone and everything. There was the living room—a fold-up camp chair and an overturned box. One Huricane lamp and the generator. The bedroom was a simple sleeping bag and lantern. The kitchen had the camp stove and a rock to sit on. At the entrance, the generator with a compressor, leaning pneumatic hammer and coils of rope. After Stan explained the layout, they sat.

"He was Spartan, wasn't he?" said Pierre.

Stan looked at the cave pictures again. "All the comforts of home. Don't know how he did it."

"Could you live like that?" asked Pierre.

"Oh, I suppose if I had to. Come to think of it, with a little more heat, not much different than Brooklyn last year."

They both laughed. "But, could you really live without much of anything the rest of your life...and have to be my eyes as well?"

Stan hesitated for just a moment, but it was long enough.

"That's a heavy one, isn't it?" said Pierre as he turned to the ocean, letting the continuing updraft of mist cover his face. "You need to think more about that."

Stan gathered his knees up under his chin and gazed at Pierre, who held his head up high as if standing under a showerhead. "Not that it's such a heavy thought," said Stan. "Just hadn't pictured it like that."

"Like what?"

"Like, I don't know. A cave? You thinking of living in a cave or are you just yankin' my chain?"

Pierre moved closer beside Stan. "It's a good metaphor for what might be ahead of me. One-room apartments, no apartments, who knows? Blind artists aren't getting the big opportunities last time I checked."

Stan reached over and took Pierre's head and cradled it on his shoulder. "I do a lot of thinking, just like you. What's this going to do to our lives? I mean, we're hardly your everyday couple, right? Never have been. But, now, we have to do a lot of extra thinking, don't we? You always worrying about me having to be your eyes. Me, knowing you hate being dependent on anyone, but also knowing…we sure as hell couldn't call it love if I packed up and left, right?"

"Maybe," murmured Pierre. "People sometimes…"

"Stop. You're being an asshole now."

"You could though, couldn't you? I mean, nothing stopping you from moving on with your life."

Stan squeezed Pierre's shoulder. "If this is what you wanted to talk about, it's done. Okay? I'm not going anywhere. And if you want to live in a cave, like I said…"

"Not much different than Brooklyn," finished Pierre. "I'll try and not make it harder than it is. I'll try hard."

"You can stop trying so fucking hard. Not necessary."

"Feel that cloud pass over?" asked Pierre.

Stan looked up. There wasn't any cloud. Only the hovering wingspan of a seagull floating with the updraft. "Just a seagull." He looked to the left and saw a double wedge of the flock passing over. "Just a bunch of birds. It's a clear day, Pierre. Clear day."

Chapter 96

After weeks of agonizing over his options, Stoppard knew the offer was unexpected and generous. Very generous. Even so, he couldn't shake the discomfort that gave him nightmares right up to the day. It wasn't the money. It wasn't the challenge. It was the realization of change. *Men, my age, don't change, God damn it!*

The surprise meeting was arranged by Terrence Kensington through Sol Berkowitz, a straight request for a business meeting to discuss something of prime importance to Echo Life and OST. Sol informed Derek, Terrence informed Stoppard that his request had been accepted, and the four men met in the boardroom atop OST at 10 AM on May 3, 2007. Coffee, bagels, bottled water and Churchill cigars, pad and pen made up the individual settings for what Stoppard told his staff was going to be *the deal of the year*.

After everyone was seated, Stoppard stood. "I want to thank you gentlemen for taking this meeting on such short notice. I think we will all realize it was most important to not delay it." Stoppard picked up four sealed manila envelopes. "Inside these envelopes are duplicate contracts for the non-negotiable opportunity for OST and Echo Life to co-exist in harmony and—what my stock holders will appreciate—potential profits that will set a new standard for expectations in the world of sight and sound entertainment. Although there will be dissenters among the share holders and our industry is always full of hard core traditionalists, like me, I think that can all be overcome with time." He motioned. "Please take a look at the summary sheet and you can determine how much of the boilerplate my illustrious legal department put together is necessary to wade through today."

Still mulling over the "non-negotiable" utterance in their minds, Derek and Sol hesitated, then glanced at each other and opened their envelope. The room fell silent for maybe five minutes as Derek and Sol read, while Stoppard and Terrence exchanged hushed small talk about their plans for summer vacations. Derek opened a bottle of water and took several swallows. Sol fingered through the forty-page contract, comparing references to the summary page. Finally, both men closed the contract.

Derek nodded to Sol who cleared his throat. "I think I understand this," said Sol, "but let's be clear what your offer really means."

"It means," said Stoppard, "that in all likelihood, one set of troubles are over for Echo Life, and a new set begins."

Sol continued. "You are actually giving Echo Life *full* autonomy?"

"Completely. You have some substantial benchmarks to address, but no one will interfere. You either win or lose on your own merits."

"And do I understand that you, Mister Denning, are financing this with your own money? You are making Echo Life an independent division of OST with all profits split 50/50, your end not going to you, but to the stockholders of OST? Do I understand that correctly?"

"Much to the chagrin of my attorney. That is correct."

"That's one hundred million risk capital per year for two years. That's a lot of money."

"That represents financing capable of bringing Echo Life up to the profit ratio that all my other divisions enjoy—twenty-one percent minimum net profit, per year. Condition one. We take it a year at a time."

"Risk capital. Recoup?" said Sol.

Stoppard allowed a half grin. "Oh, recoup or not, that's much better than letting you boys play havoc with my bottom line every quarter. You know the old saying, to make money, you have to spend it."

Sol's eyes met Derek's, which dropped to the summary page in front of him. "What's the catch, Stoppard?" asked Derek.

"You insult my integrity, Derek. No catches. You have been a competitor. I make you a part of OST and that disappears. Simple Business 101."

Derek looked again to Sol.

"We'll need to talk about this with our group," said Sol.

"Of course. Understood. We'll meet back here in one week and sign the papers. That's fine with me." Stoppard stood and lit a cigar. "You are comfortable with condition two, yes?"

Derek looked again at his summary page. "Don't see a mention of it here."

"Oh, my apologies. It's on the attachments—last page, I believe."

Both Derek and Sol fingered through the document to the last page. NON-COMPETING CLAUSE "Failure to achieve twenty-one percent net profit on any given year, the contract at the sole discretion of Stoppard Denning can be declared null and void. In any such event, Echo Life, or any facsimile created by any and/or all principals of Echo Life, must cease to exist for a period of ten years."

Derek looked up. "Rather heavy penalty for failure."

Stoppard held his eyes steady. "One hundred million dollars of risk capital per year helps insure against that, doesn't it? I'm willing to take *that* risk. Are you?"

***

Neither man spoke for the twenty minutes it took to walk from OST's boardroom to Sol's office on Broadway. Sol sat behind his desk and looked across at Derek. "You haven't said a word since we left."

"You don't like it, do you?" asked Derek.

"It's a ballsy offer. His risk is a hundred million and it keeps you under his umbrella for at least a year. Your risk is failure and the dissolution of all you've—any of us have worked for, not to mention our own investors' risk up till now."

"And like I said, you don't like it."

"I hate it."

"Hate it?"

"Derek, full autonomy, standard profit goals, financing laid in your lap—although we need to read the details carefully, and fifty percent of the profits. It's perfect. Too perfect to be true. He's not the fifth richest man in the world because he throws a hundred million around daily. There's got to be more to it. Has to be."

"So we turn it down?"

"Hell, no. We look between the lines with a fine tooth comb. We find his hidden agenda, if there is one."

"And if we don't—if we don't find any hidden agenda?"

"Be damn fools if we didn't take it. This may prove to be one of the biggest ego pacifications in entertainment history. If Echo Life is what he needs to rub elbows with... we can handle that, can't we?"

Derek looked off. "Hope so, Sol. Hope so."

***

Theo sat and waited on what he knew was Tito's park bench. The spring in New York was always a time for people to fill Central Park, people who for the most part had stayed huddled for months in their winter cocoons high above the now lime green trees and pockets of water that dotted the centerpiece of Manhattan. One cannot live in the city and not have a special attachment to the park, whether it is a once a year excursion or the habitual daily walk that many, young and old, religiously catalog in their mental diary of Manhattan life. Although the park was void of the homeless — thanks in large part to Mayor Giuliani's efforts years before—there remained the occasional reminder that even for the disenfranchised, the open skies and clean air of forest and lake were, by law, free to all.

Far from being the typical vagabond of the park, Tito nonetheless enjoyed the anonymity the park afforded those whose appearance usually caused a *look-away* by adults and an innocent curious *look-toward* from the young. *Just the way I like it.* Tito smiled back at the inquisitive eyes as he fastidiously worked his mouthful of sunflower seeds, sorting the shells to the left cheek, and the meat to the right.

He sauntered up to a bench and sat a few inches away from Theo. He pulled an inch-thick stack of Theo's tattered handwritten pages mixed in with Pierre's recently typed pages and placed them on the bench next to Theo. Theo looked down at the manuscript. Tito reached behind him for a rock and placed it on the stack.

"Well?" asked Theo.

Tito shook his head and pointed to his mouthful, his food processing not yet completed.

Theo nodded and turned his gaze back to the lake in front of them.

After a few moments, Tito swallowed and heaved a sigh. "Lot of work eating those damn things. Addictions are addictions, though. How are you today, my friend?"

"A little anxious."

"Oh, come now, Theo. Not for my assessment, surely?"

"Of course, you old coot. Think I show my work to just anybody?"

Tito sucked on his teeth. "Don't happen to have a toothpick, do you?"

Theo impatiently shook his head, reached in his coat pocket, retrieving his notebook and a packet of Post-its. "Here. These work better than toothpicks." He lifted off a few of the one-inch squares. "Fold one in half, and pick to your hearts content."

"Novel idea. Hadn't thought of that."

"Cute trick I learned from an old acting teacher."

"Really."

"Long story. So, what did you think?"

Tito picked his teeth, pulled a water bottle from his pocket, gargled, swirled, spit and said, "You ready to get sued?"

"What's that supposed to mean?"

"Means…you take the fifth richest man in the world, according to Forbes, and you suggest, no, tell us, that he's a no good son-of-a-bitch, then mess with our heads by suggesting later he's a saint. Uh huh."

"The novel is a work of fiction, for God's sake."

"More properly, a docu-novel. Big sellers today. Wise genre choice. Risky character choice."

"And?"

"And? Oh, you're going to get sued, for sure. A slam-dunk. Might have helped if you'd left out all the details in the Jamaica sequence. Hell, it's only been a couple of months since Pierre's opening. Blind painters are big news anytime, you know. And, blind painters who have an anonymous super-rich benefactor willing to rescue them from a gangland torture in Jamaica—Theo, not very subtle. That story, the actual real-life hard print story, was picked up by the wire services around the globe. Homeless are still sleeping under daily papers giving updates, and front-page coverage at that. Till Pierre decides to come out of hiding, that's going to keep up. And you try to disguise the facts with a phony character name like Clinton Rogers? Incidentally, not much of a name for the owner of the biggest media conglomerate in the world." Tito paused and stared out at the lake. "Kane would have been interesting, but its already taken."

"And?"

"You want it all, now?"

"Now is fine."

"You dedicate the book to 'The blind painter.' You really think he's going to stay missing forever? What happens when he *does* resurface? You think the publisher isn't going to worry about that and another potential law suit?"

"He's not going to resurface and sue me. Besides, I don't have any money."

"Whoever publishes this does. You think a publisher is going to indemnify you for this? And if it becomes a bestseller? Money, money, money."

"Jesus, Tito. It's not the first time a story about a celebrity has been couched in some fictional license."

"You have three in your book. I forgot to mention Derek."

"Okay. So there are some references to events similar to some headlines. I've tweaked the hell out of the plot so there's no question, this is a work of fiction. I even project out two years from now. Serge, the Derek character, is dead from a fall climbing in the Alps—the colony continues under the leadership of Benjamin. Clinton is in a mental institution. Alonzo, the blind painter, is living in seclusion with his mate in Spain."

"You asked my opinion, and I gave it. Incidentally, you have a publisher lined up for this…'Time Remaining'? Not a bad title at least."

"Yes."

"Who?"

"OST Publishing."

"Cute. Oh, yeah. That's cute."

"The truth. Stoppard said he'd publish it. He read it two weeks ago, just before you."

Tito feigned a sniff at Theo. "What've you been smoking?"

Theo didn't blink.

"You are kidding? He'd have to be nuts to print this."

"He said the same thing…about himself, and then laughed…at himself. He did want some changes, though."

"Obviously."

"He hated 'Clinton' too."

"That's it?"

"He prefers his character not be committed to an institution, but just disappears, never to be heard from again."

"He is nuts," said Tito as he rose and stretched. "Might be gettin' to be like us."

"Otherwise?"

Tito looked down at Theo. "Otherwise, you, him, the book…just crazy enough to make you very rich."

PART 3 – IRONY'S WILL

CHAPTER 97

One year later

A bus passed Tito as he sat on the curb, engaged in his usual pastime of feeding the carriage horses. The side panel read:

PBS SPECIAL - STOPPARD DENNING – 2008 LIFETIME ACHIEVEMENT AWARD May 17 – AVERY FISHER HALL, LINCOLN CENTER – 8 p.m. Sponsored by "America's most trusted financial magazine, THE ACHIEVEMENT QUARTERLY." A picture of Stoppard filled the background.

***

Earlier in 2007, the one stipulation missing in the Echo contract that Sol agonized over for weeks, was any proviso for the oil crisis and lack of fuel and oil getting to the island. Without regular deliveries, the contract could become jeopardized and as advised by Sol's attorneys, possibly fall into a force majeure argument, thus a risk of rendering the contract null and void. "Not a way to start off," Sol had lamented. But, anxieties over oil prices were short-lived. Within three weeks, regular ferry service was magically reinstated and the island was flooded with more tourists than its inhabitants could accommodate. The summer and fall reservations were off the charts as a result of the media's coverage of this most unusual move by OST.

During that same year, with artists returning to the island, Simon's broadcasts were filled with new segments, and the interactive popularity grew faster than anyone anticipated. Before the fall was over, Stoppard, not wanting to be "hind tit," as he called it, to the other entertainment conglomerates buying up the YouTube and MySpace look-a-likes popping up all over the web, insisted Derek accept another ten million to initiate Echo Life's own amateur video and audio site. With the built-in subscription base of hundreds of thousands, its success was guaranteed. So much so, that during the winter months, most of the artists were booked into lecture and demonstration tours around the globe, experiencing "rock star" status wherever they travelled. Naturally declining to buy into the inordinate attention to limousines, hotel suites and entourage escorts, the artists, instead, toured with carefully planned and executed anonymity, driving the paparazzi crazy and delighting the subscribers, who were involved with hands-on workshops and small projects with the limelight distractions minimized.

Among the artists on tour was Leonard Paxton. After realizing his bank account was being helped along by Tina's *honest* work, and unable to remain competitive with the normal professional world of musicians, he agreed to travel and teach trumpet improvisation. Horn students in many major urban centers in Europe flocked to learn his approach. Tina managed to learn video recording and recorded his sessions with students for broadcast on Simon's show. Leonard very quickly realized a new career. By late fall and winter of 2007, he was gathering accomplished amateur players and working, via Skype and computer net cams with Samara, to form a global community of musicians that hopefully would someday perform an original work playing from all parts of the world, locked into a simulcast, as if they were all in the same concert hall.

***

Stoppard, in spite of his elation with the progress of Echo Life, suffered drinking bouts and sleepless nights over the continued silence of Pierre. For the first few months of the contract period, Stoppard continued to hunt for him by hiring private investigators. When his efforts became apparent to Tanika, she called him and explained Pierre's request to be left alone and allowed to just be with Stan. After much objection, Stoppard agreed to call off the search and allow Pierre to have his wishes respected. Retiring to his workaholic life style, he stayed busy, rolled up his sleeves and took a hands-on interest in the daily workings of OST. Vacations were shelved. Siebert was given his full yearly pay for but a couple of hours a day. By the spring of 2008, Stoppard was wearing himself out, and—feeling young again.

***

In early May of 2008, Derek and Aretha stood before a five-foot high circular wall of marble surrounding her house. Its front walkway and backside opening, like a split letter C, allowed house access and the sea to be seen. As the sun began to drop toward the horizon, Derek stooped and touched the sculpted image depicting the dawn of man. "Amazing. To feel about with his left and sculpt with his right with such detail…amazing."

Aretha nodded. "He says he'd like to come back someday and sculpt the other side of the wall with the history of the universe—with my help, of course."

"Of course," said Derek with a grin. "Who would have thought the shipping of fifteen thousand pounds of rough marble slab would convert to this." He rose and stood in awe of the yearlong work. "The history of the planet etched and carved into three hundred feet of circular wall."

"With the Ode still in the middle of it all," said Aretha. "Rather fitting."

"I don't know, Aretha. My work pales in comparison."

"Nonsense. Yours is from another place of imagination and serves a different purpose completely."

"Purpose? You've never used that word before."

She took his arm and they walked the perimeter, stopping now and again to study the detail and touch Pierre's work. "Without the Ode," she said, "there may have never been Echo Life. Your *Echosis* may have never caught on."

He turned to her. "Echosis. Echo's coining of that word, God…seems so long ago, was prophetic, eh? *'Put a world of echoes together and you have its essence: Echosis.'* He chuckled. "I'm sure to some, it sounds like a malady."

"To some, I'm sure it *is*. Realizing one's inner self and resurrecting imagination; that's frightening to many. Perhaps Linda would still be here today, save for her fear of allowing the echoes of the past do their work. You and I know we can't run away or bury that which has happened. We can only put it in its place and understand it can't be changed. The past works different ways with different people. Nothing profound about that thought." She picked up her pace. "Oh, listen to me. I sound like a bad philosophy lecture."

"Hardly," said Derek.

"But, the Ode…" she continued, "there's something magical about standing in the presence of the Ode, reflecting one's *own* image. Difficult to explain, but vanity aside, it can be transforming." She grinned. "And, anything that can transform this crusty old

617

buzzard has got to have some power. It got me thinking one day and eventually it helped me see that we are but a beginning—an imagined *illusion*. Our past, present and future manifesting now, if you will. Paradoxically, the supernatural aura of Ode taught me *reality*, Derek. It allowed me to spend time in the light of any given day and perceive another layer of my own Echosis—'malady,' as you suggested some might perceive it."

She leaned down and touched a part of the wall. "Since Linda's passing, it's been so difficult. Oh, you don't know. Just to stand before this work and accept…see my condition and process that perception with some action, has been…" Aretha lifted her head and took a deep breath.

"Has been what?" asked Derek.

"Has been a bitch." She ran her hand over more details of the wall. "What was I to hope for? I was a vain member of the species always looking for others to mirror my self-worth, validate my existence. But, with the help of Stanton making me face it, well…. God, Pierre is so special, like you. But…other people can't be our reflection, Derek. Only we alone can mirror us…alone. The Ode taught me that. This wall is a confirmation. We are our personal echoes…in a particular history that is exclusively ours."

She burst forth with a celebratory smile. "How do you think Pierre was able to conceive and execute this miraculous work? In the darkness of his own Echosis, that's how. I would guess there's a bright light reflecting within that young man that will never be extinguished."

Derek squatted and rubbed his fingers over the fine detail of fossil after fossil engraved in the marble leading the eye further toward the next period of the earth's evolution. He grinned. "Beethoven would be proud, yes?"

"Beethoven? As in kindred spirits? Oh, yes," said Aretha.

They stood up and walked a few more feet. "Did he say when he and Stan would be back?"

"No," answered Aretha. "He was vague and private about it all. Before he left, he couldn't stop thanking me though, you as well, as he polished the final five feet that last day. He'd polish, stop, say a few words of gratitude, polish, stop. He said to tell you he was very grateful for all your teaching and help, and that he'd call you often from wherever he was."

"Curious," mused Derek. "Leaving without a forwarding address or anything. Didn't say which way he was heading?"

"All he said was, 'when the money runs out, we'll stop and figure out our next move'."

"Well, as frugal as he lives, that could be a few years from now."

"The commission for this wall, *your* generous payment, well, that will buy a lot of traveling," said Aretha.

"A few years at best," said Derek. "I hope he… I mean, I hope Stan reminds him often enough just how incredibly gifted he is."

Aretha nodded and smiled. "Good chance for that."

She turned at the gazebo and sat down, pouring some iced tea for each of them. "Stan was always there encouraging him, you know, even after almost eleven months. You were here in the beginning, when the slabs were delivered and excitement was high. Toward the end, Stan had to pump Pierre up from time to time. His hands were raw. Even during the winter, save the days of snow-cover… sugar?"

Derek didn't respond, his eyes fixed on the ocean.

"He was out here chipping away," Aretha continued, as she stirred her tea. "Had all ten fingers bandaged, save the tips for feeling, but still he hammered, and chiseled and drilled…it was something to watch."

"Doesn't surprise me what you're saying. When I was teaching him the fundamentals, he couldn't put the tools down."

"You disappointed?"

"Disappointed?" He pulled his eyes back to the table. "About?"

"I mean his not calling you before he left—seeing you in person."

"No. I kind of expected it. We had a long talk the day the slabs were delivered. I asked him to always remember the seagull he often heard moving her wings overhead, and that it was the only entity he needed to never forget. We talked of Echo and I suggested that maybe we were merely vessels through which powers beyond our understanding expressed creative ideas—and that we would probably inspire and spawn more vessels to take the time and express the imagination they might have lost in childhood. His tearful 'thank you' at that moment is all I'll ever need as a goodbye." He shook his head from the reverie. "May's still a bit chilly here, isn't it?"

"Here, have some sugar."

"Yeah, I was going to ask you."

Aretha nodded and scooped him a spoonful, catching her reflection in the Ode. She smiled.

Chapter 98

Successful hitchhiking of the Baja Coast in Mexico is not without its perils. Cars willing to pick up two men with backpacks are far and few between. For Pierre and Stan, however, it was just another leg

619

of their extemporaneous venture. Only thirty days removed from the yearlong wall project, walking was an agreed upon mode of life for the next little while. If an occasional car offered a ride, they were grateful, otherwise, the warm sunshine, and time for conversation, served them well. Stan assumed his role as guide, and Pierre gratefully found his partner's interest in the nomad life no less compelling than his own. So far, their wandering adventure was going well, albeit only a few weeks old.

"Read it again, would you Stan?" asked Pierre.

Stan, with Pierre's arm hooked in his, turned back the dog-eared pages of the novel and began reading again as they walked the shoulder of the highway. As Pierre heard the familiar section for perhaps the tenth time, he thought back once again when he first read the novel based on the life of a famous actress. It had been the character of Sailor, an old blind seaman living in a stone hut on the edge of the ocean that had caught his imagination. Now, with the same darkness Sailor spoke through, he was anxious to meet the man the author's agent said did, in fact, exist. Stan's patient research resulted in their trek down the Mexican coast to where they could find the hut that, according to the novel's story, and the agent, was perched high atop a plateau overlooking the Pacific.

Two hours later, they climbed out of the back of an old pick-up as the driver, Manuel, a gardener reporting for work at The Castle, a luxury resort, stopped at the guardhouse entrance.

"Muchas Gracias, Senor," said Manuel when Stan gave him five dollars for the ride. Manuel drove off through the fifteen-foot iron-gate entrance to the exclusive resort. The man in the guardhouse watched as Stan pulled out a map and turned it around several times, obviously confused where to go. Curious, the guard stepped up to them. "May I help you?"

"Looking for a dirt road to the coast, actually. A stone shelter...guy named Sailor."

The guard took another look at the two, then smiled and pointed to a path outside the perimeter of the property. "No road. Just a path. Two miles."

As the two wearily walked the last hundred yards of the path, Stan continued reading: "'She squinted at the silhouette standing at the edge of the rise, waving his stick above his head and almost singing his greeting, 'Welcome. Welcome. Please join me for tea.'

Were it not for the real sky and ocean dropping off behind him, thought Samantha, I'd swear I was hallucinating. Tea? It must be a hundred out here'."

Stan wiped his forehead. "She got off easy. Got to be hotter than that today." He lifted his eyes from the book and stopped in his tracks. Ahead of them, just as in the book, stood a man waving a stick and yelling, "Hello. Hello."

"Hey, Pierre?"

"Yes. I hear him. Just like he was described?"

"Unbelievable," said Stan.

Pierre raised his hand. "Hello."

Sailor waved his crooked stick again. "Please. Join me for tea."

Stan tried to keep from laughing. "Shit, Pierre. This is spooky."

"More like fun. C'mon." Pierre stepped forward; feeling the road with his own carved stick.

"Hey, wait up," said Stan as he pocketed the book and followed. "This guy could be a nut."

"Yeah," grinned Pierre. "Let's hope so."

After the small talk of greeting one another, the three started walking the long path down to the stone hut. "Just like in the book," whispered Stan to Pierre.

Old Sailor shuffled along, asking about their finding him. Stan filled him in with all the details while Pierre ruminated over the story of Sailor from the book, a tale he had all but perfectly memorized by now.

> "Inside the Sailor's Castle, as the spindly old man chose to call it, the temperature was ten degrees cooler, beckoning a longer visit than anticipated. The surroundings were stark and bare of any superfluous comforts. In the corner stood an old potbelly stove. Standing in the center of the stone and dirt floor was an old galleon bunk bed and three small barrels that served as chairs. The hand carved side panels of the bunk carried the inscription, "One hundred days of storm and no end in sight – June 2, 1784." The lower bunk had planks spread across it providing a level table for things such as eating, chatting and now…tea. As they exchanged niceties and sipped their tea, Samantha found his strong angular face with its weathered skin fascinating as it framed incredibly clear and beautiful eyes, eyes she had just realized were blind. The revelation made the décor of the 18th century lookout shelter all the more intriguing. Both her and Max's attention was pulled to the books, hundreds of books stacked against the walls. Okay, she thought, he's blind

and likes books. My kind of imagination. Max was the
first to pose the question.

"You certainly have a fine collection of books."

Sailor smiled and lifted the old teakettle from the
stove, quickly finding his way back to their barrel seats.
"Oh, those. Can I freshen your tea?"

"Thank you," said Samantha.

"No more for me," replied Max.

Sailor gestured toward the walls, "Those, my friends,
are such rich memories. Occasionally, a traveler will
visit and read to me. Such pleasure, books. Don't you
agree? Many years ago, I served as the ship's
librarian...a rather unique position on a salvage boat..."

Breaking Pierre out of his reverie with the book, Sailor said, "You
like books? I've got books. Books and books. Yes?"

"Yes," said Pierre.

As they stepped inside the thick walls of the hut, the temperature
was thankfully a few degrees cooler. "This is very nice," said Pierre.
"Thank you for inviting us in."

Sailor pushed two barrels over for Stan and Pierre to sit on.
"Been slow this year. Good to have visitors. Here. Sit. Tea with
sugar?"

Stan nodded. "Oh, yeah. Please. Both with sugar."

"Milk?" asked Sailor.

"Milk?" repeated Stan.

Sailor put his fingers between his teeth and let out an ear-
piercing whistle that brought a scrawny goat trotting through the door
opening. "Fresh," Sailor announced proudly.

Stan smiled, eyeing the wrinkled body. "Yeah. Gotta be fresh,
alright. No. Just the sugar." He elbowed Pierre.

"Yeah, just the sugar will be fine," said Pierre.

"Off you go, Mary. Not today."

Mary gave a couple of ba a a a's and loped back out the door as
Sailor stepped up to Stan. "May I?"

Stan leaned back as Sailor put his hands toward Stan's face.
"May you, what?"

"You sound like a kind man. What do you look like?"

"Oh...sure." He leaned forward and placed Sailors hands on his
cheeks. "Pierre here has the same need sometimes," said Stan.

As Sailor explored Stan's face, he asked, "Pierre? You are blind
also?"

"Yes," said Pierre, his hand gripping his stick tightly, feeling
strange with another blind man in the same room. *What is this going*
to be like?

What started out as a genuine visit about being blind and how Sailor had handled it, turned quickly to Sailor's reversing the direction of the conversation.

"My time and how I've handled being blind will come to an end soon. You, however, have a whole life ahead of you that I'm sure will be different from mine. This is the way I chose to be, but it's not as romantic as that novel put it."

"You know of the book," asked Pierre.

"Oh, yes. *Mind Puppets*, right? Last year an attorney made the trek to see me—one of those modern day 'ambulance chasers' I think you call them. Wanted to know if I'd signed any release papers and if not, was I interested in suing for invasion of privacy and a long list of other possibilities. Bunch of poppycock. I had Mary chase him back down the hill. He left behind the book, so the lady who brings me food and provisions began reading it to me. Interesting, but clearly a work of fiction based on some facts."

"Really?" asked Pierre.

"Yes. A man and a woman like the fictional Sam and Max actually did visit me," answered Sailor as he finished his exploring of Stan's face, head, shoulders and hands. As he moved to Pierre, he said, "You don't mind, do you?"

"Beg, pardon?"

Stan spoke up. "He wants to touch your face."

"Oh...of course not," answered Pierre. "Mind if I..."

"Touch?" said Sailor with a smile. "Hope so. Not much fun if you don't know the other person, is it?"

Stan watched as both men felt their way over each other's faces and hands, pausing now and again, then moving on.

"Not much different," said Sailor.

"From?" asked Pierre, as he finished and placed his hands back in his lap.

"From a white man. You're black features are very subtle."

"I'm part white."

Sailor nodded and sat back on his barrel. "Could you tell I was part black?"

Stan took another look at Sailor. Pierre sat motionless, but replied, "No."

"Not many can. Actually, Brazilian and Dutch. My widowed grandmother when she was young would love-up anything that would have her—so the story goes."

Stan burst out laughing. "Sorry."

"Don't be. Mary and I laugh about it often. So, young man, you've come to visit. Where did you come from?"

"New York."

"All this way to talk to the old Sailor. What's on your mind?"

"Nothing, really. Seemed like the right thing to do for a beginning."

"What are you beginning?"

"Stan and I are partners."

"Yes, I could tell. Men don't allow love in their voices very often. Yours was refreshing."

Stan looked at Pierre, who smiled. "That's kind of you."

"Truth, my friend. That's all. Speak the truth and all is well."

"Someone else said almost the same thing to me not long ago."

"He or she was right. You and Stan have known each other for a long time?"

"Quite a while," said Pierre.

"Before or after your blindness? Your scars feel recent." He rose. "Ah, the tea is ready." Stan sat on the edge of his barrel, prepared to jump to the rescue of a spilled cup, but Sailor poured with deft precision.

"Before. The accident just happened a little over a year ago."

"And?" said Sailor as he passed the cups to Stan and Pierre.

"It just happened. That's all."

"My, my. You come all this way to talk about blindness and you refuse to talk about blindness. You'll find the sugar in that can next to you, Stan."

Stan reached to his left and lifted an old coffee can with packets of sugar with the imprint, *The Castle.* As he opened a couple and dumped the contents in Pierre's cup, Sailor continued.

"I had a hard time in the beginning too, but...your hands say you like to work with them. That will help."

"I sculpt now."

Sailor tilted his head as if to hear something. He rose and went to one of his makeshift bookshelves. "There was a story I had..." He felt along the spines of the books. "Yes. Here it is." He pulled a book out and returned to his barrel. As he handed the book to Stan, "You must take this, a gift, and read this to Pierre. He is not alone."

Stan looked at the cover showing a blind sculptor carving a log. "Thank you," said Stan.

"And now," answered Sailor. "We shall go watch the sunset. Come."

Stan looked at his watch. It was only 4 p.m. "But..." he looked outside to just be sure his watch hadn't stopped. "It's 4 o'clock."

"Yes," said Sailor excitedly. "For a blind man, it's anytime you want, yes? Pierre? Ever swim with a dolphin?"

"What? A dolphin?"

"Of course not," said Sailor. "Today you shall. Come."

As the three walked the few hundred yards to the shore, Pierre ran through his mind again the end of the story of Sailor in *Mind Puppets:*

> *Sailor led Max and Samantha along a rocky path of fixed-ropes that had obviously been man-made. It wound down the hillside, passing rusted relics of a past era including rowboats, anchors, propellers, capstans and bollards. The maritime walk ended in a small cove, protected on three sides by volcanic rock.*
>
> *Sailor paused and raised his arm, whispering. "Shhh. We must be careful not to frighten them away."*
>
> *Max and Samantha stopped and waited to hear more. Below, the waters were undisturbed, save for the gentle lapping of waves brushing against the cold porous rock with its blanket of mussels and other mollusks.*
>
> *Sailor turned his head from side to side, listening. He cupped his hands and softly squealed a sound like that of dolphins. Again, he turned his head from side to side. He smiled and whispered, "They are farther out than usual. Might take them a few minutes to come in, but..." he gestured for Max and Samantha to sit down, "... we can sit on the rock here and enjoy the cool salt air. I come here often. Isn't it beautiful?"*
>
> *Samantha had been holding Max's hand on the short walk to the cove, but now she gripped it tightly, as if in fear of something.*
>
> *"Yes... very," answered Max as he turned to Samantha and quietly asked, "What's wrong, Sam?"*
>
> *Continuing to grip Max's hand, Samantha fixed her eyes on Sailor, "How do you do it?" she asked.*
>
> *"Do it? What?" replied Sailor softly.*
>
> *"Stay so happy...here...this desolate place. No one to relate to. No one to be with."*
>
> *Sailor turned his head from side to side once again and smiled. He took her hand and placed it on his chest. "Feel it?"*
>
> *"Feel it... what?"*
>
> *"Happiness, my dear. That wonderful sound "within" where the real thing resides. Where no matter the interruptions in life, no matter the place or time when the unknown, the unseen, the unexpected, can surprise you, the happiness of life comes from little else but honesty with oneself...and perhaps a small amount of intelligence to help one understand the quiet voice inside*

that keeps you company…keeps you from thinking
you're alone or without someone to relate to." He patted
her hand once again. "And of course, it's always a
special treat to have visitors like yourself to add to the
sounds." He pressed her hand tighter to his chest.
"Now, do you hear it?"

   She drank in his kind expression, his wrinkled eyes
that sparkled even brighter with the water's reflection.
"Of course I hear it."

   "Good. That is good. From me to you. From you to
your husband and the unborn I hope you will realize
someday. An honest heart deserves other honest
hearts." He turned back to the ocean. He slowly rose
and turned his head again. "Yes…they have heard the
happiness as well." He cupped his hand once again,
using the soft squeals of his voice to bring the dolphins
to the surface. One, two…seven in all. They came and
played with the three of them with the same love and
calm as had beckoned them…the same peace and
tranquility that now ushered in a tear to both Samantha
and Max's eyes. To Sam, it was as if a new dimension,
a higher self had been introduced, an appreciation that
would challenge forever her stubborn resistance to the
honesty Sailor had asked her to believe in. To Max, a
fortuitous experience that he knew would help keep the
fragile and vulnerable woman he loved from succumbing
to a world that would use her up without any thought of
its cost. To Sailor, it was just another sharing, a simple
everyday experience with two strangers in need of…"

"Pierre! You hear them?" shouted Sailor.

Startled, Pierre turned to his left and his right, but shook his
head. "No. I'm sorry."

"Well, your hearing will get better with time. Come, we'll walk
down a bit further to the grotto. They love the calm water there. Like
a big bathtub, you know." Sailor started unbuttoning his shirt as he
walked. "Not shy are you? Don't have any bathing trunks."

Once inside the massive grotto, the size of an Olympic pool, the
three men donned their "xxx" bathing suits, as Sailor called them,
and prepared to swim with Sailor's family of dolphins. For both
Pierre and Stan, the experience was beyond their imagination. As
the light shimmered across the water from the low rock opening at
the ocean's edge, Pierre naturally migrated to where the warmth of
the light rose up the wet walls of the cave.

"The waves of heat are very pleasant, no?" said Sailor as he stood upright, letting the reflective ripples of sunlight cascade up his naked body.

Stan gently urged Pierre into a like position and watched as both men smiled the gift only they could appreciate. After a few moments, the old man of the sea raised his chin and chirped the language of the dorsal wonders of the deep.

Four dolphins leaped from the water, arcing high and diving under. As Sailor shouted with glee, "Yeowwweee! Come...quickly. Casting off!" he shouted. "Here, Pierre, paddle next to me. They know how to play the blind like a fiddle," laughing at his own joke.

As they waited, Stan looked all around him, his face turning child-like as the dolphins lined up, their snouts reaching out in unison, nudging Sailor's arm. As if choreographed and rehearsed, the dolphins guided the three from one end of the grotto to the next, at times becoming saddles for their playmates. Hoops and yells echoed through the damp crevasses and ledges of the walls, as Sailor whispered and cajoled his dorsal friends into giving his guests an experience they would never forget.

It was several hours later when, past the playtime with the dolphins, the sunset, and a final cup of tea, Pierre and Stan bade farewell to their friend.

"You'll come again, I hope," said Sailor.

"Perhaps," said Pierre. "We don't know where we'll be one day to next at this point."

"Well, you are always welcome. Not often I get to share the good life with another man of darkness. Here," he said as he handed his smooth worn walking stick to Pierre. "Let me offer you reason to return. This old piece of cedar has seen many things few people see." He took hold of Pierre's stick. "May I?"

"You want to trade?"

"Only until you return. You take mine on your journey and when you return, we'll exchange again. Perhaps you will find, as I did, that seeing comes in many different forms. The eyes of my staff never sleep, but experiences here are limited now. You will add years of life to the old crook. Please. May we?"

Pierre's hands studied the knotted and twisted branch for a few moments. "It is so smooth."

"Many years of guiding me in the darkness," said Sailor as he felt the fresh cut knobs and shaved edges of Pierre's. "This is a fine young stick. Some youth in my life is long overdue. With youth, there is always the joy of the unknown, the surprise of the unprepared." He reached for Pierre's shoulder. "Use yours well."

He turned and gripped Stan's hand. "And you, my friend, trust the stick. It will let him be more of who he is—let him make mistakes where you would prevent them. Mistakes, stumbles on the road—all are important. So..." He stood back and lifted his new stick above his head. "Enjoy your journey."

Pierre stepped forward and feeling Sailor in front of him, took his shoulders. Stan watched as the two men held their blind gaze of each other. He wondered what was going through each of their minds at that moment—*what kind of connection were they experiencing?* For Stan, the smile on their lips confirmed the wisdom of Sailor's words. Blindness possessed its own value, a mystery worth just allowing to exist. He too smiled. *There are many ways to see.*

CHAPTER 99

Stoppard didn't have an answer for it as he walked through Avery Fisher Hall's backstage. A sense of slow motion, everyone moving toward, then past him—the impressions stretching and abandoning him as if morphing into something else—left him feeling strange, as if he were supposed to remember this as an interminably slow and gradual experience. After a career of many awards, accolades, and personal high points of accomplishment, he was dismayed at what he was now living through. *This is the night of nights, an acknowledgement like no other, and the opportunity to announce the most far-reaching gesture of my career. Why is everything so death-like?*

"Mister Denning? Sir?"

Stoppard blinked at the reflection of his personal mirror and pulled himself back into the moment. Over his left shoulder was Gerard, the make-up supervisor for the show, fussing over every remaining hair on his head. "Yes, I'm sorry. You were saying?"

"Nothing yet sir, but I do want you to feel your best, so—how do you like it?"

"What?" said Stoppard.

"I just touched the ends with pomade. It will catch the light and..."

"I'm sure it's just fine, Gerard. Am I finished?"

"Yes, sir. You might want to keep the Kleenex over your collar until the show starts. Frankie, would you escort Mister Denning back to his dressing room? I'll come in and touch up after we clear up in here, Okay?"

Stoppard nodded. "Sure." He rose from the chair, looked around him at the other make-up and wardrobe people scurrying about tidying up their tables and sorting costumes, and walked out with Frankie, the assistant stage manager, as the dancers began to invade the room for their makeup.

As they walked between the flats and heavy cable crowding the wings of the stage, Frankie asked, "Can we get you anything, Mister Denning?"

"No. No, thank you. Just need a little peace and quiet for a few minutes."

"Yes, it can get hectic as you well know. Right here, watch your step around these cables. Fine. This way."

As Stoppard re-entered his dressing room flanked by two security guards, he said, "What's this?"

"Oh," said the senior of the two armed guards. "New policy. V.I.P.s like yourself have to have two of us."

Stoppard smiled. "Times, they are a changing, eh?"

"Rock stars get two, plus one at each end of the hall."

"Yeah, well..."

"I'll give you a fifteen and a five, Mister Denning, so just relax," said Frankie. "If there's anything you need, water, food, you just pick up the phone, okay?"

Stoppard nodded and Frankie scurried off. After closing the door, Stoppard stood before the multiple floral arrangements and stacks of well wishing e-mails and gift-wrapped boxes from Tiffany and other impressive 5th Ave. stores. He leaned onto the dressing table and stared at himself. After a few moments, he stepped over to the couch and lay down, careful, as Gerard had insisted, to keep the Kleenex tucked over his collar. He closed his eyes and indulged in the dead quiet of the room.

Minutes later, Stoppard was escorted from back stage to the mezzanine and his honorary box, still experiencing the uncomfortable slow motion effect, making the walk seem in some respects like a walk to the gas chamber. As he passed familiar competitive faces, looking like hit men with their hands firmly at the ready to fire a fatal shot, his mind raced back to all the plateaus he had conquered, all the buttressing and fortification he had created to get where he was now about to sit. This place of honor, notoriety and fame, where few others had been able to reach, was waiting; its façade of burgundy and gold velvet ready to enfold him in its addictive grip.

As he finished shaking hands and exchanging good wishes with his invited guests, Tanika, Derek, Samara, Theo, Sol, and Siebert flanking both sides of his guest of honor chair, he turned to the orchestra floor, noting the many faces looking toward the guest of honor. Their patronizing smiles took him back to the many awards in the past, where most were received from those who would have him dead, or awards from those who would beg his favor for programming and publication—and of course the awards that many had spent time dreaming up in order to bring attention to *themselves.*

He turned to the balcony audience that was part of twenty-seven hundred that filled the hall. He nodded in the politically correct fashion and wondered for the first time, *what's it really all about?* Awards. In the world of entertainment, there would never be enough awards to accommodate the minions of bottom feeders. There were so many who groveled daily in the leftover slop and remains of failure's humiliation in order to pay their dues and maybe someday be in the same company, or at least have an audience with those that could make and break careers. Stoppard Denning was well aware he was one of *those* who could make or break a career without even making a phone call. Silence was his greatest weapon, and with it, he could alienate, maim, or kill any ambition he chose. For if one of OST's many entertainment news magazines or gossip reports on its TV or radio broadcasts didn't mention your name, you began worrying. If your name went more than two months without a reference, you could be living on *worse* than borrowed time.

And so it was with a sense of relief and closure that he stood at the velvet railing of his honorary box, overlooking the first few rows of the orchestra, and raised his hand to graciously accommodate the patronizing applause that, like a sea of fluttering scavenger wings hovering above a death scene, awaited his every move. This was the countdown.

The outside papers and gossip columns had carried rumors for some time that as a result of pulling Echo Life into OST's stable of subsidiary companies—and the publication of the phenomenal success, *Time Remaining*, Theodore Donnaly's controversial novel— this award night would be the natural time for him to step aside and let the new blood of Echo Life's proven entertainment paradigm proceed to revamp OST as a whole. *Me, step aside? Keep them guessing.* As the applause subsided and he sat, it was with relish that he reviewed in his mind the last hurrah he had prepared for all the jackals and vultures to feast upon.

The evening began with a standard "award" dance routine, followed with a comic routine by the show's host, OST's late night talk show star, Jerry Beemer. He lobbed a few *Roast* worthy shells across Stoppard's bow before ushering in the evening's entertainment tribute to honor his boss's accomplishments. As he took in the many accolades spoken, danced and sung from the stage, as well as the video clips of his past accomplishments, he couldn't help question how much of the decision to honor him was predicated on Donnaly's number one best selling novel depicting a character many believed was based on him.

As the giant screen on stage brought the PBS special into its primary award minutes with "man on the street" interviews praising the man who had poured millions into Darfur and made headlines with his funding to save the *Ivan-Scape* in Jamaica, along with medical help for Pierre Haweisi, he ruminated on Donnaly's creation of a Jeckle and Hyde persona for his character, a persona that defied the presumed singular monster image many had of him. *Did "Time Remaining" pique the public's imagination that much?* Knowing it had jumped to the number one slot on the Times Bestseller list for the past thirty-six weeks brought a smile to his lips. *After all, I know all about giving the people what they want, don't I? The public loves an anti-hero turned hero—especially a rich one. They also give him awards.*

Stoppard was quietly ushered by a production assistant from his seat to the outer halls and backstage for his entrance to accept the award as the final video montage played out on the big screen. As they made their way through the familiar labyrinth of cables, flats, equipment and stage hands, he once again experienced everything passing him in slow motion, even slower than before, giving him the eerie feeling that something overwhelming was about to happen.

Following the final words of praise from Jerry, he stepped up to the all glass lectern and received from Spencer Harding, President of "The Achievement Magazine," the platinum miniature world globe. "It is with great pleasure and honor that Achievement Magazine awards the 2008 Achievement Award to Stoppard Denning, a man of immense talent, public awareness, and daring."

The audience rose and gave him his first of many a standing ovations.

TV sets around the country, and as far away as the space station high above the earth, remained tuned in as the applauding audience calmed and took their seats. Stoppard smiled toward his box of personal guests, and began his speech.

Derek sat watching Stoppard deliver a customary acceptance speech with recognition and thanks going to OST's staff and executive team for making such an award possible. He cited his father, his teachers as a youngster, and his professors later in college. There were even some unexpected mentions as well.

"…and to the ever faithful security company, the janitorial services, the cooks, chefs and dishwashers, all part of the building that continues to provide the public with devoted media service and entertainment, let me also say *thank you*. Without them, there wouldn't be the OST you've so faithfully supported over the years."

Feeling as if they were in a *State of the Union* address before congress, the audience rose once again, applauding until Stoppard, with his inimitable timing, put the cards in his pocket, waited until the last cough was stifled, and then said, "I wish to say a few words regarding the changes in our world that I've witnessed during my years at OST. Some, incidentally, I'm proud to say were as a result of our leadership in the field of providing news and entertainment to a global audience.

"Perhaps it's appropriate to use Darfur as an example of my concerns. As you may know, I've dedicated a considerable amount of time and resources there over the past two years. During that time, I've witnessed military and political genocide of a large number of people. Among the many impressions and questions concerning this sad historical period—a period of time that continues as we sit here tonight—is one that begs to be better understood, and the single most demanding question I've been left with as I receive this award tonight: How do we stop what appears to be a global breakdown in the area of caring?

"Simple word that—caring. And, as a society, we care about many things, but we're caring less and less about the other person and becoming more and more lost in our self-interests. Now, I'm not here to lecture, or create a political platform for some kind of reform, but I am here to raise a question about this word 'achievement.' This wonderful tribute you've staged for me tonight is about my past achievements. For that, I'm very grateful, but I question what the achievements of the future should be about. Mine. Yours. The world's. As a global society, we need to ask ourselves what is the price of achievement? What price am I willing to pay for achievement? As they say, *nothing is free.* Everything has a price. We need only look at the Iraq war and the price we pay right here in America for the peace and prosperity we enjoy. But is there more we should be thinking about? I ask you that tonight. Is there more?

"I for one have done very well in the eyes of the average person. I took a small opportunity and developed it to what it is today, but—I too paid a price. No, it wasn't the financial price. And it wasn't the loss of my life or health—knock wood. But..." Stoppard hesitated and looked up at the guests seated in his box. "The price I paid is the price I'm hoping the rest of the world will cease paying. I, at one time, gave up caring. Yes, Stoppard Denning spent many years not caring about the very people I've acknowledged tonight. What I did care about was making OST the world's largest media conglomerate, at any price. Yes, I have some regrets. I regret that as I look around, I see others creating their achievements paying the same price as I paid. People who learned from me."

He glanced around the room with a sad smile. "We're so good at covering up the truth, you know. And the *truth* of the matter is, here in America we have placed achievement above all else in our quest to live the good life…at any price. We have been taught that the pursuit of happiness is really the pursuit of comfort and the stuff that gives it to us…at any price. As a result, our comfort zones are far above the rest of the world. Even our poor—not to make light of their situation—enjoy middle class comfort compared to many parts of the world. But, there is a balance that was lost… a balance during the recent years I had to be willing to learn…at any cost.

"So, before I bore you any longer with a plea for caring, let me enter my plea of guilty. Guilty of ruthless ambition at times. Guilty of greed. Guilty of duplicitous behavior. Guilty of attacking anything that threatened my comfort zone. Guilty of ignoring my family. And finally, guilty of giving the people what they wanted, with no regard to my responsibility to listen carefully and provide a platform for them to discover what they needed." He glanced up at his booth, and smiled. "I'm stealing that phrase tonight, with your kind consent."

Derek nodded ever so slightly, but enough that Stoppard not only received the gesture, but clearly made out the vertical line glistening on Derek's cheek.

"I have several sitting with me tonight who helped create the atmosphere of my epiphany, but one in particular is Derek Turrel."

The hall acknowledged Derek's presence with a few moments of respectful applause.

Stoppard continued. "His Echo Life project—although originally perceived by me as a nuisance, then as competition, then as a nemesis to OST—is now our flagship image and leading profit center. And for everyone's information, an honest profit center, with a new policy dedicating twenty percent of all gross profits to a funding organization designed to enable thousands of professional, as well as amateur artists of every discipline, to create more programming that stimulates our faithful followers with an honest desire to pursue their imagination and creation… to once again spend some time with their inner child…as I have of late."

The audience arose and applauded for two straight minutes.

Stoppard motioned the Trooper spotlights be taken off him and directed over to his box, flooding Derek and other Echo guests with the limelight. "And then there are the books to be published that carry Derek's integrity and that of his friend, and OST's number one best-selling author, Theodore Donnaly. Please stand up Theo."

Another standing ovation finally brought Theo to his feet for but a moment of humble acknowledgement.

Stoppard smiled, and then went on. "Yes—2007 was OST's greatest year not because Stoppard Denning knew how to cash in on the new digital age, or publish more best selling books, or even play the game of ratings and audience manipulation better than the next guy. It was because Derek Turrel, laboring through years of trial and error on his part, knew things about life and people that I had only been seeing as fiction, his steadfast mission of bringing the people what they need, as well as what they want, has given a rebirth to imagination and creativity for the masses. He has courageously lifted the bar to heights I could only dream about. Congratulations, Mister Turrel. To your colleagues, Mister Berkowitz, Mister Donnaly, Ms. Jennings—your symphony premier last year in this very hall was incomparable—to all of you up there, many thanks and much appreciation from me... and the world."

As the applause once again rang out, Stoppard graciously rolled a kiss from both his hands to the Echo Life guests.

"Now, during this maturation process of caring, I've had the good fortune of knowing certain people apart from the day to day business. In particular, my good friend Siebert Collins. He's sitting up there, as well. Siebert and I have known each other for many years, and I consider him my most trusted confidant. Were it not for his calm patience and understanding of my special kind of ignorance, I wouldn't be standing here tonight. Thank you, Siebert."

More applause.

"Last, and certainly not least, let me thank my family. Yes— much to the chagrin of the tabloids who will feel cheated for not breaking this first as a clandestine *inside scoop* on their front pages—I do have a family." Stoppard once again looked up to his box. "Ms. Haweisi, would you please stand up?"

Tanika hesitantly looked to Derek who smiled and nodded. As she stood, a courteous, but hesitant applause filled the hall.

Stoppard continued, "I don't wish to embarrass Ms. Haweisi, but she is not only the proud mother of Pierre Haweisi, the artist who I'm sure most of you are aware of by now, but also one who bears the cross of a secret we've both kept...the unplanned birth of Pierre Haweisi many years ago, and one I now publicly and proudly take full responsibility for. My lack of caring perhaps started back then. Who knows? But tonight, I wish to renounce that kind of behavior and make an effort to set in motion some important changes—some important caring, for Tanika Haweisi, for my son Pierre Haweisi, and to a public that is going to expect more from me and the OST organization."

Stoppard paused amidst the silent hall and sipped some water. "I've had a fantastic ride. I've earned the right to do with my time and money that which I choose. So, come Monday morning, I will be instructing my attorneys to draw up documents for the transfer of the bulk of my estate, fifteen billion dollars, to the Haweisi/Echo Foundation where further support and funding for..." He paused as the hall momentarily became a cacophony of hushed whispers and muffled gasps. "...support and funding for artists and creative minds whoever, and wherever they may be. For, as Mister Turrel has trumpeted for some time now, 'we are all creative'. I will ask Derek Turrel to share the responsibility of managing the funding with Tanika and trust he will accept. As for myself, effective as soon as possible, I will take retirement from the day to day chores at OST, but remain Chairman."

Some started applauding, prompting Stoppard to put his hand up. "Finally, my son Pierre has been on a quiet journey of late with his life-companion Stan. If you're watching tonight, I send you my love, and I wish you well." Clearing his throat, he continued, "I...I look forward to your return so that we might enjoy some time together." He held the award in his hands once again. Raising it to the audience, he said, "If the truth really be told, Pierre's accomplishments far outweigh those of myself. May we all continue learning our lessons in life with less selfishness and more caring. Thank you."

Sustained applause, less any hooting or whistles, echoed through the hall as Stoppard graciously bowed his head, mouthing "thank you, thank you," several times as he walked into the wings, smiled at the stage hands and crew, continued up the backstage stairway to his dressing room and entered, still hearing the applause as he closed the door. He looked again at the award in his hands, then sat, closed his eyes and wept. It was some time later when he brought himself out of the purge. He looked about his room; a sense of bewilderment overtook him. There wasn't any more applause— no more footsteps outside. He went to the door, opened it to see darkened halls. Stepping back into the room, a note affixed to his door. It read, "Didn't want to disturb you. We'll be at The Renaissance when you're ready to join us." He looked up once again. Silence. He turned his head slightly, trying to make out the familiar screeching sound in the distance. *A seagull in Avery Fisher Hall?*

Chapter 100

Later that night—after attending a celebratory dinner for Stoppard that Derek had arranged—the famous vertical fountains at Lincoln Center continued to rise and fall every few seconds, reminding the dark figure sitting motionless at their edge that water was wet. Stoppard's hair dripped down his face and onto the globe he held in his hands. Parked at the curb was the limo with the motor running. Siebert, ever patient, ever professional, ever the friend, watched Stoppard's insistent gestures to *give me a few more moments.*

Stoppard let his chin continue to rest on his soaked bowtie. *And so if it's possible—if there is some power up there that sends messages out—let him know his father is trying to become a bit less of an enemy...a jerk. I miss you. I miss you, Pierre.*

***

By dawn, Siebert was approaching empty on the gas tank. He glanced into the rear view mirror at Stoppard, still wet, still motionless in the corner. "If you want me to keep driving, Mister Denning, I best go for some gas."

"Huh? Oh. What do we have left?" mumbled Stoppard, looking out the window at the sun starting to break through the trees.

"Less than a quarter and you know how finicky the tank is around the empty zone."

Stoppard sat up, stretched and slumped again. "Know what, Siebert?"

"You're tired, sir?"

"No."

"Want to get out of your wet clothes?"

"No. Heavens, no. Not what I was thinking. I'm going to take a walk around the lake. You go get some gas and then find yourself a nice parking spot and catch a few winks if you want. I've got my cell phone. I'll call you when I'm done. Give me a chance to dry out, you know?"

"Very good, sir."

Siebert pulled to the side and stopped. "You want me to bring you some coffee, sir?"

"Actually, I'm okay. Thanks."

"Dry clothes. I can stop up at..."

"No. I'm fine this way...for a change." Stoppard stepped out, his shoes squishing as he walked across the road and made his way toward the lake. He looked up at the skyline. Only the tops of the buildings were getting the first rays of the day. All was quiet, save for the cyclists and joggers now beginning to appear.

As he neared the lake's shoreline, he caught site of a few ducks and a swan. Lifting his eyes skyward, he saw a formation of seagulls in the unusual double "v" formation. As they passed he brought his eyes back to the water. He squinted at the child kneeling at the lake's edge on the far side. *Strange for a child to be out this early*, he thought. He loosened his soggy bow tie and cummerbund, shoved his hands in his pockets and shuffled around the lake to the other side. As he approached the boy's backside, he noticed he was dressed rather shabbily and had a worn brown grocery bag resting at his side. On a closer look, he figured the boy to be about 8 or 9 years old. "Hi," said Stoppard.

The boy turned his head and looked up, undisturbed by the sudden intrusion. "Hello." He turned back, hovering over something he was involved in.

"What you doing?"

"Fixin' it."

"Fixin' what?"

"My boat."

"What's wrong with it?" said Stoppard, craning his neck to get a peek.

"It's broke."

"Okay. Need any help?"

"Won't stick, that's all."

Stoppard moved around to the boy's side where he could see the six-inch boat made out of Popsicle sticks. The boy had a small bottle of white glue and was trying to apply it to the underside. Stoppard watched as every time the boy applied it, and pressed the connection, he'd hold it a few moments, then let go, and the stick would fall. "Not cooperating, is it?"

"My mom usually repairs it for me, but she's busy."

Stoppard looked around, but there was no one in sight. "Is she close by?"

The boy paused, then looked up at Stoppard. His eyes examined the still wet satin lapel and satin stripe down the side of his pants. "My mom told me a long time ago to not talk to strangers."

"And she was right. Especially strangers in wet tuxedos."

The boy went back to his routine of glue, hold, fall. "She'll be back with our food pretty soon."

Stoppard sat down cross-legged on the walk a few feet away and looked out over the lake.

The boy looked up again. "You homeless?"

"Nope. Just a guy who can't sleep tonight."

"It's morning, mister."

"Well, last night. Just thought maybe if I walked a bit, I could get sleepy." He glanced again at the boy's struggle to get the repair done. "You sail your boat here?"

"Sometimes when I can get here early enough."

Stoppard nodded. "Yeah, it's nice to sail when there's nothing around. Just you and the water. Guess it gets crowded here in the summer, eh?"

"Sometimes." The boy looked across the lake at the entrance. "You know what time it is?"

Stoppard looked at his watch. "Comin' up on 7 o'clock."

The boy cringed. "Only got a half hour 'fore they get here."

Stoppard looked across the lake at the entrance as well. "Who's they?"

"The stuck ups"

"Stuck ups?"

"Kids from some private school. Bunch of bullies with remote controlled boats. They get here around 7:30 before class and..."

"And..."

The boy paused. "I'm not supposed to talk to strangers."

"Well, I'm not going to offer you candy or anything. I sure don't want to scare you. But, I like boats. I've actually got a big boat I sail around in."

The boy slowly turned and eyed Stoppard's clothing again. "You're all drippy, mister. You don't look like you could own a big boat."

"Oh, these?" He pulled his bow tie off and stuffed it in his pocket. "Just show. When I'm on my boat, I'm *cas* like you."

"*Cas*?"

"Casual. You know, I put on my boatin' clothes like yours."

"Lucky."

"How so?'

"This be my boatin' *and* my dress up clothes."

Stoppard nodded, a bit embarrassed. "Well, makes it convenient. I know I hated to change clothes when I was a kid."

"Hey mister, my mom's gonna have a fit she comes here and I'm talkin' with you."

Stoppard rose. "Sorry. I'll leave, but—here, let me help you with that first. May I?"

"What time is it?"

"After 7 now. Movin' toward 7:30 pretty fast."

"Okay. If you think you can. But hurry up."

Stoppard stepped up, turned the boat over so the underside was on top. He dabbed the stick with a little glue and held it. "Well, if we're gonna be partners on this, my name's Stoppard. What's yours?"

"Stoppard? Never heard that name before."

"Well, you can call me Stop, if you prefer."

"Better. Zorn's mine."

"Zorn. That's a nice name."

"C'mon, mister. It's as bad as yours. 'Stop.' What kind of name is that?"

They both exchanged a chuckle. "You know about gravity yet, Zorn?"

"Kinda."

"Well, you see, when you try and do it the other way, with the bottom down, gravity takes over and—kerplunk. Won't hold. Flip it over. Now the gravity is working for you. You know, if you let it, everything falls to the ground. Ever see an astronaut float around in their space capsules?"

"Sure."

"That's lack of gravity. In space, there isn't any gravity. Down here, on earth, that's what keeps us from floating up, up and away."

"Mmm."

Stoppard turned the boat over. "There. Give it a couple more minutes and I bet it floats for you." He crossed his legs and sat next to the boy.

"Thanks." The boy crossed his legs as well and the two of them watched as it dried in the sun.

"How big is your boat, mister?"

"Well, it would pretty much fill this lake."

The boy burst out with a laugh. "Wow. Make *their* boats look pretty puny."

"Their?"

"The bullies' boats."

"Oh, well, big is relative."

"What?"

"Oh, nothing." He pointed to his boat. "Yours is more special than its size."

The boy looked at his boat again. "What? This? Only thing special about this boat is that my mom stole the Popsicle sticks from the mission so I could make it."

"Mission?"

"Yeah. They had a bunch. They didn't miss them, she said."

Stoppard paused a long moment. He flashed back to the nails, hammer and old ship planks he helped his father construct into "Jerry's Bar."

"Mister, I mean, Stop?"

Stoppard pulled himself back to the moment. "Yeah?"

"You stick around for a just a few more minutes?"

Stoppard chuckled. "First you want me to go, then..."

"They're comin' and they'll probably want me out of here."

Stoppard looked toward the entrance where the boy's eyes were fixed. Running down the slope was a group of 10 or 11 year old boys, all dressed in private school uniforms, each carrying a fancy sail or motor yacht with remote control. They were followed by their teacher who was in obligatory Brooks Brother's summer sharkskin pants and blue blazer, topped off with a captain's hat. Striding down to the lakeside path, he appeared to Stoppard as a parody of Admiral Nimitz going ashore. "Let's look lively, boys," shouted the teacher. "Winds are up. Tide is perfect."

The boys fanned out, each staking a twenty to thirty foot arc of the lake to sail. Three boys made their way quickly to Stoppard's side of the lake as he and Zorn placed the boat in the water. Zorn held tightly to the roll of kite string that kept it from drifting too far away. "Yeah," shouted the boy. "It works. It's floating again. Thanks, Stop."

The first of the three boys stepped up with the expected attitude. "Hey. We're from St. Mathews, and this is our time on the lake."

"Oh, we'll be just a few minutes," said Stoppard as he and Zorn eyed the yard-long fiberglass yacht in the boy's hands. "Just a few."

The second boy, hefting an equally large sailboat and remote yelled across the lake, "Mister Broadbank. We have a problem here."

By the time Mister Broadbank walked around the lake, all the boats were in the water, except the one boy with the yacht whose designated spot was where Stoppard and Zorn were enjoying their brief sail. "What seems to be the problem, Mister Evans?"

"This is my spot. How am I supposed to motor my rig with that stupid Popsicle thing in the way?"

Mister Broadbank reached over to shake Stoppard's hand. "Sorry for the mix-up." He leaned further, surreptitiously saying, "Mister Evans is a bit high strung."

Zorn started easing his boat to shore. "I'll get it out, sir. I'll get it out."

Stoppard leaned down and touched Zorn's hand. "No. I think Mister Evans can wait another five minutes while you enjoy your sail."

Mister Broadbank took a closer look at Stoppard's dress and the echo of his stern message and was nonplussed for the moment.

"Mister Broadbank?" said the older boy.

"Well," stammered Mister Broadbank. "I'm sure we can accommodate another five minutes. Now, you be patient, Mister Evans. Just sit over there on the bench and—be patient." Mister Broadbank gave another surreptitious look at Stoppard, and said, "This is just a nice man assisting his son with a few moments on the water." He tipped his hat as if to ask permission to go ashore and exited much livelier than he arrived.

Mister Evans huffed and stepped back to the bench, sitting and straddling his thirty-six inch craft on his lap. Stoppard moved to Zorn's side. Both were stifling a laugh. "See," said Stoppard, "size doesn't mean as much as you thought."

Five minutes later, Zorn wound in his boat and Mister Evans angrily placed his yacht in the water, only to find that his remote control was malfunctioning and the boat went nowhere. "Mister Broadbank? Mister Broadbank?"

Zorn picked up his brown bag and walked to the bench with Stoppard. "You okay?" said Stoppard.

"Sure. My mom just started down the entrance. You better skedaddle, Stop. Thanks for the fix."

Stoppard looked toward the entrance to see an overloaded shopping cart being pushed down the walk by a shabbily dressed woman in her thirties. He paused a moment, then reached into his pocket and palmed a few bills. "Say, let's make sure you've got everything," and he reached down, opened the brown bag, stuck his hand in, feigning a check of its contents, and folded the bag back up. "Yeah. Think we got everything. You make sure you put another coat of glue on that piece when you get home. You know, the glue in your bag...just in case."

The boy looked up perplexed. "Just in case of what?"

"I don't know. Just in case. That's all. You have a good day and thanks for letting me sail with you."

"Sure. I'm here every couple of days."

"Okay." Said Stoppard. "Good. See ya."

As he walked away, he couldn't take his eyes off the woman pushing her wobbly cart. *Wonder if I could fix that wheel if I came back another day? Another day.*

CHAPTER 101

Derek remained in bed contemplating the previous Award night. "It's just that his nationwide announcement of dropping it in my lap leaves little room for me to say no."

Samara paused, then rolled out of bed. "Coffee?"

"No comment?"

She turned and in hushed and loving tones, said, "I've been commenting all night, my darling, and you've been asking me the same question a little differently for hours now. 'No comment'?" You're the one that put 'You're all creative' out there. How creative are *you*?"

"You don't know how hard it is to believe Stoppard, to...to..."

"Trust him? Oh, I think I know a little about his duplicitous nature. But he just might be past that, now. He tried to hire me once, you know."

"You never told me about that."

"I obviously didn't buy into it, so there was no reason to upset you any further than you've been for... how long as it been? Three years?"

"I still don't understand why you never even mentioned it."

"Sounds like you need to hear the whole five minute story."

"Yes. Yes I do."

"Mind if I make the coffee first?"

"Make it strong, okay?" mumbled Derek as he stared up at his "Family" rock suspended above him.

* * *

The darkness of Stoppard's curtain drawn bedroom was interrupted with what sounded like the crack of a window somewhere in his apartment. His eyes shot open as he listened for any further noise. The LED light on his alarm system remained constant, a sure sign that no entry into the apartment had been made.

He rose cautiously and walked to his windows, pulling back the heavy drapes. A bright sunny mid-day greeted his bleary eyes, and he turned away. The empty wine bottle and glass at his bedside explained the headache. He moved guardedly through the penthouse rooms, checking windows and doors. By the time he reached the living room, he was convinced he had imagined the noise, until he saw the sliding glass door to the terrace. There was a jagged crack running the full vertical length. "Son of a bitch," he grumbled. "Son of a bitch."

He walked closer to examine. The door was still locked. The sun was beating directly on the glass, giving him his answer. He shook his head and reached for the wall switch that electrically unfolded the terrace awning. He shuffled over to the telephone and called the concierge desk, still staring at the cracked glass. "Nathanial, I've been fucked. No, I mean, the fucking sun has cracked my window. What? I forgot to open the awning, that's why. How the hell hot is it out there? Hundred, huh. What's with this fucking heat? What time is it anyway? Two? Well—hell. Serves

642

me right. At any rate, get me a replacement ASAP. Eh? Yeah. Extra tempered glass. Good idea. As much temperin' as they make. Good... Well, as quickly as you can. Looks like shit, you know. Thanks. Hey, didn't mean to sound so grumpy, okay?"

He hung up and noticed another empty bottle of wine next to his TV chair. *Bad, Stop. Bad.* He squeezed the bridge of his nose. *Should have stayed at the lake instead of doing this to myself. Could have fixed that other kid's boat, little bastard. Should have fixed the wheel on that shopping cart, too. What the hell's a matter with me?*

He shuffled into the kitchen and put on his coffee. *Servants' day off. Fuck me.*

***

"And if I don't? If I fail? Then what? You want me back on the couch forever?"

Samara's calm face was the only grace he felt at the moment. They remained in bed after a few hours sleep, sipping coffee and staring up at the hanging sculpture. He was beating up on himself, unmercifully. "Derek, you don't have to take the offer. It's something you can graciously decline."

"Oh, you think he's made it possible to decline? My God, Samara. He lets Echo Life sit down at the high stakes table and he supplies the chips, lots of chips, and he says, 'just keep playin' the card you've been playin' and everything will be fine.' That's a free ride. Nobody gives a free ride."

"Your old paranoia is creeping back in again. A few years ago you drove me nuts reminding me you weren't a 'normal person.' Well, like I said to you over and over, abnormal isn't necessarily negative, unless you choose to make it so. You think he's got something he's not telling you, and I say you're right, but it's probably not what you think."

"Oh, so you do still see his scheming nature."

"I didn't say anything about 'still' scheming, Derek. Maybe what he's not telling you is he's tired. He's wanting to rest. He's probably wanting to return to the womb like all you guys, but..."

"Jesus, here we go."

"But...he's trying to change his life for the better. That's what is confusing you. You wanted to change yours the same way not long ago, and it wasn't until you 'did it,' went out and put Echo Life together that you understood that. Asking you to manage the foundation is his way of *doing it* too...for you, Derek. That's all he wants. He sees what you did for his son, and he doesn't even know you gave all your stock sell-off money to Pierre."

"And he never will. You promised."

"I know. Don't worry. But, back to the point. Derek, he's not going to do anything to hurt you. He wants you to succeed."

"Okay. Okay. Let's assume you're right. Samara, even if his motives are squeaky clean, if it's not what *I* want to do, then it doesn't matter if he thinks he's doing me a huge favor by putting me in charge of fifteen billion dollars." He went silent and took a sip of coffee. "Samara, I'm scared. Is that the kind of person that should be writing checks from a fifteen billion dollar account?"

"Can you imagine anyone with that kind of responsibility not feeling a little scared?"

"Yes."

"Who?"

"Stoppard."

"No jokes," said Samara.

"Not a joke. Why doesn't he do it? Why ask me?"

"I already suggested an answer for that."

"I want to sculpt again. I want to see if I really still have it."

Samara sighed and took a sip of her coffee. "You've never let any *other* artist intimidate you. Why Pierre?"

"So that's what you think?"

"Well?"

"Hell..maybe. I don't know."

"We need to find that out."

"You're the doctor. Tell me."

"You have to answer that yourself…maybe with a little help from the other woman in your life."

Derek didn't budge from his continued gaze of the Family rock staring back at him. *What is it about women and other women?*

***

Sitting back down in the living room with his coffee, Stoppard flipped on the TV. As usual, the news was bleak with more catastrophic threats coming from the Middle East. He flipped it to a classical radio station and sipped his coffee. After several minutes of staring at the cracked window, he nodded to himself. *Why do I think I can fix that? I bet. I bet I…*

***

As I exited the loft, my mind was consumed with Monday morning being just two days away. I knew Stoppard would be with his attorneys to start the funding documents that would alter the remaining years of his life—and possibly mine.

Samara gazed down through the loft window and lifted her hand, wishing me well as I was about to stride off in the mid-day for a final decision. She had been supportive, but there was the persistent memory of her words, many years before, that drove me this morning to face my worst enemy, *doubt*. "When are you going to do it?" had been her war cry, one that was repeated over the years as I plodded through the self doubt that my life would amount to nothing more than a piece of sculpture here and there.

I looked back and waved. As I paused a moment to throw her an uncustomary kiss, I worried she wouldn't realize how impactful her words were to me. It was because her advice was taken seriously that I now stepped out onto the street, jammed my hands in my pockets, and walked towards the Battery.

The idea of managing fifteen billion dollars is daunting to say the least, and the challenge it represents is out of my realm of experience, for God's sake... just as starting Echo Life was years ago. Maybe history is trying to repeat itself. Maybe, I need to once again use some courage and that confidence I once had to "do it." But what will happen to my sculpting life? Will it get swallowed up in administrative work? Is that more important now? More creative? With the self-imposed feeling of ineptness Pierre's work has given me, it's easy to call Stoppard's opportunity a calling—perhaps even a great excuse to avoid taking the responsibility of ever again having to say something important artistically. Fuck! The temptation is great. I caught myself looking up, but there were no gulls. As I walked, I looked everywhere, but colored scarves were not to be seen.

Chapter 102

The shopping bag was lifted from the counter. "Will there be anything else, sir?" said the clerk.

"No, thank you." said Stoppard.

With his purchase held securely to his side, he left the crafts supply shop, shuffling along the sidewalk, dodging the crowded afternoon foot traffic rushing about in every direction. By the time he reached his apartment, he was ready for a second shower.

He placed the bag on the coffee table and stepped to the thermostat where the setting read, 72. Lowering it to 68, he stepped up to the vent and stood immobile, letting the icy air bring him back to life.

***

From Battery Park, the Hudson River entryway glistened with the afternoon sun. With the Statue of Liberty and the Jersey shore in the distance, I stepped up to the bench I had sat upon that day long ago when I first witnessed the strange behavior of seagulls and the girl in the rainbow scarves that began feeding and leading them up the street.

Making its way into the river current was tug loaded with the city's weekend spoils and as usual, seagulls taking up positions alongside for their lunchtime feast. I glanced over my shoulder at the subway entrance across the road, but unlike before, it was void of any birds or multi-colored scarves floating up from the exit. I smiled at myself for thinking I could just imagine my muse and she would be there for me. At this point in my relationship with Echo, I knew there was always the unexpected to happen. But, not today. I turned back.

The barge was now straightaway from me. The gulls grew to several dozen and, as they swooped, dove and pecked at each other over the piled refuse, I focused on the tugboat maneuvering the load. I'd never seen a boat painted like a cubist mural before and it brought more smiles to my face. *Creativity and imagination is still alive and well in New York.*

"Do you really think so?" came Echo's voice.

I jumped and turned around. "Damn, wasn't expecting that."

"Sure you were."

I took a moment to look at her. "Different scarves."

"Didn't want to bore you."

"Been awhile."

"Yes it has. You've been busy."

"You noticed."

"Hard not to."

"Yeah." I rested on my elbows and nodded toward the tug and even more seagulls hovering as it made its way further along the Hudson. "Your friends deserted you."

"They always come back—just like you."

I hesitantly nodded, peered back out at the gulls, and then smiled to myself. *Naw. Jesus. I'm really letting my imagination get away from me.*

"Are you, really?" said Echo, stretching her arms out on the bench.

I was tempted to try and touch her for the first time, but—

***

Standing up to the window with a small crafting tool and a can of liquid lead, Stoppard carefully applied the gray metal to the crack. As he finished, he stood back, looked, sighed and sat back down facing the window. *Shit. Now it's a train wreck.* He stared, turned his head left to right, picked up pencil and paper and started drawing the line depicting the crack. From there, a few more turns of his head, left to right, and he began giving the crooked vertical line offshoots, first bringing on a sense of tree, then he found himself making more and more crooked lines. He stopped and held the paper up next to the glass. He wasn't sure it was appropriate to smile, but then, *what the hell. Just me and the glass, right?*

***

I paused and looked over at Echo. *Just your usual Muse.* "Where do you get *your* confidence? Mine seems to have taken a sabbatical."

"Is that why the last time we chatted, you asked me to leave?"

"Maybe. I'm sorry about that."

"Don't be. You were in a pissy mood. Wasn't much fun to be around. But, to answer your question. My confidence is born out of the same cloth as yours. You just need to rinse, and hang it out to dry sometimes."

I looked back out at the Hudson. "Is that what I did that day?"

"Hardly a rinse. More like a turbo wash. What's it been, a year? More? You've gotten along pretty well without me. Big wash, long dry, great confidence. Got you fifteen billion, right? Not a bad payday."

I looked out to the river. "Hardly a pay day, and the offer has nothing to do with my confidence."

"So you think Stoppard is dropping his fortune in your lap because he thinks you lack confidence to manage it?"

"Oh, come on. He knows I'll turn to Sol for business decisions. I'm just decoration and maybe bait to get his son back. That's all."

"Boy, you've got a lot on your mind, don't you?"

"How'd you guess?"

"You want my opinion?"

"You're going to give it to me whether I want it or not."

"Yup. You're catching on."

***

By late afternoon, Stoppard was covered with smudges of liquid metal, his jeans and t-shirt looking more like the dress-up attire of an artist rather than the rarely worn work clothes of a billionaire. As he reached into the shopping bag and retrieved a number of small cans of glass paint, a grin of pride came across his face.

As he opened the cans and arranged the colors in front of him, he flashed back to the boy at the lake and then his own early childhood at the bar, pounding nails, creating the walls from old boat planks. All he could think was *where did the time go?*

He brushed a preparation liquid to the glass and then began to apply the stain-glass paint. As he picked up the brush and applied the dark blue to the upper shapes, he paused, wondering how foolish and childish this all was. *Why don't I just let the glass people replace the window?*

647

He thought of Pierre and how he had distinguished himself by being—even more foolish and childish than me? He continued painting, gradually working his way down the pane with lighter shades of blue, then dark green that progressed to lighter green and finally, earth brown. As he stood back and stretched his back, the sun was leaving long shadows across Central Park. His stained glass window with its *space* blue to *sky* blue to treetop green to lawn and finally earth brown at the bottom stood vertically beside the other half of the sliding glass door. It wasn't until he pulled a bar stool to the window, sat down, and lit up a Churchill that he noticed the horizontal planes of the real sky and park landscape seeming to match the planes of his own repair. *Will you look at that? Will you look at that?*

Like a kid that had just discovered he could create magic with finger paints, he jumped up and anxiously opened his last bottle of '82 LaFite Rothchild. As he lifted the glass to the light, his eyes moved to the stained portion of the window again. The last low rays of light finding their way between the buildings and across the park were bearing down, slipping under the protection of the awning. The refracted light of the stained glass bathed his living room in multi-colors. He felt like he was standing in the middle of a carousel, the bright colors around him like the brass poles and ponies of his youth.

He walked to the sliding glass door, opened it and stepped out onto the terrace with a Churchill in one hand, and a glass of Rothchild in the other. The air would start to cool soon. Summer evenings overlooking the park were one of his favorite quiet times. He moved to the railing and inhaled deeply. He raised his glass to toast—not knowing to what, or caring, for that matter. He was somewhere else, somewhere only his imagination knew. He felt happy, really happy, for the first time in a long while.

***

"So, couple of good hours. We're caught up now, aren't we?" said Echo.

I nodded wearily and looked at my watch, then up at the sun dropping quickly now behind the new high-rise apartments on the Jersey side of the Hudson.

"So," she continued, "as you—I—see it, Pierre's got you thinking you're nothing in comparison, and that's bad for the ego. Stoppard, on the other hand, has got you thinking that if you just maintain the status quo, he'll continue to fund. That's good for the ego."

"And?" I asked.

"And what?"

"And—my *confidence*. Good for my ego and my *confidence?*"

Echo fingered the scarves she had been weaving into a complex heptagon design. "Most likely. Yes. I just spent an hour addressing that. You handled Echo Life for two years while you nurtured the Rock to completion, kept your love life together...barely...and helped bring a young artist of enormous talent into the cross-hairs of the art world and an innocent public. Oh, you also did something to merit the handling of a billionaire's bequeathing of fifteen big ones. Not bad for a guy worrying about his confidence. Like the design?" She lifted the scarves for me to see.

"Yes. Pretty. Thanks for the analysis, but you've got it all wrong."

"*I've* got it all wrong?" She lowered the scarves and began to make some adjustments in the thatching.

I got up in a huff, stepped to the railing and hunched out over the water. "I don't want to let anybody down. You're right. I almost lost Samara because I was letting her down. I could have lost Echo Life a long time ago. Came very close to letting a lot of people down. Now this."

"You're worried that even with the confidence, the ego boost, the m-o-n-e-y, you might succumb? Become another Stoppard. *Is that it?*"

I turned around. She was gone.

***

Sitting on his terrace and watching the colors of the trees below change as the sun continued to drop, Stoppard looked at his gray stained hands and the final glass of his '82 wine and smiled. With a sense of pride and peace, he rose from his lounge chair and turned to gaze back at his stained glass window one more time. His eyes narrowed. His head extended. *What the...? What's that?*

He stepped to the jagged crack and stopped. Reaching up to the top where the crack began, he removed a short gray and white feather snagged in the crack. Like a bullet or a nail or a beak—there was a small round fracture that had caused the break. "Fucking bird?" He plucked the feather and flicked it over the edge of the terrace and watched as an updraft held it to a slow motion hover that refused to falter.

***

"Don't do that again," I shouted at her as I walked back from the rail and dropped down on the bench, giving her the evil eye as she chose to perch on the railing.

"Do what, leave for a few minutes while you come to your senses?" responded Echo.

"Yes!"

"Works in all good domestic debates," she chortled.

"Fine." I said and sighed, thinking it was time to leave.

"Before I get myself back to normal, are you going to ask me?"

"Ask you?

"About the heptagon."

"Oh, you noticed."

"You watching me weave it? Uh, huh. Made you think, didn't it?" she said.

"Kinda"

"Well, it's simple actually. You used to call on it subconsciously a lot, so I thought I'd remind you that's it's been awhile since you visited the answer."

I had to grin. "Okay. I'll bite. What answer is that?"

"As you learned back in the 7th grade, in all cultures, myths and legends the number seven represents: completeness and totality, macrocosm, perfection, plenty, reintegration, rest, security, safety, and most importantly, synthesis. Philosophically, you always understood it, but it wasn't until now that you wrestled with its practicality. Derek, your seven is the combination of thesis and antithesis in the Hegelian dialectical process whereby a new and higher level of truth is produced."

I shook my head. "In the what process?"

"Hegelian dialectical. Run it past Theo. He'll clear it up for you. For now," she held up the heptagon, "know it's *you*." She flicked her wrist and the ribbons opened back to their flowing freedom about her neck. "You're about to realize the 'completeness and totality' of it all."

"Easy for you to say, but if I screw it up... Oh boy. Don't even want to think about it."

"Then don't. Derek, don't want to rush you, but here's what you've been trying to talk yourself into for what, three hours. Spend it fast. Buy the island. Sell off lots on the far side to The Vineyard and Nantucket bores. Save the best lot for Stoppard. Give it to him. He'll love keeping up with the you-know-who's while he tries to retire, which he'll never succeed in doing. Buy your own ferry service and a couple of shuttle planes. Consider it an insurance policy to guarantee tourism. Put up a half dozen buildings for the arts campus. And to top it off, see what one of those Freighter Cruises companies will sell you a long-term passenger lease for. Make a dandy floating Echo Life extension campus and artist-exchange program around the world." She flung the ribbons over her shoulder and pointed to her head. "Gotta use that imagination even more now, Derek."

She paused and chuckled. "Hey, that's seven again, if you count the ways to spend it. Oh, by the way, there's twenty-four hours in the day, so as far as your sculpting life is concerned, your imagination is pretty good, and there's lots of rock around. Now..." She turned on her perch and looked toward another tugboat and barge with the customary flock of seagulls. "I see they got their bellies full. Gotta go. Let me hear how that works out for you and— not so long a dry spell next time, okay?"

I dropped my head to my chest. "You're crazy, you know," I said, as I shook my head—my eye catching the dog to my left, who had wandered up some time ago, sat, and perked his ears at my talking to myself.

"Aren't we all," was the last thing I heard before I looked back at the rail. She was gone again, but this time, I knew it would be for a while.

I stood a moment, peered back at the dog, still holding vigil for my madness, and turned to the sky where a flock of gulls started moving into a double "V" to head across Manhattan. I turned and walked off, shaking my head. *Accept it, Derek. She's never going to leave you alone. Never."*

From behind, I heard a bark. I turned. The dog barked once more at the gulls—disappearing to the north.

CHAPTER 103

12 YEARS LATER
2022

Derek having accepted Stoppard's request that he manage the foundation considered his responsibilities carefully. With Sol having analyzed both Derek's and other's suggestions on how best to use the fifteen billion, the foundation went ahead and purchased the island, renaming it Echo Island, followed by the construction of the arts campus and artists' cottages, as well as the parceling off of lots for private purchase. Stoppard not only purchased the largest lot— refusing to take it as a gift—but also spent his recreational time indulging in his newfound creative outlet of staining glass windows around the house, just as he had done with his Manhattan penthouse. Echo Island over the next few years became an artist's mecca, accompanied by extraordinary tourism. A long-term lease on a freighter allowed for the floating annex, and Pierre, having returned to New York after traveling around Europe for three years, was immediately encouraged by both Stoppard and Derek to create his "Scape" approach to similar salvage and junk sites in other countries, which he did. Using his uncanny sense of touch to determine colors, he soon discovered and transformed giant mounds of destruction into art installations all over the world.

***

In spite of Stoppard Denning and OST's goodwill and desire to create a better service to the people of the world, other powerful influences continued to flourish as well. Middle Eastern extremists continued in their quest to terrorize and destroy the West. Increased acts of terror made not only the United States, but also the rest of the Western world feel precarious, continuing to remind everyone of the insidious nature of a jihadist mindset. The impact of OST and Echo Life's new paradigm of expression on the world's population was beginning to create a different kind of international harmony. Where politics and economics had been the antagonistic factors of past terrorist activities, it was this new western influence on independence through creative expression that became Terrorism's newest enemy. Since 2001, eleven years had passed where the world had staved off any other major disasters of the 9/11 magnitude. But, on June 3rd of 2012, al-Qaeda made a major attempt to change that.

***

While many on the eastern seaboard enjoyed typical clear blue skies and the mild temperatures of early summer, the inhabitants of Echo Island found themselves looking to the skies and asking, "Why?"

At 9:07 AM, a twin-engine crop dusting plane took off from Bangor, Maine, heading west. Within minutes of take off, the plane banked toward the east and passed over the coastline and into the Atlantic Ocean air space. Thirty minutes later, it was flying low across the waters leading up to Echo Island. As tourists, villagers and artists alike looked skyward, it began dusting the island with a mist. After several passes, it banked west and headed back toward Bangor, crossing over Stoppard's beach home on the northwest side of the island for one last misting. Smoking a Churchill and caught up with early summer temperatures and sea breeze, like the rest of the island, he gazed up nonplussed, unaware of what was really happening.

America was once again under attack.

The effect was not immediate. No one felt ill, but everyone was fearful that the incident spelled something horrible. They had never been dusted before. What for? Their apprehensions were soon born

out when within 24 hours; many on the island began to feel sick. Nausea, headache and itchy skin were the primary symptoms of what—they didn't know. Everyone speculated, but no one could figure out why a crop duster would be spraying the island. Tourists returning home, as well as islanders, became severely ill a week after the dusting. Lesion patches on their skin quickly swelled into massive disfigurement. Further diagnosis determined that they were infected with a leprosy-like virus that the medical world had no cure or treatment for.

Echo Island become an incubator for what was later described as a modern 21st century leprosy, a contagious disease that had already, through the tourist population on the island returning to their homes, become a biological dirty bomb of the highest magnitude. America, in an effort to quell the potential disaster, gave the former tourists two choices: return to the island and live out their days while a cure is sought, or be placed in a confined area of Alaska. Thirty-three chose Alaska, three hundred ten chose Echo Island, and two committed suicide.

Because the virus was an airborne contagion, no one was allowed to leave the island, and for the following 10 years, food and other provisions were airdropped weekly. Fortunately for the rest of America, the unique viral characteristics were determined, and through a revamped Homeland Security and special border scanners at air and seaports, further infiltration of the deadly biological warfare had thus far been thwarted. As time went on, however, no cure was found, and the cancerous disease on Echo Island mutated from disfigurement to the slow crippling of arms and legs.

Early on, as Tito's newspaper editorial cited, Echo Island's center for creative freedom had become the extremists' primary nemesis. Fostering the liberation of dormant creativity and individual expression as fuel for independance among millions of people, Echo Life's influence made in increasingly more difficult for terrorism to break down people's will. No longer was it as easy to conquer a country and make it subservient to dictatorship. Gone were the days when everyday people would willingly allow their emotional and intellectual needs for creative freedom to be quashed.

Now, on the tenth anniversary of the island's quarantine, an armada of fifty-four helicopters representing the Alliance of Nations against global terrorism surrounded the island in a salute, each one bearing the flag markings of its respective country. In the lead chopper was OST's prime-time anchorwoman, Elinore Hardy. Sitting next to her was Pierre Haweisi, now a cultural ambassador for the UN. Behind him was Siebert, a faithful guardian-like friend, who whenever necessary, carried out the custodial needs Stoppard had financed via a generous trust fund. Siebert's emotions had always been easy for him to handle...'til now. The bottled water in his hand had little effect in covering up the swallowing gesture he was fighting back.

As cameras rolled from inside their chopper and from the other hovering aircraft, Elinore finished her televised tribute carried via loud speakers to the islanders below and accompanied by, as in previous anniversaries, Samara's symphonic music.

The lone stooped figures of Stoppard and Derek stood atop Echo Rock and waved their respective canes. Several helicopters, holding above the island and Echo Rock released the now traditional shrouding; a cloud of white rose petals.

Wearing a headset, Pierre asked Elinore, "Do you see my father or Derek?"

Elinore lifted her binoculars and answered into her mouthpiece, "Yes. They're both standing on the top of Echo."

"How does he look...my father?"

"He's waving his cane. He seems fine."

"And Derek?"

"Same. He's waving as well."

"Good. The other artists... do you see many of them?"

She raised her binoculars and scanned further up the peninsula to the village shoreline. "Yes. I'd say there are a dozen or so on the beach near the village and back at the campus, many more."

"I'd like to wish them well. Is that okay?"

"Of course," said Elinore. She leaned toward the instrument panel and adjusted the music level on the loudspeakers. "The on/off switch on your head set is now live. Anytime."

Pierre paused a moment, then began. "This is Pierre, everyone. I hope you're doing okay and that your work is progressing. The last broadcast where you showed Lanagra's latest, as well as the performance of 'Angels in America' by Wollzak's troupe of actors, well, just hearing the many comments on Greco's show was enough to convince me that creative hope and reward is still alive and well on Echo Island. I just want you to know as I travel the world, I hear more and more thanks and appreciation for what you continue to provide. It seems that amidst all the pain and sorrow you've sustained, the inventive spirit prevails, carrying the message that imagination is all powerful and that by allowing our innate need to express, the world continues to become a little better place, a more peace-minded place, a more creative place. Thank you for all you continue to do. Dad, thanks for the digital photos. Yes, I know you must have thought I was mad asking for them, but the digital gurus have now invented a brail language for art, as strange as that might sound. I'm sending you a tape of my description of the new stain glass panes you've created. Bet I nailed the colors. Derek, Samara wanted me to let you know, the whole island for that matter, that just last night she completed her 5th Symphony. She wanted me to tell you that she titled it Echosis."

Pierre turned his mic off a moment while he cleared his throat and wiped his eyes. He flipped it back on and continued. "So…that's about it. The world is grateful for you in spite of the separation. Don't ever stop." He pressed the off button again.

Elinore reached up and adjusted the music once again, and turned to Pierre. "I'm sure they appreciated that, Pierre."

"It's the least I can do, isn't it?"

As helicopters banked and headed toward the coast of Maine, Elinore gripped his hand. Samara's music became distant, as time and space was once more placed between *life on the run*, and the *endless life* of Echo Project.

Derek and Stoppard watched the final moments of the helicopters retreat, and then sat down on the rock. "Damn," said Stoppard. "You'd think this fuckin' disease would at least numb one's ass for sitting on rocks, wouldn't you?"

"Hey, give it a rest. Just stop! You're worse than an old lady. You know that? You bellyache, bitch and moan about everything." He reached down and grabbed some tufts of grass. "Here."

"And you don't?" said Stoppard as he shoved the grass under his backside with his right hand, his left now showing the advanced stages of the disease's crippling effect.

"Me? When the hell did I last complain about anything?"

"That steak I cooked for you last night, for starters." He gestured toward the grass. "Gimme some more of that stuff."

"God. That was horrible." Derek grabbed another handful and handed it to him. "You burned every last ounce of juice out of it."

"You're so full of it. That was char-broiled."

"That was *burn*-broiled. Theo even said it was worse than homeless grub."

Stoppard rose up. "Grass's not worth shit. Not gonna let that rock bother my ass any longer. You comin'?"

"I'll be along in a while. Need a breather from you."

"Yeah, well…" He strode off. After a few steps, he paused and turned. His face was enveloped with the kind of smile he hadn't felt since being with Zorn in Central Park. "Pierre keeps growing into quite a man, doesn't he?"

"Of course. What did you expect? His mother's got good genes."

Stoppard nodded and smiled through his disfigurement. "At least we agree on one thing." He turned and continued up the path mumbling, "Char-broiled. You're so full of it."

Derek looked around. Even though the disease had rendered his hands stiff and crooked, he was still of high spirit. To the real him, the *him* he'd spent a lifetime finding, nothing had really changed. The sea continued to batter the rock below. The sky was blue as the Azure Sea. The air was clean as always—excepting that one bleak day many years before.

He took a deep breath and stared at the shoulder of his Echo rock. He tilted his head to the right, studied the rock a moment and then took a pen and piece of scrap paper out of his pocket. As he struggled to hold his hand steady and sketch a seagull now perched on Echo's carved shoulder. *I can do that. I can.*

"About time. Of course you can," replied Echo.

Fin

www.ingramcontent.com/pod-product-compliance
Lightning Source LLC
Chambersburg PA
CBHW020452020726
47493CB00001B/3